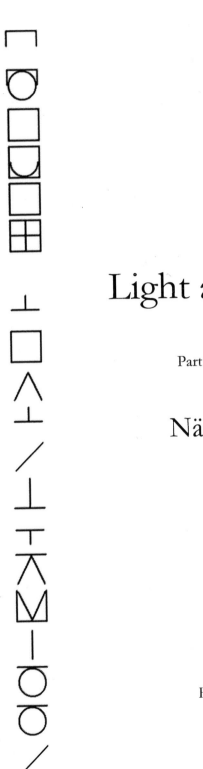

Light and Glory

Part One of Eight
of

Närdamähr

First Edition

This is a work of fiction. All characters and events appearing in this novel are fictitious or used fictitiously.

LIGHT AND GLORY

© 2006 by Justin M. Sellers

All rights reserved. No part of this book may be reproduced or transmitted in any form or by any means, electronic or mechanical, including photocopying, recording, or by any information storage and retrieval system, without written permission from the author.

WhiteFire Publishing
10015 Old Columbia Rd., Suite B
Columbia MD, 21046

www.whitefireprinting.com/publishing

ISBN: 0-9765444-4-X

Cover design by Paul Clark and Justin M. Sellers.

First Edition, 2006

Pronunciation Guide

This book contains words that originate from fictional languages. I've transcribed the words into Roman letters that approximate their proper pronunciation, and modified them to make them appear less intimidating to pronounce.

The Roman vowels used in these words are pronounced in the following way:

A – like "a" in "sat"
Ä – like "a" in "father"
Ē – like "ea" in "eat"
Ĕ – like "e" in "egg"
Ō – like "o" in "nose"
Û – like "oo" in "boot"
Ŭ – like "u" in "up"

Consonants in these words are each pronounced individually. For example, the word "Pp'm'tärnhär" is a five-syllable word: p-p-m-tärn-här.

When conjugations make words hard to read, I have placed apostrophes between the conjugations and the words. For example, the "n" conjugation of "Närdamähr" is written "N'närdamähr."

Justin M. Sellers

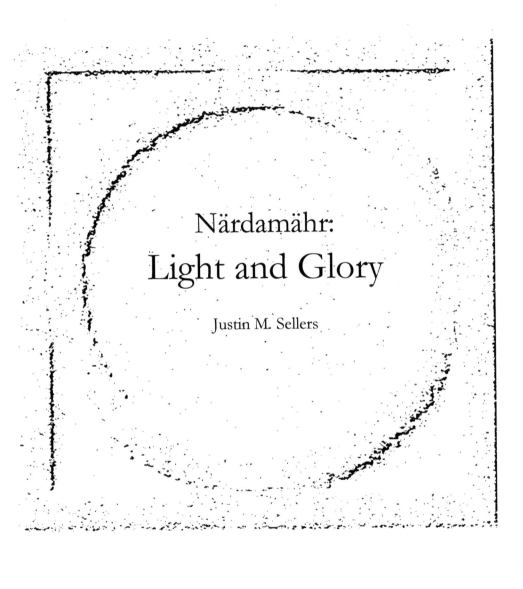

Närdamähr:
Light and Glory

Justin M. Sellers

Ōhä-Ä'ähänärdanär!

Contents

1   Horrors and Hopes – 1

2   Vanguard – 18

3   Nrathĕrmĕ and Nŭährnär – 34

4   Fantastic Realities – 53

5   Nōhōnŭäär – 70

6   Answers and Questions – 85

7   The Light of Life – 106

8   Ämäthōär - 125

9   The First Moves – 144

10   Hearts of Heroes – 155

11   Sarah's Will – 169

12   The Simple Truth – 190

13   A Perfect Sense – 206

14   Training Begins – 222

15   Ärthähr Logic – 239

16   Initiation – 254

17   The Decisions of Peter Garcia – 268

18 On the Genealogy of Victory – 282

19 The Deeps of Infinity – 299

20 Transcendent Encouragement – 318

21 Rally – 340

22 Hero of Nŭährnär – 360

23 The Faithful and the Fearful – 376

24 Light and Glory – 392

25 Heritage of Ähänär – 413

26 One of Those Times – 428

27 Outguessing Thahn – 444

28 Blaze of Glory – 455

Närdamähr:

Light and Glory

Chapter 1

Horrors and Hopes

From "About Forms" by Thomas Pratt:

...those kinds of obstacles were needed. We missed each other, definitely. Of course we did!

Let me stop here. I have been writing so much about Antär; I should put it all in better perspective.

So I think I ought to record for your reading a full version of the war between Antär and Sĕrĕhahn. I'll do it chronologically this time. Events like these deserve to be seen in their proper light.

Events like these! What amazing, wondrous, archetypal events! What awesome adventures, shadowing the Great Adventure, I have been allowed to enjoy! Really, life in Ōmäthäär-hood is a life unlike and greater than all others, life as life has always, ever, been meant to be life!

I say that these events shadow Eternity, but give me any event, and give me time, and I can show how that event reflects totally the whole of Ä'ähänärdanär. But I have experienced these events. I've been able to ponder and muse about them. So I'll use the story of these events to demonstrate the perfect interweavingness of Är's Full Story, as much as I can in the time that I have to give to this.

This conflict of light against false light, reality against error, intelligence against destructiveness, these wars as I still call them, of Ōmäthäär against Sĕrĕhahn, are excellent fountains of so many themes of the Eternal Epic. The natures of good and evil, and their infinitely varying hues, and the ways in which they're recognized and the ways in which they are mistaken for each other, were shown profoundly and so thoroughly through these events, these endeavors and glorious endurings.

And how much the character of Infinity was displayed throughout that terrible but glorious adventure! How much the dangers of self-inflicted ignorance, of masochistic rejection of ubiquitous opportunities for growth and betterment, of self-inflicted naïveté, of stubborn cowardice of life and love and everything that's worth living and being for, how much the dangers of prideful mulishness were displayed! And how much the glory of bravery and of progression was shown too! The awesomeness of moving forward, of being! And the confident mistakes of even the wisest of people, and the simple success of the unpretentious!

And these events are a better sermon than any that I can design, on the need for dedicated Ōmäthäär in Ä'ähänärdanär!

And that's motivation enough for me to record the whole epic in chronological order. Instead of trying to explain what I want to explain, the character of Är and the perfection of Ärthähr, directly, I will let you live the events that explained those things to me in ways that few words could ever have done. Archetypal principle can be better apprehended if it's seen in the context of the events all around it.

I am not going to analyze principles here, unless it is absolutely necessary and flows with the telling. Analyses of the applicability of most of these events can be found in my other writings, and especially in the writings of people like Räröähr and Ûnrĕ. And Mär.

I want this account to provide a profitable overview of these wars. Conclusions can be found in other sources, and earlier in this book of course, and I hope you'll draw new conclusions as you live these things, as you're personally inspired to. What will strike me, or has struck Mär, or whomever, as profound will not necessarily strike you in the same way; what people harvest is relative to what they need, and to what they already have. It's a waste of time to try to explain didactically every single principle. This account, I hope, will provide a springing-off point for you to glean everything that's applicable to you, just by living these events yourself....

…and that was right about the time that Ōhäthäär and Thahn met one another. Think what you will, but I do not believe it was a coincidence. The West called that year 1942.

The Nazis were less careless than Razar and her minions. I think they resemble M'razar more than they resemble R'bathĕrŭ. But Ōhäthäär was tremendously more subtle than Adolf was. Adolf was more like Razar, I think.

Now, Razar had the M'tärnhär, the Ranrĕĕlĕrĕ as they dared to call themselves, and even the bitterest of Adolf's allies were not anywhere near as darkly potent as the M'tärnhär were. But I think the profundity of the Axis-Allies War lies more deeply. Adolf did not wield M'tärnhär the way Razar did. Adolf's campaign against the Jacobites was less terrible, and less comprehensive, than was Razar's campaign against the Nōhōnŭäär. Nevertheless, his campaign was more potent in that it struck at the heart. Razar was more terrible, but Adolf was positioned at the core.

Ōhōnŭäär's history was more profound than was Närdamähr's. It is a perfect archetype that the diminutive Earth should be so overshadowed by Nrathĕrmĕ's grandiosity, while she, all along, held power over that great, mighty one!

But I, for one, owe an infinite debt to Närdamähr. It was Mär's Ōmäthäär, who are from Närdamähr, who made my life worthwhile! Who made me more than a grey shadow of unrealized possibilities! Who gave me life, and light, and the keys to everything I can want!

Consider what you know of my life before I met Mär's Ōmäthäär: I had been, for the most part, content in my meaningless mundanity. I had had plans for what I thought was all the education I really needed; I had had plans for what I thought was a

1: Horrors and Hopes

worthy career. I planned to entangle myself in the sophistries of that society's temporal governing. I planned to achieve what I believed to be success. I had sated the expectations of my blind educators to a point of special distinction. I had good friends, I knew many who would help me achieve my small-sighted goals, I had a fine family, I enjoyed the company of a wonderful woman.

Brittney.

A wonderful woman. I believed I had a bright future.

But my life was cold. It was dark. It was blind!

Imagine the horror of living a life with no final goal, no victory at its end, chasing after fickle pleasures and evading chilling woes! The only thing that kept me sane, aside from my family and Brittney, was forcing the reality of my life's ultimate pointlessness continually out of my thoughts!

Compare that to Ōmäthäär-hood! Compare that to Är! To Ä'ähänärdanär! To everything the Ärthähr is and everything it can make anybody! To Ä'ähänärdanär and joy!

How much I know now that I didn't know then! O, how much I am now, that I could never have imagined being then! What awesome things I have been able to do! What I have seen! What wonderful things, that I could never have imagined before!

I was shallow and small. I was merely a bystander, an oblivious extra, in the Grand Epic of Är. I knew nothing of the glories that were happening even as I lived my pointless existence.

So glory for gallant Ōmäthäär!

Glory to Mär.

Still, while Mär attempted to show me how to let myself be a hero instead of an extra, how to allow myself to take part in and revel in the awesomeness of the Great Perfect Plot, while I had been as unknowing of that Plot as extras are wont to be, his explanation was not sufficient, not for my blind self. Not until I lived both horror and hope would I apprehend what he wanted me to understand.

That's why it'll be better for me to go on with the chronological recounting; this way you can live what I and others have lived. This way you can learn more easily, and I won't use my time attempting to convey everything that I want to convey in these uncommunicatively straightforward words.

That Axis-Allies War then led the faction called the Union of...

...by that time, I was nearing my twenty-first birthday. I had no way of knowing that I would not finish that year before everything I knew, and everything on which I had so stupidly placed value, would be flipped upside down.

November twenty-first was when it started for me. The sun was rising over Austin when the pirates struck. I love the sunrise of that day; I love looking back at it; it signifies to me the rising of real light, finally, into my life.

Light and Glory

Isn't it right that pirates served as my preliminary introduction into the world of Närdamähr, and, consequently, of Ä'ähänärdanär? Räröähr contends that it was Är's idea of a practical joke. I think, this time, he's right about Är.

The N'nŭährnär acted quickly. Äthähäth had been waiting for a plain sign that the pirates were working with the Ämäthöär. Many of the pirates struck at Earth together. The N'nŭährnärs' hold on the planet saved it from breaking apart, but the pirates were soon aware of them. Now that the pirates knew that they were not alone, a quick active scan revealed all of Äthähäth's vessels to their sight.

The stealthy division that had slid in to stabilize the planet split apart. The pirates pursued many of them, but the tactic bought the N'nŭährnär the crucial time that they needed.

Äthähäth's main force, waiting just outside the range at which the pirates might have spotted them, bore down quickly upon the pirates. The pirates realized their mistake in time, and gave up pursuing the smaller, stealthy ships.

Many of those stealthy ships had been destroyed, but their splitting apart and scattering ensured that, while the pirates engaged some of them, the others were yet free to continue to keep a stabilizing hold on Earth in case the pirates should strike at the planet again.

Äthähäth's fleet was nearly one-and-a-half times the size of the pirate fleet. Sěrěhahn had not compensated the pirates yet; he did not want unusual technology to insinuate a possible connection between the pirates and Nrathěrmě. Thus Äthähäth's fleets were almost as able as the pirates' were. Being outnumbered by such a significant margin against equally well equipped foes, the pirates' odds of defeating the N'nŭährnär and completing their job were manifestly slim.

Sěrěhahn had intentionally selected a particularly degenerate, cowardly clan of pirates to annihilate Ōhōnŭäär for him. Such an act of senseless barbarism could easily have been put to the charge of the pirates alone. Who would suspect that the pirates had acted under employment of someone from Nrathěrmě itself?

According to N'zärnär, these pirates feared death supremely. In their minds, no reward that they believed Sěrěhahn could offer them for the completion of the job was worth the risk of death with no hope of revival.

As soon as the pirates were aware of the strength of the N'nŭährnär forces, they attempted to flee. Äthähäth had prepared for this. His ships were positioned in a wide sphere around the pirates, just outside the pirates' range of passive visibility. Äthähäth, wisely, was terrified of letting escape anyone in league with the Ämäthöär.

Many of the pirates were cornered by the N'nŭährnärs' swiftly closing encirclement. The majority of the pirates, however, flocked together in a tight pod and charged through a more sparse area in the collapsing sphere.

The N'nŭährnär nearest the escaping pirates broke away in pursuit. The pirates were faster, and they spared no energy from accelerating to the retreat. The

1: Horrors and Hopes

N'nüährnär did not pursue the pirates far, lest they reveal themselves to any of the other nations near that area.

Meanwhile, Äthähäth insisted that some few of the pirates be left alive, in order to be questioned. Sĕrĕhahn had covered his tracks well; the pirates knew little that the Ōmäthäär were able to find significant.

Nevertheless, Äthähäth, not yet knowing the extent of the pirates' knowledge, commanded the pirates to surrender. The N'nüährnär corralled the survivors together, who, knowing they were outdone and seeing their enemies' desire to preserve them alive, promptly obeyed the command....

Tom placed the last of the four mismatched plates at the head of the small, scratched kitchen table. Straightening up, he surveyed the orderliness of the sparse tableware for his family's daily breakfast.

"Tom!" Lewis Pratt barked impatiently at his son.

Tom looked up at his disheveled father as Lewis flipped another darkly browned pancake onto a plate beside the stove.

Lewis cursed under his breath, then turned to Tom, taking the smoking pan from the heat. "Go see what's taking—" he began, then stopped himself, moderating his tone. "Please, tell Andrew and Terry that breakfast is waiting."

Tom barely had time to step around the small table before his brother Andrew emerged from the hallway into the kitchen, having obviously heard Lewis from his bedroom. Beginning to smile to himself at Andrew's promptness, Tom quickly suppressed the impulse, seeing Andrew's even more sullen than usual demeanor that morning.

Andrew sighed wearily as he flopped into a chair beside the table, dropping his backpack beside him. He was already wearing his coat, ready to escape the house and his father's compulsory breakfast gathering as quickly as possible.

"Juice," Tom muttered, realizing the missing piece of his table setting and turning toward the fridge.

Terry then emerged from the hallway, brushing briskly at her back-length red-brown hair. She took her seat beside Andrew as their father brought the steaming plate of pancakes to the table. Tom followed close behind Lewis with a jug of store-bought orange juice.

Lewis set the plate on the table, and Andrew reached for a small pile of pancakes as Lewis sat himself down at the table's head. Both Andrew and Terry, who chose only a single cake, deliberately avoided the more burnt ones, though every one of the pancakes had been browned or blackened to varying degrees.

As Tom reached the table with the orange juice, he noticed the time on the clock above Andrew's head. It was already almost seven-thirty. He hesitated, realizing he had to leave at that moment if he was going to make the bus to the city. But then he moved forward again and set the juice on the table, pretending not to have seen the time.

Lewis instinctively glanced at the clock as Tom paused to check it, however. "Tom!" he said. "Get going! You're going to be late again!"

"It's alright," Tom said dismissively as he sat himself down across from Andrew.

"Tom, this job is important," Lewis said intently.

"I know," Tom said, still attempting to sound unworried. "I can catch the next bus."

"You need a better work ethic," Lewis chided him.

That struck Tom in a soft spot. Tom had only wanted to stay at home as long as he had so that he could serve as something of a moral support to his despairing father. He loved his new internship, but he found himself wanting more to be there for his father. He opened his mouth to respond, but then just assumed an attempted casual smile and a shrug. Then he snatched up a few more severely burnt pancakes, carefully avoided by Andrew and Terry, as if to seal his determination to stay.

Lewis stared at Tom for a moment, then shook his head helplessly. He grumbled some more about Tom's lack of responsibility as he took a couple pancakes for himself. Inwardly, however, Lewis Pratt was thankful to be able to have breakfast together with his children.

Andrew shook his head again as he bolted down his pancakes, wishing Lewis would tell him to "get going," rather than insisting on these morningly rituals together. The sooner Brent got there, the better, he thought to himself.

Terry, finishing her pancake, swiftly disappeared back down the hallway to her bedroom.

After an uncomfortable silence, Lewis, swallowing his last bite, joked shakily, "Andrew, be careful, you'll choke!"

Andrew continued shoveling down his breakfast, as if his hurry would cause his ride to arrive sooner.

But hurry or no, hardly two seconds had passed before a loud horn honked from the street outside.

Andrew sprang up, knocking his chair back and shouldering his bag in one quick motion. "See ya," he said, swallowing his mouthful as he waved bye to Tom.

Tom waved back, his mouth too full to return Andrew's farewell.

1: Horrors and Hopes

Andrew halfheartedly extended his goodbye wave to his father, but didn't look at him as he maneuvered his way around the table toward the front door. Terry then came striding out of the hallway in a bright sweater, her books in her arms and a distinctly cheerful expression suddenly pasted onto her face.

"Bye, Dad! Bye, Tom!" she said, following Andrew to the door.

"Bye, have a good day!" Lewis called after them. He wanted to add, "I love you!" but restrained himself, knowing that they would find it awkward.

Tom waved again after Terry, and then went back to his breakfast as she closed the door behind her.

Lewis stared silently at the closed front door for a few moments. Then he sighed, and looked back at the clock. "Now, Tom," he began, hoping Tom could now be persuaded to leave too, though Lewis did enjoy his company.

But Tom suddenly sprang up. Nearly tripping over his own chair, he twisted around toward the front door. Spewing orange juice out of his mouth, he bellowed, "Stop!"

Before Tom could understand what had so suddenly come over him, and before Lewis could register surprise at his son's senseless outburst, a glaring white burst of light blinded them both. Tom felt a tremendous weight crash into him, bowling him over. Lewis felt a sudden crushing force thrust him into the back of his chair and smash him into the wall behind him, just as his ears seemed to explode and his entire body burn with a sudden concussion of air and heat.

And everything fell immediately to blackness.

...but, whatever the case would have been, there would have of necessity been survivors. Äthähäth and his company were the right people in the right place at the right time; Är always knows what he's doing.

It was a miracle that the planet was not destroyed. The N'nüährnär's stabilization of the planet's core saved it, but the Nōhōnüäär on the surface suffered awfully.

The strain caused on Earth's interior ripped the surface crust layers. Magma burst through the surface in scattered fissures all over the Earth. Many lofty cities of the fragmented Earthmen were toppled and burned. Millions of people died within the first few minutes as a result of the seismic and volcanic reactions of the assaulted planet.

The pirates had also fired a few bolts of rantha at Earth. I see no reason why they should have; their tearing of the planet's interior would have destroyed it immediately, had not the N'nüährnär intervened to stabilize it. N'zärnär has speculated that the rantha was nothing strategic, but was just twisted, malicious overkill. These cowardly, small-hearted pirates wanted to take as much pleasure as they could afford to take in their annihilation of the helpless civilizations of Earth.

The rantha was significantly slowed by the N'nŭährnär's protective field in and around Earth. But though the planet was not shattered by the volleys, the rantha was still moving at such speeds as to demolish what remained of the Earthmen's pretentious empires.

Upon contacting Earth's atmosphere, the rantha instantaneously heated the gases around it. Though it had been slowed by the N'nŭährnär's field around Earth, much of it was still moving quickly enough to shatter atoms in the air and especially on the surface. Energy released from the broken atoms tore across the land, wiping away the Earthmen's cities like dust in a sudden gale.

The vast majority of the Nōhōnŭäär were annihilated by the rantha, and then most of the survivors later perished in the earthquakes and volcanic inferno. Only those who were sufficiently distant from rantha impacts and volcanic rips had any small chance of surviving, but many of those were killed in the quakes.

I was just on the outside edge of the burst of a rantha impact. I lost consciousness as a result of the blast and the heat, and managed to remain unconscious through the rampaging earthquake that convulsed my home, which ironically remained standing.

All, all this destruction, by the command of Sěrěhahn.

Quantitatively speaking, the destruction caused in this instance by Sěrěhahn's mercenary pirates was insignificant. Mere billions were killed, and most of them were later revived. The eradication of the Earthmen's civilizations could have been deftly repaired by the N'nŭährnär.

But still, this attack inaugurated the destruction of so much! So many lives, so many dreams, so much happiness that might have been, had it not been for the nefarious, twisted evil of Sěrěhahn and his associates!

And Earth was its own world! A whole world with its own history, and all the wonderful things that good men and women have done there! The Josephs, the Moseses, the Muhammads, Buddhas, saviors of men! The thousands upon thousands of heroes! The magnificent blood of nobility that again and again, progressively, lifted Earth from the ashes of evil men!

Evil men like Sěrěhahn.

He cared no more for life, except for his own. Every living act he did, everything that outwardly made life, was bent by his poisoned, deeper desires. The destruction that day at Earth was minimal quantitatively, but, having sought, and temporarily achieved, the destruction of so many real people in his effort to exalt himself, Sěrěhahn sealed his downfall. No one can destroy life and glory without reaping his own destruction.

Sěrěhahn's illusionary day of power was already beginning to set...

The first thing Tom realized he was aware of was a horrible searing feeling all over his body. It felt like the worst sunburn, yet burning everywhere at once. Only after a few seconds of dim awareness of the biting pain did he notice that he was lying on his face on the floor.

He tried to open his eyes, but then immediately shut them; they burned with a worse pain than the rest of his body as soon as they began to open. Lifting himself up painfully on his hands, he realized that something wet and warm covered the floor underneath him.

"Dad?" he croaked, his throat stinging.

He heard no answer other than a shrill ringing in his ears.

"Dad!" he said more desperately, rising gingerly to his knees and feeling around frantically with his right hand. It grazed something sharp, sending a spasm of pain up his arm as he felt his palm split open. He jerked his arm back, but in doing so lost his balance, and fell back onto his front. He heard the tinkle of glass and felt another piece of it cut his right cheek as his face hit the floor.

"Dad! Lewis!" he screamed, beginning to cry with fear and pain. "Lewis Pratt!"

Lewis returned to consciousness hearing his son's screams but not registering what he was hearing. All he was aware of was the searing burn all over his body and a throbbing pain in his head. Then he began to feel an intense pain in his stomach. And finally, he realized that Tom was sobbing his name right there beside him.

He tried to open his eyes, but they stung, and he shut them again. "Tom!" he said.

"Dad!" he heard Tom's shaking voice in the stinging darkness.

"I'm here," Lewis said. "I'm right here."

Lifting himself onto his hands again, feeling even more stinging pain now in his right hand, Tom reached wildly toward Lewis's voice with his left hand. After a couple seconds, it landed upon something soft, and warm and wet, Tom guessed despite himself, with his father's blood.

Lewis felt Tom's hand grope about his calf. He tried to lean forward to touch his son's hand with his own, but a sudden shock of pain pierced his right side as soon as he made to move.

"That's my leg," Lewis said as Tom called out to him again. "But I can't move, son."

Tom quickly wiped blood and tears away from his eyes with his left hand, and tried to open them again. The pain was almost unbearable, but through the searing sting and through blotchy, blurred vision, he saw a flickering image of his father crumpled unnaturally against the wall. Lewis's chair was broken underneath him, and the table looked as if it had been hurled into Lewis's abdomen. Even through the blur, Tom could see that his father's face was red and raw, and his clothes were becoming increasingly soaked with blood.

Tom closed his eyes again, more out of horror than out of pain. "What's happened?" he moaned.

The only response he heard from his unmoving father was a low groan, followed by what sounded like a tearful whimper. He forced his eyes open again.

He found it a little easier to keep his eyes open this time. The rising sun was shining through the empty frames of the shattered kitchen window across from where he now lay. He could see that many of the thinner branches of the trees outside had kindled; almost all their leaves were gone. The chairs, dishes, and table inside had all been apparently hurled in Lewis's direction.

Turning himself painfully to look behind him, he saw that the rest of the kitchen looked the same: pans and dishes thrown to the floor, all gathered toward the northern side of the house. The closet door by the entryway was swinging open, its hinges visibly contorted. And as the door swung slowly back again in the wind that was whistling steadily through the house, Tom saw that the front door had also been wrenched open, and was drifting slowly back and forth in the breeze.

He remembered Andrew and Terry. Whatever had just happened, he realized, Andrew and Terry had been outside for it.

He began to lift himself to his knees, wanting to find his siblings, though he had no thought as to what he might be able to do for them. But he was knocked down again onto his face as the ground shivered violently underneath him. Crashes sounded from other rooms, and the house creaked dangerously around them.

"What was that?" he said, growing more terrified now.

Lewis gave a choking whimper, and Tom saw his eyes flicker slightly open, only to instantly shut again.

"What is going on?" Tom coughed, feeling panicked tears dribble down his face. He pushed himself up onto his knees again. His skin felt like it was ripping with every movement.

He heard his father mumble something about Andrew and Terry, then saw him slump forward limply.

"Don't worry," Tom said to him, trying to keep himself calm. "I'll go get help." He turned and stumbled across the broken floor toward the swinging front door. The yellow sun cast shadows behind the scattered dishes and

1: Horrors and Hopes

utensils and into the dents all over the wall, and reflected off of the ubiquitous shards of broken glass, making the mess seem more chaotic and jagged to Tom. He realized he was shaking before he managed to reach the front door.

Some part of Tom had hoped that whatever had happened had affected only his house. But as his stinging eyes adjusted to the light shining in through the doorway, he felt his chest seize up with despair.

The street outside was cracked in several places. Every house he could now see looked plainly as damaged as his own. Roof tiles had been ripped off, every window he could see was shattered, and many of the taller houses seemed to be leaning noticeably to his right. Water was gurgling up from a fire hydrant across the street. A few of the houses and many of the cars were smoking. He could see flames beginning to lick up from the side of one house.

He fell to his knees in the doorway, the pain of his burned knees striking the ground only a dull shock to him now. He slid over sideways, resting his head against the doorframe, staring unacceptingly at the destruction all around him.

The car in the driveway across the street was smoking. Tom almost wanted to turn back into his house. He didn't want to see any more. He didn't want to find out that his neighbors were dead.

But he lifted himself up again, ignoring the continual pain all over his body. He began to stump forward, his knees aching with every step. As he made his way past the garage, he saw that a large portion of the horizon to the south was a towering pillar of black smoke. He choked on an emerging sob. It seemed clear to him now what had happened: Austin had been struck with a nuclear bomb.

The cloud of smoke towered indefinitely away into the sky, rising from some place far over the horizon. And then Tom saw Brent's car.

His brother and sister's ride was lying on its side in the middle of the street just before the stop sign at the corner. He could see from where he stood that its windows were all broken. Smoke rose from its front.

He stumbled toward it, crying more fully now. He wanted desperately to get to that car, to find his brother and sister alive, to take care of them, to make sure they were okay. But he was terrified that they would not be. Even as he jerkily approached the dented rear of the car, he realized that no one was moving inside.

Tom's right leg suddenly seized up with the pain of walking so quickly, and he fell to his face again. Forcing himself back up, he shouted, "Terry! Andrew!"

No sound more than a dull hissing came from the battered car. Tom continued staggering toward it, but his hope was already gone.

"Terry! Andrew!" he shouted again.

He fell to his hands and knees. The pain of walking was unbearable. His eyes were starting to sting more severely again. He pulled himself forward for a couple meters more, then looked up toward the car. He could now see two unrecognizably burnt and battered forms slumped in the back seat of the car through the broken rear window.

"NO!" he screamed.

He crawled forward more quickly, his right palm piercing him with pain every time it touched the cracked pavement. Upon reaching the car, he reached his left hand in through the shattered window and began violently prodding the burnt, bloodied bodies.

"Terry!" he shrieked madly. "Terry! Andrew! It's okay! Wake up! It's okay!" He began screaming more and more loudly, as if his unrecognizable brother and sister would revive if he screamed louder. "Wake up! It's Tom! Wake up!"

Tom lost track of how long he remained there, shaking the lifeless bodies and shouting their names. But all of a sudden, a very firm hand came from behind him and pulled him back.

Tom shouted out in surprise, then saw a tall man crouching in front of him. He swung his right arm wildly at the man, who calmly ducked out of the way and pulled Tom down into a sitting position on the broken street.

"Tom," the man said familiarly, "Leave Terry and Andrew alone."

"Who are you?" Tom demanded fiercely.

"I am a friend."

"How do you know us?" Tom shouted, not caring to hear the man. "*Did you do this?*"

"No." The man's voice shook with a strange passion. "I can help you, Tom, and Andrew and Terry, too."

Then the man reached forward again toward Tom. Tom shouted and kicked out at him, but the man's hand managed to touch Tom's head.

The first thing that struck Tom as strange then was the lack of the intense pain he had come to expect as a result of moving his leg like that. He felt his foot connect with the man's left side, but the man didn't seem to notice it.

And then he realized that the pain in his skin was gone. His joints didn't burn anymore. And his head was clear, and his eyes were clear and painless, too.

The man stood and moved to the roof of the sideways car. Tom didn't see if the man touched the car or not, but the next thing he knew, the roof was

1: Horrors and Hopes

disconnected from the rest of the car, and the man was setting it gently down onto the ground. Tom watched dumbly as the strange man stepped onto the roof of the car, reached in, and then lifted a blinking and perfectly whole Terry Pratt out of the car.

"Terry!" Tom screamed in elated disbelief. He leaped to his feet with agility that would have surprised him had he not been overcome with the sight of his once mangled sister now standing in perfect health. He leapt forward and scooped Terry up in his arms, now truly sobbing.

"You're okay! You're okay! You're okay!" Tom babbled, squeezing a totally disoriented Terry in what was becoming a painfully tight grip.

She managed to extricate herself enough to say, "What's going on?" before Tom shrieked again with delight as he saw the man lift an unscathed Andrew out of the car.

Tom dodged around Terry to go embrace Andrew, but then stopped dead, looking with fearful suspicion at the man who was now bending into the front seats of the car.

"Who are you?" he asked the man again.

The man stood and surveyed Tom, but before he could answer, Brent Young, whom he had just lifted from the car, began shouting.

"What ha—Stacey!"

Brent lunged down toward his girlfriend's body, but the man caught him with a surprisingly firm arm across his chest, holding him back.

"Brent," the man said, "Wait. Watch."

Brent struggled against the man's unmoving arm as the man reached down and touched Stacey's head.

The blood and burns faded off of Stacey Brown instantaneously. She looked up, confused and obviously alarmed to find herself in the crumpled wreckage of the car and to see Brent screaming hysterically above her.

The man released Brent, who swooped down on Stacey, kissing her and asking her if she was alright.

"What happened?" Stacey asked, more worried now, but glad to have survived their apparent crash.

Brent bent down to help Stacey out of the car, but found that her legs were pinned down.

"It's okay," the man said from behind him. And just then, Brent saw the twisted metal retreat away from Stacey's legs, as if of its own accord.

Brent jumped in surprise, and Stacey looked to where he was staring just in time to see the bleeding cuts in her legs close up, as did the tears in her jeans.

Brent let go of Stacey and stepped back, looking uncertainly at her.

"Don't worry," the man smiled, placing a hand on Brent's shoulder.

Brent backed away from the man as well. The man reached toward Stacey, and she floated out of the car without him touching her.

"Don't worry," the man said again as Stacey screamed in surprise before touching down on the cracked pavement. She ran immediately to Brent, looking nervously at this strange man.

"There is a lot to explain," the man said quietly.

"Yeah," Tom said impatiently. *"Who are you?"*

"Tom! Andrew! Terry!"

The three Pratts spun around to see Lewis sprinting toward them. No longer bloodied, no longer injured at all now, they could see that he was crying with apparent joy to see them all safe and alive.

"Dad!" Tom shouted euphorically, running toward his father. "You're okay too!"

Lewis embraced Tom, then let go of him to see if Andrew and Terry were alright.

The two younger children had only then become aware of the desolation surrounding them. Both of them stood rooted in horror as Lewis embraced them, weeping.

"What's happened to our house?" Terry gasped as Lewis embraced her.

"What happened to everything?" Andrew said.

Lewis looked past them to where the man was talking to Brent and Stacey. A young woman was now standing between them and the man, as if she had appeared out of thin air.

"I'll take you to your families," the man was saying to Brent and Stacey. Then, without another word, the man scooped Brent off his feet with one arm and Stacey with the other, and glided gracefully into the air.

"What the—" Andrew shouted as Terry screamed. They watched as the man picked up speed and disappeared with a screaming Brent and Stacey over the rooftops.

"It's alright," the woman in front of them said, grinning slightly. "I'll explain everything."

"Who the hell are you people?" Lewis said to her.

"I am here to help," she said. "That's all." Like the man, she looked very young. She was dressed very plainly, in what looked to the Pratts like some sort of robe. But her grey, shimmering clothing had no discernible edge; it just seemed to fade right into the air a few inches from her body.

"Why don't we go inside?" she said, addressing Lewis.

Lewis put his arms around Andrew and Terry. "I am not letting you

1: Horrors and Hopes

inside my house," he said. "Not until you explain to me what is going on here."

The woman sighed and sat herself comfortably on the pavement. Lewis remained standing, as did his children around him.

"I think you'll want to be sitting down for what I have to say to you," the woman said.

Finding that easy to believe, Lewis guardedly sat down on the curb, keeping what he thought was a safe distance between this person and his family.

"Call me Liz," the woman said as the Pratt children sat down on the curb as well.

"Liz," Lewis said untrustingly.

Liz looked at Lewis as if considering him. Then she said, "We, that man and I, represent a group of people called Nüährnär."

"Did you do all this?" Lewis demanded. "Who are you people?"

Liz's voice was soft but forbiddingly firm as she said, "We did not! I didn't, neither did any of my friends in Nüährnär! This was a despicable, cowardly, evil thing that Sĕrĕhahn did to your world!"

"Sarah who?" Lewis said.

Liz's abrupt anger softened as quickly as it came, and an understanding smile smoothed her already smooth, young face. "All this, that's happened to your world, this was all the result of an unprovoked attack instigated by a man who calls himself Sĕrĕhahn."

She sighed again, then looked seriously at them all. "We, Nüährnär, we're not from Earth," she said simply.

Lewis began to laugh dismissively and derisively at such an idea, but something about Liz's easy expression made the laughter swiftly die in his throat.

"You don't believe me?" Liz asked conversationally, looking at them all. "I can change that. Look down."

They had been sitting right on the curb when she said that, but then, as soon as they did glance at the ground, they saw that it was more than a hundred meters below them. The cold November wind whistled around them as they found themselves suspended high above their house in thin air.

All four of them screamed, flailing around in the air. Liz, sitting comfortably cross-legged in the air in front of them, laughed at them all in what was clearly a good-natured way. Then Lewis felt the surge of adrenaline disappear that had filled him at the sight of the ground so far below, and he felt his shaking self suddenly calmed somehow.

Liz smiled amiably and extended a hand to Lewis, uncrossing her legs to float more relaxed in the air.

"Lewis," she said, her unraised voice somehow perfectly audible over the whistling wind, "It's alright."

Lewis swung his arm desperately forward to take Liz's outstretched hand, and stretched his other arm out for his children. Andrew and Terry grabbed onto it, but Tom, being closer to Liz, reached out for her other arm. Liz took Tom's flailing hand as well, and then the Pratts found themselves plummeting with terrifying speed back to the ground.

They stopped just as their dangling feet touched the burnt grass in front of their house, then collapsed to the ground as Liz let go of Lewis and Tom. The trip downward took only a fraction of a second. Tom felt like he should want to throw up, but, even after such a drop, his body didn't seem to have any need to.

The Pratts then all felt themselves lifted into sitting positions there on the grass by some invisible, but rather pleasant, force. Liz had sat down cross-legged again on the ground.

"Sorry to scare you," she said, understanding laughter still twitching at the corners of her mouth. "But do you believe me now, Lewis?"

Lewis rose to his feet. "Get away from my family."

The laughter faded from Liz's face, but her tone was still comfortable as she said, "I'll get away, and leave you forever, if that's what you want. But only if it's still what you want after hearing what I need to explain to you."

Lewis hesitated. Liz's flying prank had begun to convince him. At least he was certain now that Liz was no regular person. But it had also frightened him. He did not want this person to hurt his family.

Suddenly, Liz was standing. "Lewis Richard Pratt," she said levelly, "Neither I nor any of my friends of Nŭährnär had anything to do with Sěrěhahn's attack on your world." She sounded almost offended then; her voice shook with fury as she said Sěrěhahn's name. "I don't want to hurt you. I won't hurt you! You cannot hurt me, and I'm not going to hurt you. But Sěrěhahn *will hurt us all!*"

Lewis had no idea who this Sěrěhahn person could be, but still he felt some unspecified dread creeping up his spine as Liz referred to him.

"If you don't want to be destroyed by Sěrěhahn," Liz continued, now speaking more quietly, "Then my people of Nŭährnär are the only ones who will protect you from him."

Lewis was surprised. He gazed speechlessly at Liz for a moment. He looked down at his children, still seated on the grass, only Tom's face not white with fear now, and, the thought of protecting them overpowering his apprehension about Liz, he nodded, not looking at her.

"Fine," he said, sitting back down. "Tell us what you have to say."

Chapter 2

Vanguard

...as ambassador of Reality. Sometimes, many small things lead to wondrous ones. But I wouldn't have thought at the time that the destruction of everything that I knew was a small thing!

Such disasters do help to awaken people to the things that really matter. The things that eradicate the petty distractions that stand in the way of lives remind us what life is for! That's the way it was with me. The destruction of everything that I thought I knew opened a window for me to learn everything that there really is to know! Disaster and horror drew me from the illusions of pretended, hollow "life" to what Life really has always been.

To Ä'ähänärdanär.

This was a tremendous, pivotal event in my life. Don't think that it wasn't. But it was also just the first, and one of the smallest, of the terrors and pains that I was about to endure. I had no idea who Sĕrĕhahn was back then. I had heard of Pp'm'tärnhär, though I didn't realize it, and I didn't take seriously what I had heard, anyhow. I knew nothing of...

...and Ämäthöär. Lhĕhrha's strain notwithstanding, few things reflect the epitome of evil, in its worst, most mixed, most potent manifestations, than they did. Evil, and destruction, and the terror of endless regression! Good is good, but so much of the good that they did served as mere host to their evil intentions!

But I ought to continue with the chronological version of the story, as well as I can give it here and now. This story! This microcosm of Ä'ähänärdanär! But that's what all stories are.

More than a billion N'nŭährnär were now reviving and orienting the fallen Nōhōnŭäär. The proportion of dead who turned out to be revivable was remarkable; nearly two-thirds.

My dear counter-Antär was...

An unseasonably warm breeze swept through the circle of kneeling Trotters outside their house as Scott Trotter finished his prayer with a quiet, "Amen."

"Amen," his present family agreed around him.

Scott put his arm around his wife beside him.

"I hope they're okay," Rene Trotter wept as she leaned into Scott's embrace.

2: Vanguard

"Of course they are," Scott said comfortingly. "How big can an earthquake be?"

"I bet Aaron's watching this on the news right now," their son Joseph said, reclining, still shaking, on the lawn.

"I bet," Scott smiled. "He's probably wondering if we're all okay."

The slouching house creaked and snapped behind him.

"Dad, I'm freezing!" Kathy said, clutching her nightclothes closer to her. "Can't I just run in and get my coat? It's dark still!"

"No," Rene said sharply. "No one is going close to the house, at least until help comes."

The house abruptly stopped creaking altogether. "Good morning," a pleasant voice said from the broken sidewalk.

The Trotters looked up to see a smiling young woman walking toward them.

"Good morning," Rene said, quickly looking over the girl to make sure she was unhurt. "Are you okay? Do you need help?"

The stranger's smile deepened. But as she sat down near them she said very capably, "At the moment, I'm here to help you."

"Who are you?" Kathy asked. She was staring at the woman's glowing white gown, if it was a gown, which cast shadows behind them all in the grey predawn.

Just as she was speaking, a man descended swiftly from the sky, carrying a shaken Aaron Trotter in one arm.

"Who—" John Trotter shouted.

"What—" Joseph said at the same moment.

"Aaron!" Rene exclaimed, leaping to her feet and running toward him. "What's going on? Who is this?"

"Aaron, let go," the man was saying, gently prying Aaron's clutching arms from around his neck.

Aaron seemed to become aware that he was standing on solid earth again, and leapt away from the man, tripping and falling to the grass.

Rene scooped him up in her arms. "Are you okay?" she asked tearfully. "Why...who are—" she began, looking up at the strange man. But he was nowhere to be seen.

"Rene," the young woman said, standing again slowly.

But Rene's attention was drawn quickly away by Kathy's squeal: "Sarah!" just as John shouted, "Whoa, look!"

Another woman touched down on the grass, carrying Sarah Trotter in her arms.

"Mom! Dad!" Sarah cried, running and embracing Scott without a second glance at her rescuer. "Here too?" she said, horrified, catching sight of her family's leaning house.

"I'm afraid so," Scott began, confused but happy to see all his five children safely there with him.

"Aaron!" Sarah said, springing away from Scott and running toward her mother and still shaking brother. "How—"

Then, seeming to get a hold of herself, Sarah turned back to the woman who had brought her to her family. But she too was gone.

"She's gone to help other people," the glowing white woman said as Sarah looked around.

"Gone?" Sarah said blankly.

"What are you people?" Aaron choked from where he still crouched on the ground.

"It's alright," the woman said to Sarah, correctly reading her expression. "She knows you're grateful. I'm certain she'll be getting thanked by a lot of other people today. And," she said, grinning first at Aaron then directing her words to Scott, "I obviously have a lot to explain to all of you."

"You most certainly do," Scott said, with almost a trace of laughter in his voice.

The woman sat down once more. "Come here," she said to them all. She leaned back casually on her hands.

The Trotters, led by Scott, obligingly moved into a tight clump in front of the woman.

"Alright," the woman said, looking at each of them and then back at Scott. "The first thing you have to know is that I and those others are not from this Earth.

"Don't worry," she said quickly to Scott and Rene's flummoxed expressions, "This will all make sense to you soon."

She paused, but none of the Trotters challenged her. Every one of them was staring wide-eyed and uncomprehendingly at her, but they were still listening. After what they had all just seen, most of them felt ready to hear almost anything from this strange, glowing girl.

"The earthquake you've all just been through—and yes, it was here, too," she said particularly to Aaron and Sarah, Aaron just now beginning to notice the contortions of the mountains around them and the ruin of his home neighborhood. "It affected everywhere on Earth. Sarah, you were just in Arizona?"

Sarah nodded, even more amazed now.

2: Vanguard

"Sarah was lucky to survive," the woman said complimentarily to Scott and Rene. "The land there was affected far worse than your mountains here have been."

"And fires," Sarah breathed. "And lava..."

The woman looked sadly at her. "Yes." She sighed, then said, "All these worldwide earthquakes were caused intentionally. Aaron," she said, looking at him, "You saw things much worse than earthquakes over in Florida, didn't you?"

Aaron looked fearfully at the woman. "How do you know that...you don't know me..."

"I know what happened to Florida," she said. "I saw it. And—"

"How?" Aaron demanded.

"I'll explain," the woman smiled. "But, for now, just know that my people stopped what was being done to Florida, and to everywhere here. This was not natural. This was done by people who wanted to destroy your world."

"I can't believe that," Rene said breathlessly.

"I know your names," the woman shrugged, "Because...well, we know about a lot of things about Earth. But I'll explain all that soon.

"But Aaron," she said kindly, "I saw what happened to Florida, because I helped stop the people who did it."

"I think it was an atom bomb," Aaron said darkly to his family. "Or some worse kind."

"It wasn't a bomb," the woman answered him, "But it was a much worse kind. Like a lot of atom bombs, being set off from the sky to the ground."

"In Florida?" Rene gasped, becoming very white now.

"And in a lot of places," the woman said. "But it's over now. For now."

"For now?" John asked, going white too.

"We're here to protect you, in case you get attacked again."

"Attacked?" Scott said. "Who attacked us?"

The woman paused for a moment. "There really is so much to explain."

"But who," Joseph said. "And why?"

"And where are you all from?" Sarah asked.

"Bad people did it," the woman said, "From our old world."

"Why?" Joseph asked again.

"'Old world?'" Kathy repeated.

The woman smiled in an almost overwhelmed way at Kathy, then looked wordlessly at Joseph for a moment. "To be honest," she said then, "I don't know why they did. But my parents, and others of our leaders, knew the attack would be coming before it came. So they must know something about why you got attacked."

"Your leaders?" Scott said. "Are they here?"

"No," the woman said a little sorrowfully. "But," and she visibly brightened as she spoke, "I hope they will come here soon. You might get to see some of them."

Kathy crept closer to her mother. She wasn't sure if her family should be listening to this glowing person, and wasn't sure if she wanted to see still more people like her.

"But, if you're going to meet anybody," the woman was continuing, "I need to explain a whole lot more to you first."

Sarah noticed her father nod slightly, showing he was listening. She smiled unconsciously as she looked back toward the woman. Whoever this person was, whatever she was, Sarah wanted to hear whatever she had to give them.

...what a marvel she was even then!

That same general scene of introduction was happening all over the Earth, the noble vanguard of Nüährnär attending to every family or individual who would revive on Ōhōnüäär.

Some received them remarkably well. Like Scott and Rene Trotter. Some others took a great deal more convincing. Some, like dear Rod Hawke, made themselves pests to be reckoned with! But, sadly, many of those never were so wise as Rod eventually became. They left Nüährnär quickly, and the Ämäthōär made ghastly use of them.

Then there were Peter and Annie Garcia: heroes in beautiful archetype! And John and Kōrhas Fleming were, of course, intertwined in the Garcia legacy. John may have died thinking his efforts to save Nüährnär were a failure. He was no more of a failure than I was in that catastrophe. His efforts rescued and dignified so many who might, otherwise, have suffered the baseness of heart that is so much more incapacitating than mortal death! John, Peter, Rodney, all heroes to the uttermost extremity!

Rod's welcome to Nüährnär, as represented to him by Hōrdaädr, was characteristically far more violent than Peter and Annie's, much less to mention John's! Peter was suspicious, perhaps insensibly so. But when Rod...

"Where are they?" Peter Garcia muttered crossly, looking over his shoulder at the ruin around them.

"Who?" Annie choked between groans.

"Ambulances, Search and Rescue," Peter said, turning back to her. "Anyone."

"They're probably helping other people," Annie said, shifting her weight

2: Vanguard

in the rubble.

"Don't move!" Peter said, and he tightened a filthy rag that he had tied around Annie's left arm.

"Peter," Annie said, then winced. After a breath, she continued, "You need to take care of yourself."

"I'm fine," Peter curtly lied.

Annie Baker was lying in the rubble of what had been their apartment complex. Peter had tied tourniquets on her left arm and leg, and bore one himself on his right leg. The moans of suffering neighbors filled the smoky air on every side.

"Adam! No! Adam!" a voice shrieked from beyond one of the heaps of twisted wreckage.

"Adam?" Annie said.

"Don't talk," Peter urged her quietly, dabbing her severe burns with a wet cloth. Water was everywhere, spewing from a ruptured pipe nearby.

"Not Adam Morris?" Annie said. "That's Katie Morris screaming!"

"Come back!" Katie's voice wailed in their ears over the groans of everyone around them. "Don't leave me here! Adam! Come back!"

Peter was becoming all too used to those kinds of cries now.

"He's..." Annie began, tears emerging and falling down her blistered cheeks.

We'll all be just like him, Peter thought hopelessly to himself, *If real help doesn't get here soon.* He wrung the wet cloth out into the broken metal and plaster underneath them.

"Here," he said, gently lifting Annie's head and placing the wrung-out rag underneath it. "I'm going to the...to where the office was. There may be something better than dirty towels in there."

"Peter," Annie said sharply. She forced herself to sit up, awkwardly raising herself with her unbroken right arm. "You can't go off digging through...through all this. You're bleeding! You take care of yourself first!"

Peter didn't respond, but just eased Annie back down onto her back in the wreckage of their shattered home. He wiped away blood that was falling down the side of her face.

Annie pushed his hand away, then snatched the cloth out of it.

"Hey—" Peter said, but Annie lifted his untucked shirt and pressed the cloth against his skin. Peter winced, but Annie pressed the cloth more firmly against him.

"Annie, I will be alright," Peter said, gasping from the sudden renewed pain.

"No, you won't," Annie said firmly. "I will be alright now; you need to take care of yourself!" Peter's entire body was red, his freshly ironed clothes now torn and splotched with blood and grime. Painful blisters covered the right side of his face and his right hand.

Annie's night clothes were just as filthy as Peter's clothes, though less bloody, as Peter had tended to her wounds promptly after the blast. Her blistered left side was less burnt than was Peter's right side, though both looked the worse in the eyes of the other.

"I'll be back," Peter grunted, standing as pain pierced his right leg.

Annie's hand with the towel slid out from underneath his shirt, and Annie yelped as she saw how quickly the towel had become soaked with blood.

"What are you doing?" she demanded, then winced again and fell back onto the rubble.

"Just...just stay here," Peter said, ignoring the burning pain in every joint as he turned toward the center of the ruins.

The apartment office had been a good hundred feet from where Peter and Annie's apartment had been. Less than half an hour ago, Peter thought shakily, he would have just walked down the stairs and over to the office within a matter of seconds. Now he faced a long and painful distance over a mire of jagged wreckage and between the bodies of slain and suffering neighbors and friends.

But Peter saw other people standing amidst his apartment's desolation. They did not look injured. Peter wondered for a moment if they were some sort of rescue team. But their dress was unlike anything he had ever seen. They were scattered throughout the destruction, apparently talking to the suffering survivors. But they weren't dressed like any rescue personnel of which Peter was familiar: their clothes were long, flowing, and shimmery, almost luminescent.

"Peter," a man's voice said from behind him.

Painfully he turned on the spot, to see one of the oddly cloaked people standing right there near him and Annie. A similarly dressed woman was kneeling beside Annie behind the man.

"Who are you?" Peter demanded impulsively. "Are you medically certified?"

"Yeah," the man smiled.

The man was dressed in what looked like an amazingly thin, light robe, but Peter could not tell where the man's skin ended and the robe began. Nor could he even tell where the robe ended and the air began; the man's clothes just seemed to shimmer like a defined cloud of flowing blues and whites.

2: Vanguard

Then, as he watched, Peter realized that the blues and whites of the man's robe were constantly drifting and changing through each other. Were these members of some kind of charity, Peter wondered? Where were their medical kits?

Then he saw that Annie was lifting herself up from the pile of debris. "Annie!" he shouted, alarmed. "What are you doing?"

But Annie didn't seem to be in any pain at all as she stood.

Then Peter felt the man beside him lightly touch his arm. Peter jumped despite himself, and fell over backward in the sharp rubble. He felt his hands get cut on shards of bricks below him, but then the pain instantaneously vanished. And then Peter realized that he was no longer in any pain at all.

He looked at his hands. There was no trace of any cut or scratch on either of them. Then he registered that his burns were gone; the blisters on his right hand were gone, and the skin of both hands was as healthy and tan as it had been before. It was even healthier, cleaner somehow.

He looked up in wonder at the man in front of him, hardly even noticing as the bandage on his leg unraveled itself and fell limply to join the refuse around him. Annie was standing all the way up now behind the man, her tourniquets and wounds and burns gone too.

Peter scrambled to his feet. "Who are you?" he said again. He stumbled through the wreckage toward Annie, who was looking amazedly at her woundless left arm.

"That will take me some time to explain, Peter," the man said casually.

"Who are you with?" Peter said, staring at the robed man and woman. "How do you know my name? Why are you here?"

"Sit down," the man invited. "I'll tell you everything."

The pillar of smoke towering out of the Atlantic over the horizon had already conjured into Peter's mind fears of international war. Were these members of some radical terrorist group? Had Washington been bombed as well? Peter glanced quickly to the southwest, but the dusty sky there was pillar-free.

"What is going on?" Peter demanded, turning to the strangely dressed people. "Was it a meteor?"

"I'll take you home, Annie," the woman said kindly.

Annie backed away from the woman, looking fearfully at her.

"This is her home!" Peter said with even more suspicion, and he put his arm around Annie. "And her parents live a thousand miles away; what are you trying to pull here?" He was becoming increasingly afraid of these people.

The man chuckled in what struck Peter as an out of place, but no less comforting, way. "A thousand miles isn't far, Peter, as I want to demonstrate. But neither of you have to go anywhere if you don't want to." He turned to the woman. "I'll help these two."

"Okay," the woman said conversationally. Her tone too seemed to Peter not to fit in the ruins of such a disaster. "Good-bye," she waved to Peter and Annie with unfitting familiarity. "I hope to see you again soon."

Peter was sure he caught a mischievous smile glint across the woman's face, just as she launched herself straight into the air. She accelerated in the blink of an eye and vanished in a swirl of dust.

Annie screamed beside Peter, who stumbled backward in shock. He noticed a particularly sharp shred of twisted metal out of the corner of his eye. Stooping quickly down, he grabbed it up and pointed it threateningly at the man standing in front of them.

"Keep away!" he shouted as he put his arm around Annie again. "Whoever you are."

"Peter Garcia," the man said patiently, appearing totally unperturbed. "If you want to know what's going on, then sit down and put that ridiculous thing down. I'm going to tell you everything."

Peter stepped forward, brandishing the strip of metal more threateningly. "I think I can guess enough," he retorted. "Get away from us!" He glanced around, afraid another terrorist might attack them from behind.

The man calmly put up his right hand, and, as he did, the piece of metal was yanked from Peter's hand. It soared slowly up into the air and came back down to land in the man's outstretched left hand. Then Peter felt his muscles seize up, and realized he was sitting down despite himself. Annie sat down beside him, terror on her face.

The man sat down in front of them, looking at Peter with an entertained, chastening expression. "I hope you'll listen," he said, holding the piece of metal in front of him, "Because what's just happened here," and the piece of metal began to droop in his hand, "Concerns both of you." The metal turned clear like glass, then fell from the man's hand, splashing into his lap, no more now than so many droplets of water.

"What I have to say is extremely important to you both."

Peter tried to open his mouth to resist, but found that it would not respond.

"Your whole world has just been attacked. This disaster was not caused by me, or my companions, or by anyone from your world. People acting under the direction of a man whom we call Anhar tried to destroy Earth. My countrymen and I thwarted them, but Anhar will try again. We, obviously, are

2: Vanguard

not from your world, and neither is Anhar. He will try again. I and my countrymen are here to protect Earth from him."

Peter still found himself unable to speak, yet he realized that sneering in contempt at such a yarn was unhindered.

The man, still untroubled, looked down at the rubble in front of him. Peter instinctively looked down too. Tiny drops of water were racing up into the air from between broken bits of brick and plaster and wood, collecting in a quivering glob held somehow between two of the man's fingers. Peter watched astonishedly as more and more drops leapt from the rubble to attach themselves to the lengthening strip of water in midair, held up by only the man's fingers. Then before he knew it, the water had gone opaque, and the man was again holding the same twisted strip of metal that Peter had been pointing at him seconds ago, just as twisted and sharp and dirty as it had been before.

Peter was staring unblinkingly at the man, when the man spoke, snapping Peter out of his dumbfounded gaze.

"Peter," he said, "You're not too bright are you? You refuse to believe that I and my companions aren't from Earth, in the face of having been wholly healed, of having seen Mänrŭ fly, and still in the face of what you've seen I've been able to do with your powerful weapon."

Peter had been snarling venomously at the man for some seconds before he recognized that his mouth was his own again: "Bright! You stupid, brash idiot! Do you have any idea what my IQ is? Here you are, destroying things and blowing up towns, and you're here calling me stupid? I don't care what gadgets you people have, it doesn't give you the right to kill people, and to come here and keep Annie and me from talking, and I see no proof, I don't see any reason why I should think that that means that you're some kind of extraterrestrial! You could be anyone! *You're* stupid if you think cheap tricks will fool—"

But the man's hearty laughter overrode Peter's furious outburst. "You see?" he was saying, laughing as if at a shared jest, *"You don't know what's going on.* I could be anybody. Why rule out the truth, if you don't know what it is yet? But you do know that I'm not what you're used to seeing as ordinary. And," he said, adopting something of a mock-censuring tone, "Don't you think you should be a lot more grateful to someone who has saved both your lives?

"I cannot expect either of you to believe anything yet. But, after what you've both just been through, I'd expect that you'd be prepared for what's unexpected!" The man paused, then said, almost as if to himself, "You're going to have to be." He sighed thoughtfully. Then he focused back on Peter

Light and Glory

and Annie, and said, "I'm going to give you both more proof than even you could ask for, Peter, of everything I'm going to tell you, and of what I've told you. But before I can, before I can *show* you what I need to, you both are going to have to take one thing on trust. You're going to have to let me—"

"I don't trust you," Peter interrupted. He would not have been still listening to the man if he had had any control of his legs.

The man smiled understandingly. "I am sorry that we healed you without forewarning you," he said. "I need to do something more for you, however."

Peter felt his muscles return to his control. He stood, taking Annie's hand. He nodded curtly to the man, then said, "We're going."

The man floated lightly into the air, crossing his legs under him. "Where?" he asked.

Peter didn't answer. He put his arm around Annie and turned away from the man.

As soon as they turned, the man was floating in the air right in front of them.

"What are you?" Peter cried, his voice shaking suddenly.

"Let me tell you all about that," the man begged sincerely. "Please, just sit down. Hear me out."

"Peter," Annie said fearfully, but then trailed away.

Peter looked at her. She was white and clearly terrified. Looking up hatefully at the man blocking them, he said, "Do we have any choice?"

"Here's your choice:" the man said, "Don't talk to me, and remain in the dark while everyone else helps one another against Anhar's next attacks, or just hear me out, and thereby know enough to help everyone. We need to work together here!"

Peter snorted. "You'll really just let us leave?" he said doubtfully. "What do people as gifted as you need my help for, anyway?"

"Peter," Annie said, staring at the man with apprehension. "Let's just listen. We can at least listen."

"Please, Peter, Annie," the man said, still floating firmly in midair.

Peter looked untrustingly into the man's light blue eyes, then sat down again in the ruins. "Alright then," he said. "Talk. We're listening."

"Are you?" the man asked dubiously. But then he rose a couple of feet and soared gracefully around Peter and Annie, first on his front, then on his back. He smiled at them both, and asked, "How would you like to be able to do this?"

Peter stared stonily at the man as he came to hover in front of them. The man stared straight back at him. Finally, Peter said, "Sure. Of course I would.

2: Vanguard

Annie?"

"Who wouldn't?" Annie said timidly.

The man smiled a small smile. "I can give you what I have, what lets me do this."

"What?" Peter queried.

"Your clothes," the man said. "You're dressed for work and you for bed, but you're both wearing clothes."

Peter stared uncomprehendingly at him.

"Manifestly, your clothes aren't part of you, but they help you. They cover you, keep you warm, make you look sharp," he said, nodding at Peter. "When they're not torn, that is," he smiled friendlily. Peter's mouth did not so much as twitch back.

"They give you more than you are without them. They're yours. They add to what you are yourselves, especially for warmth.

"Now, I'm not any different from either of you, physically," the man began, but then Peter cut in.

"Hold it!" he said, pointing at the man. A triumphant grin creased his face. "I thought you said you weren't from Earth!"

"I did," the man began, raising his hand placatingly.

But Peter overrode him. "An extraterrestrial who just happens to be no different from ordinary people?" he sneered. "Who are you? What do you want?"

"Peter, I do not understand that," the man said forcefully. "How it is that you are no different from us. But we are no different biologically from one another. I still have plenty of questions about that. But if you want to know more about what is going on, why we're the same, then hear me out. Once you understand what I am trying to tell you, then you will get to talk to people who are a lot more knowledgeable about all this than I am."

"Who?" Peter asked.

"My leaders," the man replied simply. "The Ōmäthäär."

"The who?" Peter said.

The man laughed a little, saying, "Listen to what I'm telling you now, and then you'll be able to understand everything.

"But clothing. It can be a good addition to us that lets us do things that we can't do without it. That's what I've got. I have clothing inside my body as well as out, and that lets me fly, and do all sorts of things."

"*Inside* your body?" Annie said apprehensively.

"Inside, through, interwoven with it, everywhere," the man said comfortably. "You've both been immunized against many diseases. It's somewhat like that. Nothing of my body has been harmed, or changed, or taken away. But there are other things within it that help it function better.

"I never need to eat, because I have better stores of energy within me that my body gets to use. Of course I love to eat! But I never *need* to. I never need to sleep. I cannot get naturally ill or aged. I am not anything near as frail as I would be without what I have within me. And I can fly. Much faster than you would believe," he smiled. "And, I can do all sorts of things..."

The next thing Peter knew, the man had glided straight toward him, then passed, like a ghost, straight through Peter's middle and out his other side.

Both Peter and Annie shouted with surprise, but the man started laughing again.

"What I want now is to give you both the same 'clothes' that I have, so you both will be able to participate in all that we all must do to thwart Anhar."

Peter shook himself. "Thanks," he said, "But we said that we'd *listen*. Are you finished?"

The man looked wordlessly at Peter. Then, before Peter could register that anything had happened, the man had leaned forward and taken Peter's hand in his.

"Wha—!" Peter shouted, outraged, trying to wrench his hand away. But it was like trying to pull it out of a steel vice.

But then the man released him.

"Get away from—" Peter began, but then stopped dead.

He suddenly realized that he knew the man's name: Mäōhä. And he understood, as if it were English, that it meant, "One Who Lives for Truth."

As he looked around, he realized that he automatically knew the names of every stranger around him: Ōhärthär, "Perceptive;" Räszad, "Sorrower;" Äpäōthärkahn, "Rock Heart;" Ŭdtas, "Icy;" Tärnär, "Victory"...

And he knew the full names of every neighbor there in the wreckage. He could see straight through the wreckage as if it were transparent. He could see through his neighbors.

He could see into himself.

And he could see all this, he realized within himself, he could see it all without having turned his head or even so much as moved his eyes. It was as if he suddenly possessed some kind of omnipresent sight, letting him see every side, and inside, of everything around him.

But he could not see through Mäōhä, nor through any of the strangers, whom he termed "N'nŭährnär" without thinking why he did. And his skin was opaque, he realized, though his clothes surely were not anymore. But nonetheless he was *aware* of everything going on within his body.

2: Vanguard

He knew that a great system of infinitesimal weaves had sprouted on top of and underneath and all through his skin. He knew it as if he were seeing it through his impenetrable skin. Everything inside of him, he knew suddenly, had been changed.

Not changed, he understood, but added on to. Like clothes, he realized despite himself.

All this he realized within the tiniest fraction of a second. He looked at Mäöhä without moving at all. Then, without pausing to consider how, he unleashed a burst of raw momentum furiously at him.

All Annie saw was the man release Peter, then yelp as if in sudden pain, jolting violently in the air, which snapped loudly. A burst of wind instantly whipped her side, knocking her roughly to the ground.

Peter reached out to lift Annie with something other than his arms. It was gravity, he understood, or something like it. Inertia. And as Annie was righted by his invisible force, he realized that the energy, whatever it was, was being generated by every part of the adamantine weave running through him. Through his skin, but also through his bones, his capillaries, his brain, through every organ, through everything.

His brain, he saw, or all but saw, was fortified within a shell of greater density and strength than the weaves of the rest of his body, running through and around the bone of his skull. But his brain itself was totally interwoven with miniscule bridges and connections, the nerves coated with entire complexes of microscopic, even subatomic, subphotonic, mechanisms that he knew made his thoughts and his reflexes unfathomably fast. At least, he would have thought it all unfathomable before.

The mechanisms within his brain were moving more quickly than light, he realized utterly disbelievingly. Peter recognized that his long-believed Planck Distance clearly had nothing on the tininess of the myriads of objects now racing through every part of him.

And a great mesh of energy, or inertia, or momentum, Peter realized, was now coursing through every part of him. He knew that that made him practically indestructible, and also that he could send it out in order to move anything, or manipulate it in order to move himself.

He recognized then that Mäöhä had started laughing. The last second had felt like an hour to Peter's quickened thoughts.

"Well," Mäöhä was laughing jubilantly, "You're a regular N'närdamähr now, Peter!"

Annie was looking from the man to Peter, wondering what was going on.

Närdamähr, Peter knew instantly. That was Mäöhä's culture. So a

Light and Glory

N'närdamähr was someone from Närdamähr.

"How dare you!" Peter snarled, feeling more and more violated the more he comprehended how much Mäōhä had done to him. "You had no right to—"

"Peter," Mäōhä said lightly, "I am sorry that I helped you again without forewarning you. But don't you see how much there was for me to tell you? And don't you believe me now?"

Peter didn't want to believe this person, this thing. Yet he couldn't deny that he did know now so many things, as inherently as he knew his name or how to speak English. He knew that Mäōhä's people really had come to help them, that they really were not from Earth. He knew everything about their culture, their world of Nrathĕrmĕ, their history, everything. He had to believe Mäōhä, and his "countrymen" of Nŭährnär. He did not want to believe, but now he found himself feeling that he had no choice.

...and by then they were all just trying to calm him down! And then Rod said, "Easy on, mates! Let's not get argy bargy! If youse'll get to the duck's guts, she'll be apples; I'll be all ears flapping!"

And they believed him! Frail old Rod hoodwinked them! So then Ärōärōbät released him.

And as soon as he had control of his limbs again, Rod dove to the ground, threw himself forward, and then launched himself off the cliff!

He told me that he knew what he was doing. He said there was a very inconspicuous ledge a few meters down, with a small cleft in which he had hid countless times.

But Hōrdaädr saved him the trouble. He caught him in midair, then soared out to talk with him there, floating hundreds of meters from the valley below. Rod said that that was when he recognized himself temporarily beaten. Temporarily.

And others reacted still differently. Suliaman and Elaben Naidu at first...

...needless to say, Lydia too reacted far more cognizantly than I and my family did!

Consider my father's reactions to Brä'äōdädankat. He would not accept the simple truth until it was staring him in the face! When people let petty distractions alienate them from the juice of life, it becomes all too easy for simple realities to seem fantastic to them, and for untenable philosophies, usually fearful ones, to seem bluntly undeniable. But my dad caught on quickly enough, once he let himself wonder if the truth could be true. It's unsettling how much fear can distort any evidence. It's all too easy to believe something when I'm afraid of it being true. But understanding flushes fear away.

How fearful we all were back then! Brä'äōdädankat never knew, I think, how great *a service she did to my family.* She led me to Ōmäthäär-hood and Ä'ähänärdanär! And, ultimately, to…

Chapter 3

Nrathĕrmĕ and Nŭährnär

Liz grinned at the Pratts seated in front of her. Lewis was examining the plate of food that Liz had just conjured for him, a further demonstration of the possibilities she was trying to impress them with.

"Is it...real?" Lewis asked, poking at the edge of the plate, which was sitting securely in midair in front of him.

"Taste it!" Liz invited enthusiastically.

Lewis eyed her with distrust.

Beside him, Tom picked up an elegant silver fork from where it sat in the air beside his own plate. Taking up the knife as well, he tentatively began to cut into the steaming filet mignon that Liz had made for him. Andrew, on Lewis's other side, had been given a pizza covered with pepperoni and bacon and sausage and any other meat that Liz suspected he would like. And Terry was gazing suspiciously but still hopefully at a tall chocolate parfait dangling in the air over her lap.

Lewis picked his plate up out of the air. Liz had given him rib-eye steak with potatoes and gravy, all the plates of deliciously smelling food having been generated out of thin air before the Pratts' eyes. Andrew passed his hand under his plate once, and then again. He bent to take a better look underneath it, checking to see if it really was levitating without any evident support. Terry had now taken her parfait in her hand. Glancing uncertainly at Liz, she placed the parfait back in the air, but in a different spot. It remained exactly where she left it.

Tom cut a piece from his filet mignon. It was a perfect red on the inside, not any redder than he would have wanted it to be, and it was surprisingly tender and easy to cut. He examined the piece of meat for a second, then put it in his mouth. The sudden flavor was overwhelmingly wonderful. None overpowering any of the others, the tastes of the beef and the bacon and the fantastic blend of spices intermingled in his mouth. It was tender, yet firm, more than any meat he had ever eaten. For a moment he was unaware of anything other than the pleasure of the incredible taste of it all.

"Tom!" Lewis exclaimed, noticing his son chewing, "Don't eat that!"

"Lewis," Liz said in a definitely friendly way, but with a hint of waning patience, "Do you really think that I couldn't have killed all of you already if that was what I wanted?"

3: Nrathĕrmĕ and Nŭährnär

Lewis instantly felt his muscles leave his control. He launched himself backward in a spectacular backflip right out of his sitting position, spun a somersault in the air, and landed gracefully on his feet two meters behind where he had been sitting. But then, eyes wide with shock, he hurled himself forward again, vaulted over on his hands, and landed, sitting again, exactly where he had begun. His hands shot down to brace his landing, stopping his seat just as it brushed the burnt tips of the front lawn. Then his miraculously strengthened arms lowered him softly to the ground.

Lewis's heart was beating madly. He was not as afraid this time as he was when Liz had lifted them all into the air above the house, but he was still surprised.

Tom's mouth was sagging open in wonder, a bit of mauled beef still in his mouth. Then both Andrew and Terry began laughing uncontrollably. Andrew doubled over howling, his pizza retreating out of his way, while Terry started wiping mirthful tears from her eyes as she looked from Lewis to Liz.

Liz giggled a little too, but then said, "Quite obviously, I could do whatever I wanted to do to you. So don't bother with this skepticism."

"What do you want, then?" Tom asked sincerely.

Lewis looked sharply at her, more of a challenge in his eye.

"I've come to explain to you what is going on here," she said obviously. "And, I think, the leaders of Nŭährnär want your help."

"*Our* help?" Lewis asked.

"Everyone's help from Earth," Liz said. "I think. At any rate, I am here to explain to you what is happening. I think that we'll all need each other's help. So I need you to trust us all."

"Tell us what's going on, then," Lewis commanded.

"I could spend days on end trying to explain everything to you!" Liz said. "And, even then, you probably wouldn't understand so much of it!" She smiled a little. "You'd probably understand me less, and trust me less, the more I tried to explain to you!"

"But—" Lewis began, confused.

"I want to show you everything rather than waste time trying to tell it to you. Give me your hand," she said to Lewis.

Lewis hesitated. Her point with the backflip had been well taken, even if it had been infuriating. And she did look trustworthy, really. He took Liz's decisively extended hand.

Liz released his hand almost as soon as she touched it. Then she sat back, a harmless look of satisfaction on her face. Before Lewis could be very confused, though he was getting more and more used to this person being confusing, Liz said, "Now, Lewis, you know that my usual name obviously is not Liz."

As soon as she said that, Lewis realized that, somehow, he knew Liz's real name. "Brä'äōdädankat," Lewis said, the six-syllable name rolling off his tongue as easily as if it were "Liz."

His children stared at him. "How did I know that?" Lewis blurted.

"I told you it," Liz said, "When I touched your hand."

"'Thunder Woman?'" Lewis translated the name.

Liz laughed hard. "Something like that. 'Feminine Thunder' is probably closer. That one touch was enough to tell your brain that one bit of information. That's now in your mind, permanently. I want to explain everything to you that way; it'll be a lot faster than talking. But you do need to trust me, Lewis, to let me."

Lewis answered by emphatically extending his hand to her.

Liz smiled with clear surprise. "It is more complicated than just that, though," she said as she pushed his hand gratefully back. "If I were to tell you everything now, it would be too much! Too much for you to digest yet. You could spend days thinking about it, and you still would have trouble making sense of everything. I can give you the information, but accessing it, really understanding it, your own brain has to make those connections. And it would take a long time for your brains to make sense of even a part of all this. I do not think that we have that kind of time.

"I want to tell you all a whole lot more than just my name! But, in order for you to be able to comprehend it all, I have to make some changes to your brains to prepare them to be able to handle it all."

Lewis planted his hand quickly beside him again. "You don't strike me as someone who asks permission of us," he said with half a smile. Then he asked, "What are you talking about, changing our brains?"

Liz smiled understandingly, then reached forward to touch Lewis's arm.

"Don't!" Lewis shouted, recoiling, afraid she was about to change him right there.

But Liz's fingers touched his hand as he jerked back. She sat back again. "Look at your arm."

Lewis realized that his right arm was glowing, and changing colors like a rainbow. Frightened, he lifted the sleeve of his bed shirt. The changing colors faded to his regular skin below the elbow.

"Dad..." Terry gasped as Lewis's arm faded from red to blue, and then to purple, and then on to yellow.

"What," Lewis began, stammering. Then he looked at Liz less fearfully, and asked, "What have you done to my arm?"

3: Nrathĕrmĕ and Nŭährnär

"You don't like it?" Liz asked casually. "Then make the colors stop."

Lewis looked questioningly at her, but she just smiled confidently back. He looked at his hand, then, as soon as he willed it, the colors stopped shifting, stopping at a light green. He paused, thinking. Then at his thought his arm turned red. He raised his hand in front of his face. Blue, yellow, grey, black, white, he cycled through colors more and more quickly.

"What have you done to it?" he asked again, not afraid anymore, but wonderstruck.

"I've gotten your attention," Liz smiled. "Does it hurt?"

"Hurt?" Lewis asked, looking past his silvery hand at her.

"No," Liz smiled, answering her own question. "Because I didn't hurt it."

Lewis's children gasped as their father's arm disappeared. Lewis laughed. "Unbelievable!" Then his arm reappeared out of his sleeve, glowing white. It changed back to its normal skin color. Lewis looked thoughtfully at it, then turned it silver like chrome again.

"I didn't change it either," Liz said, watching him happily. "I added to it, but I didn't change what was already there. When I touched your hand, I sent a lot of tiny things into you. They built a whole new structure in your arm that lets it change colors like this."

"I didn't feel anything," Lewis said, flexing his metallic fingers.

"I mean *tiny* things," Liz grinned. "You believe in atoms?"

"Should I?" Lewis asked, grinning a little too.

"Basically," Liz answered. "But there are things much smaller than atoms. Smaller than most Earth thinkers seem to think is possible."

"Like what?" Tom asked, interested.

"There is a lot to explain," Liz said, "If you'll let me," she added to Lewis.

Lewis looked at his metallic hand. He turned it normal again. Part of him wanted to ask Liz to undo whatever she had done.

"I can undo it completely, if you want me to," Liz said as if she had read his thoughts. "But I didn't hurt you. I added to your arm; I didn't hinder it or change what it already was.

Lewis looked at his hand, then chuckled as it and his arm faded into a vivid, glowing green.

Liz looked at him for a moment. Then, looking at all of them in turn, she raised her arms and said, "Shall we?"

Lewis's attention was pulled from his glowing hand as he realized that he was rising swiftly into the air. His children were rising with him, as was Liz in front of them.

They stopped several meters above the rooftops below. Tom noticed a few of their neighbors looking up at them, while others robed like Liz pointed at them from the ground far below.

Liz smiled at them all as they looked expectantly at her, hardly struggling at all this time. She left them suspended where they were while she soared up higher into the sky. The Pratts watched as Liz rocketed higher and higher, then fell backwards, slowly turning feet over head as she plummeted downward.

Tom saw her put her arms out as she gained speed, and she began spinning playfully, spiraling down toward them. She dove a little lower than where they were floating, then pulled up to arrive dramatically in front of them.

"I can give all of you what I have," she said, looking extremely comfortable as she relaxed in the windy air. "I can add to your bodies, so you'll be able to fly like me, and do everything that my people can do."

"Just let me fly like that!" Terry said.

"Me too," Tom said. "That looked amazing!"

Lewis smiled at his children. But then he looked at Liz. "I would love that, Liz. I'll let you give us all that. But I don't want you to alter our minds one bit."

Liz nodded, then swept suddenly toward Lewis. Lewis felt a thrill of fear, afraid Liz might change his brain anyway and horrified of what that could mean. But he didn't feel like his mind changed as Liz clasped his hand.

She let go, then glided over to Tom to take his hand as well. Acting on terror, Lewis struggled toward her, not wanting her to harm his children.

The next thing he knew, he was charging through the air toward Liz, then abruptly stopped as Liz put up her hand.

"Don't worry!" Liz laughed delightedly. "I've only done what you asked me to, yet. I haven't changed your brains yet." She moved toward Andrew and Terry, Terry reaching her hand out eagerly.

Lewis moved again in the air, drifting slowly after Liz, just getting used to being able to fly so naturally and effortlessly.

No sooner did Liz touch Terry's hand than she zoomed off and up into the air, laughing excitedly. Tom whizzed past her, then banked around to fly back alongside her.

"This is great!" she squealed.

Tom laughed and flipped in a barrel roll. He saw Andrew climbing and diving a few hundred meters away. And then he saw his father streaking toward them.

"Can you believe this?" Tom laughed over the rushing air as Lewis came

3: Nrathĕrmĕ and Nŭährnär

up level with them.

"Does that matter?" they heard Liz's unraised yet oddly audible voice from above them. They all three looked up, and saw Liz shooting down toward them from out of nowhere.

"Apparently not," Lewis yelled back. He let out his arms, loving the feeling of the wind racing past them.

Liz swept past again, then turned to them all and beckoned them toward her. "Andrew," she called. Her voice did not sound loud, but Andrew apparently heard it anyway, as he turned back toward them.

"Now, I've given you what I could," Liz said to them all as Andrew flew up to join them. "You can change colors now, if you want to," she grinned.

Andrew's skin instantly turned red. Terry gave herself her old summer tan. She rolled up her sweater sleeve to admire her perfect skin as Andrew went invisible beside her, only his clothes still visible. Tom changed his hands from blue to glowing white, then to silver like Lewis's arm had been. Andrew changed entirely silver as Tom admired the reflecting blues of the morning sky in his hands.

Lewis, his hands silver once more, smiled at his children, then took a double take at what he saw now.

Liz had vanished, and in her place Lewis saw himself!

"Hi, kids," the other Lewis said in Lewis's own voice, "I'm overbearing and paranoid."

Tom snorted with laughter, but Andrew and Terry didn't seem to know how to take that.

"Thanks, Liz," Lewis said sarcastically as the other Lewis morphed instantly back into the young woman. "What on earth are you people?"

Liz drifted lazily back and forth. "Believe it or not, Lewis, we're mostly the same as 'you people' are. As far as I know, we're exactly the same."

"But I can't do that..."

"Be paranoid?"

"Nice," Lewis said, in a "that's enough" voice. "What you just did. I can change color, that's fun, but—"

"There is still a lot to give you," Liz said. "Brains like yours can only handle so much. You still can't fly as quickly as we can. Your brains aren't built to keep track of everything that goes on in our kinds of bodies."

"But, you just said that we're the same as you," Tom said.

"Essentially, yes. And don't ask me how. I have my suspicions, but you should talk to one of our leaders about that. But we all have more added within our bodies. We are just like you. But we have helped our bodies be able to do better what they already do."

"Like fly?" Tom smirked.

"Like manipulate our surroundings," Liz answered, waving her fingers. "Manipulating forces of energy lets us fly.

"And that's all that I am proposing giving you all," she said to Lewis. "I want to *add* to your brains. Then your brains will be capable of directing the tools I'll give you, and you also will be able to assimilate everything that I still do need to tell you! There still is so much to tell you!

"Adding to your brains will not affect your personalities or your thoughts," she assured Lewis.

"How?" Lewis asked doubtfully. "If you're changing our brains..."

"I am only giving you more," Liz explained. "Helping nerves conduct faster, repairing decay, and also modifying nerve connections when I give you all the information I need to give you."

"I understand," Lewis said reluctantly.

"I will not hurt you," Liz insisted.

Lewis looked away, trying to think through his fear.

"Here," Tom said, gliding forward and extending his hand to Liz. "Give me everything!"

Lewis shot between them. "No!" he said to Tom. He rotated toward Liz. "I go first."

"I promise you," Liz said, extending her hand to Lewis, "You have *no reason* to be worried!"

Lewis's silver hand reflected the blaze of the morning sun into his eyes as he began to extend it. And then he felt something very strange. He wondered if Liz had done it, but it seemed deeper than anything like that. All at once, he felt superbly confident and at peace, in a way he hadn't felt for more than three years. He took Liz's hand.

Liz smiled at him and squeezed his hand pleasedly. And then Lewis felt himself inundated. Lifetimes upon lifetimes of information flooded into his consciousness. He knew everything. Everything about Liz's people, Nüährnär, everything about the attack that had just happened, everything about Nüährnär's history and culture, everything.

But he had no idea what to make sense of first.

He found himself staring blankly ahead. Noticing Andrew and Terry's worried expressions beside him, he shook his head as if to clear it, then smiled reassuringly at them.

"Take a look at this," he smiled, looking back at his silver hands. Slowly, and fairly grotesquely, they were sucked backward into his arms.

3: Nrathĕrmĕ and Nüährnär

His children gasped around him, staring at the stumps, but Lewis laughed loudly and his hands promptly returned to normal.

"This is unbelievable!" he cried, looking back at Liz. "I can do *anything*!"

"Well, not *anything*," Liz smiled, but Lewis wasn't listening to her. He had already enthusiastically clasped Tom's hand and now turned to dart over to Andrew and Terry. They had only just enough time to worry about their father's overflowing excitement before he took each of their hands. Instantaneously they were aware of the incalculable amounts of information, knowledge, know-how, and skill surging into them.

"Oh my gosh!" Terry said, her face shocked as if she had just tasted something very spicy.

Lewis let go of their hands, smiling with wild enthusiasm at them both. "You were telling the truth," he said, almost incredulously, turning back to Liz. "Sĕrĕhahn, Nüährnär, all of it, it's all real!"

He noticed a cloudy silver robe appear around Tom behind Liz. Then he realized with horrible consciousness that he could see through everything except for the others and except for Liz and Tom's misty robes…

"We've been naked this whole time?" he said, outraged, to Liz as a silver covering radiated out from him as well.

"Don't worry," Liz laughed, "There are many worse things! But of course I was telling the truth!" Red and white robe-like layers appeared respectively around Andrew and Terry at that moment. "Do you understand why it would have been impossible for you to understand everything before?"

"I know kung-fu," Andrew said solemnly behind Lewis.

"It still is too much for me for keep track of," Lewis said to Liz.

Tom glided toward Andrew, his silver robe suddenly changed to a totally opaque white martial arts uniform.

"You will have an infinitely easier time making sense of things now," Liz was saying as they heard Tom laughing, "Who cares about kung-fu? Check this out!"

"I'll help elucidate some of the basics to you," Liz said to Lewis.

Terry was doubled up with laughter; Tom and Andrew's arms and legs were no more than white and red blurs punching and kicking harmlessly at one another.

"You have learned well," Tom was whispering dramatically, "Grasshopper!" Then, as Andrew flipped him in a whirr of color toward a shrieking Terry, everything went black all around them.

They stopped instantly, to see Lewis standing in front of them, facing Liz, who was smiling widely at them. They all looked around, all of their surroundings nothing more than empty blackness.

"Sorry," Andrew said hastily to Liz, turning his attention to whatever she was showing them now.

"No reason," Liz smiled. She gestured around them.

"That was awesome," Tom whispered to Andrew.

"This isn't real," Liz was saying, gesturing at all the blackness. "We haven't gone anywhere; I'm just going to show you some of what you need to understand." As she said that, the blackness became a field of seemingly innumerable stars.

Just to make sure, Andrew attempted to see past Liz's illusion. No sooner did he try than the stars disappeared, and he saw them all back suspended high above his house.

"You'll want to watch this," Liz said lightly to Andrew.

Andrew sheepishly returned to the illusion, somehow intuitively knowing how to tune back in to what Liz was showing them.

"Are we in space?" Lewis asked, gazing around at the deep sea of stars.

"I'm showing you space," Liz said.

The Pratts gazed around at the stars. There was no sun or planet anywhere that they could see.

"Wow," Terry gasped, pointing, "What's that?"

A vast cube was in front of them. It reflected the stars perfectly; Terry wondered if she would have been able to spot it against the stars before Lewis had changed her.

"That's Nrathĕrmĕ," Liz said. The cube was getting larger and larger as they realized they must be approaching it. It quickly filled their entire field of view.

"Nrathĕrmĕ, that's your world," Lewis recognized.

Liz paused. "Yes. I like to say so," she said then. "This is where my people came from. And Sĕrĕhahn lives here."

"Sĕrĕhahn?" Tom said. "You said he tried to destroy the Earth?"

"Some minions of his," Liz said spitefully.

They were racing along, far above the surface of the cube, but still it seemed to stretch away endlessly in every direction.

"It doesn't look much like a planet," Andrew commented, as Lewis wondered aloud, "How big is this place?" But as soon as he thought, he remembered, as if he had known for years, that the cube was more than a million miles across on every side.

Tom swore quietly as he apparently realized the same thing.

"Where are all the people?" Terry wondered, thinking Nrathĕrmĕ, whatever its enormity, was very ugly.

"Inside," Liz said.

The next thing they knew, their surroundings had changed totally. They knew they must be inside Nrathĕrmĕ, but what the Pratts saw surprised every one of them.

This was no industrialized waste, no cloistered habitat. It was magnificent!

They found themselves soaring through the air of a brilliant blue sky, brighter and cleaner than any earthly sky, above a verdant, rolling landscape. They knew that they were within a closed area, but they could see no boundary other than the ground for hundreds of miles. Andrew was only slightly surprised to realize that he could see that far. But his far sight in no way lessened the glory of the shining blue sky.

Liz laughed, but her voice seemed to them to shake slightly, and she pitched downward toward the ground. The Pratts followed her; billowing, fluffy, shining white clouds rushed past them as the wind whistled freshly through their ears and hair.

Lewis zipped up and away from the others, sweeping over the surface of a bank of towering white clouds. Terry plummeted like a rock to the sprawling sea of trees below them. She dove underneath the canopy, then shot through the trees, zigzagging at breakneck speed, laughing with the exhilaration of it. The trees were enormous, and thick branches and drooping vines burst continually out in front of her, but she found her new reflexes to have no trouble dodging anything in her path. Faster and faster and faster she flew, screaming now at the excitement of banking back and forth so nimbly.

Andrew and Tom had gone on to a clear, grassy, hilly area. "Whoa," Tom cried out, pointing at an approaching hillside.

Andrew followed Tom's finger to see a sprawling herd of grey animals, which were marching carelessly through the grass. "What are those?" he asked, looking at the creatures' sleek grey coats and lopsided front and back legs.

"Called Ĕ'anakĕz, aren't they?" Tom answered, both of them touching down some meters from a few of the animals. A couple of the Ĕ'anakĕz looked curiously at them, but otherwise ignored them. They really were beautiful animals, Tom thought, taking in their chestnut eyes and stubby, hanging ears.

"Where are all the people?" they heard Terry's voice ask. They looked around for her, then realized she was miles away in a nearby forest. Her voice sounded as if she were right beside them.

Tom realized, as if he were remembering, the answer to Terry's question even as he heard Liz's voice answering it. "Nrathĕrmĕ is full of people," Liz said, again sounding as if she weren't also miles distant. "As recently as a few days ago, there were more than one hundred sextillion people living in and around there."

"One hundred how many?" they heard Lewis's staggered reply.

Tom realized that that meant one hundred billion trillion. He jerked his head toward where he knew Liz was, and Andrew followed him straight through the solid hills toward her.

Liz was chuckling. "About a hundred seventeen and a half sextillion, as of four days ago. That will have changed by now."

Tom and Andrew joined Liz, just as Lewis swooped down from among the clouds. She was gliding lazily along above a winding, muddy river, one of her hands skimming along the surface of the shining water.

"But Nrathĕrmĕ has more than enough space for them," Liz continued, "And they're always adding more to it. There are places that are full of people. But there are also wide open areas like this! Nrathĕrmĕ has wide oceans, and deep oceans too. There are majestic mountains there, wonderful ones, of all kinds of sizes and forms. Plains, rivers, rolling deserts, oceans of sand and stone, icy lakes, jungles just bursting with vitality...everything any of us could ever want!"

"And Sĕrĕhahn lives *here*?" Lewis asked.

Liz paused. "You know that my people call themselves N'nŭährnär," she said.

Now that Liz said the word again, Lewis realized that it didn't sound strange to him at all. He knew exactly what Nŭährnär meant: "Refuge," which meant that N'nŭährnär meant people from the Refuge. Then he noticed that none of them had been speaking in English at all since Liz had changed their brains, and that this new language felt more natural and comfortable to him now than English ever had.

"Nŭährnär fled Nrathĕrmĕ more than a year ago. One of your years; we haven't used any measure longer than weeks in a very long time."

"Why?" Terry's voice asked.

"No need," Liz shrugged parenthetically.

"Seven-day weeks?" Lewis asked.

"Yeah," Liz smiled. "Strange, isn't it?"

"Nŭährnär had to leave, though, more than a hundred of our weeks ago; about fifteen of your old months."

"You don't use anything longer than weeks?" Terry pressed.

"The planet Nrathĕrmĕ was taken apart to build this," Liz explained, "Along with thousands of other star systems, so we don't need to measure by

3: Nrathĕrmĕ and Nŭährnär

seasons or days or nights anymore. And life moves so quickly, weeks are the biggest measure we need. We still use days, just to measure things by I suppose, and then weeks are seven of those; a little more than four and a half of Earth's days in all.

"Think about it like you measuring archaic things in thousands of years instead of in millennia; you rarely measure life in millennia; years, and maybe decades, are the largest measures you need."

"Life moves that fast in Nrathĕrmĕ?" Tom asked.

Liz smiled knowingly at him. "You've only been speaking N'närdamähr for ten minutes now. And an hour ago, you didn't suspect that I or any of this ever existed!"

"Yeah," Tom nodded, "That's right; it feels like it's been a lot longer than that. A few days, maybe."

"There is so much for you to get used to," Liz smiled at them. But her smile faltered as she continued, "But my people don't live at Nrathĕrmĕ. I've never been there; I was born after they left, about sixty weeks ago. But I've been shown what happened enough to feel almost like I was there myself."

"You—what?" Andrew stuttered. "You were born—"

"Sixty weeks ago, nine of your months," Liz said simply.

"You look closer to Tom's age," Andrew said, trying to make sense of this. But then he realized that Liz's age was nothing unusual at all.

"I taught you everything I know about all this in an instant, and you just need to put it all together," Liz reminded Andrew, as his mind began to do just that. "I got all this taught into me when I was born; then I decided that I wanted to look the way I do. But," she said, smiling reminiscently, "I think you will get used to things much more quickly than I did when I was first born."

Tom stared at Liz, amazed to think that the capable, confident adult before him was no older than a tiny infant.

"Watch this," Liz said, getting their attention.

The three of them looked at her, and then saw that their surroundings had changed again. There were people everywhere! And even they could hardly discern the furthest boundaries to this wide open area; Lewis could see that they were in a vast hallway, like a tube more than a thousand miles across, stretching away endlessly in either direction. The distant walls were covered in forests and oceans, and even a gigantic system of glaciers in one area.

Terry was standing beside them again in the air. She was looking around in awe at the sheer number of people around them. There were millions upon millions of people racing to and fro along the cavernous highway, shooting by at speeds that Terry knew her eyes would not have been able to see before. Still more people were drifting more lazily along, farther from the corridor's heart, and others, millions of them everywhere, were grouped in crowds of all kinds of varying sizes, while others seemed to be playing on and around the land bordering the great hallway.

"This is a memory," Liz was explaining. "My grandfather's grandmother gave it to me." She gestured to a young-looking blonde woman in the nearest group as she spoke, whom Terry inherently knew was Liz's great-great-grandmother, a woman called M'děrětěnhě.

"This happened a few days before Nŭährnär fled Nrathěrmě," Liz said. "About one hundred three weeks ago now."

"She's so young—" Terry began, but Liz shook her head quickly, gesturing for them to watch M'děrětěnhě.

Nothing happened for a few long seconds. Lewis wondered for a moment why he could not hear any of the conversation that appeared to be going on in the group, but then realized that the people must have been communicating from mind to mind. That only struck him as strange for a fleeting instant, before he remembered that that was exactly how they had all been communicating together ever since they had been fully changed.

Tom glanced at Liz as the memory continued uneventfully. He was surprised to see the look on her face: there was anger, and sadness, mixed with what looked like apprehension of whatever was about to happen. And, Tom thought, there was a trace of a vague dignity about her as she watched.

Suddenly Liz started slightly, and Tom brought his attention back to the group in front of them. M'děrětěnhě and a young, extremely handsome man, who Tom knew was Liz' great-great-grandfather Û'ědnōděn, seemed to be starting to leave the group. Another woman glided sociably after them, putting her hands warmly on each of their shoulders.

Tom just had time to understand that this woman was known as Ûtōash before Û'ědnōděn cried out in apparent rage. Tom watched, stunned, as Û'ědnōděn and M'děrětěnhě dodged instantly out from under Ûtōash's hands and turned to stand with unmistakable hostility before her. At that precise instant, Ûtōash screamed in apparent agony.

And then everything seemed to go dark. Tom could see that nothing visually had changed, but everything around them all seemed to have been filled with a frozen, weighty darkness, blacker than anything Tom had ever imagined. He felt seized with a paralyzing, undefinable but completely enveloping fear.

Û'ědnōděn and M'děrětěnhě were screaming now as if in lethal pain. A blast of blazing white light, which was entirely overshadowed by the crushing fear of darkness, burst from Û'ĕdnōdĕn's left hand at Ûtōash.

The terror of the others in the group at the invisible darkness turned to shock that Û'ĕdnōdĕn had just tried to murder Ûtōash. But Ûtōash stood unharmed. Tom realized that that was not right, that that light should have annihilated her, but then that thought was crushed out of him as the darkness grew still heavier.

Ûtōash was grinning a horrible, hating grin at Û'ĕdnōdĕn. Tom felt sure that the darkness was actually radiating from out of her. A few of the others in the group apparently recognized the same thing, as half a dozen more blasts of the deadly white light burst from them into Ûtōash. People were screaming everywhere, but their voices sounded muffled by the fear that Tom felt was freezing his mind.

Ûtōash ignored all the others, more of whom began pounding at her with the bolts of stifled light. Û'ĕdnōdĕn, screaming with apparent pain and fury, dove toward Ûtōash. All Tom saw was a flashing movement of both Û'ĕdnōdĕn's and Ûtōash's arms, and the next thing he knew, Û'ĕdnōdĕn was drifting lifelessly past Ûtōash. Then Ûtōash cried out in sudden pain as M'dĕrĕtĕnhĕ shouted as if in powerful exertion. In the same moment, three of the continuing bursts of light struck Ûtōash.

Instantly the darkness evaporated. A shadow of the fear still lingered, but Tom's senses no longer felt clouded, and his mind no longer seemed compressed. He could see no trace of Ûtōash, whom he assumed must have been destroyed. Why hadn't the previous bursts of light annihilated her, he wondered.

Lewis's mind was reeling, his heart pounding. He looked at Liz, overwhelmed and utterly confused by what he had just witnessed, but she didn't respond. Her face was grave as she continued to watch the memory.

He turned his attention back to see M'dĕrĕtĕnhĕ slump into a sagging position in the air, her body curling limply. Several people rushed to her side, but she did not move. Others of the group had intercepted Û'ĕdnōdĕn as he drifted inertly on past where Ûtōash had stood.

Lewis then heard the people speak, shouting, calling out to everyone around: "He's dead!" "Û'ĕdnōdĕn is dead!" Then: "He's not coming back!"

"M'dĕrĕtĕnhĕ is alive," he heard another man call. "But she isn't moving!" a woman cried out, clearly panicked.

"Ûtōash!" someone else was screaming.

"She tried to kill Û'ĕdnōdĕn and M'dĕrĕtĕnhĕ," another man said in obvious shock.

Light and Glory

"What was that...that feeling?"

"Did you feel it?"

"Û'ĕdnōdĕn tried to kill Ûtōash!"

"It came from Ûtōash!"

"No!"

"She was trying to kill Û'ĕdnōdĕn and M'dĕrĕtĕnhĕ!"

"Not Ûtōash!"

"I'm certain it was coming from Ûtōash!"

"She *did* kill Û'ĕdnōdĕn!"

"M'dĕrĕtĕnhĕ's not moving!"

"What was it—"

The frantic group, which had now been being joined by other alarmed people from all around, disappeared. The Pratts found themselves above the muddy river again.

"What was that?" Lewis asked in horror.

Liz was openly weeping. After a few seconds, she said, "That thing that killed my grandfather, Û'ĕdnōdĕn...it was a minion of Sĕrĕhahn's."

"Like the people who tried to destroy the world?" Andrew asked, his eyes wide still from the indescribable terror of Ûtōash.

"Oh, no," Liz said. Her whole demeanor seemed saturated with grief and hatred. "No. Those could be called people. But this," her lip curled loathingly, "This was not a person! Not to me."

"What was she?" Tom asked. Though the memory had ended, the fear and the darkness still seemed to press in over him.

"Evil," Liz said simply. "And that same scene happened all over Nrathĕrmĕ around that time. Nŭährnär had to flee Nrathĕrmĕ because Sĕrĕhahn was going to kill them all."

"Why?" Terry asked.

"Û'ĕdnōdĕn and M'dĕrĕtĕnhĕ were Ōmäthäär," Liz said.

Tom tried to think what Ōmäthäär were.

"That means they knew something that Sĕrĕhahn didn't want them to know," Liz was continuing.

"What?" Tom asked.

Liz shrugged, dragging her hand through the water again. "All I know is that they called themselves Ōmäthäär, and they knew a lot about Sĕrĕhahn and his minions. But M'dĕrĕtĕnhĕ has never told me about it. I don't ask."

Lewis stared at Liz. That was not the kind of answer he had expected.

"The Ōmäthäär who survived the first days of Sĕrĕhahn's attacks fled Nrathĕrmĕ. Much of their family and friends joined them. We've called

3: Nrathĕrmĕ and Nŭährnär

ourselves Nŭährnär ever since. And Sĕrĕhahn and his minions still hunt us."

She looked at Lewis. "I believe my grandmother. The less I know, the happier I am. I have already seen too much..." her voice trailed away, and she started weeping again.

"I have lost twelve brothers and seventeen sisters to those things," she sobbed then. "And—" she began, but then stopped, softly shaking with tears now.

She stopped above the river and looked levelly at them all. "You need to understand this. You must understand how bad things are. You have got to understand that the same Sĕrĕhahn who led those...*beings* in killing the Ōmäthäär is the man who tried to destroy your world!"

Lewis's augmented mind was spinning with all of this; being reminded of the destruction of everything he had thought he had known made it yet more jarring to him.

"Who exactly is he?" Lewis asked. "Sĕrĕhahn?"

"He has killed hundreds of people that I love," Liz answered, her voice rising slightly. "His followers killed them." Her voice then rose in a fire of fury that startled Lewis. "Sĕrĕhahn is terrible. His followers are terrible! Whenever I've met them, they have filled everything with darkness! I hate them!

"All that I care about Sĕrĕhahn is that he has murdered hundreds of the people that I cared for! He wants to murder everyone I know and care about— and he wants to destroy your world, too! for what reason other than soulless murder, who can tell?"

She breathed viciously for a couple of seconds. Then she seemed to gain a hold of herself. "He's Anhar," she said at last.

That statement supplied Lewis with the kind of answer he had been asking for. Only half an instant's searching in his mind revealed to him who Anhar was.

"No!" Terry exclaimed, realizing who Anhar was at that same moment.

Anhar was the leader of all Nrathĕrmĕ, Lewis knew. Every one of those hundred seventeen sextillion people honored Sĕrĕhahn as their leader! And the more Lewis thought about Anhar, the more he understood what a wonderful leader he was. The people of Nrathĕrmĕ, the N'nrathĕrmĕ, loved their Anhar, and Lewis could see why they did. Everything good in Nrathĕrmĕ seemed to come from Sĕrĕhahn. He was the greatest kind of leader that anyone could ever want; he helped his people in any way he could, he loved them, he gave everything for them. He taught them, and governed them loosely yet competently. Everything he did bettered the lives of everyone he could influence. In less than a hundred years, Nrathĕrmĕ had changed from a small, lonely planet bound by illness and mortality to the great unaging paradise that had spread to harvest so many thousands of worlds! And Anhar had been the prime mover all along. Anhar was not a dictator or a tyrant. He ruled benignly, benevolently, and ingeniously, presiding for people who knew how to govern themselves. He was merely the keystone of Nrathĕrmĕ's beautifully self-run society.

"How," Terry was asking Liz, "Can Anhar be Sĕrĕhahn? A murderer?"

Liz smiled subduedly at her. "It is incredible," she said. "But he is. I do not understand him. I know that he is Anhar. But I also know that he is repugnant, despicable."

"How could such a man lead Nrathĕrmĕ?" Lewis asked. "Why doesn't anyone else know what he is?"

"You've got it," Liz smiled gravely at him. "Sĕrĕhahn heads Nrathĕrmĕ because nobody knows what he is. They haven't seen what awful things he does to those he fears; they only know him as the Anhar who, really, is more responsible than anyone else, almost more responsible than everyone else combined, for making Nrathĕrmĕ what it is."

She turned away and flew a short way up, taking in the panoramic beauty of the illusionary land all around.

"Nrathĕrmĕ is more wonderful than anything I have ever seen in real life," she said quietly. "Even though we N'nüährnär try to mimic it." She turned to face them as they glided up after her. "But it's more than that. The N'nrathĕrmĕ are genuinely happy. They're productive, informed, and progressive. Life is a continually deepening joy in Nrathĕrmĕ; everyone is constantly learning and growing and just enjoying everything! They love each other. It is the greatest, best adventure anyone could wish for, being able to live and grow and love, every day deeper and faster and faster and deeper than the day before, always!"

Tom thought that that last sentence sounded recited.

"And Anhar, *Sĕrĕhahn*," Liz spat venomously, "Really is responsible for Nrathĕrmĕ being such heaven." She looked past them at the rolling green land. Then she added, "People in Nüährnär are happy. But N'nrathĕrmĕ don't have to fly from Sĕrĕhahn their whole lives."

"What if Sĕrĕhahn isn't evil?" Andrew suggested. "What if Nüährnär is wrong? I mean," he said, daunted by Liz's surprised, disbelieving look, "If Nrathĕrmĕ is so great, maybe Sĕrĕhahn in fact isn't—"

"I used to be married," Liz said with forbidding flatness. "I am married! But Bäd'r'när is dead, and he will *never* come back, because of Sĕrĕhahn."

3: Nrathĕrmĕ and Nŭährnär

Tears were rolling down her again enraged face. "His horrible followers killed him!"

Andrew wanted to apologize, but Liz continued, and he didn't dare say anything else.

"Andrew," she said, "You were dead less than an hour ago, but Näb'n revived you. These things, these minions of Sĕrĕhahn, are horrible. They can almost never be killed by normal means. Those whom they kill can almost never be revived. They are inhuman abominations." Her voice was steady now, but tears continued to wash down her face. "Bäd'r'när will never, ever, ever come back. All of my children but one are dead. And they will never, ever come back! My great-great-grandfather will never come back. Never!"

She seethed for a second, her features now taut with fury. "Sĕrĕhahn, Andrew, is a monster! A deceiving monster, but therefore a monster all the more!"

"Sorry," Andrew mumbled sincerely.

Terry hesitated for a moment, then glided toward Liz and put her arms around her. Liz smiled at her, then fell into silent tears. Lewis shot Andrew a chastening look as Liz put her arms around Terry, who tightened her grip.

"You were thinking the same thing," Andrew said impudently and privately from his mind to Lewis's. Lewis scowled and shook his head impatiently.

"Thank you," Liz said softly to Terry. She looked at the men, smiling an appreciative and also understanding smile, as if to say she understood how much they were trying to comprehend. "I'm sorry," she said, and her smile lingered toward Andrew.

"I know what I know," she said resignedly. "I know that Sĕrĕhahn is behind the disaster that your world has had to suffer. I would think that that would be enough for all of you." She looked amicably but pointedly at Lewis.

She shook her head, as if disappointed with her own emotion, and Nrathĕrmĕ's magnificent halls disappeared around them. Tom felt a little disoriented to find that they were still floating above their ruined house, on Earth.

Liz drifted wearily down to the Pratts' front yard. Lewis and his children followed her, noticing that many of the neighbors were floating and soaring around above the houses.

Touching down on the scorched grass, Liz looked up at the battered house. The house lurched more upright as the Pratts landed behind her, its damaged and burnt areas healing before their eyes. The lawn turned vividly green under them. Liz walked along the ground toward the front door, which opened by itself. The inside of the house, which they could view right through the walls, was perfectly whole and clean, as if no catastrophe had ever happened.

Liz looked around at the pristine house in front of them. Tom could detect something of nostalgia on her face, and she said, "I've never been to Nrathĕrmĕ." She turned more fully toward them. "Everyone who I know that has gone back has ended up caught by Sĕrĕhahn." She sighed. "That's how Sĕrĕhahn has still been able to find us, and kill *so many* of us!" Liz's young face sagged with a weariness as of an old, war-worn veteran.

"I love my family," she said. "And I do trust them. And I love Nŭährnär. And I know, as horrible as it really is that Anhar of Nrathĕrmĕ could be what he is, I know that Nŭährnär is right. We have no choice but to stick together. Anhar is to thank for that."

She smiled again at them. "Well," she said to Lewis, "I promised you that I would leave you forever if that was what you wanted after hearing what I needed to explain to you." She stepped aside from the front door, waving her hand up as if presenting the house to them. "Your house is yours. I envy you, that you have a home." She looked seriously and gratefully at Lewis. "I will leave you alone, forever, if you want that."

Lewis actually considered that. But as he looked at the old house standing in the morning sun, he saw how weak and pathetic it was. That shoddy pile of wood and glue would never protect them from what, he knew despite his hopes, was coming. From Sĕrĕhahn and calamity.

Knowing he could not yet grasp the magnitude of what he was doing, Lewis smiled back, terrified but confident. "No. We will go with you. I hope we can save one another from whatever may come."

A tear trickled down Liz's cheek again, and the door closed softly behind her.

Chapter 4

Fantastic Realities

...we did have some. We had crude atomic power, airfoils that flew under special conditions, electronic tools, that sort of thing. We had dabbled experimentally with biological systems. Of course, factionalism, selfishness, and general short-sighted cynicism retarded our society's progression. Our moral knowledge was, largely, embarrassing, with the exceptions of such as the Ä'ähärnhär's Ōmäthäär.

Which is where the greater disparity lay between Earth and Närdamähr. Nrathĕrmĕ's understanding of macro objects was godlike in comparison with those of the fragmented Nōhōnŭäär tribes, but it was the Ōmäthäärs' understanding of Är that truly changed everyone who would let it. It changed me. More than any technology, it was Ä'ähänärdanär that changed the world for everyone who let it. Understanding of Reality from the inside out.

But chronological storytelling will help illuminate that, so I ought to continue with explaining the technological changes that my friends and I had to handle. First the technology from the outside in, then I'll get to Ärthähr; from the inside out.

Sarah's family, as I mentioned, was first met by Ähänär. As soon as Ähänär had given them the tools to participate in Nŭährnär, and in the imminent struggles, the Trotters assaulted her with questions. They wanted to know about the Ōmäthäär. They wanted to know why Ä'ähänärdanär had fled Nrathĕrmĕ. They wanted to know why N'närdamähr and Nōhōnŭäär were identical. Really, they were interested in Är; they did not know yet how kindred the Ōmäthäär were to that desire!

Sarah was typically interested in Sĕrĕhahn and the Ämäthōär. Scott and Rene were interested in everything. And so trusting! So credulous! Scott and Rene knew what they were trusting. But anyone else would have thought them supremely foolish to be that prepared to believe such things that were so entirely foreign to them!

Of course, that's a wonderful part of why I love that family so deeply...

"I really am sorry. I wish I knew more that I could tell you about that..." Ähänär shrugged helplessly.

"Okay," Scott smiled, waving his hand dismissingly. "I understand."

"But my parents do know more about this than I do," Ähänär reminded him. She and the Trotters were still gathered outside the Trotters' now mended house. Scott and Rene were sitting on the vibrant lawn with Ähänär, all of them now clothed in robes like hers, as their children floated or swooped around nearby.

"But I have seen enough of Ämäthōär myself to know that they're worth fleeing from," Ähänär added, a hint of sorrow mixed with the loathing in her voice.

Sarah, who had been floating idly in the air beside them, shivered unexpectedly as Ähänär again referred to Ämäthöär. She looked away from her hair, with which she had been experimenting various lengths and hues, and said, "Ähänär, you said that those Ämäthöär are 'terrible.' Why? What are they?"

Ähänär looked hard at Sarah for half a second. She seemed to steel herself then. "Alright," she said. She gestured to her right, where appeared an unmoving man standing on the grass.

The man was clothed like the rest of them, wearing a borderless cloak of artificial inertia. His was decorated with simple, orderly patterns of white triangles and circles over a deep green field. His bare wrists and ankles were visible outside the green covering. His hair was a pleasant rust red, flowing thickly down just past his shoulders, and an equally thick and elegant mustache and beard adorned his hearty face.

"This," Ähänär said bracingly, "Is an Ämäthöär that I saw not too long ago."

Sarah looked inquiringly at her. Ähänär seemed to hesitate at first. Then she looked up at the Ämäthöär, and said, "Watch."

Instantly the lawn and the Trotters' house disappeared. They all found themselves standing or floating amidst a sea of large green plants. The sky was clear and blue above them. They could see thousands of people racing in all different directions through the sky. The Ämäthöär floated a few meters above them, his face relaxed as he watched the thousands of people soaring past.

Rene was just looking around disorientedly at the wide leaves of the plants all around them when her attention was pulled to the shouts beginning to sound above them.

"It's an Ämäthöär!"

"Ämäthöär!"

"No! They've found us!"

"Ämäthöär!"

Rene was surprised to find that she could hear every one of the increasingly alarmed shouts, even though hundreds of voices were now calling frantically out to everyone nearby.

"Get out of here!"

"Call the Ōmäthäär!"

"Where is Mär?"

4: Fantastic Realities

"Are there more of them?"

"Ämäthöär!"

"Quick, fly!"

Rene wondered what about the man showed that he was an Ämäthöär, but then she saw the strange position he had just assumed. His arms were extended in a relaxed but vaguely active position. Even though she was below him, she was aware that his eyes were flicking now from person to person. They had an odd, half-seeing look in them. His fingers were flexing in a rhythmic way, and his arms and elbows were also flowing in apparently unconscious ways. He looked dispassionately from person to person above him, his body arcing shallowly and gracefully backward.

And then Rene realized with horror that people were dying above them! Every time the Ämäthöär set his eyes on one of the now madly scattering people, that man or woman fell instantly dead in the sky.

Immediately she felt freezing cold. But it was no normal cold; temperatures had no effect on her augmented self; it was as if it were coming from her uttermost heart. She felt as if she were shaking terribly, but she knew that she was not.

"Wait!" Ähänär hissed, her voice sounding eternally distant amidst the inaudible throbbing that so suddenly filled Rene's senses. Rene realized that she had begun to flee from the murderous man above them, but Ähänär had restrained her with her own momentum. Scott and the children, she saw, had tried to flee as well; they were all pointed out in different directions, held back by Ähänär.

Throbbing cold seemed to cover all her senses. More and more people were dying. She could see as they froze suddenly as they fled, as if an invisible but no less powerful darkness had clouded over them.

Then the Ämäthöär's body tensed. Rene only then realized that the darkness had been filling everywhere, since at that moment twelve nexuses of light shined out from it. Twelve invisibly shining people were actually hurtling *toward* the Ämäthöär. Rene found them extremely comforting to look at against the Ämäthöär's darkness.

Rene was only partially aware of Sarah's scream of horror as one of the charging people fell abruptly dead in his charge, his light extinguished in a thrill of darkness. The eleven were almost on the Ämäthöär. The light and darkness were vying for supremacy. And then the Ämäthöär shot toward them.

All the air seemed to Rene to vibrate as the Ämäthöär and the eleven attackers met. Their arms were little other than blurs as the eleven, and now ten, grappled with the Ämäthōär and the Ämäthōär with them. The darkness was waning. The ten were screaming as if exerting consummate strength, and the Ämäthōär began screaming wordlessly in their defiance. The Ämäthōär's hands managed to grasp another of his foes, and she shivered and died.

Their arms raced madly, the Ämäthōär blocking the others' hands with both his arms and his inertia as he struggled to penetrate their parries and blockings. Everything was shuddering with the darkness that seemed to actually push back the light and with the continual shouts of the furious battlers. The Ämäthōär's hand struck the shoulder of another of them, he too dying immediately.

And suddenly it was over. Three men had simultaneously struck the Ämäthōär's body, and with one great bellow had all expired as the Ämäthōär fell dead with them. The darkness retreated from the light of the five surviving saviors, but it lingered immediately around the Ämäthōär's body.

Scott was staring transfixedly at the dead Ämäthōär. The five remaining attackers began darting to their fallen companions and touching their heads. Two of them revived, shuddering as if awakening from a dark dream, but the others remained unresponsively dead.

Scott realized that Ähänär had flown up to the dead Ämäthōär. She beckoned for them to follow her, but he was grateful that his body did not seem to want to move.

Ähänär gazed back at them. Her eyes were wet as she smiled unsettledly at them. "It's alright," she said empathetically. "Come here."

Scott thought he meant to move, but still he remained riveted where he was. His heart was thumping in his baffled terror.

Ähänär's smile became sadder and more empathetic. Everything disappeared except for the Ämäthōär's body, which now lay contorted on the front lawn.

"That wasn't real," Ähänär softly reassured them.

Scott stared at her.

"That was something that I saw. About eighty-nine weeks ago. I was one of the people passing when the Ämäthōär revealed himself."

"It felt real to me!" Joseph shuddered, staring at the very solid-looking body lying beside Ähänär.

"Come here," Ähänär beckoned again, moving closer to the body.

No one moved.

"I wanted to show you what Ämäthōär are," she said sadly. She looked from Sarah to Joseph. "Joseph, this was a memory. That terrible feeling would have been a lot worse if this had been real."

4: Fantastic Realities

"What are they?" Rene asked revoltedly.

Ähänär looked at the body at her feet. "They're people. Just people. But I think they've been taught something, some things, by Sĕrĕhahn that make them like this."

Scott stared at the body on his lawn. It was bent as if in ultimate suffering; its muscles were all taut, its eyes bulged wide.

Ähänär looked at Scott, and a tear began to fall from her shimmering eyes. She looked at the body, and it disappeared. "I wanted you to see that they are just people," she said. "But also that they are terrible." She looked back at Scott. "They, as much as I know, are why we have fled Nrathĕrmĕ. And the Ämäthöär still pursue us."

Scott looked up sharply from the body to Ähänär. "They still pursue you..." he repeated. "That means that if we join you, the Ämäthöär will pursue us!" Ähänär put up her hand calmingly, but Scott declared, "I'm sorry, Ähänär, but I will not put my family into such a situation."

The ground underneath them shook suddenly. The Trotters' repaired house creaked, several of the windows cracking as other crashes sounded from inside. Ähänär looked grimly and significantly at Scott as the shaking died away.

"*I* am sorry," Ähänär said honestly, "So sorry, that, no matter what you choose to do, Scott, the Ämäthöär are already after you."

Rene whimpered. Kathy had started crying with fear, and she huddled close to her mother. Ähänär looked at them with clear sympathy and regret.

"So," Aaron said falteringly, "It was the Ämäthöär who made the explosions? And the earthquake?"

"Oh no," Ähänär said. "We are all very lucky that no Ämäthöär were involved here. That was just weapons, normal firepower, the kind that we have."

"That wasn't technological, you're saying," Aaron shivered, "What the Ämäthöär did."

Ähänär looked unsettled. "No." She shook her head slightly, as if shaking something off. "Now, I don't know why the Ämäthöär sent the brigands that they sent, but I, and many of our leaders, suspect that it was the Ämäthöär who sent them. It is the Ämäthöär who want Earth destroyed."

"Why would they?" Rene questioned.

"I don't know," Ähänär said. "But my parents, and others, know more about Ämäthöär than I do. Whatever their reasons may be, I do not doubt that it was the Ämäthöär who directed Earth to be destroyed."

Scott didn't know what to say. His children were no longer gliding around; they had all gathered silently on the grass around him and Rene. Joseph was still gazing unconsciously at the spot of lawn where the Ämäthöär had lain. Rene hugged Kathy tightly to her side. Scott looked at his wife and daughter beside him, and he put an arm around them both. Terror coursed through him. Terror for his family.

Rene looked up at Ähänär, who was still standing. Ähänär said nothing, though her expression was one of unhappy sympathy.

Scott looked unseeingly down at the ground. He tightened his embrace around Rene and Kathy. "What," he began in a voice of fearful resignation, "What can we do?"

Ähänär's reply was noticeably reluctant. "We must stay here. At Earth. Here we'll prepare against the Ämäthöär."

"Here?" Joseph said incredulously. "Right where they know to find us? But they can destroy the whole world anyway!"

"We have to stay and fight," Ähänär exhorted them, though Sarah thought her tone sounded like she meant to convince herself as much as them. "We have the same weapons that Nrathĕrmĕ has. We can protect Earth from anybody." Her voice noticeably faltered as she said that.

Joseph nodded. He casually made the house behind them mend itself, as if to reassure himself of their abilities.

Scott looked up, no less fearful but emboldened now with determination. "But what can *we* do? What can the Trotter family do?"

Ähänär smiled appreciatively at him. "The Trotter family should meet Nüährnär's leaders. *Our* leaders."

"Who are they?" Aaron asked.

Ähänär's smile deepened through the sad empathy that remained. "Meet them, and find out for yourselves," she said fondly. She rose a couple of meters from the ground.

Sarah and Joseph stared up at her. John rose from the ground, floating expectantly above the others.

Scott looked up at Ähänär from where he remained sitting on his lawn. Still filled with worry and with shock after everything that had happened to them in the last hour, he smiled back at Ähänär. He nodded, squeezed Rene and Kathy in his arm, then arose up from the ground. He looked back at his beloved wife, and smiled with frightened confidence.

Rene smiled in agreement. She arose to follow, and took Scott's hand in her own. The rest of their children glided up behind them. Sarah moved toward Kathy and grasped her hand.

Ähänär then continued rising higher into the air. She picked up speed as the Trotters rose with her, but Scott had the impression that she was moving slowly so as to enjoy the ascent.

"Wow, look!" John cried excitedly as the mighty mountains shrank below them.

They pierced the morning cloud cover. The ground was still visible to them, stretching out in every direction.

Kathy almost forgot her fear when she saw the incredible view. She realized that it was icy cold; she could actually see the air growing thinner. But she didn't mind. She felt the cold more acutely than she had ever felt cold before, but she felt no discomfort from it. The thinning air raced past her eyes, but she felt no pain from it as she followed her family faster and faster into the sky.

She could see the air changing. She could see flowing currents of gases that she knew her eyes would never have been able to see before. There were clouds and rivers of air, layers and beautiful systems, interflowing in patterns of heat and density more wondrous than any clouds that she had ever seen before.

"Sarah, look at the air!" she exclaimed, gesturing around at the perfect currents far below them.

"Oh my gosh!" they heard Scott whisper as the air, almost in one instant, gave way to an unending panorama of space.

There were more stars, and the stars were fantastically more brilliant, than Sarah had ever seen on the clearest of clear nights. The sun was blazing in what she would have called the southeast before. She looked straight at it unflinchingly; even from that distance, she could see its surface boiling and churning, flares and cooler patches and outer gases blending in a mosaic more perfect than anything she had considered before.

"Now," Ähänär was saying impressively, "Look at your world!"

Kathy turned from where she had been gaping at the stars and Sarah from the sun. The Earth glowed blue, the land of North America stretching majestically out below them. Sarah couldn't comprehend that anyone could want to annihilate it.

"I can see our house!" John was joking.

"No, really," Aaron said, "I *can* see our house!" He pointed, and Sarah realized that she could actually see their house, even from miles and miles above it. She could see every shingle, every piece of dust on the dawnlit roof, every room straight through the roof.

"I can see everything!" Aaron said. "I can see *inside* the Earth! I can see straight through all of it!"

Light and Glory

Sarah realized that he was right; she could see anywhere on Earth that she wanted. She found it hard to imagine not being able to see that much detail.

"Aaron, we can hear each other! In space!" John cried enthusiastically. "Look at us! We're just sitting here in outer space!"

Ähänär was smiling glowingly.

"So," Scott asked her quietly, "Which one is Nrathĕrmĕ's?"

Ähänär pointed away to a golden star shining brightly above the glowing Earth. "That was our sun. It was taken apart to build the city Nrathĕrmĕ, but it will be thousands of weeks before the light stops reaching us here."

That was it, Sarah thought, looking thoughtfully at the golden speck riding high and somehow defiantly above them. Sĕrĕhahn, the Ämäthöär, the N'nüährnärs' home, they were right there in front of her.

Ähänär turned and soared off southwest. The Trotters followed right behind her, all of them still gazing at the clouds and land and oceans below.

"There," Ähänär pointed ahead.

Scott looked where she was pointing. Something was arcing over the edge of the Earth, covering over the whole planet. Though it was still in the dark shadow of the Earth's night side, Scott could see it plainly. It was a perfect mirror, an enormous shell hundreds of miles thick covering the far portion of the planet. He could tell it was spreading like a liquid at dozens of miles every second.

Ähänär looked back at them as they sped toward the shell. "Nüährnär is setting up defenses already."

...and so little time! But, as I told them then, and after, my example in ignoring my own rights forebode nothing of my intents regarding theirs! If Ĕzhēlan tried to harm them, I would fight for them. And as such I had to.

I loved them all enough—they were my world, the only world I thought I had!—that saving them was payment in itself. Sarah, Mär, Nüährnär, I wondered if I would ever see them again; these were now my world, the only hope I had around me. If only I had known how wide reaching that desperate defense would prove itself to be! I was rewarded infinitely for all of that! Infinitely, in the persons of Räröähr and all his families.

I had never suffered so much. I did undergo far worse things, mere weeks later, and then much worse things after rejoining the besieged Nüährnär, but that does not make the difficulty of that week any less. But I would have willingly prolonged that trauma indefinitely, willingly if still grievingly, if I had known that it was leading me to Sarah.

How many times I have heard it supposed that Är was angry with the Ōmäthäär,

4: Fantastic Realities

that these circumstances were his response to some wrongs of theirs. Ignorant slanderers say as much, silly fearful degenerates who have kept themselves from getting acquainted with Är. But truth is, even if so many people are ignorant of it. The Ōmäthäär went through so much! Through all of this, and not least through that week! And what wonderful adventures their suffering became! Life is as adventurous for each as each is ready for it to be. The Ōmäthäär, through their enduring of pain and war and slander and betrayal, lived adventure and grew to glories that the backbiters, as backbiters, will never attain.

The Ōmäthäär knew what they were doing. They knew their business. They knew Är, and they knew Ä'ähänärdanär. And their love for even those who betrayed them got them victory. Their love gave them permanent success, as only love can give it. They wanted only the best, only happiness, for everyone! And that earned them so many enemies. As it did me.

As time sped on, I grew to have no enemies except for love's sake. I loved everyone, even those who hated me for it. Like Rod, many forgave me promptly! But others hated me to their self-doomed end.

Like my own Äpäda'ōvaf.

But others, who hated Ōmäthäär out of innocent lack of knowledge, lived happier lives. And those of them who lived through the clashes of M'tärnhär and Ämäthōär and Ōmäthäär got the chance to know the truth about the Ōmäthäär and got to revel in Ä'ähänärdanär.

Yet, how could any Ōmäthäär blame them for scoffing at Ä'ähänärdanär? I scoffed at it myself. And then I was forced to live it! So many people, like myself then, are totally ignorant of the amazing, prodigious epics racing on all around them! But the epics race on, whether such know about them or not.

As long as people are open to learn what they don't already know, even things that seem polarly in opposition to what they already know, then they'll rise unhindered forever! Experience can force us to see things that we'd never otherwise believe! And, conversely, as long as people parade themselves, even if only subconsciously, as experienced and knowledgeable, they'll be apt to fall into a contentious attitude that will stop them from learning anything that they don't already believe. What's left to learn, where is there room for being wrong, if one thinks he knows more than anyone around him? Arrogance is really the essential ingredient of true idiocy. But hard experience, and suffering, can melt most hearts into sensibleness.

Some of the greatest men and women that I've ever known were once embarrassingly arrogant. The naïveté of refusing to believe possible any things that one is not already familiar with cripples life, but harsh exposure to fantastic realities can remedy that. How ridiculously ironic it is that the most severely naïve people are those who are most apt to call others naïve! Those who are ignorant of the fantasticalness of Reality are the ones who mock the few who know how fantastic

Light and Glory

Reality really is! Of course there are so many genuinely naïve people who believe falsehoods simply because the falsehoods seem to them to be fantastic. But the refusal to believe truths simply because the truths seem fantastic is no less idiotic...

Peter laughed adoringly as Annie screeched with excitement beside him. He could hear his own laugh as easily as Annie's shrieks, in spite of the wind howling all around them as they rocketed through the sky. Flashes of blue erupted again and again in front of them as they shot through the dense seas of clouds, which whipped past them like white flickers.

The clouds thinned almost instantly to nothing. Canada's James Bay stretched out terrifically below them.

Peter stopped, without any need to slow first. Annie shot on past him, but stopped too when she saw that Peter was behind her.

"Look at that!" Peter cried, spreading his hands out at the panorama below them, the miniscule trees and the perfect mirror of the bay in the frozen wild.

Annie smiled back at him, even though she had passed him by a couple of miles in the instant it took her to notice him stop. Peter shot back toward her and caught her in his arms, and the two of them tumbled, laughing, down toward the bay.

Peter looked into Annie's eyes, smiled mischievously, and the next thing Annie knew they were plummeting straight to the water thousands of feet below them. She screamed playfully just before she felt herself hit the surface with more force than anything she'd ever felt in her life.

The water was near freezing, but Annie didn't mind that at all. It actually felt amazingly nice, and new. She shot out of Peter's arms under the water and glided away, and then ran right into a school of fish. She laughed again as the fish sped off in different directions, and she chased effortlessly after a few of them. The fish tried desperately to dodge away from her, but Annie just laughed more and sped on past them, loving the smooth hard pressure of the water against her as she raced through it, now at hundreds of miles per hour.

Annie realized Peter was racing up behind her, then she felt his hand clamp over hers and jerk her after him as he hurtled by. But it didn't hurt at all.

Peter nodded toward the surface, and they both burst out of it and then were almost immediately back among clouds.

Peter was laughing with the sheer pleasure of it all, but then he stopped. Mäöhä's voice appeared in his head:

"Peter, Annie," he said, "Come look at this!"

Peter instinctively blocked Mäöhä from his hearing. Annie looked

4: Fantastic Realities

inquiringly at him, but he just nodded to his left. She followed him to arc around to the west as Ontario's curved horizon crawled toward them.

They had hardly soared on for two seconds when Mäōhä appeared directly in front of them, flanked by three other men.

Peter stopped dead, and reached out to hold Annie back too.

"Leave us alone," he said coldly.

"No." Mäōhä sounded almost as if he was being deliberately annoying.

Seething, Peter looked at the others behind Mäōhä. Then he asked roughly, "What do you want?"

"You know what we want," Mäōhä said immediately.

And in that instant, dozens of images raced unbidden through Peter's thoughts: There were enormous spherical crafts arrayed facing Earth. They reached out with inertial force to tear the planet to pieces, and blazing white fire struck onto it from many of them. A cloud of smaller, flatter vessels suddenly appeared out of nowhere between the spherical crafts and the Earth, and their inertial forces shielded the world from the others' fire and force.

Then his mind flashed through scenes of toppling skyscrapers, of convulsing, quaking lands, of horrific eruptions where the white fire struck the ground. The earth gaped in volcanic cracks; mountains slid to shreds; waves hurled themselves inland.

He saw his and Annie's apartment building, resting idly in the morning light. And the ground buckled and lurched underneath it. A deafening grinding sound echoed from every direction as the building crumpled. After a matter of seconds, a blast of searing air pulverized the wreckage, followed by a wave of fire that swept over everything. The fire passed, and the rubble lay ruined alike with the rest of Trenton.

Peter knew those images. Mäōhä was still pretending to be there to save them, he knew, as he resentfully took Mäōhä's point.

But then new images blossomed in his mind. Images he hadn't seen before. Billions, trillions, more, hordes upon hordes of gargantuan ships were converging toward the Earth. Fleets that Peter understood constituted Nüährnär surrounded the world defensively. He was in those fleets. Annie was in them. And the juggernaut of assailing ships overwhelmed them, scattering the N'nüährnär and annihilating the Earth effortlessly in a flash of dust.

And one last image drove it all home for Peter. Right as the entire Earth was destroyed, he saw Annie, riding within one of the N'nüährnär vessels, and then in a flash of deadly light her vessel, and she within it, dissolved into nothing.

The images stopped, as Annie screamed in horror beside him. He wanted to shout at Mäōhä, to express his indignation and his spent patience, but Mäōhä was speaking before Peter could find anything to say that seemed sensible.

"What we want is to protect both of you and every other Earthman," Mäōhä said in an easy but unmistakably serious rush. "You just saw what *will* happen to every one of us if we do not prepare for Anhar's assaults."

No words fit. Peter stared at the men in front of them. If there was an Anhar, he realized, then who but this Nŭährnär could possibly protect Annie?

Could even they protect her?

But this Mäōhä, these arrogant people...how could he believe this?

"You want to protect us..." Peter murmured, as though turning that over in his head. Then he regained himself. "Why?" he questioned sharply, his eyes narrowing at Mäōhä.

One of the men with Mäōhä, whom Peter recognized as Gaä'ärd, stared at Peter incredulously. "Why?" Gaä'ärd repeated. His voice was urgent and dark. "Peter, do you think we would stand aside to let Anhar use Nrathĕrmĕ to destroy so many people?"

"I do," Peter countered bluntly. Simple altruism just didn't add up. Why did these people care? "What's in this for you?"

The N'nŭährnär looked wordlessly at him for a moment. Then Mäōhä moved closer to Peter.

"What's in this for me," he said quietly, "Is the company of my friends."

Peter didn't understand that.

"The Ōmäthäär," Mäōhä continued. "The greatest men and women that I have ever known of. They are about to risk everything to protect you from Anhar! You want to know why, Peter? I don't know. I don't know any more than you know now. But I do know them. Their company is enough to keep me here, even if it means I die along with them when Anhar comes to kill us all."

Peter had no answer to that.

But this story still did not add up.

"Anhar," Annie said fearfully. "You think Anhar will come here? Himself?"

A heavy shadow fell across Mäōhä's expression. "If I were Anhar," he said, "I would be on my way already."

Peter's eyes had widened unconsciously. But they promptly narrowed again, and he asked, "So, what does Nŭährnär expect out of us?"

"Nŭährnär?" Mäōhä said. "You say that like you're not part of it. Both of you are as much N'nüährnär as any of us are now, if you will help to keep everybody safe from Anhar. You have been taught everything that we know; you just need to come to grips with it now." He looked pointedly from Annie to Peter, as if emphasizing Peter's need to accept what he now knew.

"And to keep everybody safe," one of the men, Ärdhär, said hastily, "We should gather with everybody else. Our leaders will tell us what we all need to do."

Annie looked at Peter, clearly liking the sound of meeting with everybody else. Mäöhä looked at Peter as well, who returned his gaze with unconcealed dislike.

"We should go," Mäöhä said, indicating his companions. "The Ōmäthäär are waiting for us to gather, so we can do everything we need to do to save everyone. Will you come with us?"

Annie could see what was going on in Peter's head: his proud dislike of these people was contending with everything Mäöhä had told them. She looked at Mäöhä and said definitively, "We will." Peter looked at her as if he was ready to argue, but she continued with emphasis, "We don't seem to have any other *reasonable* choices."

A grin flickered across Mäöhä's face. Peter hated him.

"Then follow us," Mäöhä said, pivoting and shooting away up and to the south.

The others followed Mäöhä away into the sky. Peter watched them go, not moving from where he and Annie remained floating. He turned his head to argue, but his mouth closed again as Annie shot him a chastising look. He settled for shaking his head in exasperation, then took her hand in his again as the two of them flew on after the now distant N'nüährnär.

Mäöhä and his companions were already more than a thousand miles away. The air thinned away as Peter and Annie followed, Peter taking care not to catch up all the way. And as the Earth glowed brilliantly beneath them, Peter noticed an enormous something arcing up over the southwestern horizon. It was a defense, Peter knew, feeling distinct satisfaction at not needing Mäöhä's explanation. It was thinner near its edges, which were themselves a few hundred miles thick, and it was spreading, covering more and more of the planet.

Peter saw Mäöhä, still a good seven hundred miles ahead, reach the underside of the vast growing shell. Peter could not see through or into the great defense, but he could see Mäöhä and the other men mirrored perfectly in its smooth surface as they turned back toward him and Annie. Mäöhä smiled encouragingly at them, then disappeared up into the shell, passing through the opaque mirror as if it were mere water.

Peter halted. Annie stopped too, and looked impatiently back at him. "That way," Peter said, pointing toward a portion of the shell that was safely far from where Māōhā had entered. Annie smiled, and followed as Peter passed by her toward the shell.

Naturally, as if by reflex, Peter willed the shell to let him pass as he approached its perfectly mirroring surface. He hardly had time to be surprised that he had done so before he clearly was aware that the shell had accepted his request.

He hesitated as he drew nearer to the totally solid looking shell, but Annie's hand now closed around his as she passed him, and she dragged him swiftly straight into the mirror. He was sure they were about to crash right into it.

But they just kept going. There was impenetrable blackness for a fraction of a second, and then Annie gasped.

Annie, for her part, had been prepared to enter a gleaming complex of technological metal and wheels after having seen the hard look of the smooth shell. But instead of harsh machinery, the first thing she recognized was a towering city of coral all around her. They were in an ocean! Beautiful, brightly colored fish swooped by everywhere. Purple and pink flowers, if they were flowers, sprouted here and there on the coral spires. The taste of algae was thick in her mouth; it took her a moment to realize how refreshing that taste and smell was.

"Oh my God," Peter breathed. No bubbles accompanied the perfectly audible sound coming out of his mouth. He turned all around, though he could see all around without having to turn.

Then he flung himself forward, yanking Annie with him. "Jesus!" he screamed, pulling Annie just out of the path of an enormous, whale-sized shark. He could see half a dozen rows of jagged teeth in its open mouth as it glided right through where he and Annie had just been standing.

Annie looked startledly at Peter, then at the shark, then laughed. "Peter," she said gleefully, "What could it do to *us*?"

The shark glided past, ignoring them. Flocks of fish evaded its steadily beating tail fin, but otherwise the fish seemed completely unperturbed by the presence of the mammoth predator.

"I imagine he doesn't have to eat either," Annie smiled.

"It's a she," Peter said, staring in amazement. The shark was beating its way benignly on through the sprawling coral empire. "And I think she can understand us," he realized.

4: Fantastic Realities

"Still just a shark, though," Annie laughed. She shot like a cork straight toward the surface, which was gleaming green remotely above.

Peter followed her, and a second later erupted out of the pungent water into a clear blue sky. They coasted up a few hundred feet, enamored at the majestic scene. The light blue sea stretched on and on behind them, and in front of them, a peaked green islet marked part of a tiny archipelago poking out of the water.

"Look!" Annie pointed at the islet. "Look at all the people!"

There weren't too many people on the island itself, but Peter could see a good number of N'nŭährnär, just men and women like him and Annie, floating and flying and lying all over it. Some floated in clumps among the trees, talking apparently, others were lying or dancing (some of them dancing incredibly fast! he thought) on the perfectly golden-white sand of the flat beaches, and others sliding amidst the waves or dancing around with groups of fish in deeper water.

Annie looked excitedly at him. He could tell she wanted to fly over and meet these new people. He responded with something of a more apprehensive look, and checked quickly whether Mäōhä or any of his companions were nearby. He inherently knew that they were far away within the shell. They were moving away from where he and Annie were, he noticed gladly.

A flock of small white birds was passing underneath them. Peter had not taken any notice of them, until two of the birds broke away from the others and climbed swiftly toward him and Annie. He was just realizing that there was something odd about the two birds when, flapping up in front of him, they changed suddenly into two grown people.

"Oh my—!" Peter cried as Annie screamed and the man and woman in front of them burst into laughter.

"Sorry," the woman said through her giggles. "We didn't mean to scare you."

"Right," the man, who Peter knew was called Ähŭhan, said sarcastically to her, Ōhärkrahan. Ähŭhan smirked friendlily at Peter as if Peter and Annie had been in on the joke. "Sorry; we just saw you two looking kind of confused, and, you know, we couldn't resist."

Annie tried to smile, but Peter glared at him. He glanced warily at the rest of the flock, winging away below. Those really were just birds, he could tell now.

"Who are you?" Annie was saying.

Ähŭhan hesitated. "You can't tell?" he asked uncertainly.

"Ähŭhan," Peter answered shortly. "And you're Ōhärkrahan. Correct?"

Light and Glory

"That's right," Ōhärkrahan smiled as Ähŭhan looked mildly relieved. "Why'd you ask?" she said to Annie, seeming genuinely confused.

"Uh, just getting used to this," Annie said.

"You did get taught everything, by one of us," Ähŭhan asked. "Didn't you?"

"We did," Peter said. "And the person who taught us made quite a show about hurrying to stop Anhar." He said the name doubtfully. "Why the rest and relaxation here? Where's the war?"

Ähŭhan's smile flickered, but he seemed to hitch it promptly back into place. "We are hurrying," he assured Peter in a distinctly less confident voice. "Most of us are doing everything we can to prepare. I hope not for a war, but..." His smile stiffened. "We'll prepare for whatever may happen." He looked at Ōhärkrahan, and his face looked like it relaxed again. "We should be working, too, but..." he trailed off.

Ōhärkrahan smiled back at him, then said to Peter and Annie, "Our managers are 'making' us take more time for ourselves than feels decent..."

"I'm not complaining," Ähŭhan smirked.

Ōhärkrahan laughed. "We were married just three days ago."

Great, Peter thought impatiently.

"So our managers have had to keep telling *him* to stop working," she continued.

"All me," Ähŭhan sighed sarcastically.

Annie's warm smile at the charming newlyweds fell off her face as Ōhärkrahan asked, "When were you married?"

It felt like an awkward eternity before she heard Peter say, "We aren't married."

Ōhärkrahan looked almost as embarrassed as Annie felt, but then Ähŭhan pressed, "But you're from the same household...and you're not brother and sister...how—"

"Look, it's great that you guys have marriage too," Peter said. "But not everybody does things your way."

"*Let it be,*" he heard Annie hiss in his head. He glowered at Ähŭhan, but the look on his face suggested that Ōhärkrahan had just had words with him too.

"It's okay," Annie said soothingly. "No harm done. Congratulations!"

"Yes," Peter said, burying his irritation. "Congratulations for getting married. I hope you enjoy relaxing together."

Ähŭhan's chuckle sounded rather artificial. "We have been enjoying it. Even though I chafe at taking time off. Your orienter was right; we have to hurry to defend ourselves. I'm sure you know some about what we may have to defend ourselves against."

Peter had to admit that Ähŭhan did sound sincere there. But then, looking around them, Ähŭhan smiled in what Peter thought was a very forced way:

"And we did manage to get a lot built before our managers forced us to stop."

"Did you make all this?" Annie asked, astounded, looking out over the sea and islands with all their teeming life.

"No," Ähŭhan said casually. "I was working with the defenses on the Shell's outside walls."

Ōhärkrahan snickered. "He would have tried to direct everything if he hadn't been forced to spend more time with me."

Ähŭhan laughed, and Ōhärkrahan went on, "It's a good thing Mär came! Nüährnär might have had a new, self-appointed, head!"

"Mär?" Peter asked.

But before Ōhärkrahan explained, Annie remembered who Mär was: He was the leader and head of all Nüährnär.

Chapter 5

Nōhōnŭäär

Withered grey clouds whisked past as Mär flew at a slow rush through the Shell's wide skies, flanked by a legion of over a hundred N'nŭährnär.

"Äthähäth believes they'll have reported our presence to Sĕrĕhahn," a man at Mär's side was telling him.

Mär nodded gravely. He was not an exceptionally tall man, but it would have taken careful observation to notice that; he carried himself as if he had assumed the form of a colossus. His face was as young as most N'nŭährnärs', bedecked with a full sandy beard and thick eyebrows over his soft dawn-blue eyes. He bore no scars, no wrinkles. Yet something about his unaffected expression conveyed a sense of several lifetimes' share of burdens. His shoulder-length sandy hair flowed smoothly behind him as he and his entourage hastened steadily on.

"Särdnä and Äōdhä and their families should reach us within four days," another man informed him.

"And Ŭmäthŭ and Ōhōmhär are here?" Mär asked.

"A quarter hour ago," another person said.

"Perfect," Mär smiled.

A cloud of several ten thousand flying N'nŭährnär was coalescing around Mär and his companions as they sped onward.

"You'll have to talk to Mär later," one woman was saying to the pressing crowd.

"Not now," another man was saying.

"This isn't the time!"

Mär's companions continued on unperturbed. "Ōgändan's people should arrive within three days," one of them was saying.

Mär slowed to a stop. He grinned at the men and women around him, then glided into the thick of the swarming crowd that had stopped around them.

"Mär will address us all soon," a woman was assuring the crowd.

"Now," Mär corrected her genially as he stopped at her side.

He raised his hand for attention. The crowd froze. All eyes waited for him to speak.

"The Ōmäthäär must take some time, now, to decide how we all will counter Sĕrĕhahn." His voice, though smiling, delivered a powerful gravity; a

5: Nōhōnŭäär

definite shiver overshadowed the throng surrounding him at the sound of Sĕrĕhahn's name.

He put his hand on the shoulder of a man in front of him. He paused, looking around at all of them. "Tell your managers everything you want to tell me." His hand dropped from the man's shoulder, and instead took the man's hand, left in right, the fingers interlocking. "I'm sorry I can't be with you now," he said.

He released the man's hand and clapped him supportively on his shoulder. Smiling unconsciously then, he turned and rushed back the direction he had been going.

"Mär!" many of the N'nŭährnär cheered as he sped away.

The woman Mär had stood beside beamed. "Not even Sĕrĕhahn can hurt us now!" she shouted sincerely. "Mär's here."

"He's explained everything to Pp'ä'ähärnhär?" Mär said, flying more quickly now.

"Yeah," a man beside him nodded. "The Ä'ähärnhär is excited to see you, Mär, as are his counselors."

"Not more than I am," Mär blinked soberly.

Dense blue sky faded over the beautiful white mountains far below as Mär climbed higher and higher. They were flying in a boundless sea of blue, midway between the inner and outer walls of the Shell, when they reached Mär's objective.

A magnificent white structure loomed before them. It was a perfect, gargantuan sphere of ultimate whiteness, sitting unmoving within the frame of a perfect white cube. Neither sphere nor cube actually radiated light, but their sheen was so perfect that they seemed to glow as brightly as a sun. The unpolluted blue sky appeared dark and mottled behind the vast building's pureness. One man stood as a sentinel in the center of each of the cube's open faces, clothed in light as white as the building.

Mär approached the nearest Sentinel as his companions grouped some behind him and some before the other Sentinels. He smiled jubilantly as he interlocked the Sentinel's right hand with his left, then placed his own right hand lovingly on the man's shoulder.

"Ōhä-Ä'ähänärdanär!" he cried, ending with a tremor of laughter.

"Ōhä-Ä'ähänärdanär!" the Sentinel smiled back at him, then removed his hand from Mär's and swept his leader into a tearful embrace.

"I'm so glad we get to see each other alive," Mär whispered as he pulled the Sentinel more tightly close to him.

Light and Glory

The Sentinel grinned through his shining tears as Mär released him. "Glad to be working with you again, Mär," he laughed.

Mär clapped him on the shoulder as he passed straight into the sphere's smooth white wall, murmuring "Ōhä-Ä'ähänärdanär" relishingly as he went.

Through courtyards and corridors, past blazing gardens and pillared palaces, Mär and his trailing companions hurtled single-mindedly through the depths of the great white citadel till they emerged within a wide spherical hall. Several score unruffled Earthmen were waiting in the room, hosted there by a few of Nüährnär's Ōmäthäär.

"Ä'ähärnhär," a tall, dashing Ōmäthäär said to Mär as Mär careened toward him, "This," he indicated an Earthman floating beside him, "Is *the* Ä'ähärnhär!"

"Ä'ähärnhär," the Earthman bowed as Mär reached him.

"Don't you call me that!" Mär begged earnestly. "Not now that you're here!"

The Earthman called the Ä'ähärnhär smiled at Mär. As was usual he looked like a young man, with a smooth face and clean dark hair and beard, but he like Mär carried himself with a light dignity as of the oldest man ever to live.

"'Mär' is a finer title," the Ä'ähärnhär admitted.

Mär laughed powerfully. Without warning he scooped the Ä'ähärnhär up into a crushing hug, bursting into laughing tears as he did.

"Mär!" the Ä'ähärnhär laughed fondly, "I remind you, I still *feel* like a very frail little old man!"

Mär released him, laughing still, and interlocked his left hand with the Ä'ähärnhär's right. "And you didn't keep your well-earned wrinkles?"

"Mär," the Ä'ähärnhär said lightly and with feigned reproof, forcing his own left hand into Mär's right, "There are deeper awards than mortal disfigurement."

Mär looked from the Ä'ähärnhär's benign face to his left hand clasping his own right.

"Thank you," the Ä'ähärnhär whispered in explanation. "All of you. Ōmäthäär!"

"All of us!" Mär corrected him, beaming. He released the Ä'ähärnhär's hands, then clapped his own hands smartly together, nearly glowing with joy as he looked around the room. Thrilled voices were clamoring through the air as Mär's Ōmäthäär mingled with the Ä'ähärnhär's.

"And you are still the political head," the Ä'ähärnhär reminded him.

Mär's voice filled the room. "Ōmäthäär!"

5: Nōhōnŭäär

Despite their excitement each at seeing the other party, both orders of Ōmäthäär halted their conversations and directed their gazes toward Mär.

"Earthmen," Mär said warmly. "Has Ŭmäthŭ explained everything?"

The Ä'ähärnhär didn't answer, but looked questioningly at Ŭmäthŭ, the tall dashing Ōmäthäär beside him.

"The essentials," Ŭmäthŭ said seriously. "She helped." He squeezed the woman on his right. "A little."

Mär smiled momentarily, but it faded as he continued. "Sĕrĕhahn believes Earth to be Pp'ōhōnŭäär."

"Me too," the Ä'ähärnhär said.

"I know," Mär said. Worry emanated from him, as it did from Mär's Ōmäthäär, who had all looked at the Ä'ähärnhär as he confirmed their fears.

"This is the greatest opportunity, a greater opportunity, than I think any of us ever hoped for," Mär said to his Ōmäthäär. "And a greater responsibility!"

The room hung in heavy silence.

"Sĕrĕhahn wants to destroy Ōhōnŭäär and every single Nōhōnŭäär," Mär declared. "You threaten him, perhaps more than any other Ōmäthäär can.

"I believe that Sĕrĕhahn has other purposes for you," he said darkly. "But it is clear that he intended these mercenaries to destroy you, for starters."

He braced himself, and saw Ŭmäthŭ seem to do the same, then he said, "I propose that we stay at Pp'ōhōnŭäär, to defend it against the Ämäthōär!"

"Agreed," a few voices called from around the hall, and Ŭmäthŭ and his wife nodded, but the rest wore expressions of varying degrees of terror.

"Mär," an Ōmäthäär said, raising her hand slightly. Mär looked acknowledgingly at her.

She looked at Mär and also at the Ä'ähärnhär as she said, "I suggest that we leave this location as soon as possible. The Ämäthōär know that we thwarted their pawns here. We can take the Nōhōnŭäär and split up again."

One of the Ä'ähärnhär's Ōmäthäär raised his hand. Mär looked at him.

"In that case, the planet must also be taken. It is part and parcel of Nōhōnŭäär-hood."

"I agree with George," the Ä'ähärnhär said with startling force.

Mär nodded to another Ōmäthäär.

"Friends, we have found Ōhōnŭäär itself!" the Ōmäthäär said. "We *cannot* let Sĕrĕhahn capture it! If we take Ōhōnŭäär and every Nōhōnŭäär far from Nrathĕrmĕ, we will protect them from him, and, by the time the Ämäthōär catch up to us, we may have harnessed the Power of Ōhōnŭäär ourselves!"

The Ä'ähärnhär looked hard at Mär.

It was several seconds before Mär moved. Then he looked around at all his fellow Ōmäthäär.

"We cannot leave."

The Ä'ähärnhär grinned.

"Pp'ōhōnŭäär must not be destroyed or captured. Ōhōnŭäär is more important than Nrathĕrmĕ and all the people who live and have ever lived in it." A slight grin creased his face as he said quietly, "Nevertheless, the people in Nrathĕrmĕ are still important."

Many of the Ōmäthäär smiled bravely as Mär said that.

"I, for myself, cannot leave," Mär said concretely. "Not so long as Sĕrĕhahn has his chain over the N'nrathĕrmĕ.

"There is nothing to gain and much to lose by leaving here while attempting to stay near Nrathĕrmĕ; the Ämäthōär will be able to follow our tracks from this place.

"We must stay and fight."

Even the Ä'ähärnhär, though glowing with admiration, looked terrified.

"We cannot contend against Nrathĕrmĕ militarily," Ŭmäthŭ said with no less admiration than the Ä'ähärnhär.

"Nor can we contend against Sĕrĕhahn when he comes!" another Ōmäthäär said with more fear.

"Mär," a third Ōmäthäär said with respect, "The Ämäthōär will come if we stay here. They will come in power and in numbers too great for even all of us together to resist."

Ŭmäthŭ looked doubtfully at the speaking Ōmäthäär, but then looked to their head for his answer.

Mär was smiling concurringly. "Yeah," he said sincerely, "You're right. Neither I, nor all of us together, can stand up against Sĕrĕhahn alone! Much less against armies of Ämäthōär." He shivered. "Not against a fraction of their hosts."

He glided to Ŭmäthŭ, and placed his hands lovingly on his shoulders. Ŭmäthŭ smiled courageously back at him, putting his left hand deferentially on Mär's arm. "And if Sĕrĕhahn can get Nrathĕrmĕ to fight us," he said to them all while looking at Ŭmäthŭ, "And, I think, Sĕrĕhahn will have no difficulty arranging that; then we will be inexorably overwhelmed."

He glided back from Ŭmäthŭ with a trusting pat against his shoulder, and faced the Ä'ähärnhär. The Earthman stared inscrutably at Mär for an instant. A small yet fiery smile then emerged on the Ä'ähärnhär's face.

"When I'm in hopeless situations," Mär said with a nostalgic laugh, "I can typically tell myself that I've had worse before."

The mood lightened noticeably as Ōmäthäär from both worlds chuckled

5: Nōhōnŭäär

knowingly.

"But I can't say that now," Mär said curtly. "But I have had very, very bad." He smiled sadly at another Ōmäthäär. Then he looked around the room. "In my darkest, most utterly hopeless times, I almost never have what it would take to succeed."

A few comprehending smiles surfaced around the room.

"But Är! Är is stronger than Sĕrĕhahn and all the martial might of Nrathĕrmĕ!

"We don't have to be strong enough to fight an onslaught of Ämäthōär. Or strong enough to resist a N'nrathĕrmĕ army. All we need is to be strong enough to let Är use us to be his wonders!"

Sounds of agreement rustled through the hall. The Ä'ähärnhär raised his arm, and Mär acknowledged him.

"You speak of the 'Power' of Ōhōnŭäär," he said to the room in general. "This is it! We possess it already! My dear friends, it's Ä'ähänärdanär!"

Mär beamed at him. "Are we Ōmäthäär?" he demanded jubilantly of his peers surrounding him. "We cannot abandon the N'nrathĕrmĕ! Ōhōnŭäär is no license to leave them. But it may well be the turning of the tide!"

He breathed deeply, the room seeming to vibrate with his emotion.

"I will stay! If we trust Är, here, we will become the tools that will lead to Sĕrĕhahn's eradication and Nrathĕrmĕ's redemption!

"Närdamähr's redemption!

"If there is any other way, then we ought to take it. But I know of no other way to do what we ought to do. We have to stay, and defend Pp'ōhōnŭäär. It is Är's fault that we are in this predicament," he smiled. "If we do what we must do, Är will provide a way for us to do it!"

There was a deep silence.

"Are any in favor of staying with me to fight?" He raised his arm to signify his favor.

Every single Ōmäthäär, from both worlds, raised his or her arm in favor.

Tears trickled down Mär's cheeks as he said, "Are any opposed to staying?"

No arms rose. Scattered laughter broke the stillness.

Mär laughed loudly. He threw his arms exultantly over his head, proclaiming, "Ōhä-Ä'ähänärdanär!"

The Ä'ähärnhär was laughing as he wept.

"I wonder," one of the Ä'ähärnhär's counselors said, "How willing the rest of Nŭährnär will be to stay with us."

"That will be up to them," Mär said.

"Most of them should not be told much about our situation," an Ōmäthäär said.

"Though we should tell them all we can," another added. "Most of them will know our military danger. But they shouldn't have to know details about the Ämäthōär."

"Not yet," Mär nodded at her. "But I'm afraid that all of us will see the threat of Ämäthōär firsthand. But that will come as it will come. Now, we have to hurry to prepare to defend ourselves. We have to shoulder these responsibilities that Är's thrown us into." He turned dutifully to the Ä'ähärnhär. "We have to marshal the N'nŭährnär."

"Like...that!" Lewis Pratt said triumphantly. The wide plains below them morphed into a perfect duplication of the Himalaya mountain range.

"Wow!" Terry said.

"Perfect! Flawless! Look at it!" Lewis raved.

Tom laughed. "Amazing," he said.

"Yeah, but if we wanted to see the Himalayas, we might as well have just gone back down and seen them," Andrew shrugged, soaring around above the towering range miles below.

There was a deafening thunder as Mount Everest cracked open, spewing smoke and ash from its shattered summit.

"Andrew!" Lewis yelled as his son roared with laughter. "Don't ruin my work!"

"Work, right," Andrew snickered. "It took you all of a split second to do it."

The mountain repaired itself instantaneously and the fire and smoke vanished. "It's the Himalayas!" Lewis insisted.

"I always wanted to see Mount Everest be a volcano," Andrew sighed happily. "And now they're boring! We might as well visit the real ones."

"These might as well be the real ones!" Lewis said excitedly, spreading his hands out at the wide scene of mountains. "Every single particle, every bit of dust, every atom, it's just the same as the real ones!"

"But still, they aren't the real ones," Terry said.

"When I can make a mountain range at will, I don't ask for any more!" Lewis argued.

"Lewis!" a voice shouted.

"Look at you all!" another voice called.

Lewis's brother and sister-in-law hurtled down from the Shell's internal sky, stopping in front of Lewis and his children.

5: Nōhōnŭäär

"Who made those?" his sister-in-law asked as she stopped.

"Dad labored—" Andrew began.

"I did," Lewis smiled, flying forward and hugging his brother. "Look at you two! You're like kids again!"

"No younger than you," Daniel Pratt grinned. "Tom and Andrew almost look older than you, now!"

"Yeah, I always wanted to be older," Tom laughed as he hugged his uncle. Tom looked cleaner but only a handful of years older than he had been an hour beforehand.

"I can understand that," his aunt Ann said. "Our kids look about our age now, too."

"Where are they?" Tom asked as she hugged him.

"They scattered," Ann smiled, shaking her head. "Off to explore and meet people."

"You aren't worried?" Lewis asked Daniel. "Letting them scatter with all these strange people around?"

"I couldn't hardly hold them back!" Daniel chuckled. "They can take care of themselves. They're no less adults than we are, now! I say, let them explore."

"Adults!" Lewis said dazedly. "Taught everything we know..." He shook his head. "A few hours ago, life was life, and now..."

"I know," Daniel said, shaking his head as well. "It makes me dizzy to think about it. But I'm more than happy to get used to what these N'nŭährnär have given us! This past hour has felt like an eternity, but it's been a busy eternity!"

"Busy?" Lewis asked. "How so?"

Daniel nodded toward the mountains. "Messing around, getting used to all this stuff!"

Ann had glided over to talk with Terry. Lewis sent his words to Daniel alone: "What do you think of all this business about Anhar and Nrathĕrmĕ?"

Daniel's cheeriness faded slightly. "I believe it," he said, "But I hope...well, I hope what I know of Nrathĕrmĕ's military strength is...I hope I'm misinterpreting it. I really do."

"So do I," Lewis said worriedly.

"I don't understand why these people are staying here," Daniel said. "How can they protect us? There's no way they can stand up against what I think I know about Nrathĕrmĕ."

"Do you believe they really are here to protect us?" Lewis asked.

"Sure, I believe that much," Daniel said. "I'm just not sure about their motives."

The air rumbled as Everest erupted again, followed by every other peak in the entire range. Andrew's arms were dramatically raised, as he shouted, *"Behold, my creation!"*

The fire and smoke disappeared as the emerging magma turned solid. A thickening layer of ice began forming over everything on the ground below.

"Tom!" Andrew yelled, "You're ruining my work!"

The mountains turned normal again as Lewis said, "Andrew, leave my mountains alone!"

Tom turned to Daniel. "So where are the kids exactly?"

Daniel eyed the mountains, and a fantastic deluge flowed out of nowhere, covering everything except for the tallest peaks. Lewis sighed.

"Spalding and Heather are back on the surface," Daniel said to Tom, "And Robyn and Mark and Christina are all somewhere or other in the Shell. Just look around, you'll find them."

Tom realized he could find every one of them just by thinking to find them. His cousin Heather, he knew, was over where France had been. Spalding was deep under the Pacific Ocean.

"I'm going to go see Spalding," he said to the others.

"If you can recognize him," Ann grinned.

"He's grown up too?" Tom asked.

"Well, physically," she smiled.

"Good. Six year-olds are too good to lose," Tom chuckled.

"Take him with you," Lewis said, pushing Andrew toward Tom. "Then I'll have some peace making things."

"Alright," Andrew said, "I'll leave your mountains alone." He waved at Tom, then sped off away into the sky.

Lewis hadn't realized he was staring apprehensively after Andrew until Ann said, "He'll be okay, Lewis."

"I'll see you soon," Tom said, turning to go. "Wait, we can talk to each other just fine, no matter where we are. Okay, call me if you need me!"

He pitched forward and a second later had plunged into Daniel's instant ocean. He passed straight through the solid mountains and then out through the inner armor of the colossal Shell.

The Earth glowed lively beneath the Shell. The defense now covered the entire planet, but dawn was still creeping westward over the shining blue Pacific. Tom admired the reflection of the land and seas in the Shell's opaque underside as he hurtled into Earth's atmosphere, and considered how strong that thick, dense matter must have been. He hoped it would be strong enough

5: Nōhōnŭäär

to defend Earth from Sĕrĕhahn.

The sparkling water was rushing up to meet him. He spotted Spalding deep under the water a couple hundred miles away, swimming along with a pod of large whales.

"Tom!" he heard Spalding's voice in his head as he knifed into the surface without a splash.

"Hey," Tom said back, slowing quickly and coming up level with his cousin and the whales.

"Isn't this awesome?" Spalding said excitedly. "Real whales! And they can understand me!"

Tom glided up behind Spalding, loving the pressure of the ocean on every side. "You sound like my cousin," he joked, "But six year-olds don't need to shave!"

Spalding Pratt was to all appearances a full grown man robed in a sparkling kaleidoscope of color. But he had turned his blond hair white and given himself a beard that trailed almost to his knees.

Spalding laughed merrily, and the beard vanished. "I can look like whatever I want to look like," he said. "I turned into a shark earlier, but they didn't like it." He smiled at the whales.

Tom greeted the whales, then realized that he had simply spoken emotions into their minds. He felt a wary but interested surge as reply.

Spalding was spinning slowly away like an underwater top. "This is so cool!"

Spalding had always been Tom's favorite cousin, though Tom would never admit that in front of his other relatives. Now, as Tom saw Spalding a grown man but with no less of his pure minded charm, he forgot all about Ämäthōär and Sĕrĕhahn. All he cared about was how life had so incredibly become heaven.

"Hey," Spalding said, stopping in mid-spin with his arms out.

Tom blinked.

"Let's race!" Spalding shot off like a flash of many-colored light away through the ocean.

Tom burst after him. He passed his cruising cousin, then shot up and out of the water and within half a second was back in the cool of space.

Southern South America stretched out majestically a hundred miles below, and the shimmering Atlantic was drawing closer. He was staring awestruck at the perfect forms and patterns of the Earth's surface when Spalding blasted past him.

Tom accelerated, but Spalding had already passed far ahead. He

Light and Glory

disappeared suddenly into the reflective blue Shell. Tom followed right behind him, barely noticing wide green land drop away as he raced into the spacious interior.

Spalding was still far ahead. Tom could see him dodging the few people in their way, and then the blue sky gave way to a rolling sea of sand. It was as if they were flying downward again as Spalding ahead vanished into the desert and through the Shell's formidable outer armor. An instant later, Tom plunged into one of the dunes and through the Shell.

Emerging into open space, Tom looked around for Spalding but couldn't find him anywhere.

"Hurry up, slow poke!" he heard Spalding's voice laugh in his head. Then he spotted him, far, far ahead, nearly at the sun.

He knew he was traveling faster than light, but what was heavier on his mind was that Spalding was still going faster. Two seconds later he slammed straight into the sun, was dazzled by the sudden total immersion of light and fire, then was rocketing again out the other side.

Spalding was still far away. He was still going faster!

Tom accelerated more. A nagging feeling, stifled by Spalding's far lead, wondered how fast he would be able to go. Then he noticed he had already burned a sizeable chunk of the energy that Liz had put into him.

He shot past Spalding, who had stopped altogether. He stopped immediately, only to realize he had used almost all the rest of his energy to decelerate from such a speed. He turned back and flew, much more slowly, back to rejoin Spalding.

"Whoohoohoo!" Spalding laughed. He was away at the glimmering speck of Jupiter, Tom saw.

"I got going almost three hundred times light speed there!" Spalding gloated.

"Me too," Tom laughed. "But I don't want to do that again! I used up almost all my energy right there!" Jupiter was becoming a small disk now.

"Oh. Yeah," Spalding's voice said. "I didn't think about that."

"I guess we can still do it, since we've got less mass in us now to move," Tom said as the giant planet grew larger and closer. "But I don't want to waste it."

"Yeah," Spalding agreed.

"That was a whole lot of energy that we just used!" Tom said in awe.

"If we had gone much faster," Spalding said as he came into closer sight and the great glowing planet filled most of Tom's view, "We wouldn't have had enough energy to stop!"

5: Nōhōnŭäär

Tom had a terrifying thought of floating endlessly through space, powerless to ever return home. "Yeah, but we can get going a lot faster, more than six hundred times light, I think, before we'll have to worry about that."

"But we shouldn't waste it. We don't have that much energy to go around," Spalding said thoughtfully.

"What do you mean?" Tom asked, gazing distractedly at the massive ball of gas. "Look at this thing!"

"Didn't they tell you about Anhar, and everything?" Spalding said. "We have to make as many defenses as possible."

"Yeah...where did they get all that matter for the Shell?" Tom wondered.

"Yeah!" Spalding said. "We've got a lot of matter stored inside us. I bet they used that to make the Shell. I guess they brought a lot of matter with them."

"From where though?"

Spalding shrugged. "Nrathĕrmĕ? Or other stars, maybe."

"And we've just wasted a lot of it," Tom said guiltily. "Who'd have thought a race could be so serious?"

Spalding laughed. "We were going really fast!"

Tom looked thoughtfully at the gargantuan majesty of the glowing world. "We're going to have to use Jupiter, aren't we? To make defenses out of."

Spalding looked anxiously at Jupiter too.

"Have you two been having a good time?" a woman's cheerful voice called out to them.

Tom looked and saw a very attractive woman slowing to stop right beside them. Her name was Ōdaädŭ, he knew, then smiled unconsciously as he realized that that meant "Speedy."

"Yes," Spalding said uncertainly, looking at Tom.

"I'm sorry to get in the way," Ōdaädŭ said to Tom, "But I need to take you to a meeting, right now."

"A meeting?" Spalding said.

Tom was looking questioningly at her. "Don't worry," she smiled easily, "My friends will explain everything. But we really need to hurry."

"Okay..." Terry Pratt was muttering to Ann. "What was that all about?"

"I'm not sure," Ann said, the two of them flying rather swiftly away from a knot of N'nŭährnär. "Here's Robyn." She pointed ahead to where her daughter was surrounded by a dozen strangers. "It looks like she's having the same problem."

Robyn Pratt looked up and saw them. "Hi Terry!" she waved happily.

Light and Glory

The crowd around Robyn looked over at Ann and Terry, opening a space for them to pass in. Robyn hugged Terry as the crowd closed all around them.

"What's going on?" Terry asked her, looking around nervously.

"We've been talking about Earth life," Robyn said, clearly pleased at the attention.

"This is your mother?" a man called Rahär asked Robyn.

"Yes it is," Robyn smiled, "Ann Pratt. And this is my cousin Terry Pratt."

A smiling woman named Nŭnŭ extended her left hand to Terry. Terry looked confusedly at it, then took it with her own left hand.

Nŭnŭ stared at Terry, then smiled again. "I'm sorry," she said, and she gently took Terry's right hand by the wrist and guided it toward her left hand. She interlocked the fingers of her left hand with the fingers of Terry's right hand, as another man did the same with Ann.

"Okay," Terry said, catching on. "We're used to doing it this way." She took Nŭnŭ's right hand in hers and shook it.

The others all laughed, and Nŭnŭ said, "Then that will be fine," as she shook Terry's hand in return.

"Clasping left to right means a lot to us," a man, Ŭdähänär, explained.

"Yeah," Robyn nodded, "They were telling me about Ōmäthäär. It's really interesting."

"What do you mean?" Terry asked, as another person shook her hand enthusiastically right to right.

"You too?" a man called Ōhäräkran said, looking puzzled. "You know about everything except the Ōmäthäär?"

"I'm not sure," Terry said.

"What have you told Robyn?" Ann asked.

"The Ōmäthäär are the only people who can stop Ämäthöär!" Ŭdähänär said. "They know how to do amazing things with the Ärthähr!"

"What's 'The Ärthähr?'" Terry asked, more confused.

Robyn shrugged.

"You're Nōhōnŭäär!" Nŭnŭ said in surprise. "You don't know what Ärthähr is?"

"Maybe this isn't Ōhōnŭäär," N'mōth said softly.

"Ōhōnŭäär?" Ann asked. "What's that? 'House of the Infinite?'"

There was a small pause. A few of the N'nŭährnär exchanged meaningful glances.

"They said it's Earth," Robyn said tentatively. "But I don't know what they mean by that..."

"You really don't know what we're talking about, do you?" Ōhäräkran

5: Nōhōnŭäär

said pityingly.

"No," Ann shook her head. "I'm sorry. Can you explain it to us?"

There was another small pause.

"If you weren't already told about any of this," Ōhäräkran said, "Then maybe we shouldn't tell you. Mär always has reasons."

"Any of what?" Terry asked.

Nŭnŭ smiled. "You should talk to an Ōmäthäär. They know how to explain these things well."

"Where can we find one of those?" Robyn asked.

"Anywhere," Ŭdähänär reminded her patiently, "Just like how you'd find anyone else."

"We'll have to ask an Ōmäthäär about these things," Robyn said, looking at Ann and Terry. "Now that you've gotten us interested."

"I'm amazed you don't know more about this than we do," N'mōth said uncertainly.

"Here's an Ōmäthäär right now," Ōnōth'nrŭ said happily.

A grey clad man flew up behind the Pratts. Everyone backed away for him.

"Hi," the Ōmäthäär, who Ann knew was named Ōhäzärŭnŭz, said, extending his left hand to her. "Ann Pratt?"

Ann nodded, and nervously took his left hand with her right. The people behind her chuckled.

"What have you been telling these three?" Ōhäzärŭnŭz smiled incriminatingly at the others. "How did she know that?"

Ann, intimidated, didn't say anything.

Ōhäzärŭnŭz chuckled and squeezed Ann's hand affably. He took Terry's right hand in his left, then Robyn's.

"Ann, Robyn," he said then, "We need you to come with me."

"'We?'" Ann asked.

"Why?" Robyn said.

"Why not me?" Terry asked.

Ōhäzärŭnŭz smiled at Terry. "We'll be right back. We're having a meeting; Ann and Robyn are wanted there."

"Why us?" Ann asked.

"Mär will explain everything," Ōhäzärŭnŭz assured her. "But we don't have much time now. Daniel is going to be there, too."

Ann looked helplessly at Terry. "I suppose we'll see you later."

"See ya, Terry," Robyn waved, moving away beside Ōhäzärŭnŭz.

"Ōähŭhan," Ōhäzärŭnŭz said to the crowd, "Ŭdmŭnan. You're wanted as well."

Terry was slightly comforted to see that the crowd looked almost as confused about this meeting as she felt. Ōähŭhan and Ŭdmŭnan, on the other hand, a pleasant, sober looking husband and wife, seemed more composed as they joined Ōhäzärŭnŭz.

"I hope to see all of you later!" Ōhäzärŭnŭz said genially to the remaining crowd. Wheeling sharply around, he shot back the way he had come, the others tailing behind him as Terry watched them dwindle.

Chapter 6

Answers and Questions

Ähänär brought them to a vacant spot. "Here's our place."

Scott and Rene stopped beside her. Kathy and Sarah stopped on their other side.

"Wow," Kathy gasped.

More than two million people had gathered out in space outside the Shell. They had been arranged into a perfect hollow sphere, which shimmered oddly as people milled around near their places. And away in the center, Rene recognized Mär, standing in the midst of a swarm of official-looking people.

"Those are my parents," Ähänär said, pointing out two of the people around Mär, "Tärmäth and Ähärz'th'päöth."

"All those people make Mär harder to see," Scott commented.

"It's better for them to be there," Ähänär said vaguely.

Thousands of people were joining themselves to the developing sphere from all over. Kathy looked around interestedly at the stars and the Shell, which she had begun to think was rather pretty in its perfect reflectiveness.

Sarah glanced at her sister. It was amazing seeing young Kathy as an adult woman. She smiled to herself, and looked around at the people all over the sphere. She entertained herself for a couple minutes by thinking of the name of every person she looked at, but irresistibly her attention was drawn to Mär and his companions at the center.

Mär was looking fixedly at various of his companions; Sarah guessed he was speaking to them. The majority of his companions were simply looking outward. She watched Tärmäth, Ähänär's father. He seemed to be looking closely from person to person in the multitudinous sphere, and he looked supremely serious.

Then he locked eyes with Sarah. His serious demeanor disappeared so quickly that it shocked her. "Glad to see you, Miss Trotter," he smiled amiably. "Don't worry; we should be beginning in just a minute."

"Okay," Sarah said dumbly.

"Keep an eye on Ähänär!" he smiled more deeply. Then he broke eye contact with Sarah, and resumed somberly watching the people around the sphere. But Sarah thought she could see something of a grin linger through his solemn countenance.

The streams of people joining the sphere had soon dried up.

"Let's begin!" Mär's voice thundered abruptly.

The million conversations twittering through the sphere ceased, and all eyes turned to the leader of Nŭährnär.

"Thank you for coming. All of you," Mär's voice rang out when everyone had turned their attention to him.

"And welcome, dear, well-met Earthmen!

"Don't feel too confused," he said with a knowing laugh. "You will get used to everything before you know it. I thank you, especially," his voice heaved with warm gratitude, "For joining us here, for agreeing to help everyone in the cause of the fight against Anhar.

"I hope you have all been told something about Anhar and his involvement in the assault of two hours ago.

"I'm going to explain a little more right now.

"We all must know what we are involved in. I do not want to do anything more until you, Earthmen," he always said that title with a strange but affective degree of veneration, "Know at least a little of what we're involved in and why."

Mär looked around at them all. Then he said stoutly, "Anhar of Nrathĕrmĕ, a man we call Sĕrĕhahn, feels threatened by you."

He hesitated, as if letting that declaration sink into them.

"Though you don't have the resources or the technology to threaten Anhar..." He trailed suddenly off, then left the thought unfinished.

"Sĕrĕhahn is oppressing Nrathĕrmĕ," he said instead. "Though Nrathĕrmĕ is a wonderful place, the people there are being kept from becoming everything that they could be, everything that they deserve to be!

"Because Sĕrĕhahn wants to keep them in his grip.

"Sĕrĕhahn is feeding off of the ideas and genius of the society of Nrathĕrmĕ.

"To keep that rein over them, he has, unavoidably, ended up limiting them from what they could be.

"This is what Nŭährnär is for: to work to overthrow Sĕrĕhahn and set free the N'nrathĕrmĕ!"

Mär paused again.

"Compared to Anhar's Nrathĕrmĕ," he said pleasantly, "Nŭährnär isn't much of a threat. But you Earthmen are.

"Earth is a new world. You aren't under Sĕrĕhahn's influence.

"I am setting out to keep it that way."

Sarah felt herself smiling with Mär. She wasn't sure what to think of him, but, for whatever reason, something inside her wanted to trust him.

6: Answers and Questions

Peter Garcia noticed the woman to his right smiling. He frowned slightly; there were too many holes in this story. He found himself beginning to wonder if Mär, and the others, had been lying to them all about Nrathěrmě. At least, he was not about to swallow everything this Mär was telling them, not until he explained things a little more at any rate.

Emotion saturated Mär's voice as he pledged, "Nŭährnär will not leave you to be destroyed by Sěrěhahn, or by his followers!

"Anhar hired a clan of," he hesitated for the slightest moment, "Of pirates to destroy all you Earthmen. He could not get Nrathěrmě to use its resources against you.

"Nrathěrmě would never do such a thing.

"The N'nrathěrmě are too good," he smiled.

"That will buy us some time. The N'nrathěrmě, as of yet, know nothing about you or about Earth.

"But that will not last long at all.

"The people of Nrathěrmě would definitely embrace you if they knew about you.

"But do not underestimate Sěrěhahn. He will find a way to turn the N'nrathěrmě against you.

"He will find a way.

"Sěrěhahn used pirates so he could eliminate you once and for all and then blame it on a barbaric, soulless people. The pirates have been frustrated, but now Sěrěhahn will know that Nŭährnär is here.

"However much a military match Nŭährnär isn't for Nrathěrmě, it is more than a match for that breed of pirate. Sěrěhahn will not use degenerate clans again.

"But I do not doubt," his voice carried heavy force into even Peter's mind, "That Sěrěhahn will find another way to destroy you.

"So I and my friends aim to stay and defend you and Earth from him."

Peter didn't trust this. Mär was imposing himself on them. How was this any different, he thought, from Mär coming in and openly occupying them, like a simple warlord? And now he thought he could lure their loyalty by claiming to be protecting them? This sounded like common thuggery.

"We could flee," Mär was saying, "All of us, with the Earth too.

"But Nŭährnär also has a responsibility to the sextillions of people under Sěrěhahn's weight in Nrathěrmě.

"Nŭährnär will stay.

"You are free to flee if you want to. But know that Sěrěhahn will hunt you whether or not you flee.

Light and Glory

"You will be safest here with Nŭährnär, which will stay to defend the Earth and to stand against Sĕrĕhahn."

Mär smiled glowingly then, despite the gravity of his subject matter.

"Remember, Earthmen! This is your world! Your history, your legacy and your heritage! Defend it! No matter the pain, no matter the fear, defend your legacy, against anyone and against anything that Sĕrĕhahn may contrive to destroy it!"

Against anyone—like you? Peter wondered.

"Nŭähnär will gather as much matter as it can to build defenses. All stars and worlds that are close enough to be safely reached must be harvested and brought to Earth.

"We will not move Earth at all; we will conserve as many resources as we can. For now, it will be better to use matter as defenses than to burn it as energy.

"If we all do what we need to do, we will be prepared to stand against everything that Sĕrĕhahn contrives to send at us.

"Now, you all have been selected to lead Nŭähnär.

"You N'närdamähr," he said to the non-Earthmen, "Let me explain this more to the Earthmen."

He looked around, as if profoundly pleased at the people assembled there.

"I'm the leader of Nŭähnär.

"But the only reason for that is that the other N'nŭähnär agree to go where I go.

"And where I'm going is to fight Anhar and defend Earth. Any of you, or any of you N'närdamähr for that matter, who don't want to do that are free to do your own things.

"You will be safer with the mass of Nŭähnär, even though this is where Sĕrĕhahn's stroke will strike the hardest.

"I am going to stay. Sĕrĕhahn has struck at me before; I have learned not to cringe.

"If any of you, at any time, want to leave, you are your own people.

"But I hope you will stay!

"I need all the help you can give me! Nŭähnär, and Earth, need all that you can do!

"*Your world* is worth everything you can give.

"These people," he motioned at the men and women clustered on every side of him, "Who are standing so distractingly close to me, do more for me than I can do for myself. They head Nŭähnär.

"They will be here for you, to help you assist in leading our N'nŭähnär.

6: Answers and Questions

"Leading?" Tom Pratt breathed aloud. He had wanted to believe he had misunderstood what Mär was saying.

The man to Tom's right looked at Tom with his eyebrows doubtfully raised.

"Each couple of them," Mär was continuing, "Is assigned to eight couples. Well, those who haven't had the fortune to marry yet," he said smiling, but then his mood quickly darkened, "Or those who have lost their companions, fill the space of a couple. Each couple, or individual, of my friends here is assigned to eight couples or individuals.

"Each one of those, couple or individual, to which they are assigned is assigned to eight more.

"Every couple or one of you will be assigned to eight others.

"Those eight must help you with anything you need, and you need to make sure that life is great for the eight to whom you each are assigned.

"Your eight are *your* responsibility. Not the other way around.

"We all are working to defend Earth.

"We must establish defenses according to whatever we think is good, and to do that we need to work with our assistants to be more efficient.

"If any of you have any bright ideas, tell your managers!

"If any of you find your managers unfriendly, be sure to let your managers' managers know," he smiled threateningly.

"We all have to work together if we are to stand against Anhar.

"I want to be able to talk a great deal more about how we can work better together, but I will leave that for your managers.

"For now, the most important things that you need to know are who your assistants are and who your managers are, and that we really need to do everything we can to prepare to defend Earth against Anhar."

Mär paused for a couple of seconds.

"About building defenses," he said then, "Your managers will tell you anything you want to know. The worlds here will be harvested, and people will be sent to every nearby system to harvest them and bring the matter here.

"We all need to keep a close eye on everything that is going on at Nrathĕrmĕ.

"Some of my friends are hiding at Nrathĕrmĕ; Sĕrĕhahn knows that, but he hasn't discovered them yet. They do their best to keep us connected to everything that is happening there.

"Every one of you has access to all of Nrathĕrmĕ's usually accessible media.

"Keep up to date. We may see hints of what Sĕrĕhahn is going to do."

Mär smiled dismally. "Sĕrĕhahn knows we'll be watching Nrathĕrmĕ's media. But we may be able to glean some things."

He looked around at the sphere assembled for their cause.

"If any of you have any questions, any difficulties, anything, if you just want to talk for the sake of talking, tell your managers!

"But we do have a lot to do," he grinned.

"Talking to your managers just for the sake of it is a good idea; morale is more important than bare production—it is production!—but always remember how much we have to do if we are to survive!

"But get to know your managers, your assistants, anyone and everyone.

"I don't want to be part of a society that isn't bonded by friendship and love!"

He paused with an understanding smile. "Friendship and love can happen more quickly than we might think between us while we're working industriously to assist each other and to protect everything that's precious."

He smiled warmly at them all.

"There will be more than ninety billion of us when the rest of Nŭährnär arrives. You will not likely ever get to know each and every one of our compatriots in Nŭährnär.

"But our friendships with each other, with our managers and assistants, all through the ninety billion of us, will hold us together more than all our defenses will.

"If we do not value each other, our solid, fluid, beautiful constitution will break apart in the very times in which we need it most!

"Work closely with your assistants! Use them, make them work!

"But work harder than you work them. Any tyrants," he smiled benignly, "Will have their own managers to reckon with before long.

"The eight couples, or individuals in the place of couples, under one couple of managers are to be recognized as together having the same authority as those managers. My eight sets of assistants together have the same authority that I have; if they get together, they can overturn any decision I make. Or if seven of them and eight of their assistants get together, they can cancel my decision.

"If anyone decides not to honor that authority—Please! Honor each other! We are all in this together!—But if anyone does not, then our loose, fluid, potent system will become congested, crippled!, with force and penalties, which is exactly what Anhar wants to happen to his enemies!

"Why is Nrathĕrmĕ so powerful?

"How has our world grown from a divided planet to span thousands of

6: Answers and Questions

worlds in so short a time?

"Why is life so easy, why do we have all the opportunities that our understandings of our universe have given us?

"It's because people together are infinitely more powerful, more progressive, more potent, and more happy!, than people apart!

"The N'nrathĕrmĕ work together! They want each other to be happy, and thus they all are happy!

"Pirates generally destroy themselves. The only clans that last are those bound by friendship and respect.

"Which way are we going to go?

"We have so few recognized laws.

"Lead as you see fit. Live as you see fit.

"But, please, listen to your managers!

"But if you know better than they do, well, then do what you think is better; either you or they will have some learning to do.

"Most of Nŭährnär is not with us right now. Those of you whose assistants were not summoned to this meeting will need to let them know what is going on.

"You have come here because the heaviest portions of the load will fall on you. You are to be the head of Nŭährnär.

"So get to work! Your managers will tell you in more detail what exactly needs to be done.

"Our greatest responsibility is to one another. But, for right now, a great part of that responsibility is to build defenses.

"Get to know each other, help each other, spend time together, but, for this time, put as much time as you feel you can into harvesting and into designing and building defenses."

Mär stopped, and looked around once more at the sphere of two million leaders.

"You are amazing," he told them fervently. "We will triumph, here, at Earth."

His voice disappeared in Tom's head. Without further ceremony, Mär and the legion around him soared off through the sphere and toward the Shell standing as a bastion around the Earth.

The sphere began to dissolve as most people followed Mär and his assistants back into the Shell. Tom immediately realized then who his manager and assistants were, as if an unperceived voice had spoken it into his brain. He had only one manager, Ōdaädŭ, the pretty woman who had summoned him to the conference. And he knew he had twelve assistants; four couples and four singles; only five of them were Earthmen.

This was going to be interesting, Tom thought nervously.

Ōdaädŭ was just entering the Shell after Mär, he saw. He was about to follow her, when the man beside him spoke.

"Well," the man said, like he was trying to get Tom's attention, "What did you think of that little speech?"

Tom knew that the man was called Peter Garcia. Peter's expression was hard to read, but he seemed friendly, and in any case Tom felt relieved that he was an Earthman.

"I'm pretty confused," Tom said honestly.

A few other Earthmen had heard Peter, and they nodded.

"Yeah," "Me too," a couple of them said.

"So am I," Peter said gravely.

Sarah turned her attention to the conversation beside her. Her manager was called Nōvagähd, she knew, but it wouldn't hurt to talk about all this with these people before she reported to him.

Ähänär turned to her and the other Trotters and smiled, then soared off after Mär. Scott and Rene flew off across the disintegrating sphere, Sarah surmised to go see their managers.

Tom was feeling oddly energized by Mär's address. "We'll get used to it," he said to Peter.

Peter smiled easily.

Sarah glided closer. A woman called Elisa Rozas was commenting, "This is all pretty mind-boggling, though."

A man named Peter Garcia said neutrally, "I'm not so sure that these people are telling us the truth."

"What do you mean?" a man called Tom Pratt asked, looking interested.

"Are you sure?" Peter asked him.

"No," Tom said.

"Are any of you sure?" Peter asked the growing crowd.

A few people said no as well, also looking interested. Some others looked wary. Sarah didn't say anything.

"We should be more careful before we just trust these people," Peter exhorted them.

"I do trust them," Eva Wright said.

"I know," Peter said disarmingly. "They seem trustworthy enough. But that's exactly what bothers me. What if this is all a sham?"

"A sham?" Aziza Singh asked.

"Look," Peter said benevolently. "They come here, there's an awful

6: Answers and Questions

disaster, and they say somebody else did it, someone whom they can't produce. Someone who isn't here anymore."

"But we've seen it," Eva said.

"We've seen what they showed us, what they put into us," Peter corrected her.

"Well, why else would they be here?" Holden Dos Santos said.

"Think about it," Peter said. "We don't know for certain if anything they told us is true. We don't know if there even is a Nrathĕrmĕ."

Some people made protesting disbelieving sounds, and Peter put up his hands. "We don't know that there isn't a Nrathĕrmĕ, either. But the point is, Mär and these people come here telling us this story, and what if the truth of the matter is that Mär just wants our Earth? And he's telling us that we all have to be afraid of this person that we've never seen, and that we need these people's protection."

Sarah saw Tom's eyes widen. The others didn't seem as ready to challenge Peter now.

"Mär may very well be telling us the truth," Peter conceded, "But we should be careful. If he is fooling us, we need to know what we can do about it."

"Mär said that we can leave if we want to," Tom McInnis protested.

"But not with Earth," Peter said. "Mär gets Earth either way."

"But they don't need Earth!" Kathy said irritably. Sarah hadn't noticed her lingering beside her. "They have more than Earth could give them already!"

"That is true," Peter said, turning and looking appraisingly at her. "But why else would Mär want our world? Maybe he just likes the idea of owning an inhabited world."

"Maybe he's just telling the truth!" Kathy said disdainfully.

"But what if he isn't?" Mamadou Tandja asked.

"What about the Ämäthöär?" Kathy insisted.

Most of the others stared uncomprehendingly at her. Tom Pratt smiled appreciatively behind Peter.

"What about what?" Peter asked, genuinely bewildered.

"Here," Kathy said impatiently, beginning to extend her hand to Peter, about to show him. But then she heard a sudden voice in her head: "Don't do that!" She realized it was Tom Pratt's, who was looking warningly at her.

"It's alright," Tom's voice assured her, as Xu Li was saying, "The point is that we have to be ready, just in case we are being lied to. We have to have a way to save our world."

"Yes," Fatima al-Naqib agreed. "And now that we've been given their same abilities, we can hold our own in a fight if need be."

"Whatever the case," Tom Pratt smiled, waving his hand as if to drive away smoke, "We should be awake. Let's not be fooled by things that aren't there, whether for or against what these people have told us."

Peter turned back to him. He smiled too, though his eyes were tight. "That's right," he said.

"And," Sarah said, "We should work to build defenses around Earth, whatever the truth is about Nŭährnär." She had put her hand calmingly on Kathy's back. "I would hate to be caught divided and undefended when Sĕrĕhahn does arrive. And," she looked pointedly at Peter. Peter backed away slightly, then straightened again as if disappointed with himself. "If Sĕrĕhahn is a hoax, we still have a powerful sway now as leaders in Nŭährnär. If the worst is true, if Mär really is not sincere, we can deal with that when we know for certain. But until we do know, we should work to defend Earth."

Peter looked at Sarah for a second, then agreed. "Yes, there is no sense, none at all, in not building the defenses." He looked away from her, sweeping the eyes of everyone else. "Be alert. Tell each other if you find anything else suspicious. And make sure the aliens don't know!"

Tom nodded a neutrally disarming nod. "Shall we go to work then, and meet our managers?" he said calmly.

A few yeses were murmured, and the small crowd began to disperse.

Peter watched Tom as he turned and shot away to Earth. He sighed, then decided he should go report to his managers, some people named Mŭdhōär and Ōärnär.

Sarah took Kathy's hand as the others headed toward Earth.

Kathy shook her head angrily. "I like Mär," she said. "I like Ähänär too. I don't think that that Peter was right at all about Nŭährnär."

"We do have to be careful," Sarah shrugged. "But I really like the N'nŭährnär, too."

"People like that, like that Peter, could mess up what Mär's trying to do and turn us all against each other," Kathy grumbled. "People like that could make it so we can't work together."

"I hope not," Sarah sighed. "But not everybody was agreeing with Peter. I liked what Tom Pratt said." She patted Kathy on the back, and they both started off toward Earth.

Kathy was gazing at the stars reflected in the approaching Shell. "He told me not to show Peter about the Ämäthōär."

"What?"

"I was about to show Peter what Ähänär showed us," Kathy said, "But

6: Answers and Questions

Tom told me privately not to."

"Really?" Sarah said thoughtfully. "Maybe he was right. Maybe going into all that with Peter would have just made him more confused, and suspicious."

"I would have liked to see him shake," Kathy grinned nastily as they passed into the Shell. "I mean Peter." They emerged through the ground amidst mountainous crags.

Sarah didn't laugh, but shivered herself. "That means that Tom knew about the Ämäthöär, though," she noted. "I wonder why so few people got told about that."

"Dad kind of pressed Ähänär into it," Kathy said. "And you too."

"I wonder why they didn't tell all of us, though," Sarah said. "The Ämäthöär seem pretty important. They're what we're fighting against, aren't they?"

"Nrathĕrmĕ's military sounds bad enough to me," Kathy said.

"Maybe." The evil of Ähänär's Ämäthöär was making her think there must still be a great deal that no one was telling them about. She felt that Peter's suspicions were misfounded, but there was obviously a lot that Mär was hiding from them. But then, she thought, maybe that was a good thing for the time being.

They had stopped in a windy sky above the jagged crags.

"I envy the others, in a way," Sarah said. "I'd rather not have to think about something like the Ämäthöär."

Kathy grunted. "I'd rather there weren't agitators like Peter."

Sarah laughed then. "Don't worry," she said, stroking her sister's perfect brown hair. "You're getting pretty agitated yourself."

Kathy smiled a small smile. "I'd better go meet my managers."

Sarah hugged her before she could get away. "Bye."

"See ya," Kathy said, then flew up and away.

Sarah searched around for Nōvagähd. He was by the outer wall, she could tell.

She soared speedily over the broken mountains to where she knew he was, several thousand miles away. Mountains, ocean, desert, more ocean, marshes interspersed with drier grassy plains all passed rapidly under her. She dropped lower to skim the tips of the tall grasses, dodging trees, which were becoming steadily more frequent.

Suddenly a monumental jungle towered ahead. She banked up, flying along above the canopy, then saw Nōvagähd.

He was down among the trees, accompanied by a few dozen other people.

She guessed those must have been his other assistants. She dove down through the canopy.

"Sarah," Nōvagähd's voice greeted her vigorously as she zipped around branches and vines.

"Hi," Sarah said back as she slowed, passing around a few more gigantic trees. "What do you want me to do?"

She entered an open area around a particularly massive trunk. Nōvagähd was reclining unconcernedly on one of the tree's large boughs.

He laughed a full, hearty laugh as she drew to a stop. "Wait up for me," he laughed. "I'm still deciding that."

Twelve other people were floating nearest to him. Some were also in branches, but most of them were just floating in the thick, humid air. Sarah glided over to a bough to recline on like Nōvagähd, but the feeling of floating so effortlessly in the air was still so new and freeing to her that she changed her mind, and ended up hanging nervously in the air beside the tree's great moss-covered trunk.

"Thanks for coming as promptly as you have," Nōvagähd said appreciatively to her. He looked at the other twelve near him. "I hope all your assistants don't come too soon, or we'll be so flooded with people we won't be able to get anything done!"

So these were her fellow assistants' assistants, she realized, glancing around at the couple dozen people waiting farther from the tree.

"Anyhow, Ōpäm, Hänmäv," Nōvagähd said to one of the couples. "It's the star at 206°, -23°, 140 quadrillion athz. Harvest it and bring it all back. Be back here within no more than thirty-six days. Be ready to make it sooner if the need arises."

Ōpäm nodded with none of the nerves that Sarah was feeling.

"Take as many assistants as you think you'll need," Nōvagähd said.

"Okay," Hänmäv said.

"In thirty-six days, old buddy," Ōpäm smiled. He clasped Nōvagähd's right hand in his left, then he and his wife blasted away through the thick trees.

Nōvagähd turned to his remaining assistants. "We need to start breaking down the worlds here to make defenses. Mäth and Mähn, I need you to go among the smaller worlds, out past the gas worlds.

"Pōthäth and Thōaōaōs, Nōŭähä and Tärnär, we need you to help harvest the star.

"Rämharŭ, Artŭn, go help with the sixth world, Saturn.

"R'tähasōhän and Amōth, the second world, Venus."

The five couples nodded. "Good to be with you again," Nōŭähä waved to

6: Answers and Questions

Nōvagähd as he and Tärnär began to rise.

Nōvagähd waved wordlessly.

Rämharü and Artŭn lingered beside Nōvagähd. Artŭn touched his arm in what looked to Sarah like a consoling way, and she figured they must have been conversing privately.

Nōvagähd smiled reassuringly at Artŭn, and a few seconds later both Rämharü and Artŭn beamed at him.

"Do well," Rämharü then said to Sarah and the remaining assistants. He and Artŭn waved again at Nōvagähd, then plummeted headlong toward the jungle floor.

Nōvagähd turned to Sarah and the other couple, Edmund and Angela Muentefering.

"Where are the others?" he wondered aloud. Then he smiled. "Alright. I'll just go to them when we're done here. And then you two can help your assistants," he said to Edmund and Angela, looking over at the others waiting near them.

None of her assistants had found her yet, Sarah realized. She was about to search around for them, but then Nōvagähd began talking to her.

"I need the three of you to stay around Earth for the present. I want you to use the resources that our other assistants send back to construct defenses.

"Use your imagination in building the defenses! Thick, dense defenses like our Shell are excellent for resisting rantha, but unpredictable arrangements of defenses can confuse enemies enough to be better than just armor."

"Rantha?" Angela asked. Sarah searched in her mind for what rantha was.

"Think about it," Nōvagähd was saying to Angela. His expression had darkened somewhat.

Volumes of knowledge about rantha poured through Sarah's understanding. It was the fiery bolts that Aaron had shown her, the fiery bolts the pirates had used in assaulting the Earth. She knew what it was now, how it was made, all the thousands of different types of rantha, their common uses, the history of the conception of and uses of it.

She focused her mind on destructive uses of it.

Rantha was tiny particles, some larger than baryons, some tinier than the clouds within visible photons, moving thousands, tens of thousands, sometimes even hundreds of thousands and millions of times the speed of light. The heavier the rantha, the more frequently it could strike atomic nuclei and other, more fundamental particle clouds, blasting them apart in a reaction of horrific amounts of kinetic energy.

Edmund swore loudly.

"Yes," Nōvagähd said grimly.

Sarah understood now what Nōvagähd meant about the benefit of thick, dense defenses; it would take more rantha to blast through denser matter. Matter far denser than atomic matter, she knew. And it would take much more kinetic energy to scatter such dense matter.

"What do you mean, 'unpredictable arrangements of defenses?'" Edmund asked.

"I can teach you and give you ideas," Nōvagähd said, "But I'm sure you'll have plenty of original ideas that I don't have, too.

"Consider this: If our armor's of the same thickness and density everywhere, then it'll be weak. Only parts of the armor will typically be attacked in a battle; the rest is largely wasted."

Nōvagähd said the word "battle" in what Sarah though was an unnervingly casual tone.

"The armor that wasn't attacked could have been put in the places that did get attacked," Nōvagähd was going on, "And those places could have been stronger.

"So make the parts that are more likely to be attacked stronger than the places that are less likely to be attacked. But be careful; attackers can be surprisingly surprising! They have a knack for going straight for the places that one would think would not likely be attacked.

"So we give false leads. Try to outguess the attackers. Make them think that strong places are weak and weak places are strong. Leave traps. Set defenses up so as to snap around to surround attackers when they come for what they believe is a weaker spot.

"If we make all our defenses uniformly strong, they'll be uniformly weak. We can win battles that we would have lost if we had just had uniform defenses.

"But trying to be unpredictable is a gamble, and if it fails, it can be catastrophic.

"But if we all do our parts well, if we are able to outguess anyone Sěrěhahn sends to try to destroy us, it can turn the tide in battles in which we're otherwise outmatched."

"But how could anything stand up to something moving as fast as rantha?" Edmund asked.

"Our defenses can't stand up to it alone," Nōvagähd said frankly. "Thicker defenses and denser defenses can soften and slow down the rantha enough that it's moving harmlessly slowly after it penetrates through them. But matter alone, the best kinds of matter we can produce anyhow, cannot

6: Answers and Questions

stand up to rantha very well by itself.

"Think about how rantha's made," he said, leaning forward on his bough.

Sarah thought about it. She understood that rantha was tiny particles that were manufactured and put into extreme inertial fields. The inertia hurled them well past the barrier of light up to speeds that depended on the strength and length of the inertial field. Larger particles needed wider fields, and therefore more energy expended, but they could inflict much greater damage. Enormous hunks of matter could be used as terrifyingly destructive torpedoes. The smallest rantha, on the other hand, could slip right through atomic and even leptonic matter, and be too light to pack too much of a punch even at rantha's speeds, and be used as communication.

She had been using rantha as communication ever since Ähänär had changed her, she realized. She could hear people when their rantha passed through her internal inertial frame, the energy that let her move herself and other things and even let her make her own rantha, and that made her virtually indestructible.

Virtually indestructible.

"Oh, the energy," Sarah exclaimed.

The stable inertia of her frame would slow rantha as soon as it hit. The same inertia that she could use to make rantha could also slow incoming rantha to much less harmful speeds. It wouldn't stop it completely; it took much less energy to fire off one burst of rantha than to continually maintain a slowing field everywhere; but it would give her densely woven body a chance of surviving it.

"That's right," Nōvagähd said. "The energy does more than the matter does. But it's not enough either. It's easier to put a surge of energy into accelerating rantha than it is to constantly defend against it. Rantha will almost always be moving too fast for our energy to slow sufficiently. But with the armor behind the energy, the things that need protecting may get protected.

"But it's best not to get hit at all."

Nōvagähd glided forward off of his bough. Sarah and the Muenteferings backed away automatically. An enormous leaf detached itself from the tree and floated to sit in the air between them and their manager, its thin side turned toward them.

"It's a lot harder to hit defenses that look like this," Nōvagähd said, "Than it is to hit defenses that look like this." The leaf turned to bare its broad face at them.

"We cannot just make a stationary Shell to sit around Earth. This Shell that we already have can sustain a good bit of rantha damage, and we can generate rantha all along its surface to fire at attackers. But if we can keep this Shell from being attacked in the first place, that will be best.

"We need other defenses, separate from the Shell."

Dozens of leaves showered down on them and arranged themselves surrounding Nōvagähd.

"Consider me as Earth and the Shell, and these," the leaves spun theatrically, "Are other defenses."

The leaves began racing around Nōvagähd. Sarah couldn't see any pattern to the way they were moving; they just zipped here and there randomly. But no matter how they swooped around, they kept their thin sides always facing her and the Muenteferings.

Then several of the leaves turned abruptly, flashing their broad faces at them, and immediately turned back.

"Broad, flat defenses can turn to fire off rantha at an attacker," Nōvagähd narrated, "And then turn back to be much harder to hit."

The leaves surged suddenly forward at the three of them and began whizzing by on every side, turning unpredictably, and then returned to orbit Nōvagähd, who smiled at their startledness.

"Some defenses can attack the attackers."

"Sarah," a voice called.

Sarah looked to see two of her assistants, Ōhärthär and Änthär, flying toward her through the trees.

Sarah looked at Nōvagähd, as if to ask what she should do. Nōvagähd just smiled back with a confidence that seemed to almost audibly say, "You're the manager. Do what you want."

She smiled nervously at her assistants. They looked sorry to have interrupted. "Thank you for coming," she said. "Thank you for finding me. Can you—" But then she turned to Nōvagähd. "Can they just join in our conversation too?"

Nōvagähd smiled at her more deeply. "I'm fine with that."

Nōvagähd's trust in her was contagious; she was smiling more comfortably as she turned back to Ōhärthär and Änthär.

"Come on, listen to Nōvagähd with me," she said, motioning to her side. "None of the other assistants have come yet."

"Will you explain for them later?" Nōvagähd asked her. "I'm going to keep going from where we were. You're the one, as their manager, who really needs to know these things."

Sarah nodded.

6: Answers and Questions

"I'm just stealing your manager from you for a moment," Nōvagähd grinned at Ōhärthär and Änthär. "I've been talking about defenses and their arrangement."

He looked back at his three immediate assistants. "Make defenses that can attack attackers. Arrange them so they can confuse attackers. Arrange them so they can make traps, so they can draw attackers in to strong points and funnel them away from weak points.

"And arrange them to fool attackers. People may notice if you're trying to trap them. If you pretend to try to trap the attackers and thereby lead them to try to escape that supposed trap, you can trick them into escaping into the real trap.

"Battles are not nearly so much about rantha and armor as they are about outthinking the enemy."

Up until that point, Nōvagähd had seemed to Sarah to be a rather odd man. He had something of the air of a buffoon, in a way, in her eyes. But suddenly, as his expression darkened and his gaze deepened, Sarah was struck by what a powerful, indeterminable resemblance he bore to Mär.

"I don't like referring to anyone as my enemy," Nōvagähd said meaningfully and quietly. "I never want to think of the N'nrathěrmě as enemies!

"Sěrěhahn I largely have to consider as an enemy."

He looked at Sarah and the others. It was as if a superficial cover had been removed from over the bottomless well of his eyes. "I imagine that you will not want to consider our attackers as enemies." He sighed, looking hard at even their assistants.

"Understand that Sěrěhahn will very likely be able to get good people to fight us." He paused for a short moment. "Remember, that Sěrěhahn wants to destroy this world. Remember," he said, looking harder at Ōhärthär and Änthär, "That Sěrěhahn is stifling Nrathěrmě from what it could be. We have to fight him.

"And that is worth fighting even people from Nrathěrmě, if we have to.

"We cannot slacken! We cannot be half-hearted! We must defend this world, and we must defend ourselves, so that there will be someone left to unravel Sěrěhahn and free Nrathěrmě, and everyone else, from him!

"They are the enemy, for now. Anyone Sěrěhahn sends at us, even N'nrathěrmě, anyone who wants to destroy us or Earth, will have to be fought without reservation." No lighthearted smile remained on his face anymore. There was pain, and sadness, so much that his young bearded face seemed scarred.

"Do you understand this?" he asked softly.

Sarah didn't know what to say. She saw that Edmund and Angela beside her looked just as worried as she did, as did the Earthmen among their listening assistants. The others, however, though also silent, looked more solemn than worried.

Nōvagähd smiled sadly at the three of them. "I am sorry. This is one of the worst effects of villains like Sĕrĕhahn: That good people suffer, that conflict and loss must be endured in order to save good people from villains' tyranny. Which tyranny will cause more conflict and loss if it is not fought.

"I wish we could save everyone from Sĕrĕhahn without conflict!" he said fervently. "Especially without conflict with the N'nrathĕrmĕ themselves. And maybe we still will be able to. But we must defend Earth."

"Are we sure Sĕrĕhahn will attack?" Sarah heard herself ask. "Maybe we'll be just fine."

Nōvagähd looked quickly at her, with a sharp searching look, but it almost immediately softened into a sad but admiring smile. "I surely hope you're right," he said with a return of his light laugh. "I hope no one attacks us.

"But I'm sure Sĕrĕhahn will attack us." He glided to Sarah and placed a surprisingly comforting hand on her arm. "I hope, however, that we will be just fine." He looked searchingly into Sarah's eyes again, then patted her arm and drifted back from her.

Then he smiled more easily again. "And worrying will get us nowhere." He threw his arms up over his head. "Let's get to work! There are resources already pouring in, and that is nothing to the resources that will be coming once the harvesting gets fully underway.

"Hurry! And think! Surprise me! Use your minds to think up confusing, unpredictable defenses. Tell me about any ideas you have. Go on!" He swung his arms at them as if to shoo them away, then smiled and began to turn away.

"Where are you going?" Sarah asked impulsively.

"I have two busy assistants to talk to," he said to her, then smiled serenely. "And I want to have a word with my managers. But you can call me if you need me, but don't be afraid to think for yourselves."

He raised his hand in farewell, then turned and rocketed away through the thick jungle.

Edmund and Angela glided over to their waiting assistants. Sarah gazed after Nōvagähd for a couple seconds. Somehow everything seemed grey now that he had gone.

She took an unneeded breath and turned to Ōhärthär and Änthär. It was very odd leading N'närdamähr.

6: Answers and Questions

As if having sensed that, Änthär extended her left hand friendlily to Sarah. "It's alright, we're here to help," she smiled.

Sarah took her left hand in her right. Änthär added, "You are our manager. You were assigned to be so for a reason."

Sarah had begun to release Änthär's hand, but then she embraced her gratefully for her confidence.

Änthär was obviously surprised, but she laughed a little as Sarah drifted back.

"You're going to do just fine as a manager," Ōhärthär smiled.

"Help me," Sarah begged the both of them fervently.

"We'll try," Ōhärthär said.

Sarah nodded, trying to suppress her anxiety, and rose upward through the trees.

The three of them emerged out over the canopy. Sarah loved the grandeur of the jungle; it stretched on like a sea from horizon to horizon. And with the blue sky above, with its tall, white clouds, and the feel of the warm light on her, Sarah felt like she could have been on Earth. Peacefully. Without any worry about Sĕrĕhahn, or leading peers into war.

But there was no sun in here. Even with all the perfect light and warmth, Sarah wished there was a sun. There was just something missing without it.

And they were going to have to dismantle the real sun, she remembered with a pang. Pōthäth, Thōaōaōs, Nōŭähä, and Tärnär, had already gone to help take it apart. Soon it would be gone, forever, she realized.

She sighed, and searched about for her remaining assistants. Ōhärthär and Änthär, of course, were right there with her above the sea of leaves, gliding unworriedly as they waited for her. The rest were scattered all throughout the Shell, except for one whom she knew was on Earth, galloping on a horse where India had been.

It was going to be better to call them all to her than to go to each of them one by one, she thought. She braced herself and sent her voice to all of them:

"Good morning, er, day. My name's Sarah Trotter, I've been appointed as your manager."

"Hello, Sarah," R'nväg's voice answered.

"On my way," Bal Karunanidhi said from horseback.

"What do you want us to do?" R'tähahavaf asked.

"Hi, Sarah," Violet Malin said. "Thank you for finding me."

Sarah felt both more encouraged and more overwhelmed. "Find me outside the Shell," she told them.

Several voices said they would.

She grinned shakily at Ōhärthär and Änthär, then retraced her way back down into the trees, feeling indecisive and entirely unqualified for this.

She emerged out of the Shell, Ōhärthär and Änthär behind her. She flew out a short way. She couldn't help feeling cold and small, and the infinite deep of stars only amplified her feeling of vulnerability against the Ämäthöär.

Turning back to the Shell, she felt a little safer. Nōvagähd and Mär were in there. They would all be fine.

Her assistants were beginning to trickle out of the Shell. Despite her nervousness, she began to decide what she needed them to do.

As the last of them stopped expectantly in front of her, she smiled in what she hoped was an inspiring way. "Thank you for coming so promptly," she said to them.

"I was enjoying myself," Bal said teasingly.

"Is horseback riding still very fun, now that you can fly?" Sarah asked, grateful for his friendly spirit. "And you can run faster than any horse...you can even be a horse."

"It's always fun," Bal said.

Sarah smiled more genuinely.

"Okay," she said, "I need you to send resources back here to me, so we can all build defenses against Sĕrĕhahn."

She noticed a few of her eight N'närdamähr assistants blink uncomfortably as she mentioned him by name. Part of her didn't want to know Sĕrĕhahn the way they apparently did.

"Everything around us is being dismantled so that we can use its matter to make defenses," she reminded them.

"What?" Chang Luli said in surprise. "The beautiful planets too?"

"Yes," Sarah said, not trying to hide her regret.

"Isn't there some other way?" Luli asked.

"I don't want to lose our planets," Sarah said, "But if we don't use them, we all could be wiped out by Sĕrĕhahn. We won't get to look at them then, either."

Luli nodded unconvincedly. "I understand. But these planets...they've always been here..."

"I know," Sarah assured her. "I think our leaders know what they're doing, though." That did not sound very convincing, even to herself. "And, I will ask my manager about that," she added consolingly.

"But for now, the harvesting has already started."

"R'nväg, Är, go direct some of the matter getting harvested from the sun back here to me."

6: Answers and Questions

"Right," R'nväg said without hesitation. He and his wife bolted back into the Shell, toward the sun.

"Bal, direct matter from Mercury. Äszad, take Venus."

"Mercury!" Bal said excitedly.

Äszad smiled approvingly at Sarah before she flew away.

"And I always dreamed of going to the moon..." Bal grinned, turning and leaving too.

Sarah laughed. She was feeling slightly better about this managing situation.

"N'fävan," she said, "Take Mars. Ōhärthär, Änthär, there are a lot of asteroids out between Mars and Jupiter; send those.

"And you should use your assistants, if you need to," she said as those three waved to leave.

"Xuezhong and Luli, send me matter from Jupiter. Don't worry; I will talk to my manager Nōvagähd about this. But for now, our lives depend on you sending Jupiter's matter back here.

"Violet, you get Saturn. R'tähahavaf, Ŭdmäähär, take Uranus. If you like, send some of your assistants to Neptune, but if not, these planets will be enough to be going on with."

"We'll put them to work," R'tähahavaf said, and they all blasted away in different directions, leaving Sarah alone at Earth.

Chapter 7

The Light of Life

Sarah drifted about, feeling considerably less vulnerable, and began considering what she ought to build once resources reached her. She liked Nōvagähd's counsel about making unconnected, mobile defenses. She started rolling over in her mind various different shapes and arrangements of defenses that she could make.

She would want thicker, more spherical platforms nearer to Earth. Those would be easier to hit, but they would be hardier. And she would intersperse broad, flat platforms through them. Those would need to be thin, so they could turn to be more difficult to hit, but they would also need to be massive enough that they would have sufficient matter to burn as energy in order to maneuver about and fire off rantha volleys.

On the other hand, she could build a lot of broad, thin platforms that were not very massive. Those could use all their matter up in making one strong inertial field to fire off one powerful broadside. Those would be false targets, not intended to be strong against any attack; as soon as an attacker drew near, they would dissolve of their own accord into a blast of rantha fired at them.

She smiled to herself. These ideas were falling together so easily in her mind, she hardly even had to think. She knew just how to build these complex defenses she was imagining; she could think of hundreds of ways she could arrange their interior power veins without really trying. In a fraction of a second, she came up with half a dozen complicated schemes of how she could maneuver the defenses around one another, cornering attackers and channeling them away from the Shell.

But then she remembered that anybody who attacked them would of a certainty be more used to these things than she was. Her brilliant plans, she realized soberingly, would have been done thousands of times over before.

Looking at the Shell, she finally understood just how weak it was. In the light of the strength and experience of N'nrathĕrmĕ and their ilk, this was a comparatively frail defense.

I'll just have to be more original, then, she told herself. *I was assigned to this station for a reason.* She hoped Änthär was right. She hoped that their leaders had known what they were doing when they had chosen her for that position.

She noticed a huge cloud of dissolved, leptonic matter careening toward her from the direction of Venus, moving at a few times the speed of light.

7: The Light of Life

"Äszad," Sarah called to her. "Don't send the matter so fast! We have time. Don't use up so much energy! Slow is better."

"Alright," Äszad answered. After a couple seconds' silence, she said, "I will tell the others here, too, if their managers will agree; that's a good point, we don't need to burn so much energy accelerating this stuff just yet."

"Thanks," Sarah said. She figured she had better make sure her other assistants knew that too. "Hey, guys," she called to all of them except Äszad, "Send the matter slowly, so we can conserve as much of it as we can. It'll be fine if it takes a few days for it to reach Earth."

"Oh, alright," Violet's voice said.

"We've already begun sending it about that slowly," Ōhärthär said cheerfully.

"Ours as well," R'tähahavaf's voice called.

"Thanks," Sarah said, glad she had such capable assistants. She felt as if her load was significantly lightening.

"And if you have any ideas about effective defenses, tell me," she added.

"Okay," R'nväg said.

"We don't have any yet," Ōhärthär said, "But we'll be sure to tell you."

The cloud was getting closer to her. She directed it to slow down, then realized how much energy she had just used to do that. She directed some of the matter straight toward herself, and began channeling the rest of it to start forming itself into different kinds of platforms. The branch of the cloud hurtling in her direction began to reach her, and she absorbed it all right through her augmented skin, replenishing the matter she was burning to inertially direct the clouds.

She was directing the inertial fields deftly, guiding the subatomic matter into enormous, wide platforms, into tiny, hand-sized platforms, into paper-thin platforms a couple thousand miles across. With hardly a thought she commanded the matter to form subatomic tunnels and conduits running like nerves and arteries all through the superdense defenses. In a matter of seconds there were thousands of mirror-like platforms formed in front of her, which she effortlessly directed to glide away behind her as the cloud cascaded on at her.

Matter was continually flowing into her, compensating for the enormous amount of energy she was catapulting out to incite the inertial fields.

Sarah laughed out loud. She was actually absorbing the planet Venus into her body! She was eating the planet Venus!

She flourished her arm out as she threw another city-sized platform carelessly over her shoulder. She waved her other arm to send another behind her, then began beating her arms like she was conducting an orchestra, hurling matter this way and that, throwing platforms out and away, directing swirling clouds to coalesce and order themselves as if by magic.

She organized longer, slimmer platforms; thicker platforms; platforms like two planes at right angles, making a cross. She waved her arms more energetically. At her command, a fabulously exultant N'nrathĕrmĕ tune she'd never heard before filled the space around her, waves of harmless rantha filling her ears.

Her arms flew in time with the music. She swirled and spun and danced in the rhythms, launching matter and platforms wherever she told her inertia to carry them.

She lifted her head and sang with the music with all the power of her new lungs. An entire Nrathĕrmĕ-caliber symphony burst from her vocal cords as her eyes closed tightly.

Thousands of defenses whisked around her. She laughed even as she sang, able to see everything she was doing even with her eyes pressed closed as her mouth smiled in the polyphony.

Then she broke off singing and tumbled into a ball of laughter as the music intensified. It was all so fun, so amazing!

"Sarah," Ōhärthär's voice sounded in her head. She stifled her mirth.

"Änthär and I are returning to Earth; one of our children needs us. Our assistants are going to keep sending the matter to you."

"No problem," Sarah replied, her voice a little higher than usual.

The music flowed on as Sarah silently continued directing matter and absorbing it into herself. The sun had begun rising over the side of the Shell. She gazed at it again, admiring the patterns on and within it. A visible haze of matter was funneling away from it toward Earth, and there were hundreds of millions of people all around and even inside of it.

Soon it would be gone, she thought. Venus, beautiful Saturn, all of them. Her new powers were wonderful. She only wished that such a desperate defense hadn't had to have been part of the deal.

Our lives depend on our defense, she reminded herself. *And if Nōvagähd's right, these things will see use all too soon,* she thought as she surveyed her work. It wasn't enough to stand up to even a portion of a typical striking fleet, she knew.

The music faded into silence. She couldn't shake the growing guilty feeling, the feeling that they were destroying irreplaceable beauty to save their own selves.

"Nōvagähd," she called. She could tell he was somewhere inside the Shell.

7: The Light of Life

A few seconds passed. Then Nōvagähd's voice answered, "Yeah?"

It was as if the triumphant music had resumed playing inside of her.

"It's Sarah," she said.

"Yes, I know," Nōvagähd chuckled.

"Well...I told my assistants to direct matter back here to me. Some of them are using their assistants to help. I've been building some defenses here. One of my assistants sent me a lot of matter really quickly; I told her to slow down; but I used it to build some defenses already. She slowed down what she's sending me, though. All my assistants are sending the matter slowly, so it should get here in a few days or so. I'll, um, keep trying to think of new ways to arrange them. The defenses."

"Great," Nōvagähd said.

She was afraid of challenging the order to dismantle the worlds. They had no choice, she knew. "And I, uh, I told my assistants to help me think of new ways to arrange them. I'll need their help to outsmart any N'nrathĕrmĕ."

Nōvagähd laughed softly and grimly. "We all will need more than just cooperation to outsmart them."

A silent pause ensued.

"Very efficient, Sarah," Nōvagähd then said, apparently thinking she had said all she had intended to. "And I think you'll rise into your responsibilities a lot more than you already are. Thank you for taking our situation as seriously as you have."

Then his voice seemed to smile as he said, "Now, what was it that you really wanted to talk to me about?"

The intimate friendly tone in his voice, as if they were sharing a joke, softened her fears.

"Sorry," she said.

Nōvagähd waited.

"Nōvagähd, I don't mean to second-guess your decisions, but—"

"I'm sorry to hear that."

"Uh..."

Nōvagähd laughed, and Sarah felt even less worried. She could talk about this with him.

"What's on your mind?" Nōvagähd invited.

"I don't like that we're destroying all these worlds," she said, surprising her own self.

Nōvagähd didn't answer. Sarah waited, but when there was nothing but silence for several seconds, she called, "Nōvagähd?"

It sounded as if he was laughing softly as he answered, "Yeah, I'm still here. That's a really good concern."

He sounded sincere. "Some other people feel the same way," she added.

"As do I," Nōvagähd promised her. There was another small pause. "But we aren't destroying these worlds.

"I'm not from Earth; these worlds are new worlds to me. But I think I can appreciate their beauty.

"We do need to defend ourselves. For this time, and I hope only for a short time, it is more important that we protect Earth and every Earthman that we can than it is to let these worlds be.

"If we did have to destroy these worlds to protect the Earthmen, I think I would still do it. But, as we're doing it now, these worlds will be just fine."

Sarah didn't know what he was getting at. But he continued straight on:

"My son S'thähr was killed in battle with pirates once. His armor, his body, all of it was totally destroyed."

Sarah could definitely detect a sense of pain in Nōvagähd's voice, and she felt sorry for him, but she was surprised at how casually he referred to his son's death.

"But his body was rebuilt. I knew every smallest detail about his body, all the way down past the size of communications rantha, and I made it just the way it was before he had died. And he awoke just as alive, and ambitious, as he's ever been."

In spite of her shock, Sarah knew that this was not only possible, it was common. She wasn't sure she liked the spiritual implications of that, though.

"The last time I had seen S'thähr was before the battle, so the knowledge I had of his brain was a few minutes out of date," Nōvagähd was saying. "When he woke up, he had no memory of the battle...but he really hadn't missed much."

Sarah didn't like the spiritual implications of that, either. But she knew it happened all the time. And it felt right when Nōvagähd said it.

"I was very lucky," Nōvagähd said. "Occasionally, people won't revive after getting killed. Their bodies just won't come to life. But that is comparatively rare."

"What about Ämäthōär?" Sarah asked, before she thought better of it.

There was a tiny pause, followed by Nōvagähd's explosion of out of place laughter. "Oho! So you know about the Ämäthōär already, do you?"

"Ähänär told me about them," Sarah said, thinking the Ämäthōär were anything but laughable.

"Ähänär!" Nōvagähd chuckled. "I am not surprised."

There was another pause for a few seconds, as if Nōvagähd were speaking

7: The Light of Life

to someone else. Then he said, "You should not talk about Ämäthōär too much. The Earthmen will be told about them when they've been better prepared to handle it. I hope we can prepare them. And as for N'närdamähr, you'll find that most of us aren't fond of thinking about them.

"But, no," his voice darkened, "People killed by Ämäthōär typically cannot be brought back."

Sarah couldn't bring herself to ask if Ämäthōär had ever killed anyone Nōvagähd knew. She thought she could guess the answer.

"What I meant, though," he said after a pause, "Is that people who are killed, taken apart in humane destructive ways, can usually be brought back."

"These worlds are a lot simpler than S'thähr is."

"Do you mean," Sarah asked, sure he couldn't mean it, "That these planets are alive?"

"If anybody asks me, I think so."

Sarah hadn't been taught anything like that.

"I like these planets, at any rate," Nōvagähd said. "When we don't need defenses anymore, we'll be able to make all these worlds, just the way they were. We can even modify them, make them just the way they would be after the passage and decay of time. We know everything about them. Well, at least we know enough to bring them back completely. We never dismantle a world, even an asteroid, without recording its structure.

"And even before we put the planets back, we can still visit them."

"What do you mean?" Sarah asked. She was still inattentively directing the incoming cloud, about which she didn't feel so sad anymore.

"Many thousands of worlds have gone into making Nrathĕrmĕ. Whether those worlds will ever be put back is uncertain; I hope they will be. But if they are not, if Nrathĕrmĕ remains as it is, we still have the records of every single one of those worlds. Sĕrĕhahn wouldn't have it any other way," he said with cryptic bitterness. "If we want to visit a representation of those worlds in our minds, we can enjoy the worlds' beauty without needing the matter to remake them."

That satisfied Sarah. "Wow. I'll tell my assistants about that. Some of them were concerned about losing these planets."

"I'm glad they were," Nōvagähd said appreciatively. "If we just concentrate on building defenses alone, we will be neglecting more important things. There's nothing worth living for if to live means to destroy!

"But we will use these worlds, and keep them recorded, so that they won't be destroyed at all. If we use these worlds well, we'll be able to save ourselves from being destroyed, too.

"But Sarah, the real destruction is that Nrathĕrmĕ is under the influence of the Ämäthöär. We will use these worlds to save ourselves from destruction, so that we can unravel the Ämäthöär! And save all the N'nrathĕrmĕ from them."

"Okay," Sarah said. She empathized with the N'närdamährs' reticence to talk about Ämäthöär.

"And don't worry about the Ämäthöär," Nōvagähd said as if he had read her mind. "We've got some good people with us. We will be alright against Sĕrĕhahn."

"I hope so," Sarah said smally.

Nōvagähd laughed, and Sarah felt a little better. "I know so!" he said. "Thank you for asking me about this. And don't worry anymore about second-guessing my decisions. But if you would tell me when you do, that would help."

Sarah laughed a little too. "Okay."

"Keep working. And have fun; don't work too hard. It will be better for you to be happy than to work constantly, thinking you're being productive."

Sarah laughed more easily. "Alright." The dark feeling that had begun to creep into her when Nōvagähd had spoken about the Ämäthöär felt like it was being warmed out of her.

A few more seconds passed in silence, and she assumed he had gone.

She looked around at the tens of thousands of defenses waiting behind her. She started to think of ways she could organize them, various strategic arrangements that could trap attackers and that could let the defenses work most effectively with one another.

She was going to have to put herself inside the defenses. And her assistants too, and theirs, as many as they needed. That way, they would be able to command the defenses with less delay than if they commanded from within the Shell. She knew that even the shortest delay could make the difference between being hit or missed by rantha. The more people flying with the defenses, the better.

But she hated the idea of risking lives for the sake of better defenses. *But if our defenses fail, we'll all die.* And, she realized with dreadful finality, there would be no one left to bring any of them back.

She tried to clear her mind. Whatever she ended up planning, she would need to coordinate her plans with Nōvagähd and her fellow assistants of his, she told herself.

But her mind felt like it was tripping over itself. She was having more and more trouble thinking. In the face of all her new knowledge of military theory, and the tremendous speed of her thoughts now, and the ideas she had been

7: The Light of Life

starting to have before she had called Nōvagähd, she was feeling increasingly like her mind was spinning its wheels.

She shook it off. She resumed the energetic music, and imagined the defenses in different arrangements.

But it was as if her thoughts were being squashed. She had untold fathoms of military history in her head now, knowledge of tactics, of leaders, of thousands of battles. She thought that ought to help. Why couldn't she think of anything new?

The music disappeared and her directing arms fell limply to her sides.

"What's wrong?" she demanded, putting her hand to her head.

Images of Ähänär's Ämäthōär were flashing across her thoughts. She wanted to block it out, but it kept coming back. She could feel the darkness, the suffocating fear.

And she remembered the people who had fought and killed the Ämäthōär. Who were they?

She remembered what Ähänär had shown her. Ähänär had been one of the passing people when the Ämäthōär had started killing. She remembered the people had mentioned Mär. But Mär hadn't been in the memory. But one of the people had screamed to call the Ōmäthäär.

Ōmäthäär, she thought. Mär was an Ōmäthäär, she realized. But she found that she didn't know much of anything about them.

Those people had obviously had some power to harm the Ämäthōär. No one else had even tried to kill him. Did they have the same power the Ämäthōär had, that power that Ähänär had said wasn't technological?

But they hadn't made her feel dark or afraid. They had made her feel warm.

The way Nōvagähd did.

Nōvagähd, she thought. He seemed to know something about the Ämäthōär. Maybe he would be able, and agreeable, to tell her what Ōmäthäär were.

"Nōvagähd?" she called.

"Go ahead," he answered, so promptly he might have been waiting for her.

"What are Ōmäthäär?"

Nōvagähd's answer was slow and subdued, but he did sound interested. "Did Ähänär tell you about them, too?"

"Sort of," Sarah said guiltily. "Was that alright?"

"If Ähänär thought it was alright," Nōvagähd laughed softly, "It must have been. Ähänär's parents are Ōmäthäär."

"Oh!" Sarah said. "I saw Ähänär's father standing with Mär in the meeting."

"Tärmäth," Nōvagähd said. "One of the best men I know."

"And Mär is an Ōmäthäär too, right?"

That made Nōvagähd laugh loudly. "Yes!" he said ardently. "Mär is the most Ōmäthäär-like person I have ever known!"

"But what is an Ōmäthäär?" Sarah asked.

Nōvagähd didn't answer right away.

"What are they?" she pressed.

Nōvagähd sounded like he was smiling as he answered, "Okay. I'll tell you what I can for now.

"Don't tell anyone, not yet, anything that I tell you about Ōmäthäär."

"Okay," Sarah agreed. "Why? Is it just because people aren't ready, like about the Ämäthōär?"

"I'm very glad we're talking about Ōmäthäär instead of Ämäthōär," Nōvagähd said. "Be careful about talking about this. But don't ask me why. Not yet." He paused, as if thinking. "Don't talk about this with anyone who isn't an Ōmäthäär."

"I won't," Sarah promised. "Thank you for trusting me with this."

"Don't worry, I'll only tell you a little for now," Nōvagähd assured her. "That's safest. For you.

"So tell me, what does 'Är' mean?"

"You're asking me?" Sarah said.

"Think about what 'Är' means."

"Uh, it's infinity. Wholeness, completeness, that kind of thing," Sarah tried to articulate.

"It's also a person."

"Who?" Sarah asked, thinking of her assistant Är.

Nōvagähd hesitated. "Är," he said, "The Är, is an infinite person."

"Infinite?" Sarah asked. "Like God?"

"Yeah!" Nōvagähd's voice smiled. "Just like that! What do you think about a God, Sarah?"

"Well, I believe that God exists," Sarah said, not sure where this was leading.

"Excellent! You have an advantage on most people."

"What do you mean?"

Nōvagähd seemed to ignore that. "What do you believe about your God?"

This was odd, Sarah thought, talking religion with someone from another world. "I believe he's an infinite being, like you said. Infinitely powerful, infinitely knowledgeable, infinitely loving."

7: The Light of Life

"Doesn't that sound a little ludicrous?" Nōvagähd said.

"Well, yeah," Sarah said, "It does, really. Kind of. But I believe that there really is a God like that all the same."

"Why?" Nōvagähd asked in almost a derisive tone.

Sarah thought for a short moment. "I can't really say. But it feels really right."

"That's perfect!" Nōvagähd said happily. "You didn't say you think there's an infinite being because you think you've seen amazing things that must have been from some kind of deity. You believe it because it feels right.

"Not that there's anything wrong with recognizing 'divine intervention,'" though Nōvagähd said those words with manifest disdain. "But just keep listening to those feelings."

"So, you believe in God," Sarah said.

"I believe in a lot of things. But don't talk about God, or Är, or an infinite being, with anyone. Not for now."

"Okay. Why?"

"Most people, even in Nüährnär," Nōvagähd said dismally, "don't think about Är much. And almost everyone in Nrathĕrmĕ is certain that there cannot be such a person.

"For one thing, it's not a good idea to tell the N'nüährnär too much about Är yet. Mär does want them all to know about Är as quickly as they can, but we have to be careful. If we don't tell them the right things at the right times, they may misunderstand, and then think even more certainly that Är cannot be actual. That would cause us some real problems."

"I don't really understand what you mean," Sarah said.

"You believe that your deity is both infinitely powerful and infinitely loving," Nōvagähd observed.

"Yes," Sarah said.

"Then why are there Ämäthōär?" Nōvagähd asked. "Why does Sĕrĕhahn have so much power over so many people? Why are we even now preparing defenses to fight for our lives?"

"So much disorder. Where is Är's love and power?"

"But you still believe in Är," Sarah said.

"Believe?" Nōvagähd said. "Well, yeah, I do believe in him, if you want to say it that way.

"And I do understand some of why Är lets there be Ämäthōär, and pain, and fear. But keep trusting your feelings. That's what's important.

"But don't you see what I mean? People have to be ready to understand that Är is real, and that pain and evil does not mean that he isn't."

"But if I tell people about the infinite Är, and they're convinced that there shouldn't be evil if there is an Är, then of course they won't believe me!

"And they'll be that much more disposed against the idea of a real-life Är.

"We have to tell everyone everything we can as quickly as we can. But, at the moment, that is very little. We cannot tell them too much too soon, or else, well, we won't be able to do much at all against the Ämäthöär."

"Why?" Sarah asked.

"Never mind. But everyone in Nŭährnär does know a little, at least, about the Ōmäthäär."

"You still haven't told me what the Ōmäthäär are," Sarah said, pretending to be annoyed.

Nōvagähd laughed. "I don't really know myself. But I'll tell you what you want."

"Wait," Sarah said, "You're an Ōmäthäär, aren't you?"

"More or less. Really, anyone who believes that Är's real, and who also tries to do what they think Är wants them to do—that's essential—is an Ōmäthäär. But what people tend to mean when they talk about Ōmäthäär is more than that.

"I gather that you've seen something of the Ämäthöärs' abilities."

"Yes," Sarah said quietly. She felt dark again just remembering Ähänär's Ämäthöär.

"And the Ōmäthäär?" he asked.

"I saw something," Sarah said.

"Tell me what you saw."

Sarah explained what Ähänär had shown her family. As she finished telling how the people had finally killed the Ämäthöär, she noted, "They definitely had some kind of power that I don't have."

Nōvagähd was silent.

"If those were Ōmäthäär, why did it take so many of them to kill the Ämäthöär?" Sarah asked.

"It shouldn't have," Nōvagähd said heavily. "Anyhow, the Ōmäthäärs' and the Ämäthöärs' abilities aren't anything exotic."

"I can't understand them!" Sarah said. "And I've been taught most of what everyone else knows."

"I'm going to teach you a few things that most everyone doesn't know," Nōvagähd said.

"There is something that we call the Ärthähr. It's a scandal that most people don't know about it. The Ärthähr is what the Ōmäthäärs' power is."

"Okay," Sarah said.

7: The Light of Life

"It isn't anything special," Nōvagähd explained. "Everything comes from the Ärthähr. All life, energy, everything. Matter is a denser manifestation of it. The inertial manipulation that we all have is a rough exercise of the very same principles behind the Ärthähr that the Ōmäthäär use."

"But the Ärthähr itself comes from Är. I think everything comes from Är, but raw Ärthähr is the force behind everything.

"The inertia we use is a bigger, cruder way of using Ärthähr," he explained again. "And when we pick something up in our hands, or interact with anything at all, that's also Ärthähr.

"The Ōmäthäär can use Ärthähr on a much finer scale."

"They have better inertia technology?" Sarah asked.

"Not like that," Nōvagähd said. "It isn't caused mechanically. We just don't have the capacity to make machines that fine!

"I won't explain for the time being how the Ōmäthäär do it. But we exercise an affinity with the Ärthähr that lets us do great things." His voice swelled with pleasure. "Some Ōmäthäär have such affinity with the Ärthähr that their own capacities are more potent than our technology."

"But you won't tell me how," Sarah said disappointedly.

Nōvagähd laughed. "Not yet, at any rate. I want to tell you some other things.

"But I will tell you this: anyone can use Ärthähr the way the Ōmäthäär do. They just have to know enough about Ärthähr.

"And that can be a problem.

"Our inertial technology can be used to build and to destroy. It makes life easier, but it can also kill.

"Ärthähr is the same way. It can be a great help, but people can also use it to kill, or to do damage in other ways.

"Sĕrĕhahn is the single most potent user of Ärthähr, well, next to Är of course, but Sĕrĕhahn has the most control of Ärthähr of anyone else I know of.

"But Sĕrĕhahn uses Ärthähr for his own purposes. Now, understand that if anyone uses Ärthähr against what Är wants them to do, then they'll lose capacity to use it. But Sĕrĕhahn, apparently, still has a lot of capacity left to lose.

"And the thing about Sĕrĕhahn is that he's so good! He uses Ärthähr very closely to how Är does. I think that even Sĕrĕhahn himself may almost believe that he's doing what Är wants him to do. Almost."

"What?" Sarah asked. "I thought Sĕrĕhahn wants us all dead!"

"He does!" Nōvagähd said. "Sĕrĕhahn uses Ärthähr closely to how Är uses it. He does terrible, horrible things. But he does great, wonderful things too. But the greatness of the good things he does is turned bad by the horrible things he does. He does do good, and that brings prosperity to Nrathĕrmĕ and Ärthähr to him, there is no evading that. But the good he does is aimed to further terrible desires! It is only good in the short term. But that is sufficient for gaining hold of some aspects of Ärthähr. Yet all the 'good' he does ultimately serves to make existence worse for everyone he has influence over.

"And that is a lot of people."

"Ärthähr can do horrible things."

"But there is normally no great danger in teaching people about it. People who use it badly are usually quick to lose their affinity with it."

Sarah was rushing to take in and understand all of this. "Why?" she asked. "Why do they lose their affinity with it?"

"Because the Ärthähr *is* Är," Nōvagähd pointed out. "More or less; you can't see the Ärthähr."

"But you can see Är?" Sarah asked eagerly.

"The Ärthähr works entirely according to the way Är works. If a person tries to use it opposed to the way Är works, he'll be working opposed to the Ärthähr. And so he can't use it as well."

"But the Ämäthōär can use it," Sarah said, confused.

"Yes," Nōvagähd sighed. "Quite obviously they can. Even Mär is no match for many of the Ämäthōär in Ärthähr battle."

He paused. "Nevertheless, to use the Ärthähr in their way is to lose it. The Ämäthōär destroy themselves. They are immensely powerful. But unless they turn around, unless they stop fighting Är, they will lose more and more of their control over Ärthähr."

"Then how are they so powerful?" Sarah asked.

"The best of them are like Sĕrĕhahn," Nōvagähd said, "Which makes them formidable. They are not erratic. They are not driven by anger or outright hate or even by selfishness. Not on the surface, anyhow. They use Ärthähr well. They do deviate from it in some ways, and they lose the aspects of it that they defy. But they use it well in enough ways that when they do deviate from it, they still have a great deal of power to deviate with!

"In my opinion, they're hollow. Though on the surface they seem to increase in their understanding and ability in regards to Ärthähr, they neglect its core. They are fakes. It is only a matter of time before they topple, with or without us Ōmäthäär to topple them. The question is how many lives will be strangled before they do topple."

"But, why are the Ämäthōär so much more powerful than Ōmäthäär?" Sarah asked.

7: The Light of Life

"They aren't," Nōvagähd said firmly.

"But you just said that even Mär couldn't stand up to some of them."

"To a great many of them," Nōvagähd corrected her.

"And it took a dozen Ōmäthäär to kill the one Ämäthōär that Ähänär showed us."

"That's true," Nōvagähd said. "But it doesn't mean that they are more powerful than the Ōmäthäär.

"The Ōmäthäär are a new group. The Ämäthōär have been being tutored by Sĕrĕhahn for thousands of weeks, maybe longer. Now, Mär is the leader of our Ōmäthäär."

"Was he the first Ōmäthäär?" Sarah interrupted.

"No, he wasn't," Nōvagähd said. "But he is the best that we have left.."

"Left?" Sarah asked.

"None of us know how long Sĕrĕhahn has had Nrathĕrmĕ in his grip. I, at least, don't even know where Sĕrĕhahn learned about Ärthähr in the first place. We have no idea how old he is. We know nothing about his early life, except that he introduced himself as being called Sĕrĕhahn.

"But we believe that he was the man who originally established Nrathĕrmĕ as a world nation. You understand, Sarah, that our people have no history beyond legends before roughly nine thousand weeks ago."

"Oh," Sarah said. "That's right."

"Only we know that Anhar is the same Sĕrĕhahn who was supposed to have died thousands of weeks ago.

"We don't know how long there have been Ämäthōär. Or R'bathĕrŭ, as they themselves say it. But as far as I know, there have been Ōmäthäär for as long as Nrathĕrmĕ and the Ämäthōär have been established. Är made sure of that.

"Sĕrĕhahn trains the Ämäthōär, but Är is smarter even than Sĕrĕhahn. Är kept up training Ōmäthäär, who worked to overthrow the Ämäthōär."

"Training?" Sarah asked. "Personally? And why are the Ōmäthäär so intent on getting rid of Sĕrĕhahn and the Ämäthōär? I mean, I hated that Ämäthōär, but what makes you Ōmäthäär good and them bad?" Sarah then realized what she had just said. "I just want to know," she added hastily.

"Tactlessness is fine with me," Nōvagähd's voice smiled. "And yes, Är trained Ōmäthäär. No one else was around to train them, except for Sĕrĕhahn."

"Did Är train Mär?" Sarah asked, growing steadily more excited.

"No, he didn't," Nōvagähd said.

"Who did?"

"Mär wasn't one of the first. But Är did train the first Ōmäthäär that we have any history about.

"But Sĕrĕhahn killed them."

"What?" Sarah said. "They died?"

"Most of them. They were truly amazing people; it is not just anyone who gets personally trained by Är! But Sĕrĕhahn hunted for them and killed them. Only a few managed to keep hidden. As soon as there was technology to leave Nrathĕrmĕ, many of them fled.

"Some of them marauded near Nrathĕrmĕ, so as to harass the Ämäthöär while hiding in wide space. Some others struck out away, leaving Nrathĕrmĕ behind. None of us know where they went.

"But the reason Är trained Ōmäthäär in the first place was to deliver the N'nrathĕrmĕ. So Är, together with the remaining Ōmäthäär, trained more. We did our best to stay hidden from Sĕrĕhahn, who killed any Ōmäthäär he tracked down, while we planned how we might overthrow him.

"But about a hundred weeks ago now, the Ämäthöär found out who almost all of us were. Don't ask me how, we still don't know. There were a few million of us Ōmäthäär by that point."

"A few *million* Ōmäthäär?" Sarah exclaimed. "Where are they all?"

When Nōvagähd finally answered, it was with dark emotion, even anger. "I was there. I was at Nrathĕrmĕ. I got to enjoy the company of our arising order of Ōmäthäär. We were even then in later preparations of a plot to strike against Sĕrĕhahn and the Ämäthöär. It was to be the decisive struggle for the liberty of the hearts of the N'nrathĕrmĕ. Our leaders were setting into motion wonderfully complex plans. We would have the strategic advantage. We were going to make the N'nrathĕrmĕ notice the Ämäthöär."

"You mean the N'nrathĕrmĕ don't know about the Ämäthöär?" Sarah cut in.

"Of course they don't! Think, Sarah. You know everything about life at Nrathĕrmĕ. The Ämäthöär are the invisible strings with which Sĕrĕhahn controls every aspect of the zeitgeist of Nrathĕrmĕ. He gives them every freedom anyone could want, except for freedom of thought!

"Nrathĕrmĕ is saturated with Sĕrĕhahn's lies, the lies he orchestrates so his people will never become powerful enough to buck against him."

"I don't understand this at all," Sarah said apologetically.

"I'm sorry," Nōvagähd said. "I got ahead of us. This will help you understand why Sĕrĕhahn is bad.

"The Ämäthöär knew who all of us were. They knew what we were planning. Their plans took advantage of everything our leaders had arranged.

7: The Light of Life

The attacks started out secret, but our leaders quickly knew what was happening. We knew we had been discovered, with the exceptions of only a fortunate few.

"The Ämäthōär did their work well," he said hatefully. "Millions of Ōmäthäär, the bravest and best people I ever knew, were massacred.

"And even now, almost no one at all, in all of Nrathĕrmĕ, has any idea that anything happened! You see, the Ämäthōär have to stay behind the scenes, because—well, I will get to that. But the N'nrathĕrmĕ know as little about the Ōmäthäär, for what we really are, as they know about the Ämäthōär.

"Nrathĕrmĕ is being used by Sĕrĕhahn. He is a parasite, feeding off his own creation. He wants to feed off of the ideas and intelligence of the people of his pet empire; he wants to use their breakthroughs for himself. They are just another tool for himself.

"I think Sĕrĕhahn believes he can become infinite by himself, without Är. And he's using the collective discoveries of all of Nrathĕrmĕ to help him along.

"But he's afraid of anyone who could get in his way.

"Of course, I can only guess at Sĕrĕhahn's motivations. But it is certain that Sĕrĕhahn doesn't want anyone to know about Är, which is why he attempted, and still attempts, to kill the Ōmäthäär; we know Är.

"Nrathĕrmĕ is as near a perfect society as any of which I know. It is more powerful than all other nations and clans put together, because its people are so excellent. Sĕrĕhahn has taught them how to be great. How not to be petty—which is more than can be said for our Nŭährnär—"

"Really?" Sarah said.

"Nŭährnär is still getting on its feet," Nōvagähd answered her. "But most N'nrathĕrmĕ have been taught what it takes to be wonderful, prosperous, joyful people. Nrathĕrmĕ's atmosphere has improved magnificently in the past several thousand weeks. But few N'nrathĕrmĕ would ever seriously consider the possibility of the being of a real, individual Är.

"Sĕrĕhahn has done extraordinarily well in pervading Nrathĕrmĕ's culture with tenets that seem to prove the impossibility of an individual infinite person.

"I think he does that in order to ensure that no one except those whom he teaches or whom his pupils teach will gain sufficient mastery of Ärthähr to threaten him."

"And he's taught the Ämäthōär," Sarah observed.

"That's what we call his pupils. And Sĕrĕhahn himself, as well. He seems to look for people who he thinks are apt to communicate with the Ärthähr. Apparently, he knows enough about the principles behind Ärthähr that he can teach Ämäthöär how to handle it without having ever to mention Är."

"But why not teach his own Ämäthöär the truth?" Sarah asked.

"I don't know," Nōvagähd said thoughtfully. "I have met a few Ämäthöär who did know that Är was real." His voice shuddered with evident dread at the memory. "They knew all about Är, but that didn't change anything for them.

"Now, I would like to give them the benefit of the doubt. Perhaps, maybe, they thought that what they and Sĕrĕhahn were doing was alright. But I am rather certain that they just love the power. The power is enough for them; they don't care about any infinite Är.

"But I still hope that some Ämäthöär—in fact this has happened before—might turn against Sĕrĕhahn if they knew about Är and what Sĕrĕhahn is doing."

"But what exactly is he doing?" Sarah asked.

"Do you like all the new abilities that Ähänär gave you?"

Sarah thought he was trying to dodge the question. "I love them. But I don't understand exactly what Sĕrĕhahn is doing. I can tell he's awful, and the Ämäthöär too, but why would an Ämäthöär turn against him if they knew the truth about Är?"

"The greatness, the pleasure, and the efficaciousness of what Ähänär gave you," Nōvagähd said powerfully, "Is *nothing* compared to what the people of Nrathĕrmĕ could have if they knew about Är! If only they knew! Just how...how *perfect!* Infinity is!

"And Sĕrĕhahn is robbing them of that! Many even of the Ämäthöär, if they knew that Sĕrĕhahn was intentionally suffocating thoughts about Är, if they knew what Är was!, would see that as an intolerable crime. And they would fight him.

"But the Ämäthöär are all too often harder to convince than even N'nrathĕrmĕ," Nōvagähd said sadly, "Being in such close contact with Sĕrĕhahn.

"Sĕrĕhahn's arguments are very convincing."

He laughed sadly. "And, you know, an Ōmäthäär would need to keep an Ämäthöär from killing him first if he wanted to explain anything to him!"

"So the Ämäthöär hunt you just because you know about Är?" Sarah asked.

"You, too, Sarah. They're hunting you, too. And Sĕrĕhahn hunts us for that reason. I think. I have never actually asked him," he smiled grimly.

"But most Ämäthöär hunt us, we do know, because Sĕrĕhahn has taught them that we want to ruin their great system and take over Nrathĕrmĕ.

7: The Light of Life

"And we do want to take Nrathĕrmĕ from them," he said jovially, "And help the N'nrathĕrmĕ to be their own rulers within themselves, as well as their own political rulers as they falsely appear to be already.

"And we have and do try to tell the N'nrathĕrmĕ the truth about Sĕrĕhahn and Är and the Ämäthöär. But, almost always, they have been so thoroughly taught that any concept of an Är is ludicrous that they cannot so much as consider it.

"And those who do consider it find themselves quickly dogged by Ämäthöär.

"Nevertheless we have to help the N'nrathĕrmĕ know about Är. That's why we Ōmäthäär risk our lives staying so close to Nrathĕrmĕ. I hope the N'nrathĕrmĕ will someday finally understand everything about Är, about *everything*! Oh, how much could they be able to become, if people like them could just understand about Är!"

Sarah didn't know quite what Nōvagähd thought the N'nrathĕrmĕ would be able to become if they knew about Är, and she stayed silent. Her cloud of incoming matter was drying up, but she didn't notice that at first.

She really did love the idea of the N'nrathĕrmĕ knowing about Är, she thought.

"So, actually answering your question, Sarah," Nōvagähd resumed after his pause, "It is Är that makes us Ōmäthäär more powerful than the Ämäthöär.

"A few times, the Ämäthöär have killed nearly all the Ōmäthäär. More times than we have record of, I imagine. And few Ōmäthäär can rival many Ämäthöärs' grasp of Ärthähr.

"But Är will not let us fail. Not if we do the best we know how to do, he won't. The Ämäthöär do have formidable outward power, but they work against Är, and so they lack the single most potent aspect of Ärthähr.

"Really, they have merely a shadow of Ärthähr.

"But the Ōmäthäär are a new group. Mär has known about Ärthähr for little more than five hundred weeks. I've been an Ōmäthäär for hardly one thousand weeks, while some of the Ämäthöär have been learning about Ärthähr for thousands and thousands of weeks.

"There used to be Ōmäthäär who were very powerful, who rivaled even the best of the Ämäthöär aside from Sĕrĕhahn, but they were all killed around the time of our flight a hundred weeks ago."

"That's terrible," Sarah said.

"Well," Nōvagähd said seriously, "Being with the Ōmäthäär is more than worth anything that Sĕrĕhahn can do to me."

"I wish I could get to know them," Sarah said, impressed.

"So do I," Nōvagähd said quietly. "But for now, Sarah, we need to do everything we can to prepare to defend Earth from Sĕrĕhahn. But I hope you will meet all the Ōmäthäär someday."

"Thanks for telling me so much," Sarah said, her mind rolling with everything Nōvagähd had just explained to her.

"Thank you for being willing to hear it!" Nōvagähd said with a short laugh. "But don't talk too much about this, any of this. Especially not with other Earthmen. We really want the Earthmen to know everything about all these things, but Mär says we need to be careful in how we tell them all about it."

"Agreed," Sarah said, feeling light and energized in an oddly fatigued way. "But I've heard some people calling Earthmen 'Nōhōnŭäär.' Why?"

"I had better talk to my manager before I tell you any more," Nōvagähd said admiringly.

"Alright," Sarah said, a little disappointed. Then, in saying "Nōhōnŭäär," she noticed that it meant, "person from the house of Är."

"Keep doing well in organizing defenses," Nōvagähd was saying in farewell. "We're going to need all your best efforts."

"Nōvagähd, what do they mean by 'house of Är?'" Sarah pressed.

"They mean I should talk to my manager first," Nōvagähd said shortly. "I don't want to get into deep water just yet."

Sarah hoped Nōvagähd's manager would be as reasonable as he was. But, she realized, if Nōvagähd was an Ōmäthäär, his manager was likely to be one too.

"Be quick, then," she said.

Nōvagähd laughed. "I have all the motivation I need for that! Thank you for your time, Sarah Trotter."

My time? Sarah thought. "Bye," she said, but there was no answer.

She looked around at her idle defenses. And all at once, she realized she could think again. She couldn't say why, but her mind was suddenly on a roll. Everything Nōvagähd told her was spinning through her head, chased by more and more questions, but nevertheless she could, all of a sudden, think of ingenious, original ideas, almost without any effort.

Chapter 8

Ämäthōär

"Already done," Tom said back to Ōdaädŭ. "They're sending matter back."

"Thanks," Ōdaädŭ said, impressed, gliding toward him from the Shell. "Take a break, Tom. We'll work out tactics next."

Good, he thought. Now he could finally go see Brittney.

But there was so much to do; he would find her as soon as he finished this last idea.

"I'm alright to keep working," he shrugged amiably.

"On what?" Ōdaädŭ laughed.

"Rämhasōhän gave me some great ideas. I want to compare them with that pirate war you were talking about."

"Okay," his manager smiled as she began accelerating past him toward the sun. "I won't force you to take a break this time."

"Good," Tom grinned after her. "I won't be at it for long."

He drifted away from Earth, where he could see scattered defenses forming already. In his mind, he started cycling through reports of hundreds of different battles and skirmishes. The recorded clashes of warring pirate groups, he could tell already, were a treasury of brilliant strategies and unorthodox maneuvers. Every time he saw a tactic he liked, he made a mental note of it, and within a minute he had gathered an array of scores of beautiful and ingenious schemes. Even as he replayed other battles in his head, racing through great clashes in instants, he was planning how he could mix or combine the strategies that had already caught his interest.

The old pirates' genius was stirring up his own ingenuity. He was starting to come up with his own original ideas and new spins on the pirates' old moves. He could see in his mind how defenses would have to be arranged to accomplish his ideas. He mentally raced through accelerated simulations of battles to consider how his tactics might fare against variously disposed foes.

"Hey, Tom?" a voice broke in through his rapidly speeding thoughts. It was his assistant John Fleming.

"Hi, John," Tom answered, sending his voice away to John out at Mars. He had paused right at the deciding point of his most recently reviewed clash, an assault on the head of a drone nation.

"What do you think about all this?" John's voice said in what was clearly supposed to be a conversational tone.

"That's a hard question," Tom said with a small laugh. "There's so much! A few hours ago I was getting out of bed ready for a normal day." He laughed. "I was worrying about getting to work on time!" He thought for a couple seconds. "I can't really know what to think. I'm still in shock from it all. But I really like these people."

"I like them too," John's voice agreed.

There was silence for a few more seconds. Then John said, "One of my friends is afraid that they aren't telling us the truth."

Tom remembered Peter Garcia's suspicions of Mär, and Lewis's initial mistrust for Liz. He didn't think John's friend was likely to be any more right than they had been, but he was interested to find out. "Why?" Tom asked.

"I'm not sure what to think about it, myself," John warned.

"What did your friend say?"

"He's afraid that all this business about Anhar and Nrathĕrmĕ could be a sham," John said hesitantly. "What if there isn't an Anhar, or, if there is, what if he isn't out to kill us all? What if Mär only told us that so we'd cooperate?"

Tom waited, but John seemed to be waiting for him. "What do you think about that?" Tom asked carefully.

"I'm still thinking," John said sheepishly. "What do you think?"

"I want to keep an open mind," Tom admitted. "Here we are building defenses, getting ready to defend ourselves against this Anhar. What if the real enemy that we need to defend our world from is right here? We can't not keep our eyes open.

"But it would be just as bad, probably worse, if Sĕrĕhahn really does want to kill us and we turn against the N'nüährnär, if they really are trying to protect us.

"We still have to keep our eyes open. But," Tom's voice intensified unconsciously, "As far as I can tell, Mär and these people are telling us the truth."

"Okay," John said, sounding heartened. "But how are you so sure?"

"I don't want to be sure," Tom said slowly. "Not until I really can be sure. But I believe these people enough to fight alongside them."

He hesitated thoughtfully. "I hope Mär's telling us the truth."

"I'm not sure what to hope," John said with a baffled chuckle. "What's worse, having Sĕrĕhahn or Nüährnär as our enemy?"

"I wish it were neither," Tom said. "At any rate, I believe it will be better having these people as our friends."

John made an approving sound. "I'll tell Peter that," he said.

8: Ämäthöär

"Tell Peter what?"

"What you said," John said plainly.

"I don't think what I was saying would make much of an argument," Tom smiled, "It's just what I think."

Then something clicked.

"Wait a second—is this Peter, is he named Peter Garcia?" Tom checked.

"Yes, that's Peter!" John said, surprised. "How do you know him?"

"Dark brown hair, dark eyes, kind of deep eyes, clean shaven?" Tom clarified. "Kind of a big, straight nose?"

"That's him," John's voice smiled. "How do you know each other? I'd never met you before this."

"I only just talked to him for a couple of minutes," Tom said. "Just less than an hour ago."

"Oh," John said. "Still, that's incredible. Small world, huh?"

"It was, maybe."

"Peter and I have been best friends for years," John said.

"Wow," Tom said. "It's weird how stuff works out like this."

"Peter has been pretty worried that this is all a lie," John's voice said.

"That's what he said to me," Tom nodded.

"I hope these people are telling us the truth," John said. "I'll talk to Peter about it."

Tom had swiveled to stare at Nrathĕrmĕ's belatedly burning star. "And are you going to keep sending matter to me?" he joked. "As long as you still hope this isn't a lie…"

"Yeah," John promised. "From what I know, I'm much more afraid of Sĕrĕhahn and Nrathĕrmĕ than of everyone here combined."

"Everyone here combined is a whole lot fewer people, and less resources, than Nrathĕrmĕ is, by a long shot!" Tom reminded him.

"I know," John said in a subdued tone. "How do you think we're going to survive, if Anhar really is trying to kill us?"

"I'm sure Mär knows what he's doing," Tom said hopefully. "These people must understand what they're up against."

"At any rate, it'll take more than a month—or, should I say, seven 'weeks,'—for anyone to get to us from Nrathĕrmĕ," John noted.

"I want Mär to be telling the truth," Tom said, "But that doesn't mean I'm not terrified of Nrathĕrmĕ, whether it's weeks away or years away. And from what I've heard about Anhar Sĕrĕhahn…" he trailed away.

"John," he asked tentatively after a pensive pause, "Did they tell you about something called 'Ämäthöär?'"

Before John could answer, an urgent, shouting voice burst in on Tom's thoughts:

"*Everyone, evacuate the Shell, now! This is Ōhōmhär. Evacuate the Shell immediately! Ōmäthäär, Mär is under attack in the Shell!*"

"What's going on?" John wondered.

"I don't know," Tom said, but he understood "under attack" as well as anyone else.

"*Ōmäthäär, to Mär!*" the woman's voice shouted. "*There are Ämäthöär here!*"

Tom had hurled himself to speed back to the Shell before he thought that that could be a terrible idea.

"Do you know what she's talking about?" John's worried voice came in his head. "What are Ämäthöär?"

Tom felt his blood freeze. Ämäthöär. And they were killing Mär. Some mad part of him wanted to help, not at all daunted by the fact that he had no help to give against such beings.

If he could see the Ämäthöär firsthand, then he would know for sure that this was not a lie, he thought without realizing it. If Ämäthöär were as terrible as Liz had portrayed them, he would believe that Mär and his Ōmäthäär really were protecting Earth from them.

He whizzed into the Shell, but as soon as he emerged and burst out through a deserted ocean he lost nearly all desire to see Ämäthöär.

Everything was shaking with palpable fear. He knew Mär was more than a thousand miles away, but the darkness even from that distance was terrifying.

His heart seized. He wanted nothing more than to run, to run and escape this horrible power closing around him. But then he found himself hurtling toward it, as if the fear were sucking him in.

His mind was reeling. His extraordinary sight was flickering. He could not see. He could not think. Knives of fear were sawing at every piece of him.

He felt as if he was choking. His skin, his bones, his heart felt frozen, and open, and naked. He felt like he was perceiving everything through a dark, pressing mist. The bright sky was black with encompassing terror.

And in the very center of the moaning blackness ahead, he saw Mär, like a pinprick of fiery, living light. Hundreds of other islands of life blazed out of the blackness around him.

Tom's head was shaking. He could not feel his body. He could not think to slow, or stop, or turn and flee, insane with terror. No one noticed him rocketing toward them.

He could hear nothing but a horrific unearthly sound like a tremendous,

8: Ämäthōär

scraping gale. The sound of pulsating winds of audible terror filled his mind, which was fading in and out.

There was Mär. His consciousness gasped a breath of living air.

And grappling with Mär at incomprehensible speeds were two vortexes of darkness.

In the instant before Tom crashed through the battling swarm, he recognized the two fear-blazing people; they had been with Mär at the meeting. Ōmäthäär were trying to grapple them, and others tried to touch Mär, but all but Mär were being hurled back by a force that Tom's fogged eyes couldn't bear to see. And Mär's light was flickering.

Everything was winding down to slower and slower motion. Tom's heart was crushed in darkness. The last thing he saw was one of the nexuses of terror leap away from Mär, hurtling straight at him.

Tom could see the man's inhuman face, contorted with terrifyingly relaxed fury. Slowly, rising above the deafening screeching wind, Tom could hear his soul-freezing scream.

And the darkness leapt forward, and Tom was consumed.

Tom remembered all that, as if it had happened in some foreign lifetime, as the world faded back around him into reality. The air was peaceful and bright. The sky was blue, and clouds glowed white and clean.

Fourteen men and women had their hands on his body.

"He's coming back!" one of the women said in an elated, and infinitely distant, cry.

Tom couldn't talk. He was aware of his body as if he hadn't felt it in ages.

He looked more closely at the people around him. They were all Mär's people. From that meeting from some other life. They gently let go of him, and excellent, wonderful warmth filled every corner of his consciousness.

"You, Tom Pratt, are a madly brave man," a man called Arnä beamed.

Memory floated darkly back into his mind. He felt himself lifelessly mouth, "Ämäthōär."

Some of them exchanged grave glances.

"Come here with us," Arnä said, wrapping an arm around Tom. An inexplicable rejuvenation flowed into him. His senses were clearing more as he heard Arnä whisper, "Mär wants to see us."

Oh good, Tom thought, feeling more exhausted than he knew a person could feel. *Mär's alive.*

Sĕrĕhahn heaved a heavy sigh.

"They've failed."

Light and Glory

Lhĕhrha looked into his eyes. Then she nodded acceptingly.

Sĕrĕhahn smiled cherishingly at her, and pulled her in to a deep hug. "I'm going to have to go to Hĕnahr," he whispered sadly.

Lhĕhrha held him tightly. "I wish I could go with you," she smiled.

Sĕrĕhahn laughed through manifest downheartedness, backing away and looking at her adoringly. "Why?"

"Oh, no, it's not like that," Lhĕhrha said in a dismissive, courageous way. "We need me to stay. But Hĕnahr would be fantastically exciting, even if I'd have to be with you the whole time." She snickered and kissed him.

"Heh, I'll miss you too," Sĕrĕhahn smiled.

Lhĕhrha pushed him roughly away, beaming. "Get going! The sooner you leave, the sooner we see each other again!"

Sĕrĕhahn glided right back to her and embraced her again. As he slid back away, he clasped both her hands, rights in lefts. "I love you," he said with casual power.

He whirled around on the spot and pitched straight down through the open sky.

"I love you!" Lhĕhrha's voice joyfully called in his head. "I'll be waiting for you!"

Sĕrĕhahn smiled blissfully within himself. He passed down through tall clouds, through a roiling hurricane and a raging sea, and down and came out again in a woody wilderness. He soared from ground to sky to ground again, passing through world after world in Nrathĕrmĕ's capacious interior empires, until he came down from a clear, warm sky upon a string of weathered, red peaks.

"Where's Lhĕhrha?" a cheerful woman, floating comfortably near the ground of a scrubby mountain pass, greeted him as he approached.

"Busier than you're about to be," Sĕrĕhahn said seriously, lighting gracefully on the gravelly soil.

"What did you feel?" one of two men there asked him.

Sĕrĕhahn hugged him. "You?" he asked first.

"Tĕlgad and Nĕthra," the man said.

Sĕrĕhahn nodded, hugging the other man. "Dead," he said bluntly.

The woman nodded as well, as if she had expected no less. "How, though?" she wondered aloud, touching ground by them.

Sĕrĕhahn embraced her too, and she asked, "And Mär?"

Sĕrĕhahn stepped back and smiled weakly at her. "Something's happened."

He looked at the others' expectant faces. "Tĕlgad and Nĕthra did wonderfully," he said obviously. "They're heroes; they wouldn't have died unless it was important."

"Hĕnahr?" the woman said promptly.

Sĕrĕhahn smiled broadly. "Yes," he said, putting a hand on her shoulder and grinning enthusiastically at the other two.

He looked silently at them with a solid smiling air that nonetheless compelled a profound gravity.

"We truly have found Hûhōnĕrrŭ."

"And Mär's there," the woman added.

Sĕrĕhahn sat in the red dirt. He looked out with peaceful pleasure at the valleys that sloped away from the pass, dappled with silvery lakes and gleaming, snaking rivers.

"I like Mär," he said definitively.

The woman smiled. "We all like Mär."

"And Lhĕhûnrĕ," Sĕrĕhahn added.

No one said anything. The woman moved to stand beside their Anhar. "Yeah," she sighed sadly. "I liked Lhĕhûnrĕ too."

Sĕrĕhahn looked up at her. "Thahn," he said, "We may need to kill Mär."

Thahn smiled sadly but admiringly down at him. She looked out over the living land, a tear trickling down her beautiful, brooding face.

Sĕrĕhahn patted her calf where it emerged from her shining white inertial robing. "Mär has done wonderfully well," he said quietly and comfortingly. "Death will not be a misfortune for him."

"He could have been so great," one of the other men said, sitting down beside Sĕrĕhahn. "If only..."

Sĕrĕhahn smiled lightly and rubbed the man's near shoulder. "Mär's as great as he's ready to be," he said happily. "Death is not the end for him!"

Thahn sat down too. The second man sat quietly where he was standing behind them, where he began passing his hand absently through the leaves of a tiny bush.

Thahn looked up at the puffy clouds above the valleys. They started whisking and whirling rapidly back and forth, dancing and splitting and recombining as Thahn watched, absorbed in meditation.

Sĕrĕhahn smiled, and watched the clouds contentedly. Several soft minutes passed, with the four of them sitting benignly and totally comfortably, as if without any care or responsibility to trouble them, as if they all were just basking in the joy of some perfect moment.

Then Sĕrĕhahn whispered, "Go ahead."

No one moved, but each sat, looking utterly unperturbed. The clouds

Light and Glory

continued their sweeping dances for almost half a minute more.

Then the clouds coasted back into their usual paths. "I'll need a capable army," Thahn said, "And as many R'bathĕrŭ as Lhĕhrha can spare me."

Sĕrĕhahn laughed relishingly. "You're afraid of Hûhōnĕrrŭ."

Thahn laughed too, but it was more softly. "Aren't you?"

"Only of power used wrongly," Sĕrĕhahn said sincerely. "And Hûhōnĕrrŭ could mean a lot of power, a whole lot of power!

"I love power; it can cause good. But what can do great good can also do great evil."

"Mär has Hûhōnĕrrŭ," the man beside him commented.

Sĕrĕhahn raised an eyebrow. "Mär is *at* Hûhōnĕrrŭ. And he may be able to use it."

"I wish he would come back to us," the man sighed tiredly.

"He may still," Sĕrĕhahn allowed. "But we may not be able to afford him that chance. If he might use Hûhōnĕrrŭ to do damage, then we will need to kill him, as well as Hûhōnĕrrŭ itself." Sĕrĕhahn's tone didn't reflect pleasure at the idea.

He looked silently at Thahn.

"I don't think Mär will ever come back," Thahn sighed.

"He could surprise us," Sĕrĕhahn said sadly, looking out over the valleys. "If given enough time. But if we have to kill him before then, he will still be able to grow and learn."

He stood, and walked comfortably toward the other side of the rocky red pass. He touched the other man's shoulder in a grateful way as he stepped past him. "Don't be afraid of Hûhōnĕrrŭ, Thahn," he said. He smiled out at the valleys stretching beyond the other side of the pass.

Then he turned back, looking at Thahn with intense meaning. "If everything goes well, Hûhōnĕrrŭ will fall straight into your hands.

"But," he said, looking into her eyes, "Tĕlgad and Nĕthra failed to kill Mär. They're dead, and Mär still lives. Something must have happened for them to have tried to kill him now. I'm afraid something we haven't expected is happening with Hûhōnĕrrŭ.

"I am afraid.

"You may fail like them," he said steadily to Thahn.

He swooped without warning through the air, colliding with her in a passionate embrace.

"You are more than a match for Mär and all his 'Ōmäthäär,'" he said. "If you fail, it will be because of Hûhōnĕrrŭ, not Mär.

"I don't understand everything about Hûhōnĕrrŭ," he said. "I need to go

8: Ämäthōär

to Hĕnahr and prepare for the worst."

He took Thahn's left hand in his right.

"I hope you'll go to Hûhōnĕrrŭ, scatter R'dōnĕmär, and manage to save Mär and many of his imitation Ōmäthäär.

"But I'm afraid that it will prove to be much more difficult."

"I'll do the best that I can do," Thahn shrugged bravely.

Sĕrĕhahn embraced her again. "I would have gone myself," he said, as if they had discussed this before, "If I weren't afraid of Hûhōnĕrrŭ."

He let go of her, but Thahn pulled him back powerfully. "I would rather I die than you!" she said with fiery earnestness.

Sĕrĕhahn squeezed her tight. "I hope neither of us ever need die!" He released her and moved back, looking softly at her indomitable demeanor. "But Hûhōnĕrrŭ is important. Immortality can come after death, if need be." He caressed her smooth arm.

"If Thahn fails at Hûhōnĕrrŭ," he said to the other two, "Then we will know that R'dōnĕmär has harnessed parts of it. Even I would fail against that. But we need to know what Hûhōnĕrrŭ is doing."

"We win whatever happens," Thahn smiled. "At least we make progress, whatever may come."

"I hope you obtain it," Sĕrĕhahn said. "That would be better than any knowledge your death could give. But Hĕnahr may be our only hope, now.

"And," he said with deeply affective, weighty brightness, "Even if R'dōnĕmär makes unprecedented difficulties for our progression by wielding Hûhōnĕrrŭ, if the unexpectable happens, if anything or everything happens in the means of obtaining Hûhōnĕrrŭ, we must obtain it! The Life of Hûhōnĕrrŭ is worth everything else we may have to give and endure!"

Thahn smiled at him, more completely now.

"It is time to call the others," the man at the bush said. "The ones we can trust," he smiled up at Sĕrĕhahn.

Sĕrĕhahn sighed and nodded. He glided up carelessly into the air, admiring the valleys on both sides again, as he contacted several of his assistants at once.

"We need to talk about Hûhōnĕrrŭ," he called to them. "Call all your knowing assistants."

Sĕrĕhahn spread his arms euphorically. "This is it," he said out loud.

He turned and looked back at the other three. "This is it," he grinned again.

He waved his fingers playfully, and the valleys and the skies and the mountain pass evaporated into a field of pure, radiant whiteness.

Thahn and the two men glided away from Sĕrĕhahn, stopping to stand, facing him, some distance away, the four of them standing peacefully in the perfect, complete whiteness.

They were soon joined by a few other R'bathĕrŭ, who also stood facing Sĕrĕhahn from a distance. They all stood comfortably as those few became a score over the succeeding minute.

"You came quickly," Sĕrĕhahn greeted them appreciatively. His light demeanor was tainted by a shade of solemn seriousness as more and more arrived.

At the end of three minutes, in which Sĕrĕhahn greeted friendlily his friends as they arrived, more than twelve thousand R'bathĕrŭ were gathered in a sphere around him.

He threw out his hands energetically. "Let's get started," he said in a commanding voice. "We have found Hûhōnĕrrŭ."

No one moved. Some of the R'bathĕrŭ looked entirely surprised; many others looked excited.

"But things have become complicated," Sĕrĕhahn said. He smiled a little. "As could have been expected.

"R'dōnĕmär knows about Hûhōnĕrrŭ."

An angry tremor rustled through the sphere.

"We cannot afford to underestimate Mär," Sĕrĕhahn warned them. "Don't let unwarranted anger keep you from doing what you should do.

"In an effort to keep Hûhōnĕrrŭ from Mär," he continued, his pace easy but his demeanor nonetheless conveying a consuming rush, "We paid some pirates to make a record of and utterly destroy Hûhōnĕrrŭ; Mär would have no record and no Hûhōnĕrrŭ, and we would revive it here.

"But a few things have changed. Mär found out about the pirates, intercepted them, and protected and seized Hûhōnĕrrŭ. Now the planet, and its inhabitants, are in the hands of Mär's 'Ōmäthäär,'" Sĕrĕhahn said the word with a kind of sorrowful ridicule, "And R'dōnĕmär.

"The pirates made the record of Hûhōnĕrrŭ. They claimed it was destroyed in the fight with R'dōnĕmär, but it was a lie. They were eliminated," he nodded gratefully to a few of them, "But we found no record of Hûhōnĕrrŭ.

"The record may have been destroyed when we attacked the pirates. But there is a faint chance that they had been able to pass the record on before we caught up with them.

"I am afraid there could be a record of Hûhōnĕrrŭ out somewhere in the Wild, waiting to be given to the highest payer. Whoever has that record may be able to make Hûhōnĕrrŭ for themselves, along with its people.

8: Ämäthōär

"We have to work quickly. As long as Hûhōněrrŭ is alive, anyone who uses that record will build only an unenlivened shell.

"We must secure Hûhōněrrŭ.

"And we must secure that record. We need to find everyone who has had it and destroy it.

"We need to wrest Hûhōněrrŭ from R'dōněmär before Mär is able to harness it, before he is able to influence the people of Hûhōněrrŭ any more than we can prevent.

"The record is lifeless as long as Hûhōněrrŭ remains intact. We need to get to Hûhōněrrŭ and keep it safe."

He glided aside as Thahn soared down into his place in the center.

"I am going to Hûhōněrrŭ to redeem it from R'dōněmär," she announced. "Mär will stay where he is. He won't take Hûhōněrrŭ away; he'll stay to oppose us.

"We need to free Hûhōněrrŭ from him. We may need to kill him, if he opposes us that far.

"Hûhōněrrŭ must be obtained intact if possible. But we may need to destroy it, and revive it here, if R'dōněmär uses it against us."

She glanced at Sěrěhahn. "Any moment in which Hûhōněrrŭ is dead is a moment in which anyone with a record can revive it. We will only destroy it if we need to.

"And," she said with a relishing smile, "What is the power of Hûhōněrrŭ without its people?

"The people of Hûhōněrrŭ must be spared as much as possible. Mär won't leave many people on the planet itself; when we make our record, we will not get a record of many of them. Though they will likely fight us, we must capture as many of them alive as possible.

"People from Hûhōněrrŭ may make better R'bathěrŭ than any of us.

"But unexpected things are happening. I am afraid Mär may already be using some of Hûhōněrrŭ's power.

"Tělgad and Něthra tried to kill Mär; they must have known something that Mär's planning that we don't know, which necessitated Mär be removed immediately.

"Naturally, his friends defended him, but Tělgad and Něthra were capable. They should have been able to kill Mär and escape without falling."

She looked at Sěrěhahn.

"They are dead," he affirmed.

"Mär's people should not have been able to destroy them," Thahn said. "We believe something is happening with Hûhōněrrŭ. But now we've lost our ears in R'dōněmär.

"We must work very quickly. All who want to come with me to Hûhōněrrŭ, come forward."

More than five hundred R'batherŭ glided forward into the sphere, and congregated behind Thahn as she moved back toward the edge.

"I am going to Hěnahr," Sěrěhahn said, taking the center again. "If Mär, or anyone, manages to use Hûhōněrrŭ against us then we will need every advantage we can get.

"Lhěhrha is the best qualified to head Nrathěrmě in my absence. Influence her as much as is feasible, but trust her. She's as smart as anyone I've ever known.

"She knows that Hûhōněrrŭ has consummate power, though she does not know as much as you know. But she will take care of our efforts to acquire it. Follow her.

"I will keep a watch on events here. If I feel the need, I will come back, but I want to stay at Hěnahr as long as I can.

"We will need every advantage we can have."

He stood silently. The sphere was taut with determined anticipation.

"To get the N'nrathěrmě to follow you," he resumed, "Tell them that I've been killed by assassins from R'dōněmär. I'm sure you will make it convincing."

He smiled lovingly at the R'batherŭ all around him. "Until victory," he said confidently.

Then he disappeared.

Tears were sliding freely down Thahn's face. She looked tearfully at where Sěrěhahn had vanished for several seconds. Then she looked around at her fellows. "This is it," she whispered.

Physically speaking, Tom felt perfect. But he couldn't imagine himself smiling again.

He was back in a sphere around Mär, all the nearby higher managers having been urgently summoned back, but they were within the Shell this time. Snaking rivers gleamed blue miles below, weaving their ways to a jagged green coastline under cover of cottonlike clouds. Tom stared emptily down at them; everything seemed distinctly lifeless to him now.

Thirty-four Ōmäthäär had been killed by those two Ämäthōär, he had been told. And Ōdaädŭ had been one of them. Though four of the Ōmäthäär had been successfully healed, his vivacious manager would not come back. His own manager.

8: Ämäthōär

He had been looking at her, talking to her, seeing her as alive as anything, just less than half an hour ago. He had known she had been married, but he hadn't asked her what had happened to her husband. And now she was gone. She had been totally alive, and now she was just gone.

Peter Garcia glided into place beside him. Tom didn't care. At that point, he was prepared to believe anything Mär could say.

Mär, who was looking straight at him from the center, he realized. He looked back at him, but Mär didn't say anything.

Tom didn't know what to think of the look Mär was giving him. He looked intensely solemn, almost angry; it was as if he were reading something written behind Tom's face.

"I'm sorry," Tom apologized uncertainly, "I know I shouldn't—"

"I am very glad that you did come," Mär interrupted in his head. He was smiling now. He raised his hand gratefully at Tom, then turned his head to one of his surrounding friends.

Tom suddenly felt remarkably warmer. The lingering cloud over the world seemed to pass.

He actually felt himself smiling faintly as he looked at the Ōmäthäär around Mär. The majority of them were scanning the sphere like before. This time, the impression was clear to him that they were guarding Mär, and now he understood precisely why. He wished he didn't.

Peter had cleared his throat significantly. Tom looked exhaustedly at him, and Peter said, "So…"

Tom responded by looking away.

Peter looked at the man beside him for a moment. Well, at least he was clearly making him think, Peter thought, even if he did not yet want to face reality.

He wondered what Mär had to tell them so soon. He was going to keep an open mind, but he would have to see what real meaning lay behind whatever Mär had to say.

"If it is, then Peter won't be able to doubt anymore," Kathy was saying bitterly in Sarah's head.

"Maybe," Sarah said back, avoiding the eye of Peter beside her. "All the same, I hope it's something else."

"One of my manager's other assistants said there were Ämäthōär here," Kathy insisted. "And remember what that Ōmäthäär said? She said there were Ämäthōär attacking Mär."

"It may have been a false alarm," Scott shivered. "Mär is alive."

"Anyway, we'll all hear what he's called us for in a second," Rene said, fear in her voice making her sound impatient.

Sarah didn't say anything else at that point, but Nōvagähd's frantic command to her to stay far from the Shell and his long silence afterward made her afraid that Kathy was in fact right, that there had already been an Ämäthōär attack. Right there, right at their own Earth, there had been Ämäthōär just like Ähänär's. But Nōvagähd hadn't been eager to say much of anything when his voice had finally returned.

And then Mär's voice filled her head:

"Thank you for coming," he said, his voice unperturbed, even pleased. "The construction of defenses has gotten to a great start. We will need all the protection we can have.

"You all heard something about the Ämäthōär who just attacked.

"Some of you, notably N'närdamähr, already know a few things about Ämäthōär. Others of you, and most of you Earthmen I think, have not been told very much about them."

Sarah couldn't help noticing Peter's confident poker face give way a little.

"I'm about to tell all of you more about Ämäthōär than I have ever had the opportunity to tell Nüährnär. Your assistants may know as much as you elect to tell them, but the time has come for you, as heading managers, to try to understand about Ämäthōär."

Mär's unperturbed, genial air had subtly transformed into a serious, desperately earnest, yet no less genial, gravity.

"What we call Ämäthōär are a group of some of Sěrěhahn's most potent allies.

"Like Sěrěhahn, the Ämäthōär want to destroy us. Now they know where to find us. We should expect more Ämäthōär to attack us.

"If any Ämäthōär attack us again, *do not fight them*! Flee from them! They cannot frequently be harmed by any means that most of you have. Flee from them as soon as you spot them, and call one of these people," he motioned to the guard clumped around him. "These people standing with me will keep you safe from Ämäthōär.

"Let the Ämäthōär come."

He paused, then said with a clear shade of regret, "It is difficult to spot Ämäthōär until they show themselves as Ämäthōär."

He paused again. "When Ämäthōär show themselves," he continued, "you will feel unexplainable fear. If you feel *anything* like that, even if you think it isn't anything, tell one of these people! We know that Ämäthōär are terrible. We will be extremely grateful if you call us at any time that you so much as think you feel any kind of fear like that.

8: Ämäthōär

"Keep your eyes open for them, tell us about them, and flee from them!"

He seemed to shrink then back to normal size. He smiled, like a friend in a regular conversation, and observed, "You want to know what happened."

He sighed. "Two of my closest friends were in fact Ämäthōär." Sarah could see tears trickling down Mär's face as he talked. "They'd been disguised for hundreds of weeks, since before we fled Nrathĕrmĕ. I had loved them! They knew much of what Nǜährnär is planning."

He waited, then said simply, "They showed themselves as Ämäthōär do, and they tried to kill me. My friends and I killed them."

Tom realized that Mär was looking right into him again. His expression was still inscrutable, but it seemed softer. But then the instant passed, and Mär directed his eyes elsewhere.

"We must prepare ourselves against the armies of Sĕrĕhahn," Mär said. "He will find a way to use Nrathĕrmĕ's martial capacity against us. Prepare for that; my friends and I will deal with the Ämäthōär.

"Leave them to us."

He looked around at the frightened sphere of managers. "Do not fight them. Call us. False alerts are better than late ones."

He smiled sadly. "Thank all of you," he said emotionally. Then he shot away through the sphere and into the strangely dimmer sky, flanked by the swarm of Ōmäthäär.

Sarah noticed Peter's loosened composure tighten back into haughty assurance as soon as Mär left. And she also noticed Tom Pratt on Peter's far side.

She thought for a second. Then she ducked around behind Peter, calling, "Hi."

Tom recognized Sarah, and Kathy tailing her, from what felt like eons before.

"My name's Sarah Trotter," Sarah said.

"Hi," Tom smiled feebly.

"Of course we already know each other's names," Kathy said, stopping beside Sarah. "We're sisters," she told Tom. "And our parents," but then she saw that Scott and Rene had already sped off back to work. "Well, our parents were right here."

Peter noticed Tom, Kathy, and Sarah conferring privately to his left. He decided they weren't worth talking to just yet; let them work things out themselves first, and then they might be ready to face facts. He rocketed off to find Annie.

"What do you know about these Ämäthōär?" Sarah was asking Tom.

Tom didn't answer. His expression seemed to cloud over.

"Are you okay?" Kathy asked, concerned.

Tom shook his head sharply. "I'm fine," he said, sounding anything but that.

He looked from Sarah to Kathy. He might as well just tell them. "I saw them," he said.

"The Ämäthöär?" Sarah asked, surprised.

"Yeah. I don't know why I did it. I went to go see them."

"What were they like?" Kathy asked with a sort of frightened eagerness.

Tom shuddered involuntarily. "Mär's telling the truth," he said fervently. "They were terrible. Worse fear than I've ever had before."

Despite his shaken appearance, something about Tom's manner struck Sarah as uncommonly friendly. Especially in comparison with Peter. Something about the easy way he looked at them made her feel like she was talking to an old friend. She felt herself loosen up too.

"Of course Mär's telling the truth!" Kathy said. "You didn't believe that idiot earlier, did you?"

Tom smiled weakly. "No," he said calmingly. "But now, I can't doubt at all."

"Did you tell Peter?" Kathy asked.

"No," Tom said. He actually managed an extremely exhausted laugh. "It's not nice to think about."

"Maybe this isn't the best thing to be talking about," Sarah observed.

"Yeah," Tom nodded, still smiling somehow. He stared blankly ahead, then whispered, "Those Ämäthöär were the worst things I have ever seen."

"Leave it," Sarah said privately to Kathy, who she could tell was itching to ask for more details.

"Could you tell us about them later?" Sarah asked kindly.

"Sure," Tom answered, his eyes refocusing. "I could tell you now; I'm really okay. But," and he seemed to think better of it, "Maybe it would be better to talk later. Better to think about other stuff for a while."

"Okay," Kathy said, trying and failing to mask her disappointment.

Sarah smiled slightly at Tom. It was nice to talk to him, even if they were talking about Ämäthöär.

"Thanks for asking me about it," Tom said. "I mean, not Ämäthöär, but thanks for caring. But I better get back to work. Back to thinking about normal things." He laughed more healthily. "'Normal things'! If this is normal..." He smiled. "But thanks." He waved as he turned and coasted toward the sea below.

8: Ämäthōär

Sarah was still smiling a little as she watched him shrink into the misty sky.

Kathy noticed that, and grinned, "That Tom is a lot nicer to talk to than Peter, even if he didn't say much."

"You can hardly blame him," Sarah shuddered. "Real Ämäthōär..." She tried to shake off the creeping, cold feeling chilling her.

"I would love to hear what he can tell us about them," she said. "Later."

Peter found Annie out past the planets, corralling matter from tinier worlds.

"Hey," Annie called to him, swooping toward him as he siphoned some comet into himself.

"Hey, you," Peter smiled. Annie hugged him.

"What did Mär have to say?" Annie asked after kissing him.

Peter took a breath, then reported to Annie a brief overview of Mär's statements about Ämäthōär.

"So there could be a real Nrathĕrmĕ," Peter said then, "And a real Anhar. Or Sĕrĕhahn, as Mär calls him. That makes everything make more sense.

"Apparently, Mär's men found some spies of Anhar's and killed them.

"Mär did say that the spies had tried to kill him," Peter admitted, looking out at the stars. "That may be true. If there is a Nrathĕrmĕ...and Mär is obviously not a part of it...Mär may be some kind of outlaw. And if so, Mär may have been telling the truth; Anhar's spies would have ample cause to kill him."

Annie was listening wordlessly. Peter's assertions made sense. But something down within her did not latch on to his explanations as readily as she wanted to.

Peter thought for a moment. "We may need to run away from Mär," he then said quietly.

"And from Earth?" Annie asked anxiously.

"Maybe. Maybe enough of us will oppose Mär that we can save Earth from him."

He looked back at Annie. "There may very well be a Nrathĕrmĕ, and Anhar may attack Nüährnär. Because Mär is a criminal, not because Anhar would for any reason want to destroy *us*.

"I've been looking over what my managers claim are N'nrathĕrmĕ media." He nodded his head, as if to say that what he saw looked legitimate enough. "Nrathĕrmĕ's never found another intelligent civilization before. Assuming that what they showed me was from an actual Nrathĕrmĕ.

"From what I know, the people of Nrathĕrmĕ would be overjoyed to find an intelligent civilization. Nrathĕrmĕ's supposed to have explored hundreds of thousands of worlds, and we're the first civilization they've found. They would not attack us.

"I am...almost certain...that the disaster that almost killed us this morning was done by Nŭährnär, so we would be afraid and actually believe all this. Mär is using us, and most of us," he said disdainfully, "Seem to be playing right into his hands."

Annie was feeling more and more alarmed.

"I am convinced that Mär is duping us. I wonder," he said darkly, "What Mär will do to us if armies from Nrathĕrmĕ do arrive to destroy him. Maybe he thinks he can fool us so much that we'll actually fight for him.

"It's a perfect plan! N'nrathĕrmĕ won't want to harm us; he can hide behind us! He's just a petty terrorist who's fooling our whole world into being his hostages!"

"Are you sure about this?" Annie asked worriedly.

"I'm sure," he said. "I'm getting more sure all the time." He bowed his head in thought, while Annie was feeling increasingly frightened.

"They all seemed so nice..." she said breathlessly.

Peter looked up. "Mäōhä? And that Ähŭhan, and Ōhärkrahan? They seemed so fake!

"These people have been with Mär for a long time, if what we've been told is true. But many of them don't know everything he's doing. He may be fooling them too, or they all may be in the know, working with him to fool all of us."

"So, what do we do?" Annie asked, summoning her courage.

"Don't tell anyone else about this. If the wrong people find out what we know..." He trailed away ominously. "Just don't tell anyone except people we know we can trust. I've already told John. He's keeping an eye out. Only tell people from Earth for now, until we know if these people know what Mär's up to."

"Okay," Annie nodded bravely.

"I'll try to warn as many people as I can," Peter said. "We may be able to save Earth. But be ready to run if it comes to that."

"Okay," Annie nodded again, feeling her courage falter. "Where would we go?"

"Nrathĕrmĕ, probably," Peter said. "But we should take it slowly. First we need to get enough people to oppose Mär." He kissed her again. "And we need to keep working. To keep up appearances. We can't let anyone suspect

8: Ämäthōär

that we know Mär isn't genuine."

"Okay," Annie nodded again. "I wish we could work together."

"I talked to my managers about that," Peter said with noticeable bitterness. "Only married couples get to work together."

Annie looked significantly at him.

He didn't seem to notice. "I need to get back, before my managers start asking questions."

"What would they ask?" Annie laughed. "You have every reason to talk to me!"

Peter laughed too and kissed her again. "Be careful," he whispered.

Chapter 9

The First Moves

"Alright, alright," Nōvagähd's voice gave in, laughing at her. "You can tell him. But don't go too far!"

"Thanks," Sarah said back. She was floating out far from Earth with her small squadron of defenses, the armored planet just a glowing speck amid the stars, reflecting the sun's diminishing light. "I think I can trust Tom."

The better part of an Earth day had passed, and it had been the longest twenty hours of Sarah's life. With no need of eating or sleeping, no need to go to work or to her classes, and with her superhumanly fast thoughts, she felt like she had been with Nŭährnär for the better part of a month.

"Be careful what you tell him," Nōvagähd advised her, but with only a touch of sobriety. "But if he's the one who saw the Ämäthöär... Well, he must be an immensely foolish person!" he joked.

"You were there too," Sarah accused.

Nōvagähd's laughter dissipated. "That was not at all pleasant," he assured her, though his manner implied that it had not been particularly strange for him either.

And then he laughed again. "Go ahead! Go talk to him. You probably won't be able to tell him anything that can surprise him, after what he's seen."

Sarah smiled unknowingly as she thought of talking to Tom Pratt again. "Thanks," she said to Nōvagähd.

Nōvagähd didn't answer, and Sarah assumed he had gone again.

Sarah glided around amongst her platforms, brainstorming new strategies, as she searched around for Tom. He was over inside the shrinking sun, she realized.

"Hey, Tom?" she called.

He didn't answer at once. Sarah continued gliding thoughtfully through the defenses. But after several seconds, Tom still hadn't answered.

She didn't want to be rude; she waited a couple more seconds.

She was about to call to him again, when a voice that wasn't Tom Pratt's called to her.

"Hi, my name's John," the voice said. "Tom's tied up helping his manager at the sun. What do you need?"

Tom must have sent his assistant to talk to her, Sarah realized disappointedly. She could see John approaching from the Shell.

9: The First Moves

"I just wanted to talk to Tom about—" She paused stupidly. "About some things my manager told me."

John flew up to Sarah through the sea of motionless defenses. He had thought he had been getting used to the beauty of people in Nüährnär, everyone looking as they pleased, but this woman struck him momentarily dumb. She was pretty, yes, but something in the way she was holding herself dazzled him somehow.

"Erm, if you tell me," he managed to say, "I'll tell Tom for you."

Sarah remembered Nōvagähd's warnings. Talking to Tom about Sěrěhahn and the Ämäthōär was one thing, but she had never spoken to this John before. And she did want to talk to Tom again; he seemed like a good guy.

And talking to him face to face would be nice.

"Thank you," Sarah smiled at John, "But I'll just try him when he's less busy."

John laughed in what sounded embarrassingly to Sarah to be a very nervous way, and he shrugged with an overly nonchalant grin. "I'm not sure when that will be. Tom's always working."

He looked around at her defenses. "You've been very busy, too," he said.

"I got some matter early," Sarah said noncommittally. "So I've just been playing with ideas. Could you please tell Tom I want to talk to him?"

"I will," John nodded. "You could just tell me," he pressed.

"Thank you, but I don't think I should tell anyone except Tom for now." That was rude, she thought. "It, uh, it has to do with Ämäthōär," she added, hoping that would explain her reticence.

John's eyes momentarily widened. "Tom would know about that," he agreed. "But he hasn't wanted to talk about it."

"Do you know what happened with him and the Ämäthōär?" Sarah asked.

"I know he saw them," John said, sounding eager for a continuance of conversation.

"Yeah," Sarah nodded. She had hoped John had known more. "They were apparently trying to kill Mär."

"They were?" John asked, sounding sincerely surprised.

"Well, yeah," Sarah said. "Weren't you told?" She realized John would not have heard Mär's address firsthand, but she had told all of her assistants about it.

"Tom told me something like that, now that you say it," John said. He was looking away, his brow furrowed. "So...people like that, as terrible as Tom thinks they were...they want to kill Mär."

Sarah was staring at him, trying to see what was so significant about this.

145

"Mär's an Ōmäthäär," she said slowly. "Of course the Ämäthōär want to kill him!"

"What are Ōmäthäär?" John asked, looking back at her quickly.

So much for not going too far, Sarah chided herself. "They are really great people," she said, hoping she was safe. "They can fight Ämäthōär; no one else can, but they can. Mär is one of them."

An astute thought came into her mind.

"What, didn't you trust him?" she inquired.

John looked startledly at her. "Yes," he said quickly. "I did. I do. But it would be nice to know for sure."

"I'm sure Mär's a good person," Sarah said. "A really good person. That's why the Ämäthōär want him dead. I think Tom trusts Mär, too," she added.

"He does," John agreed. "He told me he does. But some of my friends aren't so sure."

"What do you think?" Sarah probed.

"I like Mär," John admitted. He smiled, as if saying it made it truer. "But I don't want to jump to conclusions."

"What conclusions are there to jump to?" Sarah asked, a little challengingly.

"I don't know for certain that Mär isn't lying," John said defensively.

"Okay," Sarah said, catching herself and backing down. "Bother Tom, then, until he tells you more about what he saw," she said more friendlily. "That will help you trust Mär more."

John was intimidated, and thus even more attracted. "I do trust Mär," he said, "But I want to be able to be certain."

"And, please," Sarah added affably, "Tell Tom that I want to talk to him about both the Ämäthōär and the Ōmäthäär. Whenever he has time, I mean."

"Sure," John said, "I—" But he stopped. Then after a couple seconds, he smiled less nervously. "That's Tom right now." He was silent for a few more seconds, in which Sarah imagined he was responding to Tom. Then he said, "He needs my help at the sun."

Sarah wanted to tell John to just tell Tom right then. But she was afraid that that would be rude, and a little too aggressive.

Aggressive? she thought. *This isn't anything like that...*

"It's been nice talking to you, Sarah," John smiled. "I hope we see each other again."

"Thanks for talking to me," Sarah smiled gratefully back.

John turned to leave, and she reminded him again, "Tell Tom!"

"I will," John said, looking back at her. He stood there, as if waiting for her

9: The First Moves

to keep talking. But then he turned and darted off toward the sun.

Sarah stared at the sun, thinking of Tom Pratt.

She shook her head. *What's the big deal?* There was no sense in her being disappointed that Tom had delegated her to John. Sure, it would have been nice to tell him what Nōvagähd told her, but how did she know he would even be interested?

Odds are, I'll never see him again, she told herself. Really, in the overall scheme of things, it didn't matter at all if she never talked to him.

"Nōvagähd," she called. "I've got some new ideas."

Mär looked at Ŭmäthŭ with grim humor. "This is one of those times that I hate saying, 'I told you so.'"

"We should have seen this coming," Ōhōmhär sighed beside Ŭmäthŭ.

A few more than three dozen Ōmäthäär were gathered back within their brilliant white headquarters. They were all sitting in a flat, round room, watching an image of Sĕrĕhahn's wife Lhĕhrha addressing Nrathĕrmĕ.

"In memory of everything that he has done for us," Lhĕhrha was saying in level fury, "In memory of our peace, of our freedom, in memory of the glory and the sweetness of our society all of us one with another, and in memory of his love for us all, I announce that our Anhar, my husband!, has been taken from us!"

"Each time we've watched this," Ŭmäthŭ noted, pointing thoughtfully at Lhĕhrha's still speaking image, "I've noticed more clearly that she never once says that Sĕrĕhahn is *dead.*"

Mär made a sound of comprehension, and Ŭmäthŭ skipped the record forward several minutes.

"Here," Ŭmäthŭ said, "She says that the assassins took her husband from her."

He jumped the address forward farther.

"And here..." he prompted. He watched Lhĕhrha's powerful demeanor as she spoke on.

She was weeping unabashedly. "My husband is gone. Our leader is gone." She paused, then said, "We have tried to bring him back. But we must accept that our hero is gone."

She smiled handsomely through her tears. "He must be happy where he is."

"Here, she refers to him as being 'gone,'" Ōhärnäth, an Ōmäthäär, finished for Ŭmäthŭ.

"...Anhar lived great and taught us all how to live great..." Lhĕhrha was saying passionately. Her demeanor was remarkably affecting.

"In the context, it certainly makes it sound like Sĕrĕhahn's been killed," Mär said appreciatively.

"But it may well mean something completely different," Ŭmäthŭ added.

They watched Lhĕhrha for a few minutes more.

"…We can still cherish his memory, and live by everything he taught us! I do not believe we deserved such a leader and friend. But we can try to deserve him by going forward, by remembering what he showed us, by living more closely to the way he lived!"

"Some of the others did say unequivocally that Anhar's dead," Ŭmäthŭ commented.

Some of the others nodded.

"Ämäthōär, probably," Anŭsths observed.

Mär nodded. "Maybe. Many of them may not be, though."

"…Anhar was innocent of any crime," Lhĕhrha was saying. "His passing was only accomplished by the conspiracy of the contracted hearts of small people. Innocent in life, he has been innocent to the end. His voice was always for peace…"

"She's making me love Sĕrĕhahn," Ŭmäthŭ joked.

Mär smiled only slightly. "I've very rarely known Lhĕhrha to intentionally deceive anyone," he said thoughtfully. "Though I have known her to tell only half the story, and people whom she doesn't deem able to understand the full truth get only half of the idea of what she means."

"I wonder who that reminds me of," Ōhōmhär grinned at him.

Mär smiled back at her, then looked back contemplatively at Lhĕhrha. "If I know Lhĕhrha, then everything she's saying here will fit the true story, whatever that may be.

"Sĕrĕhahn cannot be dead," he added, almost as an afterthought.

"Can we be sure of that?" Ärdhär asked, as Lhĕhrha continued revering Anhar.

Mär turned and looked at Ärdhär. His expression was as soft as usual, but deeply serious.

"No one we know of could have harmed Sĕrĕhahn," Ŭmäthŭ said.

"Lhĕhrha is clearly avoiding saying that he is literally dead," Mär added.

"That is some very close avoidance," Ährnär said admiringly. "I wouldn't likely have noticed that she hadn't actually said it if you hadn't pointed it out."

"I would really know it if Sĕrĕhahn were dead," Mär smiled at Ärdhär.

Ŭmäthŭ had cleared Lhĕhrha's address, and a different speaker had taken her place in the middle of the room.

9: The First Moves

"...which implicates them as spies from R'dōněmär," the man was saying.

"Here's another one," Avhä said darkly.

"The other seven were killed in the act of the murder," the man said. "They may yet have accomplices at large at Nrathěrmě.

"They have been positively linked to R'dōněmär."

"I don't know any of them," Mär said of the supposed murderers.

"They're not from Nüährnär," Ŭdbän said obviously.

"...whom his followers call 'Mär,'" the man continued, "The self-appointed head of R'dōněmär, has been charged with hundreds of murders over the past four hundred fifty weeks."

Ŭmäthŭ cycled to another speaker.

"...that we have met this foreign world! An independent, living civilization!" the woman said. "The very R'dōněmär that murdered our Anhar has laid claim to it. It has declared ownership of their world and is dominating its people."

No one spoke for the next several minutes, as Ŭmäthŭ skipped through other speakers. Many spoke about Earth, others about Anhar, others about the assassins and R'dōněmär. The tone of them all, however, revealed Nüährnär, which the N'nrathěrmě continued to refer to as R'dōněmär, as an upstart, insurgent group that had long opposed and had now murdered their leader, and which yet opposed Nrathěrmě's managers. And now it was oppressing the precious, newly discovered world that the N'nrathěrmě obligingly called "Těra."

Finally Ōhōmhär broke the silence: "Well," she said, still gazing at the current addresser, "Here we go."

No one said anything for a few more seconds. Then Ärdhär said to Mär's back, "Mär, we are all with you."

Mär smiled without turning. He didn't take his eyes off the speaker as he breathed, "Sěrěhahn's plan is in motion." He watched for a moment more, then said, "I have no idea how far into motion his plan is...

"Sěrěhahn found a way. Now all of Nrathěrmě wants to destroy us."

There wasn't much for Lewis Pratt to do, but watching the dismantling of Jupiter was engaging enough. He gazed from the blazing gas planet to the mammoth rivers of matter stretching out away from it.

"This is remarkable," he called to his manager. He turned back to watch the cloud flying from the moon Ganymede's now churning face.

"Jupiter was beautiful as it was," his manager Zämŭth's voice said, "But it's got a whole other kind of beauty now that its gasses are coming away."

149

Lewis looked back at Jupiter. It was considerably smaller than it had been, but its characteristic colors had given way to new bands of gases. Zämŭth was far away beside the great world, directing harvested matter in the direction of Earth, but Lewis could see him without trouble even from that distance.

He swooped nearer to Ganymede, watching the planet diminish slowly but steadily, a cloudy stream of matter whipping away from it toward Earth. Jupiter could have been harvested already, he understood, along with all of its moons, but moving the matter that quickly would have taken tremendous amounts of energy. And he was happy with this way of moving it; he got to enjoy watching this amazing work in action.

"I already miss the Great Red Spot," he half-joked to Zämŭth.

"Of course, you can visit a representation of the Spot whenever you want to," Zämŭth said.

Lewis smiled with pleasure, enthralled by all of it. There he was, flying through open space, feeling the icy tingle of space without any pain. He was actually at Jupiter! He could remember seeing the planet through a telescope when he was younger, but even now with much of its gases stripped away, the view was incomparably more wonderful than the blur he had gawked at then.

They were actually taking apart a planet! But he could still visit a perfect representation of it in his own mind, whenever he wanted to.

"This is remarkable!" he said again, with even more feeling.

He heard Zämŭth chuckle a little, and noticed him flying toward him.

"Yeah, it is pretty amazing," Zämŭth said reflectively as he glided up to him.

"It takes a lot of the wonder out of it, though, knowing that we're going to have to use all these worlds for defenses against people who want to kill us," Zämŭth added.

The mention of defenses shook Lewis out of his enjoyment a bit. "I was wondering about Nrathĕrmĕ," he said, trying to sound brave.

But then Zämŭth's wife Zad's voice called in both of their heads. "Hi Lewis," she said as she swept toward them from Jupiter. "Okay, I'm taking a break," she said to Zämŭth.

Something that had been bothering Lewis ever since Liz's mention of Bäd'r'när stabbed at him yet again. "Seems like everyone's married here," he commented with failed jauntiness.

"I'm glad for that," Zämŭth smiled, "For my part."

But then he looked harder at Lewis. He glided right up to him and struck him hard on the arm. "Don't worry," he told him. "You won't last long; just give it time, you won't be single for long!"

9: The First Moves

Lewis's attempt at a smile failed even more readably.

"Or, do you want to marry again?" Zämŭth asked perceptively.

The words tumbled from Lewis after being held in for so many hours now: "It could be possible to bring back Mary, couldn't it? My wife."

"Well, it could be," Zämŭth said slowly.

"When did she die?" Zad asked.

"Three years and five months ago last week," Lewis said quickly. "Earth years."

Zad frowned sadly.

"I don't think we will be able to bring her back," Zämŭth said.

"Why not?" Lewis asked with transparent casualness.

"People rarely come back if they've been dead for long," Zämŭth said.

"Why?" Lewis demanded. "If they're restored just the way they were, why wouldn't they?"

Zämŭth hesitated, as if caught between answering and forbearing.

"There's a lot more to them than just flesh and nerves," Zad said.

Lewis looked disbelievingly at her. "Would it hurt just to try it?" he asked.

"It might," Zämŭth said reservedly.

"What?"

Zämŭth still seemed to be debating with himself. Then he smiled uncomfortably. "Hey, we won't make any rash moves yet, okay?" He looked at Zad. "We'll talk to our managers about it."

"I might be able to do it myself," Lewis insisted. "I remember her perfectly; I'd just have to find—"

"You've lived without Mary for three and a half years," Zämŭth said. "You can wait a few more hours."

Lewis smiled back, his smile even more worried than Zämŭth's. The combined weight of forty-one months was falling on him all at once now that he felt so close to having his wife back.

Zad smiled understandingly, then swept forward and hugged Lewis.

Lewis hugged his manager back, feeling grateful but also very awkward. He wished, more than he could remember wishing in three years, that he could have been holding Mary there in his arms, that he could see her again, that he could see her smile at him and hear her laugh again. That he could enjoy her company, at last, again. He forced his augmented eyes not to moisten.

"Thanks," he said as Zad released him with an encouraging pat. "Couldn't I just try—"

But Zämŭth put up his hand, he and Zad waiting as if listening. A moment later, Zämŭth said, "That was our manager Äthäanhō. Mär's called a conference for all Nŭährnär."

"All of us?" Lewis asked.

"We can stay here and listen," Zad said.

"I'm interested to hear him," Lewis said.

"I wonder what's happening," Zämŭth said. "It must be important, for us to stop everything like this."

"We'll find out," Lewis said, feeling a little excited at hearing Nŭährnär's leader.

Mär was standing in the center of a much wider sphere within the Shell. He looked out over the millions waiting for him.

He wished he could have called them together for a happier reason.

"Ready," he heard Ōhōmhär's voice.

He waited. The N'nŭährnär were very pleasant to look at. He hoped hopelessly that that wasn't about to change.

Then Ŭkan's voice said, "Ready."

"My friends," he called to all Nŭährnär. He paused, enjoying the sound of that word, and hoping his friends did too.

"I told you that Sĕrĕhahn would find a way to get Nrathĕrmĕ to fight us. Well, he's found a way.

"The reports you may have heard that Nrathĕrmĕ's Anhar has been killed are false."

He smiled understandingly. "I imagine many of you may have thought it wonderfully great news to hear that Sĕrĕhahn has been killed. He has not been killed," he assured them. "This is some of the worst news we could have received from Nrathĕrmĕ.

"I don't know why Sĕrĕhahn has staged this. But, for one thing, it has succeeded in stirring all Nrathĕrmĕ up against us.

"Like you know, Sĕrĕhahn was adored by his people. His supposed assassins were 'proven' to be members of our Nŭährnär. So, capable, resourceful, ambitious sextillions of N'nrathĕrmĕ will employ much of Nrathĕrmĕ's power to eradicate us, and to liberate you Earthmen from us. The Ämäthōär would take you from there, I'm sure."

He let that sink in.

"We have some time. Even the fastest fleets of which we know will take many weeks to reach us here.

"Sĕrĕhahn will not be careless. The onslaught that he has spurred Nrathĕrmĕ to send at us will be made to be unsurvivable.

"So we must do more to survive it."

9: The First Moves

He paused again. He knew what he had to say; he owed it to them. But cowardice was the last thing any of them needed in the fight to save themselves and Ōhōnŭäär.

"You are free to leave!" he said seriously. "I, for one, will not force anyone to stay here with me. I am going to stay. I am going to protect the Earthmen's world.

"But know that we will not be able to militarily match a miniscule fraction of what Nrathĕrmĕ will send at us."

He looked around at the N'nŭährnär grouped there. No one had fled immediately, he thought with guarded hope.

"But I do need your help!" he cried passionately. "I cannot defend this world from Sĕrĕhahn alone. Everyone who will stay will need as much help as anyone—*anyone*—can give!

"We can survive this. We have advantages that even Nrathĕrmĕ does not have.

"But we need to work, quickly and brilliantly. Resources are not enough. Should Nrathĕrmĕ come with armies thousands of times our strength but without intelligent plans, our weaker resources will turn the tide against them. But Nrathĕrmĕ's leaders are greatly intelligent. They'll be original.

"And they are determined.

"The N'nratherme believe that Nŭährnär is tyrannizing you Earthmen and subverting Nrathĕrmĕ's leadership; they will not come after us half-heartedly.

"This does not mean that we will not win against their onslaught. It means that we *cannot* be half-hearted.

"I hate fighting N'nrathĕrmĕ. But the Earthmen's world, its history and legacy, are worth warfare against them; what Nrathĕrmĕ gets, Sĕrĕhahn's Ämäthōär will get.

"We are doing everything we know how to do to persuade the N'nrathĕrmĕ that we are not tyrannizing you Earthmen and that we do not want to fight Nrathĕrmĕ. But that's difficult to do, since we must actively oppose Sĕrĕhahn, whom they love as their, now past, leader.

"It is more than good, it is more than worthwhile, to defend ourselves, even when it means war against the great people of Nrathĕrmĕ, to oppose Sĕrĕhahn and to preserve Earth from him.

"We *need* to win! We need to protect this world, our loved ones, and the truth about Sĕrĕhahn, and about the Ämäthōär!"

He let that word sink as deeply as it might.

"No matter the tremendous disproportion between our resources and Nrathĕrmĕ's, we will, we must, survive. *We must win!*

"And we can. But to do it, we will need all the ingenuity and imagination that all of us can bring out of ourselves. We need to plan traps and snares that even experienced, cunning attackers will not be able to foil. We need to build strong defenses. We need to plan. We need to work together. We need to work flowingly and seamlessly all of us together, so we can work to confound even the most resourceful, potent, and prepared attackers."

He paused. Then he threw out his arms as he added, "And, we need to relax!

"Work hard. But among our greatest advantages will be our relationship one with another! Genius comes best when we enjoy the energy of our friends. Don't just burn yourselves out thinking yourselves in circles.

"Work hard, and enjoy each other. Plan hard, and take it easy."

His smile receded partially. "Those sent to harvest nearby stars will not be called back yet. That means," he said heavily, "That any smaller attacks that come upon us before the full bulk of Sĕrĕhahn's killing blow hits us will have to be resisted with only the resources we have from the worlds here.

"It is very likely that smaller nations who favored Anhar or who sympathize with the supposed plight of the Earthmen will attack us. Such could reach us long before Sĕrĕhahn's stroke from Nrathĕrmĕ.

"So prepare. The first pieces have been moved forward. Now we need to prepare our plan to preempt Sĕrĕhahn's designs. *We must not fail here!* We will not, as long as we do everything we can."

There was nothing more he could say. But there was so much to say! But not just then.

He looked around one last time at his silent friends. Then he hurled himself forward. A subdued cheer followed him through the sphere as he called, "Äthääōhä, Ährnär, meet me outside the Sanctuary."

Chapter 10

Hearts of Heroes

Hours of watching hadn't made the wonder of Jupiter being whittled away any less for Lewis.

Zämŭth and Zad had gone back to the Shell to enjoy themselves. But Lewis was perfectly content to watch Jupiter and its moons dwindle slowly. He could see the different layers of the planets, gaseous and solid, each getting gradually exposed.

The core of Io was glowing in front of him. A thick cloud of fine matter was shooting away from it off to Earth, the clouds of particles in it incomparably smaller than the tiniest bits of matter of which he had been taught in his life beforehand.

He smiled to himself, then careened down at the planet. He passed dozens of others who were directing the harvested matter, but they weren't disturbed at all as he shot through their streams. A cloud of tiny particles was radiating off the planet as other N'nŭährnär leisurely dissolved its matter into more uniform, fundamental elements.

The energy in and around him repelled the lethally speeding swarms of particles as he slid through the blazing cloud, and he laughed out loud as he dove right into the moon's glowing, exposed core.

The moon's solid matter glowed brilliantly in his eyes as he burrowed through it as effortlessly as if he were still out in open space. He flew slowly enough that it took him a handful of seconds to reach the planet's center. He loved feeling the increasing light and heat, then watching the intensity of the energy about him diminish again as he burrowed on past the center.

He knifed to the left, aiming to come out right in the path of the rushing stream of particles heading to Earth. Bursting out of the raw surface, he found the energy and heat in the shining stream to be even more than at Io's center, the speeding particles crashing with explosive power into natural matter soaring benignly through.

"Lewis!" someone called to him.

He soared out of the fiery river. He could tell it wasn't Zämŭth or Zad calling, and felt a jab of guilt that he hadn't yet contacted any of his assistants. Apparently they had decided to come to him.

But it wasn't an assistant whom he could see flying toward him from Earth.

It was Mär himself.

Lewis seized up a little with nervousness. He had been so interested to hear Nŭährnär's leader just hours ago, but why was Mär calling to him?

But Mär did not seem imposing. "Lewis," Mär called again, waving this time. The leader of Nŭährnär rapidly drew level with him.

"I want to talk to you," he said easily, as if he and Lewis had always been friends.

Lewis had expected any introduction but one like this, but he found himself feeling surprisingly comfortable already.

"Uh, yes, sir," Lewis said submissively.

Mär smiled, and Lewis suddenly thought Mär knew exactly how he was feeling.

"I've been told that you, for some reason, miss Mary," Mär grinned.

Even Lewis's augmented mind took a second to register that Mär had said what he had. Had he not been so surprised about the head of Nŭährnär knowing about his personal life, he might have told him to nose out.

Mär's smile became smaller yet deeper as Lewis floundered for words.

Then he heard himself ask, "Is it possible to bring Mary back?"

Mär looked at him for a second. "It may be," he said. "That's what I want to talk to you about."

Lewis looked closely at Mär, making sure that this really was Mär the leader of Nŭährnär. This man was not talking like the leader of a nation. He definitely carried himself in an easy but decisively kingly mien, but where were his bodyguards? Why did he care about Mary? Kingly or not, Mär did not behave himself in a very official way.

Mär was looking intently yet unimposingly at Lewis. "I imagine you love Mary," he said with a playful grin. "A lot."

Lewis stared at this complete stranger whom he had just heard commanding a nation. How could he talk to Mär about Mary? About more than three years of pain?

But his renewedly intense feelings got the better of his reluctance.

"I love her more than you can know."

Mär seemed extremely satisfied. He patted Lewis's shoulder, pulling him forward a little as his hand connected. He motioned for Lewis to follow him past Io.

The moon passed by under them, and the gargantuan orb of Jupiter rolled into view. Its colors were still more beautiful now than they had been those few hours ago. The enormous funnel streaming away from it, its matter glowing more and more blazingly the closer it was to the giant world, gave

10: Hearts of Heroes

Jupiter an even more majestic look.

"Mary's been dead for three and a half years?" Mär asked Lewis, who had tentatively slid up beside him.

"How do you know all this?" Lewis asked.

"Zămŭth and Zad," Mär said lightly. "They told their managers, who told their managers, and, luckily, I found out about it at the end."

Mär smiled, as if reading Lewis's mind. "No, my assistants don't tell me everything. People tend to pass on only the most important things to their managers, to keep the managers sane.

"I'm very glad that all the managers between you and me were smart enough to see your feelings about Mary as one of the more important matters.

"Look at this planet!" Mär exulted as Lewis thought about what Mär had just implied. "Look at the size, the beauty of it! It's so perfect.

"No human I know, and I have known some incredibly able people, has ever created anything that matches the thorough beauty of nature. Look at the colors, how they flow through each other! The beauty isn't in the randomness of it, it's in the incredible complexity of it! There is order there, deeper than even we can see! Down to the smallest limit of our vision, the colors flow through one another in order so complicated and fine that we can perceive its magnificence, even though we cannot understand all the ins and outs and depths of its patterns!"

Lewis was staring at Mär; he was only slightly aware of the planet.

"Look at those stars," Mär said, waving his arm grandly. "On and on and on they go. Where do they end? Galaxies and chains and worlds without end! The order of them all, the panorama of different shades of light cushioned in the blackness all around them! They're so beautiful! The fantastic design of nature is, well, so fantastic!

"But love like yours," he said, turning abruptly to Lewis, who blinked self-consciously, "Is greater than all of those."

Mär was talking about him and Mary, he realized. But how could he say that?

But, Lewis admitted in his heart, he did like what Mär had just said. Even if he didn't know if he could take it literally.

"I mean that," Mär said affectingly. "Your love for Mary is of more worth, it's of more magnitude and greatness, than this wondrous planet and all the stars and every other glory of nature. Love, and marriage! Marriage is among the greatest of nature's wonders."

Lewis hoped this meant Mär would help him bring Mary back, but he seemed to have lost his voice.

Light and Glory

"But," Mär fixed him with a serious and unarguable look, "You should not try to bring Mary back here."

"What?" Lewis sputtered. "What do you mean?"

"It—" Mär began, then seemed to change his mind. "There are ways to insure, Lewis, that you and Mary will *always* be together." He paused momentarily.

"Mary will not come back to life in this way."

"Why?" Lewis asked, horrified.

"Well, few people who have been dead for a long period of time are ever able to be brought back," Mär said matter-of-factly.

Lewis was sure Mär wasn't explaining something.

"And you need to move forward," Mär exhorted him.

"I can't," Lewis pleaded.

"Do not move forward *past* her," Mär smiled gently at Lewis's devotion. "Move forward, see what life has to offer you, find out what wonderful people there are! But that doesn't mean you need forget Mary, nor let go of her."

Lewis was staring at Mär again, trying to decipher what he meant.

"You will see Mary again," Mär said with a savoring look.

"How?" Lewis burst out. His distress was overthrowing his fear of rudeness to Nüährnär's head. "How will I ever see her again if I don't bring her back?"

Mär looked silently into Lewis's eyes. Lewis was too enveloped in his feelings of wavering hope to realize the pain evident through Mär's steady features.

"Mary is dead—" Mär said.

"Of course she's dead!" Lewis interrupted. "But I *can* bring her back."

"But," Mär continued undisturbed, "What do you mean by 'dead?'"

Lewis had trouble answering such a ridiculous question. "She's gone!" he said. He felt like bursting into tears as Mär made him discuss this, but he told his body not to. "Her body was wrecked! She's dead."

Mär just looked at him.

"Her body stopped working, her brain failed, her heart stopped, her body's rotting in the ground!" Lewis choked, having to keep a stronger check on his tears.

Mär still just looked inscrutably at him.

"That's death! And Mary's dead! My Mary, my wife! She is dead! Do you understand? She's gone! My wife!"

He fumed, feeling his mind heave with passion.

"I have to try, at least, to bring her back."

10: Hearts of Heroes

Mär suddenly clapped Lewis in a solid hug. It was unexpectedly comforting, much more comforting than any embrace Lewis had ever felt from a man.

"See?" Mär said, drawing back slowly. "I told you that love and marriage are among the greatest of all things!

"But there's more, a whole lot more, to Mary than just her body that's died. How else do you think people can be revived? *The people themselves always exist*," he said with emphatic warmth.

"There's more to Mary than just her memories and her body, though we need a record of both of those to even attempt to bring her back."

Mär stopped and looked silently into Lewis's eyes again.

"What, are you talking about a soul or something?" Lewis asked, taken aback.

He couldn't tell if that was a grin or a grimace that crossed Mär's face, but it was gone in an instant.

"More than a soul," Mär said.

Lewis was about to ask what he meant by that, but then Mär added, "In a way, Mary is a whole lot more alive right now than you are."

What was this person talking about? Even if he was the leader of Nüährnär, Lewis wondered whether that meant Mär couldn't entertain some rather odd beliefs.

"Lewis," Mär said impressively, "You have to realize that there is more to know than what you already know! You had no idea that I existed a matter of days ago! But I did no less. I was me, even though you were totally unaware of that reality. How many other things might there be that you just do not know about?"

Mär's demeanor softened; it was as if Lewis could breathe more easily. "I can't expect you to understand everything I'm saying just yet. But, I promise you Lewis, Mary is not dead at all.

"Yes, her body's stopped working," he said to Lewis's flabbergasted look, "But," he paused for the smallest moment, "That body never was Mary. *Mary is not dead.*"

Lewis didn't know what he could say. He looked desperately at Mär. "I wish that were true," he pleaded. "But I need her here with me!"

Mär didn't seem to be trying to restrain his tears; some formed around his eyes as Lewis said that.

"She's almost more a part of you than you are yourself," he commented.

"Then why can't I bring her back?"

"Because you love her!"

"What are you talking about?" Lewis demanded, emotion filling him.

Mär's tears were falling freely. "If I thought in any way that you could succeed in bringing Mary back, then I would not be here talking to you right now. She will not come back."

"How can you know that?" Lewis demanded more angrily.

"Lewis, you can believe me, even though you know it's hard, and avoid hurting yourself and your memory of Mary. Or—"

"How could trying to bring back my best friend hurt my memory of her?"

"Or," Mär pressed on, seeming desperate for Lewis to understand, "You can try to bring her back when she does not want to come back and cause yourself more pain and make it even more difficult for you to be prepared to understand that she has not left you! And need not ever leave you!"

Lewis had no idea what Mär meant by that. But he could gather that he was saying that trying and failing to bring Mary back would be painful and make it more difficult for him to move on.

"I cannot forget about her," Lewis insisted.

Mär smiled more sadly. "Don't! Don't try."

Lewis looked helplessly at him.

Mär seemed to diminish then. He looked peacefully back at Jupiter. Then he looked at Lewis.

"I can't force you to listen to me," he said with affecting serenity. "And I can't force you to believe me. But, please, believe me! I don't want this to be hard for you." He looked intently into Lewis's eyes. This time it was clear there was pain in his face.

"Why does this matter so much to you?" Lewis asked.

"Does it matter to you?" Mär asked quietly.

"It matters to me," Lewis said fervently and defensively, "And it should only matter to me. You have no place here."

Lewis was mildly surprised to see Mär, the governor of everyone there, nod a little.

"You are right," Mär agreed. "This is your province. But it *is* my province to tell you what I think will make you happier."

"Mary," Lewis said heatedly. "Mary will make me happier."

Mär looked wordlessly at Lewis for a moment more. Then he said, "Don't you think there could be anyone who could also make you just as happy as Mary did?"

"Mary's my wife!" Lewis answered.

"And I can tell quite obviously," Mär grinned, "You both made each other very happy."

10: Hearts of Heroes

"No one else could be that for me," Lewis said defiantly.

"What, was Mary born your wife?" Mär's voice rose in an unabrasive roar. "Or did you marry her, and she marry you, because, *before* you were husband and wife, you loved each other? Because you already helped each other, made each other happier, made each other better?"

Lewis was startled by Mär's sudden force; his reference to his and Mary's premarital courting made his words penetrate more deeply.

"Lewis," Mär said, "What if you had turned away from Mary when you had first met her, just because she was not already your wife?"

"What?"

"Yeah, it's ridiculous!" Mär said. "If you had refused to consider marrying Mary for only the reason that you hadn't already married her!

"How much would you have lost if you had never married her in the first place?"

Lewis stared at Mär.

"Yes, almost everything!" Mär said for him. "But you didn't. Of course you didn't. You found Mary, fell in love with her, and you married each other. And your children, your life together, your love for one another, which still continues, all of that came because you were open to fall in love with her."

"You're saying I can find another Mary," Lewis said.

"Never," Mär declared. "I am sure of that. You should never expect to find any Mary except for Mary herself.

"But, then, you didn't marry Mary because you were looking for someone named Mary Pfeiffer. You married her because you made each other more wonderful than you could possibly be without each other!

"I am not saying that you should look for another Mary. But if you don't think that there are thousands of different people who have their own capacity to make you just as happy, just as much more than you are without them, then I think you are keeping yourself from seeing the greatness of all the wonderful people around you."

"You don't understand," Lewis sighed. "You don't have a wife."

Mär looked at the glowing gas giant. Then he said, somewhat guardedly, "No one, no dear friend, can fill the place of a wife." He looked back at Lewis, but it was as if he were looking through him.

"No one.

"Do not deprive yourself of the power of having a wife again. Not Mary, not a replacement for Mary. There are so many people out there who, as themselves and not as replacements for Mary Pratt, are the kind of people with whom you can be and enjoy and love far more than you are and do now."

Lewis started to reply, but Mär overrode him. "Not a 'second wife,' not a runner-up nor a replacement, but a *wife*!"

Lewis saw despite himself that what Mär was saying was more right than he wanted it to be.

But he ignored that. Mär may have been right, there may have been other people whom he could love just as he loved Mary. But he wanted to see *Mary* again!

Mär was looking earnestly at him.

He knew Mär was right. He could be happy if he was open to look for the love he hadn't found yet. But then he ignored that too; it was far too painful.

He had to try. Who was Mär to tell him not to?

"What right," he asked softly, "Do you have to tell me what to do about my wife?"

Judging by Mär's expression, Lewis could have just punched him. "I don't have any right to force—"

"If it's so easy to move on," Lewis said, "Then why haven't you?"

Mär looked at Lewis in silence. Lewis was slightly pleased to see almost as much pain in Mär's expression as he was feeling himself.

"How long has it been, Mär," there was a distinct challenge in Lewis's voice now, "That you've been single?"

Mär just looked at him. No more tears, just a look of deepening devastation with every word Lewis spoke.

"Why haven't you married again, then?" Lewis was about to go on, his indignation mounting, but sudden apprehension stopped him.

Mär had backed decisively away. His eyes were as sad as Lewis had yet seen them, but his entire countenance was nevertheless severe and forbidding. It was like an invisible power had sprung from his every feature and, wordlessly, without argument, had struck Lewis with startling shame.

"Lewis, you know what I have told you," Mär said in formidable softness. "I will not force you, not to do anything. You know what is right. It's in your hands. It always has been."

The unspecifiable power radiated thrillingly from him.

"Please! Remember what I've said!"

"I have to go." The power throbbed all about as Mär smiled with distinct worry at Lewis. "I hope I will see you plenty of times later."

He turned and was away.

Ŭmäthŭ passed through the glorious white garden and into the next room. Mär smiled at him as he entered, tears slowly trickling down his face. He

10: Hearts of Heroes

glided to meet Ŭmäthŭ, extending his right hand.

Ŭmäthŭ took Mär's hand lovingly, then pulled him into a tight hug. He then pushed back enough to look queryingly at Mär.

Mär responded by pulling him in and embracing him more passionately, bursting into fresh tears. They floated intertwined that way for nearly a minute.

Mär released Ŭmäthŭ, his tears having slowed, but now tears were leaking from Ŭmäthŭ's concerned eyes.

"Is there something I can do?" he asked.

Mär laughed softly through his tears. "Isn't there always?"

"You just talked with Lewis Pratt, didn't you?"

"Yes," Mär said. "I hope he does what he knows is best."

"I hope so too," Ŭmäthŭ breathed.

"As for what you can do," Mär smiled, "Just do better what we're already doing for these people!"

"Ah," Ŭmäthŭ said. "What did Lewis say?"

Mär smiled. "We were talking about Mary Pratt; you can guess."

"What did you say to Lewis?" Ŭmäthŭ asked.

"Nothing."

Ŭmäthŭ looked with admiring sorrow at him.

Mär glided around, enjoying the beauty of the bedecked room. "It wasn't important," he said.

"You will find someone," Ŭmäthŭ assured him.

"If I live that long," Mär said casually.

Ŭmäthŭ frowned, but nodded. "Är never loses, though."

Mär smiled broadly at him. "That's all that keeps me going sometimes. Most of the time."

"All the time," Ŭmäthŭ smiled.

Mär nodded, chuckling softly.

"Look," Ŭmäthŭ said, gliding up to Mär again. "If Sĕrĕhahn does destroy Nŭährnär, it's not the end."

Mär sniffed tearfully. Then he whispered, "I hope Sĕrĕhahn never will destroy all our Ōmäthäär.

"But if he does, we'll be okay." He smiled, tears rolling more quickly down his face.

"Ä'ähänärdanär will be okay."

"Exactly," Ŭmäthŭ said.

Mär closed his eyes. He floated peacefully there, tears dripping quietly into his beard. Ŭmäthŭ closed his eyes too, enjoying the spirit of the room and of his manager beside him.

Several minutes passed.

"Have you checked up on Lewis's son Tom?" Mär asked Ŭmäthŭ out of the warm silence.

"Yeah," Ŭmäthŭ said, his eyes still closed. "Harhahär assigned Härtärnär and Nan to him.

"And Nōvagähd mentioned him, too." He opened his eyes to look significantly at Mär.

"Sarah Trotter is with Nōvagähd, isn't she?" Mär looked back at him, a grin tugging at his wet face.

"They've met," Ŭmäthŭ said. "Tom and Sarah."

"I wonder," Mär said, his smile deepening.

"Yes," Ŭmäthŭ smiled back. "Är is up to something."

"Well, one can hope," Mär said. He laughed quietly.

"But who knows?" Ŭmäthŭ said. "I don't."

"What if…" Mär began.

Ŭmäthŭ sighed. "I hope so."

"Tom Pratt saved my life," Mär said.

Ŭmäthŭ's eyes darkened. "Hōnhŭ."

Mär closed his eyes, but in pain rather than relaxation.

"I had no idea," Ŭmäthŭ said in self-reproach.

"None of us did," Mär said sorrowfully. "They were our friends! Hōnhŭ and Ämharŭ.

"They were beautiful!"

He opened his eyes again, and rage shined through the sadness. "And they had been Ämäthōär the whole time."

"I don't think there are any others," Ŭmäthŭ said judiciously. "Not here at Pp'ōhōnŭäär, at any rate."

"No," Mär agreed, shaking his head emotionally. "I imagine they all would have helped fight if there had been more."

"A lot of us were there fighting for you," Ŭmäthŭ said pleasedly. "But we can't be sure."

"Never," Mär sighed.

He smiled sadly, as if remembering something.

"But I believe there are no more Ämäthōär with us at the moment," Ŭmäthŭ said.

"Not Sĕrĕhahn's Ämäthōär, at least," Mär amended, his face falling grimmer. "And I doubt we'll see any more of his until his full blow hits us."

Ŭmäthŭ looked away.

10: Hearts of Heroes

"We've got Är," Mär reminded him. "Sĕrĕhahn forfeited that."

Ŭmäthŭ looked back at him. "And we've got each other," he smiled courageously. "I am so thankful for that."

"Tom, though," Mär said, closing his eyes again. "He survived Hōnhŭ's first blows, for one thing, and Hōnhŭ must have seen something in him that was significant enough for him to let off killing me."

Ŭmäthŭ nodded knowingly. "Nōvagähd said Sarah's been asking some notable questions about Ä'ähänärdanär."

"Like what?" Mär asked.

"Nōvagähd told me it was very easy to talk to Sarah about Ōmäthäär, Ärthähr, Sĕrĕhahn, Ämäthōär. Even Är." Ŭmäthŭ said.

Mär smiled, his expression relaxing more.

"She seems to believe everything he told her," Ŭmäthŭ continued. "Even about Är. He said her beliefs about Är were impressive."

"That is encouraging," Mär said. "Let's hope there are enough others like that."

"You remember what the Ä'ähärnhär said," Ŭmäthŭ noted.

"Yes!" Mär said emphatically. "This is an incredible world."

Ŭmäthŭ sighed appreciatively at that.

"A world like this could give us the kind of people I've had trouble spotting among the N'nŭährnär," Mär said.

Ŭmäthŭ frowned. "You know I've always admired how you've carried on without her."

A tear leaked from Mär's closed lids. "I tried to help Lewis understand that. Carrying on. I've never really had to be without Lhĕhûnrĕ. I still don't.

"But," he said, opening his eyes and looking at Ŭmäthŭ, "You know that I would be able to do so much more if I could marry again!"

"What exactly did Lewis say?" Ŭmäthŭ asked, concerned.

"Well, from what he knew, what he said was understandable," Mär said fairly. "He accused me of not following my own advice.

"He pointed out that I haven't remarried yet."

"And you said nothing," Ŭmäthŭ said.

"Well, I said a great deal! To myself. But no, not to Lewis."

There was silence again.

"I know what you're thinking," Mär smiled.

"Perhaps he had something," Ŭmäthŭ suggested.

Mär looked sadly at him.

"Perhaps you can take your advice more than you have."

Mär's look asked him to explain.

"I know you're not looking for a Lhĕhûnrĕ," Ŭmäthŭ said, moving closer. "But could you be looking for someone too much like her? Do you think there are Ōmäthäär perfectly suited to you, even if their personalities aren't like Lhĕhûnrĕ's?"

"Who do you have in mind?" Mär grinned.

"You know I don't have anything," Ŭmäthŭ said wearily.

Mär looked thoughtfully away.

"Two of my dearer friends just tried to kill me," he said after a pause. "Lhĕhûnrĕ was killed because of me. Our children were killed. Because of me."

"Because of Sĕrĕhahn," Ŭmäthŭ corrected him firmly.

"Sĕrĕhahn had them killed so he could get to *me*!" Mär said shakily. "You, and all of us, are continually in danger from Ämäthōär because of what we are."

"We've chosen to live this way. Opposing evil means we're opposed by evil."

He laughed bitterly. "How easy would it have been for me to marry if I could have simply lived peacefully at Nrathĕrmĕ? Knowing nothing about Är. Or Ämäthōär."

Ŭmäthŭ bowed his head.

"I could be very happy married to just about anyone," he said quietly. He smiled. "No matter how different, or similar, her personality might be to Lhĕhûnrĕ's."

Ŭmäthŭ smiled knowingly a small smile back.

"But I do know about Är," Mär said. "And that is worth it. But it does make marrying a lot harder."

Ŭmäthŭ expelled a heavy breath. "Yeah."

Mär smiled at him. "I need someone like Ōhōmhär. An Ōmäthäär. One who's as mad as I am."

"There are a lot of amazing single Ōmäthäär women," Ŭmäthŭ teased.

Mär laughed more freely. "'Amazing' does not begin to say it!

"But I need to be careful. When I mentioned that about the Ä'ähärnhär's people, Hōnhŭ and Ämharŭ tried to kill me, and just me, before any other Ōmäthäär.

"I could be consummately happy with any valiant Ōmäthäär girl, but..."

He looked at Ŭmäthŭ with desperate meaning.

"I cannot ask any good woman to live this kind of life!

"Simply being an Ōmäthäär is difficult enough; what would life be like as my wife?

"No; I need someone willing to endure leading our Ōmäthäär against

10: Hearts of Heroes

Sĕrĕhahn."

He grinned seriously. "You know I seem strange sometimes."

Ŭmäthŭ smiled sadly. "Working for Är does make a person seem a little strange to everyone else."

"Even to other Ōmäthäär," Mär said.

"Ōhōmhär's pretty strange," Ŭmäthŭ argued jokingly.

"I need someone who won't see me as strange," Mär said fervently. "Someone strange enough to fight beside me."

"We don't think you're strange," Ŭmäthŭ said lightly. "Just a little off, occasionally."

Mär's smile was subdued. "I envy Lewis. A lot. He needn't consider that to marry a woman could be to doom her to death by Ämäthōär.

"But don't worry; nobody's looking for a wife for me more desperately than I am.

"Except Är. I hope."

"I wonder," Ŭmäthŭ said thoughtfully, looking away.

"A Nōhōnŭäär?" Mär said for him.

Ŭmäthŭ looked contemplatively back at him. "Maybe."

"Maybe," Mär agreed openly. But his eyes were growing moist.

"Look at us. Here we are, telling the Nōhōnŭäär themselves that we're here to save them.

"I think they'll be the ones who save all of us."

Then Mär dissolved all at once into overpowering sobs.

Ŭmäthŭ, unperturbed, leapt forward and took Mär's right hand in his left. Mär smiled at him through continuing heaves of weeping. Ŭmäthŭ looked into his eyes intently and encouragingly.

Mär squeezed Ŭmäthŭ's hand.

"I am...so afraid for us," his voice shook.

Ŭmäthŭ nodded.

"We'll do fine," Mär said, still gasping through unrestrained sobs. "As long...as the Ōmäthäär follow Är.

"But...we must tell these people as much as we can...as soon as we can!

"I don't want Nŭährnär to be destroyed. These wonderful people."

He let go of Ŭmäthŭ's hand with another loving squeeze.

"We are doing everything we can," Ŭmäthŭ said quietly.

"We will not survive here..." Mär whispered powerfully, "Unless we rely on Är."

"This isn't because you're afraid we can't match the Ämäthōär," Ŭmäthŭ checked.

"Nah," Mär smiled through his unabating tears. "I've gotten used to that. The Ōmäthäär…must live up to our title better, though. As must Nŭährnär." He shuddered with tears.

"I'm not worried," he said unfittingly.

"I'm not ever really worried.

"But the thought of the N'nŭährnär, or our Ōmäthäär!, keeping themselves short…of what they can be…out of their own petty…petty foolishness…" he managed a wet laugh, "Is enough to make me a little sad!"

Ŭmäthŭ hugged him warmly. "As long as we listen to someone as mad as you," he said, "Not even Sĕrĕhahn can defeat us."

Mär still was shaking with tears. "As long as we never forget Är."

Ŭmäthŭ slapped Mär confidently on his back, and forced his left hand back into Mär's right.

Mär pulled Ŭmäthŭ in like a vice. "Thank you," he whimpered fervently.

"Sarah Trotter," Ŭmäthŭ said as he extricated himself, his eye gleaming.

"What about her?" Mär asked, his tears beginning to slow.

"A Nōhōnŭäär, who is just glowing with potential already. She's stood out to us after only a matter of days. And you don't think Är may be pointing you to an equal counterpart at last?"

Mär burst into choked laughter. "Now, *that* is encouragement against Sĕrĕhahn! Just to know that there are people like her.

"No," he said flatly to Ŭmäthŭ's growing grin. "Somehow I think that Sarah is too strange for me. Too much for me. I won't be able to live the kind of life that a husband of hers will have to live."

"You haven't met her," Ŭmäthŭ said in surprise.

Mär looked surprised at his confusion. "I may not have seen well enough to see through Hōnhŭ and Ämharŭ," he said with pretended defensiveness, "But I can see already that Sarah's more than a match for me. At least, she has it in her to be.

"I hope she will be."

Chapter 11

Sarah's Will

"Xuezhong, pull to the rear!" Sarah commanded. "Violet, forward! Charge!"

A raging tide of vessels not unlike Sarah's defenses was racing toward them. Sarah had covered herself in a large spherical platform; billions of other vessels whizzed around her.

Far away on the left of the field, a swarm of flat vessels surged toward her forces.

She pulled her own vessel swiftly backward, willing millions of others to follow her. She noted how much matter she had already used in maneuvering. She couldn't use too much, or she would find her armor dangerously weakened.

Violet's arm of platforms shot toward the right side of the enemy vessels that were pursuing Sarah's withdrawal. Sarah saw rantha blaze from Violet's swarm at the column of charging attackers, many of whom banked to the right to engage Violet's fleet.

"Ōhärthär, Äszad!" she shouted. "Bring yours around on top of them!"

"Sarah, watch down below!" Ŭdmäähär called.

A larger wave of attackers was charging up from below the swarm that Violet had distracted. That charge had been meant as a diversion, Sarah realized.

"Violet, up!" She threw her own fleet downward.

Her swarms dodged under the column of attackers that had turned to engage Violet.

"N'fävan, flank the right of that bottom fleet!"

Her ships unleashed a storm of rantha at the fleet driving up from underneath. She immediately directed her flat vessels to swivel to the side, presenting only their narrow edges to the rushing attackers. Many of them didn't turn in time and were caught by the attackers' rantha; almost every struck platform dissolved in a burst of light.

Violet's fleet had splintered into half a dozen swarms, and were making what looked to be an effort to confuse and envelop the divertive fleet; it was racing around after her, twisting and running into itself.

N'fävan's fleet swooped down from the right, crashing through the fleet charging at Sarah. Then his group broke into no less than twenty smaller groups as it wove through the faltering attackers. His assistants seemed to be working fluidly one with another, banking around one another to confuse and scatter their opponents.

Sarah threw an arm of her fleet at the attackers, piercing right into their charging mass.

N'fävan was scattering them from the right.

Sarah's arm of ships started breaking the enemies apart from each other, but she was losing much of her fleet in the process.

Then, before she got the words out to tell him to do it, Bal thrust a few divisions of his forces forward from the left, scattering the splintering fleet even more.

"Perfect timing!" Sarah called to him.

She directed more platforms after those that had broken apart the swarm of attackers, and simultaneously drew the matter from pulverized ships of both sides into her own vessels.

She sent most of her fleet up to help Violet as she deftly directed more of the broken matter to form new vessels.

Bal and N'fävan's forces were routing the lower attackers. Sarah was bearing down on the swirling battle around Violet's fleet above.

"I just died," Violet's voice called disappointedly.

"R'nväg," Sarah ordered, "Take Violet's assistants!"

"Don't worry," she called to Violet. "Just watch now."

She felt much less shaken this time than she had the first time one of her assistants had been destroyed in a battle, but the suddenness of the mock-deaths of these simulations was still foreboding.

"N'fävan, Bal, remember what I told you," she called, trying not to think about Violet.

Nearly half of N'fävan and Bal's fleets arced upward through the scattering attackers; the rest of their ships stayed behind to complete the rout of that portion of the attackers. Both their fleets had swelled considerably as a result of the matter they had cannibalized from destroyed platforms.

"R'nväg, keep them busy! Bait them, but don't scare them off!"

"Xuezhong, accelerate now, around below them all!"

"I know what to do," Xuezhong's voice said.

Sarah accelerated forward and upward, as if to relieve R'nväg's fleet, which was letting the attackers hammer desperately at it.

She felt a thrill of pride as her assistants worked in perfect coordination:

Xuezhong's fleet shot past below the attackers, then abruptly banked back and up, cutting off their rear.

11: Sarah's Will

Just as he did, Bal and N'fävan slammed their charging fleets into the attackers, blocking them on the left and underneath.

Öhärthär's fleet swooped after Xuezhong but then veered away right at the last moment, blocking the attackers' escape from that direction as well.

As Sarah's divisions swooped down upon their foes from the top, the only escape open to the surrounded ships was straight back out from where Sarah's fleet had come. And R'tähahavaf and Äszad's fleets were there waiting just near enough there to eradicate any who came at them.

R'nväg's stalwart fleets shot out that way. The attackers surged after them, panicking in their encirclement and desperate for any opening.

As they had practiced, Sarah's assistants did not surround their enemy too tightly. A matter of seconds in that position demolished almost a quarter of the surrounded attackers.

R'tähahavaf and Äszad's poised hordes scattered in coordinated nets to herd the panicking attackers continually back together, while still keeping them disjointed.

Sarah's assistants' fleets were using their tactical head start to direct the drifting debris that had been so many millions of attackers into new ships of their own.

The loose encirclement provided all of Sarah's forces the advantages of surrounding their enemy without tightening enough to drive them to suicidal fury.

The attackers were swooping and firing madly, buffeted about by R'tähahavaf and Äszad's ships, while Sarah's other assistants closed in, pushing and tearing at them inertially.

By the time the attackers seemed to see that they had no chance of victory or escape, any chance of either had long since passed, as had the opportunity of the surge of valor that might have occurred as that point of no return approached.

"Peace!" the voice of the attackers' commander sounded then in Sarah's head. "Hold! We surr—"

His words were cut short as the fleets and even the stars disappeared.

Sarah and her assistants were standing in the middle of more than twenty-six thousand people: her assistants' three following tiers of assistants. Many of them were sitting or reclining in the wind-swept tall grass of the plain stretching out to the horizon, while others hung idly in the air.

Sarah took a happy breath, and launched herself up from the damp ground to stop a hundred feet up, where all her many assistants could easily see her.

"That was great!" she said. Her nervousness about leading so many had been diminishing day by day, she having chosen to work too hard to remember to be intimidated.

"Bal, thanks again for coming to intercept that column; that was perfect!

"We did a lot better encircling this time. So much better! There were hardly any attackers who got away this time!

"That's the way, well, a way, to do it: keep their morale stilted on false hope until there's no real hope left to support it. Then they'll just surrender like this, without ever getting driven to the stonewalling we've been running into before every victory!"

She sighed pleasedly. "But this is all the exercising we'll do for now. You probably could use some time to relax. Just take it easy, like Mär said. Nōvagähd told me that sometimes the best thing we can do for progress is to postpone working."

The rustling laugh that replied around her bolstered her confidence still more.

"For the future, think more about communication and independence.

"Violet, when you let your assistants take independent control of individual groups, that worked great to confuse the attackers!

"And N'fävan, that was incredible, that twenty-headed spiraling attack you guys did!

"Let's do more of that. We'll be harder to predict, harder to trap, and harder to avoid. If we all keep in touch with each other while working independently, all managers directing your assistants while assistants execute managers' ideas, and your own ideas, in your own ways, then, and only then, we'll have the fluidity to contend against N'nrathĕrmĕ.

"This next time, we'll fight a smarter army. We did great this time, but our enemy was about our same size. I'm going to put us up against a much bigger force next time.

"But we're doing so well! Already, we can defeat an army like that one in less than six minutes!

"So thank you all, for all your work and dedication.

"Your managers will tell you when we'll be practicing again. That's all for now!"

She waved her arms as if to scare them off.

"Go away now!"

The thousands of assistants began rising off into the sky or disappearing through the ground.

"Thank you guys, again," she said privately to her immediate assistants.

11: Sarah's Will

She flew back down through the grassy plain, and an instant later had emerged outside the Shell.

The Shell's armor had thickened in the past few days. Most of the matter that arrived, however, had been being put into the great field of defenses stretching farther and farther out around the planet. Earth was now but a spot in the middle of a zoo of all different kinds of vessels, all sitting immobile but ready to dance in and out of one another like ingeniously directed wasps should Nŭährnär be attacked.

But this was only the beginning of the matter that had begun to arrive from the surrounding worlds. Millions of N'nŭährnär were out directing construction, just as she had been days before.

We did do very well, she congratulated herself, flying out through the ships. Nōvagähd was right: their connections with one another were their most powerful asset.

She found herself hoping that the N'nrathĕrmĕ weren't as congenial and cooperative with one another as she thought. But from what she knew of life in Nrathĕrmĕ, she imagined its armies were going to be far more fluidly one than she and her assistants could ever become.

And they have Ämäthöär, she thought, and shivered suddenly. She wondered how Ämäthöär would affect a battle. The thought sent a chill through her as she tried to guess what they might do.

She checked quickly over her shoulder; she felt like someone sinister was standing right there.

There was no one there, just Earth and the Shell. She tried to ignore the dark, heavy feeling, but then jumped. She looked back more closely at Earth.

The armor around the world looked just as it should have.

She didn't know what it was. She had thought she had seen something, or felt something, about Earth that had chilled her again.

Stop being stupid.

She gazed back at the pretty light of the clouds of matter being slowed and stopped by the others, and the steady shining of the multicolored stars.

She should tell Tom Pratt what Nōvagähd told her, she thought.

Sarah was a little surprised at herself. She hadn't thought about Tom since she had talked to John; work had driven Ämäthöär pleasantly out of her mind.

It isn't worth the trouble, she told herself. *Tom's probably busy working. Anyway, he'll find out about the Ämäthöär soon enough.* After all, Nōvagähd had said the Ōmäthäär wanted to tell everyone about Är and the Ärthähr and everything as quickly as they could.

But he was nice to talk to. Sarah didn't notice as the cold fear brought on by worrying about Ämäthöär disappeared.

And he had said he would tell her about the Ämäthöär he had seen, "later." This was later.

She wondered where he was. *If he's close, I'll go try.*

"Bye," Spalding waved to his manager Raōthä.

He thought about going to see his brother Mark. But then, he thought, he hadn't seen his uncle Lewis in what felt like a long time.

He searched around, and found Lewis back on Earth's surface.

He pitched upward into the sky, heading for the Shell's inner wall.

Lewis was back in Austin, Spalding realized as the blue sky started to fade into rolling green hills. He was back in his old house. Spalding smiled that his uncle still preferred his own house in place of all the amazing things and people around.

He came out of the Shell, Earth glowing blue and protected in front of him. Austin was on the other side.

"Woohoo!" he whooped as he accelerated straight at the surface. Clouds flashed past him right before he plunged into the ocean. The water rushed by; he put his arms out and laughed in its growing pressure, then shot into the ocean floor.

The pressure was building, and the light and the heat. He put on another little burst of impatient speed.

Then he stopped himself all at once, emerging exactly beside Lewis through the floor of his undamaged house.

The cheerful "Hi," died on his lips.

He had expected to find Lewis relaxing in his homey house, content and happy to see him.

He had not expected to find him sprawled on the floor, crying over a dead body.

His uncle looked up with a shout. There was an almost insane look in his eyes as he stared wordlessly at Spalding.

Spalding didn't know what to do. He had been so pleased with how he had stopped right on target after rushing so fast through Earth's core, but now he just looked on in horror. Who was the woman lying dead in his uncle's house?

"Lewis?" Spalding said.

Lewis's tears disappeared as if they had evaporated. He looked away.

"Lewis," Spalding said, thinking he recognized who that woman was, "Is that—"

11: Sarah's Will

Lewis may have nodded, but it was unclear, as he threw his face into his hands and fell into wailing tears again.

Spalding was trying not to panic. Tom! he thought. He'd call Tom; Tom would know what to do. This was his father. And his mother.

He searched wildly for Tom.

There he was, away among asteroids past Mars.

"Tom!" he called. "Come here! Hurry! It's Lewis! And—" He hesitated. "And Aunt Mary."

"What?" he heard Tom's excited answer. "Aunt Mary?"

"I think Lewis tried to revive her," Spalding said, staring at his wordless, sobbing uncle.

"Really?" Tom said, sounding elated.

"No, Tom," Spalding said woefully. "She's dead!"

"Oh no," he heard Tom say. There was a momentary pause, then Tom called, "I'm already on my way."

"Hurry!" Spalding urged. Lewis was shaking, cradling Mary's head in his arms, and not seeming to care about anything else.

Spalding knelt down beside him and touched one of his hands.

Lewis shouted something utterly incoherent. He bowed his face out of sight.

"Lewis!" Spalding shouted.

Lewis violently batted at him. Spalding shifted back and out of range. He felt helpless. He hoped Tom got there soon.

There he is, Sarah saw. Tom Pratt was careening straight toward her from out in the asteroid belt.

"Tom," she called pleasantly.

He didn't answer.

She could tell he was moving extremely fast. Several hundred times the speed of light, it looked like.

"Tom," she called again. "It's Sarah Trotter. Could I talk to you?"

He still didn't answer.

Was he ignoring her? she wondered. *Maybe he just doesn't want to talk about Ämäthöär.*

She saw him whiz past not too far away and disappear into the Shell. She thought she could tell he had stopped on Earth's surface somewhere.

She was feeling frustrated and a little hurt; she realized she really had wanted to talk to him; when another voice called into her head.

"Hello, my name's Yulia Yavlinskiy. My manager Tom Pratt told me to tell you he's sorry, but he'll have to talk to you later."

Sarah grunted disgustedly.

"Can I help you with anything?" Yulia asked.

"No. Thank you, Yulia," Sarah said. "I'll just talk to Tom later."

"Sorry," Yulia said, and her connection stopped.

Again! Sarah thought.

She hesitated for a moment, then shot toward the Shell.

I'll just go straight to him and ask him if I can talk to him as soon as he finishes whatever he's doing.

She shot into the Shell and through and out of it again in a matter of seconds, then veered toward Tom, whom she could spot on the surface.

Slowing down, she saw the ruins of a large city approaching. Tom was in a house away on the outskirts.

She felt more apprehensive; was this Tom's old house? If he was with his family, she'd feel really rude about interrupting.

Maybe this was why he wouldn't talk to her at the moment. She hesitated again, stopping a few hundred feet over the cracked suburban street in front of Tom's house.

But he was so friendly before, she thought. Even when he seemed uncomfortable talking about the Ämäthöär. He hadn't seemed to have minded talking to her then.

She'd just go try. She'd be quick, and just tell him she would like to talk to him as soon as he got a chance. That wouldn't be too rude.

And she would really like to talk to him.

She had glided down to stop on the perfect lawn in front of the small house, which stuck out amidst all the damaged houses and graying lawns around.

She would just be quick.

She had stepped up to the front door. The cramped building seemed so foreign to her, after the past few eternally long days. She raised her hand awkwardly to knock, then noticed the doorbell. She pushed it, feeling supremely foolish.

The shrill, discordant chime of what a few days ago would have sounded to her like a modestly melodic doorbell sounded through the paper-thin walls. A little playfully, she looked at the doorbell and changed the ring to something much more tuneful. Then, horrified at her own presumptiveness, she quickly undid the change.

No one was moving inside, she could see, though she felt uneasy looking through the Pratt family's walls. Tom and two other people were in there—

11: Sarah's Will

And then she felt her emotions freeze. There was Tom's father, Lewis Pratt, and another called Spalding Pratt. But on the floor, just below Lewis Pratt, whom Tom was even then wrenching to his feet, was a dead woman that Sarah didn't recognize.

Someone had been killed! No wonder Tom wouldn't talk right then!

Before her nervousness could make her think about what she was doing, she launched herself straight through the wall of the house, cutting across a corner of the garage and through two more walls, to emerge into the room with the Pratts and the dead body.

"What's happened?" she asked, staring at the dead woman on the floor.

Lewis spun around, apparently taken totally by surprise. Only then did Sarah realize she had done a terrible thing intruding like that.

Tom and Spalding both looked at her in surprise too, though Tom's expression lightened her embarrassment a little; his surprise was mixed with a little sheepish apology, and also what looked like relief.

"What are you doing here?" Lewis Pratt demanded.

Sarah stumbled for words. Tom nodded shortly, and she understood to wait. "I'm sorry," she began nonetheless, mortified to be standing there. "What happened?"

Spalding glided forward, standing between Sarah and Lewis. "What do you need?" he asked privately.

Sarah was staring at the body on the ground. "Who died? What happened?"

"No one's died," Spalding said quickly.

"But," Sarah began.

"Oh," Spalding said dumbly. "That's my aunt, but she died a long time ago."

"Your aunt?" Sarah said. "His wife?"

"Yeah," Spalding said. "Um, you shouldn't be here right now."

Sarah nodded, feeling more and more embarrassed. She didn't register the absurdity of his saying that his aunt had died a long time ago, watching as Lewis collapsed into tears in Tom's arms. She glided past Spalding to stand in front of Lewis.

Tom seemed to be saying something privately to him. Sarah, aware that this man was mourning his wife, gently patted him on his back. "What can I do?" she asked familiarly.

"Who are you?" Lewis asked weakly as Spalding came up uncertainly beside Sarah.

Tom smiled reassuringly at her. "Sarah Trotter's a friend of mine."

Lewis didn't seem to hear him. "Would you be so kind as to go out?" he said acidly.

"I'm sorry," Sarah said, backing away, but something kept her from leaving.

Tom had grabbed his father by the shoulders, saying something inaudible to him.

"What would you have done?" Lewis moaned aloud at Tom.

"I would have listened to Mär!" Tom said.

"To what?" Lewis shouted. "That man didn't tell me anything helpful! He only told me not to bring back my wife!"

He looked down miserably at Mary's body. "Why didn't he tell me this would happen?"

Sarah finally thought she understood what had happened: This man had tried to revive his wife the way Nōvagähd had revived his son. But it didn't work. She felt a surge of pity for him.

Lewis had fallen to his knees by his wife's body.

Tom knelt down beside him. His own heart felt like it was going to explode as he whispered, "Mom is gone."

"I know that!" Lewis said tearfully.

"Let me..." he said, stretching his hand out to dissipate Mary's body back to dust.

"No!" Lewis cried. "Don't!"

"Dad," Tom said, quietly but more firmly, "She is gone!"

"I know that!" Lewis shouted. He bowed his head. "I know you can't understand, Tom, what it feels like to lose your spouse. This is very hard."

Tom didn't answer, but his heartache at seeing his dead mother right in front of him was close to Lewis's anguish over his wife.

He put an arm around his father.

"I don't deserve Mary back," Lewis whimpered.

"That's not true," Tom said quietly. "You know it."

Sarah swooped down then. She took Lewis's hand, smiling comfortingly at him.

Lewis looked at her, then looked away again, closing his eyes. Tears continued to leak out and stream down his tortured face.

"She was always better than I was," he said.

Sarah felt tears rapidly forming around her own eyes.

Tom squeezed his father tightly.

"She was always there for you kids," Lewis said. "And I—" He broke off, quivering with tears.

11: Sarah's Will

"You," Tom said softly but with definite force, "Were here for us so much that Andrew and Terry hated it!"

Sarah looked up at Tom. He smiled at his father, a tear trickling down one of his cheeks.

"I need her back," Lewis said.

"We all need her," Tom answered.

"She never should have died," Lewis choked bitterly.

Tom didn't say anything. He looked at his mother's unmoving body. She looked as young as everyone else in Nŭährnär. He realized sadly that this must have been about how she had looked when she and his father had first met.

"She never held it against me," Lewis said, smiling sadly at Mary's face below him. His mouth trembled. "I watched her die."

Tom knew what Lewis was getting at. "It wasn't your fault."

"She just smiled at me," Lewis went on, "And told me how much she loved me."

He was silent for a moment.

"I'm sorry about this," Sarah heard Spalding's voice.

"No," she said privately back to him. She rubbed Lewis's hand consolingly.

"I was a drunk!" Lewis burst out, as if saying it to Mary in front of him. "And she never held it against me. Even after...even in her last hours."

"When I found out about that car, that man who hit her..." he said, tears cascading down his face as he pulled his hand out of Sarah's and took one of Mary's in both of his. "My own wife...she died because of a drunk! I should have died! Never her. Never my sweet Mary."

"Dad," Tom said. "This isn't helping you."

"It should have been me!" Lewis said.

"It should have been neither of you!" Tom said, feeling more unnerved. "It should have been nobody!"

"He died when he hit Mary's car," Lewis said miserably. "*I* was the drunk who should have died!"

"I love you!" Tom said fervently. "Don't talk stupid!"

"I still drink it!" Lewis moaned. "I did, until, well..."

Tom knew he was referring to Liz's transformation.

"*I know!*" Tom said. "I know! I don't care!"

"You know?" Lewis said, looking back up at Tom blankly.

"It was kind of obvious," Tom said. "And I don't care. I love you. And Mom loved you."

"She still does," Sarah's small voice said on Lewis's other side.

Tom looked a little surprised at her. Lewis smiled in a distraught way at her.

"Dad," Tom said. "Let me take her body away. I loved Mom, but this is not helping you."

Lewis closed his eyes as he squeezed the lifeless hand in his own. He pulled himself out from under Tom's arm. He bent forward and kissed his wife. "I love you," he whispered.

Then the body disappeared.

Sarah held in the deluge of tears she felt like releasing. She glanced at Tom, but he was looking singly at his father.

"Mär was right," Lewis sighed.

"But how can I carry on without her? I feel like I've lost her all over again." He absently patted the floor where Mary's body had just been.

Tom scooted forward and hugged his father again in a tight hug. Then a storm of tears he hadn't expected burst from him.

"It's alright," Lewis whispered to him now.

Sarah felt embarrassed again. She stood up slowly. She looked at Spalding. It was as if a spell had lifted; she was feeling more and more out of place every second.

But Spalding was looking gratefully and somehow approvingly at her.

"I should go," she said, not looking at any of them.

"What? Why?" Spalding said.

Sarah looked back at Tom and Lewis. Tears were still shining down Tom's face, but he was helping Lewis up.

Sarah looked back at Spalding, feeling so awkward she wished she could just evaporate. "I just wanted to talk to Tom about something," she said privately. "I shouldn't have intruded." Even Ärthähr and Ämäthöär didn't seem as important as her getting away.

But Spalding seemed pleased to hear that. "Oh, okay!" he said, starting to turn to Tom.

"No, never mind," Sarah said. She just wanted to fly out of there, but she didn't want to be any ruder than she had already been. "I'll just talk to him later."

"Tom," Spalding said out loud. "Sarah wants to talk to you. That's why she came here in the first place."

Tom looked over at Spalding and Sarah, still looking fairly shaken. Lewis beside him looked considerably better; he was even smiling, apparently at something Tom had been telling him.

11: Sarah's Will

"Yeah," Tom said, grinning apologetically. "I know."

"I'm so sorry," Sarah said. "I can wait till some other time."

"No," Tom shook his head, "I'm sorry I didn't talk to you last time."

Sarah still felt embarrassed, but at least Tom seemed to want to talk to her.

"Sorry for barging in," she said to Lewis.

"You're a friend of Tom's?" Lewis asked, looking very embarrassed himself.

"I told her I would tell her about," Tom began, but then paused, as if it hurt him. "You know, those Ämäthöär."

"Really?" Spalding said, sounding excited. "Like what?"

"Just, uh, what I saw," Tom said uncertainly.

Lewis shuddered a little. "Hearing that once was enough for me."

"What did you want to ask him?" Spalding pressed cheerfully.

"Uh, only…whatever you're comfortable talking about," Sarah said to Tom.

"Yeah," Tom said. "I can—"

"Yes, he can tell you plenty about that," Spalding cut in. He was gliding around Sarah and Tom over to Lewis. "Why don't we go back up to the Shell?" he said stiffly. "So we don't have to hear it."

Lewis looked a little startled. But then he seemed to catch on. He pulled himself away from Spalding, though, who was tugging a little at his arm, and hugged Tom again.

"Thank you, son," he whispered.

Sarah was also startled at Spalding's eagerness to leave. And she didn't know what to do when Lewis let go of Tom and took her hand in both of his.

"Thank you," he said, shaking her hand. Then he looked away ashamedly.

Spalding looked without subtlety at Lewis, then shot up through the roof. Lewis waved at Sarah, then followed his nephew.

"I am so sorry," Sarah said again. "I didn't mean to barge in and interrupt like that."

Tom seemed to recover himself from Spalding and Lewis's sudden departure. He shook his head kindly. "No, I'm glad you came." He looked embarrassed enough himself, Sarah realized. "Thanks for helping my dad," he said.

"Did I help?" Sarah asked. "I—"

"Yeah," Tom nodded forcefully. "You did. Thanks." He looked nervously at the ground. "This was really hard for him."

"That was your mother?" Sarah asked, then immediately wished that she hadn't.

But Tom just nodded dejectedly.

Sarah didn't know what to say. "I'm sorry," she said again.

Tom smiled sadly. "Thanks. We will be okay; he really is a great father."

Sarah looked down at the floor. Then, realizing she was looking where Tom's mother had just been, she looked abruptly up again, looking around the room.

"This is where I used to live," Tom said. "It seems like forever ago."

"It does," Sarah agreed. Tom was looking around the house too as if he had never lived there. "I had some things I wanted to tell you," she said awkwardly. "About the Ämäthōär."

Tom cringed, but he said, "Really? Like what?"

Sarah remembered what Nōvagähd had told her, about the Ōmäthäär and the Ämäthōär. But she couldn't figure out where to start.

She backed up and sat down on Lewis's old bed to give herself time to think.

Tom sat on the bed too, facing her casually, leaning back a little on the headboard. She was really very pretty, he thought. But then he dismissed that; everyone in Nüährnär was good-looking.

"My manager told me a lot about the Ämäthōär," Sarah said, "And about the Ōmäthäär."

"The Ōmäthäär?" Tom said. "What about them?"

Sarah liked the casual way Tom was looking at her, but still she felt lost for words. She wasn't feeling so embarrassed about Lewis now; her nervousness was all for herself.

"Um, what do you know about them?" she asked.

"Just what everyone knows," he said, "Which isn't much. But they're the leaders of Nüährnär, aren't they?"

"Yeah," she said.

Tom sat peacefully, as if waiting for her to go on.

Ōmäthäär, she reminded herself. "Anyway, my manager told me that the Ōmäthäär have the same power the Ämäthōär have."

Tom shifted uneasily, and didn't look at her. "It didn't seem like that to me."

"What do you mean?" Sarah asked, surprised.

"Well, the Ōmäthäär, Mär and the other leaders, they weren't so dark and awful, like the Ämäthōär were. They were nice."

Sarah didn't bother to say that that wasn't what she meant. "What happened?" she asked quietly. "When you saw the Ämäthōär?"

"Yeah, I told you I would tell you," Tom smiled. He thought for a moment. "I don't know what there is to tell. They were awful, like I said before.

"I heard that Ōmäthäär telling everyone to get out of the Shell and calling the other Ōmäthäär and saying there were Ämäthōär there. I wasn't in the Shell, I don't know why I did it, but I went to go see the Ämäthōär.

"I guess I wanted to know for sure that what I had been told about the Ämäthōär was true. That Mär had been telling us the truth."

He partly expected Sarah to criticize him for listening to Peter the way Kathy had. But she just sat quietly, looking expectant.

"As soon as I got back into the Shell," he said, "I just felt afraid."

He paused, and Sarah waited silently.

"I can't explain it. I was just afraid. I felt naked, and cold." He shivered, remembering it.

Sarah remembered how she had felt when Ähänär had shown her the Ämäthōär. And she remembered how Ähänär had said it would be worse in real life.

"Anyway," Tom said, "And I have no idea why I did this, but I went to get a closer look. At the Ämäthōär.

"I'd think I would have gotten out of there as soon as I felt that fear. But it was weird. It was like I wasn't in my right mind. It was like something was pulling me toward the source of it all.

"I remember getting closer and seeing them. There were hundreds of people, hundreds of Ōmäthäär, and Mär. And two different people.

"Mär and the Ōmäthäär with him made me feel less horrible. But the other two people were horrible. It was like the fear; and it felt like everything was dark; it was like all of that fear and darkness and coldness was coming from those two people."

Sarah was watching him, feeling more dark and cold herself as she listened.

"They were fighting Mär. Those two. They were fighting Mär with their hands." He looked up at Sarah. "Why would they fight with their hands?"

Sarah didn't answer. She was feeling colder, and remembering Ähänär's Ämäthōär grappling with the Ōmäthäär.

Tom noticed the fearful look on Sarah's face. He was only then aware of the cold fear that had crept up inside of him too.

"Maybe we shouldn't talk about this," he said with a small smile.

"What were the Ōmäthäär like?" Sarah asked him.

"They were nice, like I said," Tom said. "Mär and the other Ōmäthäär made me feel more like myself.

"Being around the Ämäthöär was the worst feeling I've ever felt.

"There were so many Ōmäthäär. But they just seemed like little bits of warmth, or light or something, in the middle of all that darkness."

Sarah remembered what Nōvagähd had said about so few Ōmäthäär having the capacity to stand against the Ämäthöär. "And the Ōmäthäär killed the Ämäthöär," she said.

"I think they did," Tom said. "That's what Mär said."

"You didn't see?" Sarah asked.

"I got closer to them, and then I remember the Ämäthöär charging me. One of them. One of them charged me as I passed through the Ōmäthäär." He tried to remember what happened after that.

"All I remember is the Ämäthöär charging at me, and then the next thing I can remember, some Ōmäthäär had their hands on me, and the Ämäthöär were gone."

"Did you die?" Sarah asked, wide-eyed.

"I don't know," Tom said. "Maybe I did. I don't remember at all."

Sarah couldn't believe she was looking at someone who had died.

Tom shook his head a little, as if to shake off the dark mood. "At any rate, that's what happened."

"My manager told me some about the Ämäthöär," Sarah said. "And about the Ōmäthäär," she added quickly, wanting to talk about something less dreadful.

Tom sat back again against the headboard and looked quietly at her, clearly waiting for her to say more.

She felt lost for words again. Nōvagähd had told her so much, she thought, and now that she was actually talking to Tom she couldn't remember any of it.

"Uh, well, my manager, he's named Nōvagähd, he told me that the Ōmäthäär and the Ämäthöär both have the same abilities. Sort of."

She was afraid Tom would think she was contradicting him. "The Ōmäthäär don't cause that kind of fear, I don't think," she said quickly. "But they have powers that no one else has, and that the Ämäthöär also have."

"What kind of powers?" Tom asked, interested.

"My manager, Nōvagähd, told me about some kind of force that makes everything happen," Sarah said.

"*Makes* everything happen?" Tom said skeptically.

"I don't know," Sarah said. "That's not what I mean, I guess."

"I didn't think anyone made me do anything," Tom said conversationally. "How could they?"

11: Sarah's Will

"Yeah," Sarah agreed. "I don't understand it; I'll probably just make a mess of trying to explain it."

"Okay," Tom smiled back at her. "I'll keep an open mind."

"Thanks," Sarah said. "But you should probably talk to an Ōmäthäär instead of me."

"I will," Tom said, still smiling. "But tell me what you can remember."

"Well, like I said, Nōvagähd said there's a power, or force; you know what I mean," she said at Tom's entertained smile. "He talked about God, too."

"Really?" Tom said, sounding very surprised. "Nōvagähd, your manager, talked about God?"

"More or less," Sarah said. "But he called him 'Är.'"

Tom's eyes were widening now, and he was leaning forward some. "That's interesting," he said.

"Yeah," Sarah agreed with a little laugh.

Tom looked down at the bed. "That's really interesting." He looked like he couldn't understand how what she was saying could be true.

"Nōvagähd said that that power comes from Är," Sarah said. "He called it the Ärthähr."

"Really?" Tom said, more interested.

Despite the strange subject, Sarah could feel her nerves at talking to Tom ebbing away. "Yeah," she said. "Nōvagähd said that people who know enough about it can use it to do things that we can't do."

"Like what the Ämäthōär did," Tom said. He looked deadened as he said it.

"And what the Ōmäthäär do," Sarah said.

"Like how they were fighting the Ämäthōär," Tom said, looking back up at her.

"Must be," Sarah said. "Mär said that most people can't hurt the Ämäthōär."

"But this Ärthähr can?" Tom asked.

"Yeah, that's what Nōvagähd said," Sarah nodded. "At least I think that's what he meant.

"Did he tell you how it worked?"

"No," Sarah said.

Tom looked disappointed.

"Yeah, I know," Sarah said. "I hope Nōvagähd will tell me more."

"I'll ask my managers, too," Tom said.

"Nōvagähd said that most people who aren't Ōmäthäär don't know much about Ärthähr," Sarah said. "He didn't seem very happy about that, though," she remembered.

"My managers are Ōmäthäär," Tom said. "Härtärnär and Nan."

"Really?" Sarah said. "I wonder how many other people at our level have Ōmäthäär for their managers."

"There can't be too many who do," Tom said. "There aren't enough Ōmäthäär here. Not that I know of, at least. There are barely fifteen hundred that I know of, and there'd have to be more than two thousand for even half the people at our tier to have Ōmäthäär managers."

"Well, I'm glad I have one for a manager!" Sarah said.

"One?"

"He isn't married," Sarah explained. "But," she remembered, "He did say he had a son. I wonder what happened to his wife."

Tom thought he could guess, but he said hopefully, "Maybe she's just away for now. Nan said that hundreds of Ōmäthäär are off at other places, spying on Sěrěhahn or something."

"That would be scary," Sarah shuddered. "Being an Ōmäthäär right under Sěrěhahn's nose."

"Yeah," Tom said, feeling scared just thinking about such a situation. "But Nan wouldn't tell me for sure if that's what the other Ōmäthäär are up to." He shuddered too. "If Sěrěhahn is anything like the Ämäthōär I saw, I would not want to be sent to spy on him."

"But the N'nrathěrmě love him so much," Sarah said. "At least from what I can tell."

"I don't blame them," Tom said. "Have you thought much about what Nrathěrmě's like?"

"Yeah, I have. That's what Nōvagähd said, that Sěrěhahn seems really, really good on the outside."

"That's frightening."

"What do you mean?" Sarah asked.

"If Sěrěhahn can fool the people of Nrathěrmě," Tom said, "And if he's really as evil and awful as we've been told, then how can we really trust Mär? Or anybody? It's scary, that anyone could really be such a sinister villain but seem as benevolent as Anhar does."

Sarah nodded. "But I think Mär really is good."

"Yeah," Tom said with a bit less certainty. "I think he is too."

"Aren't you convinced now?" Sarah said with a small laugh. "That's what you told Kathy and me before."

"Yes," Tom said, a little more certainly but still not completely so. "Yeah, after what I saw. And what I felt! But how do I know for sure?"

11: Sarah's Will

Sarah shrugged. "I'm only feeling more and more sure all the time. I'm sure we can trust the Ōmäthäär."

Tom smiled at her. "I hope you're right." He sat up more and scooted back against the headboard again, as if waking himself up. "Yeah, I'm sure you're right.

"That is a scary thought, though."

Sarah could definitely see that. It was a frightening thing to think about; what if they couldn't trust Mär?

But somehow that just didn't sit right with her. She remembered what Nōvagähd had said about trusting her feelings, that that was what was important.

That felt right to her.

But there had been so much she had wanted to tell Tom about the Ōmäthäär, and the Ärthähr! And now she couldn't think of anything more to say.

She remembered what Nōvagähd had said about the Ōmäthäär being trained by Är, and about the Ämäthōär driving them from Nrathĕrmĕ. She remembered what Nōvagähd had said about Sĕrĕhahn's desire to keep anyone from knowing about Är. She remembered what he had said about Sĕrĕhahn stifling the people of Nrathĕrmĕ. She remembered so many things.

But somehow the words just would not come now, when she wanted to explain it to Tom.

"What else did Nōvagähd tell you about the Ōmäthäär and the Ämäthōär?" Tom asked.

"A lot!" Sarah said. "A whole lot."

"Like what?" Tom said eagerly, ready to sit and hear a whole lot.

"Erm..." Sarah struggled. "I don't know," she said lamely.

Tom looked surprised at that.

"I do know!" she said quickly. "I just don't know how to explain it."

The words had been coming so easily just then. Why couldn't she talk now? she thought in frustration.

But then Tom smiled again, as if he knew just how she felt. "I should still talk to Härtärnär and Nan about it."

"Yeah, maybe you should," Sarah said, smiling apologetically back at him.

"Thanks for telling me this, though," Tom said, his tone implying that she hadn't had to.

Sarah was sure she would have blushed if she hadn't had control of her body. She felt embarrassed with herself just to realize that. "I just thought that you of all people should know, since you saw the Ämäthōär."

Tom felt the darkness try to creep into him again. But it seemed somehow diluted. "I am glad I saw them with my own eyes and felt them firsthand," he said, "Even though..."

"Even though they were that terrible," Sarah finished for him.

"Yeah. It feels worth it in a way."

Sarah realized she was smiling absently at him. She quickly stopped herself; he didn't seem to have noticed.

"Does Kathy want to know about the Ämäthōär too?" Tom asked.

"I think so," Sarah said. But then an odd twinge pulled at her stomach. "But I can tell her what you told me," she added.

"Okay," Tom said. "But I'd be happy to tell her if she wants."

"No," Sarah insisted. "I don't want you to have to relive it too much." She felt a lurch of guilt, as if she were lying to Tom; she really knew she just didn't want Tom's attention directed away from her.

"Thanks," Tom said gratefully.

"I wish I could remember more of what Nōvagähd told me," Sarah said.

"Well, just tell me later sometime," Tom said. "I really am sorry I wouldn't talk to you before."

Sarah smiled. "Don't even think about that."

"I wanted to talk to you," Tom assured her, "But the first time..."

"No, really, it's okay," Sarah said, feeling deeply satisfied now about getting to talk to him. Her former frustration had been more than paid for, she thought.

"And you understand why I didn't want to talk to you just now," Tom said.

"Completely."

"Thanks a lot, too, for helping my dad."

"I'm glad you think I helped," Sarah said.

Tom laughed. "You really did, really."

Sarah smiled gratefully. "Thank you."

"I mean, I did want to talk to you," Tom corrected himself. "I felt bad that I didn't talk to you before. But it didn't seem like a good time at all."

"I understand," Sarah said, smiling more.

"But it's worked out just fine," Tom said. "It's worked out very good. So come talk to me whenever."

"I will. Thanks for talking to me this time."

"I'm glad you tried again," Tom said. "I'll talk to Härtärnär and Nan and find out how badly you messed up telling me about the Ōmäthäär and everything."

11: Sarah's Will

Sarah laughed. "I'll tell you more later."

Tom smiled at her. "I should go back and talk to Härtärnär and Nan anyway. I had to get away quickly to help my dad. They could use me back."

"Oh, alright," Sarah said. "I didn't mean to keep you from going back."

"No," Tom said, "I really enjoyed hearing about Ärthähr and Ōmäthäär. You should come tell me more whenever you get the time. If nothing else, if we're both working, we can still talk from far away."

Sarah liked the idea of talking face to face better. "Okay," she said anyway. "I don't want to keep you, though, if you're trying to get away. And I should probably go get more done too."

"I'll talk to you later." Tom smiled again and waved bye to her, then shot away through his house's ceiling.

Sarah sat there for a few minutes.

It had been great being able to talk to Tom. Finally.

She stood up, hoping Lewis was going to be alright. Then she realized she was standing alone in the Pratts' house, and was about to fly away immediately, embarrassed at her intrusiveness.

But she didn't. She sat back down, smiling to herself as she looked around the house. Looking through the walls, she could see everywhere. It was a nice house, she thought. It was cozy, but it felt nice.

She leaned back a little on the bed, smiling around. So this was where Tom grew up, she thought.

She stood again. What did it matter to her where Tom Pratt grew up?

She shot away through the ceiling as well.

He had been really good to talk to, though, she thought before she could stop herself. *Yes, really good to talk to*, she told herself more firmly.

She hoped Tom had enjoyed talking with her at least half as much as she was finding she had enjoyed talking with him.

She had passed into the Shell. She didn't want to disturb her assistants; she'd let them rest. She could go out past the major planets and harvest matter out there, she thought. That would be good and restful and mindless. She continued upward toward the outer wall.

An hour ago, Sarah would not have wanted to let her mind wander; it would almost always lead to thoughts of the impending doom of Nrathĕrmĕ's military might. Or, worse, to thoughts of the Ämäthōär.

But now her thoughts were very well occupied.

Chapter 12

The Simple Truth

A few hours later, Sarah's thoughts were still warming her, way out beyond the orbit of Neptune.

She had found, to her annoyance, that Peter Garcia was working fairly close to where she had decided to go. She had already told some others that she was coming to help harvest; she didn't want to let them down, even if Peter was close by. But she had tried to keep her distance from him, and that hadn't been proving very difficult.

She looked over at him, gathered with a large group of people in the distance. "What are they doing over there?" she asked Sōha, who was herding matter to her from a giant comet. "They've got almost a whole planet's worth of matter around them. They're not sending it anywhere."

"I don't know," Sōha said unconcernedly. "Can you take this one?"

"Oh," Sarah said, looking back at the comet far below her. "Sure."

Sōha swept away into the stars, in search of other tinier worlds.

Sarah reached out, stripping more matter from the comet's frosty crust, but she was hardly paying attention. She looked back over at Peter as she hurled the matter off toward Earth.

There were more than a hundred people with him, she could see. And they were all Earthmen. She felt a plunge of disgust as she realized what they were probably up to.

She kept peeling matter from the comet, dispersing it into tinier elementary clouds. She was tempted to just fly over there and ask what they were talking about.

I'll tell Nōvagähd, she thought instead. *Just in case.*

"Nōv—" she began, but then a frantic scream sounded in her ears.

"*Help!* I'm being attacked!"

Sarah searched quickly for the owner of the voice. She found the woman not too far away, and to her horror saw that she had been serious: About a hundred thousand platforms were racing all over, releasing rantha at harvesting N'nüährnär and taking harvested matter into themselves.

Sarah scooped the rest of the massive comet into herself all at once and hurled herself toward the strange attackers. "Nōvagähd!" she called. "Someone's attacking us out here!"

She hurled matter out of herself, expending incredible stores of energy as

12: The Simple Truth

defenses swirled immediately into form. She gratefully noticed that Sōha and scores of others were streaking to the attackers, clouds of matter coalescing around every one of them.

Hurtling toward the attackers, she ran through a series of feasible tactics in her head.

The attackers were scattering, as if to engage more people at once.

She commanded her ships to generate randomly flowing inertial fields on their surfaces, so as to scatter any rantha the attackers might send at them to try to sense them. She knew that those stealthy fields wouldn't be able to scatter rantha enough to keep the vessels from being hit, but they would keep sensing rantha from reflecting off them directly enough to give the attackers much knowledge about them.

The attackers, however, seemed to have even more powerful stealthy fields than her platforms had. All she could see of them was a hail of translucent blurs, fading in and out of her vision.

But she felt a bit of hope at the attackers' foolish decision to scatter as they had. She would be able to engage only a part of their numbers, thus helping the others to repel them without having to risk being overwhelmed by them.

She directed more matter to condense solidly around herself. She looked just like one of her defenses now; she hoped the attackers would not be able to discern which platform held her inside. She was almost in range to hope to hit some of the nearest branch of dancing, advancing attackers.

"Thanks, Sarah," Nōvagähd's rapid yet jarringly calm voice called back. "We already know. Help is on the way. Come back to Earth, and get as many to follow you as you can. But don't come so quickly that you leave yourself open to be hit. Fight the pirates, but bring the fight back toward the fleets coming to you from here."

Sarah didn't take the thought to answer. So these were pirates, then.

She was in range. She sent a large portion of her brand new fleet arcing around to spread out behind the arm of nearest attackers, and threw a weaker portion in front of them. That mock-encirclement, she hoped, would entice the pirates to break through the weaker side and come on faster toward Earth.

She wished her assistants were with her; had they been manning parts of her fleet, her tactics could have been more complex and unpredictable.

At least this way no one was at risk of dying except for her, she thought unconsciously, as the pirates she had hoped to lure eradicated the junction she had left unknowingly too weak between her front and rear wings. They had just broken her fleet into two disjointed parts without her having seen it coming.

Her feelings turned to lead as she realized that this was real. People might actually die. These could be her last moments.

Then she remembered Peter, as the pirates scattered outward with surprising speed. He had his hundred people and his vast collection of matter. The pirates had shot straight out through the wings of her fleet.

They were about to encircle her, she realized.

And then the genius of the pirates' attack became clear as she realized with horror that their scattering hadn't been a foolish decision at all. The pirates had succeeded in enticing what looked to be all the N'nŭährnär nearby to engage their seemingly disconnected arms. Now, without Sarah noticing, she and the others had been corralled into a few dozen clumps around which the pirates were suddenly swooping in rapid enclosing arcs.

"Peter, help!" she called desperately. She hoped he and his companions had not been encircled too.

She made her ships dance around one another in patterns she hoped would be difficult to predict, firing rantha at the pirates and then attempting to turn their narrow edges on them.

But the pirates were on all sides. As soon as her ships turned away from one attacking group, they almost always ended up facing another group.

Almost a quarter of her fleet had already been eradicated. The pirates had clearly not yet figured out which vessel was hers, but she wondered how long she could be so fortunate.

She directed most of her ships to condense to become more spherical, to avoid being hit on broad flat sides and to be able to fire rantha all around equally easily. The vessels on the outer edges of her surrounded fleet morphed into flat-faced hemispheres and began hammering the pirates with unceasing rantha.

"Peter!" she screamed, "*We need help!*"

There was an opening. Some of her ships had been trying without much success to tear the pirates' platforms apart with inertia, but they had managed to push a tiny chink in the encirclement. Sarah sent a huge burst of energy to push some of the pirate vessels off course.

It worked. The chink became an actual opening in the pirates' shifting patterns, and Sarah combined rantha and inertia to force her ships' way through.

The pirates were confused for just enough of an instant for Sarah to throw most of her fleet out of the gap, burning much of her energy in the leap of acceleration before the pirates could counter her.

She was soaring free, the collapsing pirate encirclement dropping quickly

12: The Simple Truth

behind her.

She wanted to run to Earth. Even if the pirates didn't follow her to Nŭährnär's armies, she knew she had to get far away if she didn't want to die.

But, now that she had freed herself, she wrenched her fleet around to go back to the other N'nŭährnär fleets being crushed within the pirates' traps.

She grabbed up some loose matter from destroyed pirate and N'nŭährnär ships and set it to forming more ships as she unleashed blasts of rantha and waves of inertia at a weaker spot in a horde of pirates around one of the larger N'nŭährnär clumps.

Then a voice called to her. "Hi, Sarah, my name's An'ntä." His voice was maddeningly carefree in the face of the life-and-death struggle Sarah was engaged in. She spiraled her fleet down and to the right, avoiding a surge of responding pirates.

"My manager, Peter Garcia, told me you needed something," An'ntä was continuing obliviously. "What c—"

"*We're getting killed!*" Sarah screamed back. "*There are pirates killing our people!*"

She spotted just barely in time another horde crashing toward her fleet, and banked sharply up to avoid getting caught between them and the pirates she had just tried to attack.

"*Tell Peter to help!*"

"I—I'll tell Peter!" An'ntä's surprised voice said.

Sarah hoped Peter got the message and came to help before too many of them were killed. She saw that she had managed to weaken the pack she had just assaulted, though. A large portion of the entrapped N'nŭährnär fleet had managed to break free. But the rest was still trapped by the pirates, and was being rapidly annihilated.

"Help! I'm still trapped!" a woman's voice called to her from the still surrounded ships.

Sarah pulled her ships up and around to blast the pirates apart from another weaker looking area.

"If you—" the woman's voice began, but it was harshly cut off, and the ships in her fleet hesitated slightly in their maneuverings.

Sarah felt a shock of dread as she realized what just happened. As if to drive the horror of it deepest, she only at that moment recognized the woman's name.

M'hōnŭ's fleet started executing new maneuvers by itself, but Sarah was sure the ships' own intelligence would not be enough to outthink these pirates.

She seized control of M'hōnŭ's remaining ships, which recognized her as a friend and submitted to her directions. Her fleet almost doubled in size but her spirits severely shaken, she raced away from the pirates, who were surging after her.

She realized just in time that the pirates would have expected her to try to escape. She pulled off upward just before an arm of the pirates' fleets spiraled down to intercept right where she would have been.

She stabbed her fleet into the spaces between the splintering branches of that arm, breaking it apart and making again to put distance between her fleets and the pirates' while the pirate fleets recovered from her unpredicted move.

It was as she was soaring terrifiedly from the battle that she saw Peter and his hundred other Earthmen. They were far away, traveling fast toward the faint glimmer that was Saturn.

"Peter!" she called. He was still close enough that he could come back and help.

But Peter didn't answer.

"*Peter!*" she shouted again, indignant fury creeping into her voice.

Still he didn't answer. He and the others kept on their course toward Saturn.

Sarah pulled her fleet around again to strike back. A few other N'nüährnär fleets, she saw in relief, were already streaking away to Earth. But the others still needed their help.

"Come back with me!" she called to them as she spurred her ships faster back to the battle. "Help me save—"

"Hi, Sarah?" another untroubled voice broke in. "I'm—"

"TELL YOUR MANAGER TO COME BACK AND NOT LEAVE US TO DIE!" Sarah snarled as soon as she recognized the man's name.

The pirate fleets were speeding toward her more quickly now than she was toward them. There were still a few N'nüährnär trying to evade the pirates in the rear, she could see, but dozens had already been killed, their fleets adding to the strength of the pirates'.

Then she realized that enormous armadas were racing up from behind her: real military strength from Earth. Even if Peter didn't help, she thought with relief but also savage bitterness, they might be able to save the others.

The pirates were arcing up. She pitched her ships down and left.

"Sarah, get away!"

Sarah pulled back and around. That was Ärdhär, she realized. An Ōmäthäär.

"Get out of here!" Ärdhär commanded. "We'll drive them away."

Sarah hesitated. They could use her.

12: The Simple Truth

"Sarah, get out of here!" Ärdhär's voice said unopposably.

The pirates had changed direction at the sight of the approaching mass of Nŭährnär's strength.

"Take my ships!" Sarah called to Ärdhär.

The N'nŭährnär fleets began to blast past her, and she realized how inconsequential her ships comparatively were. But then she felt Ärdhär take the offered control of her fleet, and her ships hurtled past her as well.

She wanted to help, but, remembering Ärdhär's command, she let her vessel melt off of her. She flew out of the way, watching and hoping and praying that the fleets would be able to save the others still embattled with the pirates.

And as her mind cleared from the clamor and fear of mortal battle, the first thing she thought of was Peter Garcia.

He was still headed for Saturn with his companions. Sarah pitched toward them, accelerating as fast as she dared.

How was Peter any different from a murderer? she thought in fury. How many people had just died because of his cowardice?

She was already catching up to them. They were not moving very quickly; they seemed to be slowing down.

Now that the danger's past, she thought angrily, *Now they're stopping.*

Then she wondered if it hadn't been cowardice at all that had made Peter flee. She remembered what he had said about Mär being the real enemy.

But how could he still believe that now?

She would find out in a moment, either way, she thought grimly. She was too angry to decide what she wanted to say.

Peter and his companions had stopped.

"Sarah," Peter's voice said genially in her head. "You want a word with me?"

Sarah tried to convince herself that, somehow, Peter might have had a good reason for doing what he had done. Tom had had good reasons for not answering her. Maybe Peter hadn't intended to let innocent people get killed.

She forced herself to be calm as she asked, "Why didn't you answer before?"

Peter glided forward to meet her, making her stop short.

"What just happened here?" His question was not one of innocent bewilderment. It was as if he was leading her to notice something obvious.

"What just happened?" Sarah asked in incredulity, though still maintaining her calm. "We've been attacked, Peter! People have died!"

"Why?" Peter asked forcefully.

Sarah knew what he was insinuating. She waited, working to contain the anger surging at his stubbornness. Then she asked, as if it were an ultimatum, "Do you believe Mär, or not?"

"Oh, Sarah, wake up!" Peter said.

Sarah noticed that her fists had balled. She released them, but just looked angrily at Peter, unable to say anything that seemed fitting.

"Think about it," Peter said more friendlily. "Those people were obviously trying to stop Mär. Mär had Anhar killed, and he's keeping us all under him. I do not believe for one minute what Mär claimed about Anhar somehow not being dead."

He waited for Sarah to oppose that. She just stared at him with her mouth half open.

"Why would Nrathĕrmĕ say Anhar is dead if he isn't?" he continued. "It really is a feeble lie; Mär could have at least said that the assassins weren't connected with Nŭährnär. That would have been less ridiculous than to say that Nrathĕrmĕ's just pretending that its venerated leader is dead."

Sarah's mouth had opened a little wider in wordless disbelief. She could not believe how certain Peter was about these things about which he knew so little.

"That, Sarah, is why these people have attacked Mär's faction. He calls it Nŭährnär, 'Haven,' but haven for whom? Do you really believe Mär is protecting us?"

Sarah wanted to gesture to what had just happened, but she figured it would be useless. And Peter showed her to be right:

"Why would Nrathĕrmĕ ever want to harm us, the 'Earthmen' as these people call us? Haven't you been following Nrathĕrmĕ's media? The people of Nrathĕrmĕ are ecstatic about us, an alien civilization! They don't want to destroy us!

"These people only attacked here because Mär has had their leader murdered and is holding us all as captives at our own world!"

"Captives?" Sarah repeated with more venom than she had intended.

"That's one thing Mär has done intelligently," Peter said. "He hasn't forced us to stay here. That makes us feel free. But look at the facts: there's a terrible disaster that destroys the world as we know it, and then these people appear and tell us that was caused by someone hired by Sĕrĕhahn. But why would Anhar hire anyone to destroy a new world?

"Don't you see, Sarah? *Mär's* people caused that disaster. He keeps telling us to be afraid of Anhar, and these Ämäthöär. But we've never seen them."

Sarah started to protest, and Peter said smoothly, "It is likely that someone

12: The Simple Truth

did try to kill Mär earlier. But this nonsense that Mär thinks he can feed us about the Ämäthöär being some kind of monsters is ridiculous, too. But, of course, Mär does not want us to talk to any of Anhar's spies, since they would tell us what he really is."

"You want to hear about Ämäthöär?" Sarah said in a quiet, deadly voice.

"What?" Peter said imperturbably.

Sarah found herself wanting just to yell at him, to tell him everything Nõvagähd had told her, everything Tom had told her. The idiot! But she did not think that that would do much good.

Instead, she said softly, "The Ämäthöär are more than just spies. Have you seen them, Peter?"

"Have you?" Peter asked.

Sarah hesitated, and a triumphant grin emerged on Peter's face. "I know someone who saw them," she said.

Peter waved his hand disparagingly. "Sarah, listen to yourself."

"No, I saw one!"

Peter paused, his grin flickering.

"The person who taught my family about Nŭährnär showed us her memory of an Ämäthöär, and it was exactly what Mär says they are, Peter!"

"A memory!" Peter exclaimed. "How do you know that was real? I could invent a memory right now and show it to you and make it feel realistic enough."

"You don't know what I saw," Sarah said.

"That's true, I don't," Peter said. "And if I did I'm sure it wouldn't somehow prove to me that Mär and these people are telling the truth.

"But, Sarah, don't you see? Mär tells us that Anhar's going to kill us and that our only hope is to rely on him to 'protect' us. We're captives here without him having to force us at all! He's holding us here by fear!

"And when Nrathĕrmĕ or anyone else comes to free us from him, and make him pay for what he's had done to Anhar, he has us all ready to believe that they're coming to destroy *us* and not him! He's going to get us to fight the people who want to save us!"

"And that's why you wouldn't help fight these pirates," Sarah said scornfully.

"Pirates," Peter said mockingly. "How do we know they weren't about to be our liberators, or justified reprisals against Mär's terrorist group?"

"Perhaps they were," Sarah said. "That is what Mär said, isn't it? That Anhar's so-called 'death' has spurred not only Nrathĕrmĕ, but smaller nations too to try to destroy us."

"But you believe Mär that it's all a great hoax," Peter said longsufferingly.

Sarah ignored that. "Though the pirates may very well have meant to 'liberate' us," she said, "They're doing it because they're playing right into Sĕrĕhahn's hands, who wants Nŭährnär and the Ōmäthäär destroyed. And I will die if I have to, to fight for the Ōmäthäär."

Peter was shaking his head, smiling, his longsuffering air thickening.

"Which sounds more plausible, Sarah?" he asked. "Which is more simple? That Anhar of Nrathĕrmĕ, Nrathĕrmĕ being so enormous compared with Mär's faction here, is hellbent on destroying Mär and his friends, but for some reason can't use his own nation to do that, and so elaborately fakes his own death, fools sextillions of people that he's dead, and wants to destroy Earth which he didn't even know existed until just now? Or, that Mär is just a common thug who is using fear and lies to get us to do what he wants, and who has finally managed to have Anhar killed, and whom Nrathĕrmĕ says has been defying Nrathĕrmĕ's higher leaders for years, and that *that's* why everyone else wants to destroy him now?"

Sarah seethed for a few seconds. Then, without thinking to say it, she heard herself say, "If only you knew more of what's happening, then what you're calling simple would be obviously ridiculous, and what you're calling ridiculous would be plain and simple."

"You say that as if you know," Peter said dismissively.

Some of the others had glided up behind him. A woman, Annie Baker, was standing at his right elbow, looking at Sarah as though Sarah were being unreasonable.

Sarah couldn't believe this. All these people believed Peter. If only they could hear Nōvagähd, or Tom Pratt!

"We are staying, Sarah," Peter said, "But we are going to resist Mär. Not so he notices yet. But we have to all gather together if we are going to save ourselves. If enough of us help, we will be able to save Earth too. We cannot let this madman dictate over Earth!"

Sarah looked at them all, at Annie, whom she guessed must have been his girlfriend the way she was leaning on him, then back at Peter.

"You ignorant, arrogant, blind—" she began. "If only you knew! If only you would let me let you know!"

Peter sighed outwardly and shrugged, exchanging significant looks with some of the others who had come up beside him.

"You're like children!" Sarah said. "You're so sure you know what's going on. You have no idea!"

Annie was still looking disapproving, but she had stopped looking at

12: The Simple Truth

Sarah.

Sarah shook her head, then looked Peter straight in the eye. "You do what you want," she said. "I hope you'll listen, but you do your thing." She looked around at all of them. "I will stay and fight for the Ōmäthäär. And Mär. I know that Mär is a great man. And if you insist on constricting your minds, if you actually fight the Ōmäthäär, then I, and some others, *will fight you.*"

Peter sighed again and looked around at the others.

Sarah looked at them too. Then, with one last disgusted look at Peter and Annie, she turned and bolted away back toward Earth before any of them could say anything more.

She had not noticed it, her feelings had been too intent against Peter, but Annie Baker was not looking quite so certain about Peter's assertions now.

Tom had been told by Nan to stay at Earth when she and Härtärnär and most of his fellow assistants of theirs had gone to drive off the pirates. But as soon as he had found out what was going on, he had heard that Sarah Trotter was one of the people mortally engaged with the pirates.

So he felt tremendous relief now that he could see her flying safely back to the Shell.

"Sarah!" he called as she approached.

She didn't respond for a moment. "I was contemplating passing you off to one of my assistants," she said at last.

"Well, you sound fine," Tom laughed, passing out of the Shell.

"No, not really, I'm not," Sarah called. "You remember Peter Garcia?"

"Yes," Tom said warily as he flew to meet her. "What about him?"

She explained to him what Peter and his companions had done, abandoning her and the others as soon as the pirates had appeared.

Tom was coming up closer to her. She slowed down.

"Then I went to go talk to him," she said, "To see if he had a good reason."

"Somehow I imagine he didn't," Tom said as he slowed to a stop in front of her.

"No, he didn't at all," Sarah said.

Tom could tell by the look on Sarah's face that Peter Garcia had only gotten worse. "What did he have to say?"

"Nothing intelligent," Sarah said sourly. "He said that Mär's a madman. He said that Mär and the Ōmäthäär are lying to us about Sĕrĕhahn's not being murdered, about Sĕrĕhahn wanting to destroy us, and about the Ämäthōär, among other things…"

"I should talk to him about Sĕrĕhahn and the Ämäthōär," Tom said darkly.

Light and Glory

"You should try," Sarah said with a hopeless laugh. "But, well, you'll have to try and we'll find out if you can manage to get him to see reason. For me it was like talking to a rock."

"Did you tell Nōvagähd about what Peter did?"

"Oh, no, I haven't yet," Sarah said.

"Don't let me bug you, then!" Tom said. "You should tell him right now!"

Sarah had actually been about to call Nōvagähd when Tom had called to her, but the amount of concern in his voice had driven that important thought from her mind.

"Nōvagähd?" she called. She felt a little sheepish, but also glad in a way that it had felt more natural just to talk with Tom about what had happened than to talk to Nōvagähd about it.

"It's good to hear you less panicked," came Nōvagähd's fond answer.

"Alright. Thanks," Sarah said awkwardly, not sure how to respond to that. She told him a somewhat more detailed version of Peter's treachery.

Tom was waiting quietly, looking unconcernedly at the stars as Sarah talked with Nōvagähd.

"Well, I can completely understand Peter's opinion," Nōvagähd said lightly when Sarah had finished.

Sarah's temper had risen again just at recounting Peter's accusations to Nōvagähd. "But it's nonsense!"

"Oh, it is," Nōvagähd agreed. "Even Peter should be able to tell that. But if he's not letting himself see reality, then his arguments really do make a whole lot of sense."

Sarah didn't know what to say to that.

"Thanks for telling me this," Nōvagähd said. "Tell me if you hear anyone else expressing those kinds of opinions, or anything more from Peter, or anyone at all. Everyone in Nüährnär must be let to think and believe whatever they want to, but I want to know what notions are becoming more common among us."

"I'll tell you everything," Sarah said.

"Thanks," Nōvagähd said brightly. "Now get back to talking to Tom. We're keeping him waiting."

Sarah blushed as Nōvagähd's voice went away. Tom noticed that before she could make her body stop it, and he laughed a little.

"What, what did he say?" he asked.

The impulse to blush returned, but she stopped it in time. "He, uh, didn't seem surprised by any of it," she said evasively.

"Really?" Tom said. "Maybe the Ōmäthäär have already heard about this

12: The Simple Truth

kind of thing."

"Yeah, I bet they have," Sarah said, not looking at Tom and looking at the stars to her left instead. "I hope there aren't many others like Peter."

"So do I," Tom said. "But I imagine there would be, wouldn't there? Let's just hope those kinds of people get to know what's really going on before they cause any kind of trouble."

Sarah snorted. "I almost got killed! And Peter left me to die!"

"Okay," Tom amended, "Any worse trouble than that."

Sarah looked back at him with half of a disbelieving smile on her face.

"I'll stop talking now," Tom said.

Sarah laughed and smiled at him. But her smile faded as she commented, "It seemed so impossible to get him to consider anything but what he already 'knew.'"

Tom didn't say anything, remembering what John had told him about Peter.

"If many others are like that, then there will be, um, 'worse trouble' real soon," Sarah said.

John! Tom thought. "Sarah, one of my assistants is a good friend of Peter Garcia's. I'll have to talk to him. Maybe he'll be able to get to Peter, get him to understand what's going on."

"What?" Sarah said. "One of your assistants?"

"Yeah," Tom laughed, seeing the half surprised, half thrilled look on Sarah's face. "John Fleming."

"Oh," Sarah said. "*That* assistant."

"What?"

"You sent John to talk to me when I was trying to talk to you a few days ago," she reminded him.

"Oh. Sorry."

Sarah smiled at him. "John didn't seem nearly as inflexible as Peter," she said.

"He isn't," Tom said. "He's been bugging me a lot about the Ämäthöär."

"Oh, that's my fault," Sarah said. "That's exactly what I told him to do: to bug you, so he could be more sure that Mär is telling the truth."

"Thanks, then," Tom said. "John's been talking to me a lot about the Ämäthöär. I've told him, at least half a dozen times, all about every moment I can remember from when I saw the Ämäthöär. He still doesn't take it seriously when I tell him that I get scared talking about it too much.

"But he believes me. And he believes Mär. He hasn't mentioned Peter in a while, though."

Light and Glory

"Hopefully that's a good thing," Sarah said.

"He said that he and Peter have been friends for years," Tom said. "I bet they're still close, but I don't think John's going for what Peter's saying about Nüährnär."

"I hope he isn't," Sarah said. "Do you think Peter will listen to him?"

"We'll find out. I'll talk to him about it," Tom said.

"Thanks, Tom," Sarah said.

"Thanks?" Tom laughed. "This affects all of us."

"I know," Sarah said. "Thanks all the same."

She really was beautiful, Tom thought. He couldn't put words on what it was, but something about Sarah made her seem to shine in a wonderfully comforting way.

It was the better part of an hour that they stood there in open space, talking about their families and their old lives, before Tom said he needed to get back to his assistants.

"I'll see you later," he waved cheerfully, turning and speeding back to Earth.

Sarah stayed riveted in the vacuum as she watched him go.

Though she had been able to fly and float for the past interminably long days, she now felt more weightless than she had ever felt before.

John swerved around another of the gigantic pockmarked pillars. The forest of colossal towers stretched on into the distance as he weaved in awe between them, breathing in the warm grey fumes that flowed out of their dark surfaces.

"Hey, John?"

He recognized Tom's voice. It was even more amiable than usual as he called, "What're you doing?"

The forest of immeasurable towers disappeared. John was resting on a misty hilltop overlooking a fog-filled valley.

"I was just exploring Nrathĕrmĕ," he said. "It's an amazing place."

"Is it?" Tom's voice said, as if he weren't paying much attention.

John saw Tom come hurtling down out of the Shell's cloudy sky. He plunged down into the valley, then pulled up spectacularly, skimming the tops of tall trees poking like spikes out of the fog as he soared up and stopped gracefully on the moistened sod in front of John.

"Yeah, it is," John said, watching Tom's dramatic arrival. "It's so enormous! I could spend forever there and never visit the same place twice. Or see the same person twice."

12: The Simple Truth

"I wish we could go there," Tom said vaguely, not looking at John.

John sat there on the ground for a while. Tom seemed to have forgotten he was there.

"So," John said.

Tom jumped a little.

John laughed. "What's on your mind, Tom?"

"Nothing," Tom lied automatically. "Well, no, plenty," he said, "But never mind. I want to talk to you about your friend Peter."

"What about him?"

"Have you heard about the pirate attack yet?" Tom asked, sitting himself down on the wet grass beside John.

"What?" John said. "Attack? When?"

"Just barely an hour ago."

"No," John said in surprise. "What happened?"

"I was just talking to Sarah Trotter." Tom smiled unconsciously. "You remember her?"

"Yeah," John said.

"She was there fighting the pirates, before stronger fleets came to fight them," Tom said. "She said that the pirates surprised them. They were really outnumbered. There were a good number of them there, but there were a whole lot more pirates."

"I hadn't heard anything," John said.

"Well, the pirates are gone now," Tom said. "One of my managers, Nan, told me the N'nüährnär fleets chased them off.

"But several people got killed."

"But they'll be revived?" John asked.

"I hope they will be," Tom said. "But the thing is, Peter was there too."

"Is he alive?"

"Yes, he's alive," Tom said. Then he told John what Sarah had told him, about Peter abandoning Sarah and the other N'nüährnär.

"But he must have had a good reason," John said.

"Um, well, Sarah went to talk to him then," Tom said, "And she told me that Peter said he wanted the pirates to be able to get in, and destroy Nüährnär."

John didn't say anything.

"Does that sound like something Peter would do?" Tom asked.

John sat quietly for a couple of seconds. "Peter might," he said, "He might go that far."

Tom wanted to say, "He did go that far," but he thought that might not have been the wisest thing to say to Peter's friend just then.

"Did he really do that?" John asked.

"Well, he had his justifications," Tom said. "How much has he told you about what he thinks about Mär?"

"I haven't talked to Peter in a long time," John said. "Whoa, it's just been a few days! We've just been busy. I've been meaning to get together with him and Annie, though."

"Annie?"

"Annie's Peter's girlfriend," John explained. "But I haven't talked to either of them about Mär since I talked to you about it."

"Sarah tried to tell Peter he was wrong about Mär," Tom said, "But she said he didn't think that was possible."

John laughed a little. "I can imagine that," he said with a faint knowing smile. He stared down into the valley.

Tom was about to ask if John thought he could get Peter to understand what was going on.

But then John said, "The thing about Peter is that he's usually right. Oh, I don't think he's right this time," he added quickly. "But he's really, really smart. He's used to being right."

Tom didn't know Peter very well, but still he found himself thinking that the arrogant way he seemed to act did not seem very smart to him at all.

"I need you to talk to him."

John laughed quietly. "I doubt I'll be able to convince him if his mind's made up."

"You'll do better than I or Sarah would," Tom said positively.

"I'll talk to him," John said. "At least I'll find out what he thinks Mär's up to."

"Peter is just one man," Tom said, "But he, or other people who share his point of view, might do worse than just run away when we're attacked."

"I hope not," John said. "Peter's a good guy."

"Good."

"I'll tell Annie what you and Sarah told me," John said. "If she believes me, then she'll have a better chance of getting Peter to believe it, too."

"Thanks, John," Tom said. "I am sorry about this. But I'm worried. I don't want us to fight each other and play right into the Ämäthöärs' hands."

"By the way," John said flatly, looking across the valley, "I wanted to ask you something about the day you saw those Ämäthöär."

Tom visibly braced himself.

"Tom, I'm just messing with you!" John laughed.

12: The Simple Truth

Tom sighed with clear relief. "Don't joke about that."

Chapter 13

A Perfect Sense

Lewis pounded down the vaulted stone hallway. Tall, thin torches flickered blue from steel brackets in the cold windowless walls.

"Lewis! Wait!" his niece Lucy Breslin shouted.

Lewis had nearly reached the great iron door. He turned, waiting for his eight relatives to catch up, then raced forward again with the others at his heels, a long, notched, bloody sword held firmly in his right hand.

"Open it!" he shouted as they reached the door, panting under his armor.

Daniel Pratt dropped a bloody flail on the flagged floor as he plunged his hand into his battered mantle. He pulled a large sack from his belt.

Lewis stepped aside, his sword ready in front of him and a wide green shield on his left arm.

Daniel shook a carved stone hourglass, glowing eerily blue, from the sack into his hand and slammed it into an hourglass shaped socket in the center of the iron door.

A blast of blue flame exploded from the hourglass. Daniel was launched backward and Lewis was thrown into the wall as the door burst open. Lewis put up his shield as the door swung heavily into it.

"Daniel!" Ann screamed, rushing to where he lay unmoving on the ground.

Her son Mark grabbed her arm and pulled her toward the door. "We'll come back for him!"

Lewis hurled himself around the door, roaring, "*Tasirak!*"

Miles Breslin and Spalding had already charged through. Lewis rushed in after them, Terry and Daniel and Ann's daughter Heather running after him.

Miles and Spalding had run straight into the knees of three enormous stone creatures. Towering more than five meters above them, the three golems swung their vast arms right at Miles and Spalding's heads.

They ducked beneath the lethal blows, but one of the golems' arms collided with Miles's sword, wrenching it from his grip and hurling it across the room.

A jet of blue flame shot out from behind the golems, throwing Spalding past Lewis back through the door and knocking Miles sidelong a few meters through the air.

Lewis ducked down and rushed between the golems, his shield out in

13: A Perfect Sense

front of him.

Past the monsters, he raised his sword with a yell as he raced at a man in purple silk robes.

Another blast of blue flame erupted from the man's hand, but Lewis had his shield ready. The flame hit the shield and seemed to be absorbed straight into it.

Tasirak the sorcerer lowered his hand. "You have the Heart of Adamant," he observed coolly.

A golem swung at Lewis from behind and he dropped and rolled on the ground. Tasirak shot another jet of fire at him, but he had already put up his shield. The flame was absorbed harmlessly into it.

A small black sphere embedded in it glowed faintly blue, then went black again.

Another golem's foot came crashing down toward Lewis. He rolled away just as the foot smashed into the flagstone floor. Fragments of floor pelted Lewis's back.

Miles dashed out from between the two other golems. His sword forgotten, he hurled a long, sharp knife at Tasirak.

Tasirak caught the knife by the blade. He fired another bolt of fire from his left hand at Miles.

Miles leapt aside but some of the fire caught him. He was knocked to the ground, but he wasn't finished yet. He looked around for his sword.

Lewis could hear the frantic shouts of the others on the other side of the golems. His golem was trying to squash him as he darted around it, his shield raised, but the other two were still swinging and stomping at his family.

He saw Terry dodge out from under a blow just as the other golem hit Heather. She was thrown into the wall, then lay still on the floor, blood trickling from her brow.

Mark was hewing at the golem's rock legs, but his sword was just glancing off harmlessly, as were Lucy's arrows. Even Ann's wizardry wasn't seeming to faze them.

Lewis knew what he had to do. But it was going to leave him vulnerable to Tasirak. He ducked and slid forward under the golem's swooping arm.

Tasirak was no longer looking at him. A stream of blue blood was falling down the sorcerer's right arm, which was raised, the knife blade now raised in his hand.

It had to be now. Lewis dropped his sword and yanked his shield from his arm, then rolled, the shield in his hands, away from the golem's stone fist as it crashed into the floor.

The knife in Tasirak's hand burst into blue flame.

Lewis put his hand on the black sphere in his shield, the Heart of Adamant. It glowed bright blue as he pulled it out.

Tasirak threw the knife.

Lewis hurled the Heart after the knife, straight at the golems and his family.

The Heart hit the back of one of the golems just as the knife exploded in midair beyond them.

But the knife's blue explosion was nothing to the eruption of white light that blazed from the Heart of Adamant. All three golems shattered into thousands of tiny shards. The blast of blue flame from the knife was blown harmlessly away by the Heart's light as if it were in a wind.

The light vanished as quickly as it came. The Heart of Adamant hit the floor with a sharp thud.

Tasirak was laughing. The others were standing stunned. But at least they were safe from the golems, Lewis thought.

"Hedan died to keep the Heart of Adamant from me!" Tasirak gloated at Lewis. "And now you've thrown it right into my hands!" He raised his bleeding right hand and the ball raced up from the floor and landed in it. The stream of blood down his arm retreated back away into his hand, the cut sealing.

Tasirak switched the Heart of Adamant into his left hand and raised it high. His right hand blasted fire at the others.

Ann dodged out of the way, but Terry, Mark, and Lucy were all hurled into the wall.

Miles reached his sword. He stumbled around and charged at Tasirak.

Tasirak shot another blast of fire at him. It hit his shield and burst right through it, throwing him backward.

"Ann, heal them!" Lewis shouted.

Tasirak turned and blasted fire at Lewis. Lewis dodged, but his shield on the ground behind him erupted apart in flames.

"I can't!" Ann called desperately. "I need time!"

Tasirak fired another blast at her, but a jet of ice flew from her hand, dissipating the blue flames before they hit her.

"I can't!" Ann said again. "He'll kill me if I stop!"

Tasirak raised his hand, and Miles's sword flew up into it.

Ann took the pause to hit Tasirak with a small bolt of red flame. The fire was absorbed into him, apparently harmlessly.

Tasirak laughed derisively. "Finally! This precious Heart finds an owner

13: A Perfect Sense

who truly can wield it!"

"Now!" Lewis shouted at Ann, running at Tasirak. "Now!"

Tasirak turned toward Lewis, his lip curling indifferently. He raised Miles's sword.

"Lewis! No!" Ann was shouting.

But Lewis didn't care. He saw the sword in Tasirak's raised arm burst into blue flame just before he hurled himself into the sorcerer.

He felt indescribable pain as the sword struck his left shoulder. His armor seemed useless against the flaming blade. It felt as if his entire left side was on fire.

But his hand had found its mark. As Tasirak had brought the sword in his right hand down into Lewis, his left hand had relaxed its hold on the Heart, and Lewis's outstretched hand had knocked it out.

Tasirak stumbled.

The Heart of Adamant was rolling away across the floor.

Lewis was in so much pain he couldn't see. "Now, Ann, *now!*" he screamed horribly. Then everything went black.

And then the blackness and the pain completely disappeared. The room came back into full view, but now Spalding, Miles, and all the others were standing behind Ann, watching the action.

There was silence as Lewis looked up quickly to see a bolt of red fire envelop Tasirak.

"YES!" Daniel cheered as some of the others started clapping.

Tasirak had fallen onto his back. He raised a scorched hand toward the Heart of Adamant, sitting on the floor meters away.

Ann shouted an incantation, and a larger blast of red fire burst from her hands.

Tasirak was hit again, and was rolled harshly into the room's towering back wall. He fell limply into an unmoving heap.

Everyone was clapping and cheering excitedly. Ann raced forward and scooped up the Heart of Adamant.

"Yeah, Mom!" Mark and Spalding shouted.

Only Andrew, who had been standing in the center of the room, had kept silent, as if in focused concentration. But as Ann's final blow had hit Tasirak he had let out a deep whoop of satisfaction. He started clapping with the others.

Lewis glided up behind Andrew. All of their bodies, except for Andrew and Ann's, were lying where they had fallen on the floor; he could see his own armored body lying on Miles's sword near where Tasirak had landed.

Ann was straightening up. She tossed the Heart of Adamant casually into the air and caught it again. "Well, Andrew," she said windedly to the walls, "Is there any point in me healing the others?"

Andrew laughed, and the room, the bodies, and Tasirak all disappeared.

They were standing in the air high above a brilliant ocean within the Shell. Thousands of other people were racing by above and below them.

Ann's armor and weapons had melted off of her. She heaved her fist into the air. "Yes!" she cheered, apparently only just then able to see or hear Andrew and everyone else. "We did it!"

"That was awesome, Andrew!" Mark was saying, hitting Andrew on the back.

"Lewis, that was amazing," Daniel said, "Throwing the Heart at the golems!"

"Thanks," Lewis smiled. "It almost didn't work."

"No," Andrew shook his head pleasedly, "I was setting it up so you'd have to use the Heart sooner or later."

"And sorry about that door," Lewis said to Daniel. "I didn't know it was going to do that."

"That's okay," Daniel said. "I was disappointed, but this way I got to see you all in action at the end."

"Whew!" Andrew exhaled. "I'm glad it's done!"

"Yeah, right," Spalding said to him lightly. "When are you going to do another one of these?"

"Me?" Andrew said. "No! It's someone else's turn now."

"But that was so good!" Heather protested.

"Yeah, it was," said a woman there that Lewis didn't recognize.

"Thanks," Andrew said. "But do you know how long it took me to think that all up? No, we'll have to get someone else to make up the story for next time."

"Let's make Tom do it!" Spalding said.

"Yeah," Miles laughed. "Get his mind off work."

"Oh, be nice," Terry said. "He's got more to do than any of us do."

Lewis had noticed that Zämŭth was there standing beside the new woman, whom he recognized was called Tävna.

"Hey, Zämŭth!" he said, trying to sound lighthearted. "What are you doing here?"

"Watching you!" Zämŭth laughed. "That was really exciting!"

"It was," Lewis said. "How long have you been here?"

"Nine hours or so," Zämŭth smiled. "Since the dragon."

13: A Perfect Sense

"I just got here a few minutes ago," Tävna said. "I've never seen a story like that!"

"My son Andrew designed it," Lewis said. "It's taken us almost a day and a half to get through it."

"Oh, I've played stories before," Tävna said. "But those stone rooms, and the magic, and all. That was amazing!"

"We have a lot of stories like that, or, we had a lot like that, on Earth," Lewis said.

"I should see those."

Spalding had flown up to them. "Who are you?" he asked friendlily.

"This is one of my managers, Zämŭth," Lewis said.

"I'm Tävna," Tävna smiled. "I just came to see Zämŭth, and I got caught by your story. You better tell me when you're going to do another one!"

"Okay," Spalding said.

"This is Spalding Pratt, my nephew," Lewis introduced him. "And that," he pointed to the others, who were still talking, "Is my brother, and his wife. They're Spalding's parents, though you'd think they were his siblings," he smiled.

Spalding laughed, but Tävna didn't seem to get the joke.

"Uh, those two flying off are two more of their children," Lewis said. "Those following them are another nephew and a niece of mine. And these are my children." He motioned for Andrew and Terry to come over to them. "Andrew and Terry. My other son, Tom, is with his managers.

"Andrew, Terry, this is Zämŭth, one of my managers."

"And I'm just Zämŭth's friend," Tävna said.

"You aren't married?" Terry asked.

Tävna laughed loudly. "No! Never! To this guy?"

"You think any couple you see has to be married?" Andrew said to Terry.

"Around here..." Terry said defensively.

"No, it was a good guess," Zämŭth laughed. "My wife is called Zad, and we're never apart. Except for times like this; she had someone to talk to."

"See?" Terry said with feigned smugness.

"She just left a few minutes ago," Tävna said. "You'll have to tell her how it ended, Zämŭth. That Tasirak..."

"Really, it seems like everyone's married here," Terry said to Zämŭth, as if determined to justify herself.

"She's got a point," Spalding said mock-seriously to Andrew.

"We are, me and Zad," Zämŭth smiled. "That's enough for me."

"Yeah, well," Tävna sneered at him with something of a grin, "Others of us aren't so lucky."

Then Spalding thought of Lewis. "So," he said deliberately, "What did you think of that ending?"

"I didn't know if you were going to beat Tasirak," Tävna said.

"Neither did I," Andrew shook his head. "I made him too tough, I guess."

"But they got him in the end," Zämŭth said. "When they finally found him. Your sister got him," he nodded at Lewis.

"Yeah, but Dad was the one who really saved the day," Terry said. "Giving up the Heart of Adamant like that! And after everything we did to get it in the first place!"

"I'm glad that worked," Lewis said gratefully to Andrew.

"Hey, I didn't cheat for you!" Andrew said. "I was wondering if I should, but you got out of it all on your own."

"Yeah, that was intense and brave," Spalding said to Lewis. "How you just ran at him and let him kill you."

"Come on, the way you say it, it makes him sound stupid!" Tävna smiled at Spalding. "He sacrificed himself to get the Heart of Adamant away from Tasirak! That's the only way Ann could kill him."

"You really got into this, didn't you?" Andrew said to her.

Zämŭth laughed.

"I want you to put me in next time," Tävna said to Andrew.

"Hey, come with us now," Terry said to her, starting to drift away. "Heather and all were going down to the dolphins."

"Yeah, let's go," Andrew said.

That sounded great to Tävna. But then she heard Zämŭth's voice in her head: "I may need you here to get rid of Spalding."

"I can't right now," Tävna said. "Thanks."

"Next time, then," Terry said. "Are you coming?" she said to Spalding.

"Uh, no," Spalding said. It had been he who had convinced Andrew to give Lewis such a prominent place in the story, hoping it would lift his spirits. He hadn't spoken a word about Mary, but he wanted to talk to Lewis, even if only to make sure he was fine.

"Go on with them," Zämŭth said lightly.

"Yeah, we're fine here," Tävna agreed.

"I'll meet up with you later," Spalding waved to Andrew and Terry.

"See you," Andrew said before pitching down toward the ocean.

"Yeah, see you, Tävna," Terry said, then followed after Andrew.

Zämŭth's voice came into Tävna's head again: "I need to talk to Lewis alone."

13: A Perfect Sense

"Come on," Tävna said to Spalding, jerking her head away.

"I want to talk to Lewis," Spalding said.

"It'll just be for a minute," Tävna said aloud, while privately she told him, "Zämŭth wants to talk to Lewis alone."

"Oh, alright," Spalding said fakely out loud. "I will tell you more about the story."

"Thanks," Tävna heard Zämŭth's voice. She led Spalding quickly away.

"That was really amazing," Zämŭth said to Lewis. "Spalding was right; you were incredibly brave, sacrificing yourself like that."

"Thanks," Lewis said. "It was just a game."

"You were all acting like it was real enough!" Zämŭth grinned.

"I know," Lewis laughed. "More than a day of that and you start to forget real life."

"I wouldn't mind forgetting, sometimes," Zämŭth said.

"I know," Lewis said. He looked out quietly at the sparkling water.

"Well," Zämŭth said, "That's actually why I'm here."

"What?" Lewis said. "Why?"

"Mär talked to me," Zämŭth said. "A few days ago. I just haven't known how to talk to you about it."

Lewis didn't say anything. His first fearful though was that Zämŭth somehow knew he had tried to revive Mary. But how would Zämŭth or Mär know that? he reminded himself.

"Mär told me you failed to revive your wife, Mary," Zämŭth said baldly.

Lewis stared at him. He wanted to think he had misheard him.

Zämŭth smiled understandingly. "I don't know what I'm supposed to say."

"That's fine," Lewis said. "Don't worry about it." He was quiet for a second. "How did Mär know about that?"

"I have no idea," Zämŭth said. "The Ōmäthäär always know more than I expect them to."

"Mär knew I was going to try. Of course you know that," Lewis said with a weary smile at Zämŭth. "That's why he came to talk to me."

"Mär came to talk to you?" Zämŭth said, impressed.

"He didn't tell you that?"

"No," Zämŭth said. "I'd have thought Mär would have been far too busy."

Lewis's feelings toward Mär softened a bit as he realized that Zämŭth was right; it should have meant a lot that Mär had taken the trouble to talk to him personally.

"That's true," he said. "I'm afraid I was not very kind to him."

"He told you not to revive Mary?" Zämŭth asked.

"He did," Lewis said. "He said I should look for another wife."

"That's really good advice," Zämŭth said.

Lewis didn't answer. He floated away a little, looking down at the shining slab of ocean stretching from horizon to horizon.

"Lewis," Zämŭth said, "I haven't ever had to remarry. I don't know what it means to lose a wife. But I think I know something of what it's like."

Lewis just looked down at the water.

"Zad and I have had more than four hundred children—"

"Four hundred?" Lewis looked up incredulously.

Zämŭth smiled. "The more children we have, the more we want to have," he shrugged.

"That's unimaginable," Lewis wheezed.

"Try it," Zämŭth smiled. "It's a lot more imaginable than you know."

"I...I can't," Lewis said. "Can't try it."

"Sorry," Zämŭth said quickly. "But what I mean is..." He glided over to look Lewis in the face. "What I mean is, Zad and I have lost thirty-five of our children."

Lewis looked up into his manager's face. He could tell Zämŭth was fighting back pain.

"Thirty-three of them were killed by Ämäthöär at Nrathĕrmĕ. Five more of our children were killed by pirates. Zad and I revived three of them. Ûfōth and Van wouldn't revive."

"I'm sorry," Lewis said.

"Let me tell you, Lewis," Zämŭth said. "Having more than four hundred children does not make the loss of thirty-five of our own sons and daughters any easier. They were our sons and our daughters!

"My father and my mother were killed at Nrathĕrmĕ. Eighteen of my brothers, and four of my sisters, were all killed by Ämäthöär. Three more of my brothers and five more of my sisters wouldn't revive after being killed by pirates.

"And I've lost dozens of friends besides."

"I'm really sorry," Lewis said. "I didn't know."

"It's alright," Zämŭth said. "Well no, it isn't alright! But that is the way it is for too many of us here.

"Terry thought everyone here was married." A grin showed through the grief on his face. "Well, she would have been more correct to say that everyone here has lost someone.

13: A Perfect Sense

"So I can understand some of what this feels like for you."

Lewis nodded. "I don't know if I can possibly understand what it's like for you."

"I hope you never will."

Lewis looked out at the ocean again. He tried to imagine what it would be like to have lost so many loved ones.

"I won't forget them," Zämŭth said. "I can't."

Lewis looked at him, smiling sadly.

Zämŭth paused, as if considering Lewis. "Neither Mary," he then said, "Nor my parents or children or any of them are really gone, though."

Lewis nodded vaguely, looking out over the boundless ocean again.

"This life," Zämŭth explained, "It's only a phase."

Lewis didn't say anything.

"My parents and children are still alive. Their bodies are dead, but there's more to them than just their bodies. I will see them again, after this part of life."

Lewis smiled a little at him again.

"Like in the story," Zämŭth said. "Even when you died, you were still alive. And you were still there, cheering on the people who were still alive. It's just like that!"

"Yeah," Lewis said unenthusiastically.

"That's how I get along," Zämŭth said. "I know I'll see them again. And I know they're watching us here while we're fighting Sĕrĕhahn, and cheering for us."

Lewis liked the sound of that. "Thanks," he said sincerely to Zämŭth. "It's nice to think of Mary as being still here with me."

"It makes all the loss easier to handle, seeing it in its right perspective," Zämŭth said.

"At least, it cheers a man up," Lewis sighed. "And no wonder." He looked at Zämŭth. "I was a little surprised that you were all so...well...spiritual. But it makes sense."

"What do you mean?" Zämŭth asked.

"How much loss you all have suffered," Lewis said. "Even you people, with all your knowledge, need to invent some kind of religion."

"But it is nice to think about. Even if it is just a nice thought, a nice thought is a nice thought."

"Uh," Zämŭth said, looking at Lewis with misgiving, "What I'm saying is a lot more than just a nice thought."

"I know," Lewis smiled understandingly.

"No, Lewis, this is serious."

Lewis looked at him, trying to understand what he meant.

"This is real. My friends and family would not be dead if it was not. We would be living safe at Nrathĕrmĕ if it was not."

"I don't understand you," Lewis said doubtfully.

Zämŭth looked away. "I don't know how to say it, really."

He looked back at Lewis. "Well, I'm no Ōmäthäär. Not like Mär, I mean. But...well, Lewis, you don't know about Ärthähr, do you?"

"No," Lewis said, a little curious now.

"It's what the Ämäthōär use to kill people," Zämŭth said, "And what the Ōmäthäär use to fight them."

"Oh!"

"Now, me," Zämŭth said, "I don't know enough about Ärthähr to do what the Ōmäthäär do with it. But I know enough that it's not just some nice thought to me."

"So does that Ärthähr have something to do with Mary, and your family and friends?" Lewis asked.

"I think it does." Zämŭth stopped again, thinking.

"Lewis," he said then, "You have to understand that this is the way life has been for me and Zad. For all of us who used to live at Nrathĕrmĕ before Sĕrĕhahn drove us away.

"Ärthähr, the Ärthähr, is an essential part of our lives. And so is Är, and Ä'ähänärdanär overall."

"I have no idea what that means," Lewis said. "I thought I had been taught everything."

"And I don't have time to explain it all," Zämŭth said. "Here," he raised his hand to Lewis. "I'll just give you what I know, and then I'll explain some of it."

Lewis naturally put his hand in Zämŭth's, and instantly a wealth of memories poured into him. Memories of life at Nrathĕrmĕ. Memories of thousands of Ōmäthäär meeting frequently. Joyful, warm memories of Ōmäthäär. And also memories of fear, memories of hiding, and of pain. Memories of Ōmäthäär friends being killed. And memories of having to leave a cherished home, knowing he might never see it again.

He didn't know what to make sense of yet.

"Alright," Zämŭth said, taking his hand back. "Now I can explain it more easily.

"So, Ä'ähänärdanär," he prompted.

"Is your society," Lewis said for him, "The society you all had back at

13: A Perfect Sense

Nrathĕrmĕ."

"Yes, our society, and also what we as a society knew about," Zămŭth said. "Because Är..."

"Är," Lewis said. He thought. "What is he?" he asked in an amazed voice.

"You have my memories now," Zămŭth smiled. "What is he?"

"Infinite!" Lewis said. "How can one person be everyone and everything?"

"That has to do with Ärthähr again," Zămŭth said. "And that aspect of Är is what drives so many of us to be foolish enough as to think we can fight the Ämāthōär," he grinned.

"Explain that a little more," Lewis said apologetically.

"The Ämāthōär may wield Ärthähr," Zămŭth said, "But Är has all the Ärthähr that they make use of. So we're safe."

"I still don't understand," Lewis said.

"Är's infinite. So he knows us. He knows everything else, but he knows more about me than I do. And he can't help but be involved."

"So..." Lewis smiled, catching on to the pronoun, "Infinity is a man?"

"No!" Zămŭth laughed. "I don't know. Most of us refer to Är as 'he,' even the Ōmäthäär. But they've said before not to take that too far."

"That makes more sense," Lewis said.

"I don't know," Zămŭth said. "It makes most sense to me to say, 'he.' I know people who talk to him, and they refer to him as a Man. But, like I say, people say not to take that too far."

"People *talk* to Är?" Lewis asked, amazed.

"How wouldn't they?" Zămŭth said. "If Är's Infinity, he's everything and everyone. How can he not interact with his own self?"

"But I've never seen him," Lewis said. "If there's an Infinite Someone, shouldn't I be part of it? And everyone and everything else?"

"That's about Ärthähr again," Zămŭth said. "Är is everyone, but no one but Är, 'an Är' as the Ōmäthäär say it sometimes, is Är. What I mean," he said at the bewildered look on Lewis's face, "Is that everything is a part of Infinity, but only a part. Infinity is everything, but nothing except for Infinity himself is Infinity."

Lewis nodded.

"So you'll only perceive as much of Är as you are," Zămŭth continued. "I surmise, then, that to see or talk to Är, you'd have to be enough of Infinity to perceive him that much."

"Wow, that makes sense, I guess," Lewis said. He laughed. "So, you and I are very, very small bits of Infinity, aren't we? Can a person become more, a bigger part?"

"Talk to an Ōmäthäär about that!" Zämŭth said. "I mean, yes, anyone can. But talk to an Ōmäthäär about that.

"But about death," he said, and Lewis pulled his mind back from everything Zämŭth had just given him.

"Parts of Är don't just disappear. Är, as Infinity, cannot not be. If he isn't, if there's no Infinity, then there's no anything."

"Why's that?" Lewis asked.

"What I mean is," Zämŭth said, "Är is everyone and everything. If there is no everything, then there's no anything! Even if there were nothing at all except for you and me, well, then you and me together would be everything, and that would be Är."

"But Är's a person himself, isn't he?" Lewis asked.

"He is," Zämŭth said. "An Ōmäthäär would be able to explain this better. But anyway, one of them told me that everything that can be, is. What I mean by that is that people cannot just disappear. When Mary died," he said, looking Lewis suddenly deeply in the face, "Her consciousness, her self, didn't just end.

"Some Ōmäthäär told me," he said, looking out over the ocean again, "That my parents never died. They said that their bodies were broken, so, as bodies, they died; they were not working bodies anymore, so they, as bodies, had ended.

"But my parents," he said, looking back at Lewis, "Were using those bodies. But those bodies never were my parents. Not really. So my parents never did die. As who they are, they're still just as alive as any of us are."

Lewis thought about that. He looked up into the blue sky. "You know, Mär said that kind of thing to me. It sounds better the way you said it."

"I find that hard to believe," Zämŭth laughed. "But anything good sounds better when you hear it again after you've had to think about it."

"Maybe," Lewis said. He sighed. "So, you're saying that Mary is a part of Infinity, of Är, and that means she can never die?"

"That's exactly what I'm saying."

"I like that idea a lot, Zämŭth," Lewis said quietly. "But the fact is that Mary's gone. I can't see her or talk to her. What good is it if she still exists in some other state?"

"At least," Zämŭth said, "It means you know you will be with her again. And," he paused, then grinned a little. "And sometimes those who we think are dead do come and talk to us."

"What?" Lewis said.

13: A Perfect Sense

"A few of our children visited Zad, at least one time. That's what she told me, at least. And I believe her. Children of ours who were killed by Ämäthöär at Nrathĕrmĕ."

Lewis wasn't sure whether he should take that seriously.

Zämŭth was smiling savoringly. "I won't tell you the details of what she told me, but they were extremely happy. Our children were.

"And it is not just a nice thought," he said, as if he had guessed Lewis's thoughts. "Think about the memories I gave you. Everything about the Ämäthöär, and the Ōmäthäär, and the Ärthähr. This is serious, this is real. No one who's been close to Ōmäthäär or Ämäthöär, especially when they're fighting," he shuddered, "Can dispute that these are not just artificial ideas.

"I guess what I meant to say all along is that Ōmäthäär, the ones who do talk to Är; and from what they say, some of them talk to him just like how we're talking to each other right now; those Ōmäthäär have told me, and most of us who were with them at Nrathĕrmĕ, that people, as themselves, never do die. Those Ōmäthäär said that that's what Är taught them. And Zad and I have seen the Ōmäthäär use Ärthähr enough to know that it's all real."

"I understand," Lewis said. "But, how do you know there really is an Är? I mean, how do you know that the Ōmäthäär really have spoken to him? They could be lying to you—although I don't believe they would do that!" he said at Zämŭth's protesting look. "Or they could be mistaken. I'm sorry, but it's just too fantastic, too impossible."

"I know that Är is real," Zämŭth said soothingly. "I believe the Ōmäthäär, but it's more than that. I don't know how to do what the Ōmäthäär do with Ärthähr, but I can use it a little. Ärthähr can tell me if something's true or not. I've felt the Ärthähr enough about Är that I can't doubt that he is real. And that the Ōmäthäär are right in what they've said about death."

"But," Lewis said, "Don't you have to wonder if that's just because that's what you want to feel?"

"Not at all," Zämŭth said relishingly. "Not with Ärthähr."

"Okay," Lewis said uncertainly.

"When I was first being taught about Ärthähr," Zämŭth said, "An Ōmäthäär described it to me like this. She told me to imagine that I was blind, and that everyone everywhere was blind, except for a few people. Everyone can hear and feel and smell and everything, but almost no one can see."

"Okay."

"But it's just because almost everyone has their eyes closed," Zämŭth went on.

"Not that that matters," Lewis smiled.

"That's actually pretty new, using rantha for sight and hearing," Zämŭth said. "A lot of old Ōmäthäär could remember when our eyes were just the same as yours were before we came. But you know what I'm getting at."

"I get it," Lewis said.

"So everyone's eyes are blindly closed except for a few people. The blind people don't even know that they have eyes. So the people with their eyes open can see things far away, but no one else can. They just have to feel their way around."

Lewis had a strange image of thousands of people wandering around with their eyes shut, running into things and into each other.

"She asked me to imagine what it would be like for a seeing person to try to explain sight to a blind person," Zämŭth was continuing.

"Okay," Lewis said. "How would you?"

Zämŭth laughed resentfully. "I'm not very good at it."

"What?"

"Think about it," Zämŭth said. "There's a set of people with a natural sense that's more powerful, more effective, more wide reaching, than any other sense, but that most people don't have. That's the Ōmäthäär!"

"Oh," Lewis said, suddenly comprehending.

"The use of Ärthähr is a sense, a natural sense," Zämŭth explained. "It lets you perceive things that are far away, much farther than even our kind of sight, if you can use it well enough. But how do you explain what it's like to someone who's never used it? It's just like trying to explain sight to someone who's never seen, who's always relied on nothing better than hearing and feeling."

"Can you use it?" Lewis asked.

"That's what I said," Zämŭth said. "Enough to know things even if I haven't seen them. It's just like you knowing something because you can see it, regardless of whether or not you can hear it. Which would you be surer of, something you could hear but not see, or something you could see but not hear?"

"I see what you're getting at," Lewis nodded. "I'm surest of things I can see. But you're saying that Ärthähr is better than seeing?"

"For me it is, sometimes," Zämŭth said.

"Imagine, though that a seeing person started teaching a blind person to open his eyes," he continued. "It would hurt, accustoming his eyes to light. The Ōmäthäär told me that most people don't like to open their eyes once they try it. It's too scary, too uncomfortable."

"Disorienting," Lewis said fervently.

13: A Perfect Sense

Zämŭth smiled at him. "But, at first, when a person's getting used to opening his eyes, things will be out of focus. He won't be used to light. It will be hard for him to see. That's the way it is with Ärthähr; you get better at it if you keep using it.

"So I am sure that this is true, that Är's real, and that our loved ones are still alive as themselves."

Words failed Lewis. Zämŭth smiled.

"You know," Lewis said finally. "I wish it were true. I hope it's true. It ought to be true."

"Then find a real Ōmäthäär," Zämŭth said. "Get him to teach you."

"I should. What if it were really true?" He said it as if he were just entertaining an enjoyable idea.

"And," Zämŭth began, but he hesitated. But then he said, "And, Lewis, be open. To marry again, I mean."

Lewis looked back down at the ocean. "Okay," he said at length. "At least...well, I will. But I want to find out more about this Ärthähr and Ä'ähänärdanär first."

Zämŭth was staring at him as though he were having trouble believing what he was hearing.

"What?" Lewis said.

"That was really easy."

"What was?" Lewis said.

"You, your accepting what I said about Är," Zämŭth said. "Is everyone from your world so open-minded?"

"I never thought of myself as open-minded," Lewis said.

"Some Ōmäthäär, even, wouldn't accept such new things so quickly."

Lewis felt awkward. But he also felt markedly light and content, as if the conversation had energized him.

Zämŭth smiled appreciatively. "I hope other Earthmen accept things about Är so well."

Chapter 14

Training Begins

"And that all led us here," Spalding said to Tävna. "But the workshop's deserted."

They were standing amid hot raining ash on the rim of a volcano, outside of a low stone building. Spalding walked forward along the uneven, ash-covered ground, and pushed open a heavy iron door in the side of the building.

"This is so neat!" Tävna said, following Spalding inside.

The inside of the workshop was scorched. Burnt remnants of chairs and books littered the room. A metal chandelier lay twisted in the center of the stone floor. Pieces of glass and of strange silver and glass instruments were visible on the floor through the blackened doorway into another room.

"Of course, Tasirak's goons searched this place a long time before," Spalding said. "They didn't find what they needed, but Tasirak had them burn it all, so no one else could find anything either."

Tävna was looking all around, enthralled.

"But Hedan told us what to do," Spalding said. He bent down and dusted some ash of of the charred floor. "Hedan gave us his key," he said; a tiny, flat stone eagle materialized in his hand; "And with the other keys we already got," four other flat stones appeared in his hand: a fish, a lion, a lizard, and a beetle; "We found what Tasirak's guys couldn't."

He placed the five stones at the five corners of one of the floor stones. The floor stone dropped slowly away, and then the floor stones around it dropped away also, arranging themselves as the first steps of a steeply winding staircase that plunged into blackness below.

Tävna squealed with pleasure. "This is awesome!"

She rushed down the staircase into darkness. A torch materialized in Spalding's hand, and he ran down after her.

"We couldn't see in the dark when we did it!" he reminded her.

Tävna looked up at him, and a torch appeared in her hand too. "Well, come on!" she said, and started running again down the winding stairs.

"You're more excited than we were!" Spalding laughed at her.

Tävna leapt aside off the stairs and plunged straight down the black shaft in the center.

When she landed lightly on a hard floor more than fifty meters down,

14: Training Begins

Spalding was already waiting for her.

"Do you know how tiring those were?"

"No," Tävna said. "It wouldn't be fun tiring myself out, though, unless I was really doing the story."

Several other torches had sprung to life around the wide, low-ceilinged chamber. A red light shined up from another stairway that led down away from the far side of the room.

"Here it is!" Spalding said, gesturing to a shining steel stand. The Heart of Adamant was perched on top of it.

"And that leads down into the volcano, doesn't it?" Tävna asked, taking a few steps toward the other stairway.

"Yeah," Spalding said. "There was something more rewarding about exploring when we had to work for it."

Tävna gazed around at the roughhewn stone of the walls and ceiling of the room. "I love it. You've got to tell me when you do another story like this one!"

"You do one," Spalding grinned.

"Me?" Tävna said, looking uncertain. "I don't know this kind of story."

"I'll help," Spalding said.

"Okay," Tävna said smiling. She looked around the room again, as if looking for ideas.

"Can we go on with Andrew's?" Spalding asked.

"Yeah. What did you do next? After you got to the Heart of Adamant?"

"The Alchemists had put a few booby traps around it." Spalding pointed to the Heart on its stand, being sure not to touch it.

"Oh! Wait," Tävna said abruptly.

Spalding waited. After a few seconds, Tävna said, "I have to go." Her voice made it sound like a crushing tragedy.

"Work?" Spalding asked.

"Yeah," Tävna said. "I usually like it, but now that I have to leave something like this…"

"Go on," Spalding said happily. "I'll think about story ideas while you're gone. I'll get some work done, too."

"I think I already have some ideas," Tävna said. "I'll tell you when I'm done."

She disappeared.

Spalding reached forward and touched the Heart. A bolt of lightning flashed up through the stand and Heart into him. He laughed, and let go of it.

"It doesn't hurt anymore," he laughed.

The room disappeared, leaving him standing on the surface of the ocean.

"Ōŭähä, Raōthä, I'm ready to work," he called.

He would see if Sarah wasn't busy, Tom thought, as he sped away from what remained of Saturn. He had only seen her a couple times since the attack those few days ago.

"Tom," his manager Härtärnär called.

"Yeah?" Tom replied.

"I'm really sorry to call you right back," Härtärnär's voice smiled ruefully, "But Harhahär just called. Mär wants to see you."

"Me?" Tom said. "Alright, I'm going."

He searched for Mär. He was in the Shell, so Tom kept flying that way.

What could Mär have to say to him, he wondered. And why hadn't Mär just had Härtärnär tell him whatever he needed to tell him? Why did Mär need to talk to him personally?

He was afraid for a moment that he had done something terribly wrong without having known it. Maybe that was why Mär himself had sent for him; he was going to be reprimanded, or punished.

But Härtärnär and Nan had all the ability to reprimand or punish him, he thought, if he had done something wrong.

He didn't think he had done anything very wrong. He had been working hard. Had he taken some kind of liberty that he shouldn't have? Should he have relied more on Härtärnär and Nan to know what defenses he should build, and how he should coach his assistants?

Härtärnär and Nan are both Ōmäthäär, he reminded himself. *I suppose I should have taken them more seriously than I have. I should have worked more closely with them. I've been too self-willed in my planning and my leading.*

What was Mär going to do to him? he wondered, more and more apprehensively. If that even was why Mär wanted to see him. But what other reason besides administering a penalty could someone as important as Mär have for seeing him? Would he be taken away from his assistants? Would they say he needed to learn to follow better, and put him in a lower tier?

At least I'd be able to spend more time with Spalding and Andrew and everyone, since I wouldn't have so much responsibility. He would miss his managers, and his assistants. And he probably wouldn't be able to talk to Sarah much anymore either. But he might be able to visit them when they weren't too busy.

Those thoughts were multiplying faster and faster in his mind, when he heard John's voice.

14: Training Begins

"Tom!" He sounded anxious, and urgent.

"What's wrong?" Tom immediately asked.

"I need your help. Right now. With Peter." It sounded like John was trying to carry on another conversation while calling to him.

"Ask somebody else," Tom said regretfully. "I'm sorry, I can't come right now. Call Härtärnär or Nan."

There was a short silence. Tom was coming closer to Earth.

"I really need you, Tom," John insisted then. "Right now. Please."

Mär himself wanted to see him, Tom thought. But John sounded like he meant that he needed him.

He searched around for John. He was way out in an open area of space, past the orbit of Neptune on the other side of the solar system.

He was almost to Earth. He couldn't make Mär wait. *I'm already in trouble,* he thought. Maybe.

But he couldn't do it. He swerved and accelerated more quickly toward John.

"Härtärnär," he called, "Tell Mär I will be late; one of my assistants needs me right now."

"Okay," Härtärnär said, sounding unperturbed.

"I'm coming," Tom called to John. "What's going on?"

After a few seconds, John's voice called, "Hurry." Then he said, "Can't. Talk. Now. Come quick."

If he had been being too willful, Tom thought as he put on more speed, this would not help.

Sarah could see Mär up ahead, in the middle of a bunch of seven other Ōmäthäär. They were floating high in the bright blue sky, close to a strange, huge structure, like a stunningly white sphere encased in a cube.

She was more than nervous about talking to Mär personally. What was she going to say? She hoped she wouldn't have to say much.

Mär waved to her as she slowed. He was smiling, she saw with tiny relief.

She stopped in front of the group of them. The seven other Ōmäthäär backed away deferentially, which made Sarah feel small and embarrassed. She noticed one of them smiling encouragingly at her.

Mär swept forward and reached for Sarah's left hand with his right. "Thanks for coming, Sarah."

Sarah's voice was gone, but she took his hand naturally.

Then Mär gave her his left hand. She took it uncertainly.

Mär smiled and released both of her hands. "How have you been?"

Sarah stammered soundlessly before she finally heard, "I've been alright," emerge from her mouth.

"Good," Mär said warmly. He looked quietly into Sarah's eyes for few seconds, making her want to look away, but she forced herself not to. Mär smiled.

"Thank you for coming," he said again. "And thank you, a lot, for helping Lewis Pratt."

Sarah was more embarrassed than she was surprised. "Thank you," she said back. She wondered what else Mär knew.

"That was really a great thing you did."

"Thank you," she said again.

Mär's smile deepened. He looked at some of the other Ōmäthäär. They looked at him; Sarah guessed they were talking. Were they talking about her? she wondered. She didn't know what she was expected to do, so she just waited nervously for Mär to say more.

"Yes," Mär was saying privately to Ärdhär. "Let's get started."

He turned to Sarah, clapping his hands loudly together, and smiling at her trepidation. She just glowed, he thought.

"Let's get started, then," he said out loud to her.

"Wait!" an Ōmäthäär called Ŭkan said suddenly.

"What is it?" Mär asked.

Sarah looked startled at Ŭkan.

Ŭkan held up a hand and didn't say anything. Then he said, "Tom Pratt's having trouble with Peter Garcia."

"What kind of trouble?" Mär asked pleasantly.

"Guess," Ŭkan said. "Nearly half a million people have gathered with Peter, and it sounds like Tom's arguing with them."

"Excellent!" Mär said, clapping his hands again, his eyes gleaming. "So that's what's kept him."

Kept him? Sarah thought. Had Mär sent for Tom too? Why would he have sent for both of them? Were any other people coming?

What did Mär know?

There was laughter on Ŭkan's face as he suggested, "Should I send Härtärnär and Nan?"

"No!" Mär said. "Don't!" He looked around at the others. "Tell all your assistants to tell everyone to let Tom do this by himself. No Ōmäthäär are to interfere, no matter what happens. And Särdnä, tell Anŭsths and Tärnär. Äōdhä, tell Ŭmäthŭ and Ōhōmhär. Avhä, tell Äthääōhä and Ährnär. And Ŭdbän, tell Bävän and Thas."

14: Training Begins

The Ōmäthäär smiled without apparent confusion.

Mär turned back to Sarah, smiling in a satisfied way.

"What's wrong with Tom?" Sarah heard herself asking.

"Nothing Tom won't fix," Mär winked.

Sarah realized she had no idea what Mär thought he meant by that.

"So we'll go on without him," Mär said. He looked silently at her again, smiling offhandedly. "Nōvagähd has talked with you about Ä'ähänärdanär?" he observed quietly.

She couldn't remember Nōvagähd mentioning that. She shook her head slowly, afraid of contradicting Mär.

Mär grinned understandingly. "You talked about Är, and Ärthähr, didn't you?"

"Yes," Sarah said quickly.

"Good enough," Mär smiled. "Give me your hand."

Sarah extended her left hand to Mär's open right hand. Mär beamed at her as he took it.

She had expected another rush of information, but she didn't notice any. But, all of a sudden, she felt extremely warm and comfortable, deep within herself. It was as if her heavy insides had been replaced with nothing but buoyant white light.

Mär was staring into her eyes. "I want to tell you just a little bit more about the Ärthähr."

Then came the blast of information. It felt like far more knowledge than Ähänär had given her almost two weeks ago. Knowledge about the Ärthähr. Knowledge about the society of Ä'ähänärdanär, and about Är. Knowledge of the history of the Ōmäthäär. She suddenly had memories of hundreds of battles between Ōmäthäär and Ämäthōär.

And she knew how to use Ärthähr.

Her mind was reeling. She was looking at Mär but not really registering that he was there.

Mär released her hand. He was still smiling a little, but his face was now profoundly serious.

"Sarah," he said.

Sarah looked at him more cognizantly.

Mär smiled at her. "You should take your time in thinking about all this. Take your time."

Sarah nodded, staring partly through Mär.

"I will send for you again before long. Until then, you should just think about what I've given you. Don't worry about making sense of it yet," he smiled. "Just let it sit in your mind for a while. You'll only understand what I've given you if you just let it sit."

"Alright," Sarah said.

Before she realized it, Mär had dived forward and picked her up into a solid, powerful embrace. She felt the wave of warm tranquility surge through her again.

Mär drifted back again. "Sarah, don't tell *anyone* what I've just given you. Not anyone for now. Nōvagähd will know not to ask. Do not tell anyone anything about this for the time being."

"Okay," Sarah said.

"Just for now," Mär said. "Think about this. If you have any questions about any of it, call me directly."

"Okay."

Mär smiled adoringly at her. "Thank you for coming," he said, as if she had done him some great service.

"Thank you," Sarah said in a small but emphatic voice.

Mär smiled in a deep way that unequivocally told her that their business was through. For the present.

But she didn't want to just leave rudely. She half nodded, half bowed to Mär, then turned and flew away, though she was careful not to fly away from them too quickly.

Mär watched her go. He was feeling apprehensive despite his joy at having been able to teach such a promising Nōhōnŭäär what he had.

"I like her!" Ärdhär said definitively.

"She would be a terrible Ämäthōär," Mär said softly.

"Yes," Ōhärnäth agreed soberly. "Or, what an Ōmäthäär!"

Mär smiled again. He looked around at them. "And you still believe it's worth the risk?" he asked, much more lightly.

"I do," Särdnä said fervently.

The others smiled, showing their agreement.

"Yes," Ŭdbän said. "For her, yes."

Mär beamed at them and clasped his hands loosely together in front of him. "For her."

Deep down, Tom was terrified, but his anger overshadowed that. All he was aware of was a greater indignation than he had ever felt, despite the fact that he, John, and a handful of others were surrounded by a few hundred thousand hostile people with their arranged legions of ships.

"So, you're just using them," Tom said in a flat furious voice.

14: Training Begins

"Tom," Peter said amiably, standing in front of Tom in the center of his army. "I'm helping them. Aren't I?"

It was as if Tom could actually feel the thousands of unfriendly eyes glaring at him from all around.

"Explain to me how you're doing that," he said in the same quiet, opposing tone.

"Tom, all these people *want* to follow me," Peter said. "That's enough as it is. But they are following me, we are all working together as one, in order to free ourselves and everyone else from Mär."

Tom glowered at Peter for a couple of seconds, then said slowly, "That is anything but help to anyone but the Ämäthöär, and least of all to the people you're using."

"How can you say that I'm using these people?" Peter asked. "Tom, don't you see, it's Mär who's been using all of us to effect his seditious obsession against Nrathěrmě! He's had Anhar killed; why would Anhar suddenly decide to fake his own murder? And he's lying to us about the Ämäthöär, and about Anhar. He is inciting us all to be afraid of Nrathěrmě, but he is the enemy whom we need to fight! Tom, don't you understand? He is the enemy."

"Mär?" Tom said softly.

"Yes, Mär! Not Nrathěrmě, not Anhar, not Anhar's spies. This Mär has come and taken over our world, but we must fight him. Even his own people," Peter gestured to the throngs of N'nüährnär around them, a great many of whom Tom could see were N'närdamähr, "Know that we have to free ourselves from him. They know that Mär's a fanatical madman. They know that he has gone much too far now."

"Yes," Tom said with a sneer, looking away from Peter at the armies around them. "They know that Mär's gotten into a situation that could cost him his life, and they're afraid it could cost them their lives along with him. They aren't fighting for you because they feel some noble need to free us from some tyranny of Mär's. They're fighting for you because they don't want to fight Nrathěrmě. They want to leave, and they want to justify themselves in doing it. Or have I not understood part of what you've said?"

Peter shook his head wearily. "Yes, Tom, like I said, they are afraid. They should be. They should all be afraid of bearing the consequences of the crimes of someone like Mär. *We* all should be afraid of staying near him."

Tom was baring his teeth without realizing it.

"We have to be afraid," Peter continued, "Of what Mär plans to do with us when Nrathěrmě's armies do come. We have to be afraid of being his shield, of being his hostages! Yes, Tom, we should be afraid, every one of us. Any one of us who isn't will fall right into Mär's hands. Tom, we must save our world, our people, our lives! And we must not aid this criminal!"

"The less we aid Mär," Tom growled, "The more we help the Ämäthöär and Sĕrĕhahn, and the more we will have to really be afraid of. Unless I'm misunderstanding things deeply, Sĕrĕhahn will not leave us Earthmen alone, no matter how far we put ourselves from Mär.

"And *that* is why Mär is here, Peter. Because Sĕrĕhahn does want to destroy us! Or do some thing worse to us. And without Mär and the Ōmäthäär, we don't have any chance against the Ämäthöär. So, please, don't do this to yourselves!" he said to them all. "Don't do this to us all!"

Any fear in him of the menacing armies had quietly evaporated.

"Tom, there are no Ämäthöär!" Peter said. "Not the spooky way Mär described them. You're buying the lies he's using to use us—"

"Shut up."

Peter looked deliberatingly at Tom. He glanced at the host of armed men and women around him.

But Tom couldn't care enough about himself to feel threatened at the moment. "Mär isn't lying, and you're just ignorant of the truth," he snarled, his voice rising sharply. "You ignorant imbecile! Don't tell me there are no Ämäthöär! There are!"

Peter put up his hands appeasingly, but Tom continued.

"Peter, you really have no idea what you're talking about, do you?" There was acidity in his voice that Peter hadn't expected of him. "You say there are no Ämäthöär. What proof do you have, Peter?"

Peter's mouth opened, but he quickly closed it again and adopted a superior expression. But Tom cut off his words before he could form them.

"Tell me, what proof do any of you have that Mär is a liar?" Tom looked up at the horde around him. "How are you sure that he's not telling the truth?"

He looked back at Peter. "Can you prove any of these things that you're so sure of?" he said with mocking indignation.

Peter shook his head and sighed. Then he looked at Tom confidently. "Can you?"

"Prove that Mär is telling the truth?" Tom asked.

"Yes, that's what I'm saying," Peter said, his confident air seeming slightly strained. "What proof do you have that we're wrong?"

"Ämäthöär!"

Peter rolled his eyes.

14: Training Begins

"Ämäthōär!" Tom said again, and though he felt dark again as he remembered them, a tingling warmth subtly filled him at the same time. "I know that Mär is not lying about them. If anything, he understated how terrible they are! I saw them!"

A slight tremor, as of hundreds of thousands of heads turning to look at one another, shivered the sphere around them.

"I saw them trying to kill Mär!" Tom said. "There is proof that Mär was not lying about that! I saw them fighting the Ōmäthäär!"

His voice had become passionate and intense. "You cannot tell me that there are no Ämäthōär. I saw them, and I felt them! They were terrible, Peter! *You have no idea what you are scoffing at!*"

He stopped, his eyes glaring at the multitude around him, which was rustling a little more. He looked indignantly at the fleets they had organized to oppose the Ōmäthäär.

"You N'närdamähr," he called, "You know very well that you aren't thinking of abandoning Mär because you believe this slander about him. I have not been with him as long as you have, but I cannot believe what Peter Garcia is suggesting about him, or about the Ōmäthäär! I have seen them fight Ämäthōär, and I know that they are not criminals, or liars, or oppressors or tyrants.

"But you all know, don't you," he continued, ignoring Peter's affectedly exasperated sighs, "That you want to leave Mär because you're afraid of Nrathĕrmĕ! You're afraid of giving your lives for the Ōmäthäär. And for my world!

"Whatever these ignorant guessers guess, I know, from what I have seen, that the Ämäthōär are terrible. They do want to destroy my people! And if you run to save yourselves, you will be abandoning us, abandoning my world!"

He looked at Peter, his eyes flashing, his voice rumbling with anger, but he still addressed everyone there. "You all think about what you know is right! What I know your parents and their parents have taught you."

He turned to leave. He smiled smally at a staring John Fleming, his fury melting away a little.

"Do what you know is best!" he said again to the crowd. "I'm out of here; I've been keeping Mär the liar waiting."

As soon as he said that he wished he hadn't. Surely they would not let him go to Mär, knowing what they were planning.

Fear of the firepower around them tightened inside him again.

But no one moved. Even Peter, who was standing there appearing unruffled, didn't offer any rejoinder.

John smiled weakly and very impressively back at Tom.

Tom shot away back toward Earth before anyone could decide that they did want to stop him. He hardly noticed that many of the people moved aside for him.

John looked back at Peter. The others with John gathered more firmly together.

John and Peter stared at one another.

"I can't believe..." Peter began quietly. "John, you betrayed us."

John gazed at Peter for a moment more. He had to banish unexpected tears as he said, "Peter, you are wrong. This time."

"John..."

"No," John said, forcing himself to look his best friend in the eye. "Peter, any enemy of Mär's is an enemy of mine."

Peter looked at John, incredulous.

No other words would come. John turned away and shot after Tom, people clearing out of his way more.

John's companions flew off after him, a few of them giving Peter or others nearby significant looks.

Peter stared after them. He felt the hundreds of thousands of pairs of eyes gradually flicking back toward him.

Naïve, he thought scornfully, coming back to himself.

But his armies around him were already starting to disperse.

"I'm sorry I'm late," Tom said as he hurtled toward Mär and the other Ōmäthäär in front of the majestic white Ōmäthäär headquarters.

"I'm glad you are," Mär smiled at him as he stopped abruptly in front of them. "I want you to tell me everything that just happened."

"Just when?" Tom said, confused.

"With Peter Garcia, just now," Mär said. "No, of course that's not why I called you here originally," he said, grinning at the baffled look on Tom's face. "But tell me everything."

"Gladly," Tom said, his disgust at Peter overcoming his nervousness about speaking to Mär.

"Well, I came right when you called for me," Tom said.

Mär grinned.

"But one of my assistants called to me just before I arrived. He said he really needed me. I told him I couldn't come over there. I told him to call someone else. But he said he really needed my help with something about

14: Training Begins

Peter Garcia.

"So I went to go help him," Tom said apologetically.

"That was John?" Mär said.

"Yes, John Fleming," Tom said. "How did you know...you knew?"

"John's a great person," Mär said. "You're lucky to have him as an assistant."

"I didn't know he knew you," Tom said, impressed with John.

"Neither does he, unfortunately," Mär said. "Go on, Tom," he smiled at Tom's expression.

"Alright," Tom said. "Well, I went, and I found John and a few other people arguing with Peter. Peter's raised an army. Mär!" He felt stupid for not telling Mär first thing. "They're going to try to take Earth! They want to leave. They say we can't fight Nrathĕrmĕ."

"They're right about that," Mär said simply. "But don't worry, Tom, Peter won't be starting any fights for now."

Tom didn't understand why Mär wasn't disturbed by this news of civil war in Nüährnär.

"It's because of you, Tom," Mär said on cue.

"What? Me?"

"Peter won't be making any major moves now," Mär said, "And it's because of what you and John just did."

"How do you know all this?"

"Well, I still need you to tell me what you did," Mär smiled. "But whatever it was, it's worked."

"How do you know?" Tom said again.

"Tell me what I want to know, and I'll tell you that," Mär said.

"Sorry," Tom said.

"Peter has an army, though, like I said. He's convinced a lot of your people, a lot of N'närdamähr I mean, to follow him. From what he was saying, it sounded like he's using their fear of Nrathĕrmĕ to get them to help him fight you."

Mär was watching Tom, but it didn't make Tom feel uncomfortable at all. In fact, it made him feel more at ease. His words started coming more easily.

"John and a group of other people were arguing with Peter and his supporters. Peter thought John would join him, but when John found out what Peter was planning, what Peter was doing, he wouldn't go along with him.

"So Peter was trying to convince John to help them when John called me.

"John's told me about Peter's ideas before, but I guess this was farther than he thought Peter would go.

"John stopped talking to Peter after I got there, and Peter asked me what I needed. I asked him what was going on. He told me that they were working together to free everyone from you.

"I couldn't believe that Peter still thought..." but then he trailed off. "What he told me before."

"That the Ōmäthäär are using you and lying to you about Sĕrĕhahn and the Ämäthöär," Mär said.

"Yeah, that," Tom said. "Peter says that Sĕrĕhahn is dead, and that you caused the destruction on Earth, and that Nrathĕrmĕ isn't going to try to kill us."

"I can see why he could think that," Mär said casually. "I do not think he has any good reason to think that we lied to him that the pirates were the ones who nearly destroyed Earth, but I can understand why he would believe that Nrathĕrmĕ would have no desire to hurt you Nōhōnŭäär. I'm sure most N'nrathĕrmĕ don't want to hurt you. But I'm also sure that Sĕrĕhahn has other designs."

"Like what?" Tom asked.

Mär smiled. "I'll tell you later. But his Ämäthöär are resourceful, and brilliant."

He looked at Tom expectantly then, and Tom knew he was waiting for him to go on.

"Peter's sure you're lying to us," he said.

Mär just smiled tranquilly.

"I didn't think he would have been able to convince so many Earthmen," Tom said, "But I think there were a few score thousand of them there. But I was surprised that there were a few hundred thousand N'närdamähr there.

"I think Peter's got the N'närdamähr to follow him because he can give them a reason to leave Nŭährnär." His anger was returning slightly, though he found it pleasantly hard to feel angry in front of Mär.

"Well," Mär said thoughtfully, "I'm really glad that they won't leave without a reason." He smiled as if to himself.

"So I told them that it would not be a good thing for them to leave," Tom said after a small pause. "I said it would help the Ämäthöär, that if they fought you they'd abandon their only defense against the Ämäthöär.

"Then Peter said there are no Ämäthöär. At least not the way that you described them to us."

Mär was smiling knowingly.

"I got pretty angry at that."

Mär's eyes were glowing.

14: Training Begins

"So I told him I had seen Ämäthöär, and I tried to say what they were like. Peter didn't say much after that."

"And I told the N'närdamähr that they were being cowards."

"Did you really?" Mär laughed.

"Yeah," Tom said, feeling a little ashamed now, but also encouraged by Mär's reaction.

"Why did you say that?" Mär asked.

"Well, because they wanted to leave. They were afraid for themselves and didn't care about defending their families and friends. They weren't loyal...I don't know, it just felt really selfish to me. They wanted to latch on to any justification they could get, even Peter's, to give themselves a reason to leave and not defend Nŭährnär."

Mär didn't say anything.

"I told them they were abandoning the Ōmäthäär and Earth. Then I left."

"Did John go with you?" Mär asked.

"No, he didn't."

"Don't worry, he's safe," Mär smiled at the suddenly fearful look on Tom's face. "I told you; what you said, and whatever John did after you left, confounded the armies of Peter Garcia. For now."

"It must have been John," Tom said ashamedly. "All I did was get angry."

Mär laughed. "And you said some really great things to them."

Tom didn't want to argue with Mär.

"Now, I told you I would explain how I knew what had happened with you and the others, if you would tell me what I wanted to know first." Mär looked placidly into Tom's eyes, then asked, "What do you know about Ärthähr?"

"I know a little," Tom said. "A friend of mine told me some about it."

"What was her name?" Mär asked conspiratorially.

"Sarah Trotter," Tom said. "How did you know it was a she?"

"I figured it was Sarah," Mär said satisfiedly. "She was just here, in fact."

"Oh. Why?" Tom asked, before he realized he was being nosy.

"For the same reason I called for you," Mär said.

Tom remembered fearing punishment, but that did not seem very likely anymore.

"But things happened so I couldn't meet with you both together," Mär said with cheerful disappointment.

Tom thought, for a fleeting moment, that he had seen a couple of the Ōmäthäär smirk at one another.

"What did Sarah say about Ärthähr?" Mär asked.

"She said that you, the Ōmäthäär, you guys, use it to fight the Ämäthōär. She said it's a force but that most people don't know very much about it."

Mär's cheeriness wilted, and his face looked suddenly fatigued.

"And she talked about a God," Tom said. "That's what she called it. Är."

Mär looked quickly into Tom's eyes. Then he smiled a little, the fatigue seeming to melt down into him.

"Well, I'm going to tell you more about Ärthähr," he said. "And about Är. If you want me to."

"Of course!" Tom said.

Mär reached forward and touched Tom's brow.

The rush of knowledge was overwhelming. But above the swirl of memories and theory and principle, all of Tom's attention was directed to the idea of Är.

"Yes, Är," Mär was saying, as if from far away, withdrawing his hand.

Tom didn't know what to say. He looked at Mär and the Ōmäthäär, only half seeing them.

"Tell me about Är," Mär said.

"It's real," Tom said breathlessly.

"He is," Mär smiled burningly. "But don't take my memories' word for it."

"What do you mean?" Tom said.

"I want, I need, Tom, for you to think about what I've given you. Be slow to draw any conclusions. Just think about it."

"There's so much," Tom said. He searched a little in his mind, recalling hundreds of Ärthähr battles. "So many Ämäthōär!"

"Yes, I gave you a few memories involving them," Mär said. "But you will be better if you concentrate most on memories of Ōmäthäär, and of Är."

Tom searched around and found a wealth of memories of Ōmäthäär. Memories of teaching other Ōmäthäär. Memories of wielding Ärthähr for good, to heal weary hearts, to encourage, to enliven, to inspire, to create.

He found he could understand the workings of Ärthähr, what it was, and what it wasn't. He knew lifetimes' worth of theory of how to use it, how to interact with it, and how to resist it. He glimpsed exciting views of what could be done with a mindful management of Ärthähr.

And he knew that the Ärthähr radiated from Är. His mind returned to Är, amazed at the idea of an actual, real-life deity.

"Now," Mär said brightly, after waiting for Tom to think for a bit.

Tom blinked and looked back at Mär. Many of the memories he had just sped through involved the seven Ōmäthäär behind Mär, and he was looking at

14: Training Begins

them now with reverent admiration.

"I told you I would explain how I knew that you and John helped to subdue Peter," Mär said.

"Ärthähr," Tom said.

"Yes," Mär said. I've been keeping an eye on Peter, so to speak. The decision to give him as much responsibility, and influence, as his tier incites wasn't an idle one. And the same goes for you," he smiled appreciatively, "And for Sarah. The Ōmäthäär who appointed you knew, though vaguely, that you ought to be given that kind of responsibility."

"That's amazing!" Tom said.

Mär laughed admiringly at him. "All we knew was that you would do well at this tier. We didn't know any more than that. But Peter has impressed and gratified those who appointed him.

"Yes, he has," Mär smiled at Tom's surprised look. "And it's because of the Ärthähr again that we're more excited about Peter Garcia now. Just about everyone at the higher tiers was appointed in that way, Tom."

"Thanks," Tom said, realizing what that implied about himself.

"You have also impressed us, Tom," Mär smiled. He fell silent for a moment. Then his smile drooped, his expression becoming somewhat more serious.

"I'm glad you came," he said.

"I want you to think about what I've given you. Don't tell anyone anything about it. Not your father, not anyone. But think about it."

"What about Sarah?"

Mär didn't answer at once. But then he grinned. "Yes, I did talk to Sarah about this too. Okay. But you need to think about it yourself, too. But only talk to Sarah about it privately. Even Härtärnär and Nan will know that they should not talk about this with you. Not now."

"I won't talk to anyone about it," Tom promised, "Except for Sarah. Privately."

"Thank you, Tom," Mär said. "I will call for you again soon enough. And if you have any questions about this before then, call me directly."

"Alright," Tom said gratefully.

"And don't worry about Peter. Maybe he'll want to talk to you more. But don't *worry* about him; he'll be fine."

Tom stared at Mär, forcing himself to believe him. He nodded.

"Well, get back to work, then!" Mär said. "But remember that thinking about what I've given you, just sifting it out, is more important than all the defenses or plans you can create."

"Thank you," Tom said. But before he flew away again, he said, "Can I ask you a question?"

"Anything."

"Did that Ämäthöär kill me? The one you were fighting."

There was no sign of fear or pain in Mär's expression at the mention of the traitorous assassins. "No," Mär said, and it seemed to Tom almost as if Mär's expression was triumphantly satisfied. "No, he did not. We stopped him before he could."

"Oh," Tom said. "I thought..."

"I know," Mär smiled. "No, you were very lucky. Unfathomably lucky." He smiled deeply at him.

"Thank you for being there," he said.

"Where the Ämäthöär were?" Tom asked.

Mär smiled. "Remind me to thank you for that better sometime. And now, get back to your managers. Remember, don't speak about this to anyone, except privately to Sarah."

"I won't," Tom promised.

Mär smiled exultantly, then grabbed Tom's arm and pulled him into a crushing hug.

"Thank you," he said quietly.

Tom was stunned. When Mär let him go, he just stood there for a few seconds, feeling confused.

"Thank you," he said then, and he turned to finally go take something of a break, his mind churning with a whole new world of ideas.

Chapter 15

Ärthähr Logic

"But I can't *use* it," Sarah said.

She and Tom were paddling about lazily in the warm shallows beside a golden-sanded island, a few days after their meetings with Mär.

"I know," Tom said, splashing the water idly.

"I asked Mär about it," Sarah said. "He didn't have much time at the time, but he told me not to worry about it. He just told me to keep thinking about it." She didn't add that Mär had also told her to talk to Tom about it; she still felt a little bashful at the enthusiasm with which he had suggested that.

Tom smiled. "That sounds like Mär."

"What about you?" Sarah asked.

"Same. I can understand how Ärthähr works. A lot of how it works, at least. But I can't do anything with it."

"I bet we don't know anything," Sarah said, smiling at her distorted reflection in the rippling water.

"Yeah," Tom said. "The next time we see Mär, I'm sure he'll tell us even more than he did last time, and we still won't know enough to use Ärthähr for much of anything."

"I hope not," Sarah laughed. "But yeah, that's probably the way it'll be."

"So," Tom looked fixedly at her, "Have you thought much about Är?"

"A little," Sarah said, but then they both heard Mär's voice come in their heads.

"This is Mär, manager and leader of Nŭährnär," his voice said. "I need all of you to listen to me for a few minutes."

Tom and Sarah smiled to each other.

"Any exercises, any construction, any relaxing," Mär said, "Ought to be set aside for now. I need all of you to give me your attention."

Tom raised his eyebrows.

"What I need to say concerns all of us in Nŭährnär.

"There are many points of view gaining influence among us. They are each different from the others; I won't elaborate on them in too much detail now.

"But the opinions of which I am speaking all draw one common conclusion: that we ought not to remain here at Earth and fight Nrathĕrmĕ's armies."

"Oh," Sarah said, thinking she could guess what Mär was about to say.

"Some of you believe that to fight anyone from Nrathĕrmĕ would be a betrayal of our very purpose as Nŭährnär. Some of you believe that it is foolhardy to remain here at Earth where Nrathĕrmĕ knows we are, and that we should flee.

"Some of you believe that I and the Ōmäthäär have been lying to you, that Sĕrĕhahn is dead and that I am deceiving you in order to gain your cooperation."

"Peter," Sarah said grimly to Tom.

Tom nodded, his eyes wide at Mär's bluntness.

"Some of you believe we owe it to our cause to abandon Earth, that we cannot prevail against Nrathĕrmĕ's military and that we owe it to our families and to our hope as Nŭährnär to leave, to hide.

"Many of you believe, for a multitude of reasons, that we ought not to fight Nrathĕrmĕ here."

Mär paused, then said, "I can understand that.

"We cannot hope to match a trace of Nrathĕrmĕ's military capacity. Were we to try, we would find that Nrathĕrmĕ is increasing in strength, in resources, and in innovation exponentially more quickly than we can hope to.

"That is part of why we as Nŭährnär have never attempted direct war against Nrathĕrmĕ."

Mär paused again, then said, "Most of us have never been to Nrathĕrmĕ itself. But those few of us who lived there, who can remember the Ämäthōär hunting us, the Ōmäthäär sacrificing themselves to clear a way for our escape, and who left friends and family at Nrathĕrmĕ, ought not to ever question our need to fight Sĕrĕhahn and his Ämäthōär.

"There are more of us born, every day, who have not experienced the awfulness of the Ämäthōär. Many of you believe that the Ämäthōär are a myth. Many of you believe that they cannot really be so horrible as those who have met them say they are.

"They are," he said emphatically.

"Only a few of us now were at Nrathĕrmĕ when we fled the Ämäthōär.

"When that happened, many of us who fled were killed. The Ämäthōär pursued us. Sĕrĕhahn pursued us."

Mär's voice filled with ardent passion. "Many of the greatest men and women I've ever known, our most wonderful and dearest friends, fought Sĕrĕhahn personally, to give us the opportunity to escape. They gave their lives in dreadful ways, so that some remnant of Ä'ähänärdanär could escape."

"Whoa," Tom said aloud, surprised at Mär's plain reference to

15: Ärthähr Logic

Ä'ähänärdanär.

"Those of us who survived those days of agony remember the dissension that arose among us as soon as we got clear of the Ämäthōär. Most of Ä'ähänärdanär wanted to leave Nrathĕrmĕ forever behind. Many of us believed that we could never again be strong enough to challenge the Ämäthōär, and that we could never stand against Nrathĕrmĕ's military power, should Sĕrĕhahn find us again.

"Many of us knew that it could only be a matter of time before the Ämäthōär found us again if we stayed near Nrathĕrmĕ to oppose them.

"And many of us believed that we had no choice but to flee far away. Ōmäthäär had fled away in the past, and no one among us knew where they had gone. But many of us believed that if we struck out away from Nrathĕrmĕ, that we could someday find a distant place where we could build anew our Ä'ähänärdanär, far from the Ämäthōär.

"But that plan was folly. Nrathĕrmĕ's innovations progress incomparably more quickly than do our own. You should all be aware that our ability to approach equaling Nrathĕrmĕ's technological understanding is due only to valiant Ōmäthäär who are even now hiding from the Ämäthōär in the heart of Nrathĕrmĕ, or who live among the pirate clans in the Wild Lands, who acquire N'nrathĕrmĕ technology and send it here to us. Those Ōmäthäär are our lifeline.

"Those who fled Nrathĕrmĕ back then have much the same technology now as we had back then. They have not progressed as Nrathĕrmĕ has. Flight from Sĕrĕhahn's Nrathĕrmĕ is at best a temporary respite. Before long, Nrathĕrmĕ will have the ability to find all who have fled. Nrathĕrmĕ will be able to search farther, and travel faster, and in time Sĕrĕhahn will overtake all who have fled.

"But here's why it was truly folly: The point of Ä'ähänärdanär was to catalyze understanding of the realities of Är."

Sarah froze in the water and looked at Tom, whose mouth was hanging open in surprise. He stared back at her as Mär kept speaking.

"The Ämäthōär and Sĕrĕhahn do not want anybody to know about Är. That, believe it or not, is why our culture is so saturated with the mindset that there cannot be a singe infinite being. And, if there were, I have heard said, we might not ever know.

"Är is.

"The Ämäthōär want to destroy us because the Ōmäthäär know a few things, quite a few things, about Är.

"To you who don't call yourselves Ōmäthäär, I am terribly sorry. Sorry to doom you to live the hunted life of the Ōmäthäär. But you cannot go back to Nrathĕrmĕ. Those who have done so, who have gone to Nrathĕrmĕ to try to live there in peace, have been taken by the Ämäthōär and forced to tell them all that they knew of us. Many of you remember that the Ämäthōär have been able to find us and kill millions of us as a result of our people fleeing to Nrathĕrmĕ.

"I would send all of you away if I thought it would be safer for you. I would send all of you to Nrathĕrmĕ without any reservation if I thought I could. But if you leave us, we will not be able to protect you from the Ämäthōär."

Mär paused, then said, "You may not know it, but your staying near us protects you constantly from the Ämäthōär.

"If you leave, they will find you. So I can't send you away from us. I love being near all of you, even if I don't yet personally know you, but I wish I could get all of you as far from the Ōmäthäär as possible. Your being here with us means you have to live in exile. And it means you have to live in fear of the attacks of the Ämäthōär. And now, it means you're in danger of Nrathĕrmĕ's armies.

"But your being here with us shelters you from the Ämäthōär. You are actually safer being here with us than if you left us.

"I am sorry to you who have been born into this. But, I really hope, your being put into this situation will mean greater opportunities for you than if you had been born safe in Nrathĕrmĕ.

"Because, like I said, the point of Ä'ähänärdanär is only to help people learn about how Reality works.

"Your living near the Ōmäthäär gives you the opportunity to know about Är, and that is a potentially limitless advantage.

"People at Nrathĕrmĕ, under Sĕrĕhahn's regime, know a great deal about the way Är works. Nrathĕrmĕ in general is more solidly established in terms of understanding the way life works, and living according to that.

"That's what Ä'ähänärdanär's about, teaching us all about how Är's Reality works. If we understand what is, and why it is, then we know better how to get anything that we want. If we don't understand how Reality works, we will not get what we want. We have to know what to do to get what we want to get, and we can only know that if we understand what we're working with.

"Ä'ähänärdanär is all about helping people know how to be solidly, peacefully happy.

"So the people at Nrathĕrmĕ have a great deal of what you have access to.

15: Ärthähr Logic

Sĕrĕhahn has taught them how to be happy. He has taught them how Reality works, and they all teach each other, helping each other understand how love and cooperation and humility work. It is because of the understanding that Sĕrĕhahn has instilled in Nrathĕrmĕ that Nrathĕrmĕ is such a wonderful, industrious, plentiful, wonderful place.

"But Sĕrĕhahn does not want them to know about Är. But knowledge of Är can help them more than anything else ever could.

"And you, being born into the lot of the Ōmäthäär, have the opportunity to learn about Är without risking anything worse than the kind of life you already are being forced to live.

"The purpose of Ä'ähänärdanär is to catalyze learning about Är. Correct knowledge can only come from Är, since Är is the infinite sum of all truth and has all knowledge; or from those who have received knowledge from him. Or from those who have been taught correctly by such people. Left to ourselves, our understanding of Reality will be full of the same holes and inconsistencies that we all have in our own minds and personalities.

"I challenge any of you to think of a situation in which you have learned, or gotten better in any way, in which Är was not involved."

Mär's voice then became very heavy and passionate. "We cannot leave the people of Nrathĕrmĕ! We cannot ignore them and flee when we have the knowledge that they lack, the understanding that will bring them incomparably more bliss and peace and greatness than they have even now, than they can ever have without it.

"Sĕrĕhahn is using the people of Nrathĕrmĕ. He wants to use their progress to help himself approach Infinity. He knows Är, but he hates Är, and he fears that letting the N'nrathĕrmĕ know about Är will lead them to oppose him. He will only let them grow insofar as he can use their growth for himself.

"We have to free Nrathĕrmĕ from Sĕrĕhahn, and from his tools the Ämäthöär! We defeat the very purpose of Ä'ähänär-danär if we leave them behind!"

There was a much longer pause then. After staring at each other for a few seconds, Tom murmured, "And he told us not to talk openly about Ä'ähänärdanär!"

But Mär's voice came back. "That was the real folly of that plan. To fly away was to abandon everything we've fought for. We might as well never have joined with the Ōmäthäär, and just lived safely and ignorantly at Nrathĕrmĕ.

"All of us have the opportunity to know about Är. To know what the Ōmäthäär know. To be and do what the Ōmäthäär are and what the Ōmäthäär do, and more than that. To enjoy understanding more and more of Infinity.

"You can stay here, and grow and learn and be more, or you can flee, and abandon what the Ōmäthäär have to give you and abandon the Ōmäthäärs' protection against the Ämäthōar and leave yourselves open to them.

"It should be an easy choice," he said brightly. "Except for the impending arrival of Nrathĕrmĕ's armies. And, I'm sure, Sĕrĕhahn will have packed along more Ämäthōar than many of us have ever seen with those armies.

"So our choice now looks like staying and facing certain death, thus making sure we will never free Nrathĕrmĕ from Sĕrĕhahn, or leaving and abandoning Nrathĕrmĕ to Sĕrĕhahn, and facing the Ämäthōar at some later time.

"We could leave here while still staying close to Nrathĕrmĕ. But the Ämäthōar will know that we were here, and our trail will be all too easy for them to follow from here. All we will accomplish by leaving here will be to burn away as energy much of the matter that we've gathered, which we could otherwise use as defenses. Now that we've all gathered together as one body, we're easy to follow wherever we go.

"We could split up as we've always done before now.

"But we must protect Earth. We will not harvest it. And we, the Ōmäthäär, will not leave it.

"The history and heritage of Earth is different from that of Nrathĕrmĕ. Earth must be preserved intact. And we must keep Earth from the Ämäthōar at all costs. The Ämäthōar want Earth.

"We must protect it. We cannot split up, lest we leave the protectors of Earth too weak against pirate clans, or against the Ämäthōar if we are not able to hide Earth from them.

"So we can either stay and fight what looks sure to be a hopeless fight, or flee and abandon everything we've always fought and lived this way for."

Mär paused again, for several seconds.

"But Sĕrĕhahn is wise, in his incomplete way, to be afraid to let people know about Är. I am sure that he has reasons for that that I do not know of. But we Ōmäthäär are reason enough now.

"We are no match, person for person, for the Ämäthōar. And Sĕrĕhahn may send more Ämäthōar than we have Ōmäthäär.

"But Är is smarter than Sĕrĕhahn is. Är is smarter than all the Ämäthōar put together.

"Though we be outnumbered, and outclassed, and outdone by the Ämäthōar and by Nrathĕrmĕ's martial power, Är, infinite Är, can provide us a way to defeat them all.

15: Ärthähr Logic

"And that is my choice, you my friends and my friends' friends: to stay, and exercise Är's miracles.

"You all know that a very small army can defeat a very strong one, if the smaller army has a potent enough strategy.

"Är knows better strategy than our foes do. We *will* come out conquerors here if we follow his plans.

"We Ōmäthäär are doing everything that we know how to do to follow Är's plans. Är has never asked more of anyone than that. But we cannot do this without you.

"Är has never forced me to do anything. He will not force you. His perfect strategies are no more than idle thoughts if we don't work according to them!

"And this much is undeniable to me: unless we stay here, and trust that Är will bear us through the rest of his plan, we will lose our cause, our dignity, and our lives.

"We Ōmäthäär will do what little we can do. But if we do our part but not all of you do yours, we may yet fail here. And Är will not hold responsible those who did their best."

Sarah's face was wide-eyed and fearful, but Tom noticed that she was smiling a little too. He felt like smiling himself for some inexplicable reason. The way Mär was talking about Sĕrĕhahn and the Ämäthōär was giving him a peaceful, secure feeling, opposite from the cold nakedness he usually felt when he would think about them.

"And now I need to say something else," Mär was saying.

"Many of you believe that we should not fight Nrathĕrmĕ. Some of you believe that we should not fight at all. Some of you believe that we should flee far away from Nrathĕrmĕ, so as to be peaceful by avoiding both pirates and Ämäthōär.

"Let me tell you about peace.

"Peace is more than a temporary avoidance of external conflict.

"Some of you have said, I know, that we cannot call ourselves Ōmäthäär if we fight, and kill, and intentionally wage war."

Mär paused for a second. Tom was surprised at how much opposition there seemed to be against the Ōmäthäär, right there within Nŭährnär.

"To be an Ōmäthäär is to want peace," Mär said.

"Peace is to be free from falsehood and misunderstanding. Peace is to be secure and to want what you get. That goes for people and for nations.

"To be an Ōmäthäär, to follow Är, is to be at peace within oneself. A nation that follows Är will be at peace in and of itself, even if all outside forces rage against it. To follow Är is to get what you want; to want what you get. For individuals and for groups.

"To be an Ōmäthäär is to want peace for everyone and everything.

"Including the people at Nrathĕrmĕ.

"And including Sĕrĕhahn and every single Ämäthōär.

"When others want our destruction, we have to seek for peace with them. There are a great many pirate clans who have helped us in ways that some of you haven't known, because we offered them cooperation when they offered us violence.

"But whenever we are beset, and have no choice but to defend what others want to destroy, then we are cowards if we do not fight.

"What is a coward? A coward is a person who is too insecure and afraid to have right priorities.

"A coward is someone who considers the avoidance of personal pain and hardship a matter of the greatest importance. He will not undergo pain or ignore fear in order to achieve things that only courage can achieve.

"Courage is putting first things first, even before personal comfort if need be. A coward puts personal comfort above all else, and thus never gets what he really wants.

"Peace, and comfort, and happiness, can only be had if they are paid for!

"Who wouldn't give up a little energy, in order to harness more inertia in return? Imagine if we never used the matter and energy that we have, and just sat still, unmoving, not playing, not making, not using the powers we have, because we didn't want to use up any of our energy!

"That's truly stupid, because using energy to incite inertial currents lets us take more matter and more energy into ourselves, in addition to playing, and building, and talking, and exploring, and living!

"That's courage. Knowing that we have to pay, that the only thing that comes from nothing is more nothing. Knowing that pain overcome leads to joy, that every mistake should lead to better understanding.

"One pirate, Ōärdhär I called him; he wouldn't want me to use his proper name; told me once that the only real happiness is to be found in oblivion.

"Some of the Earthmen, too, have a proverb, that ignorance is bliss.

"I say that ignorance may be bliss. Oblivion is surely a lack of pain. Or it may be ultimate pain, at least to approach oblivion. But blissful painlessness is also joylessness."

The smiling feeling in Tom felt like it had ignited as he heard Mär's voice go on, increasing in passion and in tempo.

"Ignorance may be bliss, and experience may bring pain. But after the

15: Ärthähr Logic

pain, if fear of the pain is disregarded and the pain is endured through, and we do not recoil from it, then comes knowledge and happiness.

"Peace is not weakness. It is not virginity to pain. Joy and wholeness is feeling pain but not heeding it.

"To be an Ōmäthäär is not, never has been, and cannot be to avoid external conflict.

"To be an Ōmäthäär is to make peace. Dethroning Sĕrĕhahn and the Ämäthōär is an inescapable first step for peace in Nrathĕrmĕ.

"And, perhaps, it is the best peace we can hope for for Sĕrĕhahn and for the Ämäthōär.

"And I, for one, cannot be at peace with myself if I do not do what I have the means and capacity to do for the people of Nrathĕrmĕ.

"I will not control or command any of you. But I will tell you what I know will work, and what I know will not.

"Abandoning things more important than ourselves in order to save ourselves can never lead to happiness. Abandoning Nrathĕrmĕ will not work.

"Opening our minds to believe those who know Är, and finding out if Är really is, and following the ways he will prepare for us, that will work.

"Find out about Är! It is about time that the Ōmäthäär be able to tell you about Är, and everything that we know about him.

"And then you will get to see Är's marvels, our tiny Nŭährnär thwarting armies many times our strength, and destroying a horde of Ämäthōär.

"Please, open your minds! Your selves! We cannot survive, not here, not anywhere, if we do not now begin to fulfill Är's plans.

"The time for lukewarmness is past. We must be as dedicated to our cause as the Ämäthōär are to theirs, and as the vengeful armies of Nrathĕrmĕ will be to destroying us.

"We have no time for selfishness. No time for pettiness, for self-centered cowardice.

"We must stand with Är, and thereby triumph no matter what Sĕrĕhahn sends at us. Otherwise, if we flee from Är and what he has coming up for us, we will fail no matter what we do. We cannot beat Sĕrĕhahn, or evade him, or survive against him in this encounter, unless we let Är show us how to defeat him."

Mär paused for a few seconds more.

"I know we can do well," he said. "I love you all. Do good. Back to work! Or play."

They didn't hear his voice anymore.

Neither Tom nor Sarah said anything at first.

When they realized that Mär was through, they just looked at each other in astonishment.

"I can see why Mär's the leader of Nŭährnär," Sarah said.

Back outside the Ōmäthäärs' headquarters, Mär smiled wearily at the Ōmäthäär around him.

He turned wordlessly and swept up to one of the Sentinels around the massive cube. "Ōhä-Ä'ähänärdanär," he said, clasping the man's right hand.

"Ōhä-Ä'ähänärdanär," the Sentinel said, staring somewhat questioningly at Mär.

Mär squeezed his hand, then passed into the side of the building.

Many walls and chambers later, he and the eight Ōmäthäär behind him emerged into the same room in which he had first met the Ä'ähärnhär two weeks before. The sound of conversation among the eleven hundred strong Ōmäthäär waiting for him quickly silenced itself as Mär glided into the center of the wide spherical room. The eight Ōmäthäär who had entered with him, joined by his other seven assistants from the walls of the room, formed a loose sphere facing him.

"I hope you know what you're doing," Ŭmäthŭ said.

A few of Mär's other assistants nodded their agreement with worried grins.

Mär smiled back at them. He looked around the room.

"Well, tell me what you think," he said fatiguedly.

There was silence. Some of the Ōmäthäär were smiling appreciatively.

"I agree with what Ŭmäthŭ said," Ōhärnäth said softly, "But not, I think, with what he means. We all hope you know what you're doing! I think you were right."

Ŭmäthŭ grinned. "What do you have to say for yourself, Mär?"

Mär smiled in a drained way at Ŭmäthŭ. "I know Är liked what I said, at least," he said.

"Then so must we," Ärdhär said lightly.

"I agree with you, too, Mär," said the Ä'ähärnhär from the wall.

"That is enough for me," Mär's assistant Thas chuckled.

"Ä'ähärnhär," Mär said wearily, "Can you confirm that Pp'm'tärnhär is here?"

"I can," the Ä'ähärnhär said promptly but apologetically.

"I wonder if Sĕrĕhahn knows that," Ŭmäthŭ said.

"*The* M'tärnhär?" one of the Ōmäthäär along the wall asked fearfully.

Mär looked at the Ä'ähärnhär.

15: Ärthähr Logic

"Their chief," the Ä'ähärnhär said heavily.

"It makes sense," Ährnär said.

"It fits," Äthääōhä said, "This being Pp'ōhōnŭäär."

"I think that is one of the reasons that Earth is Ōhōnŭäär," the Ä'ähärnhär said.

"I imagine Sĕrĕhahn would know that," Mär said quietly.

"But I have difficulty distinguishing between cause and effect with Är," the Ä'ähärnhär reflected.

Mär was floating deep in thought. He muttered, "Courage endures pain to reach victory."

Ŭmäthŭ smiled at him.

"Enduring the M'tärnhär's influence," Mär said, looking up, "Will get us the glory of Ōhōnŭäär!"

"But we do have to endure his influence," Ōhärnäth said.

"The N'nŭährnär have to know as much about Är as they can; you know that," Mär said. "But our contact with Ōhōnŭäär is changing a lot for us.

"I said what I thought was appropriate."

"And I think we're all delighted that you said as much as you did," Ŭkan said. "But you caught even us off guard. I, at least, didn't know that you were going to tell them all so much about Ä'ähänärdanär."

"I didn't either," Mär smiled tiredly. "But it came, and I knew that that was what I had to say."

He looked around the room at all the proud Ōmäthäär. "Pp'm'tärnhär will find a way to destroy us, from without or within, or both, unless we cleave together and unless Nŭährnär accepts Är now.

"We've been given the opportunity of benefiting from Ōhōnŭäär. All of Nŭährnär must rise to merit that opportunity.

"I will be extremely surprised if I, and you, don't find ourselves talking openly about Ä'ähänärdanär a lot more frequently."

Ŭkan smiled.

"We have been led here for a lot of reasons, obviously," Mär said. "I only know a few. We have to teach the Nōhōnŭäär about Är as quickly as we can."

He looked at the Ä'ähärnhär, who was beaming confidently at him.

"We cannot risk overwhelming them," Mär said, "And ruining people like them. But," he hesitated, "I think that we will not need to hold back very much."

He nodded to Ŭmäthŭ and Ōhōmhär.

Ŭmäthŭ nodded, and turned with Ōhōmhär to face the rest of the Ōmäthäär. "We have already begun teaching a few Nōhōnŭäär," he said to them. "We've found that some of their cultures are usually more open to comprehending Ärthähr than others."

"Your people, Ä'ähärnhär," Ōhōmhär smiled at the Earthman, "The ones of your people we've been teaching, are phenomenally receptive."

"Those from Europe and the Americas are more like our own people," Ŭmäthŭ sighed.

"However," Ōhōmhär grinned, "That makes it only fitting that the two most exciting Nōhōnŭäär we've met with so far are both from the Americas."

"One of them was already of your Order," Ŭmäthŭ raised his eyebrows at the Ä'ähärnhär. "But both of them look extremely promising. So much so," he said with a sidelong smile at Mär, "That Mär is insisting on training them himself."

Mär nodded gratefully at them, and they turned back to face him.

"One of them," Mär told the Ōmäthäär around him, "Thomas Joshua Pratt, is being protected by Härtärnär and Nan." He nodded, beaming, at Härtärnär and Nan. "His father, Lewis Richard Pratt, is an assistant to Zämŭth and Zad. His mother, Mary, is dead.

"The other, Sarah Rose Trotter, is being protected by Nōvagähd."

"She's everything they say she is, and more," Nōvagähd said from the wall.

Mär laughed, but it was muffled with fatigue. "Sarah's parents are Scott Joseph Trotter and Rene Melanie Fielding Trotter. They are assistants to Händhär and Härthäōt.

"We must protect Tom and Sarah at all costs. There is something about them.

"Tom saw us fighting Hōnhŭ and Ämharŭ. As soon as Hōnhŭ saw Tom, he tried to kill him. His desire to kill Tom superseded even his concentration on eliminating me."

Not a one of the Ōmäthäär so much as flinched at the mention of the traitorous Ämäthōär.

"Hōnhŭ, I think," Mär continued, "Saw something in that instant in unschooled Tom that I am only beginning to see. Pp'm'tärnhär, surely, can see the same thing. He will try to kill Tom and Sarah unless we protect them. They need to be guarded and watched and shielded constantly.

"I don't want them to know that they're being guarded, not yet.

"Tom and Sarah together have the potential to defeat Sĕrĕhahn."

He said it declaratively, but then looked just as surprised at the statement as the other Ōmäthäär did.

He laughed loudly; his fatigue had gone. "They may! If we teach them

15: Ärthähr Logic

and protect them. I will teach them as quickly as can be done.

"Härtärnär, Nan, and Nōvagähd have the immediate responsibility of protecting Tom and Sarah. You three, ask any of us at any time to assist you if you so much as suspect you might need it."

"Thank you," Nōvagähd nodded.

"We will," Härtärnär said.

Mär clapped his hands as energetically as usual. "We've spent enough time talking! Let's be done with meeting and get on with doing!"

"Thanks, Annie," John said, flying up to where she waited, far from the remains of any of the planets.

"Sure," Annie said. "I'm glad you're still talking to me."

"You didn't tell Peter, did you?" John asked.

"No, I didn't," Annie said, distinct sadness in her voice.

"Thanks, a lot," John said. "Not that I want you to think badly of Peter. But..."

"I think I understand a little bit," Annie said.

John was relieved to see her smiling at him, even though she looked worried behind that.

"I think I understand what you and Tom Pratt were saying before."

"Does Peter?" John asked hopefully.

Annie looked away morosely.

"I'm really glad you'll talk to me," John said after a moment of awkwardness.

"Won't you talk to Peter again?" Annie pleaded.

"No," John said, but he didn't say it as firmly as he wanted to.

Annie looked sadly at him.

"I don't want to be his enemy!" John said. "I don't want Peter to be Mär's enemy either, though. I *want* to talk to him."

"Then why don't you?"

"He's wrong this time!" Now John's own passion surprised him.

"I know," Annie said.

John stared at her. "You...you don't believe him either?" he asked slowly.

Annie looked away.

"I believe Mär," she said. "I think."

"All this time?" John asked.

"No," Annie said. "I wasn't sure. I'm not sure still. Peter really makes sense."

"But so does Mär," John said.

"Yeah, Mär does make sense," Annie said. "But it's not like Peter. With Peter, I can see exactly what he's talking about. It's all clear, it all makes sense. It's undeniable. That's what I though before.

"But I just can't believe that Mär's been lying to us."

"Neither can I!" John said. "Not after what Tom saw. And Tom's talked to Mär himself."

"I haven't," Annie said. "But after hearing him speak yesterday...I don't know. He makes sense, even though I don't really understand why. I don't know how to say it."

John smiled. "That sounds more like you."

"What do you mean by that?" Annie asked defensively.

"Believing things you don't understand, I mean," John said admiringly. "You didn't use to be as logical as you've been since...since this."

Annie smiled too, but the smile faded into a brooding look.

"Peter's always logical," she said with a worried smile to herself. "I like it."

"So did I," John sighed. "But he won't consider that he could be wrong."

"I know," Annie said. "He almost never is wrong. He isn't used to it. He's so smart. But this time, I'm afraid his mind may be crowding out smarter parts of him."

"You think he is wrong this time," John said.

Annie didn't answer at first. She was still looking away. But then she answered, "Yes, I do. This time."

"Then you talk to him!" John said. "He won't listen to me."

"He will," Annie said. "You're his friend!"

"Not like you," John insisted. "He won't threaten you—"

"He won't threaten you!" Annie said. "He won't *threaten* anybody."

"Okay," John said. "But can you talk to him first? If you can get to him, then he will listen better to me."

"I will talk to him," Annie nodded. "I don't know if I can change his mind, but I will talk to him. And you should, too."

"Okay. But I want you to tell me first what he says to you."

"John, this is your friend," Annie pleaded. "Just go talk to him. You don't need to wait for me to report to you! Don't you think I'm worried?"

"I know you are."

"No, John. Peter loves me. What will he think of me when I say the same things the people he's been calling blind have said to him?"

"He loves you!" John said. "What do you have to worry about? If there is anyone Peter will listen to, it's you."

15: Ärthähr Logic

"But John, I'm worried, so why should you let your worry stop you from talking to him?"

"I can't say that Peter 'loves' me, Annie," John said with a wry grin.

"No," Annie said. "I think he does, John. I think you both do. You haven't talked to him at all these past few days, but I've seen how torn up he's been that you gave him away to Tom Pratt.

"Not that I'm saying you shouldn't have!" she said quickly, as John had drawn himself up defensively. "But he cares about you more than he admits."

"He calls me blind, and stubborn," John said softly. "He's the one being stupid and stubborn!"

Annie laughed a little. "You're being plenty stubborn right now," she said warmly.

John closed his mouth and looked angrily at her.

"See?" Annie said. "You care about him. That's why you're angry. That's why you called me here."

"Do that to him," John smiled through his still sullen expression. "Make him look bad just by being annoyingly sensible and patient. I know you; you can beat any amount of logic with that."

Annie blushed and didn't say anything.

"That's why you should talk to him first," John said.

"Alright," Annie said resignedly.

"Thanks," John said.

Annie smiled at him. "Wish me luck," she said. "And soon you'll have your best friend again."

"Either that, or he'll become everything he's been accusing Mär of being," John said sourly.

"Don't say that," Annie said in a hurt whisper.

John was quiet for a couple seconds. "Sorry," he said quietly.

"Don't you become everything you're accusing my Peter of being," she said evenly.

That caught John by surprise. "What?"

"Just be nice, John," Annie said wearily, as if the conversation had caused her great pain.

John looked thoughtfully at her. But then an admiring grin found its way onto his face. "Good luck," he said.

"You too," Annie said sorrowfully.

John smiled uncertainly at her, then waved good-bye.

Annie was standing there alone for a long time before she went to find Peter.

Chapter 16

Initiation

"Whoa!" Tom said nearly three days later. "Sorry, John! I didn't realize you were coming!"

He had been hurling matter around feverishly, sending it this way and that as he made new platforms. He had been so absorbed in his designing and planning that he hadn't noticed John approaching him, and John had been having to dodge back and forth to avoid being hit by the newly formed vessels as Tom hurled them away from the cloud of instreaming matter.

"No, it was fun," John said.

He flew up to Tom, who was still directing the matter but was now being careful to direct it away from John.

"Anyway," John said, "They couldn't hurt me at the speed they were going."

"Good," Tom laughed. "Sorry, though. I guess I just got carried away with this."

"Again," John smiled at him.

"What?"

"You work too much. Tävna and Spalding are running a story right now."

"Oh, I forgot," Tom said ruefully.

"Yeah, right," John said. "You got carried away, like you say."

"Why aren't you there?" Tom asked.

"I should be," John said. "The way Spalding was talking, Tävna's really excited about this. I think she made most of it up herself."

"I should see that!" Tom said. "Wasn't she going to do something fantasy, like Andrew's Tasirak story?"

"Spalding didn't say," John said. "But I think Terry said something about time travel. You should go check it out."

"Is that why you're here?" Tom asked. "You should have just called me."

John hesitated. "No, it's not."

Tom looked more directly at him, paying less attention to the hurtling matter.

"It's about Peter," John said.

"Peter?" Tom said, sounding anxious. "What about him?"

"Oh, no, he's not doing anything," John said. "That's what I wanted to tell you. That he isn't doing anything."

16: Initiation

"What do you mean?" Tom asked.

"It's not pressing or anything," John said. "But Annie just talked to me, and I wanted to talk to someone else about it."

"And you knew I would be 'carried away' working," Tom smirked.

"Yeah, I guessed," John said. "So I am glad that you're too anal to be having fun with your friends right now."

"I just forgot!" Tom said.

"But that's what Annie told me," John continued. "She's had a talk with Peter, and she says Peter's giving up the whole thing."

"Giving it up?" Tom said, amazed.

"That's not what she said, exactly," John said. "But that is what it sounded like."

"That's wonderful!" Tom said. "But what happened?"

"Well, maybe he hasn't completely given it up," John said. "But it looks like he has."

"What happened?" Tom asked again.

"Well, a little while ago I talked to Annie," John said. "She wanted me to go talk to Peter. But I had called her in the first place because I wanted her to talk to Peter. She said she would. She doesn't believe Peter anymore."

"Why not?"

"Well, because of you, I think," John grinned. "And because of Mär."

"Me?" Tom said.

"Annie was there when you chewed Peter out, remember?"

"I didn't notice," Tom said. He searched in his memory, and realized that Annie had been there right beside Peter. And now that he saw her in his memory, he realized how very small and withdrawn she had seemed.

"She was there," John affirmed. "I think she already had doubts by then, and what you said made that worse. And then, after Mär's speech earlier..."

"Oh," Tom said, surprised but pleased that Mär's words had had such an effect on someone so close to Peter.

"She's just told me that she can't think anything bad about Mär at all," John smiled, "Much less believe that he's a liar, and oppressing us."

"Good," Tom said absently, but his thoughts were recalling that that surely must have been what the N'nrathĕrmĕ felt about Sĕrĕhahn.

"I haven't talked to Peter myself since we talked to him," John went on, "But Annie says he's not been being very active about opposing Mär since she talked to him. That was about three days ago now."

"What did she say to him?" Tom asked.

"I don't know," John smiled, "But Annie has a way with Peter. But I think that after what you said, and after Mär's speech, hearing Annie make him look like a fool must have done it for him.

"And now Annie just told me that she thinks Peter's starting to consider that Mär could have been telling the truth."

"Wow," Tom breathed.

"Annie said that some of his followers came and talked to him a few hours ago," John explained, "And he wouldn't talk plans with them. She didn't tell me exactly what happened, she wanted to get back to him and wouldn't stay talking to me for very long, but it sounds like he told them that the plan's off."

"'The plan?'" Tom asked.

"They had lots of plans," John said heavily. "To outsmart Mär and take Earth, I think."

"Good luck beating Mär!" Tom said indignantly.

"But I think he won't try, now," John said, though it sounded as if he were pleading with himself to believe it.

"Wow," Tom said again.

"Yeah," John said.

"Thanks, a lot, John," Tom said after a silent moment. "I think you and Annie may have saved lots of lives. Especially Peter's!"

"Yeah, Peter's," John said quietly. "And, I hope, some friendships too."

Sarah was sitting with Nōvagähd, Härtärnär and Nan, and a score of other Ōmäthäär in the wavy blue of Earth's Atlantic Ocean. The water stretched out in every direction, reflecting the gleaming pale blue of the sunless sky. Mär and Tom were in the center of the group, clasping hands as Mär lifted Tom up from under the surface.

"Thanks," Tom smiled brightly at Mär. "Of course, I could have gotten out of the water by myself…"

"You're missing the point," Mär said, winking at him.

"Sarah," Nan said privately, as Härtärnär glided past them toward Tom with a couple other Ōmäthäär. She motioned for Sarah to come away from the group.

Sarah floated through the choppy water after her.

"You started to ask Nōvagähd about his wife a moment ago," Nan said seriously to her as they stopped. "Ask me instead."

"Oh," Sarah said, understanding. "Is his wife…"

"Yes," Nan said in a strange hard voice. "He would say he doesn't mind talking about it, but don't bring it up."

"Thank you for telling me," Sarah said. "I'm sorry, I didn't know."

16: Initiation

"That's why Mär cut you off," Nan said, grinning and glancing up at Mär, who was touching Tom's head.

"How did he know that was what I was going to say?" Sarah asked.

"I don't ask that kind of thing," Nan smiled.

"Okay," Sarah smiled too.

She hesitated for a second, then asked, "Can you tell me what happened to her?"

"Ämäthōär," Nan said, shrugging.

Sarah stared at her.

Nan smiled. "Nōvagähd misses her, Sarah," she said. "That's why I don't think you should talk to him about her. But he isn't exactly sad."

"Why?" Sarah asked, taken aback. She would have thought that such a subject would have made Nan solemn, but instead her smile only deepened as Sarah asked.

"Pō'ärthähr, Nōvagähd's wife, is an Ōmäthäär," she said. "Nōvagähd misses her terribly. I don't think anyone could've imagined seeing Nōvagähd and Pō'ärthähr parted." Nan laughed. "They were almost the same person, the way they acted."

She looked over at Nōvagähd, who was taking his hand off of Tom's head, laughing as he said something private.

"But I can't say that Nōvagähd's worried about her," she said.

"When Ahathrĕ killed her," Nan's voice hardened again, "Nōvagähd was devastated. That was almost five weeks ago now."

"Five weeks?" Sarah said. "That's not very long at all! That's right before you got here!"

"Nōvagähd's incredible that way," Nan said. "He knows what condition Pō'ärthähr's in right now. He mourns, but only privately. He mourns not having her with him all the time. But he doesn't mourn the way he did right after Ahathrĕ killed her."

"Ahathrĕ, he's the Ämäthōär who killed her?" Sarah asked.

"We knew him from Nrathĕrmĕ," Nan said. "Nōvagähd killed him, but the Ōmäthäär had feared Ahathrĕ since before I was born.

"But Sarah, Nōvagähd mourned Pō'ärthähr's death because it was a terrible, cruel death. He could imagine what it must have felt like for her to be whittled away to death by Ärthähr."

Nan's expression had become drawn and tense. "Ärthähr is the worst pain I've ever felt. Ever imagined. When it's used by Ämäthōär.

"Nōvagähd didn't mourn his separation from her nearly as much as he mourned the pain which he knew she had had. But now, he doesn't worry about that anymore. He knows that Pō'ärthähr is just fine."

Sarah smiled, feeling a warm glow as if it were radiating off of Nan.

"But don't ask him about it," Nan said. "When an Ōmäthäär dies, the Ōmäthäär mourn the least. And that's because we envy the ones who are done."

Sarah didn't know how to take that.

Nan chuckled at her obvious confusion. "Don't worry, Sarah," she said. "Ämäthōär or no Ämäthōär, life as an Ōmäthäär is a life unlike and greater than any other! But I've tasted some of what's coming up after this phase of our lives, after we die. I think nowhere is an Ōmäthäär's valiance greater than in his courage to stay alive, when so many of us know a little of what we can expect when we die.

"I think that if some people could see what we see," she said, "They would kill themselves! Just to get to it."

"Well, if Heaven's that great," Sarah asked, "Why bother fighting the Ämäthōär?"

"'Heaven?'" Nan said. "No, Sarah, if people did kill themselves, or give up fighting for good, to get to some *place* called Heaven, they would be horribly disappointed.

"Heaven's already in you! The advantage of dying is that our current condition blinds us to a large extent to the Heaven that we already have, that we *are* ourselves, and dying removes that barrier.

"But if you aren't happy enough, 'Heaven enough' you may say, now, then the mortal condition only dulls the pain that's already in you. If you die, the pain won't be dulled like that anymore.

"Ensuring that people don't do something as horrible as kill themselves to get to a Heaven and find themselves in their own hell is cause enough to keep them from knowing, yet, what death can be," she said with a patently serious smirk.

"As for us," she added, "We fight the Ämäthōär because the Ämäthōär are keeping *so many* people from receiving what could give them so much more happiness! A lot of us struggle to stay alive only so we can help everyone else here become happier."

"How do you know, though?" Sarah asked, now full of awe at the heroes surrounding her.

"About death?" Nan said. "Well, a lot of us have had previews," she grinned. "Not that I've ever died, but, well, I'll let Mär teach you all about that.

"And that's why Nōvagähd isn't at all sad for Pō'ärthähr. But he misses

16: Initiation

her. Don't make him talk about her, unless he mentions her himself."

"Thank you for stopping me," Sarah said in a hushed voice. She found herself feeling now like she was in the company of venerable emperors and empresses, powerful and wise and righteous beyond comprehension.

"Thank you, for being open to this," Nan smiled.

Sarah looked back at Mär and the others. They all seemed to be talking privately together.

"Nan?" she asked softly. "Can you tell me something? About Mär?"

"No, not now," Nan said. She was looking at Härtärnär. He wasn't facing them; he was looking at Ärdhär; but Nan said, "I know that look. They're waiting for us. Can you ask me later?"

"Okay," Sarah said. She followed Nan back through the rising and falling waves to the cluster of Ōmäthäär and Tom.

"I thought you would never finish," was Härtärnär's jovial greeting.

"Girl talk," Mär smiled knowingly. Somehow Sarah was sure he knew exactly what they had been talking about.

"Well," Nōvagähd said to Tom, "I hope to see you again soon."

"Thanks," Tom said.

"We'll give him time," Nan said.

As the Ōmäthäär gradually drew away, Sarah realized that they all seemed to be leaving except for Mär.

"I'll see you soon, Sarah," Nōvagähd said to her as he rose out of the water.

Sarah realized she was staring at him. "Oh, yeah. Bye."

Nōvagähd smiled and shot up away.

The Ōmäthäär straggled off. Soon only Ärdhär remained, talking silently with Mär.

Tom caught Sarah's eye. He was beaming uncontrollably.

Sarah laughed a little and looked back at Mär.

Ärdhär smiled and clasped Mär's right hand. Mär hugged her, and she hugged him back. They backed away then, but Mär clasped Ärdhär's right hand, smiling gratefully at her.

Ärdhär backed away and rose into the air. "You two take good care of him," she said brightly to Tom and Sarah. Then she too disappeared into the clean blue sky.

"Tom, how do you feel?" Mär asked enthusiastically.

"Incredible," Tom said.

"I can tell," Mär smiled.

Sarah sniggered.

"So, first, what questions do you have?" Mär asked, relaxing into the water and looking penetratingly from Tom to Sarah.

Tom glanced at Sarah, still grinning deeply and apparently unconsciously. "We've had a few."

"Yeah, I have one," Sarah said to Tom. "Doesn't your mouth hurt?"

Mär burst out laughing.

Tom chortled too, though not nearly as heartily as Mär. "This is all new to me, Sarah!" he said.

"I know," Sarah said. She flicked some water at him.

"Anyway," Tom smiled, turning to Mär and deftly deflecting the water away with inertia, "Why do you hold hands that way?"

Mär held out his right hand to Tom. Tom put forward his left hand, and Mär reached forward and took it.

"What I just did isn't the best way to do it," Mär said, "As I'll explain now."

"But look at our fingers."

Both Tom and Sarah saw that Mär and Tom's fingers were interlocked, each resting on the back of the other's hand.

"Your lowest finger is on top of mine," Mär pointed out. "And your thumb is on top of mine. The right hand stands for giving, and the left hand receiving. So this means that you regard me as someone who can give something to you. It can mean anything: teaching, comfort, counsel, or friendship, or esteem, even. Anything that you recognize as me giving to you.

"So, to exemplify the symbol, the right hand should never take the left hand. The right hand can be offered, but the left hand has to do the receiving. Only the receiver can choose to genuinely receive."

"Okay," Tom nodded.

"But my lowest finger comes before yours," Mär said. "I give first, then you receive with your finger counter to mine. But that isn't enough. The process, be it teaching, or loving, or whatever, is progressive. I teach a little, you receive a little. Then I teach a little more, with the next finger. Then you receive with your finger complementary to it. Then the next set of teaching and receiving fingers.

"The thumbs are different. The other fingers represent the infinite progressions of giving and taking. The thumbs rest on top. They symbolize the pinnacle of the relationship, when all giving and taking make each other into Infinity.

"But it's not complete unless the receiving thumb is on top. I can give you everything! But you have to receive it, or it will mean nothing to you."

"Wow," Tom said impressedly, as Mär released his hand.

"Then why did Ärdhär give you her right hand? Sarah asked.

"I took it, you mean," Mär smiled. "It's okay to take a right hand if it isn't offered, though that can frighten people into thinking you expect something of them.

"I give all I know how to give to Ärdhär, and everyone, but she gives a great deal to me. I would not be here if it weren't for her."

"Why?" Sarah asked. "What happened?"

"Ärdhär happened!" Mär said. "But that's for later. One finger at a time."

"Fine," Tom said.

"You have some more questions, don't you?" Mär said.

"Yes," Sarah said, looking at Tom.

"How did Nüährnär come to be?" Tom asked.

Mär smiled. "Can you keep secrets?"

"Uh, yes, we can," Tom said, nodding at Sarah's nod. "Your secrets."

"Meaning you can't keep everyone's secrets," Mär smiled.

"No, I mean," Tom began, but Mär waved his hand unconcernedly.

"I hope you can't," he said to both of them. "A lot of secrets aren't worth keeping. But can you keep mine?"

"Yes," Tom and Sarah both said together.

Mär looked satisfied at that.

"I like music," he said. "It's beauty of sound! Good, well-fitting words are wonderful music. Rhythm, tone, rhyme, alliteration, they're all music.

"A topic such as this deserves a little more music than just fitting words, though."

He closed his eyes. A deeply peaceful smile crept across his relaxed face.

Then the water started vibrating. A mellow, perfectly harmonic hum of seven different interlacing and progressing chords started emanating from all around them. The chords rose and fell, weaving in and out of one another in an exceptionally calming yet exciting way.

Sarah sank lower into the humming water, lulled and stirred by the subdued tones emanating from everywhere.

Then she realized that Mär was speaking. But the tones and articulations of his words were inseparable from the intermingling rhythms and tones singing out of the water:

Oh, sing of Är! Ōmäthäär!
Of glory, life, and light!
Of noble ones who see afar
The pow'r of truth's delight!

Light and Glory

The waves dancing around them were following a rhythm complementary to the beat of Mär's words, but it was a complex, fluctuating rhythm. The beating of the waves seemed to accentuate both the intensity of Mär's words and the intersections of the flowing chords of song.

Who've fought, and lived, and sacrificed
To save Nrathĕrmĕ and
To see that what was done sufficed
To finish what was planned,
To reconcile the wonders whom
Foul Sĕrĕhahn has fooled,
And set alight! and all abloom
Their latent and unschooled
Potency and intelligence!
Who have not shrunk from Är,
Whose love and faith and diligence
Will stand as a memoir
Forever, though so many such
Are murdered, hunted, sought,
By recreant knaves who ever clutch
For that which they know not;
By self-deceived Ämäthöär,
And Ämäthöär who
Do not know that they serve the bar
Of all that they pursue,
Who don't know that the very key
To everything they want
Is being hid from them by the
One they call their savant.

Mär opened his eyes, and the melodies continued in a graceful, tense way, as if they were waiting for him to speak again.

"You want to know about the split of Ä'ähänärdanär," Mär observed, his quiet voice fitting perfectly with the suspended rhythms.

Sarah and Tom both nodded.

Mär grimaced faintly, and the music gradually built. Then his voice threaded its way through the exact center of the tones, coming much more quickly now, but also dignified and poised:

Banished and hunted, my family all massacred,

16: Initiation

More than four years I was waiting
Far from Nrathĕrmĕ, away from the unconquered
Paradise never stagnating.

His face was more peaceful again, his half-closed eyes staring off into the clouds away on the distant horizon.

There were Ōmäthäär there,
Fugitives hiding,
Chased from the home of their loved ones.
Long I had been with them, our
Aims coinciding,
Fighting the abominations
Whom we called Ämäthōär,
Who had gone astray,
Erring, who would not understand.
We knew the Ōmäthäär
Still at Nrathĕrmĕ
Were soon to strike at Sĕrĕhahn.

The music intensified more:

Sĕrĕhahn found them, their Ä'ähänärdanär.
Long they had hidden, but no longer.
One by one the Ōmäthäär, now discovered,
Fell to their fell foes who were stronger.

The music became frantic:

Ahntä, their leader, knew then what was happening.
The Ärthähr was raging, plainly foretokening
Sĕrĕhahn's killing stroke toward them hastening.
The Ämäthōär had caught them unsuspecting;
Their plans to strike Sĕrĕhahn were unraveling.
All hope of successful attack was darkening,
And hope of successful defense was blackening.
Instantly he ordered flight; not abandoning
Nrathĕrmĕ, but leaving its halls enlightening,
To flee the Ämäthōär, and there, captaining
Ä'ähänärdanär, and there, championing

Light and Glory

What was right, they would all bide their time, strengthening.

Mär sighed. He looked at them sadly as the music retarded.

I met them then.

But the Ämäthōär found them.

The music burst abruptly out with sudden fervor:

En masse they came:
Ämäthōär;
R'bathĕrŭ;
And Sĕrĕhahn.
A burning flame
Was Ahntä then,
With armies of
Ōmäthäär.

They overcame
A few of the
Ämäthōär,
But Sĕrĕhahn
Did not misname
By very far
The ones he'd trained:
"R'bathĕrŭ."

Ahntä they slew.
The greatest ones
Of all of the
Ōmäthäär
They overthrew,
And scattered all
The remnants of
The League of Är.

The water was trembling with the tempo of the music. Mär was openly weeping.

16: Initiation

A few of us, only, escaped.

The music softened and slowed.

The others were destroyed.
Ä'ähänärdanär was raped,
And we were left devoid
Of all our gallant, great leaders.
Those paltry few of us
Were left as the soul impeders
Of Sĕrĕhahn's jealous
Campaign to stifle Nrathĕrmĕ.
So, quickly there emerged
A desperate dichotomy.
Our outlooks were diverged:
The Ōmäthäär owned to stay
And yet fight Sĕrĕhahn.
Most others wished to flee away
To hide off farther than
N'nrathĕrmĕ or pirate bands
Could find or could pursue,
To pass by e'en the Wild Lands
And there set up anew.
Not five thousand Ōmäthäär
Were left among us then.
Two hundred thousand others were
Our fam'lies and our friends.
A tiny few Ōmäthäär
Suggested that we flee,
And they became the guiding star
Of those whose loyalty
To everyone in Nrathĕrmĕ
Was subject to their fear
Of Sĕrĕhahn and their dismay
To direly persevere.
We would not war amongst our own.
We wished our loved friends good.
And they set off to lands unknown
As swiftly as they could.
These hundred weeks and more, our band

Has fought these awful foes.
But knowing we can not yet stand
To openly oppose
The dreaded Ämäthōär, we
Have waited, planned, and sought
For any opportunity
That might avail us aught
Against this mighty enemy.
But never had I thought
That here, so close to Nrathĕrmĕ,
Lay the One World that bought
All life from death, and misery,
Oblivion and rot!
Pp'ōhōnŭäär we
Had found! Now all we've fought
For, I think, will not futile be.
Our vict'ry here, hardbought,
May lead us to the victory
O'er Sĕrĕhahn's foul plot!

The trembling waves melted out in a series of gradually diminishing swells. The music softened, still playing in the background but now almost indistinguishable from the sounds of the wind and the waves.

"I think I've given you more new questions than answers," Mär said, smiling with weary enervation that Tom and Sarah had never seen in him before.

"Can I ask," Tom said reverently, "Why did you call yourselves Nŭährnär, and not Ä'ähänärdanär?"

"And," Sarah said, glancing at Tom, "Can you tell us what Pp'ōhōnŭäär is?"

Mär smiled admiringly at them, but then his expression became strange and uncertain.

"No," he said very slowly, after an odd pause. "Not right now..." His voice trailed away, as if he had fallen off into some inmost corridor of his thoughts.

Then as if Mär had known it was coming, a frantic cry burst into their heads:

"*Pirates! We're under attack!*"

Mär looked intently at them; his eyes were blazing and earnest. "Do

16: Initiation

exactly as your managers tell you!" he commanded with mortal passion.

Without another word or glance, he rocketed past them, into the sky in the east behind them.

And just as he did, they heard Härtärnär and Nōvagähd's voices burst into their heads.

Chapter 17

The Decisions of Peter Garcia

Mär arrived in the deserted spherical room within the Ōmäthäär headquarters.

"This is it," he called to his assistants. "They're back. I'll direct from the Sanctuary."

"Ŭkan, make sure that Peter Garcia is held in the back. Make sure that he is given command of a full battalion. And that it doesn't look suspicious."

Ŭkan didn't answer, which Mär accepted as his affirmative.

He closed his eyes. Within his mind, he could see all that Nŭährnär knew about the battlefield.

Only small bits remained of the planets around them and only a dying ember was left of the sun. Streams of matter were pouring slowly toward Earth, becoming thicker and more tightly packed as they converged on the armored world.

The pirates were approaching from every angle. Mär could see already that they had almost six times the matter of all Nŭährnär.

And they'll be as skilled as ever, he thought with somber regard.

N'nŭährnär who had been harvesting matter were flying toward Earth, away from the approaching armadas. The pirates were holding together, only pursuing the closest N'nŭährnär.

"To battle," he said collectedly to his assistants.

"Remember what we practiced," Händhär's voice called to Scott and Rene, who were encased in a larger vessel among the defenses around Earth.

"Everyone hold back!" Scott said to their assistants.

"There are so many of them," Rene said fearfully beside him.

"Watch their movements," Tom said to his assistants. "Keep our patterns tight. Gennadiy, Hua-Hua, be sloppy with your movements. Make them think we're weak in places we aren't.

"Stick close together still. No one fire.

"Look for patterns in their movements as they come in closer. If you can, try to spot which ones are the commanding ships."

The pirates were coming closer, but their advance was slow and measured. They weren't using much energy on stealth, which struck Tom as foreboding

17: The Decisions of Peter Garcia

of some sudden move.

"Keep a close watch. Be ready for them to disappear. Don't worry about stealth yet."

"Let them take as much of the harvested matter as they want," Mär was saying. "I believe they expect us to try to keep it for ourselves. Make sure that no one is that reckless."

"They outnumber us already. And if I know pirates, we're going to be terribly outskilled.

"But I do not think that these pirates have reckoned on Ōmäthäär," he said with a resolute grin.

"Sarah, you hold back!" Nōvagähd said in her head.
"Everyone, hold back," Sarah said to her assistants.

"Peter, please," Annie said. She was staring in horror at the pirate armadas closing in on them, waiting for directions from her manager.

"I'll fight," Peter's voice said in her head. But his tone implied, "For now."

"I love you," he said.

"I love you," Annie said. "Be careful."

"I'm watching your fleet. I will come if you need me."

Annie smiled to herself but didn't answer. She was terrified that she would need Peter's battalion to protect her only too soon. And that that, even, would not be enough.

The pirates were drawing the harvested clouds of energy swiftly toward them as they drew closer and closer to Earth. The clouds that had been taking days to reach the planet were now being drawn to the pirates within seconds.

New pirate fleets were materializing rapidly out of the clouds' matter.

They drew still closer.

"They won't use all the matter," Mär was saying. They want us to expect them to wait to attack until they've gathered everything within safe distance of themselves. So they'll move in before then, just for the surprise of it.

"So now don't be surprised."

"Let them take it," Sarah said. "We'll get it back."
"Will we?" N'fävan's voice said darkly.
"We've got Mär," Sarah said. "We've got the Ōmäthäär. Pirates won't

beat them." The burning zeal she had felt while hearing Mär's song was ringing in her.

"Stealth, *now!*" Härtärnär's voice commanded in Tom's head.

"Everyone, stealth, *now!*" Tom said, willing his own vessels to intensify the laterally flowing inertial fields on their surfaces.

Not two seconds later, the pirates burst forward at them, their ships fading in and out of sight as they too fell into stealth. Trillions upon trillions of half-invisible vessels surged at them with a tremendous burst of speed.

"Evade them, confuse them!" Tom shouted. "Stealth!"

"Torpedoes!" he heard an Ōmäthäär shout.

A hail of miniscule crafts was rocketing toward them, flashing through the charging ranks of pirates.

Tom's vessels blasted streams of rantha at them.

"Shoot them!" he yelled.

The torpedoes crashed into several of Tom's ships. Many others streaked past them and smashed terribly into the Shell.

"Charge for the break at 130°, 54°!" Sarah said. "Ōhärthär, Bal, Xuezhong, make for the hole there at 129°, 47° to draw them off, then double back to cover our flank!"

The pirate fleets and the N'nŭährnär armies clashed in a storm of rantha.

"Hao, cut them off!" Scott shouted, spotting an overextended branch of the nearby pirate armada.

A wing of Hao's fleets arced down behind the overextended pirates.

"Surround them!" Scott said.

"Watch our back," Rene said to him.

"Evade them!" Scott shouted then. His fleets had managed to decimate many of the surrounded pirates, but not before two other branches of pirates swept in on them from above and from the left.

"Help!" Scott called to Händhär.

More pirates were diving toward them, pressing their advantage. Scott realized with horror that his assistants Rämharŭ and Krōg had just been annihilated.

A group of N'nŭährnär flotillas, spitting rantha at the pirates, pierced into the pirates' encirclement just enough to break ways for Scott and Rene and their armies to extricate themselves.

17: The Decisions of Peter Garcia

"Back!" Rene called to their assistants as Scott steered their fleets away from the answering wave of pirates. Rantha caught more of their ships as they retreated behind other N'nŭährnär.

"No, Sarah," Nōvagähd's voice said levelly in her head. "Not yet. Fall back to Earth."

"Call me if you need me," Sarah said. "Violet, let it go! Everyone, back to Earth!"

"I'm on it," Tom answered Härtärnär, charging his fleet toward a critical flaw in the pirates' formation near him.

"No!" Härtärnär said. "You sweep left to cut them off if they come from there below Pōthäth's fleet."

Tom wheeled his armies around, dropped them under a charging swarm of pirates, and pulled up to cut them off, as he made his way to where Härtärnär had ordered.

"Tom, what about that opening?" John's voice said.

"Härtärnär's got someone else to do it," Tom said.

Another, smaller fleet was attempting to scatter the pirates away from the vital chink in their formation, but Tom could see already that the pirates were gaining the upper hand over them.

"I can still save it," he called to Härtärnär.

"No, Tom," Nan called back firmly.

"No! What are you doing?" Annie screamed at her assistants. One assistant's fleet had broken away, pelting back toward Earth, and now three others were following as the pirates closed in around them.

Blazes of rantha erupted from the pirates as they arced straight toward Annie.

She pulled up and out of their path, and sent much smaller volleys of rantha back at them in answer. Her fleet was getting surrounded.

"I don't care!" Mär was shouting. "It doesn't matter! Keep Annie Baker safe! Don't provoke Peter to come out too soon!"

"Annie, we can't get out!" her assistant Juan called to her, obviously terrified but still directing his assistants' fleets to fight alongside Annie's.

Annie didn't answer, overcome with the same realization herself.

"Annie, go down, now!" called the voice of an Ōmäthäär.

She saw with transports of relief that an enormous group of Nŭährnär's fleets was arcing up from below her.

"Everyone, down, *now!*" she commanded, and buried her tattered fleets in the mass of N'nŭährnär charging past her.

I could do it now, Peter was thinking to himself. His enormous fleet was still standing near Earth, watching the pirates steadily overcome the valiantly struggling N'nŭährnär. *This is my chance.*

Maybe Mär had been telling the truth. But how could he have been?

I could get Annie and head for Nrathĕrmĕ, right now.

But what if Mär was right about the Ämäthöär?

What if the pirates will accept me if I let them know that I'm not with Mär?

But if there really were Ämäthöär like that, if Tom was right, and if Mär was not deceiving them, then he had to stay with them!

But then, Mär did not seem like the most balanced person.

"Hold them together as much as you can," Mär said as more and more of Nŭährnär's fleets began to scatter.

But his voice was anything but anxious.

The pirates were quickly breaking Nŭährnär's fleets apart from one another.

The disconnected N'nŭährnär were being driven wherever the pirates chased them.

"Bäbät, Rämhasöhän, what's happening to your fleets?" Tom said desperately.

"They won't listen to me!" Rämhasöhän called back.

"I think they're trying to make a break for it," Bäbät said.

Tom put himself through to everyone in his fleets. "*We cannot lose as long as we have the Ōmäthäär!*" he shouted. "But we can't win if we don't follow them! We'll win if we're courageous and go where they're telling us to go!"

"Anŭsths," Mär said, "If you tell your divisions to break out over there to attack the pirates from behind, they'll counter that and scatter your divisions away. Your people will flee, I think, and that could start a chain reaction."

"I'll try," Anŭsths answered.

"Through that gap!" Scott heard Händhär order.

17: The Decisions of Peter Garcia

"Down through the gap at 56°, -77°!" Scott said to his assistants. "We'll come around behind them!"

Scott and Rene's fleets seemed to be emboldened by this stroke of luck, seeing the gap in the pirates' arrangements. The order was carried out with zeal.

Some smaller fleets that had been splintering away merged back with Scott and Rene's fleets as they plunged down and around behind the pirates.

"This could work!" Rene said with terrified hope.

Rantha burst from their fleets, confusing the pirates, who apparently had not noticed the flaw in their arrangements before Nüährnär had taken advantage of it.

"We've got them!" Scott cried.

The N'nüährnär fleets soared upward and back, pinching the nearby pirates between them and the rest of Nüährnär. The pirates relented a little in their advance inward, focusing firepower and maneuvers against the new foes behind them.

"Now, make sure that Peter Garcia's given foolish orders," Mär said. "Enough to irritate him.

"And Äthääōhä, get Annie just close enough to Peter that he could escape with her. But give Peter enough space."

"Mom! Dad!" Sarah shouted, realizing that her parents were in the fleets that were so suddenly being shattered by the pirates.

For a shining moment, much of Nüährnär had thought that they might gain the upper hand over the pirates, as they watched the Ōmäthäär Anüsths and Tärnär's divisions swoop through a hole in the pirates' interweaving formations and assault them from behind.

But three swift moves by the pirates had shattered what hope they had briefly had. The enclosed pirates had hurled themselves straight into the center of Anüsths's fleets. At the same moment, two other branches of pirates had broken away from scattering N'nüährnär divisions to block off any other N'nüährnär fleets from aiding Anüsths's fleets. And then several more groups of pirates swooped down to back up the pirates who had pierced into Anüsths's fleets, cutting off the rest of Nüährnär from helping them.

"No! Keep in formation! We can counter them!" Scott shouted as half of his fleets fled madly away.

The scattering fleets didn't answer, but accelerated out away from Earth and away from the pirate hordes. Hundreds of other smaller fleets began breaking away to follow them, too.

"Loyalty won't get us anywhere if all our fleets are gone," Rene moaned.

"Sarah, what are you doing?"

Sarah didn't answer Nōvagǎhd. Her fleets were peeling away from her in panic, but all her immediate assistants followed her as she charged directly into the mass of pirates between her and her parents' disintegrating fleets.

"R'nväg, left and up!" she ordered. "Ōhärthär, straight ahead! Everyone else, follow me around below, but dance around to confuse them."

"What?" Tom breathed as he realized that those were Sarah's fleets that had just barreled past where he was looking.

Sarah's remaining ships plunged themselves straight into the swirling broil of the pirates that were scattering Anüsths's people.

Tom didn't tell anyone else to follow him. He thrust all the ships under his own control toward Sarah's fleets.

"Tom, what's going on?" came Rämhasōhän's voice, his fleets banking aside to pursue Tom's.

The others followed suit, though more and more of their fleets were deserting madly away now that they saw they were heading right into the heart of one of the densest pirate swarms.

"*Tom, no!*" Härtärnär shouted.

Tom ignored him. "Sarah, what are you doing? Get out of there!"

He hurled his fleet onward more quickly, flying straight forward. The rest of his fleets were pulling evasive maneuvers while still trying to keep up with Tom's own ships.

"Tom!" he heard Nan shout. "We need you back at Earth! Turn around!"

Tom hardly heard her.

"It's my parents, Tom!" Sarah cried back to him.

Tom shouted maniacally, plunging his fleets into the rampaging pirates.

Mär was laughing loudly.

"Don't worry about them!" he said gleefully. "Let Tom go, and Sarah too. They'll be fine. They will now!"

He could see Tom's fleets merging with Sarah's. All around them the N'nŭährnär were scattering, some of them retreating toward Earth but most fleeing out and away from the pirates and the battle.

* * *

17: The Decisions of Peter Garcia

"Divide my fleet?" Peter said back to his manager Mŭdhōär.

"We need part of it over here, but we need other parts of it at 12°, -27° to counter the pirates there, and at 215°, -18°," Mŭdhōär said.

"That's desperate thinking!" Peter said. "We can't spread ourselves too thin! Let the pirates come to us!"

"Peter, we need your fleets!" Mŭdhōär insisted.

Peter paused, uncomfortable about denying an explicit command. "No," he said firmly. "You bring your fleets to me, if you want. But I am not dividing this division."

Forget this, part of him thought. Mär's faction was finally getting what it deserved.

Annie's fleets were pulling back toward Earth. He could escort her out of this mess. And he could lead anyone else who wanted out along with them.

"Peter," Mŭdhōär began.

"I'm going in," Peter said defiantly, pretending and partly intending to go help the scattering N'nŭährnär nearby. "We have enough fleets here at Earth to manage."

"Peter's on the move," Ŭkan's voice said.

Mär watched wordlessly as Peter's fleet accelerated toward Annie's.

"Sarah, no!" she heard her father cry. "Get away!"

Her fleet converged around the remnants of her parent's fleets, as Tom's fleets and her assistants' fleets tried to fend the rantha-blasting pirates away.

But the pirates were too many, and Tom and Sarah's ships were dwindling rapidly.

The majority of Nŭährnär was fleeing the pirates, and the pirates were breaking off in every direction to pursue them. But there were still so many pirates around the Trotters and Tom and their companions that Sarah could already tell that there was no hope of escape.

"Peter," Mär said pleadingly to the walls.

There was Annie, Peter saw. He almost turned his fleet toward hers.

But what if Mär was actually telling the truth?

But there's nothing I can do about that now! he thought, and he was surprised at the despair he felt knowing Nŭährnär was on the verge of being destroyed.

Then, as if in answer to his despair, he saw it.

The N'nŭährnär were scattering. The pirates were chasing them, apparently satisfied that their prey was beaten and routing.

The pirates were breaking away from each other.

One well placed flotilla, just about the size of his battalion plus his managers' divisions, could set up for a beautiful encirclement. If only the fleeing N'nüährnär would see that and turn around quickly enough.

But Mär couldn't have been telling the truth!

Then he heard Annie's soft voice in his memory: *The real reason you don't want to believe Mär is because that would mean you were wrong.*

But Annie! He had to get Annie!

If I take this move, I could save her and Nüährnär.

But it was ludicrous! How could there be something as supernatural and evil as Mär claimed the Ämäthöär were?

And why would Anhar fake his death?

And why would Nrathĕrmĕ follow such an evil mastermind as Mär told them Anhar was?

If Mär was so good, why did Nrathĕrmĕ want to kill him?

And why was Mär so desperate to rule Earth? Why didn't he just let Nrathĕrmĕ take care of them?

Really, why would Nrathĕrmĕ ever want to destroy Earth?

What if these pirates will take us in, now that they've practically broken Nŭährnär…

How dare Mär call this "Nŭährnär," "Refuge?" It's a prison of fear and deception!

But then he heard Annie's voice again: *Peter, you know so much. How much might there be that you don't know, then?*

That hadn't made sense to him when she had said it, he thought.

But it still touched him.

I trust Mär because of my heart, Peter.

But what if she had just been being sentimental over a well rehearsed speech?

But he remembered Annie's tearful face: *Peter, I love you, but I hate being around you now. I hate who I've become. I hate the contracted, blind person that logic has made me.*

But that, too, was just emotional ignorance.

Peter, I love you, she had said. *But I hate being around you now. I hate who I've become.*

I hate who I've become.

Around you.

I hate what logic has made me.

17: The Decisions of Peter Garcia

He was crying, he realized. He could not do this.

I trust Mär because of my heart.

Peter, you really have no idea what you're talking about, do you? What proof do you have, Peter? Tom Pratt's contorted voice resurfaced in his memory.

You're so sure you know what's going on! Sarah Trotter had said. *You have no idea!*

He remembered John: *Peter, you are wrong this time. Any enemy of Mär's is an enemy of mine.*

But John had been being stupid!

Hadn't he?

I trust Mär because of my heart, Peter.

Any enemy of Mär's.

Because of my heart.

I trust Mär.

He willed himself to drive his fleets toward Annie. At least he thought he did. But then he realized that he was charging straight into the part of the vacated space left behind the pirates' dispersing patterns.

And he realized that he was the one doing it.

And as soon as he did, everything fell into glorious place in his mind.

"Mŭdhōär!" he shouted. "Get your fleets over here! This is it! We've got them! Call anyone, everyone!"

Mär whooped with delight. "He's done it!" he shouted at the walls. "Peter!"

To Peter's surprise, Mŭdhōär didn't hesitate at all. Every one of his nearby fleets charged after Peter, decisively cutting the pirates off from one another.

"The rest of Nŭährnär is already being told to close back in on them," Mŭdhōär said with startling cheerfulness.

Yes, we've got them! Peter thought.

"Mŭdhōär, send some fleets up and others forward and to the right!" he called.

His manager didn't answer, but Peter could see several large fleets already speeding in those directions.

"Come up around them!" Peter said.

The N'nŭährnär fleets that had been held back at Earth now surged forward, decisively cutting the pursuing pirates off from one another from behind. The pirates had broken away from one another to pursue the fleeing N'nŭährnär, and now many of the fleets around Peter were racing forward alongside the pirates, cutting them off one group from another.

"Out that opening, 14°, 32°!" Tom shouted. The pirate patterns around them were breaking up, some of them turning back toward Earth, the others spiraling about confusedly.

His, the Trotters', and their companions' fleets flew panicking out of the gap that he thought could be their last hope of survival.

"Pull back toward Earth!" Scott and Rene heard Händhär order. "Close in around them!"

"What?" Rene said.

"We're not attacking them again?" Scott said fearfully.

But then he realized that the pirates were fleeing away from them, toward Earth, trying to counter the masses of Nüährnär's fleets that were herding them apart from each other.

Sarah realized what was going on.

"Everyone, chase them! Open fire on their rear!"

Her scattering fleets were slowly remassing around her.

"We can surround them!" Tom said to everyone in his fleets. "Come back; we can surround them!"

He swung all his fleets forward, closing around the pirates, who were being distracted by the unexpected arrival of the divisions from Earth. More fleeing N'nüährnär were beginning to return to help hem the pirates in.

"It's working!" Peter shouted, surprised at his own ecstasy.

"Brilliant!" his assistant Äähröar called to him.

"Peter, you just saved us all!" Z'mōth, another of his assistants, said, recovering from tears by the sound of her voice.

It was the first time his assistants had expressed confidence in him in what he suddenly felt had been far too long.

Sarah was laughing and crying at the same time. "We're saved!" she cried to her assistants. She banked her fleet nimbly to the right to intercept a fleeing surge of pirates.

More and more N'nüährnär were returning as the tide of battle shifted. The chain reaction of Nüährnär's encouragement happened more rapidly than

17: The Decisions of Peter Garcia

had the cascade of its scattering.

The pirates still outnumbered the N'nüährnär, but being broken up now into more than a hundred smaller parts, and every one of those parts being more and more tightly surrounded by the N'nüährnär fleets, the pirates were dwindling quickly.

The battle ended within a matter of minutes. Nüährnär's advantage increased exponentially. The pirates lost more and more freedom to maneuver, thus allowing Nüährnär to take more and more of the matter from their waning fleets.

In the end, after the pirates had ignored numerous offers of peaceful surrender by the Ōmäthäär, they were all annihilated. The Ōmäthäär were emphatic that none be allowed to escape away, and Nüährnär carried out that exhortation decisively. A few groups managed to put up a chase away from Earth, but they were caught before getting very far.

When the storm of battle ended, Nüährnär was saved but in ruins, the pirates were all killed, and almost a billion N'nüährnär had been killed as well.

And Peter Garcia was a hero in Nüährnär.

Peter came back to himself. The pirates were almost completely wiped out, and as the intensity of mortal battle faded, the magnitude of what he had just done began to sink into him.

He had just saved Nüährnär. He'd just saved Mär. He had just turned back against everything he had been planning and believing for the past eternally long weeks that he'd been in Nüährnär.

And he had never felt more fulfilled, more right, in any decision in his life.

"Yeah!" he cheered loudly to everyone around.

His ship melted away off of him, breaking derelictly apart and floating away.

He punched his fist high out in triumph. *"Yeah!"*

"Peter!" several of his assistants cheered loudly.

"Peter!" his managers Müdhöär and Ōärnär shouted too.

"Nüährnär!" Peter shouted, punching both hands high above his head.

He felt like he was on fire. He wanted to cry, or scream for joy, or something.

"Peter!" someone else called euphorically.

He turned quickly just as Annie crashed headlong into him, hurling him backward past converging throngs of cheering N'nüährnär.

"Peter, Peter, Peter!" Annie squealed, soaking him with kisses and tears.

Peter didn't try to hold back tears any longer. He held Annie tight into himself, laughing and crying and kissing the top of her head.

"I can't believe...You saved us all! You did it! Peter!" she sobbed. "You did it!"

"Peter, you hero!" he heard John bellow just before he too crashed into them, scooping them both up into his arms.

"I'm sorry," John said, holding them both tightly in his arms.

Peter extricated himself, and looked John in the face. "No, John," he said. "You saved me."

He grabbed John into a powerful embrace then, John bursting into tears.

"Room for one more!" laughed an all too familiar voice, just before Peter saw Tom Pratt shooting toward him at top speed.

Peter moved away from John to face Tom warily.

But Tom hit Peter just the way Annie had. "Peter!" Tom shouted right in his augmented ear. "Peter! You're awesome! You saved us! You're the man!"

Peter didn't know how to react to this.

"Thank you, thank you, thank you!" Tom said, releasing Peter and gazing worshipfully at him.

"Er, well, thanks," Peter stammered at Tom.

Tom looked deeply into Peter's eyes and smiled at him. "Forget everything I said to you. Before. You know."

Peter had felt a little reluctant to find himself on the same side as Tom. Having to face Nüährnär, and people like Tom, made giving up his former accusations against them more difficult. Not only had he to admit that he had been wrong, but that the people whom he had considered naïve had been right.

But, now, even he could not think that Tom Pratt's smile was the condescending grin of Mäōhä, or the faked smile of Ähŭhan or Ōhärkrahan.

Tom never had been naïve, or small minded, he saw with a pang of recognition.

"Never," he said, but he was smiling.

Tom raised his eyebrows questioningly.

It was I who was being small minded, Peter realized within himself.

And if Tom hadn't been, a voice that wasn't his own whispered within him, if there really were such phenomenal beings as the Ämäthōär who had such terrible power, then it was he, Peter, who had been being profoundly, embarrassingly naïve.

"Tom, you were right," Peter said stoutly. "I will not forget the truth, the facts, that you tried to wake me up to."

17: The Decisions of Peter Garcia

Annie's voice came forward again in his memory: *Peter, you know so much. How much might there be that you don't know, then?*

Chapter 18

On the Genealogy of Victory

"That's the last of them," Särdnä's voice said in Mär's head.

Mär bowed his head. "Alright," he said mournfully.

"We all hate killing pirates," Särdnä said empathetically.

Mär smiled about Särdnä's peacefulness. "We did wonderfully," he said then.

"Yes, we did," Särdnä said. "Peter did wonderfully."

"I'm very glad it worked," Mär said emotionally. "I was afraid he might fail out on us there. But he was smart enough after all."

"And you risked most of our lives in the process," Särdnä laughed.

"Yes, we did," Mär said shakenly. "But it did work. Är always knows best. I'm very glad he knows Peter so well."

"For Peter's sake," Särdnä said pleasedly.

"We've got a lot more matter to work with now," came Ŭkan's voice.

"Here Särdnä and I are congratulating ourselves about Peter Garcia, and you are concerned about war, Ŭkan?"

Ŭkan laughed. "Of course, Peter's decision was the greater victory today."

"But what do we do now, Mär, about the rest of Nüährnär?" Särdnä asked.

"Revive all who will revive, draw in all the matter, encourage and congratulate Nüährnär," Mär said obviously.

"Do you think that was all the members of this clan?" Ŭkan asked.

"No," Mär said. "But I think it was their main strength. They were only testing us when they attacked thirteen days ago."

"But this was the worst of them?" Särdnä asked.

"Yes, I'm sure of it," Mär said regretfully.

"Their matter will help us against later attacks," Särdnä's wife Äōdhä said.

"A little," Ŭkan said.

"Yeah," Mär said. "But we need convicted hearts like Peter's."

"Yes," Ōhōmhär's voice came in. "This seems like a purging of Nüährnär to me."

"Let us hope that there will be few who need to be purged," Ŭkan said.

"I don't know," Mär said quietly.

"Should we call back the people harvesting other systems now?" Ōhärnäth asked.

"Yeah," Mär said, closing his eyes. He put himself through to all his

18: On the Genealogy of Victory

assistants. "The harvesters of other systems should be called back now."

"How quickly?" Bävän's voice asked.

"No more than twelve days," Mär said.

"Theirs will be all the matter we will get," Ŭkan said.

"I think courage, courage in Är, will be more important than all the defenses of Nrathĕrmĕ for us now," Äthääōhä said.

"I won't even consider calling back our people in Nrathĕrmĕ," Mär preempted, "However much courage they could give us."

"Why is that?" Ōhōmhär asked.

"I do not know!" Mär laughed.

"At least, we want to keep as many undiscovered Ōmäthäär in Sĕrĕhahn's field as we can," Ŭmäthŭ said.

"Well, we haven't heard from many of them in more than three weeks," Mär said. "I've felt forbidden from trying to contact them."

"Är has other plans," Tärnär's voice smiled.

"Yes," Mär said thoughtfully. "It may well be that our survival depends on the secrecy of whatever they're up to now."

"So we still cannot risk messages even?" Ährnär asked.

"I guess not," Mär said. "They never existed, as far as we're concerned, for now. All Är has told me is that they must remain undiscovered, as if they are under such surveillance now that even a message may reveal them."

"But if the Ämäthōär have found them out, or even suspect them," Ŭmäthŭ said, "The Ämäthōär will act on that. What do you think is going on?"

"I don't know," Mär laughed softly. "But no one send any message of any kind—not even Ärthähr; *especially* not Ärthähr—to anyone who does not first send us a plain message."

"What about the ones in the Wild Lands?" Anŭsths asked.

"Perfect maneuvering, by the way," Bävän said.

"Thanks," Anŭsths said gratefully.

"He's still shaken," Tärnär said.

"Aren't we all," Mär said quietly. "It's a miracle that so few of us got killed.

"About those in the Wild Lands, it's up to your judgment. And they aren't much more dangerous to contact than they usually are.

"But this is important," he said. "No pirates, or independents," he grinned, "Are to come to us except those who are ready to follow Är. Any Ōmäthäär among unknowing pirates may return; we may need them against Sĕrĕhahn's attack; but no actual pirates are to be allowed to fight for us unless they are pledged and oath bound to follow Är."

"Understood," Ōhärnäth said.

"Yes," Äthääōhä said. "And you should get some rest, Mär."

"This is our test, a test," Mär said. "I, for one, will not rest anymore until this part of Är's plan is complete."

"Oh no!" Tävna said, sitting up sharply amid the tall stalks of grass. "Now you'll never have time to be in our story!"

"I may," Tom said, settling himself amid the grass in the muddy earth beside them all.

"We'll show you how it goes, if nothing else," Spalding said comfortingly.

"I'm just teasing," Tävna said. "Your responsibilities are more important than this."

"Not more important than you guys," Tom said.

"Yeah, but we *are* your responsibility, aren't we?" John said. "You're laboring to protect all Nŭährnär; that includes us."

"I hope I get to be with you too, though," Tom said. "I'm not your manager anymore, either, John, so you'll be as neglected as my family."

"He is family!" Tävna said, scooting toward John and hugging him.

"Who are you to invite people into our family?" Spalding asked in pretended reproach.

Tom noticed Andrew and Terry exchange the tiniest fleeting look.

Terry saw Tom looking quizzically at them, and she moved deliberately toward John. "Well, I say he's family," she said authoritatively.

"Good," said Tävna, grinning gloatingly at Spalding.

"Uh, yeah," Spalding said.

"What?" Tävna said, looking closely at him.

"Nothing," Spalding shook his head offhandedly. He just smiled warmly at her, then turned jerkily to Tom again.

"So," he said, and his voice had an uncertainty that Tom had never heard from him before, "Yeah, we don't mind. We love you; we'll be happy to see you whenever you get the opportunity."

"I could just tell Mär no," Tom said lightly. "Tell him I don't want to move up a tier."

"Two tiers," Lewis reminded him proudly. "And I don't advise it."

"Yeah, Dad got promoted too," Andrew said.

"And so did Andrew," Tävna said to Tom. "But it's not a 'promotion,'" she said patiently to Andrew.

"Right, we don't get pay or anything," John said, "Or more fun time," he

18: On the Genealogy of Victory

said, looking at Tom, "If we go up a tier."

"It takes selflessness," Tävna said seriously, "So you can use your brilliance to help everyone else!"

"And if Tom isn't brilliant, I don't know who is," Lewis added.

"That's two reasons why I'll never have as much responsibility as you do, Tom," Tävna laughed, rolling onto her back in the mud.

"You're brilliant," Spalding said, and his voice was jerkier still.

"Ah, but not selfless!" Tävna smiled at him.

"Of course you are," Terry said for him, and Tom noticed Andrew looking with a knowing grin at Spalding, who was looking rather intently at Tävna lying placidly in the mud.

Oh, he comprehended. *I have been away too much.*

"No, I'm with Tävna," Lewis laughed. "If they want selflessness and brilliance, then I was right to resist being placed up a tier."

"Right," Tom said sarcastically.

"From what I hear, you've got selflessness down pat," Tävna said, closing her eyes.

"Ah, but not brilliance," Spalding smiled.

"Touché. Brilliance too."

"No," Lewis said casually. "But I'll do what I can for what I need to do.

"But Tom," he said, "I told Zämŭth and Zad I didn't want to go up a tier. Now, it was up to me, they said, but they said that Nŭährnär needs whatever I can give it. They said that my new managers and assistants will help me. That goes for you, too. Don't say no. Take the new tier."

Tom nodded slowly.

"And you new managers are Ōmäthäär, aren't they?" John said.

"Yeah," Tom said. "Änŭn and Härkärds."

"So I think they know what they're doing when they appoint people," John said certainly. "Take it."

"We'll see you plenty still," Terry said. "Even Mär must get out to have fun sometimes."

"You must be the only non-Ōmäthäär at that tier," Lewis said.

"I hope I'm not!" Tom said, feeling even more apprehensive.

"Yeah," Andrew said. "Up until now, at least, everyone at that tier was an Ōmäthäär. I don't know what other new appointments there've been, though..."

"Yeah, and think of it," Terry said. "There are always less than a thousand people at that tier, and most of them are couples. That means that you'll be over nearly two hundred million people!"

"Good," Tom said falsely.

Lewis laughed at him. "You're up to the challenge, Tom," he said. "Just go and get married now, so you can split the load."

"Right," Tom rolled his eyes. "I'll just go find a random girl and—"

But then, unbidden, Sarah's smiling image popped into his mind.

"—and marry her for my own sanity," he finished smoothly, though his insides felt much less steady.

"Marriage would be good for sanity," Tävna said happily, her eyes still closed.

"It's a beautiful insanity," Lewis said, gazing away at the drifting puffy clouds.

"And we're all depressingly sane," Tävna snorted. "Yeah, Tom, go get married. Show us how it's done."

"Don't worry, Tom," Terry said, smiling at the terrified look on her brother's face. "We'll be strong; even if Nüährnär is obsessed with marriage, we'll hold on to our American dignity."

"I don't know," Andrew said.

"American!" Tom said dazedly. "I'd almost forgot all about Texas, and everything."

"And Brittney?" Lewis asked slyly.

"Yeah," Tom said. "And everything!"

"You haven't talked to Brittney all this time?" Terry asked, shocked.

"No," Tom said, "I've hardly even remembered her…ever since I saw…you know…the Ämäthöär," he finished quietly. It was as if he were remembering another person's life, from long, long ago.

"Who's this, Tom?" Tävna asked, opening her eyes and sitting up excitedly.

"A girlfriend?" Spalding asked. "I guess I wasn't really aware of those kinds of things a few weeks ago."

"No, but I did kind of want her to be," Tom said unconcernedly.

"Go find her!" Terry said.

Without any conscious effort, he realized that Brittney was just over in the other side of the Shell.

"Later," he said evasively.

"Tom," Lewis and Tävna said together.

"Alright," Tom said wearily.

"Bring her back here," Tävna said.

"I'll go say hi to her first," Tom laughed. But now the Brittney he had been so charmed with back on the ground seemed strange, like and unknown

18: On the Genealogy of Victory

foreigner.

He flew up into the air, and as soon as he did he felt a deep surge of excitement at talking to Brittney again.

He put on more speed. "Brittney?" he called.

"Tom!" he heard Brittney's distantly familiar voice after hardly any pause. "Where have you been?"

"Here, of course," Tom called back friendlily. Suddenly it felt like he had never forgotten her. "I'm sorry I never came and saw you before now."

"Me too," Brittney said apologetically as Tom slowed down in front of her.

"What kept you, then?" Tom asked brightly.

"Work," Brittney said. "And all this! I'm sorry I got so distracted."

"I can't believe I didn't come see you before now," Tom said. "It feels like it's been forever, in a way."

"It does," Brittney smiled tenderly at him.

This is great!

No, it isn't, something else inside of him said.

Yes it is. Of course it is!

"What's happened to you for this past forever?" Brittney asked.

Then the first thing that came into Tom's mind was Hōnhŭ's terrible shrieking face and the heart-freezing darkness and fear. Then he saw Mär fighting him and Ämharŭ. Mär tutoring him. Mär helping him out of the water, and singing about Ä'ähänär-danär to him and Sarah. And Sarah.

Sarah was just a friend.

"A...a lot!" Tom said. He was about to tell her about the Ämäthōär, and about what Mär had been teaching him, but then he remembered Mär's warning:

Don't tell anyone anything about it. Not anyone.

But surely he could tell Brittney!

Not your father, not anyone.

"I've been working a lot," he said lamely.

"Oh," Brittney said. He could tell she knew he was keeping something from her.

"I've been doing a lot more," he said quickly, "But I can't tell you about it."

"Oh," Brittney said more positively. "Something secret, or something?"

"Yeah, I guess," Tom said. "Sorry I can't say more about it."

"You're pulling my leg," she smiled at him.

"No I'm not," he smiled back. "But that's what's been taking more of my time. Except for work."

"Don't worry, I believe you," Brittney laughed.

"What's happened to you?" Tom asked.

"Outside of nearly being killed by pirates?" she said. "I've made a lot of new friends here. There are so many people here, and we have so much time to spend with people!"

"Sorry," Tom said again.

"Me too," Brittney said.

"I would have come earlier—" Tom began.

"I would have come to see you—" Brittney said at the same time.

They stopped, and she smiled at him.

"I've come now," he said.

Brittney put her arms around his neck. It felt so nice. But something, somehow, felt wrong about it.

What about Sarah? he had asked Mär. *I won't talk to anyone about it except for Sarah.*

Why, though? he asked himself.

Brittney was leaning forward. He kissed her. It was so nice.

But no. It was wrong.

I am not the Tom Pratt that Brittney knows, a voice inside him said.

Then what am I?

The voice didn't answer that.

"What?" Brittney asked, staring into his distracted eyes.

Tom smiled at her. "It's great to see you, finally," he said.

Brittney smiled back and kissed him again.

He heard his own voice echo in his head, but it was speaking out of what he was sure was an entirely different context: *You think about what you know is right. Do what you know is best.*

He began to think that what was best was to be right there with Brittney, right then. But something he couldn't grasp refuted that decisively without him understanding how or why.

He looked into Brittney's eyes. She liked him. She was so nice, so smart, so great.

Then, out of the volumes that Mär had inserted into him, one principle floated to the surface: That happiness, and power, and affinity with Ärthähr, were bound inseparably to a person's prompt compliance with what the Ärthähr said.

This is Ärthähr! the voice seemed to bellow wordlessly at him.

No, it isn't, he said within himself.

I am, the voice said.

And immediately he felt a horrible sinking feeling all throughout him.

18: On the Genealogy of Victory

Only then did he realize that the cheerful fire that had warmed him when he had been talking to Mär and the other Ōmäthäär just before the pirates' attack had never diminished. Not until just then.

He smiled at Brittney, but she looked questioningly up at him.

"I wish I could tell you what I can't," he said.

"Why can't you?" she asked.

"Here, ask your managers about Ärthähr," he said.

"Okay," she said.

Tom kissed her again, then said, "I should go, though. I need to see my new managers."

"New managers?" Brittney said. "Why new?"

"I got chosen for another tier," Tom said.

"A higher tier?" Brittney asked, smiling.

"A busier tier," Tom said wearily.

"Well, come see me when you aren't busy," Brittney said. "And I'll come see you."

"I will," Tom said, but he felt the sinking feeling sink a little more.

Mär was staring at him again. Why? "That's what my dad said," Tom smiled.

"And what my mom said, too," Sarah said.

"So it's three to two," Mär said.

"Well, my dad backed her up," Sarah grinned.

"Four to two!" Mär said. "You're outvoted."

"Make it six to zero, then," Tom said. "If you think we can handle being at this high a tier, we can."

"Agreed," Sarah said.

They were floating alone in front of the shining white Ōmäthäär Sanctuary. They were talking privately so as not to be overheard by the six Ōmäthäär Sentinels, who were standing watching them peacefully.

"Wonderful!" Mär said, clapping his hands together.

"What about our meetings with you?" Sarah asked him. "How will we have time?"

"Well, I have time," Mär said. "And don't worry. Studying Ärthähr is an endless process. The others at your tier still study it all the time."

"But studying Ärthähr makes them better managers and leaders. That's what will make or break your progress at your new tier, both of you: how much you study or neglect Ärthähr."

Tom felt a little guilty; he hadn't been thinking about Ärthähr as much as he thought he should have.

"The more you learn, and live in accord with what you learn," Mär said, "The more clear your heads and hearts will be. To understand Ärthähr is to understand life and light.

"That's what light is. The stuff that used to let you see with your eyes, photons and other things, are clouds of smaller things, like the particle swarms we send about to cause inertia and momentum. And those are clouds of other things, and those clouds of other things. And on and on.

"And the basis of all of it is Ärthähr. The light that let you see before, and the energy that moved the air that let you hear, and all of it, was complex arrangements of Ärthähr.

"And life! Not just the energy that lets our bodies move and survive, and not just the energy that holds us, and all the particle clouds that make us, together, but the consciousness and intelligence that is life! It's another facet of Ärthähr!"

Sarah was sucking this all in, made immensely easier by the fact that Mär had already taught all of this into them.

"Ärthähr is. That's the best way to put it. It's beingness, and thus by its very nature it cannot not be. The more Ärthähr we each have in ourselves, the more intelligence, and ability to act, and happiness and peaceful tranquil wholeness and happiness we'll have.

"So the Ōmäthäär who study Ärthähr are incomparably better equipped to lead and to carry heavy responsibilities. Your Ärthähr training should be an asset to you, not an additional burden. It should strengthen you, make you more and stronger and smarter, so that all your burdens seem lighter."

"You're right," Sarah said optimistically.

"I have to think about Ärthähr more," Tom said.

"Yeah," Sarah agreed, feeling negligent too.

"Good," Mär smiled. "And the past is past. Don't demean yourselves for whatever you have or have not done."

"Like think about Ärthähr?" Sarah smiled.

"Like anything," Mär said, smiling at her. "Take time to think about it. Just turn it over and run through it in your minds. And talk about it together, too. You can talk about it with anyone at your managers' tier or higher, and definitely talk about it with one another! It's good to talk about what you're both learning; you'll learn it much better that way."

"Thanks," Tom said.

"Why weren't we supposed to talk to the Ōmäthäär about Ä'ähänärdanär before?" Sarah asked.

18: On the Genealogy of Victory

"A lot of reasons," Mär said evasively. "Among others, when you were just getting acquainted with all of this, having too many teachers could have confused you and made it all even more difficult for you to grasp.

"But I think that being able to talk with a hundred or so Ōmäthäär about Är will be a great asset to you now. You need to learn as much as you can as quickly as you can."

"Why?" Sarah asked.

"You always need to learn and grow as fast as you can," Mär said. "But, now, learning specifically about what I and the Ōmäthäär are teaching you is extremely important, because that's what the Ärthähr's saying. I don't know why the Ärthähr's telling me that; I have some good guesses, but the point is that that's what the Ärthähr's saying. And the Ärthähr always says what Är means and wants. And if Är wants it, it must be good!

"Är's Infinity. He's all intelligence. So he always knows and wants the absolute best thing, in every tiniest way, in every situation, all the time. So the more we listen to the Ärthähr, the more we make the same choices he wants us to make.

"And Är wants nothing but our happiness. And believe me, making everyone happy at the same time is possible. But it takes a mind like Är's to pull it off. I know a lot of how he does it. And a lot of it has to do with Earth here."

"Earth?" Tom said.

"Yeah, Mär, what is Pp'ōhōnŭäär, exactly?" Sarah asked.

"A consummately important thing to talk about," Mär said. "But I'm saying about Är, that if we listen to him, we'll get the utmost best for ourselves and for everyone else at the same time. If we listen to the Ärthähr.

"Do you see why affinity with Ärthähr is so great?"

"Yeah," Tom and Sarah said together.

"It's the key to everything. The only key. People cannot get total happiness without Är. And that has to do with Earth too, which I'll explain in a second.

"But do you understand some of why we *have* to let all the sextillions of people at Nrathĕrmĕ know all about Är, and therefore about Ärthähr?"

"I have some memories about the Ärthähr being a person," Tom said.

"Me too," Sarah said, looking inquiringly at Mär.

Mär laughed. "So the question of Pp'ōhōnŭäär is gone that quickly!"

"No! Tell us about that," Sarah said.

"First, about the Ärthähr, the word can refer to a person, an Är.

"There's Är, and there are Ärs," Mär said in response to their confused looks. But their perplexed expressions only deepened.

"Later," Mär laughed. "We'll go into that later. I didn't tell you about that before, and you don't need to worry about it just now. Not yet.

"But when we talk about Ärthähr, almost always when people talk about it, we aren't referring to any person. The Ärthähr I need you to learn about is a grouping of an infinite sum of infinitely small bits of being that makes up everything. The Ärthähr is the force that makes up everything that is."

"Wow," Sarah said. "'Infinitely small?' How can that be?"

"Tell me this," Mär said. "Where did Är come from?"

Tom laughed. "You tell us that! I'm glad you said it."

"Next time," Mär said. "Remind me if you still want to know. But both that and the concept of infinite smallness, or infinite bigness, demonstrate the same, essential, principle.

"But Pp'ōhōnŭäär," he said. "People have called you Nōhōnŭäär?"

"Yeah," Tom said.

"A lot," Sarah said.

"And you can tell me what that means," Mär said.

Tom looked at Sarah, who said, "Person from the house of Är, right?"

"Right," Mär said. "So what's the house of Är, then, you want to know?"

"And what's so important about it," Sarah added.

"Well," Mär grinned, "Doesn't Är's home sound important?"

"Är's home?" Tom said.

"An Är," Mär smiled. "The Är, as far as you're concerned just yet."

"An Är lived at Earth?" Sarah asked.

"*The* Är," Mär said emphatically. "Är did not live at Närdamähr, or anywhere else. Only Earth. Only."

"Är *lived* on Earth?" Tom asked.

"Where's Närdamähr?" Sarah asked.

"Närdamähr is Nrathĕrmĕ, the way it was before Sĕrĕhahn raped it," Mär said.

"Oh!" Sarah said.

"So 'N'närdamähr' just means people from Nrathĕrmĕ," Tom said.

"Who aren't under Sĕrĕhahn," Mär said. "Sĕrĕhahn's followers we call N'nrathĕrmĕ, obviously.

"And Är did live on Earth. That's as much as you need to know for now. But the One Infinite Being actually lived on Earth. And nowhere else.

"And that makes you Nōhōnŭäär very important, even if most of you have forgotten why. But there are a few Nōhōnŭäär still around who know more than even Sĕrĕhahn knows about this."

18: On the Genealogy of Victory

"How did we not know about Är himself living on our world?" Sarah asked amazedly.

"You both knew," Mär said, and he looked intently at Sarah. "Especially you."

"Oh!" Sarah said suddenly. "Yeah!"

"No," Tom said incredulously. "The only thing I can think of would have been..."

"Exactly," Mär said. "The Är you've sworn to follow is the very same Guy you and your family scoffed at before."

"I didn't scoff," Tom said. "But I didn't know...I couldn't have known..."

"You know now," Mär smiled. "But Sarah knew. There were still people on Earth, Ōhōnŭäär, who knew.

"But here's why you should keep to yourselves about this. And, I think, why so few Nōhōnŭäär know what they themselves are.

"At Nrathĕrmĕ, no one seriously thinks that Infinity can be one person. But in the Wild Lands farther from Nrathĕrmĕ, there are millions, trillions, of fascinatingly different sects and cults and religions.

"A lot of clan leaders use religion, and sometimes even use actual parts of Ärthähr, to convince people to follow them," Mär said. "Religion can be a terrible, disgusting, debasing thing.

"If the N'nŭährnär hear about Är in that light, they will think of the Ōmäthäär worse things than your friend Peter thought of us.

"And, Tom, if you ever heard of Ōmäthäär back in Austin, I think you would have thought the same about them. That they were an artificial order made to gain power over anyone who would take them seriously."

"It did seem like a lot of religions were nothing but shams to take peoples' money," Tom said.

"Some N'närdamährs' religions are made for worse things," Mär said darkly. "I would rather meet an Ämäthöär, in some ways, than some of the religionists I've met."

Tom and Sarah stared at him. "How could any liar be worse than an Ämäthöär?" Tom asked.

"About Pp'ōhōnŭäär," Mär said, obviously avoiding that. "You all have a right to know what you are. And why Sĕrĕhahn wants you. But I would rather have all you Nōhōnŭäär be prepared to know this first than to tell you when you aren't ready to understand."

Mär paused, then smiled at them. "I will tell you more later. Avhä and Ŭkan are calling me now. I have to go inside." He jerked his head toward the sphere and cube behind him.

"When can we go in there?" Sarah asked.

"Think about Ä'ähänärdanär," Mär said, "And ask me, or Ōmäthäär in tiers higher than yours, all your questions later."

"We'll have a lot," Tom smiled.

"The more the better," Mär said, drifting backward toward the Sanctuary.

"Bye," Sarah said.

"And you two talk to each other about it!" Mär said emphatically.

Sarah countered the impulse to blush, but found herself feeling very grateful to Mär for that instruction.

Tom felt another pang of guilt. Sarah was just a friend, but spending time with her reminded him of his irrational misgivings about Brittney. Irrational, but undeniable.

Mär waved at them and turned to a Sentinel, then disappeared into the great white building.

"Finally," Ŭmäthŭ said.

"At least we know that some of them are alive," Bävän said.

"I think they all still are," Tärnär said.

Six days had passed since the battle with the pirates. Mär and eight of his assistants were floating in a smaller spherical room within the Ōmäthäär Sanctuary.

"I think so," Mär said.

"No mention of everyone else, though," Thas said.

"So, as far as Zōrd and his guys at Nrathĕrmĕ know, nothing has been sent against us yet?" Avhä said.

"As far as they've *said*," Ŭdbän said.

"Yes," Mär agreed. "They are saying nothing about the other Ōmäthäär. They may be keeping quiet about other things, too. I believe that they know something that they don't want to risk transmitting to us here."

"Something more important than their own survival," Ōhōmhär said, "Since they would lose that if their messages were discovered. But they won't risk telling us about this, even when they still risk staying connected to us?"

"Something is happening," Mär said. "I wonder if the survival of all of us is dependent on what they're not telling us."

"We have time," Ŭmäthŭ said. "The soonest anyone we know of could arrive here from Nrathĕrmĕ since Sĕrĕhahn's disappearance would be another eighteen days or so."

"And knowing Sĕrĕhahn, he could send something much more quickly than that," Mär said.

18: On the Genealogy of Victory

"And we have other N'nrathěrmě to worry about," Anŭsths said. "Hōäōhä should arrive within ten days, but he thinks the uprising he saw could reach us within as little as two days. But he doesn't think they will move that quickly."

"Two days," Mär repeated.

"So now we fight actual N'nrathěrmě," Tärnär said.

"Now they make us fight them," Ŭdbän said sorrowfully.

"Hōäōhä's people have tried to tell the N'nrathěrmě out there that we are not their enemies," Ōhōmhär said. "We have no choice now but to fight them as they come."

"Those sent to harvest other stars will, hopefully, all arrive before the N'nrathěrmě get here," Anŭsths said.

"These are not pirates," Mär said. "But they will be cunning. These people live away from Nrathěrmě by choice, harvesting matter and keeping pirates in check. They will be formidable strategically, and their link to Nrathěrmě will make them more potent technologically than we are. They will be faster and better.

"This will be the worst military encounter Nŭährnär's ever experienced."

"Do you think they will have Ämäthōär with them, Mär?" Ōhōmhär asked.

Mär sat silently for a moment. "I don't know," he said.

"I doubt Sěrěhahn would send them with this group," Bävän said. "He'll send them all at once to destroy us utterly."

"Peter, what are you up to?" Annie said with feigned suspicion.

"Nothing," Peter's voice said back.

"Nothing, huh?" Annie said. "So why are you taking me away from my battle exercises?"

"You're good enough," Peter said. "Missing the end of an exercise won't change that at all."

"Well, that is high praise, coming from the hero of Nŭährnär," Annie said, speeding toward Peter, whom she could see soaring through the sky toward her.

Peter laughed lovingly at her. "I was just in the right place at the right time."

Annie met up with him in the air. "You were marvelously brave and smart," she said. "You know it."

"I know that I love you," Peter said, kissing her.

Annie kissed him back. "Is that why you called me away?"

"Yes," Peter said simply.

Annie stared at him, then smiled.

"But, as an afterthought, I want to show you something," Peter said.

"Ah," Annie smiled.

"Come on," Peter said, and he took her hand and shot upward into the sky.

Annie flew up alongside him. The blue sky gave way to a flowing green and golden grassy plain as they shot toward the inside floor of the Shell.

Everything had looked a hundred times more beautiful to Annie ever since Peter's heroism against the pirates. Now as they soared toward the rapidly approaching plain in front of them, the rippling grass and the snaking brooks and the creeping animals filled her with warm delight. And having Peter with her in every free moment of every day, Peter even more caring and smart and dashing now than he ever had been before, made even the threat of impending war seem insignificant to her.

They hit the plain, then an instant later emerged out of the Shell over Earth.

"Down there," Peter said, turning toward what used to be the southeastern United States.

"What is this, Peter?" Annie pressed.

"It's called a surprise," Peter smiled at her.

"I think I can guess what it might be," she said as the ground of her native North Carolina rushed up to meet them.

They landed lightly in the middle of a narrow street in a neighborhood of small houses.

"It's my house!" Annie squealed. A low, off-white house was right in front of them, its lawn perfectly manicured, its garden glowing with a swirl of different brightly colored flowers. The trees in the yard were in full leaf. The windows were clean and clear, shining into the house where Annie grew up from childhood to her college years.

"Do Dad and Mom know about this?" Annie asked excitedly.

"Not yet," Peter smiled. "But it wasn't hard, you know."

"That doesn't matter!" Annie said, gliding up and over to the front door. She fingered the old door knocker lovingly.

Peter glided up beside her. She turned to beam at him, and he kissed her deeply.

"Thank you," she said in a small, grateful voice.

"Go on in," Peter said.

Annie touched the doorknob with relish. She turned it, and the door

18: On the Genealogy of Victory

swung open with its familiar squeak.

She saw the welcoming warm interior of her old house, complete with its worn furniture in the living room.

A high pitched barking greeted her ears, and a golden cocker spaniel galloped around the corner from the dining room, its stunted tail waggling excitedly as it charged toward Annie.

"Mango!" Annie shrieked, opening her arms and making the small dog swoop upward into them.

Mango licked her face franticly, her tail jiggling from out of the space between Annie's arms.

"How does she recognize me?" Annie asked as Mango continued soaking her cheek.

"I just told her that this is what you look, and smell, like now," Peter beamed at her.

"I haven't seen you in years!" Annie said babyishly to Mango.

Mango seemed to understand her, and wagged her tail still more turbulently.

Peter turned and retrieved a well worn book from its perch on the back of the nearest couch.

Annie was still occupied with Mango. Then she noticed the book in Peter's hand. "What's that?"

"Nietzsche," Peter said, a meaningful grin creeping across his face.

"On the Genealogy of Morals," Annie read. Then comprehension lit up her eyes. "Is that—" she began.

"Yes," Peter said softly. "You were walking Mango..."

"And you were sitting on the park bench reading that," Annie said. "You were visiting friends here."

"And Mango stopped to be a dog..." Peter smiled.

"And you started talking to me," Annie said. "You thought I was cute."

"I thought you were beautiful," Peter said glowingly.

He took her hand. "Let's go," he said.

There was a whiz of color as houses and trees shot past instantaneously, and then Annie saw that they were standing on the dirt path by the bench where they had first met, so long ago it seemed.

She dropped Mango on the ground, and the dog capered around excitedly. Peter had sat himself down on the bench, the book on his knee.

"Peter, this is amazing," Annie said, gazing around at the leafy trees around them, shading the path and the bench. She sat down on the bench beside Peter.

"And we got to talking then..." Peter said.

"For an hour..." Annie smiled.

Mango was bounding off into the trees on the other side of the path. She turned and barked earnestly at Annie, as if to get her attention.

Annie got up and walked over to Mango. Mango galloped back to her, and Annie was about to bend down to pet her, but then she noticed that Peter was right behind her.

And he was kneeling.

Annie spun around to face him.

Peter's eyes were tearing up as he smiled adoringly up at her.

"Peter..." Annie began disbelievingly.

Peter took her hands in his. "Annie Kimberly Baker, will you marry me?"

Annie burst into tears. Mango raced around them barking energetically.

Peter waited, looking up into Annie's streaming face.

"Peter!" Annie sobbed. "Yes! Yes! Of course I will! You don't need to ask!"

Peter leapt up and grabbed Annie into an ecstatic hug. They kissed for nearly a full minute without a break.

Chapter 19

The Deeps of Infinity

"It's wonderful!" Mär said to Tom and Sarah not an hour later, leaning back satisfiedly in the mountain's brilliant white snow.

"John just told me," Tom said. "How did you know?"

"The gossip line of managers," Mär said happily. "Both Peter and Annie told their managers, who told their managers, since they thought the Ōmäthäär would want to know this kind of thing. They were more than right, of course," he grinned.

"Why?" Sarah asked.

"We like Peter and Annie," Mär said. "And we like marriage. We like true love. We like all of it. What's the point of working to help people if we don't enjoy the great things that people do and are?"

"You set Peter up," Tom accused admiringly.

"Yes," Mär said. "Partially. Är and Peter did most of that. We just put him in the right place during that battle. He had to make a decision. It had to be *his* decision. He had to have the option of carrying out what he wanted to believe or facing what he knew was really right."

"What would have happened if Peter hadn't made that decision?" Tom asked.

"Most of Nüährnär would have been destroyed, and I don't know what the Ōmäthäär would have had to have done to defend Ōhōnŭäär," Mär said without worry.

"Oh," Sarah said, surprised at his attitude.

"But I didn't think that would happen," Mär smiled reassuringly at them. "Setting Peter up was not our idea; it was Är's. We could never take such a chance, manipulating real people, ourselves. People like Peter are too complex. But we knew, through the Ärthähr, what we ought to do. Peter had to have an opportunity to do what he knew, in his heart, was wrong, and not take it."

"I wasn't sure that Peter would make the choice that he did," Mär said, running his hand across the perfect surface of the snow, "But I hoped he would. And I knew that Är knew what he was doing in any event. It wasn't very worrying for most of us. We've had to trust Är in stranger, far more desperate situations before."

"I hope we can listen to Ärthähr that well," Tom said. "It's been hard for me. It's hard for me to tell what's the Ärthähr and what's just me thinking I'm feeling something, or me imagining things."

"Good," Mär said.

"Good?" Sarah asked.

"It means you're differentiating more between Ärthähr and yourself!" Mär said thrilledly. "That means you must be getting more conscious of it. The fact that you noticed that it was hard means that you're growing and being able to notice where you need to improve next."

"Okay," Tom said.

"What have you thought you've felt?" Mär asked.

"Just good or bad feelings about doing different things," Tom said.

"Like what things?" Mär asked shrewdly.

Tom felt suddenly naked, as if Mär could read right on his face everything about Brittney and his anxiety over breaking away from her.

"Lots of things," Tom said. "Like where to go, sometimes, when I have free time." That was true enough; he had felt good about going some places without knowing why. "Or sometimes I've felt bad right as I've been saying something that I shouldn't have been saying." But those things were far less prominent in his heart than was his worrying about Brittney.

Mär looked at him significantly, and Tom felt suddenly like a liar.

But Mär smiled appreciatively at him. "Keep listening to those kinds of feelings. Follow them, test them out. That way you'll get to know by hard experience how to distinguish Ärthähr from your own thoughts, or from other feelings.

"But think about what I've taught you, too. You should have a lot of memories of what real Ärthähr may feel like and what it does not feel like. But you've made great progress in only a matter of days' time already.

"So keep thinking about what I've given you."

Mär looked at Sarah, and she thought he knew that she hadn't been thinking about it as much as she should have been.

"Now, I think you had some questions for me from before?"

"About who made Är," Tom said.

"And about how parts of Ärthähr can be infinitely small," Sarah added.

"You should know about that," Mär said to her. "The origin of Är isn't nearly as important to you right now. But they're two things that demonstrate one principle, so explaining them both will help you understand the principle you need to understand.

"Think about what I've given you as we talk about this; you'll find things that will help you understand this better."

19: The Deeps of Infinity

"Okay," Tom and Sarah said as one.

"First, tell me this," Mär asked, "What's under us right now?"

"The Shell," Sarah said.

"Yeah," Tom said. "Why?"

"The Shell, under the mountain, under the snow, I could say," Mär said. "What's under that?"

"Earth," Sarah said.

"Yeah," Mär said, "But the Earth doesn't hold up the Shell. What does?"

"Inertia," Sarah said.

"The Shell itself," Mär said. "But why doesn't the Shell fall down?"

"Where would it fall?" Tom said.

Mär smiled. "Down!"

"But down here is up on the other side," Sarah protested.

"What?" Mär asked with an entertained look of pretended confusion. "How could up be down?"

"They're relative," Tom said.

"Yeah," Sarah said. "Down is just where gravity pulls, and we make our own gravity for the Shell. There's no down for it to fall to!"

"Yes!" Mär said, jabbing an emphatic finger at Sarah. "It's relative," he said to Tom.

"What's under the Earth?" he asked then.

"There is no under," Tom said.

"Well, under the surface there may be rock," Mär said, "And other configurations of rock under those. But what's under those?"

"More rock, molten rock..." Tom said.

"What's under those?"

"You just keep going down," Sarah said, wondering where Mär was going with this.

"Forever?"

"No, till you come out the other side," Sarah said.

"Then it's up and not down," Mär said. "Where's the *bottom* of the Earth?"

"There's no bottom," Sarah said.

"Just a center," Tom said.

"Just a center," Mär repeated, as if that was what he had been getting at all along.

"Up and down are relative concepts that gravity impresses us with. But if we understand about gravity, then we understand that up and down are not absolute, not universal, and they don't stretch out forever.

"There's a lot more to the universe than just up and down from the point of view of a person on the surface of the Earth."

Mär paused, looking intently at them. He played absently with the snow a little more with his hands.

"Now," he said, burrowing his bare feet into the snow, "What about before and after?"

"They're relative too?" Tom asked.

"If you knew nothing of gravity, if you did not know that your planet was a ball, the concept of up and down being relative would be appalling, and incomprehensible. It would seem as if reality would have to fall apart for up and down to be relative!"

"It does seem hard to imagine before and after being relative!" Sarah laughed.

"Like Einstein's Relativity?" Tom asked.

"Tom, you've been flying around at dozens of times the speed at which what those men called photons typically move. Have you noticed time flowing any differently for you?"

"No," Tom said. "I hadn't thought about that. So what about Einstein?"

Mär smiled. "He was a man. His ideas were much more accurate than a great many other ideas, which have taken much stronger holds in both your culture and Nratherme's culture, have been.

"I would never presume to manipulate Peter Garcia on my own. Nor would I presume to say anything of myself definitively about the way light and life works.

"But I do both," he smiled.

"But not of myself.

"I know what I'm talking about because Är has told me, or the Ärthähr has shown things to me.

"Good people make mistakes.

"I like Al Einstein. A lot. And I think he would have been less surprised than you are, Tom, to find that his surmisings had missed the mark.

"How much theory has been based off of half-correct interpretations of what people have seen with their eyes and ears, but not with anything else?

"How many lives have been squandered, how many peoples have putrefied, how many opportunities have been lost because people trusted their own imperfect interpretations of Är's perfect world?

"It is mortally dangerous to trust your own understanding, or any imperfect person's understanding," he said to both of them. "Always, *always* be ready to learn something new that turns everything you have learned yet upside down. And test it out. See if it turns out to be good.

19: The Deeps of Infinity

"People reject a lot of things that they think conflict with what they already understand, while those things actually support and dignify and embellish what they already understand. They just don't do it in the ways we may expect them to do it," he smiled.

"We need to make decisions. We need to pass judgment regarding what is good and ought to be pursued, and what is not good and ought to be seen through. But just keep them tentative! Be ready to eat your own beliefs.

"But Ärthähr, Tom, once you do recognize it, is infinite."

"Good!" Sarah breathed. "I was starting to think we couldn't believe anything!"

Mär laughed loudly.

"So we can trust Ärthähr," Tom said.

"And nothing else!" Mär said. "Well, trust things only insofar as they're trustable. And only Infinity can be unrestrainedly trusted. Something that feels only mostly reliable should be mostly trusted, but with a little reservation that it could yet be faulty.

"Sarah," he then said, fixing her with a serious but entertained look, "Why have you sworn to follow Är?"

"Because I know he loves me," Sarah said.

Tom felt a surge of something toward Sarah that he was afraid to put a name on.

"You 'know?'" Mär said. "How could you say that, Sarah? Don't you mean you *believe* that Är loves you?"

Sarah was quiet for a few seconds. "No," she said. "I know, I think. I mean, I know I know."

"Have you ever seen Är?" Mär challenged.

"No."

"Have you seen him?" Tom asked eagerly.

Mär grinned a very odd grin. He started to look back at Sarah, but then he turned to Tom. "Don't tell anyone, as usual."

"You...you have?" Tom asked, amazed.

"I've talked with him, counseled with him, and just enjoyed seeing him. Just as we're talking now. But a whole lot better.

"But Sarah," he said. Sarah was staring at him. "I knew Är was there long before I saw him. Because of Ärthähr."

"Oh," Sarah said. "So I do know!"

"Do you?" Mär asked.

"Through Ärthähr, like you said. I can just feel it. It's not like my own feelings. It..."

"It's solid," Mär finished for her. "And the more you two get acquainted with it, the more you'll be able to know by means of it.

"And what I'm telling you about time I was taught by someone who learned it from someone else, who learned it ultimately from Är. No person just thought this up.

"I have it from Är that before and after are relative in the same kind of way that up and down are relative."

"Okay," Tom said.

"How do you mean, 'in the same kind of way?'" Sarah asked.

"There is no ultimate down," Mär said. "There is a center, on which everything rests, but there is no bottom to the Earth. The Earth rests on itself, because that is how gravity works. Nothing holds the Earth up. That's not how up and down, which are aspects of gravity, work.

"In the same kind of way, there is no ultimate before. There is no beginning to the universe. No beginning to Är."

"So Är didn't come from anywhere?" Tom asked.

"That doesn't make any sense, does it?" Mär said. "There are rocks below the rocks under the surface of the Earth.

"And there was an Är before the Är that I'm talking about. But there is no ultimate beginning to the Ärs, just like there's no ultimate bottom to the layers of rocks. There's a center, but no bottom.

"There's a core, but no beginning."

"I can't imagine that," Sarah said.

"Time is like gravity," Mär said. "There are forces at work there, and we, I and you both, cannot understand the more general workings of time while we're bound in time the way we are. And we can only live the more general aspects of time by learning more about Ärthähr. Time's Ärthähr too.

"So is cause and effect. And so is larger and smaller.

"There is no smallest thing, Sarah," he said. "There is no one thing that is infinitely small. When I say 'infinitely small,' what I mean is the principle, the core of smallness. There is no bottom, no beginning, no smallest thing, in that sense. Just a center, a core, a principle.

"And that, you two, is a good explanation of what Ärthähr is. It's principle. The principle of being, and of comprehending in its more complex arrangements."

"Incredible," Tom said. "But it feels right."

"Good!" Mär said. "Är wants everyone to be happy; he wants everyone to become infinite. He understands things about time that mean that our happiness is his happiness, and vice-versa.

19: The Deeps of Infinity

"The Är before the Är whom I've seen led that Är to become infinite. Är wasn't always Infinity. The Är I've spoken to, I mean."

"How many Ärs have there been?" Tom asked.

"How far up can you fly?" Mär asked, grinning. "There have always been Ärs. Time doesn't have a beginning, just founding principles. Standing on the surface and only seeing a tiny portion of the extensive planet, up and down may look absolute. And when we see only a tiny portion of infinite time, before and after may look absolute.

"But there is no beginning, just as there is no bottom to a planet, even though it may seem like there ought to be one from that limited point of view.

"And, for all of the time that we three are involved in, the Är I've spoken to has been Infinity. The time when he was not yet Infinity is part of his past, but it is not that way for us."

"He lived in another time, another set of time, then?" Tom asked.

"Think of it this way," Mär said. "Loosely, mark you. Imagine that you could go backward in time, like in Tävna's story."

"You know Tävna's story?" Sarah said.

"I've only seen a little of it," Mär said. "Spalding showed me a little of what she and he were planning."

"He didn't tell me that," Tom said.

"I didn't expect to meet him," Mär said, "But I'm glad I did. I think you'll see what I mean soon enough."

"What?" Tom asked interestedly, goaded by Mär's conspiratorial smirk.

"In a few days, I hope," Mär said.

"But imagine that you could travel backward in time and go talk to yourself. You would have a lot to tell yourself, especially if you traveled far backward in time. He, or she, would not yet be you, but you would be him and more.

"As far as he is concerned, for his time, you have always been you. No matter when you travel to in order to visit him, or her, you will always be you for him. There has never been a time for him or her when you have not been you. You can remember times when you were not the you that you are now, easily, but he can't. Always, for him, or her, you are as you are.

"Now take that loosely," he said. "Time is not a loop. But I do like to think of it as a ball, but only very loosely then, too.

"Är does not exist 'outside' of our time. There is no outside of time; that's not what time is like. But he is Infinite. He is in and through all of it. Every time for us, past or future, is *now* for him, always and all at once."

Tom nodded.

"For us, the Är I've met has always been Är," Mär explained. "But that's not the way it is for him. He has an Är, who has an Är, and so on. And all of them are Är together, Infinity together!

"Imagine what a society—Infinity!—that must be!

"The principle of Ärs is the principle of everything. There has never been no beingness, because that is not beingness's nature; by being beingness, it *is*!

"There has never been no Är."

"Wow," Tom said.

"I understand, at least a little," Sarah said.

"That's plenty to start off with!" Mär smiled excitedly at the two of them.

"Now, you two, think about all of this, and take the time to talk about it. You, and Nüährnär, will be better served if you ponder about Ä'ähänärdanär than if you focus only on building and planning.

"Ärthähr is intelligence. It is better to draw closer to the sum whole of all intelligence, and thus get some of it rubbed off onto you, maybe a lot of it onto you, more and more the more you get in touch with it, than it is to just use what intelligence you yet have to plan things."

"Okay," Tom said with a guilty smile.

"We will," Sarah agreed.

But she couldn't help feeling worried by how Tom had been seeming progressively less willing to talk to her about anything.

"If it weren't for the Ōmäthäär," Tävna sighed to Spalding after another battle exercise, "I would have left a long time ago!"

"I know," Spalding said. "I finished a battle just half an hour ago, and we got decimated."

"But the Ōmäthäär will get us out of this," Tävna said.

"Just like last time," Spalding smiled.

"I wish Mär had told you something about this army that's coming," Tävna said.

"I've heard it's more than ten times the size of the army that just destroyed my managers and me," Spalding said, "And we were simulating all of Nüährnär fighting with us."

"So Mär's news probably would have just scared us more," Tävna smiled.

"He was more interested in other things, anyway," Spalding said, hugging her.

"Look at you two," came a man's voice. An Ōmäthäär called Äröähr swept toward them from the distant ground.

"Hi," Spalding said, still holding Tävna. "We haven't told anyone yet."

19: The Deeps of Infinity

"Well, I'm not marrying you two if your families don't know!" Äröähr said.

"We'll tell them all," Tävna smiled. "We just want to savor it ourselves first."

"I don't know about you two," Äröähr said easily. "You decide to get married less than a week after you first realize that that's what you even wanted, and three days later you still haven't told anyone?"

"We know what we want," Spalding said positively.

Äröähr laughed. "That's what Ōhōmhär told me. And I'm happy for you both. If only more people could know what they want the way you do."

"Living forever together..." Tävna said dreamily, leaning into Spalding. "It's not a very big decision."

Spalding laughed. "Sure," he said with complementary sarcasm.

"Of course, that's assuming we live through these next few weeks," Tävna said lightly.

"Do not joke about that," Äröähr said tensely.

"I'm sure we'll be fine," Spalding said certainly.

"Whatever happens," Äröähr said, "We'll be alright, as long as we've got the Ōmäthäär still. We will be fine."

"So what's up?" Tävna asked Äröähr. "Are you just here to tell us how adorable we are together?"

"Actually, Ŭmäthŭ sent me," he said. "About Tom."

"Tom?" Spalding asked. "Ŭmäthŭ?"

"Ŭmäthŭ just wants to know about Tom and Brittney Jensen."

"I see," Spalding said. "Mär helps me work up to say I'm in love with Tävna, and now Ŭmäthŭ's going to help Tom with Brittney?"

"Maybe," Äröähr said. "But I don't think so."

"What, then?" Tävna asked, more interested.

"I don't think Tom wants to marry Brittney," Äröähr said simply. "Or anything like that. But I think Ŭmäthŭ, or maybe Mär even, wants to help Tom figure out what he wants."

"So, it is like Mär and me," Spalding said.

"What does Ŭmäthŭ want Tom to want?" Tävna asked, a slight shade of disapproval in her voice.

"Oh, it's nothing like that," Äröähr said. "I think Ŭmäthŭ's just worried about Tom. He says Tom has some idea of what he has to do, but Tom does not seem to understand how to do it. I think Ŭmäthŭ's just worried that he will do something rash, and hurt himself and Brittney in ways that he should not."

"Does he want to split up with Brittney?" Spalding asked slowly.

"I was hoping you could tell me," Ärōähr smiled. "How long have they been courting each other?"

"I know they had spent some time together before Nŭährnär got here," Spalding said. "But I think they only started seeing each other again barely a week ago."

"Six days ago," Tävna said.

"I've only seen Tom twice since then," Spalding said. "And Brittney wasn't with him either time."

"He did seem a little preoccupied," Tävna remembered.

"But he seemed really happy to go talk to her again when he went to see her before," Spalding said.

"What about Sarah Trotter?" Tävna wondered.

"She's not anything more than a friend, is she?" Spalding asked her.

"*We* weren't anything more than friends, Spalding," she beamed at him.

"Yeah, maybe," Spalding said thoughtfully. "If I could choose someone for Tom, I'd choose Sarah. No question."

"Well, Ŭmäthŭ's not about to choose anyone for anybody," Ärōähr said. "But do you think Tom could be divided between Brittney and Sarah?"

"If he is, he hasn't said anything to me about it," Spalding said.

"If he is, he owes Sarah a big apology," Tävna said a little tartly.

"Why?" Ärōähr said.

"Sarah said something about Tom not wanting to spend much time with her alone," Tävna said. "She likes him, but I don't think she knows it yet. But it's pretty obvious."

"Do you think Tom cares about her?" Ärōähr asked.

"He risked his life for her!" Spalding said. "When the pirates attacked us. I've never seen him do anything that reckless before."

"Which would explain him shunning her," Tävna said.

"Tom's had a lot to be preoccupied about," Ärōähr said charitably. "Mär's been teaching him and Sarah a lot of things that he won't say much about. I would be surprised if Tom knows if he's avoiding his friends."

"I'd like Sarah to be more than a friend," Spalding said brightly.

"But this is what Ŭmäthŭ seems to want," Ärōähr said, "To try to make sure Tom doesn't hurt himself, or Brittney, or anyone else."

"You would have to ask Tom himself," Spalding said. "We haven't seen him much."

"Or ask Sarah," Tävna suggested.

Ärōähr floated silently there for a moment. "Very well," he said then.

19: The Deeps of Infinity

"Thank you both. And tell your families about yourselves!"

"Alright, we should now," Tävna said, winking at Spalding.

"This will be fun," Spalding squeezed her.

"I'll see you two lovers soon," Äröähr said. He turned and flew back from where he had come.

Tom looked at the rugged black rock in front of him.

The Ärthähr could be used to move things, he remembered. Just like inertial currents.

Better than inertial currents, if it's used skillfully enough, he told himself.

The intelligence in the object had to agree with the intelligence being communicated to it, by means of Ärthähr, from the person trying to move it. *The intelligence in this rock will have to allow me to move the rock,* he thought. *I need to feel the Ärthähr enough to be able to discern the nature of the rock.*

He could see the clouds of particles within the rock's atomic clouds, and the clouds within those clouds. But he knew that that alone was not enough. He had to understand the miniscule, reticent intelligence of the rock, the Ärthähr that made it and all the cloud particles within it.

What am I going to say to Brittney? his own thoughts said to him again.

He tried to concentrate on the rock again.

This would be easier to understand if he were talking to Sarah about it out loud.

No...I shouldn't be around Sarah too much, not when Brittney wants to be with me. And I have to tell her I can't be with her.

But why can't I?

But he already knew a good enough reason why he could not. He could feel the Ärthähr a lot better now than he could those days ago when he had felt restrained from talking to Brittney, and there was no denying that Är did not want him to keep Brittney as his girlfriend.

And he understood enough to understand that doing what Är apparently did not want him to do could only end in pain.

But how could being with her possibly cause him more pain than knowing he had to break away from her had already been causing him?

How much pain would it cause Brittney if he told her that he couldn't see her anymore and then couldn't give her any real reason why?

And he wanted to be able to see her! He wanted her to be his girlfriend.

I love her, he realized.

The rock. The intelligence in the rock, he tried to think.

May be greater than mine, he thought miserably.

Why did the first, strongest message he got from the Ärthähr have to be such a terrible one?

The impulse to listen to Mär had been a pretty strong one, too, something inside him thought.

And the impulse to go see the Ämäthöär.

And to comfort his dad.

And the impulse to rescue Sarah from the pirates.

Sarah. He remembered her comforting his father too. He remembered her first telling him about Är and the Ärthähr.

He remembered her smiling at him.

She's wonderful, but what does that have to do with Brittney?

Sarah was wonderful.

But I love Brittney!

Because you've known her longer than you've known Sarah, came the unworded reply.

And for Brittney's own sake, I must not carry on with her this way, part of him added.

Am I just rebounding to Sarah? he chastised himself.

He had loved being around Sarah before his friends had reminded him about Brittney.

Whom was he rebounding to?

But there's nothing between Sarah and me for me to rebound from!

It's the nothing between you that you're rebounding from.

"Hi, Tom," someone said from behind him.

Tom snapped out of his anguished debate. Ŭmäthŭ, one of Mär's own immediate assistants, was touching down on the black, smoking rock near him.

"This is an interesting place to meditate at," Ŭmäthŭ said quietly.

Tom had chosen the smoking, sweltering fields of cooling magma around a boiling volcanic vent as a place to rest from battle simulations.

"I wanted to be by myself," Tom shrugged.

"And a burning volcano is not indicative at all of any internal uneasiness?" Ŭmäthŭ questioned, sitting on the edge of a glowing stream of magma and dipping his feet into it.

Tom smiled painedly. "I should have known to be frank with an Ōmäthäär like you."

Ŭmäthŭ smiled at him. It was an immensely comforting smile.

"Come on over here," he said. "Sit by me. Melted rock's fun to play with."

Tom glided over from where he had been seated in front of his

19: The Deeps of Infinity

contemplated rock, settling down beside Ŭmäthŭ.

"What about Brittney?" Ŭmäthŭ prompted, as if he and Tom had been talking about her for hours.

Tom wasn't surprised. He plopped his feet into the burbling magma. Its hot, gooey texture did feel very nice on his skin.

"I love her," he said after several seconds.

Ŭmäthŭ smiled a sad but admiring smile.

"But I know I can't be with her."

"Why not?" Ŭmäthŭ asked.

Tom looked up at him in surprise. "You don't feel it?"

"I feel a lot of sorrow and distress in you," Ŭmäthŭ said sympathetically. "I don't feel the things that are your responsibility, Tom. But I can also see that you feel that you need to not pursue marriage with Brittney."

"I hadn't thought about marriage!" Tom said. "I just love being with her."

"And she loves you too, doesn't she?"

"She's never said that," Tom said.

"She does seem to think very highly of you," Ŭmäthŭ said softly.

Tom didn't even think to ask how Ŭmäthŭ would know that.

"I do not think that you need to break all ties with Brittney. You love her. That is a powerful, precious thing. It is too good to just throw aside."

Tom stared at him. He suppressed his arising tears.

"But you cannot lead Brittney into an inferno that she should not be made to bear," Ŭmäthŭ said with imposing gravity.

"What do you mean?" Tom asked.

"You are an Ōmäthäär, Tom," Ŭmäthŭ said. "Yes," he said to Tom's protesting expression, "Even if you don't call yourself an Ōmäthäär, you have sworn an oath to follow Är in every aspect of your life.

"And Mär is teaching you about Ärthähr. No one has told you what Mär's life has been like. But I am afraid that yours will be yet more trying than his has been."

Tom didn't know what to say, what to think.

"Brittney is not ready for that kind of life," Ŭmäthŭ said.

Then how am I? Tom thought.

"You are ready for more than you're aware of yet," Ŭmäthŭ said. "I think, and Mär believes, that neither I nor he knows yet what you may be ready for.

"The life of an Ōmäthäär is not only war with Ämäthōär. The strain alone of doing what Är wants us to do, often in opposition to what our friends, our families, and so often, ourselves, want us to do, is enough of a burden to grind many people to emotional dust."

Tom grinned morosely.

"I think, Tom," Ŭmäthŭ said earnestly, "That you will soon rise up underneath burdens that make your present agony appear trivial."

He looked at Tom with sad empathy.

"But Brittney deserves to be loved by you. Don't take that from her."

"But I have to," Tom groaned.

"You do not have to estrange yourself. You do not have to cheat yourself of the glorious feelings you have for her.

"But, for Brittney, you must not pursue her as a companion. She deserves to keep you as a friend. A friend who loves her greatly. Who loves her enough to protect her from the pain that living a life with you would bring to her."

"Thanks," Tom smiled with pretended hurt. But he knew what Ŭmäthŭ was saying.

And suddenly, most of his despair disappeared.

He no longer felt torn about Brittney. He could love her, and be with her, and let her know always how much he loved her. And that while still freeing her of the relationship that Ŭmäthŭ flatteringly termed an inferno.

"I felt that," Ŭmäthŭ said happily.

"Why are you married, then?" Tom asked. "And why are so many of the Ōmäthäär married, if being an Ōmäthäär is so painful?"

"Painful, yes, but joyful!" Ŭmäthŭ said. "No pain is wasted. The hardship of living for things that so many forces are working so hard to destroy is made into joy and victory for us who do all we can for them.

"But it is better to not endure that pain if a person isn't ready yet to endure it through to the joy of triumph," he said. "But if you are ready, there is nothing, *nothing*, that is in any possible way more worthwhile than gaining that peace and joy!

"That's why Är is so prompt in giving every one of us as much conflict as we are ever ready for at any given time," he said with a grin, "Whether internal, or external, or whatever. The opposition incites us to step up to better ways, which make us better, and happier, and more in every way.

"Marriage is one of the greatest things there is, in all. Marriage, linking people living for Är and glory and courage and life, is incomparable. It's amazing.

"But marriage in which one is ready to bear a great deal more pain than the other will result in the one not being allowed to suffer as much as he or she would, and thus not grow as much as he or she should, and the other being made to suffer more than he or she would, and too much suffering strangles peoples' spirits."

19: The Deeps of Infinity

Tom nodded silently. He felt on fire again, as if the heat of the magma had intensified several times over and filled him all up.

Ŭmäthŭ twisted toward him and embraced him.

"Thank you," Tom said.

Ŭmäthŭ smiled at him. "You love her. That's all you need; you'll do fine. Love her, make her happy."

The fire filled Tom more powerfully.

Ŭmäthŭ held out both his hands to Tom. Tom took his right hand, then looked questioningly at him.

Ŭmäthŭ smiled and took Tom's right hand in his left. "If you are not an Ōmäthäär, no one I've ever known is."

"I'm not," Tom said before he could stop himself.

Ŭmäthŭ smiled more deeply. "You're a great man, I say, Tom." He pulled his hands away and rose up from the smoking black lava.

Tom smiled, wanting to say something to Ŭmäthŭ, something to express his gratitude, his awe. Ŭmäthŭ really was like Mär, he thought.

"A lot like Mär," Ŭmäthŭ was saying to him.

"Thank you, Ŭmäthŭ," Tom said again.

"Call me at any time," Ŭmäthŭ said with forceful sincerity. He raised his right hand in a wave and then shot up and away.

Tom watched him soar away.

He paddled his feet around in the magma a little more. Then he smiled with the feeling of confident peace that had been deepening within him.

He changed the stream of magma into a rippling brook of clear, cool water. The black lava around him transformed into thick, pungent sod, bursting with shining green grass and herbs.

He admired his reflection in the water as a few slender white trees with lively green leaves sprung upward behind him. He looked just the same, but something about that reflection struck him as much more appealing than any reflection he'd ever gazed into before.

He smiled, and raised himself up from the spongy bank. Enough Ärthähr for now. Brittney was more important than contemplating how to move all the rocks ever made.

He found her with several ten thousand other people a few thousand miles away.

They must have been doing a battle exercise, he thought.

He felt a bit of anxious fear resurface in him, remembering what he'd been told about the size of the approaching N'nrathĕrmĕ armies.

He shot off toward her. He ought to tell her now, and he'd been avoiding her too much already anyway. Ŭmäthŭ was more than right, he thought. Brittney deserved his time, as much time as he could give her without his difficulties of trying to do what Är wanted him to do becoming an annoyance to her.

I am not the Tom Pratt that Brittney knows, he recalled as he slowed to a stop near her.

She was standing motionless in the clear, breezy air in the midst of a swarm of others.

But I love her, he said silently to himself as he saw her there. For the first time it struck him as remarkable that he felt so powerfully toward her after only six uncertain days, after having almost completely forgotten about her for more than three weeks.

Brittney smiled at him, but didn't give any other indication that she'd noticed his arrival, still engrossed in the battle, her eyes closed in concentration.

He started to think of how he was going to say what he needed to say. But not only would nothing good come to him, he also felt the slight sinking sensation that had been becoming all too familiar to him now, a warning that whatever he was engaging in was not a very good idea.

So he let his thoughts relax.

And just relaxing in the air and looking at her filled him with peaceful contentment. He realized that his feelings for her had never been anywhere near this powerful when they had been tentatively dating before. How was it that he had fallen in love with her now?

She was still concentrating on the battle. Tom started to feel sorry for her, and annoyed at himself, because of what he knew he was about to do to this dear, good person.

But then he recalled Ŭmäthŭ's words: *You do not have to cheat yourself of the glorious feelings you have for her. Brittney deserves to keep you as a friend who loves her enough to protect her from the pain that living a life with you would bring to her.*

A friend who is in love with her, Tom thought, and smiled to himself with confidence as he did.

Still, how do I express this to Brittney, when she can't know why I can't be her boyfriend?

Just at that moment, Brittney opened her eyes.

"We've lost," she said. "But we did do a lot better this time."

"How big were they this time?" Tom heard himself ask.

"A little less than twice our strength," Brittney said. "But we did do very well."

19: The Deeps of Infinity

"We'll be fine," Tom said. "We are doing a lot better in our battles, and Mär will get us through it."

"You've been spending some time with Mär, haven't you?" Brittney said slyly. "Your dad told me you've been to see him a few times."

"Yeah, several times," Tom said.

"Why didn't you tell me you were meeting with him?" she asked. "What have you been doing with Mär?"

"What I couldn't tell you before, remember?" Tom said with a sorry grin.

"Ooh," Brittney said, her eyes widening. "Now I really want to know."

Tom laughed, and said, "I really want to tell you! Really! But Mär made me promise not to tell anyone, except for the head Ōmäthäär."

"Hold on," Brittney said. She turned her head toward the center of the crowd. After a few seconds, she said, "Let's go. The battle's finally really over; the last of us died or just gave up, and now our managers are going to recap the battle."

"Okay," Tom smiled at her.

"Yeah," she smiled back, catching the knowing gleam in his eyes. "I've done enough battles. I don't care if I don't listen to a review of this one."

Tom laughed, and they flew down toward the ground.

"Tom," Brittney said after a few seconds' hesitation. "I'm really scared."

Tom felt a surge of love toward her. He wanted to put his arms around her and keep her safe, from death and from everything.

But should he?

A friend who loves her, Ŭmäthŭ had said.

They drifted down toward a shady wood on a knoll overlooking golden-green fields. Tom put his arms around her as they settled in the underbrush between the trees.

"We keep losing in these exercises," Brittney said worriedly. "So many people keep dying. We are doing better, and fighting big armies is teaching us what we need to do. And they are just exercises."

"I know," Tom said, knowing what she was feeling. Knowing what she was feeling far more clearly than he had ever used to be able to.

Brittney leaned her head on his shoulder. "I'm so afraid I'm going to die," she said.

The fear of approaching annihilation had been diluted for Tom by his concentration on learning about Ä'ähänärdanär. But the possibility of his loved ones being massacred had not hit him seriously until just now.

"I love you," Tom said to her.

Brittney looked up quickly into his face, staring surprisedly into his eyes.

"You do?" she asked. Tears started emerging around her eyes.

"I do," Tom smiled warmly at her. "I will not let you die." He thought those were pretty impotent words; what could he really do against the armies of nearing N'nrathĕrmĕ? But, for some reason, those words felt like a promise that he knew he had the power to fulfill.

Brittney smiled at him, and tears began to trickle down her face.

"I won't," Tom said, with firm strength that he hadn't expected.

Brittney rested her head on his arm. She closed her eyes peacefully, tears still trickling over her cheeks.

Tom's chest was on fire. He could not do this.

"I don't want you to stay with me, though," he heard himself say, feeling partly horrified and partly satisfied to hear himself say it.

Brittney looked up at him queryingly.

"I don't want you to die," Tom said.

"Wait, what are you saying?" Brittney asked him warily.

What do I say?

I do love her.

That's why I'm doing this!

"I don't want to lose you," he said. "And if you're my girlfriend, I will."

That sounded stupid.

And apparently Brittney didn't understand him either. "What do you mean?" she said.

"Mär."

"Mär?" Brittney asked, more confused.

"You know, the things he told me not to tell anyone about. I cannot be here for you the way I wish I could. The other things I'm doing...the Ōmäthäär are teaching me things. Teaching me how to be," he hesitated, "How to be like them."

Brittney was looking searchingly into his eyes, not saying anything back to this.

"And I don't want you to get hurt," Tom said. "I want to be there for you, be here for you. But as a boyfriend, I know I'll just disappoint you."

Brittney smiled at him, and he felt confidence swoop back into him.

"Why can't you tell Mär no?" she asked.

Why not? part of him thought.

Because Är loves both Brittney and you, the wordless voice said. *If you turn willingly against what you know is right, you will be turning against Brittney's happiness as well as your own.*

"I can," Tom said. "But what he's having me do it bigger than just Mär. If

19: The Deeps of Infinity

I don't do these things that I can't tell you about, if I give them up because I want to be with you—"

"Do you want to be with me?"

"Yes," Tom said meaningfully, and Brittney nodded.

"But I want you to be happy more than I want to just be with you," Tom said. "I can be with you! Just not as your boyfriend."

"Okay," Brittney said, looking down and moving away from him a little.

Tom actually laughed. "I'm not a boyfriend, but I'm still in love with you!"

"Tom," Brittney said, suddenly looking angry.

"Brittney," Tom said more quietly. "I love you—"

"I need to go," Brittney said shortly.

No! Tom cried out within himself. *What have I done?*

"Thank you for telling me, Tom," she said. And she smiled at him, but he could tell she was frustrated, angry, and hurt. "Bye," she said, then flew up through the trees and away from him.

Tom rose up to follow her.

Let her be, a comforting feeling seemed to say in him.

Tom fell to the ground. He put his face in his hands.

He stopped himself from crying.

"*I did what I knew I needed to do!*" he cried out angrily.

Mär had said something about testing feelings out, he remembered. About learning by hard experience how to distinguish Ärthähr from other, unreliable feelings.

"I guess it wasn't Ärthähr that guided me now," he whispered bitterly.

Wasn't it? a small voice suggested through the roil of his anguished thoughts.

And as if it were from somewhere deeply remote within his own soul, he sensed a tiny feeling of satisfaction, almost as if someone far away were saying pleasedly to him:

Well done!

Chapter 20

Transcendent Encouragement

"Tom, pull up!" his manager, Änŭn, called to him.

"Everyone, up!" Tom shouted. "Äszad, Amōth, watch your right flanks!"

"They're going for the Shell again!" someone shouted.

"Let them," Tom said. "Kadrŭthä, move in at 13°, -2°!"

Tom's assistant Kadrŭthä's fleets spiraled around a few prongs of a N'nrathĕrmĕ battalion that had tried to cut them off.

"Good!" Tom called.

Meanwhile, he and three others of his assistant couples had begun chasing a wedge of N'nrathĕrmĕ away from a charging surge of Nŭährnär's fleets.

"Tom, let's fake an encirclement," came an Ōmäthäär's voice.

"To the divisions at 14°, 4°!" Tom said. "Ōfha, around back behind them on their lower right. Amōth, upper left, Mamnaf upper right, Ŭdmamnaf lower left! Together! Kadrŭthä, charge their underside, like the stab-and-snare last time!"

Tom's fleets moved seamlessly along with two Ōmäthäärs' armies.

"Keep the pressure on them!" Tom said. "It's our tempo, not theirs."

The N'nŭährnär armies encircled the N'nrathĕrmĕ divisions, communicating with and playing off of one another as though controlled by one mind, yet each ship dancing and maneuvering around in its own way, and each group of ships in their managers' own ways, the multiplicity of minds at work combining in a fluid unpredictability.

Fifteen N'nrathĕrmĕ battalions had been hammering rantha mercilessly at the Shell. The Shell had been sending a continuous hail of rantha at them in return, but the N'nrathĕrmĕ were beginning to blast through it, despite the high cost of their own numbers. Now, seven of those battalions broke away to counter the N'nŭährnärs' encirclement.

That bought us a little bit of time, Tom thought. He saw with pleasure but without surprise that his assistants needed no word from him; every division under him broke swiftly and independently out of the way of the incoming N'nrathĕrmĕ.

"No one try to encircle them again," Tom said emphatically, "Unless you can feint without being caught in their snares."

He already had his next score of moves prepared in his mind, each with at least a few backup variations.

20: Transcendent Encouragement

"Now, spread out, way out," Tom said. "Mamnaf, Rähnathä, spread out and come with me toward the Shell!"

"Tom," Änŭn called happily to him, "I'll take control of your fleets; Mär wants to see you."

Tom smiled to himself. The battle disappeared, and he was sitting on the edge of a cliff over a steel colored cloudy sea. His assistants would know what to do, he knew.

He looked pleasedly at them, seated or floating motionlessly in the midst of a crowd of a couple thousand higher managers.

He rose from the cliff, enjoying the complicated percussion of the waves against the rocks far below.

Mär was back at the Sanctuary, he saw. When would he get to go inside there? he wondered again as he accelerated off toward it.

We were doing a good deal better that time, he thought.

I hope Brittney's okay.

Every time he had considered going to see Brittney over the past hour since he had tried to tell her what he needed to do he had felt unmistakably restrained. It was no feeling of fear, which Mär's memories warned him against, but a nice feeling of benevolent waiting.

I am getting the hang of this, he sighed to himself as he stopped in front of the Sanctuary and Mär. The past days that Mär had been teaching him about Ärthähr had felt like they had been long lifetimes in themselves.

"I am sorry I took you away from the others in the battle there," Mär said.

"I'll follow your schedule," Tom said. "You're the one teaching me."

"Both of you," Mär smiled, as Sarah came to a sudden halt by them.

"Hi, Tom," Sarah said with noticeable unease.

"Hi Sarah," Tom said cheerfully.

Whom was I rebounding to? his thought echoed in his head. *Whom from?*

Mär didn't say a single word about Ŭmäthŭ in front of Sarah, though. Instead, he said:

"Inside!" His face reflected the anticipation that Tom and Sarah felt as they realized what he had said.

He led them to one of the Sentinels, a man called Manhō.

"Don't try to get in without the leave of one of these men," Mär said lightly, though there was a definite hint of seriousness in those words.

"The password isn't a secret," Mär said. "But it is profoundly important and special." He nodded to Manhō.

"It's 'Ōhä-Ä'ähänärdanär,'" Manhō said.

"'The Order of Är Forever?'" Sarah paraphrased it.

"That, and a whole, whole lot more!" Manhō smiled. "How much do they know about Ä'ähänärdanär?" he asked Mär.

"Ask them."

Manhō looked at Tom and Sarah.

"It's the name of your order, before you fled out of Nrathĕrmĕ," Sarah said tentatively. "And the sum total of all you believe about Är."

"'Our' order?" Manhō smiled at Mär. He looked back at Sarah. "I can't let you in here if it isn't your order, too!"

"Oh, yes," Sarah said embarrassedly.

Manhō just smiled understandingly at her. "I know," he said. "But we called our order Ä'ähänärdanär after other things that we already used that term for."

He glanced at Mär, who took over.

"Remember what I said about the whole of time that we are in?" Mär said.

Tom and Sarah both nodded.

"That time, the whole of it, from beginning to end if you want to think of it that way—"

"But it really has no beginning or end," Sarah grinned at him.

"No more than Earth has a top or a bottom," Tom said.

Mär laughed. "But you do understand what I mean," he said. "Just like referring to the whole Earth, from top to bottom."

"Yes," Tom said.

Sarah nodded.

"That whole time is one perfect story. The Perfect Story. Every good thing you can get in one of Terry's or Tävna's or Andrew's stories is a reflection off of the archetypal forms of The Perfect Story. The Infinite Story, infinite in depth and scope and magnitude, and perfect.

"That Perfect Story is Ä'ähänärdanär.

"To want to do what Är wants us to do is to become more of a protagonist of the perfect plot of Ä'ähänärdanär.

"Är is the core protagonist, and all our tributary plots build together to the succeeding climaxes of the transcendent Plot."

"What is the transcendent Plot?" Sarah asked.

"Something like this: The virgin, vacant universe of all that is and all that can ever be undergoes progressively more horrible storms of darkness and doubt and pain and horror. But after every storm, the sun of comprehension and fulfillment and light and power and glory glows progressively stronger. After the greatest infinite storm, the sun of fullness shines infinitely and perfectly. And that's the culmination of that time's plot. That is Är's Plot,

20: Transcendent Encouragement

essentially; now just extend it over infinite years and infinite worlds and peoples."

"And that Story is Ä'ähänärdanär," Manhō said.

"There is more to Ä'ähänärdanär than that, still," Mär said. "But I can tell you that later.

"But one interpretation of Ōhä-Ä'ähänärdanär is a wish that that Story be fulfilled," he continued. "It's an oath that everything we do is to further Är's plans along, to bring happiness to everything."

He looked back at Manhō.

"So," Manhō grinned at Sarah and Tom, "Are you ready to make that kind of a commitment?"

"We already promised that," Tom said.

"Yes," Manhō said. "You're understanding what you've promised. That's more than can be said for some people. Now the promise is just made again in a more emphatic, more informed way."

"Alright," Sarah said.

"I'll go in first," Mär said. "I will meet you inside."

"Okay," Tom and Sarah said.

Mär glided to Manhō. He took Manhō's right hand with his left. "Ōhä-Ä'ähänärdanär," he said, then glided, with a smile back at Tom and Sarah, through the spotless side of the great white Sanctuary.

Manhō then turned to Tom and Sarah. "Are you ready?"

"Yes!" Tom and Sarah said together.

Manhō laughed. "Enthusiasm means 'yes.'"

He extended his right hand to Sarah. "I hold the authority, as the Sentinel, to let you pass," he said. "So I give you my right hand to give you the power to pass inside."

"Okay," Sarah said. She took his right hand with her left. "Ōhä-Ä'ähänärdanär," she said, timidly but sincerely.

"I hope so," Manhō smiled.

Manhō released her hand, and moved aside for her to pass by.

Sarah moved toward the shining whiteness, and then passed through.

She had emerged into a great courtyard. There was another enormous cube and sphere in the center of it, but the spherical courtyard was large enough to enclose a vast, spacious area outside of that inner sanctuary.

And growing all along the walls of the spherical courtyard were blooming and abounding gardens of gorgeous plants. No plants touched the inner cube and sphere, but every other surface was covered by teeming vegetation.

But they weren't ordinary plants. There was not a trace of green anywhere within the Sanctuary. Everything she saw, including Mär smiling to greet her, was a brilliant, luminous white. And Sarah had never seen any plants so beautiful, any flowers so colorful, as these glowing white ones all around her. It was as if every fair color was simultaneously shining for her to enjoy, in a deepness and completeness of whiteness that she had never pictured in any imagining of her own.

"Welcome to the Sanctuary of the Ōmäthäär, Sarah," Mär smiled, giving her both of his hands.

A trio of gleaming white birds glided toward them from one side of the vast courtyard as Sarah took Mär's hands. Mär smiled, and released her hands as Tom entered through the plants behind her.

"This is the Sanctuary of the Ōmäthäär," Mär said to Tom, taking his hands as well. "This is our nüährnär within Nüährnär. This is where we counsel, where we teach, and where we laugh and talk and rest. And this is where Är, most often, comes to talk personally with us."

He smiled as Tom and Sarah both looked around, as if expecting to see Är standing right there amongst the wheeling white birds.

"He comes when he needs to," Mär said with a fire that felt to Sarah as if it filled the courtyard.

"What's in there?" Tom asked, gesturing at the opaque white building in the center of the room.

"The deeper rooms of the Ä'ähänärdanär order," Mär said. "But in here is all we need for this time."

"Alright," Tom said, feeling nosy.

"The more you want to see what's in there, the better," Mär smiled. "Just don't let yourself in without being let in."

"Okay," Tom smiled back. "Let me in as soon as I'm ready."

Mär laughed. "Ready you are, I think. But I want to use all our time now to teach you other things. If I teach you what is expedient now, there will still be a later in which you can learn everything else you want to know."

That sounded ominous to Tom, and he didn't say anything.

Mär looked from Tom to Sarah, then back to Tom, then to Sarah again. His hands were clasped loosely together, and his eyes were flaming as if he were holding in some tremendous, marvelous surprise.

Tom and Sarah didn't know what to expect.

Mär's hands flew apart jubilantly. "Let's get Ärthähr moving!"

Tom and Sarah looked uncomprehendingly at him.

"You've thought about Ärthähr enough. It is time that you start to use it! I want you to try, in here, to move other beings by means of Ärthähr alone. No

20: Transcendent Encouragement

mechanical inertial currents, no touching with your hands. Just the communication and empathy of working by means of pure Ärthähr."

Tom remembered the unresponsive lava rock. And then he remembered Brittney. And Sarah there standing benevolently beside him. And he wondered, without intending to wonder, whether it had been Är's Ärthähr that had brought Sarah both into his life and repeatedly into his mind.

His mind was immediately occupied with many other thoughts, none of which involved moving rocks or birds or anything through Ärthähr.

"Do you think we're ready to do that?" Sarah asked Mär.

"I can see it plainly," Mär smiled at her. "Even if you haven't done it yet, there is a point at which future things end up as past; there is a point at which things you've never been able to do end up done by you. I think this is one of those points, for both of you."

Sarah smiled back at Mär's incontestable confidence.

"I would have you move plants in here," Mär said, "But I think it will be better, and more pleasurable for me, for you to try to move me around."

"You?" Tom said, calling himself back from him musings.

"As long as you don't try to hurt me," Mär joked.

"How would we hurt you?" Sarah said.

"You may be surprised," Mär said vaguely.

"But I think I can make it easier, much easier, for you to move me. The plants and animals in this Sanctuary are very intelligent, and I'm sure they will be more than accommodating to you, as they are to all Ōmäthäär. But I think I will likely open myself to you more than they will. And that will make it crucially easier for you to notice results."

"What do we do?" Tom asked.

"You've thought about it," Mär said. "And I've given you plenty of memories of other Ōmäthäär moving things through Ärthähr. Just try, now, what you already know."

"Okay," Sarah said.

"Both of us together?" Tom asked him.

"No!" Mär said, then laughed. "Unless you can communicate to one another exactly how you want to move me, that could be rather painful for me; one of you moving me one way and the other moving me another way! Ärthähr can communicate things with that degree of exactness, but we'll work on that."

"But you want us to communicate with every particle of you enough to move you?" Sarah asked in an overwhelmed voice.

"No," Mär said. "Not in this case. You only need to communicate with the core of me, the essence of me, and convince those bits of Ärthähr to make me move."

"So we're possessing you?" Tom asked, appalled.

"No," Mär said, with a sudden flash of grimness.

A brief shadow made the white glow around them seem to flicker for a fleeting instant.

"No, you are communicating with me," Mär said, and his voice returned to its accustomed lightness. "You are not forcing me, nor attempting to force me.

"Sometimes Ōmäthäär must attempt to force things, and people," Mär said heavily. No shadow this time, but an affective somberness seemed to Tom and Sarah as if it were radiating off of Mär. "That is how we kill Ämäthōär.

"The Ämäthōär, almost always, have to be killed. There is no other way, for many of them, to stop them in their destructive aims than just to kill them and remove them from this state of life.

"But few Ämäthōär will ever agree to that," he said with a grim smile.

"So we communicate with things that will listen to us, like many of the particles within the Ämäthōär, even the energies that sustain them with life, and get them to kill the Ämäthōär for us. A strong enough influence of Ärthähr can force someone to move against his will, just as a strong enough inertial force can move a person against his will. And Ärthähr can physically disrupt the fine forces of energy that keep a person alive.

"But I don't want you to try to force me!" he said. "Just communicate with me. I'm sure that the core aspects of my body will be more than happy to do what you want them to."

"Okay," Sarah said with a great deal less confidence than Mär was demonstrating. "I'll go first," she said, cocking a glance at Tom.

Tom smiled an encouraging smile at her. That made her feel confident much more than Mär's words had.

She tried not to think about Tom's smiling confidence, though, and labored to recall everything that she'd been taught about Ärthähr.

Just feel Mär, she thought. Feel him. Be aware of him. Feel him. Empathize with the energy in and through him. Empathize. Be aware of it. Let it trust me. Be one with it. Be one with it.

She was looking straight at Mär. Something unseen, but almost visible somehow, was radiating fiercely off of him. It was comforting, and beautiful.

Feel him. Be aware of his light and life.

It was as if Mär was glowing brightly from deep within himself. It was a powerfully comforting light. The invisible light was to Sarah transcendently more beautiful than all the wonderful plants there in the courtyard.

20: Transcendent Encouragement

Be aware of his life and light. Be aware of it. Ask it to move upward. Don't force it. Be aware of it. Sense it. Feel it. Light and life. Enjoy it. Admire it. Enjoy it.

Ask it to move Mär upward. Don't force it.

Tom was watching with excited anticipation. He glanced from Sarah to Mär, and then back at Sarah.

Mär was opening himself to Sarah, letting her sense him, leaving himself open to any suggestion that might come from her.

Sarah was concentrating, feeling, willing.

But nothing happened.

Sarah kept willing, kept sensing. Kept feeling out the invisible glorious light all in and through Mär.

Mär kept opening himself to Sarah. He could feel the light and power glowing off of her. He could see it invisibly.

But still nothing happened.

"You're not moving," Sarah said disappointedly.

Mär didn't say anything.

"I could feel it, I could feel a lot," Sarah said. "It was great. But you're still not moving."

"Yes," Mär said slowly. He looked doubtfully at Sarah. Then he grinned at her. "I'll move you both around a little," he said. "That may help you become more used to how it works."

"Okay," Sarah said.

Mär smiled at them, and then immediately they both felt a tremendously pleasant warmth course through them. Tom felt himself eased away from where he was floating in the air.

Tom and Sarah glided in a leisurely circle around Mär, neither of them either resisting or causing the motion.

Sarah felt overcome with unexpected emotion. She felt suddenly like weeping for pleasure.

It was as if every part of Tom's being was ablaze with a cool white fire. Everything around him, the plants, the birds, Mär, and the cube in the center, was radiating an intense, pleasurable glow.

Mär brought Sarah and Tom around in front of him again and released them. Sarah could still feel an aftertaste of the warm peace that had just been filling her, but it was only a sweet shadow of the preceding surge of joy.

Both Tom and Sarah were lost for words.

Mär grinned at them. "The fact that you liked it that much says a lot about your affinity with the Ärthähr already.

"And I felt a great deal about you both, just now. In communicating with you like that. There are many Ōmäthäär who routinely move all kinds of things through Ärthähr who do not possess the strength of Ärthähr that I just felt in you two.

"So don't be nervous," he said reassuringly. "I can see as plainly as anything that you are both capable of moving me, at the very least, if not also of moving every plant and animal in this building!

"So let's try again," he said, clasping his hands loosely in front of him again.

"Tom, you move me."

"Wait," Sarah said.

"What?" Mär asked.

"I remember, Ähänär showed my family an Ämäthōär she'd seen." Somehow, in that place, it felt a great deal easier for her to shrug off the now faint darkness that crept up within her. "And he was doing something with his hands and his arms, and his body too. Like a rhythm or something."

"You don't need to do that," Mär smiled. "I know whom you're referring to. Many Ämäthōar and Ōmäthäär move their bodies in response to finer sensations of Ärthähr. It helps concentration.

"That man, Akĕz, had the luxury of time to concentrate like that as he directed Ärthähr to kill N'nŭährnär. But I didn't do that just now to move you two; I didn't need to.

"Don't worry about this yet. But dancing; it really is a dance; is a great way to sense Ärthähr more thoroughly.

"If you want to dance to what you feel," he smiled at both of them, "Do it! Just don't take on too many new skills at once."

"Okay," Sarah said. "Thanks."

"Tom?" Mär said invitingly.

"Okay," Tom said, absently stretching out his hands as he fixed his eyes on Mär.

But, though Tom felt a thin resurgence of the tranquil warmth that had enveloped him when Mär had moved him around, he too did not move Mär at all.

"I'm not resisting," Mär said with subdued humor.

"I can feel that," Tom said uncertainly. "Do we just need to practice more?"

Mär laughed. "Always!"

"It sure felt nice, though," Sarah said optimistically. "Even if we can't move you yet."

20: Transcendent Encouragement

"Yeah, really," Tom agreed.

"Wonderful," Mär said. "You're both getting closer and closer to the Ärthähr. Keep pondering and meditating about this. But don't try to move things except for when I or a leading Ōmäthäär is there with you."

"We'll try to do better," Sarah said apologetically.

"You've done wonderfully!" Mär said. "You have been learning about these things for less than two weeks now, and look at you!"

"It seems like it's been a lot longer," Tom said.

"Learning about Är will do that to you," Mär smiled.

"You have to go, then?" Sarah said sadly, correctly reading Mär's posture.

"I should," Mär said. "And you both should, too. But remember, thinking about Ärthähr is consummately more important than battle exercises."

Tom and Sarah nodded.

"Don't worry," he said to them. "We will do well enough here, against this coming army."

He glided forward and hugged them both, clasping both hands with each of them.

"Actually," he said, "Stay here as long as you want to. It's a great place to think and to talk, and you're as welcome here as any other Ōmäthäär are."

"Alright," Tom said.

"Thanks," Sarah said.

"Do good," Mär said, smiling. Then he passed through the plants and out of the solid Sanctuary wall.

Manhō smiled at him as he passed by. Mär waved back at him, but his thoughts were elsewhere.

Why hadn't they been able to do it? They were ready. Cleary they were ready. And capable. More capable than many experienced Ōmäthäär were.

But, as he soared toward Äthääōhä, the only response from Är that he felt was an unspecified comforting exhortation to not worry.

Now that Mär had left, Sarah felt uncertain and nervous again.

"I guess we should go too," Tom said.

"We ought to talk about Ärthähr more," Sarah said. "Later," she added quickly. "When you have the chance."

"I have time now," Tom said.

"Okay," Sarah said, and smiled a little.

But then something seemed to seize up inside of him.

"But I just came from a battle exercise," he said. "I do need to go see my assistants again."

"Oh," Sarah said, her disappointment returning.

What am I doing? he thought. *I should stay and talk to her. I owe it to Sarah. I've been being a jerk, avoiding her like this.*

But I already said I should go!

"Well, call me later, then," Sarah said, giving up.

"I'm really sorry, Sarah," he said abruptly. He wanted to tell her all about Brittney, and his pain and preoccupation about her. Sarah would understand.

His avoiding her had nothing to do with her, he thought, wanting to assure her of that.

But the thought of telling Sarah about Brittney filled Tom with apprehension.

You're intimidated by her, an unsettlingly accurate voice seemed to say from deep within him.

"Sorry about what?" Sarah asked; a little too hopefully, she thought.

"Sorry I haven't been there to talk to you," Tom said.

"Oh, I just wanted to talk about Ärthähr," Sarah lied.

See? She's just a friend.

The wordless voice did not dignify that with a rebuttal.

There was still a lingering glow around Tom from his attempt to use the Ärthähr, Sarah noticed. He looked visibly just the same as he always did—

Charismatic, gorgeous, and unpretentious, she felt herself think.

—but there was something about that residual aura all around him that made him seem infinitely more attractive.

She was just as fine as ever, but that shine, or whatever it was that he was noticing glistening off of her, made her appear to him as the single most beautiful being he had ever seen.

And he was aware of, first, a powerful desire to just stay right there with Sarah forever, and then a much louder urge to get as far away from Sarah as he could as quickly as possible.

"Uh, right," Tom said. "That's what I meant. I'll talk to you later."

What did I just say? Sarah thought terrifiedly.

"Call me soon," she said desperately.

"I will," Tom said, without thinking whether he meant it at all. "I, uh, need to get back to my assistants. Bye."

"Good bye," Sarah said miserably as Tom wheeled around to disappear through the plants behind him.

What did I just say? she thought forlornly.

It doesn't matter, though. He had apologized about not being there to talk to her. That didn't mean he did want to talk to her. It meant the opposite, didn't

20: Transcendent Encouragement

it?

Did it?

"I hope I never see him again," she said quietly, though her feelings were crying out for just the reverse, but with the added fantasy of Tom actually enjoying her.

"How soon, at their speed?" Mär asked.

Nearly two days had passed. Mär and Bävän and Thas were conferring within one of the inner rooms of the Sanctuary.

"Three days," Bävän said.

"And we've spotted nearly half a million separate battalions among them," Thas said. "They rallied together some twenty-two hours ago, then set off toward us. Hōäōhä did not want to follow them after they converged to come toward us."

"Good man," Mär said. "It's a wonder he stayed unnoticed as long as he did."

He thought for a few seconds. "Alright," he said then. "No active scanning of them until they come within our usual range. They should not know that we know they're coming."

"That was very good, Sarah," Mär said sincerely.

"I still didn't move you," Sarah said, becoming more irritated.

"But you are doing better," Mär said. "Both of you are. I can feel it more strongly now whenever you try to move me."

"But we still can't move you," Tom said.

"Have you talked much about last time?" Mär asked them.

Tom looked distractedly at the shining white plants along the walls. Sarah looked sadly at Mär for a moment, then looked away too.

The beauty of the room was dimmed in both of their eyes, as if seen only dimly through smoke.

"You two," Mär said in a hurt voice, "You need to talk about this! This is more important than planning or practicing. More important even than personal worries."

Sarah looked up into Mär's eyes. His gaze was more understanding than she had expected.

"The N'nrathĕrmĕ armies will reach us within three days. I wish I could be with you and practice this with you constantly, but I cannot. But you cannot lose any time. You have to learn these things as quickly as you can!"

Tom looked up at him, and Mär smiled concernedly at him.

"I will see you both at the wedding tomorrow."

"You're going to be there?" Sarah said excitedly.

"I plan to be," Mär said heavily, "Depending on how many preparations we can finish before then."

"I'll tell Spalding and Tävna!" Sarah said, then fell quiet again.

"Or, um, maybe you should, Tom. Since he's your cousin." It was one of the few things she had said to him throughout that practice.

"Okay," Tom said awkwardly, looking at Sarah for an instant but then looking away again.

"Talk about this," Mär said again, and the emphasis of it intensified the divide inside of Tom.

Mär smiled comfortably at them despite his weariness, then passed out through the wall of the Sanctuary.

"Oüähä," he called as he accelerated through the air. "This is Mär. I need Spalding for a little while."

Äröähr smiled at them. "And you're both sure about this?"

"They're sure," his wife Änŭn said beside him.

"I am," Spalding said, beaming at Tävna and not looking at Äröähr or Änŭn.

"Tell us the terms again," Tävna said, gazing glowingly but teasingly at Spalding.

"It's for ever, like you said before, Tävna," Äröähr said humoringly, but still with heavy sobriety. "Everything else is up to you.

"But I suggest," he said with a smile, "That, being together forever, you be good to each other."

"Can we handle that?" Tävna grinned at Spalding.

"Can't we?" Spalding smiled back enthusiastically.

"The two of you together, if you're good to each other," Äröähr said, "Are much more than the two of you apart could ever be."

"Much happier," Spalding added.

Tävna beamed at him.

"But it is forever. Or until death, if death should come to either of you."

"I won't let death stop us," Tävna said.

"I'm with her," Spalding said to Äröähr.

"So, do you both accept my authority to marry you?" Äröähr asked. "Knowing that this is permanent and irreversible and unalterable except in the case of the most extreme of difficulties? Are you willing to spend forever bound and sworn to serve each other, and to work as one in everything that

20: Transcendent Encouragement

you do?"

"You know," Spalding said, "The thought of living forever has always scared me."

He leaned forward and kissed Tävna, who reached out and wouldn't release him for a considerable while. When she finally let him go, he laughed euphorically:

"It doesn't anymore!"

"Me neither," Tävna said, not taking her eyes off of him.

Spalding smiled at her, then said, still gazing at her, "We accept it."

"Yes, we do," Tävna said.

"Then so let it be recognized!" Äröähr said jubilantly. "Spalding Andrew Pratt, the son of Daniel Allen Pratt and Ann Victoria Burrows Pratt, and Tävna, the daughter of Räkran and Brōzängat, are now married!"

He threw up his hands celebratorily. Daniel and two of Spalding's sisters, Christina and Robyn, began clapping their hands loudly.

Spalding and Tävna embraced each other and kissed again as more of the Nōhōnŭäär in the water around them joined in clapping. Mär joined in quickly too, and soon everyone there in the water with Spalding and Tävna was clapping loudly like the Earthmen.

Ann rushed through the dancing waves toward Spalding and Tävna, followed closely by Räkran and Brōzängat. Spalding and Tävna were still laughing and kissing each other, and Ann had to settle for hugging them both together, getting subsequently embraced by both of Tävna's parents.

"Congratulations!" Brōzängat said to Ann.

"To all of us!" Ann said.

Daniel had come up behind them. "Alright, let them go," he was laughing. "They only married *each other*."

"Yes!" Spalding said, looking exultantly at his father. "We are married!"

"Forever!" Tävna said, hugging Spalding's middle.

"If you weren't so happy," Andrew said, gliding up through the sparkling blue water toward them, "I would still think you're both nuts."

"Seventeen days!" Terry said.

"I've seen worse," Mär smiled, gliding up from behind Äröähr and Änŭn.

"The seventeen best days of my life!" Tävna said.

"And a day is so long now!" Spalding said to Terry.

"I know," Terry said.

"Yeah, it feels like we've always been in this place," Andrew said.

"Even so, he's still just a baby," Spalding's younger sister Heather said, punching him lovingly in his back.

"Hey, six years is older than my grandparents' parents," Tävna said.

"Yeah, but who are you to talk?" Spalding said to Heather, turning around and punching her in the shoulder.

"You are a baby," Sarah said, punching him again.

"What is this?" Spalding laughed. "Now I'm married, so now you can all beat on me?"

"No, just me," Tävna said.

Sarah and Heather laughed. "That will certainly be more than enough," Sarah said.

"So, when are you going to get someone to beat on, Sarah?" Aaron said beside her.

Sarah could have really punched him.

She kept her tone cheerful as she said, "Let he who is without sin cast the first stone."

"Okay," Aaron said. "Spalding—"

But Spalding just laughed. "She may not kill her brother, but I'm not taking my chances."

He gave Sarah a strangely knowing, reassuring look, and she felt a rise of unexpected gratitude toward him.

It was more than ten minutes before Spalding and Tävna could extricate themselves from their family and friends around them. Spalding noticed Tom keeping his distance from Sarah, and also noted Tom's obvious avoidance of engaging in any conversation in which she was at all involved, despite a few valiant efforts on Sarah's part to force him to respond to her.

Then Mär caught Spalding's eye, and he was sure that that was a signal to move.

"Keep them busy," he said privately to Tävna.

"Will do," Tävna said back.

Spalding edged out of the slightly dissipating crowd, and caught Tom's eye.

"Over here," he said privately to him, moving away. Tävna was attracting everyone else's attention with another loud tale of her mischievous and accident prone sisters, Gändan and Üdmäth.

"What?" Tom asked, attempting to sound jovial.

Spalding made sure that Tävna was occupying everyone else's attention. Even Mär was looking raptly at her, his booms of laughter sounding amongst the others' chortling at the antics of his new sisters-in-law. Then he noticed Sarah glancing curiously at them.

Well, it's sort of right that she notice something, he thought.

20: Transcendent Encouragement

Then he rounded on Tom.

"What on earth do you think you're doing?" he said furiously.

"What?" Tom said, taken aback.

"Mär told me how you've been acting toward Sarah."

"How I've been acting?"

"Yeah," Spalding said, "How you've been being an arrogant jerk, and not talking to her or giving her the time of day!"

"Mär said that?" was the first thing Tom could think to say.

"Well, he took a lot more time to say it," Spalding said.

Tom knew, though, that, whatever Mär had said, what Spalding had just said was true. He had been being an awful jerk to Sarah.

"She's crazy about you, Tom!" Spalding said. "And I thought you were crazy about her, too, but…"

"Sarah?" Tom asked. "About *me*?"

Spalding looked disbelievingly at him. "You can't tell? Are you serious?"

"Why?" Tom asked, realizing that he really should not have felt so surprised about this revelation as he did.

"You've got me," Spalding said viciously. "The Tom I knew, well, I can see Sarah falling in love with him. But you…I don't know why Sarah still wants anything to do with you."

"Why?" Tom said.

"Because you won't talk to her! You won't look at her! She wants to be around you, and you're always avoiding her!"

Tom took that in, knowing he had already been aware of all of it.

"Why?" Spalding demanded severely. "What are you thinking?"

"I don't…" Tom began slowly.

"What is there not to love?" Spalding said.

What is there not to love? Tom thought thunderously.

"Nothing," he said after an internally roaring pause.

"Is it Brittney, or something, Tom?" Spalding asked more quietly. "Because if it is—"

"No," Tom said.

"Good. Sarah's better."

"Hey!" Tom said. "You don't know about Brittney. She—"

"So it is Brittney!"

"No," Tom said again. "But it was, I guess."

"What does that mean?" Spalding said, a little less angrily.

Tom was only now understanding his own actions over the past several days. He didn't say anything for a couple seconds, then asked, "You really think that Sarah likes me?"

"'Likes?'" Spalding repeated. "Like a childish crush?"

"Well, she doesn't really know me very well, does she?" Tom said.

"She used to, didn't she?" Spalding hissed. "She knew the Tom we all knew and loved. She loves you, or I don't love Tävna!"

Tom stared at him. Spalding wasn't kidding around.

"How..." he said. "We've only known each other for—"

"For twice as long as I've known my wife!" Spalding said.

It had been an incredibly long time, Tom realized.

And you fell for Brittney pretty fast, Ärthähr said in his heart. *Sarah is, just a little bit, like you.*

What have I been doing? he thought.

"I was afraid," he said out loud.

Spalding's anger changed slowly to puzzlement.

"You're right," Tom said. "There isn't anything not to love about Sarah. And I think I knew that."

A faint grin was emerging on Spalding's face.

"And that's why I went for Brittney," Tom said, partly horrified at his own actions but also relieved at his confession of them.

"I do love Brittney," he said quickly. "But I think I was afraid of Sarah. I don't think I would have been so excited about Brittney if I wasn't afraid of Sarah. I don't know what I would have done about Brittney.

"I love her," he said to Spalding's increasing grin. "But, I think I went after her all the more because I wanted to hide from Sarah."

"Sarah is imposing," Spalding smiled, "But why on earth were you afraid of her?"

Tom smiled a little as he said, "Because there is nothing not to love about her." His smile deepened. "I guess I already knew that. And I was afraid of being around her, because I thought she would never be more than a wonderful friend."

He paused.

"I was a coward. Just like Mär said: I was afraid of enduring pain to get something great. I knew Sarah was great, but I guess I was afraid that she would never be more than a great friend.

"And I guess that just isn't enough for me."

"Well, you're wising up now, finally," Spalding grinned.

Tom didn't answer. Now that he had said it, he realized that, all this time, he had been enamored with Sarah. And his response to that had been the most nonsensical, ridiculous thing he could have done.

20: Transcendent Encouragement

"So, what about her?" Spalding said.

Tom looked back inquiringly at him.

"What about Sarah?" Spalding grinned with anticipation. "Go talk to her! She's been feeling like you don't want anything to do with her."

"You don't seem to care about Brittney at all, do you?" Tom smiled wryly at him.

"Well, I don't know Brittney very well," Spalding said. "But, Tom—"

"It's okay," Tom said with returning weariness. "I hope you'll get to know her better. But Brittney isn't very happy with me right now."

"Why?" Spalding asked with forced disappointment.

"Because I can't let her be my girlfriend," Tom said, looking down at his rippling reflection in the water around them. "Because I can't bring her along with me, with everything Mär's having me do."

"Oh," Spalding said, trying to sound commiserating.

Tom smiled knowingly at him. "You'll get to like her," he said.

"As your friend," Spalding said happily. "But in the meantime—"

"I love Brittney," Tom said firmly. "I don't want you to think anything other than that."

"But you can't have her as your girlfriend," Spalding said simplistically. "She can't cope with all your responsibilities, and all."

Not yet, Tom felt in his mind.

"She's not like you, Tom," Spalding said. "Not in this way. You saw the Ämäthöär."

"Spalding," Tom said warningly.

"You're also always off having tea and crumpets with the big guy," he said, looking at Mär in the midst of the cackling crowd, "Talking about, what, I don't know. You're in a higher tier than half the Ōmäthäär. As high, at least. And whatever it is you're doing with Mär, it's always making you so exhausted.

"Or maybe it was just being around Sarah that's been making you exhausted," he grinned.

"And Brittney's smart, and cheerful, and nice, for all Terry and Lewis have to say," he pressed. "But she's not like you like this. You're right: she can't cope with your kind of life. You haven't told her what you do with Mär, have you?"

"I can't," Tom said with sad resentment.

"But Sarah!" Spalding said. "Sarah's right there with you! She's meeting with Mär just like you are! She's right at the same tier as you!

"And she looks even worse right now than you do."

Tom glanced over at Sarah. She was laughing, but he noticed for the first time the sadly subdued shade about her.

"So," Spalding said patronizingly, "She's smart, nice, cheerful; even when you shun her; capable, energetic, ambitious, and more and more; everything you are," he smiled at him. "She can live your kind of life. Everyone's waiting for you two to wake up and get together. Oh, and she's head over heels for you."

"But I guess that's not good enough."

"Spalding, it isn't like that," Tom said.

But he smiled too. "She is wonderful," he said.

And as soon as he said it, all his repressed feelings for Sarah Trotter came crashing into him. He knew her better than he knew even Brittney. Easily. And only now did he finally acknowledge that. She was greater than he thought a person could ever be.

And he realized with a sudden thrill that he felt more strongly, much more strongly, for Sarah than he did for anyone else he knew. And that he had for a long time.

"I might want to just get to know Sarah better if it was just that I thought she was wonderful like you're saying," he said to Spalding. "But I've known her for a while.

"You cannot just expect me to dive into a relationship with her just because she's impressive and may want a relationship with me." But then he grinned deeply at him. "But you're right. I've been hiding from the Tom that you knew. But not anymore."

He looked back over at Sarah. Sarah looked at him, then looked away quickly.

"The Tom that you knew was already, totally, in love with her," he said, and he felt something rush into him that was remarkably like the supreme feeling of when Mär had moved him with Ärthähr.

He didn't say another word to Spalding, but streamed through the water, around the still laughing crowd, toward Sarah.

"Mission accomplished," Spalding smiled privately to Tävna and Mär, rejoining the crowd.

"Keep their attention," Mär's voice said to them, just as he loudly asked Tävna, "But where did Ŭdmäth get the lizards to begin with?"

The eyes that had strayed toward Spalding and Tom's arrival turned to Mär and then back to Tävna. Not even Aaron noticed as Sarah slipped out of the group toward Tom.

20: Transcendent Encouragement

* * *

"What, Tom?" Sarah asked, a little more coldly than she was really feeling now that he was actually speaking to her.

Tom looked into her eyes for a moment, then said, "I'm really sorry for how I've been acting recently."

Sarah felt a rise of hope. But she said, "What do you mean?"

Tom grinned a little, seeing through her feigned ignorance. "I've been avoiding you. I've been avoiding talking about Ärthähr with you. I've been avoiding talking to you at all."

"Oh," Sarah said. "I hadn't noticed."

Tom stared at her.

A small smile managed to emerge on Sarah's face. "Sorry. I mean, I did notice something."

"I noticed a lot, at any rate," Tom smiled regretfully. "I'm really sorry, Sarah."

Did this mean Tom was going to be her friend again?

"Don't worry about it," she said.

So she didn't care, something said inside of him. Spalding was wrong.

Yeah, right.

"Thanks," Tom said. "You've been really great to me, even though I've been being a jerk to you."

"It's okay," Sarah said, smiling a little more.

Tom smiled knowingly at her. "You really have been annoyed with me," he said, almost declaring it.

Sarah laughed a little then. "Okay, I was annoyed, I was hurt that I thought you were ignoring me."

She couldn't believe she'd just said that.

But Tom just smiled more deeply. So she hadn't scared him away by saying she had been hurt by his negligence, she thought more encouragedly.

"So you did notice!" he said.

Sarah was more than relieved to feel the old easiness of talking to Tom coming back, finally.

She laughed more fully. "Yeah, yeah I definitely noticed. I wondered what was going on. With you."

Could he say this to her? But if Spalding was right, then she'd be happy. *It doesn't matter. She's Sarah. She'll understand.*

"I was becoming more and more scared of you."

"Scared?" Sarah asked, puzzled. "Why?"

Tom looked into her eyes again, the eyes of maybe the best friend he had ever had. Whom he had almost thrown away.

"Because," he said, and suddenly felt like this took a great deal more courage than sneaking a look at Ämäthöär. But he would not be a coward now. "You're such a great person. You're such a great friend. And—"

His voice gave out.

"I have fallen madly, frighteningly, in love with you?" Sarah suggested.

Tom was dumbstruck for a few seconds.

But Sarah wasn't. She knew what she had to do, regardless of what Tom might have been trying to say. But she waited for him to respond.

Then Tom's surprise changed quickly into an understanding, laughing, incredibly admiring smile. "Yeah!" he said. "I have fallen completely in love with you. As a friend, at least."

"No, no," Sarah said with exaggerated seriousness. "I was speaking for myself."

Tom laughed loudly. A few of Tävna and Spalding's viewers glanced over at them.

"You're serious," Tom said, feeling unparalleled joy flooding every part of him.

"No, Tom," Sarah said blandly. "I've been spending more time with you every day, you're nicer and in every way better than any person I thought I would ever meet, you're more than I—"

But she was cut off as Tom snatched her into a loving embrace and a deep, adoring kiss.

"—ever hoped for," she finished breathlessly, smiling brilliantly, as Tom released her. "No, I'm not serious."

She kissed him again, throwing her arms around his neck.

It took a few seconds for either of them to become aware of Spalding, Tävna, and Mär's thunderous clapping, now spreading to everyone else in the surprised group.

"Yeah!" Spalding was shouting.

"Finally!" Mär laughed, clapping his hands enthusiastically.

Tom could see his father and Andrew and Terry laughing with surprise, Spalding and Tävna cheering, Spalding whistling, and the Trotters sweeping quickly toward them.

"I was wondering when you were going to get a move on it," Scott Trotter smiled as Kathy hugged Tom around his torso.

"So everyone was in on this, except for me?" Tom laughed.

"Yeah," Sarah said accusatorily to her family. Tears were streaking her euphoric face.

20: Transcendent Encouragement

"Come on, Sarah," Aaron said, punching Tom idly in the shoulder, "Like you would have let anyone make up your mind for you."

"It was already made up," Kathy said seriously to Tom. "She just needed you to make the first move," she added critically to Sarah.

"I just needed to wake up," Sarah beamed tearfully at Tom.

"Me too," Tom said.

"Excellent matchmaking," Mär said privately to Spalding.

"Thanks," Spalding said, still a little intimidated at Mär. "It was your master plan. I just talked to him."

"And did him the greatest service I think he's ever had done for him," Mär said, watching Tom and Sarah kiss again, and feeling more hopeful than he had ever felt in all his life and adventures. "And me, too."

Chapter 21

Rally

"I should have expected this," Mär said heavily.
No one said anything.
"Thahn," he breathed acidly.
"What do we do?" Ährnär asked.
Ŭkan and Ärdhär entered the spherical white room. "What is it?" Ŭkan asked.
"Thahn," Mär said. "She left Nrathĕrmĕ more than four weeks ago."
"Four weeks!" Ŭkan said.
"And it's Thahn," Ŭmäthŭ said darkly. "After four weeks' time, she could already be right on top of us."
"We just found out," Mär explained. "Apparently she left secretly. It just became common knowledge in Nrathĕrmĕ yesterday."
"How large is her force?" Ärdhär asked.
"Typical Thahn," Ŭmäthŭ said. "From what we've been able to find out, almost four hundred star systems went into it."
"But Zōrd didn't tell many details," Ōhōmhär said.
"What do we do?" Äthääōhä asked Mär.
Mär was totally silent for a few moments.
"We wait and see what Är is doing," he said at last.
"She'll have legions of Ämäthōär with her, if I've ever known Thahn," Särdnä said.
"We cannot win against Thahn, Mär," Ŭmäthŭ said conversationally.
Mär smiled significantly at him. "When has that ever stopped us?"

"Well done," John said to his assistants after yet another battle exercise. "We all did our part very well."
"Even if we still lost," his assistant Xiushi Hao said.
"Even if everyone else lost," John said. "We did well. Especially against an army that size!"
They were floating out beyond most of the rebuilt defenses around Earth, John having wanted to practice out where they could enjoy the stars.
"Is it true, John?" another of his assistants, Häähr asked.
"Is what true?"
"Thahn," Ŭfäfävahn said.

21: Rally

"Yes," Ruben Cavallo chimed in. "Is it?"

"I don't know," John said. "I assume it is. I can ask my managers."

"I hope it's not true!" said Klavdia Zyuganov.

"I think it is," said Ayad Jawad. "But what are the Ōmäthäär thinking? If it is true, we can't fight an army like that!"

"No one can," Ruben said.

"I believe that the Ōmäthäär can," John said.

"Then why are they having us go through these exercises?" Thōhaŭ said. "They aren't all-powerful, John."

"I know," John said. "But some of my friends know some of them. They'll get us through this."

"But what about the Ämäthōär?" Ŭfäfävahn said. "Thahn is an Ämäthōär, isn't she?"

"Yes, she is," John realized for the first time.

"And she will bring more Ämäthōär with her," Ämharŭ said.

"But John's right," said Kōrhas. "The Ōmäthäär are smart. They won't keep us here if we can't win."

"Maybe Mär is ready to sacrifice all of us if it means he can keep Ōhōnŭäär from the Ämäthōär," Päm suggested.

"Mär knows what he is doing," John said, used to hearing that word but still not understanding very much of what it meant. "He won't give Earth up if he can save it, but he isn't dumb."

"Then we'll have to give Earth up, won't we?" Dmitriy Zyuganov said. "We were almost beaten by those pirates who were less than ten times our own strength. How can we survive against an army like Thahn's?"

"I didn't think we could possibly survive against the pirates," John said. "Not after the battle got going badly. But the Ōmäthäär knew what they were doing all along."

And Peter won't let me down, he thought with confident peace.

The change in Nŭährnär over the next eight hours was incredible.

The confidence that had returned after the miraculous victory over the pirates seemed to shatter all at once. Thahn was universally known among the N'närdamähr, whether through firsthand experience or by notoriety, and among the Earthmen her name was one of vague dread. Both the rumored vastness of her fleet and her anticipated company of unguessed hosts of Ämäthōär were overshadowed by Thahn's personal reputation among the N'nŭährnär.

But the Ōmäthäär had been expecting such alarm in Nŭährnär. And they were ready to work against their companions' panic.

One after another, some of the higher Ōmäthäär addressed all of Nŭährnär, inviting all to listen who wished to.

Äthääōhä and Ährnär were the first to speak with the panicking nation:

"...We do not want to die any more than you do. We will not fight a losing battle. We cannot afford to fight a losing battle...

"...We knew Sĕrĕhahn would try to destroy us. We all knew that he would send a blow that he thoroughly designed to be unsurvivable.

"But we are greater than Sĕrĕhahn knows. Far greater. Far greater than Thahn. Do you seriously believe, can you believe, that it was military strength alone that delivered us against the pirates?

"There is strength among us that not even Sĕrĕhahn has ever counted on..."

Then Bävän and Thas made a somewhat bolder sequel to their words:

"...Thahn is coming here for a reason. That gives us an advantage...

"...Thahn is afraid of Earth. Sĕrĕhahn is afraid of what the Earthmen might do...

"...Why stay to defend Earth, if it's just going to be taken, whether we defend it or not?

"Such cowardice isn't worth our time to answer.

"But we don't think we will have to give our lives here. Earth is not going to be taken if we defend it.

"Why?

"Because we know Thahn. We know her better than most any of you do. Anyone who has any objections, come tell us.

"And we have Ōmäthäär...

"...What power is there at Ōhōnŭäär? A lot of the same power that Sĕrĕhahn wants.

"And which he is terrified of Ōmäthäär using against him....

"...We have the advantage in this fight..."

Neither Ŭmäthŭ nor Ōhōmhär enjoyed this aspect of their address, though they both knew it needed to be said:

"...If you want to leave, leave! You know what will happen if you go where the Ämäthōär can take you. You have choice. Go!

"What if the Ämäthōär make you tell them our secrets? We don't care anymore. Anyone who is ignorant enough to leave Nŭährnär now must not know very much about what it means to be an Ōmäthäär, anyway...

"...Our location is known to pirates and N'nrathĕrmĕ alike now. Go. Tell the Ämäthōär everything; though, in that, you will not have much choice...

21: Rally

"...We will triumph by our bravery. Cowards may poison that.

"So don't be cowardly!

"There is so much more to be done here. We will triumph over Thahn. We would triumph over Sĕrĕhahn himself here at the World of Är!"

They did enjoy that aspect of their address.

"Why has Sĕrĕhahn not come here himself," they continued, "Now that he knows where we are? He fears this world! *We* will triumph here…

"…But if any of you are not foresighted enough to take heart about this, you may go. We wish you wouldn't, but you are your own responsibility.

"And those who stay will enjoy the safety that will come with our conquering of Thahn. And those who flee will suffer Ämäthōär and pirates and isolation and the chafing cling of guilt of knowing that you forsook good to let evil triumph.

"So choose. It is an easy choice.

"We tell you now that if you stay with Mär and the Ōmäthäär, who know Thahn and who know how to fight her, you will be supremely happier than if you had fled.

"If the Ōmäthäär say to flee from Thahn, then you can trust that that is the right course against her.

"And if the Ōmäthäär say to stay, and watch the magic, you can trust that we are not suicidal!

"As one, every Ōmäthäär here has agreed to stay.

"Now, watch the magic!"

"Thanks," Peter said to Mŭdhōär.

"You're sure about this?" Mŭdhōär asked.

"Oh yeah," Peter said. "Put me through."

Mŭdhōär was silent for a few seconds. Then he said, "You're on."

"People of Nŭährnär," Peter said boldly. "My name is Peter Benjamin Garcia, the son of Charles David Garcia and Amelia Jennifer Smith.

"I am not from Nrathĕrmĕ. I have never seen it with my own eyes. I have never met Thahn. I have never seen an Ämäthōär kill a man. I have never seen, whether in borrowed memory or waking sight, any military force to rival the alleged size of the army that now approaches us.

"But I have as much reason as any man.

"But I did not have reason, nor comprehension of what was true and what was erroneous, a matter of days ago. I did not trust Mär. I did not trust the Ōmäthäär. I did not believe that Nŭährnär should or could defy the might of Nrathĕrmĕ. And I was certain that the Ōmäthäär did not have the best interests of the rest of us in mind.

"I was wrong.

"Have I seen our future victory? Have I seen the Ämäthōär which the Ōmäthäär have warned us against? No.

"But there are braver parts of men than their eyes. Smarter things than our minds. Not foolhardy, not ignorant. Courageous.

"I believe that the Ōmäthäär have the best interests of all of us in mind. Because I faced up to have the courage to believe that. I stopped being a coward and let myself see that.

"It is very easy, and self-justifying, to believe that the Ōmäthäär are foolish, or negligent of us. Because to believe that is to believe that we should leave them, and not fight for them.

"Now, I have been told that the Thahn who approaches is an Ämäthōär. I have also been told that she is known publicly throughout Nrathěrmě as one of the more brilliant military minds alive. Sensibly thinking, how can we imagine succeeding against that kind of an enemy?

"I am no Ōmäthäär. I do not know Mär as well as many of you do.

"Yet I am sure that Mär is not leading us to doom. I am sure that he knew what he was getting himself as well as us into when he set up base here at Earth.

"And I believe that none of us has any comprehension of what Mär has been through to defend us all, and Nrathěrmě, from the Ämäthōär.

"But I can comprehend this one thing: That Mär knows what he is doing.

"Thahn may be an Ämäthōär.

"But Mär knows what he is doing.

"Thahn may have amassed an army larger than anything Nrathěrmě or Earth has seen.

"Mär knows what he is doing.

"A fleet of indignant N'nrathěrmě is approaching. I guess it will reach us within fifteen hours. So far as we can tell, they outnumber us by about ten to one. And their weapons and defenses and speed will be better than ours. In fifteen hours.

"But Mär all along has known what he was doing.

"And here is what I know.

"I know that Sěrěhahn wants nothing good for my world. I know that because Mär has said it. I have had my fill with those who believe the Ōmäthäär are in any way stretching the truth.

"Here is what I, Peter Benjamin Garcia, know:

"That I will sooner be killed in the defense of my Earth than abandon it to

21: Rally

the Ämäthöär.

"I will not run just because I do not know what the outcome will be. I will not run from what could be my victory. I will not save my own life at the cost of losing everything that is worth me living for. Like not giving up. And like working, and striving, and knowing that excellence can only be achieved through conquering my fears and my weaknesses.

"I will sooner die a martyr for dignity than live a coward.

"And I will follow Mär.

"He knows what he is doing. The Ōmäthäär know what they are doing.

"Mär himself said in the very beginning that Sĕrĕhahn would try to crush us with an unsurvivable blow. He knew what he was getting us into. He has always had a way out, in everything that has happened thus far."

He paused, smiling. *Even for me.*

"If we do not stand with Mär, we will stand by default with Sĕrĕhahn.

"If we flee from Mär, Sĕrĕhahn will find us. He will not leave us alone. If we run away, we will die later. If we stay, we will understand, if we don't already, that Mar knew what he was doing. We will 'watch the magic.'

"And if I die in accomplishing the triumphant defense of Earth, I will do so proudly, fighting so that those whom I love can be safe and free!

"Do not ruin yourselves with cowardice! Do not do that to yourselves! Do not do that to your families, your beloved ones!

"I have no authority to direct Nüährnär. But I have authority to direct Peter. And I, Peter, will stay, come armies, come Thahn, come hell or heaven. I will stay, and strive for what and for whom I love."

He meant to end the connection. But then he said, "People of Nüährnär. Do what you have been taught by your parents. Courage, sacrifice, selflessness, love. Love. For our families and our beloved ones.

"And for Mär, who has done so much for us."

He ended the connection quickly.

Mŭdhōär didn't say anything.

Peter turned to go back to Annie.

"Peter," Ōärnär said, floating beside Mŭdhōär.

Peter looked at her.

Ōärnär just smiled wordlessly at him for a moment. Then she said, "You really are a hero of Nüährnär."

Peter nodded gratefully to them both. "Thank you, Mŭdhōär, Ōärnär."

"Thank you," Ōärnär said.

Peter nodded again, then shot off and away toward Annie.

* * *

"Okay, let's get this stuff organized!" Tom said to his assistants.

The matter from many of the surrounding systems had begun to arrive at Earth. Most of Nŭährnär was rushing about to slow the hurtling matter and to direct it quickly into defenses.

"I wish we could have sent it slower," Tom's assistant Ōfha said. "We're having to burn so much of it as energy just to slow it all down!"

"This will be enough," Tom said casually.

"I hope it will be," Ōfha said.

"I didn't think I would get to see you before the battle," Sarah said to Tom as he slowed down next to her.

"How are you feeling?" Tom asked, kissing her happily.

"Very differently about Peter," she laughed.

Tom looked at the defenses swirling around them. "We'll be good. This new matter makes the odds more like twelve to one."

"And that's good?" Sarah smiled.

"I love you," Tom said powerfully to her, and he kissed her again. "And I promise, we'll talk all you want about Ärthähr, after the Ōmäthäär get us through this day."

"Okay," Sarah laughed shakily. "I'll remember that."

Tom swept forward and hugged her. "I won't let anything happen to you," he said through rising tears.

Sarah kissed his jaw. "I know." She pulled away, smiling worriedly at him. "We will be good."

"Four billion?" Peter breathed with cold fury.

"Yes," Z'mōth, his assistant, called to him. "Four billion total. But I don't think very many more are going to leave. I think most everyone who's going to run has run."

"That's five times the number that we lost in actual battle last time!" Peter said. "And more than half of them were revived!"

"Yes," she answered. "I imagine people are afraid that, this time, there will be no one left to revive anyone."

"Thank you, Z'mōth," Peter said.

"I'll get back to practicing."

"Only if you think you still need it," Peter said. "I want everyone to rest their minds before the battle."

"Right," Z'mōth said, and her voice went away.

But I can't rest just yet, Peter said to himself as he remembered the various strategies he had thought up. He ran through each of them in his head, considering any possible counter moves that he could imagine the N'nrathĕrmĕ using against his ideas. Encirclement of any kind would be extremely difficult against these odds. Decoys would be useful. Anything to distract the N'nrathĕrmĕ; anything to keep them from using all their resources at once against the outgunned N'nŭährnär armies.

These N'nrathĕrmĕ probably would not want to destroy Earth, he figured. But then they might go that far, seeing as the Earthmen would be fighting them. Would any Earthmen still try to defect to the N'nrathĕrmĕ?

If anyone goes over to Sĕrĕhahn because of what I've done, he thought, but then he stopped himself. *Then it will be their fault. I have made it clear where I stand. It will be their fault for believing nonsense.*

Could a trap be made by fooling the N'nrathĕrmĕ into thinking they were defecting to them? That would be difficult. It might just serve to break Nŭährnär into two disjointed portions. Yes, and the Earthmen being shielded by the N'nrathĕrmĕ would find themselves surrounded if they attacked their would-be liberators.

What if they made it look like they had fled, and fooled the N'nrathĕrmĕ, or used that to lure them into a better position for Nŭährnär? But that would be difficult, and it would take a great deal of matter to move everything, much less to stage a false trail of retreat. But there might be a way to make that work.

How could they get the N'nrathĕrmĕ to divide themselves? And how could they win unless the N'nrathĕrmĕ did divide themselves?

Overconfidence might be the key to victory here, he thought. The N'nrathĕrmĕ outnumbered them. If they could entice them to be sloppy until the odds were more even and it was too late for them to recover...

"Are you busy, Peter?" Mŭdhōär's voice called.

"Not terribly," Peter answered.

"Hold on," Mŭdhōär said.

Peter waited for a few seconds. Then another voice came.

"Peter, this is Mär."

Mär! Peter thought. "What is it?" he asked. He thought for a moment that Mär had called to thank him about his speech. Or perhaps Mär had another plan that he wanted him in on.

"You and Annie."

"Me?" Peter said. "And Annie? What do you need us to do?"

"Even more than you're already doing," Mär said gratefully.

Peter didn't respond yet, waiting for Mär to elaborate.

"How long have you and Annie been together?"

That question surprised Peter. "Six or seven years."

Mär laughed. "That's half as long as I've been alive!"

That stunned Peter, before he remembered that his venerable managers were both less than three years old.

"Well, it may have taken six years," Mär said, "But I'm glad that you finally proposed to her."

"You know about that?" Peter said.

"You told Mŭdhōär and Ōärnär, and they told Bäbän and Panth, and I found out about it soon enough. People seemed to think that you and Annie agreeing to marry was a very significant matter."

"Why?" Peter asked.

"We're odd that way. The Ōmäthäär."

Was this why Mär wanted to personally speak to him? Peter wondered. To chat about him and Annie? He would have thought that Mär would have been inhumanly busy at a time like this.

"Have you and Annie decided when you want to be married?" Mär asked in a businesslike way.

"Yes," Peter said. "About twenty-nine days from now. Mamōth is going to marry us."

Mär didn't answer at once.

"It is soon," Peter admitted. "But four weeks in Nŭährnär is plenty of time for us."

"I agree," Mär said softly.

Peter waited for him to go on.

"What about sooner?"

"Sooner?" Peter said.

"Yes. You are both certain that you want to marry each other?"

"We are," Peter said.

"Then do it," Mär counseled. "Don't put it off."

What? "We will do it," Peter said. "We would like some time to get used to the idea."

"I understand," Mär said. "But I promise you that you can get used to being married after you are married. You are both sure that you want to marry each other, Peter. Do it now."

Why did Mär care when they got married? And why now, of all times?

"Now?" Peter repeated.

"Yes."

"Why?"

21: Rally

Mär paused for a few moments. Then he said impressively, "Because we are about to enter mortal combat. Should one or both of you die and not revive, it will be better if you died married than merely planning to marry."

"I will not let Annie die," Peter said.

"I believe that."

Peter thought for a moment. "Should one of us die and not revive, what will it matter if we were married before we died?"

"You believe that I never lied to you about the Ämäthöär," Mär observed warmly.

Saying that to Mär himself was more shaming than saying it to anyone else. But he found it remarkably easy. "I do."

"You believe that they display powers beyond technology?"

"If that is what you say. Yes."

"And beyond what you believed to be real?"

"Absolutely."

"There is a great deal that exists that most people do not know about," Mär said with light potency. "There are ways that your marriage union can weld you together forever, even after death."

"Are you speaking of an afterlife?"

"Yeah," Mär said. "The next phase of it, at any rate."

Peter wondered whether he ought to say this to the leader of all Nŭährnär. But Mär did seem easygoing enough. Too easygoing for a leader.

"I believe everything you tell me about Ämäthöär," he said. "But I cannot believe even you about heaven if you have not yourself seen it."

"I can accept that," Mär said unfazedly. "Believe me. I have seen a lot. I have seen this."

Peter was stunned. "Seen heaven?"

"I have seen that marriage can be perpetuated after this part of life. I have seen what comes after death."

"How?"

"One of the perks of Ōmäthäär-hood. In addition to being hunted by Ämäthöär," Mär said pleasantly.

Peter didn't know what to think about that. But he was done with thinking that Mär was deluded or a liar. So there really was something after death. And he and Annie could be together even if they died.

"I don't know what is going to happen," Mär said. "I do know that you and Annie have very little reason to wait, and a lot of wonderful reasons not to."

"I will not put it off," Peter said. "I will talk to Annie about this."

"Do not put it off until after this battle."

"We would have to arrange and have a wedding within twelve hours, Mär."

"Mamōth is ready to marry you right now, as soon as the three of you can get together. Get married now, have a wedding later. The celebration is not essential. It will be essential tomorrow. Not today."

Peter thought about that. "Alright. I will call Annie and have her tell Mamōth."

"This is essential, Peter."

"I understand," Peter said.

"If you love Annie, marry her now! Do not wait. Not until tomorrow. Not for an hour. Nothing you can do now, even if you were to save all of Nŭährnär singlehandedly, will have any shade of the importance that this will have!"

"I understand."

Mär was quiet for a second.

"And Peter," he said. "Thank you. For what you said about me, and about Nŭährnär today."

Mär seemed to have saved the most appropriate thing to say for the last. "It was my pleasure."

"I know it was," Mär said adoringly. "I will talk to you soon."

There was a small pause, then Peter felt the connection end.

That was interesting.

He sat thinking about what Mär had just said to him.

"Mŭdhöär," he said then, recalling himself to the here and now. "We don't have a lot of time left, but I have had some other ideas that we could use against the N'nrathĕrmĕ."

"They are not giving very much thought to stealth," Anŭsths observed. "Not the ones we can see, anyway."

"Exactly," Äthääōhä said. "Hōäōhä reported about ten times this many N'nrathĕrmĕ."

"It's a trap, I think," Mär said. He floated toward one of the gleaming walls of that inner room.

"They're trying to make us overconfident," Ōhōmhär said.

"So whatever happens, we cannot attempt an encirclement," Mär said, absently fondling a shining white leaf. "We cannot take this bait."

"But where are the rest of them?" Bävän asked.

"If we searched actively, we might be able to find them, if they are lurking

21: Rally

nearby under stealth," Ŭmäthŭ said. "But won't it be better if we make them think that we have fallen for the bait? If we let them think that we think that these few divisions are all that there are?"

"Lead them to be overconfident," Avhä said.

"Yes," Ŭmäthŭ said. "Make them think that we are going for the bait, but be ready for them."

"So we should attempt an encirclement?" Ōhōmhär asked.

"Committed enough to be convincing, but not too much," Ŭmäthŭ said. "As much as we can commit without really taking the bait."

Mär smiled, stroking the plant's stem. "Alright."

"All the same," Thas said, "There's no way we'll win without outside help."

"We've done our best," Bävän said. "I think Är wants us to win."

"That's not enough," Mär said, turning back toward them. "Enough for Är, sure, but maybe not for Nŭährnär. I don't want to be left behind when Är wins."

"I think we have time for one more address," Ŭmäthŭ grinned.

"My dear friends who call ourselves N'nŭährnär."

Mär's voice radiated in the hearing of everyone.

"I am delighted to be with you now. Today. On the brink of this terrible conflict."

Throughout Nŭährnär, within the Shell and among all the defenses surrounding the fortified world, tens of billions of minds focused on Mär's broadcasted voice.

"A mass of N'nrathĕrmĕ," Mär said, "Whose combined strength is greater than everything we have here, will reach us within less than two hours' time.

"Another army, ten times the size of that one, is waiting invisibly right outside the range where we could detect them.

"We are outnumbered," he said with level, piercing force.

"It seems clear that the N'nrathĕrmĕs' inertial control is more precise than ours. They will be faster. Their rantha will be more powerful than ours, their stealth better, their resistance to our attacks stronger than our resistance to theirs.

"These are N'nrathĕrmĕ.

"N'nrathĕrmĕ warriors.

"These men and women live away from Nrathĕrmĕ, fighting pirates, harvesting stars, and exploring and enforcing the Wild Lands far from their home.

"These men and women are no strangers to war.

"These are not pirates or renegades, who must leech technology from Sĕrĕhahn's society. These are members of Sĕrĕhahn's society. They outclass us in numbers, in equipment, in resources.

"And in unity. And love, and bravery."

A pregnant pause followed that statement.

"Nrathĕrmĕ's solidarity is a result solely of the selfless wisdom of the N'nrathĕrmĕ," Mär's voice continued, echoing throughout the populous reaches of the Shell.

"Sĕrĕhahn has had more than ten thousand weeks, as far as I have been able to discover, to teach Nrathĕrmĕ how to prosper and progress. The people of Nrathĕrmĕ understand the value of love in society.

"They understand that two people together are better than two people apart. They understand that true knowledge leads to correct action, to achievement of desired results; desired emotional, internal results; and to happiness.

"The people of Nrathĕrmĕ understand that it is not true that any person can be unaffected by the actions of any other person. They understand that everything in the universe interacts with everything in the universe.

"They understand that working for one's self alone is ignorant. They understand that to help their selves they must help everything else.

"They understand that selfishness will get them nowhere.

"Now, these N'nrathĕrmĕ believe that they are helping other beings by their attacking us. The Ämäthöar have told them that Nŭährnär wishes to poison the solidity of Nrathĕrmĕ's wise society.

"And now they have led the people of Nrathĕrmĕ, in understandably convincing ways, to believe that Nŭährnär has murdered their Anhar and has claimed despotic rule over all life from Earth.

"And they know us as 'R'dōnĕmär': 'Mär's people.'

"If we are *my* people, then I see no way that we can survive against this onslaught.

"But we call ourselves Nŭährnär.

"I often like looking at 'nŭährnär' as being a combination of the words 'ähr' in the 'nŭ' mode and 'Är' in the 'n' mode.

"Of course that's etymologically wrong as well as grammatically questionable, but consider the combined meaning of those two modified words:

"An enduring, finite entity that originates from Infinity.

"That may not give you the usual connotation of nŭährnär, safety, but

21: Rally

what it conveys to me is worth sharing.

"Our Nŭährnär is finite. We are finite.

"We cannot win every fight. We cannot endure forever.

"But the very sense of 'nŭahr' is something finite that does endure forever!

"We, by ourselves, cannot win this battle. These N'nrathĕrmĕ are too smart. Too well equipped. To well coordinated."

Through his seriousness, Mär sounded almost cheerful as he said this.

"But you know that our Nŭährnär has sprung from a clandestine group that once thrived at Sĕrĕhahn's Nrathĕrmĕ, which called itself 'Ä'ähänärdanär': 'The Light of Är.'"

Mär's voice hesitated.

"Är is infinite," he said finally.

"Ä'ähänärdanär was no manmade organization. Är himself established it.

"He only invited us to be part of it. Ä'ähänärdanär is infinite, though our own branch of it is finite.

"Any R'dōnĕmär," he said with disdain, "Any organization established or led by or for me, or by any other finite people, will never endure forever.

"But a Nŭährnär, a limited people who originate from the unlimited Är, a finite branch of an infinite Endeavor, Är's Infinite Endeavor, need not ever fail!

"Är's Endeavor does not fail!

"Are we Nŭährnär, or are we R'dōnĕmär?"

He paused. Almost all labor had ceased now throughout all Nŭährnär, a mixture of fear and newly rising hope filling the hearkening N'nŭährnär.

A rising hope that Mär would give them a reason to hope.

"Most of us, thus far," Mär's voice continued, "Have fought for our families. We stay together because those we love are here.

"The Ōmäthäär will always fight Sĕrĕhahn and the Ämäthōär. Many of our families, loving us, have hitherto fought alongside us. Even when they have not known what we fought or why. And their families have fought with them, and theirs with them.

"A *lesser* degree of the same love that binds Nrathĕrmĕ as one has, hitherto, bound us as one.

"But now love meets love across a field of outright war."

Mär's voice rose.

"The N'nrathĕrmĕ who want to destroy us want so because they believe that we threaten people they love: their Anhar, the rest of Nrathĕrmĕ, and the Earthmen, the 'St'tĕra' as they call you.

"We want to destroy these armies because we know that they threaten people we love: our families and our friends.

"Our beloved ones.

"Can there be any victory in this kind of a conflict?

"Lives will be ended today.

"Families will be destroyed.

"Husbands will cry for their wives within a matter of hours. Wives for their husbands, parents for their children and children for their parents, and siblings and friends for siblings and friends!

"Plans, and dreams, will be shattered within these next few hours!"

Mär's voice was level, but its emotion was palpable.

"Can there be victory in war?

"Whether the N'nrathĕrmĕ destroy us all or whether we destroy them, dreams and hopes and cherished companionships—people!—are about to be lost!

"That's the way of evil!

"A little evil, left unopposed, leads to the wreckage of so many wonderful things!

"We have already lost, partially. Sĕrĕhahn and the Ämäthöär have been allowed to fester, strengthening their hold on all the people and families and dreams and lives of Nrathĕrmĕ.

"They have been allowed to do this much damage already because of the apathy of those who could have opposed them in the past.

"It must stop.

"It will stop! Here!

"We *must live!*"

He paused for several seconds this time.

When his voice reverberated again throughout the fleets of Nŭährnär, it shivered with feeling.

"You must understand that this *is* a battle of good against evil.

"This conflict is not about us-against-them. We must live, or no one will live anything worth living!

"No life will matter if it is trampled by Ämäthöär. If we do not break Nrathĕrmĕ free from them, who will remain to?

"Here is Nŭährnär's choice, right now:

"To risk our lives here and destroy the lives of these innocent N'nrathĕrmĕ who do not know that they intend to destroy the only people who can deliver the world from Sĕrĕhahn's destructive rule, or to lay down and let ourselves be destroyed by them and leave Nrathĕrmĕ in the Ämäthöärs' hands.

"We have no other choices!

"We cannot flee. These N'nrathĕrmĕ are too fast.

21: Rally

"We cannot negotiate. The only negotiation these will accept now is rejection of the Ōmäthäär—the leaders of this so-termed R'dōněmär."

Mär waited, then his voice returned with quiet power.

"If any wish to reject the Ōmäthäär," he said, "Then the N'nrathěrmě may well accept you.

"But I hope that none of you will. I don't want any of you to turn against us.

"And," he said bitterly, "I know that the Ämäthōar will make any who flee to the N'nrathěrmě regret it.

"We can end the well lived lives of these people whom Sěrěhahn has blinded, or we can give our own lives in order to save theirs. And in so doing give up the hope of Nrathěrmě.

"There are no other choices today. If we do not destroy these people, Sěrěhahn will further destroy Nrathěrmě.

"It is good to give one's life for those who can be saved by it.

"And the purpose of the underground Ä'ähänärdanär was to give our lives to save everyone; not, of necessity, giving our lives in death, but giving our lives totally over to *living* for the sake of those whom we can save!

"But it is one of the worst of all things to give a life for nothing.

"Including one's own life.

"And it is good, I know," he said with emphatic energy, "To *take* the lives of even good people who have been deceived into fighting against the very things that might save them!

"I do not wish to take any life. I wish we could save these people without them fighting that.

"Yet it will not do for me, or Nŭährnär, to let our families and the hope of *all* the people at Nrathěrmě be snuffed out."

His voice built in tempo, echoing off of the hills and waves within the bulwark of Nŭährnär's Shell.

"Can there be victory in war?

"Can there ever be victory, after what the Ämäthōar have already done?" he said passionately.

"Can the world ever be clean again?"

He paused, but the silence echoed throughout Nŭährnär like a muted rumble of a storm.

"The nature of genuine good is that it heals," his reverberating voice said.

"We must succeed here!

"We must, in the end, destroy the Ämäthōar!

"We must wrench their corrosive influence from Nrathěrmě!

"Only when Nrathĕrmĕ is rid of their darkness will we be able to heal our world of all the damage that Sĕrĕhahn and his minions have caused!

"Are we my frail R'dōnĕmär, or are we Är's Nŭährnär?

"All who will fight, and are willing to die, to save Nrathĕrmĕ from Sĕrĕhahn's stifling sophistries are fighting for Är!

"Regardless of whether or not you mean to be. If you are fighting for the love of your fellow men, you are fighting for Är!

"So both sides in this conflict, driven by love, are fighting for Är.

"If only we could fight together, not opposed!

"But Sĕrĕhahn, the orchestrator of this conflict and manipulator of the N'nrathĕrmĕs' love, is using their good to execute his destructive intents.

"The N'nrathĕrmĕ are on our side. On Är's side. But their martial might, the dark direction of their pure intentions, to destroy us, *is not.*"

His voice ceased like the withdrawal of a surf before the onslaught of a thunderous wave.

"Oh, you people who think you are a Nŭährnär, *do you know what this planet is?*

"Pp'ōhōnŭäär! The very Seat of the Life of Är!

"The Light of Är, Ä'ähänärdanär, would not be were it not for *this* world!

"Let me tell you that Är is real!

"The Light of Är, the pervasive bedrock that makes and sustains, and *is*, the Ōmäthäärs' Ärthähr, comes from this world!

"Believe it," Mär said frankly.

"The theory of an ōhōnŭäär, I have been taught, is one of the older notions of the Ōmäthäär.

"It is the theory that all order and vitality, and intelligence, and even all matter and energy, is upheld by a single, comprehensively infinite Event that takes place at a single place and time.

"Only a few Ōmäthäär, to my knowledge, have ever taken the theory of an ōhōnŭäär seriously.

"And very few indeed were the Ōmäthäär who considered that the truth or error of that theory was a matter of any remotest priority.

"But I have met very few Ōmäthäär who do not agree that the Ärthähr that we wield is based in a force that upholds all life and progression.

"The reality of our state is that things fall apart.

"And we as people make mistakes.

"Good can heal, but there is no good without the sum whole of all good: Är! The healing power to turn corrosion into growth and to turn ignorance into progressive learning, the pervasive foreign force that gives flawed people,

21: Rally

and unstable things, the knowledge and stability that they simply did not previously possess, is the comprehensive power of the Comprehensive Är!

"The ōhōnŭäär theory was that that force, transcendent of time and space, did have to be made, it had to be put into motion, by Är, in some specific time and place. That time and place would be *the* Pp'ōhōnŭäär.

"This 'Earth' *is* Pp'ōhōnŭäär!

"This world did once serve as host to Är himself!

"And it was from this world that Är set in motion the transcendental Central Pillar of all being and vitality!

"Look at the stars! Think of Nrathĕrmĕ! Think of the infinite multitude of galaxies and of galactic chains!

"The infinity of the universe!

"It all depends on *this little planet*!

"No, let me amend," Mär said quickly. "It all does depend on the Light of Är that was unleashed by Är while he resided on this planet.

"And that Deed is done. The universe is headed unpreventably away from disorder now. The Ämäthōär cannot defeat that."

There was peaceful relief in Mär's voice as if he had just made safe a loved one from a horrible enemy.

"But the execution of the Light of Är left its mark on this world.

"And on its people.

"That is why people who listen to the Ōmäthäär have been calling you Earthmen 'Nōhōnŭäär,'" Mär's voice seemed to smile. "The power of that universally dominant Event has influenced all of you.

"It is in your flesh, in your hearts and spirits.

"And Sĕrĕhahn wants that.

"He wants to wield you. He wants to use your world. He wants to harness the transcendental force of the Light of Är.

"I think," he said, "That he believes he can command all Eternity if only he can study you and study Earth."

He paused again. All of Nŭährnär was utterly silent. Even the waves and the winds in the Shell seemed to be caught in a reverent quiet.

"Now," Mär's voice smiled, in a distinctly wry tone, "Do you see why we Ōmäthäär are bent on defending Earth?

"This is a battle of good against evil!

"But the tools being used by the powers of good and evil in this conflict, the nearing armies of N'nrathĕrmĕ and the unfortunate majority of Nŭährnär, were all until now unaware of that. In terms of a battle of N'nŭährnär verses N'nrathĕrmĕ, this would be a battle simply of us against them. Of good, intelligent, living, loving people against other good, living, loving, intelligent people.

"But the directing force behind these N'nrathĕrmĕ is Sĕrĕhahn and the Ämäthōär.

"And the directing force behind Nŭährnär has been the Ōmäthäär.

"This is a battle of good and evil. But evil has disguised its tools as decent and upright, and good has been obliged, up until now, to keep its tools ignorant of its true virtue."

Mär's voice hardened. "I am afraid that many of you would leave Nŭährnär right at his moment, thinking me and the Ōmäthäär deluded fanatics for our assertions that this world is the centerpiece of an actual Är, were you not faced with imminent destruction by these N'nrathĕrmĕ should you leave the main strength here.

"Be that as you want it to be."

But then his voice lightened again.

"And now, in this battle, Nŭährnär finally knows what it is fighting for.

"I invite any of you who doubt me to take our victory today as a signal that Är exists, and that he will deliver us if we fight for his Ä'ähänärdanär.

"If the forces of evil fight blind to their real cause while the forces of good, here, do not, then we will have the power of good, of Är! behind us!

"You Earthmen really are Nōhōnŭäär!

"This world, out of all the worlds in all of infinity, is *the* Pp'ōhōnŭäär!

"We must know what we are fighting for, if we are to see Är's wonders here! What greater cause can there ever be than to defend the power of Är from evil, and to work to deliver the hosts of N'nrathĕrmĕ from the blindness induced by Ämäthōär?

"We will see Är's power here, *if* we fight here for Är's World and for the people of Nrathĕrmĕ!

"If we fight for only ourselves, if this is, in our hearts, an us-against-them conflict, then we will be left to only ourselves.

"Yet if we fight for what Är is and will be fighting for, he will fight with us!

"Choose your sides. You can fight with Är, and enjoy the glory that we are trying to bring to the people at Nrathĕrmĕ. Or you can fight for yourselves, and never see or feel or love the awesome lightness and power of heart that comes from fighting alongside the Perfect Är!

"So choose your side.

"I, and the Ōmäthäär, have chosen ours.

"This battle marching upon us is effectively unwinnable.

21: Rally

"These N'nrathĕrmĕ are too many, too strong, too intelligent, and too united.

"But Är never loses.

"He can lead us to win.

"Do you want to see Är's power?

"Är will help us win.

"But Är will not, he never will, force us to win. Är will not *make* good win.

"Good has to *want* to win! We all have to *be* good, we have to want good to win!

"Är is about to give us all the help we need to win this unwinnable fight.

"Är *is* going to give us all the help we need to fight Sĕrĕhahn, and to save everything that is worthwhile.

"But he will not make us take his help.

"And I will not either."

He paused emphatically.

"I am going to watch the magic here. You must all do what you feel is right.

"But let me tell you this, like what Peter Garcia told you:

"If we abandon all that's good and worth living for, that's worth existing for, we will be infinitely worse off than if we had died!

"But if we die fighting to make a better world for everyone else, then, I can tell you by experience, death will be no ending for us.

"And I can tell you that Är is perfect.

"I know him. I know this. Perfection does not fail its own.

"Är will not fail us, if we do not fail out on him.

"Glory to Är and Ä'ähänärdanär!

"Now. Let's watch the magic."

Chapter 22

Hero of Nŭährnär

"They're being pretty reckless," Kōrhas's voice observed in John's head.

"Yes," John said back distractedly, remembering what his managers had told him. "Don't be drawn in by them. Our place is to wait here on Earth's far side. Remember, there are a whole lot more N'nrathěrmě hiding out there."

"They want us to think they're being reckless. I think they think we'll be reckless if we think they are."

"To think we can fight these N'nrathěrmě is reckless already," Päm said.

An extremely convincing part of John echoed the same thought, as he watched the sprawling fleets of the N'nrathěrmě hurtling ever closer.

"Hardly any stealth at all," Kōrhas said, ignoring Päm. "That is reckless."

"Mär knows what he is doing," John said unconvincingly. "Be ready to follow my commands instantly."

"If you get us through this alive," Ŭfäfävahn said hollowly, "I promise you, John, I will do whatever you say for the rest of our lives."

"Keep moving!" Peter called to Antonio and Marcela Ngonda. "Don't be afraid to spend energy; confusing them is where we'll beat them, not in brute force."

"Pete, you meant what you said yesterday?" Äszad asked hopefully.

"I meant that this is worth fighting for," Peter said with soft power as he stared calculatingly at the approaching N'nrathěrmě horde.

"I want Sarah Trotter with me," Tom said flatly to Änŭn.

"That's fine," Änŭn's voice called back to him.

Tom banked his fleet in a shifting, changing pattern down to the left, his ships' stealth making their erratic dance appear even more confusing to any N'nrathěrmě who might have been watching for weaknesses in their formations. His assistants were completing other distracting maneuvers as they organized the strategies of the continuing tiers under them.

"Sarah," he called.

A few moments passed before Sarah answered. Tom continued maneuvering and watching the inbound N'nrathěrmě, Sarah's delay being no surprise to him. Being only three tiers below Mär himself, Tom and Sarah were almost continually occupied with the orchestration of the effectively

22: Hero of Nŭährnär

hopeless battle.

After a comparatively short wait, Sarah's voice responded. "Yeah?"

The sound of her voice banished much of the building fear inside of him.

"Let's flank them from beneath," he said.

Sarah didn't answer again for several more seconds. Then she said, "We'll be there. We'll sweep around from the far right; make it look like we're trying to confuse them."

"Excellent," Tom said. "I'll meet your fleets just as you hit them."

"Take care of yourself, Tom," Sarah said anxiously.

"We'll be flying together," Tom said seriously. "Nothing can hurt us."

Mär was streaking in a tiny platform through the lines of Nŭährnär's defenses.

"Encirclement to commence in sixteen seconds," Ŭmäthŭ's voice broadcasted in his head.

"Är, save us!" he said conversationally to the open vacuum as he gazed at the N'nrathĕrmĕ. They were nearly in range.

The N'nrathĕrmĕ armadas were approaching at terrific speed. Their formations were flattening into a widening circle facing the N'nŭährnär fortifications around Earth, a plain preparation to attempt an encirclement of their own.

"Twelve seconds," Ŭmäthŭ announced.

Mär stopped in his progress, floating among the defenses with Earth at his back.

He waited.

"Eight seconds."

He let his fear and self-concern drain out of him. He could feel the N'nrathĕrmĕ.

He could feel the Ärthähr, surging forward behind him with the sense of an unstoppable giant wave.

He smiled, slightly, as power filled him.

"For Pp'ōhōnŭäär," he said out loud.

"Four—*now!*" Ŭmäthŭ gave the command prematurely as the N'nrathĕrmĕs' formations abruptly broke apart. Some of them swung outward, as if to swoop back in to surround all of Nŭährnär's defenses, but the bulk of the N'nrathĕrmĕ pelted forward, instantly achieving a speed beyond the reach of any N'nŭährnär vessel as they charged straight into the thick of Nŭährnär's defenses.

* * *

Tom's assistants knew what to do.

As the N'nrathĕrmĕ charged at them, they hurled themselves downward as if to evade, releasing token blasts of rantha behind them.

Tom saw vast collections of fleets arcing around to the right as if to flank the N'nrathĕrmĕs' side: the dancing armadas under Sarah's command.

"Back toward Earth, slowly," he ordered. "Here we go!"

The bulk of the N'nrathĕrmĕ had charged straight past Tom's fleets, heading directly for the armor around Earth, but many divisions had broken off downward to charge after his divisions.

Tom's assistants closed around the charging divisions, and he directed his own forces to close in on the underside of the passing N'nrathĕrmĕ.

The N'nrathĕrmĕ were moving much faster than his fleets could, but his ships connected with the bottom rear of them, beginning to pin the N'nrathĕrmĕ between the Shell and his fleets.

He could see tides of rantha erupting from the Shell and blasting into the charging N'nrathĕrmĕ, and then saw a hail of speeding ships, Sarah's fleets, come crashing into the underside of the N'nrathĕrmĕ from off to the right.

"Now!" he heard Änŭn command.

"Break!" Tom shouted desperately to his assistants.

The N'nŭährnär fleets had only begun to complete their encirclement. Then, all as one, the formations of N'nŭährnär surrounding the foolishly charging N'nrathĕrmĕ scattered out in every direction. Tom saw Sarah's fleets break away from the N'nrathĕrmĕ they had just surrounded just as his own forces scattered.

And hardly an instant later, he saw the rest of the N'nrathĕrmĕ charging in toward them.

He was immediately glad of the matter they had gotten from the pirates, and that the matter from the surrounding systems had arrived in time. The N'nrathĕrmĕ were over ten times more numerous than had been that terrifying pirate army.

They were pouring in from every direction. John had never seen ships move that fast.

"Prepare for battle!" he heard his manager Nhōath shout.

"This is it!" he called to his assistants. "They've taken our bait; they thought we were taking theirs!"

But what difference will that make? he heard himself wonder as he watched the seemingly endless hordes charging into attack range.

*   *   *

22: Hero of Nŭährnär

Well, if there were ever a time to leave Nŭährnär, Peter thought, *This would be it.*

The N'nrathĕrmĕ might well accept Annie and him, he knew.

No.

I know what I am fighting for.

He tightened his will and gazed out at the terrible charging hordes sliding into visibility.

"There!" he said to his assistants. His gaze had fixed on one portion of the newly appeared N'nrathĕrmĕ hosts, their stealth no longer totally veiling them at that distance.

He extended his voice to Mŭdhōär and Ōärnär as well. "See, at 45°, 67°! They're loose there. We can shoot through and come around their rear!

"Abdul, Äszad, you take the front! Make as if we're heading for the opening at 51°, 50°! We all will follow behind you! Go, go, go!"

Peter's fleets lunged forward.

"Watch for them to counter us!" he heard Mŭdhōär shout as a great portion of Mŭdhōär's divisions hurtled after him.

Rantha spurted from the N'nrathĕrmĕ as Peter's armadas closed in on them. The N'nrathĕrmĕ had better range than his ships did.

"Äährōär, Ähänär, N'näth, Antonio, all of you use your energy to push them away from the opening at 45°, 67°! But not too soon; don't forewarn them!"

His ships were being pulverized. The N'nrathĕrmĕ were closing in around them. Their rantha was too powerful, and their shields too strong.

"Don't get caught!" he shouted. "Now! Make for 45°, 67°! Now!"

His fleets changed direction instantaneously. Several tentacles of N'nrathĕrmĕ divisions had swooped around to surround them and clutch them into the swirling hordes of the rest of the N'nrathĕrmĕ, but his armies dodged left and up. Many of them slipped free of the N'nrathĕrmĕ encircling, but far too many were surrounded and eradicated with terrifying swiftness.

"Mŭdhōär," Peter shouted, "We need more to block that fleet at 42°, 67°!"

Then Peter realized with a jolt of horror that his communication could not find its target.

"Mŭdhōär!"

The N'nrathĕrmĕ were sweeping in toward him from the left.

"Go, go, go!" he shouted madly to his assistants. "Out the break!"

He couldn't sense Äährōär anymore.

"Push them away from the hole!"

The N'nrathĕrmĕ swarmed toward them as the hole ahead of them rapidly contracted. He could see his ships dwindling rapidly.

"We're out!" Antonio Ngonda called panickedly to him.

Peter could see Abdul Karzai's fleets burst out through the hole and begin harassing the N'nrathĕrmĕ from behind.

This might yet work, he dared to realize.

He hurled his own vessel down as a pod of N'nrathĕrmĕ ships sliced through his division, tearing his fleet to pieces.

"Don't help me!" he shouted, terrified that the N'nrathĕrmĕ would realize that his was the commanding fleet.

The N'nrathĕrmĕ were closing in. His opening was almost nonexistent.

He banked abruptly to the right, then charged forward, screaming. His ships unloaded continuous volleys of rantha as they spent their energy to create inertial currents to push the N'nrathĕrmĕ out of the way, making a new opening for him.

He was through!

"Spread out, don't let them surround us!" he commanded.

He was amazed to find himself still alive.

That was 38 percent of all his forces destroyed, he realized, despair growing unignorably.

There were so many of them! *What can we possibly do?* he thought with sinking realism.

"Väth, keep your forces around Earth!" Tom shouted. "The rest of us, we have to get out of this!"

"Tom, we'll make a big impression if we both use our forces to make an opening," he heard Sarah say.

"Thanks," he called back; her timing couldn't have been more perfect. "Ready now?"

"I am," Sarah said.

"Then let's go!" he shouted to her and to his assistants.

"Everyone," Mär called to his immediate assistants as he sped alone through the boiling masses of N'nüährnär attempting to hold the N'nrathĕrmĕ off from Earth.

"Nüährnär's quite capable on its own, strategically."

As he said it, more N'nüährnär divisions all around earth were forcing passages out of the N'nrathĕrmĕs' crushing encirclement.

"Now," Mär said imperiously, "It is time for the Ōmäthäär to look to their part!"

22: Hero of Nüährnär

And, not slackening in either his speed or his maneuvering, he let his tiny vessel fall off of him. He stretched his arms out wide in an all but unconscious movement.

His fingers began flexing rhythmically.

"They're breaking through!" Annie shouted to Mamōth, her manager, as she saw the N'nrathĕrmĕs' rantha begin hammering the Shell.

"Annie, Yi, you bring your fleets around on their front side!" Mamōth called.

Annie pushed her fleets forward, as she saw her fellows' fleets swoop around above her. Hundreds of other small N'nüährnär fleets were flanking the massive N'nrathĕrme hosts who were bombarding the slowly weakening Shell.

"Annie, they're breaking through the Shell!" Abani Kalam called to her.

Annie didn't know what words of encouragement to give. She was certain that they were all watching their lives' final moments pass before them.

Everything seemed to be moving more and more slowly. The Shell was pummeling the N'nrathĕrme with unceasing storms of rantha, but every N'nrathĕrme vessel that burst apart in a flash of light and rantha was promptly replaced by another.

A deep indentation was being gouged into the Shell by the unrelenting hail of rantha crashing into it.

It would only be a matter of moments before their beautiful living spaces were destroyed, she thought. She felt as if she had lived there forever. And now it was all about to be destroyed.

Maybe the N'nrathĕrme would spare the Earth itself. But the dirty planet hardly seemed to matter to her anymore at the prospect of everything else being annihilated.

"Come around to the left," she said half-heartedly to Abani.

Then she got a better hold of herself. "Come around to the left," she commanded again, she hoped more firmly this time. "Ruth, guard Abani from above."

But, seeing the growing hordes of N'nrathĕrme, she realized with surety that they were all going to die, regardless of whatever maneuvers they attempted against this N'nrathĕrme juggernaut.

A blaze of homey light shined out from within the Shell as its armor was finally breached.

Ährnär knew the N'nrathĕrme would not be able to detect her; better than any inertial stealth, Ärthähr itself was shielding her from the eyes of all except the five Ōmäthäär around her.

She flew straight into the crossfire of rantha pouring between the rupturing Shell and the unrelenting N'nrathĕrmĕ. The deadly particles were absorbed painlessly into her.

We can't stop them entirely, she felt Nōvagähd say beside her.

But we can give our friends some help, she willed back to him.

Tom saw more and more N'nrathĕrmĕ divisions descend upon the Shell. Three, four, six breaches had cracked open through its dense armor.

They could divide the N'nrathĕrmĕ, he realized. The N'nrathĕrmĕ had devoted too many forces to the Shell. If his forces seized this opportunity to divide apart the N'nrathĕrmĕs' neglected rear forces, they might create a strategic edge over their attackers.

"Let's hit them now, hard, from behind!" he called.

Hundreds of millions of N'nŭährnär rained down upon the N'nrathĕrmĕ from behind, finding crevices and chinks in the N'nrathĕrmĕs' formations, forcing them apart from one another.

Tom's division spiraled around behind the N'nrathĕrmĕ, harassing them with rantha, then pulling away again as the N'nrathĕrmĕ banked back to reply.

But there were still so many N'nrathĕrmĕ, and so few N'nŭährnär.

If nothing else, we will make them pay dearly for destroying Nŭährnär, he thought as he swung his division up and to the right, pulling the N'nrathĕrmĕ after him away from another developing hole in the Shell.

"They're pulling away!" Annie called incredulously.

She couldn't believe her eyes as she saw the N'nrathĕrmĕ being shunted away from the Shell's growing breach by the ridiculously smaller N'nŭährnär divisions. It looked as if the N'nrathĕrmĕs' maneuvers were continually failing and intertangling one with another.

"Be careful, this has to be a trap," Mamōth called.

Ährnär lowered her arms amidst the diminishing tempest of rantha. She instantly felt drained.

Well, we confused them, she said to the others there with her.

"Hääbr, Kat," she called to her assistants. "We've scrambled the brains of these N'nrathĕrmĕ; send our forces in to carve them up!"

"This isn't enough," Mär observed to his assistants as he careened

22: Hero of Nŭährnär

undetected right through a dense bunch of N'nrathĕrmĕ. A wave of fear and uncertainty and ensuing miscommunication was radiating from him through the billions of N'nrathĕrmĕ nearby.

"Even confused, these N'nrathĕrmĕ are just too many," he said.

"We are doing all that we can do," Ōhärnäth's voice said with calm exhaustion.

"We're waiting on someone," Anŭsths said. "I can feel that."

"He's right," Ōhōmhär said. "This is somebody else's show now. We're doing all we can do."

Mär continued on serenely toward another gargantuan N'nrathĕrmĕ swarm gathered around a widening gap in the Shell as N'nŭährnär behind him slowly began gaining the upper hand over the befuddled N'nrathĕrmĕ.

"Yeah, you are right," he agreed as he felt Ärthähr complement what Anŭsths and Ōhōmhär had said. "Let's be ready, though, to move in, in case whomever we're waiting for doesn't step up."

Go there.

There was nothing over there, Tom thought half-consciously.

Over there, the feeling seemed to nag more strongly.

"Hährthär!" he called, not realizing he was ignoring the nagging impression. "At 289°, -23°! Scatter then, distract them, bait them; just stop them from getting into the Shell!"

Fine. Now, get over there.

There was nothing over there, Tom thought offhandedly again, hardly aware of it.

"S'zahahn, at 320°, -46°!" he shouted desperately, seeing too late the massive wing of N'nrathĕrmĕ looping around behind them.

"Vhōnag, D'rnär, pull up and left with me!"

I am serious, Tom! the wordless Ärthähr said with suddenly very noticeable impatience.

The tugging feeling inside of him finally rose above the fear and intensity of battle to draw his gaze to a patch of empty space away behind the rampaging N'nrathĕrmĕ horde in that area.

Those fleets are lost, he said deliberately to the feeling inside of him, noticing the almost entirely overcome N'nŭährnär near that area struggling to escape from a vice-like encirclement where they had obviously been attempting to defend the Shell.

Nevertheless he thrust his fleets toward the empty patch.

"Z'vaf, come with me! Vhōnag, D'rnär, forget that last command!"

Light and Glory

He hurtled toward the empty area. Coming in behind the conquering N'nratherme, he saw fearfully that the N'nratherme were breaking away from their encirclement of the other N'nüährnär and charging toward his fleets.

He suddenly realized how very small his fleets were as the ranks of N'nratherme cascaded toward him, thwarting what they evidently thought was his attempt to flank them.

At least he was diverting the N'nratherme from eradicating those few surviving N'nüährnär, he thought, wondering if he had just gotten himself killed.

He hurled his fleet back, postponing engagement with the charging armies and hoping to draw them farther from the still surrounded N'nüährnär.

He directed his voice to the commander of the few remaining N'nüährnär being surrounded near the Shell. "Get out of there! Just get away! To the left!"

He pulled his forces spiraling up to the right, the N'nratherme being surprisingly stupid and easy to draw away.

The N'nüährnär were still having a difficult time of it, he could see.

They weren't gong to make it out of there alive.

But if he went in again, that wouldn't do any good. He would just get his own people killed needlessly!

But these N'nratherme were being very foolish.

Was it a ploy?

It doesn't matter, a harsh voice said within him. *Go in there, now!*

"On it," Tom said out loud to the vacuum.

"Z'vaf, in!" he shouted as he jerked sharply down and around the following N'nratherme, charging back toward the Shell.

The N'nratherme still demolishing the encircled N'nüährnär seemed to see Tom's fleets bearing down toward them, but they also apparently saw the great wave of N'nratherme gaining on his fleets. They broke away from the surrounded N'nüährnär, evidently secure that their companions would catch all the N'nüährnär when they reached them.

Not if I can help it, Tom thought, seeing that.

But the N'nratherme were catching up to them very quickly.

And then the pieces finally came together in his racing mind: That commander he had just called to was Hui Yi.

Brittney's manager.

Then it struck him just how very few N'nüährnär were left in this division in front of him.

"No!" he shouted out loud to open space.

22: Hero of Nŭährnär

"Tom!" he heard Brittney's voice call to him before the shout was fully formed in his mouth.

She was alive! he realized with sudden euphoria. She was alive!

And just at that moment, an engulfing storm of rantha seared into his fleets from the charging N'nrathěrmě behind him.

"Tom, what do you think you're doing?" he heard Sarah's terrified voice shout.

A great mass of N'nŭährnär fleets, half of Sarah's fleets, was sweeping down from above.

"Sarah, take these, Hui Yi's division!" Tom shouted.

"Tom, we're doomed!" Brittney moaned forlornly.

"Go with Sarah Trotter's fleets!" Tom called to both Yi and Brittney. He banked his fleet left, just as a great arm of the N'nrathěrmě, fully as large as his entire fleet, crashed down toward him from above.

"Get out of here!" he called to Brittney.

"No!" Brittney shouted back decisively. "If you get out, then I'll get out with you!"

It was as if the fear and clamor of battle had been altogether muted.

"You will get out!" Tom promised with passionate power.

"Z'vaf, head out right to 199°, -3°!"

"If you say so," Z'fav said with frightened humor.

But just as he directed his fleets in that direction, the main body of the N'nrathěrmě moved directly in front of him. Rantha pelted his fleets, tens of thousands of ships getting struck instantly.

"To 192°, -2°!" he shouted more anxiously.

But then the dense core of the N'nrathěrmě in front of him began scattering apart, as if at the charge of a fleet far larger than Tom's.

Even if this was a trap, it was a way out, he thought, thunderstruck at the N'nrathěrměs' unexplainable cowardice and stupidity.

"Back to 199°, -3°!" he shouted.

He hurled his fleets around again, burying them in the mass of Z'vaf's forces, and the N'nrathěrmě continued to scatter.

"Why are they fleeing?" Z'vaf said suspiciously.

"Trap or no trap, we're out!" Tom replied, just as their fleets burst free from the enormous mass of now scattering N'nrathěrmě.

And Brittney was still with him, he could see, with a tiny few of Yi's other forces.

He wanted to tell her to get away to some place safe, but there was nowhere safe to go to. And he knew that she would never leave the battle if she could still contribute to it.

But the N'nrathĕrmĕ had scattered away from them, gathering together farther away in disorder.

"Have you noticed," Sarah's confused voice said, "The N'nrathĕrmĕ seem like they're half asleep?"

"You have too," Tom said. "But half asleep of all asleep, there are still too many of them!" He realized that he'd lost more than half his own forces already.

"We cannot win this," he recognized.

The regrouped N'nrathĕrmĕ were swinging back around toward them.

"Peter!" John called in relief.

Peter's fleets had swooped down upon a horde of N'nrathĕrmĕ who had nearly eradicated John's fleet.

"Get as many as you can and head upward!" he heard Peter yell.

"Kōrhas, up toward 181°, 5°!" John shouted. His other assistants all killed, he contacted the rest of his fleets directly. "To 181°, 5°!"

"John, I think we can win this," Peter said.

John pushed his fleets up and past Peter's armadas, which were struggling to hold the surging N'nrathĕrmĕ back.

"That's one of us," he replied frenziedly. "You've got to get out of there, Peter!"

But Peter had already released his fleets from holding back the N'nrathĕrmĕ.

"Keep moving, John!" Peter shouted, his fleets hurtling desperately toward John's demolished forces, the N'nrathĕrmĕ pursuing right behind him.

"To 179°, 47°!" Peter called.

"No! Don't you see them there?" John said frantically, staring with horror at the enormous sprawl of N'nrathĕrmĕ hammering larger and larger breaches in the Shell.

"I see them," Peter said, much more steadily than John. "They're almost through the inner armor. I want to drag these N'nrathĕrmĕ behind us over there."

But sandwiching themselves between two forces that were double the strength of all of Nŭährnär combined did not strike John as a brilliant strategy.

"Sarah, bring those N'nrathĕrmĕ over here!" Sarah heard Peter Garcia call urgently.

She swooped her fleet downward. Then she saw three tremendous

22: Hero of Nŭährnär

divisions of N'nrathĕrmĕ sweeping toward her from opposite sides. She changed direction instantly, pulling up and ahead, but the N'nrathĕrmĕ followed close behind her, spitting rantha as her vessels fell rapidly.

"If you want them!" she called back.

"Mäŭg, Tärnär, Änrŭ, Nōth'nrŭ, get everyone to 178°, 47°!" she shouted to her assistants. "Get the N'nrathĕrmĕ to follow us!"

"*Are you insane?*" Tärnär cried as he pulled his fleets around after Sarah, facing the teeming mass of N'nrathĕrmĕ far ahead.

"Someone must be," Sarah smiled shakily as she responded. "Let's hope he knows what he's doing."

"Now what?" John demanded of Peter.

"Now, get out, fast!" was Peter's rushed reply. His fleets soared back away from where they had come. The newly gathered mass of N'nrathĕrmĕ, more than a match for three times Nŭährnär's strength, was demolishing the Shell without much apparent thought for Peter's divisions.

"What is Peter doing?" Mär heard Ŭkan wonder aloud.

Mär stared at where nearly half the N'nrathĕrmĕ forces were now gathering, over toward the other side of Earth.

"He's stepping up," he said quietly.

He closed his eyes for a moment, then opened them again.

"We have to attract all the N'nrathĕrmĕ to that breach!" he commanded then. "Äthääōhä, Avhä, get in there and keep them from hurting Ōhōnŭäär!"

Mär hurled himself forward, closing in on a fiercely battling army of N'nrathĕrmĕ.

If he could just influence their minds to join the fray near that breach…

"'Watch the magic,'" he heard Ŭmäthŭ laugh emotionally. "I wonder if Peter knew how much of the magic he was going to end up as."

"Or already was," Mär said. He could feel rising tears reflecting what he was starting to feel, as he hurtled into the midst of the swirling N'nrathĕrmĕ.

"Tom, to the breach at 179°, 47°!" Änŭn called.

"Good, you're still alive!" Tom said frantically. "I just lost Z'vaf and Raōthä!"

He shot his fleets upward.

"Everyone, get over here!" he said to his few remaining assistants.

"I'll be there," he called back to Änŭn.

"Get the N'nrathĕrmĕ to follow you," Änŭn said.

He hardly had any choice, he thought as he steered around toward the sprawling horde of N'nrathĕrmĕ attacking the Shell in the distance.

"It'll only work if we surround them on the inside as well as the outside," Peter was saying to John.

"But whoever's on the inside will be massacred!" John's voice said back.

"I've already contacted Bäbähn," Peter said, dodging upward, keeping his distance from the charging company of N'nrathĕrmĕ. "He's going to send several divisions of unmanned ships in—"

He stopped talking as he banked quickly to the left. The N'nrathĕrmĕ were taking more notice of his fleet.

"Is everyone in position?" Peter shouted to Bäbähn. The Shell below them was breaking to pieces, revealing the no longer glowing Earth sitting naked in front of them.

Gathering the unmanned ships was taking too long!

"Annie! To the right!" Mamōth's voice cried.

Annie looked desperately around. There was no way out.

Chasing the N'nrathĕrmĕ away a little too ambitiously, she was finding herself trapped as the N'nrathĕrmĕ soared back toward the disintegrating Shell.

"Bäbähn, we're losing our window!" Peter shouted furiously. "We don't have time! We'll all be dead before we can get into position!"

He plunged down and forward, more N'nrathĕrmĕ joining the pursuit following hotly behind him.

"Bäbähn!" Peter called again.

No answer.

He burst out through an opening serendipitously made by three interweaving N'nrathĕrmĕ armadas, but those N'nrathĕrmĕ instantly banked back to flank him. He hurled his ships up as many of them were caught by the N'nrathĕrmĕs' ubiquitous rantha.

He noticed a sizeable group of N'nŭährnär down far below him near the Shell, right in the thick of the rampaging N'nrathĕrmĕ.

As he offhandedly concluded that those N'nŭährnär had, if possible, less hope at that point than he did, he realized that Earth was still untouched, though the enormous Shell was now falling to pieces in powerful eruptions of light and rantha.

Annie! he recognized. Those N'nŭährnär were Annie's people!

22: Hero of Nŭährnär

He immediately broadcasted his voice to every higher manager in the area.

"*Get in position! Now!*" came Peter's deafening shout in Tom's hearing.
"Position?" Tom shouted to Änŭn. But then he saw what Peter was doing.
A great mass of N'nŭährnär, all under Peter's command, had plunged itself right into the heart of the surging throngs of N'nrathĕrmĕ.
"Send all you unmanned ships in there!" Änŭn commanded fiercely.

"Peter, get out of there!" Peter heard Mōŭhär, a higher manager, call to him.
"Annie!" he shouted as he wheeled his ships around to a weaker part of the N'nrathĕrmĕ. "We have no time! 171°, 30°, *now!*"
Peter's ships were dropping with horrifying speed. Several powerful bursts of rantha weakened the horde of N'nrathĕrmĕ directly in front of him, which Annie's fleets plowed into and through.
He made to follow her, but he already knew that both he and Annie would be slaughtered along with everyone else unless they could somehow execute this last ditch maneuver.

"Peter!" Annie shouted hysterically.
Her fleet had managed to extricate itself miraculously from the clutches of the N'nrathĕrmĕ. But now she saw that, instead of following her, Peter had wheeled around to engage the densest portion of the armies that outnumbered him by a hundred to one.
"Peter! Get out of there!" she sobbed. She turned her fleets back toward the N'nrathĕrmĕ, but she knew that that would not be any help.
And just then, the rest of Nŭährnär closed in around her, bearing down on top of the N'nrathĕrmĕ.

Sensing only foolishness, the N'nrathĕrmĕ clamped down around Peter's fleets, which were now swelling with the reinforcement of hundreds of billions of self-driven unoccupied vessels.
And like clockwork, the tattered remnants of Nŭährnär swarmed around the outside of the densely thronging hosts of N'nrathĕrmĕ.
No encirclement could have lasted long against such enormously superior numbers. But Peter's desperately battling fleets within their very heart were occupying the abruptly trapped N'nrathĕrmĕ horde, allowing the scanty, demolished divisions of Nŭährnär to seal their sudden strategic gain over them.

Light and Glory

* * *

"Peter!" Annie's voice moaned forlornly.

"I love you, Annie!" Peter yelled back. He had never expected to cry twice in one day.

He dodged left, then down, then left again, then up. The N'nrathĕrmĕ were all around him. Rantha seemed to cover all his vision.

He pulled around back in a swerving loop, willing all the unmanned vessels to spend themselves completely in releasing rantha.

He broadcasted himself to everyone under his command still with him:

"This is Peter Garcia. I am terribly sorry I led you into this!"

He banked quickly down.

"Know this: We have just saved Nŭährnär!"

His tears were coming more quickly. He could see the N'nŭährnär forces outside whittling down through the still encircled N'nrathĕrmĕ legions.

He swung his vessel with those nearest him in a spiraling pattern to the right.

"We have just saved our friends, our families!" he shouted triumphantly. "Our loved ones!"

The last thing Peter saw was Annie's smiling face as he shouted out to her: *"Annie, we win!"*

"NO!" John shouted. He could see Peter's vessel, caught in the middle of a sweeping upward drive, annihilated in a horrendous glare of austere white light.

Everything froze for Annie.

The battle didn't matter anymore. Earth didn't matter anymore.

Peter was gone.

Peter, her Peter, was dead.

Her Peter.

He was gone!

"Annie," came Mamōth's abrasive voice.

Annie didn't register that he was calling her.

"Go out to 78°, 0°," Mamōth told her softly. "We will be alright here."

"They killed Peter," she mumbled lifelessly.

"Come with me," Mamōth said more firmly.

Annie saw his fleet disengaging from the now desperate N'nrathĕrmĕ and flying off away from the still roaring battle.

She didn't care.

22: Hero of Nŭährnär

"They killed Peter!" she said again.

Her assistants were still battling valiantly, leaving her farther behind as the N'nrathĕrmĕ were slowly beaten apart.

She didn't care.

"Annie, he saved us all!" Mamōth said earnestly. "He died to save you—"

"No!" Annie shouted at him. "Back, Mamōth, back to the N'nrathĕrmĕ!"

She hurled her vessel and her own ships forward, straight into the swirling storm of struggling N'nrathĕrmĕ and N'nŭährnär.

Her platform slowed down despite her urging it onward.

"Annie, no!" Mamōth yelled. "Come away!"

"Let me go!" Annie roared, hazily realizing how much energy Mamōth must have been spending to hold her ship back so firmly.

"Annie, *you have done enough!*" Mamōth hissed emphatically.

Annie stopped willing her ship forward and dissolved into miserable tears. She felt Mamōth pulling her ship back from the flashing, churning battle. She could not bring herself to care anymore.

Chapter 23

The Faithful and the Fearful

"Annie?"

Annie opened her eyes and looked around.

John was standing in front of her, in the middle of pleasant, bright light.

John didn't say anything. He just looked at Annie with a kind of forlorn jubilation on his face.

"John?" she asked vaguely.

She looked around. She was up in the foothills of what she recognized were the Pocono Mountains, slouching in a raised cleft of rocks like a throne in the middle of a sizeable crowd of people. Her parents were there, and one of her sisters, and Peter's parents...

Peter's parents.

Suddenly she remembered everything.

Amelia Smith, Peter's mother, swept forward to embrace Annie as Annie fell into tears again, closely followed by Annie's own mother Adrian.

"Annie, Peter saved everyone," John said with quiet fervor. "Again!"

Annie looked up from the two weeping mothers and smiled shakily at him.

"What happened?" she asked Adrian, closing her eyes, part of her not wanting to hear anything about that vicious battle.

Neither mother answered for a few moments. Amelia backed away to let Adrian hold Annie.

Then she heard Mamōth's voice from her right. "You just went blank. I thought you might have died."

"It was like you were asleep," John said. "We could tell you weren't dead," he said with a patronizing glance at Mamōth. "I didn't know we could still faint."

"No," Annie said. "I meant, what's happened to Peter?"

John looked at the ground.

Adrian stepped apart from Annie, caressing her back.

"We tried to bring him back," Amelia said, her voice cracking.

Annie stared at her, unable to believe this.

"Our son died like a man," Charles Garcia said, failing in his attempt to keep his tone steady.

"No!" Annie wailed voicelessly. Her mother stroked her back more firmly.

23: The Faithful and the Fearful

"Annie, he saved all of our lives!" John said pleadingly. "He died so you would live!"

"He won't come back?" she whispered.

"He lived a worthwhile life," Amelia said softly.

"A worthwhile life?" Annie moaned, tears reemerging from her wide eyes. "He didn't even live to be thirty!"

"In any case, he is satisfied to finish the way he did," Amelia said, almost as if she were trying to convince herself.

"'Satisfied!'" Annie said. "He's not satisfied to be away from me! He's dead! Our...our 'technology,'" she said bitterly, "Can't bring him back, that's all!"

Amelia turned away, crying. Charles Garcia was notably avoiding looking at his ex-wife.

John looked hopelessly at Amelia for a moment, then said, "No, Annie, Peter's mom's right. You should hear the Ōmäthäär talk. Peter's not dead."

Annie smiled appreciatively at John, but then looked down, away from him.

She didn't move for a moment, then lowered her face down into her knees and fell into silent sobs. Her mother put her arms around her again.

John didn't know what to say. He stood miserably, watching Annie weeping into her mother's shoulder now.

It was more than a minute, Annie weeping silently and indifferent to everything around her, before an unfamiliar voice gently said her name.

Everyone looked to see Ärdhär the Ōmäthäär, Mär's own assistant, standing thus far unnoticed at the back of the group.

The crowd immediately parted deferentially for her. Ärdhär didn't react to that, but waited for Annie to acknowledge her.

Annie looked up, still weeping silently, and then recognized the commanding Ōmäthäär in front of her. She sat up quickly and banished the tears from her eyes, looking at once prepared to receive whatever order Ärdhär might have for her.

A weak smile passed across Ärdhär's face. Then she bowed her head in an unmistakable gesture of reverence.

Annie didn't know what to do. "What is it?" she asked awkwardly.

Ärdhär moved quickly toward her, then looked at Adrian, as if begging permission to talk to Annie.

Adrian nodded, wide-eyed, and moved away.

Ärdhär smiled more deeply. "I think she wants you to stay by her," she said meekly. "But I have a message for you," she said, looking squarely at

Annie.

No eyes but Peter's had ever filled Annie with such sudden serene warmth. She stared speechlessly at the venerated Ōmäthäär in front of her.

"Mär wanted to talk to you himself," Ärdhär said. "But I'm glad I have to come to congratulate you in his place."

Congratulate me? Annie thought. But she was too overwhelmed to respond to Ärdhär.

"Yes," Ärdhär said clairvoyantly.

"Why?" Annie asked tentatively.

Ärdhär looked benevolently into Annie's eyes, but didn't say anything.

Annie understood. She looked down again, but forced a mournful, "Thank you."

"I have heard the Ōmäthäär talk," Ärdhär grinned, and John felt slightly sheepish. "You deserve a congratulation." She looked around at everyone there. "You all deserve to be more than proud of Peter."

The way she said his name somehow comforted Annie.

"Adrian's right," Ärdhär said, looking significantly but obligingly at Charles. "I think she's right, anyway.

"Any technology that had the capacity to revive all the dead, without regard to their desire to return to our situation, would be a terrible tyranny of a device!" she said informally, turning to Annie again.

She hesitated, then said, "Seventy-one billion N'nüährnär were killed today. And almost two hundred fifty billion N'nrathĕrmĕ have been killed today, too."

The effect of those words was to make Annie feel insignificant, even petty, in her agony over Peter, and also to provoke an upsurge of pity for the billions of others mourning like herself, which somehow lessened her own lonesome pain. Her mother whimpered quietly beside her.

"We can't risk reviving the N'nrathĕrmĕ," Ärdhär sighed. She stood quietly for a few seconds, staring at the mountains behind Annie. "Of the fallen N'nüährnär, barely a third have been revived.

"I can't say why so many will not revive after this battle," she said heavily. She looked Annie softly yet directly in the eye. "But I'm ready to say that Peter is one whose life has been brilliantly lived. He will not revive," she said impressively, "Because Peter has no need to come back to this shadowy mortal situation."

"But *I* need him!" Annie pleaded.

Ärdhär looked down sadly.

"You were married, at least," Amelia ventured.

23: The Faithful and the Fearful

Ärdhär's head snapped up sharply. "You were married?" she demanded with frightening intensity.

"Uh, yes," Annie said, a little taken aback. "We were."

"But this is perfect!" Ärdhär exclaimed glowingly, slapping her hands loudly together.

"I married them," Mamōth said from behind Ärdhär.

"We had no idea!" Ärdhär exulted, positively beaming at Mamōth.

"I have not told my managers yet," Mamōth said guiltily.

Ärdhär seemed to get a hold of herself. "Yes. That's fine, Mamōth. We all have had a lot of concerns today.

"But Annie!" she began, turning toward her again. But she seemed to catch herself, and her thought went unsaid. She smiled benignly for a second, then said, "That's perfect.

"I'll have to tell Mär. He'll be thrilled!"

Annie remembered what Peter said about Mär's sentiments on marriage after death. Now, after Mär's premonition had turned out to be so horribly accurate, she hoped more than ever that she could believe him as much as she had after the pirate attack.

And he had been right about one unbelievable thing: Nŭährnär had survived through the day!

She hoped he was right about Peter and her.

"Daniel and Ann!" Lewis shouted, his head in his hands. "And Ian and Fiona and Teddy! And now *Terry*?"

Tom couldn't believe what Arkŭth was saying.

"We tried to revive her as soon as the N'nrathĕrmĕ surrendered," Terry's manager Arkŭth said to the remaining Pratts. "I'm sorry."

Lewis turned away, watching the ruined remains of Nŭährnär regathering the pulverized matter of the Shell in the distance.

Andrew was looking unseeingly out at the stars. Terry was dead. His little sister Terry.

"Have you asked any Ōmäthäär to try?" Tom asked Arkŭth with quiet urgency.

Arkŭth's eyes hardly looked alive as he stared confusedly at him. "No. What would they do?"

"Never mind," Tom said. He would have to see if Änŭn could help, he said to himself.

Arkŭth extended his left hand to Tom, since Lewis was still gazing fixedly at Earth. Tom took it obligingly in his right hand, then let go quickly.

"I am very sorry," Arkŭth said regretfully. He turned and shot straight away toward Earth.

Tom didn't move.

"Damn the N'nrathĕrmĕ!" he heard Lewis hiss behind him.

He turned toward Lewis and Andrew. Andrew's face too was drawn and deadened.

"They killed my daughter!" Lewis roared. He turned toward the delayed golden light of Nrathĕrmĕ's star. Raising his fists at it, he shouted, "They killed my brother and my daughter! They killed Mary's sister! They killed them!"

And we killed billions of brothers and sisters and fathers and daughters, Tom thought morosely. But he held his tongue in front of his father's rage.

Andrew still was simply staring into the infinite darkness in front of him.

"Sĕrĕhahn!" Lewis bellowed. "I will see you dead! I will make you pay for this!"

Tom swiveled to look at Nrathĕrmĕ's old star. *Sĕrĕhahn,* he thought. It was all because of Sĕrĕhahn.

"Damn you!" Lewis shouted, bowing his head into his hands again.

Three hundred billion actual, individual, living, breathing people were now dead, Tom thought, his sorrow too rising into fury.

Because of Sĕrĕhahn.

Lewis's hands were tight over his face. Andrew's eyes were narrowed.

"Sĕrĕhahn," Andrew echoed in a scathing whisper.

At least Sarah was alive, Tom felt himself think. But then he kicked himself, thinking he was being self-centered.

"We've killed Thahn, at least," Andrew said viciously. "That's a hurt to old Anhar, I'm sure."

"What?" Tom said, looking back at Andrew.

Lewis looked up miserably at them.

"Thahn," Andrew said. "She was leading the N'nrathĕrmĕ. Everyone was saying how terrible she was. Well, now she isn't!"

"Thahn wasn't with these N'nrathĕrmĕ," Tom said.

"What do you mean?" Andrew asked, looking closely at him.

"Thahn is still on her way," Tom said, wishing Andrew was right. "These N'nrathĕrmĕ were acting independently. Thahn is coming with a real army."

Andrew stared lifelessly at him.

Lewis looked away.

"'A real army,'" Andrew repeated disbelievingly.

"Here," Tom said, extending his arm to Andrew.

23: The Faithful and the Fearful

"Don't show me!" Andrew said.

"Thahn is coming, whether you're ready for her or not," Tom said levelly. He kept his hand extended.

Andrew touched his hand reluctantly, and Tom sent into him much of what he had been told about Thahn and her armies.

Andrew jerked his fingers back. "No!"

"The Ōmäthäär got us through this," Tom said quickly.

"Yeah? How are they going to get us through Thahn?" Andrew demanded terrifiedly.

"We were outnumbered more than ten to one just an hour ago," Tom reminded him.

"And now we're outnumbered a couple hundred to one!" Andrew said.

"Oh, no; with the matter from this battle, make that twenty to one!"

"I want to trust Mär too," Lewis said to Tom in a subdued voice. "But the man has his limits. Remember, Thahn is an Ämäthōär."

Tom stared at the two of them. "Dad," he said after a pause in which his own fear climbed up powerfully within him, "Andrew, we have to stop Sĕrĕhahn. We have to beat him."

Lewis smiled an almost pitying smile at Tom.

"I know the Ōmäthäär," Tom said. "And they know Är."

Lewis's smile faded.

"If Mär's not lying, and I know that he isn't," Tom said seriously, "Then our little Earth is that Pp'ōhōnŭäär. And Är won't abandon us if we're defending that from Ämäthōär!"

"God's abandoned people before," Lewis said, eyeing Tom with distinct pride. "But I do hope Mär is right."

Andrew looked away again.

"I need to go," Tom said. He looked at Andrew, then glided forward and hugged him.

Andrew was caught off guard by that uncharacteristic gesture from Tom.

"I am happy that we three are alive," Tom said, holding back tears more for Andrew's sake than his own.

He let go, then moved aside and hugged his father too.

"I will see you later," he said heavily.

Lewis nodded, smiling yet more proudly at his son.

Tom streaked past them off toward Earth.

"I'm back," he broadcasted to his remaining assistants as he drew slowly nearer the virtually unscathed planet. "Thank you for waiting for me."

"Tom," M'tärnär called back, "You deserve to be with your family at a time like this!"

"Thahn is coming," Tom said tensely. "I love my family; that is why I need to work now, and spend time with them later."

"Your family may not be there later," Härthär said unflinchingly.

"We must do what we can!" Tom snapped, slowing to a stop a small distance from the reforming Shell.

"We've lost Z'vaf and Raōthä, and S'zahan and Ōbäd," he said stonily to them all, watching the organization of renewed defenses. "Määrhan, can I count on you and Nartŭn to take up Z'vaf and Raōthä's responsibilities?"

"No," Määrhan answered desolately. "But we will try."

"That's all that we need," Tom assured him consolingly. "M'närdamähr, will you and Hōämhär lead for—" he hesitated, the pain at the death of his assistants searing into him.

"Yes," M'närdamähr answered resolutely.

"S'zahan and Ōbäd fought to save Nŭährnär," Hōämhär reminded Tom quietly. "I know they want us to carry on."

"Yes," Tom smiled, not holding back tears anymore. "Carry on!"

"We will!" Ōfha's voice said.

Tom knew exactly what he had to do now. He might have hesitated had he thought to do this in earlier times. But he felt sternly that he had no more time for hesitation now.

"Call me when you need me," he said to all of his assistants. "I will speak to you again soon."

He turned and began flying out toward the regathering defenses farther away from Earth.

"Yi," he called to Brittney's manager. "This is Tom Pratt. When can you spare Brittney some time? I'd like to talk to her when she has a chance."

"Ask Brittney," Hui Yi answered him with noticeably fatigued amiability. "Thank you, Tom. You saved her life as well as mine and Ding's just then."

"Thanks," Tom said, preoccupied about getting to talk to Brittney. "And you're welcome, too," he added feebly.

Drawing nearer to Yi's group, he could see Brittney darting around with her fellows, hurling matter this way and that in Nŭährnär's desperate rush to prepare for Thahn's unstoppable arrival.

"Brittney," he called.

"Tom!" Brittney shouted back, plainly happy to see him now. But he noticed a definite note of uncertainty in her voice.

Brittney left the whirling construction of defenses and glided, with measured slowness, toward him.

23: The Faithful and the Fearful

"Tom, thank you! Thank you! You saved my life!"

Tom glided more purposefully toward her. "I'm glad I was there right then," he said. "Really glad."

Brittney had slowed to a stop in front of him, clearly trying not to act awkward.

"You said you wouldn't let me die," she said tenderly to him. A loving smile was emerging on her face. "And you didn't! Not even though there were more N'nrathĕrmĕ than I thought we could possibly escape from."

She made an obvious, awkward movement.

Tom felt like his heart was going to break under its weight. He just wanted to hold her, to make her happy. He wanted to keep her safe from everything, from fear, from Ämäthöär, from Thahn. And from Sĕrĕhahn.

He would kill Sĕrĕhahn for putting Brittney through this!

He wanted to embrace her right then. But he was afraid of being insensitive to Brittney's already bruised feelings. He knew that he could not let her be with him the way he wanted Sarah to be so totally with him.

He swept forward and hugged her tightly.

Brittney seemed surprised by that at first, but then she embraced him back, burying her head in his shoulder.

"If I can," Tom said, "I will *always* be here for you. Just call me, anytime you need me."

Brittney released him gently. "I've thought about what you said."

"Brittney," Tom began.

"I understand," she said forcefully.

Tom looked uncomprehendingly at her.

"I don't understand what you're not saying," she said with half a smile. "But I got to talk to Ōähŭhan; she's one of the Ōmäthäär." She smiled more completely at him. "I believe you, Tom."

Tom smiled back at her softly. "You believe that I hate having to keep you away like this?"

"Keep me away?" Brittney said. "According to Ōähŭhan, we can still be near each other. But…" she looked down, then looked back up at Tom. "You really are an Ōmäthäär?"

Tom laughed. "Not according to me!"

"According to Ōähŭhan, Mär's been teaching you how to kill Ämäthöär."

"No, he hasn't," Tom said, surprised.

Or had he been? Was that what Mär had been doing?

Sarah and he had just been learning about Är, and Ä'ähänärdanär. Mär hadn't told them how to hurt anything.

383

Brittney furrowed her brow at him.

"At least, not directly," Tom amended. "But he has taught us a little about that kind of thing, I guess."

"'Us?'" Brittney said, confused. "How many Ōmäthäär-in-training are there?"

"Oh. I meant Sarah Trotter. Mär's teaching the two of us."

"Oh," Brittney said, her voice somewhat subdued.

Tom looked sadly at her. "Do you believe that I'm in love with you?"

Brittney smiled a warm but sad smile at him. She asked, "Does that matter?"

"Of course it matters! I—"

"I love you, Tom Pratt," Brittney said, smiling a little more sadly. "That's what matters to me.

"And I believe you that you are looking out for me, like you tried to say you were.

"I want to fight Ämäthōär with you! But after hearing what Ōähühan had to say, I understand why you don't want me to have to.

"And I don't think I'm ready for that yet."

Tom was aware of a distinct self-satisfied gloating feeling that was not his own, as if Ärthähr were saying, "See?"

"I love you," Brittney was saying, her voice trembling, "But maybe you will be happier with someone who is ready."

Tom had never been more impressed with Brittney before now. "I may," he said. "But I know we'll both be happier if you don't have to suffer because of me."

Brittney smiled as if she was satisfiedly giving up a treasured hope. "Friends?" she said with affective calmness, extending her hand loosely toward him.

Tom scooped her up into a tight hug again. "More than that!" He squeezed her even more solidly. "We're friends already!"

He released her. Brittney hastily made her falling tear vanish.

"Friends who are in love with each other!" Tom said enthusiastically.

Brittney smiled at him, then came forward and kissed him on the cheek.

"Living different lives, while helping each other and caring about and enjoying each other," she recited. "That's what Ōähühan said."

Tom smiled back at her, and kissed her on the forehead. "I do love you!" he said. "So much!"

"I believe that," Brittney smiled at him. She looked smilingly, and more contentedly than he had seen her since before Nüährnär's coming, into his eyes

23: The Faithful and the Fearful

for a few seconds.

"Now, Thomas Joshua Pratt the Ōmäthäär," Brittney said with feigned seriousness. She snickered as Tom shook his head denyingly at that title. "You had better come back to me later. To talk, I mean," she said quickly. "Because right now you and Mär have billions and billions of people to save!"

Tom tried very hard to hide his fear of Thahn from Brittney and her imposing confidence in the Ōmäthäär. He hit her lightly and affectionately on the arm, and, as he did, he felt an unintentional surge of a fine, deep warmth pass from him into her.

"I'll never be too busy for you," he said, surprised at his having been able to send Ärthähr to hearten her like that. "Call me whenever," he said, drifting away from her.

"You too," Brittney said. "Just don't slack off."

Tom smiled and waved at her, then went to head back to his desperately laboring assistants.

Brittney stayed staring after him for a few minutes before she went to work again.

"Sarah!" Rene Trotter said, tightly embracing her oldest daughter.

"I would have come earlier," Sarah said with consummate exhaustion, "But—"

"We understand," Scott smiled proudly at her. "You are very important in Nüährnär now."

"We're just so happy that you're alive!" Rene said, squeezing Sarah more tightly.

"I checked as soon as I could," Sarah said, hanging limply in space as her mother released her. "I couldn't believe we were all still okay."

"See, that's why the Ōmäthäär put you where you are," Joseph said from behind her. "We were all worrying for almost an hour before Kathy realized we could just check to see if you'd lived."

"We're so grateful you're safe," Scott said.

"I died before the real force of the N'nrathĕrmĕ hit us," Aaron said quietly. "Härs'zahahn brought me back."

Sarah looked tearfully at her older brother, unable to say anything to him, overcome by her rising fear of Thahn's arrival. How was this devastated remnant of Nüährnär going to stand against Thahn's fleet and Ämäthōär?

"How is Tom?" Kathy asked quietly after a small silence.

"He's alive," Sarah said relievedly. "But I guess you know that. I haven't seen him since the fight."

"It feels so unfair," Rene said somberly, looking back at the now glowing planet behind them, already almost completely covered by the new Shell. "Our whole family survives, and Tom too. It feels unfair."

Sarah glided up behind her mother. "This whole thing is unfair. None of this should ever have happened!"

"But it is happening."

She kept to herself the fact that four of her assistants, and many more of their assistants whom she knew very well, had been killed within the past hour and would not revive.

"Why should our family be so lucky?" Rene sighed sadly.

"It isn't your fault, Mom, that other people have lost their—" Sarah began, but then Scott indignantly breathed, "It's Sĕrĕhahn's."

Sarah closed her eyes.

"If Mär is anything but a liar," Scott said more softly, pulling his wife in close to him with one arm, "Then this nightmare is because of Sĕrĕhahn. And the best that we can do is help everyone else. Everyone who has not been as blessed as we have been."

"I would consider myself blessed if I never lived to see any of this," Kathy said. "Even if I never knew Nüährnär."

Annie bowed her head as Mär finished his tearful, exultant tribute to her husband. Tears were streaking her face profusely.

Glory and honor, and life, light, and rev'rence
Will ever be to our hero and friend!
Ever remembered in brightest resplendence,
Peter Garcia's name never will end!

She rose up slowly from where she had been seated on the earth, and Mär nodded to her, sitting himself down.

Annie, Mär and several hundred family members and friends, including her and Peter's surviving assistants, were gathered around a magnificent white monument of Peter towering nobly over his father's newly repaired house in his native Virginia.

I think of you, and wish that there were heav'n!

Annie could not look at the beautiful statue as she tried to sing the pain and love in her heart. She gazed miserably into the sunless blue sky.

23: The Faithful and the Fearful

I need you here!
Life without you is just lonely prison.
I need you here!
How can I live, how can I fight or try,
Without you here? To live is just to die!

She paused, then wiped her tears with her hand. She smiled sadly but thankfully at Mär before she sang out,

I want to know that you can hear me now.
I want to know
That all the things you said are true somehow.
I want to know
That you will see my face again! Someday.
That there is heav'n, that loss will pass away.

Yet, though you live or you be truly gone,
I still love you!
Heaven or not, eternal love or not,
I still love you!
And all your life will ever live in me!
No matter what! You'll live triumphantly!

I still love you!

She broke into silent tears again, and collapsed back onto the ground.
Then, quietly, picking up the failing melodies left hanging in the air by Annie's short song, Mär's voice returned, singing strangely familiar words that none there would have expected to hear coming from him:

Oh, thus be it ever, when free men shall stand
Between their loved home and the war's desolation!
Bless'd with vict'ry and peace, may the heav'n rescued band
Praise the Pow'r that hath made and preserved us a nation!

His words became his own as his voice filled the air.

No matter the trial! No matter the pain!
Pure love, and its glory, will guide us again!
And Är's unfailing valor will atone for the slain

Light and Glory

And will answer the deeds of the noble and brave!

He glided to Annie, and placed an unnaturally comforting hand on her shoulder.

Glory and honor, and life, light, and rev'rence
Will ever be to our heroes and friends!
Ever remembered in brightest resplendence,
Our great, beloved ones never will end!

Annie smiled up at him, whispered, "Thank you," then rose from the ground again.

"Thank you all for coming," she said deadenedly to the throng of friends around her.

Mär gave her a small, encouraging smile, patted her lightly on her shoulder, which sent a heartening rush of cool warmth through her, then rose quickly and streaked away without another word.

Annie was taken by surprise by the sudden rush of Ärthähr coursing through her. She realized she was shaking without knowing why.

Hsu Yifei, one of Peter's few surviving assistants, had drifted over to her. She didn't hear what he said, distracted by the emotion of memorializing Peter and by the strange, wonderful sensation of Ärthähr. She nodded and offered him a vague "Thank you" when she could see that he had finished saying whatever he had had to say.

After considering leaving like Mär, she just surrendered to the crowd around her and drifted over to fall to the ground between the feet of the towering statue.

She became so used to nodding and noncommittally thanking well wishers and would-be comforters that it was a few minutes before she realized John had sat himself down silently near her, staring at the ground between his own feet.

She looked over at him. He was sitting on the toes of Peter's right foot, apparently lost in his thoughts, his expression worn and weary.

The crowd was thinning more rapidly now, but Annie still didn't risk entangling herself in conversation with other lingering friends by giving any committed responses to people's condolences. "Hi," she said privately to John, not moving a muscle outwardly.

John looked up at her, then couldn't suppress a small, still sad grin as he followed suit and resumed appearing unresponsive.

23: The Faithful and the Fearful

"Hi," his voice said back in her head, his tone all but lifeless.

Neither of them said anything for a couple more minutes.

Only Peter's mother and Annie's parents remained when Annie finally moved again.

"If the rest of them are anything like Ärdhär and Mär," Adrian Baker was saying, Annie only now becoming aware of the conversation going on in front of her, "Then I can't imagine why Nrathĕrmĕ wants to destroy them!"

Her mother must have been talking about the Ōmäthäär, she surmised, looking up at them.

Amelia nodded, then smiled a more peaceful smile at Annie than Annie had expected from her in a time like that. A much more peaceful expression than she had had earlier that day.

"Are you alright?" Adrian asked.

Annie didn't respond, but just looked back at her mother, surprised at the question. But then she saw that she was looking at John.

John looked up, opened his mouth soundlessly for a moment, then just shook his head.

"No," he said then. "But are any of us?"

No one responded to that.

"Well, life must go on," Annie said bravely after a pause.

"Maybe," John said.

"I really loved what you said, Annie," Amelia said quietly. "'All your life will ever live in me, no matter what; you'll live triumphantly.'"

"Life does go on. Through us."

"I really hope so," John said subduedly.

"It will," Annie said more consolingly to him.

John smiled a little less weakly at her.

"What makes you two so sure?" Annie's father Steve asked with admiration but noticeable fear.

Annie looked down at her feet.

"I trust Mär," John said, looking at Annie. "I do not believe he will tell us to stay if there is no hope. But how many of us will die, even if there is hope?"

"I wish I could trust Mär that much," Steve said.

"There is hope," Amelia said. "Even if we don't get to see it."

Annie didn't know what that meant. And John apparently didn't either; he asked, "What do you mean, don't get to see it?"

"If we die," Adrian said softly.

"Yes," Amelia said. "Hope isn't all about living and dying."

"I thought it was," John said with a shadow of a grin.

Annie looked impressedly at Peter's mother. She had always respected her, but this was uncharacteristically profound for her.

"She's right," Annie said.

"About what?" Steve asked.

"Hope is about moving on, getting happier, and better," Amelia said. "Not about not dying. If we die fighting for good things, we'll be as happy as when we live fighting for good things."

"Unhappy," John said.

"And we can hope for leaving life better for everyone else," Annie said. She tried to keep her voice steady as she said, "Just like Peter did."

"If there is anyone else left," Steve said. "I understand this Thahn intends to wipe us out."

"That is where I don't worry," John said. "If Mär says there is hope for Nŭährnär, then there is. And…if Mär says God is fighting for the Ōmäthäär, then I really have to believe that, too.

"I just don't like dying, personally."

"And having words with Peter's mother wasn't a bad thing, either," Ärdhär reflected happily.

Ŭkan smiled.

"I'm glad Mär was busy," Ärdhär said. "Though I wish it could have been for other reasons."

"A few families went anyway," Ŭkan sighed.

"They'll be the first of many, I'm afraid," Ärdhär said.

"Ŭkan," the voice of one of their assistants called to them.

"What, Äfäzan?" Ŭkan asked.

"Mänhähär is preparing to leave. Most of his family is ready to follow him."

Ärdhär closed her eyes.

"Thanks," Ŭkan said.

"He's set on it," Äfäzan said. "I am afraid that this is only the beginning."

"You talked to him?" Ärdhär said.

"And his family," Äfäzan's voice said wearily. "A lot. Which is why only most of them are following him."

"Okay," Ŭkan said. "Let them go."

"I did say that the Ä'ähärnhär agrees with Mär," Äfäzan said.

"I wish we could say that to all Nŭährnär," Ŭkan said.

"I wish more of Mänhähär's children cared what the Ä'ähärnhär said," Äfäzan said.

23: The Faithful and the Fearful

"Against Thahn's forces," Ärdhär said, "We'll be weak no matter what, whether all or none of Nüährnär decides to leave. Let the cowards go. We will have more chance without them."

"It's not us that we're worried about," Äfäzan's wife Artŭn insisted.

"I know," Ärdhär said sadly. "But, to be honest, the fewer spineless people stay, the more Är will do for the faithful people who fight here. And maybe they will come back."

"Är will take care of them," Ŭkan said. "They'll grow in their own ways."

"We will keep encouraging everyone who does want to listen," Äfäzan said. "The more people we can remind to be faithful, the more chance we'll have."

Chapter 24

Light and Glory

"What is it?" Tom asked as he slid out of the wall into the brilliant Sanctuary. The Ōmäthäär had seen to it that the Sanctuary was rebuilt and inaugurated as soon as the reconstruction of the Shell was underway.

Sarah smiled dejectedly at him.

"I don't know," she said. "He isn't here yet."

Tom flew to her and hugged her.

"I'm happy to see you too, again," Sarah said.

"I'm glad we survived."

"John told me about Terry," Sarah said shakily.

"Oh," Tom said.

"I'm so sorry, Tom."

Tom's mouth hung open, but he couldn't manage to say anything.

Sarah hugged him again.

"I guess...I mean, she is okay," Tom choked.

Sarah kissed him. The already bright room glowed much more enliveningly. He felt his chest unknot.

"Um...how is your family?" he asked, bracing himself.

Sarah's sad eyes glistened as she managed another smile. "We're all okay. Alive, and okay."

"Oh, good," Tom sighed.

Mär emerged abruptly through the white enfoliated wall.

Tom and Sarah both turned expectantly to him.

"Thank you for coming," Mär said breathlessly.

"What do you need?" Sarah asked.

Mär smiled, but his whole demeanor was exhausted and careworn. "I'm sorry we always have to be so structured," he said, "But it's training as usual."

"Oh," Sarah said.

"Yes, now," Mär said to Tom's surprised face. "*Especially* now. My assistants can run Nŭährnär just fine without me, even now. You two need to learn as much as possible as soon as possible. I hope we will have more time than I'm afraid we will."

"What?" Sarah said.

"Remember, if you learn what's necessary now, then you will have a later to learn everything else in."

24: Light and Glory

"Well, R'r'hahär said we could keep growing even if we die," Sarah said casually.

Mär blinked.

"Yeah," Tom said, though his voice made it clear that he wanted to die no more than John did.

"Well," Mär said with a weary shadow of an admiring chuckle, "The fact that you see it that way tells me that you've got everything from mortality that you need."

"What do you mean?" Sarah asked.

"Almost everything," Mär smiled, looking away at the inner cube and sphere. "But I mean that your lives may not be what will be at stake here.

"Yes, you two can keep growing and learning and becoming more and better and essentially happier, in this state or not, but not everyone is like you.

"I need to teach you everything I can, so you can help everyone else."

"But you'll still be here!" Sarah said.

"I want to be," Mär said. "But Är wants me to teach you a lot now.

"I hope that if you learn what you need to now, there will be a later, here, for all three of us. And for everyone else, too."

"Okay," Tom said.

"But it's questions first," Mär said, looking a tiny bit more lively. "What do you need to know?"

Sarah didn't say anything for a few seconds, so Tom said tentatively, "My sister's dead."

Mär's look was unreadable.

"Her manager couldn't revive her. But...can Ōmäthäär bring back the dead?"

Mär sighed. "Not even Sĕrĕhahn can force back dead who aren't to come back," he said. "And Är won't. Är can bring back the dead. But, Tom, if Terry wouldn't revive, that means she either is not being allowed to fall back to this state or she doesn't want to. Knowing her," he smiled, "I think it's the latter.

"Är can bring back the dead, and often he does act through his Ōmäthäär to do it. But, with the exception of death by Ärthähr, our tools can revive everyone who can be revived."

Tom took a steadying breath.

"She's okay," Sarah said, taking Tom's hand in hers.

"I know," Tom said.

Mär's eyes were blazing at the two of them. His shoulders were sagging a little less now.

Tom looked expectantly back at him.

"Anything else?" Mär asked.

"Uh, we still have a lot," Sarah said. "But, for right now..." she hesitated.

"What's on your mind?" Mär invited.

"How much do you know about Thahn?" Sarah asked.

Mär paused, then said, "What other questions do you have?"

He laughed wearily. "No, it's okay."

He closed his eyes for a moment, then asked, "What do you want to know?"

Tom looked at Sarah.

"Um, she is an Ämäthōär, we know that," Sarah said. "But can you tell us anything else about her?"

"She's one of the best," Mär said stiffly. "Except for her defective heart of hearts, she's one of the most skilled people I know. In everything she does."

"You know her?" Tom asked.

Mär looked away. "I don't like going in that direction," he said.

"Oh."

"But you deserve to know," Mär said, looking past them. "I think you'll need to know.

"Yes, I knew Thahn." He breathed quietly for a few seconds.

"She is an incredibly able person. She is empty in the core, but in every other way she is incredible.

"Some Ämäthōär choose to live secretly; Nrathěrmě at large has no record of them. But Thahn is very well known at Nrathěrmě. No one there knows what she is, obviously. But Thahn is well known as an ingenious higher manager of Nrathěrmě, just four tiers under Anhar himself. Or herself, since Lhěhrha's recognized as the sole Anhar now.

"But Thahn is an ingenious leader, an incredible tactician and strategist, a cunning administrator and governor, a wonderful friend..." he paused. "And a master of Ärthähr."

"You were friends?" Sarah said.

"Thahn might not call herself a master of Ärthähr," Mär continued deafly, "But it fits."

He closed his eyes for several seconds.

"Yeah, we were friends," he said finally. "At least, she was mine, and I was inexperienced enough to believe I was hers. I do not think Thahn knows what it means to have a friend." He breathed more heavily.

"You have to understand this about Ämäthōär," he then said intently. "They are fake. The blackest of them have never known what pure good feels like. But they have seen good people. They act. They act good. They think, almost in their heart of hearts, that that is all goodness is: acting good.

"Love to them is acting loving. Leadership is acting like a good leader. Wisdom is acting as the wise would act. Humor is acting humorous, friendship is acting like a friend," he hissed.

"Do you see the idiocy? They are not anything themselves; they can only mimic those who are!

"Sĕrĕhahn, you will need to know, regards us as fake Ōmäthäär, mimicking the original Ōmäthäär.

"Whom he killed, I think. But he never elaborated to me which Ōmäthäär he was speaking of."

"You've met Sĕrĕhahn?" Tom said amazedly.

"Yes. He views us as mimics. Don't forget that.

"But understand that there is a difference between doing good and acting good!

"Doing genuine good is just part and parcel of *being* good. Acting good is a failing attempt to reap the benefits of the happiness that defines good from evil but without the effort of transforming one's own self within.

"When Peter Garcia defied everything he thought he wanted so he could do what he knew he really wanted; preserving fact and the wellbeing of his loved ones; he did what he really *was*. He valued fact. He loved his friends.

"Thahn, and most Ämäthōär, values herself, period.

"But whatever they can do to raise themselves, they will do. They will help others, they will act good, they will be obedient, obliging, sacrificing, enduring, almost truly courageous.

"But they don't do good because they genuinely care about the wellbeing of others. They do good because they understand that the very nature of good as opposed to evil is that good ultimately produces happiness, while evil doesn't.

"If you want to go up, you don't fly down! If you want to be happy, you don't act against Reality! To gain wholeness, to become more of Infinity, you have to understand the awesome perfect totalness, the awesomeness, of Infinity, of Reality! Of Är!

"Good is intelligence; if you understand Reality, if you are more of Reality, everything you do will get you exactly what you want, and that will only be because you will understand and really, vitally, want what is intelligent to want!

"Happiness is *not* getting what you want *externally*. Happiness is *being* what you want internally!

"Tom, have you ever been bored since you've been here?"

Tom snapped back to the moment. "I, uh, haven't had time…"

Mär smiled. "Well, yeah. But if you had, I imagine you would not have been bored.

"I have had to make weeks long journeys alone. No contact with anyone. It was just me and the stars. But I had more than enough in my mind, that I had been given by my parents, to entertain me indefinitely.

"Solid, inner happiness is like the perfection of that. No matter what happens around you, or to you, you *are* everything you want. You are happy because you *are everything*!

"Or much of everything.

"Think of how incredible Är's life, his condition, is!

"And we can offer that, as we learn it from him still, to everyone, *especially* to the marvelously good people of Sĕrĕhahn's reined-in Nrathĕrmĕ!

"The Ämäthöär understand, with fatally flawed understanding, but nevertheless they understand that good is the way of happiness.

"So they've seen genuinely good people and have seen how happy and great and magnificent those people are, and they act good, thinking that that is all goodness is.

"Thahn acts like a good person. In terms of strategy and leadership, she acts like a genius. She is brilliant, she is, and studying other geniuses helps her act like a combination of all their geniuses. Acting is more effective in tactics than in other things, but still I wonder how much more strategically original she could be than she already is, if her whole heart wasn't set on acting and not being.

"Genius isn't about study. That's *acting* like a genius. Study can help, but only if there is a core of brilliance to cannibalize it all, otherwise it becomes impotent learning without use.

"Genius, intelligence, the capacity to make the best decision in any set of conditions in which you are intelligent, is nothing more or less than affinity with Ärthähr. Är, and his executive the Ärthähr, is the sum consummation of all intelligence, in everything; living and thinking in coordination with Ärthähr leads to doing exactly what needs to be done in exactly the best ways to do it.

"Ärthähr is a whole lot more than light and warmth and moving things and fighting.

"Remember, Ärthähr is life. Consciousness is the pinnacle of Ärthähr. The more we become, the more of Är we let ourselves become, the more of the Ärthähr we grow to be, the more consciousness we actually have!"

"Yeah," Tom blurted.

Mär smiled at him.

24: Light and Glory

"I mean...well, before you inaugurated me into Ä'ähänärdanär, it's like I remember things more dimly. Kind of."

"How do you mean?" Mär said, considerably less fatigued now.

"Uh," Tom stalled, "I...You know, I didn't know anything."

"And you do now?" Mär asked.

"A lot more than before!" Tom said fervently.

Mär grinned, nodding with more energy.

"I'm more me now than I was then," Tom said.

"Well said," Mär breathed. "And you are *becoming* more. You're not just slapping knowledge onto an unchanged interior. You, Thomas Pratt, are changing! You're becoming more, you're getting more intelligent, you're getting more conscious, you're getting more potent, more of Infinity.

"Remember, when I first gave you a little knowledge about Ä'ähänärdanär, I told you to sift it out, just let it sit in your minds.

"I did not tell you to try to use it right then. I did not tell you to force an understanding out of it. I did not tell you to make it make sense. Yet. But I told you to just let it sit, let it marinate all through you.

"Letting the words and the thoughts and the lessons and the legacies of those Ōmäthäär that I passed on to you, letting those ferment down into your centers began a gradual change of your innermost selves that you are only now beginning to notice, and which mere comprehension of or understanding of the up front meanings of those things could not have effected.

"Scholarship in Ä'ähänärdanär has not been doing that to you. You have not focused on individual memories that I gave you; you've let the whole of it sit and slide again and again through your minds, and that let it imprint its summative message in your hearts.

"You have *not* consciously been acting according to the lessons of those memories. You have just been doing what you do, but who and what *you* are has been changed! Just by constant, unforced exposure to those Ōmäthäärs' legacies. What you do has been changed legitimately by the changes of what you are. You changed your real selves first, and then your actions, your liveliness, your whole demeanors and auras followed inseparably from that!

"If you had just changed your actions, you might have duped yourselves into believing that was all that was needed, and you might never, ever, have really grown!

"A counterfeit, never realizing the awesome unparalleled perfection of the realities of goodness and wonderful tremendous great greatness!"

His excited eyes dimmed again slightly. "Which brings us," he said reluctantly, "Back to the Ämäthöär.

"And Thahn."

He shook his head in revulsion.

"So Thahn is formidable on the outside. But she is hollow enough on the inside that all her power, all her capacity to do good, all her half-baked intelligence is used to destroy good.

"That's my long, round-about answer, Sarah. Thahn is formidable. She's a match for any Ōmäthäär here. More than a match. She is more than a match strategically to take on Nŭährnär with less than one battalion. And she will have a lot more than one battalion."

Tom wanted to ask what Mär was going to do. But Sarah pressed, "And you were friends?"

Mär smiled desolately. "There's no diverting you. We were friends."

"And you knew Sĕrĕhahn?" Sarah said.

"I talked to him," Mär said. "I don't know if I ever knew him."

"How did you survive?" Tom asked amazedly.

Mär chuckled softly, but his face was sadly drawn.

"Mär..." Sarah began, her eyes widening.

"What?" Mär prompted, nodding to her.

"But, no," Sarah sputtered.

"I was an Ämäthōär," Mär said for her.

"*What?*" Tom gasped.

"But—you?" Sarah said.

"I was an Ämäthōär," Mär said firmly, almost harshly, forcing the irreconcilable statement into their ears. "The Ämäthōär taught me how to use Ärthähr."

"But," Tom stammered, suddenly fearing for his and Sarah's lives, "Those two Ämäthōär that I saw—"

"Trying to kill me?" Mär said seriously. "I am an Ōmäthäär! I am no Ämäthōär, Tom! I *was*.

"I never knew Hōnhŭ or Ämharŭ were Ämäthōär. I never knew who all the Ämäthōär were. Sĕrĕhahn made sure that few of us knew who all of us were.

"And I was one of them!

"*Was.*"

It was as if powerful warmth were appeasing the sudden horror and terror out of Tom.

"But then I found out about Är. And I wanted to know more.

"And I found more. I found where to look.

"But when I came back to Nrathĕrmĕ, Thahn knew what I had learned.

24: Light and Glory

"She and I met with Sĕrĕhahn. I was used to that. I met with Sĕrĕhahn frequently. He was my friend," Mär said viciously.

"If anyone knows how to act good and be anything but that, it's Sĕrĕhahn. We talked deeply about Är, about Ärthähr, and about his, Sĕrĕhahn's, plan for Nrathĕrmĕ. We were friends.

"He told me I had to live up to the new knowledge I had learned. I had only been an Ämäthöär for forty or so weeks then; he told me he would have waited, but apparently Är had other plans for me. He said I would have to live up to that.

"Meaning they would likely need to kill me if I did not.

"Which was, actually, understandable," Mär said as Tom and Sarah looked appalled. "It would be out of protection of the N'nrathĕrmĕ who hadn't been fully prepared for that knowledge, whom I might ruin if I told them about it in defiance of Sĕrĕhahn's schedules. Sĕrĕhahn claimed he planned to tell the N'nrathĕrmĕ everything, but all in its right time.

"As do I, for you and everyone.

"Sĕrĕhahn does not *like* killing, nor does Thahn. But if they feel there is no other way, they will kill.

"As will you," Mär said more pointedly. "The line between combat and murder can be argued by people of Sĕrĕhahn's point of view.

"I think Sĕrĕhahn knew I was disposed against him.

"Of course he knew."

"But he underestimated you," Tom said, trying to remind himself that this was still the same Mär he had thought he was starting to know.

"Sĕrĕhahn?" Mär said. "The only mistake I've ever known of him to make is the consummate mistake of the lie he lives as a fake, black-hearted Ämäthöär; on the surface, I've never known him to make any mistake. He didn't underestimate me. Sĕrĕhahn could see right into me, into my deepest heart and desires.

"He just lacked enough light in the deepest areas of his heart that the same parts of my heart were indecipherable to him. I'm saying, even seeing everything through my heart, which knew now what he was, he would not recognize himself what he was.

"It was Är whom he underestimated. Är saved me from him."

"What happened?" Sarah asked.

"If I wasn't certain you had to know about Thahn, I would not talk about this.

"I want to be open with you! But…Sarah, Tom…this is hard."

His eyes were rapidly filling with tears.

"I'd heard of the Ōmäthäär," he said quietly. "Ahntä's people. I had a very hard time finding them.

"Thahn was my mentor. She had watched me since I was less than a hundred weeks old. Before I was six hundred weeks old she introduced herself and began to inaugurate me into the Ämäthōär. R'bathĕrŭ, we called ourselves, you know. It's all the same meaning, but in their language.

"I had married when I was four hundred eighteen weeks old," Mär smiled. A tear flowed down his cheek. "Lhĕhûnrĕ.

"That was her name," he explained, looking into their eyes.

"She was perfect.

"She was everything I saw, everything I knew, everything, more than everything I had ever known I'd wanted! My dear, sweet, wonderful, beautiful Lhĕhûnrĕ!

"I had never known what true, real love felt like, until I was in love with her! Lhĕhûnrĕ was my other half, my equal and other half, in every sense of it! My indomitable love, my dear, unrealistic dream.

"I told you Thahn was cunning. She will do whatever it takes to do what she thinks needs to be done.

"I had hid from my fellow Ämäthōär. Thahn knew me. She knew what I was going to do before I did. She knew I was looking for Ahntä's renegades. I'd been told about their view of Är, and I wanted to see if they were what I hoped they were.

"I knew the Ämäthōär were not the heroes I had thought they were. But I hoped Ahntä's Ōmäthäär, as I knew they termed themselves, could possibly be.

"Thahn understood that the Ämäthōär could not afford an Ämäthōär joining with Ahntä's Ōmäthäär. She knew she had to find me, and possibly kill me.

"I was afraid I would have no choice but to make Sĕrĕhahn's Ämäthōär kill me. I could not let them find me.

"And I knew Thahn would know that. I knew what she would do.

"I tried to warn Lhĕhûnrĕ.

"She hadn't been actually inducted into the Ämäthōär yet, but I had taught her anything Thahn taught me. She could use Ärthähr so well.

"I called to her from where I was hiding, far across Nrathĕrmĕ.

"But Thahn answered. She had waited where she had killed my Lhĕhûnrĕ! She knew my rantha call to Lhĕhûnrĕ would be directed there, and she had intercepted it, and now she knew exactly where I was.

"I killed four of my old friends within less than an hour, Ämäthōär whom

24: Light and Glory

Thahn sent to kill me. By the time she caught up, I had eluded them again.

"But Thahn knew me too well. I wanted to kill her! I wanted to kill every one of them!

"They killed Lhĕhûnrĕ! They killed every single child or grandchild I had ever had! They wiped them out! All of them!"

Mär's breath was heaving, his eyes were glistening as tears rolled slowly into his beard. "And it worked. Thahn knew I would not hide for long. She knew I would want...really, I wanted revenge.

"It didn't matter to me if I lived or died!" he said passionately. "I didn't care anymore if Sĕrĕhahn was poisoning the lives of everyone at Nrathĕrmĕ! My wife and my sons and my daughters had been murdered!

"And by Ärthähr! Tom, Sarah, I wish I could hope that you will never have to know what it feels like to be attacked with Ärthähr. My Lhĕhûnrĕ had been murdered with Ärthähr!

"I wanted to fill Thahn with the pain of killing Ärthähr forever! I wanted to make her pay for my family!

"And I tried. Thahn knew me. She knew I would try. That's how they were going to catch me."

Mär shuddered with silent tears. Then he said, "Är, for whatever reason, thought I deserved one more chance.

"I should not have lived through that hour. I went straight for Thahn, my old friend, determined to make her understand what she had done, whom she had murdered. She, more than a match for me by far, and two other Ämäthöär should have killed me.

"And they almost did. Sarah, Tom, I still cannot find words to describe the total, terrifying pain of Ärthähr when it's used against you.

"Tom, you felt some of it when you saw Hōnhŭ and Ämharŭ fighting, and you both have memories of other Ōmäthäär being attacked by it.

"The fear of those memories, the heart-choking fear you felt, Tom, they are nothing to what it really feels like to have Ärthähr used skillfully against you. It is undiluted terror, and darkness, filling you; you can feel it smothering, trying to eradicate, your very self.

"That's what Thahn and the other Ämäthöär did to me.

"I was all but gone, all but ready to give in. I can't say to you how horrible the pain was, how much it took everything good and strong out of me!

"But Ahntä had been following me, too. They still hadn't let me find them, but I guess Ahntä and his counselors deemed I was trustworthy. They sent several Ōmäthäär to save me.

"Which was an enormous risk to all of their Ä'ähänärdanär. For any

Ōmāthäär to reveal himself was to risk tipping the Ämäthōär off to who other Ōmāthäär might be, which would lead them to still other Ōmāthäär; one breach of anonymity could reveal all of Ä'ähänärdanär to Sĕrĕhahn.

"But Ahntä did it anyway. When the Ōmāthäär arrived, however, seven of them, they found that they were no match for Thahn.

"Two of those seven were Ŭkan and Ärdhär." Mär smiled faintly.

But the smile fell to pain. "Thahn killed the leader of the seven, and the other six, the seven of us, were all wearing away in their killing Ärthähr. The leader had managed to kill one of the Ämäthōär before Thahn had focused and killed him, but the two remaining Ämäthōär were enough to destroy the seven of us simultaneously.

"Three other Ōmäthäär died, and Thahn and Zĕrdhŭ concentrated on us four. Then Ŭkan died."

"He—" Tom cut in, but Mär continued quickly.

"And that, I think, saved us. When Ärdhär saw her husband ground to death by Ärthähr, and when I saw in her and Ŭkan my anguish for Lhĕhûnrĕ, both she and I mastered our consciousnesses just enough to surge back, simultaneously, and knock Thahn and Zĕrdhŭ momentarily off their guard.

"As soon as our minds were freed, Ärdhär threw her momentum around all of us and shot away.

"Thahn pursued us, and we only managed to elude her and the other Ämäthōär she was sending after us after several horrifically long hours and by using every stratagem we could.

"And then I finally met Är's Ōmäthäär. I finally met the wonderful people of their secret Ä'ähänärdanär.

"I wish I could have stayed with them!"

He smiled longingly. "I would not have stayed single long among them, I think.

"But I was too dangerous; the Ämäthōär knew me. And now they knew the seven who had risked their wonderful lives to save mine.

"Är let the Ōmäthäär bring Ŭkan back. Tom," he smiled sorrowfully, "I think your father would be interested to know how much I harassed the Ōmäthäär to try to bring back Lhĕhûnrĕ.

"But only Ŭkan came back. So we four survivors were smuggled out of Nrathĕrmĕ to live among the Ōmäthäär who were stationed in the nearer Wild Lands.

"That was a good four hundred seventy-three weeks ago now."

"But you're stronger now," Sarah insisted. "You can fight her now. Thahn."

24: Light and Glory

"Thahn is stronger, too, Sarah!" Mär said. "I tend to grow more quickly than many people. Even faster than Thahn, I dare to think. But I am hardly twelve hundred weeks old. Thahn is six thousand six hundred three weeks old yesterday.

"I am not equal to fighting her."

"Then who will?" Tom asked.

"Me," Mär said. "I'm not equal to it; I'll need help; but Thahn will have to be stopped if we are to survive. I will have to try.

"Ä'ähänärdanär is not about me; the fight for light and glory can go on, as long as there is someone left to fight it.

"Someone like you.

"This is why I have to teach you right now, and as often as I can manage before Thahn gets here.

"I can risk myself.

"But, Tom, Sarah, please, for the sake of everyone else, guard yourselves!"

"What?" Tom said.

"Fight, do whatever you need to do, but save yourselves! Sacrifice of good things now may let you live to do *essential* things later.

"I don't want you to fear death. I don't fear death; I wait for it! I know what it'll be like, what my life will be like, after 'death.' I've been there, I've felt it. I don't believe either of you have anything to fear about death; I think you have much, much more to dread about living here than you do about dying!

"But I do everything I can to stay alive, so I can help people here in this moldable state, so they'll have nothing to fear either. I want you two to stay alive so you can help too, here.

"You have to learn everything you can now, so there will be a later in which you can keep helping people *here*."

"And you will be here, too," Sarah said intently.

"I want to be!" Mär said. "But this is less about me, now, than it has the potential to be about *the two of you*."

Tom nodded, unsure what to say.

"And I still have some time," Mär said. "For training right now, I mean. What other questions do you have?"

Neither Tom nor Sarah said anything, both trying to come to grips with Mär's Ämäthöär-hood.

"It's okay," Mär said with typical effective power.

Sarah smiled shakenly.

"I trust you, Mär," Tom said. "But it's just...not anything I'd have thought of you."

"Remember that, then," Mär said. "Remember that you don't know how wonderful some truly despicable people can grow to become, if they let themselves, given some time."

"Are there good Ämäthōär?" Sarah asked.

"Yeah," Mär said without hesitation. "But there are no really bad Ōmäthäär. A 'bad' Ōmäthäär would lose his affinity with Är, and have to resort to the Ämäthōärs' way of doing things."

"But Ämäthōär use affinity with Är, too," Tom said.

"You said 'Ämäthōär,' instead of 'the Ämäthōär,'" Mär noted pleasedly. "As if you recognized Ämäthōär-hood as a phenomenon separate from Sĕrĕhahn's people."

"What?"

"Ämäthōär is what Sĕrĕhahn's people call themselves; well, it's a translation; but they aren't the only such people.

"I say *the* Ämäthōär when I talk about Sĕrĕhahn's people in particular, but Ämäthōär in general are a principle, a kind of person that, I believe, exists in most cultures throughout space and time. You had, and I'm afraid still have, Ämäthōär here at Earth."

"Here?" Sarah asked.

"Sarah, you knew the Ä'ähärnhär before we came," Mär said. "You believed he spoke for Är. Both he and his predecessors say and said a good deal about evil powers and people. How is this a surprise to you?"

"I just never thought about it," Sarah said honestly. "I knew there were bad people, but I didn't spend a lot of time thinking about bad people with capacities like that..."

"Yeah, and, at the time, you may not have needed to," Mär smiled. "But I'm sure you need to now. Now you're growing to get involved, to help, to accept the reality of living Ämäthōär and to learn how to unravel them. There were Ämäthōär all along, but just now you're living selflessly enough to let yourselves become the kinds of people who can do something about it. Selfish people are too concerned with little, stupid things to be positioned to perceive, much less combat, people like Ämäthōär.

"Of course Earth's Ämäthōär didn't call themselves Ämäthōär or R'bathĕrŭ. And there have been many, many orders of Earthly Ämäthōär. Sĕrĕhahn's near monopoly of Ämäthōär-hood at Nrathĕrmĕ is, I imagine, a very special case indeed.

"Which monopoly makes him all the more formidable."

"Why haven't they attacked you? Earth's Ämäthōär?" Tom asked.

24: Light and Glory

"I don't doubt they will, if it ever favors them," Mär said. "But we're protecting them from Sĕrĕhahn, from Nrathĕrmĕ; why should they fight us yet?"

"Sĕrĕhahn won't help them?" Sarah asked.

"Sĕrĕhahn's Ämäthöär are a supportive order to one another. But Earth's Ämäthöär aren't like them. Sĕrĕhahn's Ämäthöär work together to farm the genius of Nrathĕrmĕ's population. They have a common goal.

"None of Earth's Ämäthöär shared that goal, having no contact with Nrathĕrmĕ. There are several major groups of Earthly Ämäthöär of which I'm aware. Most of them, before we came, at least, were concerned with money, political influence, or just getting more control of Ärthähr. The various orders of Ämäthöär referred to Ärthähr in their own ways, some more coherent than others. There were various plots of world domination among some of the orders. Nŭährnär's arrival foiled all of those plots, at least for now," Mär said with hateful satisfaction.

"How do you know all this?" Tom asked.

"You know the Ä'ähärnhär?" Mär asked.

"Sarah's people's prophet," Tom said.

"And yours, now!" Mär said. "And mine. He's Är's head spokesman among the Ōmäthäär, now. I had filled in as our spokesman when the rest of our leaders were killed, but since the Ä'ähärnhär's the spokesman for Ōhōnŭäär, we all submit to him.

"I lead politically, he leads really," Mär smiled.

"He knew a whole lot more about the Ämäthöär of Earth than he openly let on," Mär nodded to Sarah. "He's filled some of us in on the less perceived wheels in Earth's history. I think I understand more about the workings of Earth life through all the millennia than all but very few Earthly historians ever did."

"But, what are we going to do about the Ämäthöär here?" Sarah asked.

"Let them decide to stop," Mär said harshly. "If they don't, if they still fester away into deeper darkness, then we'll kill them. World domination by Ämäthöär can be a terrible, awful thing.

"Närdamähr was very fortunate to be taken over by an Ämäthöär like Sĕrĕhahn.

"Unfortunately, such 'pleasant' Ämäthöär are so much harder to remove!"

"You think Ämäthöär here would try to take over Nŭährnär?" Tom said.

"I think they would take over Är's throne if they could," Mär said.

"Isn't that the Earth, though?" Sarah asked.

Mär laughed. "Oh, no. We call Earth Ōhōnŭäär, house of Är, but that's only accurate in limited ways. It was his home when he lived here, but never his real home.

"It's been your home, too. But not your real home."

"What do you mean?" Tom asked.

"Ōhōnŭäär is a sort of capitol of the universe," Mär said. "But there's another one. A Real Capitol."

"Where?" Tom asked.

"Är's throne," Sarah said quietly.

Mär smiled at her. "Using the term 'throne' loosely.

"But that's less important now. I want you to stay *here*!

"Now, Ämäthōär do use affinity with Ärthähr, but not with its core. An Ōmäthäär who acted selfishly, who *acted* at all, would lose that core of genuinity."

"Oh," Tom said, "Thanks. I forgot I asked."

Mär smiled at him. "Of course, an Ōmäthäär who did that could still have fabulous power, but he would not be an Ōmäthäär as such.

"And, usually, other Ōmäthäär can see through that.

"You know the way you feel when you remember Ämäthōär."

"I hate even thinking about them," Sarah shivered.

"Even talking about them," Tom said.

"I know," Mär said. "So do I. But not everyone does."

"I've noticed that," Tom said with a weary grin.

"John isn't as aware of them," Mär said.

"How did you—" Tom began, but he gave up.

"A lot of people are like that," Mär smiled. "Unfortunately. Your state is better than blind ignorance. The light and life you have in you now, because of your living and being better, is incomparably better than just lacking susceptibility to Ämäthōärs' dark evil.

"John, and many others to much greater extents;" he said to Tom, "John is much more aware of these things than many are; but people like that don't feel as acutely as you do about Ämäthōär, simply because you are much less like Ämäthōär than they are.

"You have more light, more Ärthähr, more being and life, and everything, in you than those kinds of people do. I'm sorry, but that is the truth.

"More selflessness. Less short-sighted pettiness.

"And the contrast is what scares you.

"Tom, you said you remember things more dimly, those are the words you used, before you were inaugurated into the Ōmäthäär.

"When we initiated you as a member of Är's Ä'ähänärdanär, Är gave you,

24: Light and Glory

right then and there, a lot more Ärthähr, power and happiness and being, than you had ever had."

"I could tell," Sarah smirked at Tom.

"Yeah, I could tell," Tom said. "I had never felt so happy!"

"How do you feel now?"

"Uh, well, a lot better than I did then, if that's—"

"Exactly what I mean!" Mär said, pointing sharply at him. "You've been growing more and more!

"But you aren't grinning like a goof now," Mär smiled. "You've learned to handle that power better, that joy.

"Before I met you personally, other Ōmäthäär told me how impressed they were, with both of you. Sarah, you'd been initiated already into Earth's branch of Är's Ä'ähänärdanär led by the Ä'ähärnhär. But you didn't call yourself an Ōmäthäär then, even by another name."

Sarah shook her head.

"And Tom, you hadn't even been initiated at all.

"But both of you, already, had such light in you, such love, such peacefulness and unfaked power, that Ämäthōär frightened you.

"They frighten most rational beings, but they chilled you pretty deeply, didn't they?"

Tom and Sarah both nodded. Sarah shivered.

"Exactly," Mär said.

"Hōnhŭ and Ämharŭ," he growled, "Were adept enough at Ärthähr that no one noticed their darkness until they focused everything on killing. Then we, and you, Tom, saw the Ämäthōär-ness that they had always been hiding.

"Few Ämäthōär feel the fear the way you did.

"Tom, what would you say if I offered to take away everything you've gained, emotionally, since we first met?"

"No!" Tom said impulsively.

Mär laughed. "It's okay, only you can take that away.

"But that's just my point.

"There was a great old Ōmäthäär on Earth many many thousand weeks ago. Joseph, he was called. Now, when Joseph was first being tutored by Är, he occasionally made mistakes. Like most of us," Mär smiled.

"But he disobeyed Är so many times that he lost some of the light he had been given since he'd been introduced into Earth's Ä'ähänärdanär.

"Joseph wrote that that was his personal taste of hell.

"All that happened was he lost what he had gained. He became, almost, as 'dim' as he had been before he'd known about Är's order.

"But just going back, just losing that joy, was torment. No other Ōmäthäär could comfort him. He couldn't eat, he couldn't sleep, he cried; it was hell.

"Had it been hell before, back before he gained that happiness in the first place, before he met Är? Not for him. It wasn't like Heaven either, but it wasn't that much a hell to him. He had never tasted that much happiness back then.

"Only after he had had it for so long did the loss of it become such a hell to him.

"It's the contrast. Darkness seems darker when you've just come from a brightly lit area. Ämäthöär contrast with you.

"I'm afraid, Tom, that when you see fighting Ämäthöär again, it will be unexplainably worse than it was when you saw Hōnhŭ and Ämharŭ."

"I thought I was going to die, just from the fear," Tom said. "How could it be worse?"

"I think you'll be able to stand up to it better, too," Mär said. "But your capacity to feel it will be enhanced more than you know.

"You have grown so much.

"But others, who don't, who just do not have as much light and life and consciousness in them as you're growing to have, don't feel the contrast as badly.

"And many Ämäthöär don't notice it at all. For most of them, there is so little contrast.

"I personally think Sĕrĕhahn is among the most nefarious of the Ämäthöär. Perhaps the single most. He is the most outwardly intelligent of them, no question, but he's still dark enough that all of that intelligence is put to darkness.

"But he seems positively radiant to most of the Ämäthöär. On the outside.

"I noticed the contrast, but I wasn't cognizant of it until after I learned about Är, and realized what the Ämäthöär were doing.

"They were keeping people from getting initiated into Ä'ähänärdanär the way we have been, keeping them from getting the joy of Ärthähr that you've just recently been only beginning to taste!

"And it'll only get better, if you do not screw up."

"What?" Tom said, laughing a little at Mär.

"If you don't screw up," Mär said, "You will be able to look back on your lives now and see returning to this, now, as hell.

"And the farther you grow, the easier it is to never, ever screw up!"

"Okay," Tom said.

"Now, Ärthähr used offensively by Ōmäthäär is no less painful," Mär

24: Light and Glory

shuddered, "But it should not have that dark evil.

"But few Ämäthöär would be aware of the difference.

"And, in that much pain, few people are aware of anything, anyhow.

"But yes, Sarah, there are some good Ämäthöär."

"Oh," Sarah remembered. "Yeah."

"What are they like?" Tom said.

"Like people," Mär shrugged. "Different from each other.

"In principle, though, they tend to be good people, light enough and with talents ordered such that they're outwardly close to Ärthähr, handpicked by the Ämäthöär to progress their order.

"A sincere, good-hearted Ämäthöär will still cause the same darkness, though in a much lesser way than less admirable Ämäthöär will. The worst, darkest Ämäthöär are the foul ones who know all about Är, but don't care. Who want to do things their own, flawed, uninfinite ways.

"The good Ämäthöär don't cause the fear themselves per se; many, many Ämäthöär don't cause the fear. The fear is a side effect that some of them fail to recognize and others intentionally ignore.

"Sarah, tell me who Pp'm'tärnhär is."

"Well," Sarah breathed. She paused. "I'd rather hear how you'd tell it."

Mär laughed. "And I'd rather hear you. And saying it will help you understand it more. I haven't told Tom much about this, but you both need to understand this.

"I've been talking too much for my own comfort, anyhow."

"The Enemy," Sarah said, glancing at Tom. "That's what it means, *The Enemy*."

"Sĕrĕhahn?" Tom asked.

Mär looked at Sarah.

"He's like him," Sarah said. "Sĕrĕhahn is like the Enemy M'tärnhär.

"But the M'tärnhär's a spirit. Er…"

"That works," Mär said.

"Okay," Sarah said. "At least, I can't see him."

"That won't last," Mär muttered.

Sarah looked at him.

Mär nodded her on.

"Well, I can't see him. He's not mortal. You know what I mean. He's a he, but he's not mortal, but not immortal either."

"You're talking about the devil?" Tom asked.

Sarah looked to Mär.

"Come on, Sarah," Mär said. "You knew this before we came."

"Yes, he is," Sarah said then to Tom.

"Let me talk a bit more," Mär said. "Tom, there are very few Earth legends of which I've been taught, and I've been taught most of them, that are not loaded with factual debris.

"There are plenty of legends of an invisible, overall Enemy.

"Tracing those legends, many of which your society still had not uncovered, almost all of them funnel back to common, basic understandings had by ancient Ōmäthäär of the person whom we call the M'tärnhär.

"A 'devil' is a fragmented view of him. He is like us the way we were before we ascended into mortality."

"From where?" Tom asked.

"Är's Throne," Mär smiled, "To put it nebulously.

"He is the Enemy. There are many horrible amortals like him, but he is the de facto chief of them all; he is the least evil of them, and therefore the most truly powerful.

"He is less a person now than just a blister of envious delusion.

"He, and his undermen, contrast us much worse than any living Ämäthöär. No mortal is as dark as he, the lightest of them, is. Dark, lacking happiness, lacking peace, and consciousness, and life, and everything good. They emit fear because they have it, they are it, and we feel it so acutely because we are not it!

"Happiness is so much greater than oblivion!

"Some Ämäthöär emit fear because they are dark themselves. But some Ämäthöär emit fear just because these amortal M'tärnhär enjoy the destruction the deluded Ämäthöär cause to other, otherwise happy people.

"If that can be called enjoying.

"Ämäthöär, and any destructive people, attract the envious, bitter M'tärnhär. Less destructive people repel them.

"If you've got enough light and being in you, you can sense the M'tärnhär even if you can't see them yet.

"I thought I was happy as an Ämäthöär. But I was in hell. I had never felt what happiness was! I was surrounded by M'tärnhär, and I had actually gotten used to that kind of an atmosphere!

"We have to free Nrathĕrmĕ from Ämäthöär! And that includes however many Ämäthöär who would want to be freed if they knew what Är's freedom is."

"Which is infinite happiness," Tom said tentatively.

"To put it succinctly and unaffectively," Mär said. "Infinite happiness, and consciousness, and also infinite individuality. Real freedom, the ability, the capacity, the opportunity to be able to do whatever we want, and to actually get what we want from that.

"Not foolish hedonism; that's doing what we think we want but never getting what we want out of it! But real, infinite, freedom!"

"Yeah," Tom breathed.

"And we're not going to do anything about the Ämäthōär here?" Sarah asked.

"We're doing plenty," Mär said with a touch of weariness. "But nothing violent. I hope we never have to, but I'm afraid we will later if not sooner."

"Do you think there are Ämäthōär on other worlds?" Tom asked.

"I think," Mär said. "And I think we could have known. It's being said that Earth is the first foreign civilization Nrathĕrmĕ has ever found.

"I say that's nonsense. If I know anything about Är, there are a lot more branches of Ä'ähänärdanär near here. Or there were.

"I wonder if Sĕrĕhahn's Ämäthōär didn't just erase any other civilizations before now. Another case of Sĕrĕhahn thinking his Nrathĕrmĕ wasn't 'ready' yet.

"Meaning *he* wasn't ready to keep control of them yet under such a development as meeting a new world.

"But I believe there are Ōmäthäär on every world, at least for some if not all of its history, and that means there are likely to be Ämäthōär.

"But I think some worlds don't have to have them.

"So, before you forget, I remember you asking me this:

"Why did we call Nüährnär Nüährnär after we left, instead of keeping the title Ä'ähänärdanär?

"Well, I have a lot else to say on that subject. But it'll have to wait until I call you again."

"Oh," Sarah said, clearly disappointed.

"I'm sorry all we did was talk this time," Mär said. "I'm sorry I don't have more time.

"But next time I want to practice moving things with Ärthähr more. You'll have to understand that, at least, I think, if you're going to understand how to protect yourselves from Ämäthōär and how to fight them yourselves.

"Thahn is coming. You have to learn this!

"We will be okay. Do not worry, we will be okay.

"Ponder what you have, and remember your question for next time."

"We will," Sarah said.

"Thanks, Mär," Tom said.

"Likewise," Mär smiled. He jerked his head at the brilliantly warm wall.

Light and Glory

They followed him through into the Shell's dim blue atmosphere.

Mär looked at them, then grabbed them together into a passionate hug. "Thanks, you two."

"For what?" Tom gasped.

Mär let go of them and smiled tearfully. "I hope to call you soon enough."

Then he shot away from them.

Tom exhaled as if physically exhausted. Sarah took his hand comfortingly, then smiled up at him.

Chapter 25

Heritage of Ähänär

Tom and Sarah glided up through the ground.

"The Himalayas again," Tom observed.

"We weren't expecting you two," Lewis said gratefully, standing up out of the snow.

Tom swept forward and hugged his father. "This is worth it," he said.

"What?" Lewis asked.

"Just seeing all of you!" Tom said. "So many war exercises; I'm going to go nuts if I don't just spend some time with you!"

"I guess I'm no help," Sarah smiled.

"Yeah, Tom," Andrew said, looking sadly but welcomingly up from the snow. "You've got Sarah, what are you complaining about?"

Sarah laughed and moved to sit down with the Pratts and others gathered there.

Her mood was very out of place. Andrew was sitting morosely in the snow, beside a comparatively dark Spalding and Tävna Pratt. Spalding's four brothers and sisters were also there on the mountaintop with them, as was John and one of his assistants.

"I told him we'd be here," John said to Lewis, smiling weakly at Tom. "But I didn't expect you to come, either."

"Sorry it's been so long," Tom said, sitting down with Sarah.

"I don't want you to be here," Lewis said. "I'm happy to see you, Tom, but you don't have time for this."

"I do if I say I do," Tom said with soft seriousness.

"We might as well do what we can with the time we have," Andrew said.

"Yeah," Tom said. "This is more important than administration to me, really."

"We work enough, believe us," Sarah assured Lewis.

Lewis nodded powerlessly. He sat down again.

"So what's happening?" Sarah asked.

"Nothing," Tävna said quietly. "We found Lewis here, and the crowd just snowballed."

Tom nodded. A grey silence fell.

"Andrew and I were discussing his story," Lewis ventured.

"Just leave it," Andrew said.

"Fine," Tävna said. "I'll talk about ours."

Sarah looked questioningly at Andrew, but he was absorbed in the snow in front of him.

"Are you going to do another one?" Tom asked when Tävna didn't go on.

"Why bother?" Andrew mumbled for her.

Tävna shook her head impatiently at Andrew, but still didn't say anything.

Tom looked helplessly around. He looked at his father, who returned his concerned gaze with tired grief.

"I guess there's been a lot going on in the past couple days," Tom said slowly. "What's wrong?"

Andrew looked disbelievingly at him.

"We're scared, Tom," Spalding's sister Christina said.

"Oh," Tom said softly.

"Dad was trying to tell us we'd have a happy ending, no matter what," Andrew murmured. "Like in our happy little stories."

"He's got a point," Tävna said incisively.

"He does," Sarah said.

"Thanks," Andrew said, "But I'm willing to face this.

"This is not a story. This is real life. Real life doesn't have to have happy endings."

"Says who?" Sarah said.

"Says reality," Andrew said exasperatedly.

"Glad you came?" Spalding privately said to Tom in a gloomy voice.

"So you're giving up?" Tom asked Andrew.

"He's not," Robyn said. "But we're afraid."

"We're not leaving Nüährnär," Lewis assured Tom.

"We're not like that," Andrew said. "Those are cowards. But it doesn't mean we're not afraid."

Tom smiled sympathetically at him. "Look, Andrew, I'm not worried. And I know more of what's coming than most people do."

Andrew looked at him, and didn't say anything.

"The thing about stories," Sarah then said, "Is that the heroes always win. Well, in most stories."

"In good stories," Tävna said.

"Just because we let them win easier than in Andrew's..." Spalding said.

"We're going to win, here," Sarah continued, "Because we're with the Ōmäthäär. They're the heroes.

"This *is* a story. It's Är's story. And the Ōmäthäär are his heroes.

"I guess that's not far off from what 'Ōmäthäär' means in the first place!"

25: Heritage of Ähänär

she said. "'Är's Executives;' they're 'Är's Heroes.'"

Tom squeezed her hand. "Even if we die," he said. "Being a hero isn't about running from death. Or even beating death. Not this kind of death."

"If we abandon all that's good and worth living for," John recited slowly, "That's worth existing for, we will be infinitely worse off than if we had died."

"Yeah," Tom said. "And if we die fighting to make a better world for everyone else, then death will be no ending for us."

"You really believe Mär," Heather smiled at Tom and Sarah.

"We would," Sarah said. "We have been around him. And he says we will win here."

"When I made that story," Andrew said, "I knew they would win. I made it that way.

"But people lose in real life. Who has adventures like that? Isn't that why we have stories, so we can get excitement that our lives don't have?"

"Mär has adventures like that," Tom said. "Better than that. But real adventures are scarier than stories. In real adventures, we don't know already that we're going to win.

"But I believe Mär. I believe we will win against Thahn, Andrew. But it's not as easy as one of your stories, you're right.

"But Sarah's right too. This is Är's story.

"People like Mär have adventures because they're Är's heroes. They live so they can be heroes. He's selfless, he's ambitious in a patient kind of way, he risks everything all the time for Är."

"But so do you," Andrew said.

"Not like him."

"And Mär wasn't always the way he is now," Sarah said. "Tom's had plenty of adventures. Like this one sitting beside him," she leaned her head on his shoulder. "Är leads you into his adventures while you grow."

Tom stuttered slightly while he put his arm around Sarah. "We'll only be heroes when we're heroic. It's not the other way around. Heroes know better than to not hope!

"Trust Mär. And trust us. There is so much to hope for."

"I wish I could believe that," Andrew said sadly. "I wish it were as easy as our stories. When Tävna and Spalding were leading us through their plot, it was so much simpler. Everything happened within a day. There wasn't this uncertainty that never ends."

"You were main characters, maybe," Sarah said. "But that didn't make you heroes.

"What did you overcome, besides physical obstacles like the guardians?

415

You didn't have to overcome fear, or doubt. But now we do have to. Now, even if we're not 'main characters,' we can be heroes."

"So Lewis was a hero and a main character," Spalding said. "At the end of the Tasirak story. That looked like it really hurt."

"I think," Lewis said, "That keeping hope against Thahn would be a lot more heroic than getting hurt to win a game."

"But no less possible," Tävna said.

"I agree," Lewis said. "Anyone can be heroic when we know we're going to get what we're after. It's life's uncertainty and slow pace that make us be genuinely heroic."

Tom realized he was staring at Lewis. He blinked and looked back at his downcast brother.

"We've got to stick with the Ōmāthäär here," he said. "We can win this. Somehow. I don't know how. But Mär thinks we can."

"We believe him," Sarah added.

"Well, I am going to stick with him," Andrew said. "I'm not leaving like everyone else. But I'm not hoping yet."

"You better," John said. "People are depending on you."

Andrew sighed.

"A few of us got appointed up," Lewis said to Tom and Sarah.

"Congratulations," Tom said unconvincingly.

"Thanks," Tävna said sincerely.

"Right," Andrew smiled forlornly. "The day I lead a couple thousand people is the day we're really desperate."

"A couple thousand?" Tom said.

"Four tiers up," Andrew said in an overwhelmed voice. "But that's a lot fewer people than it would have been, since so many people are leaving."

"Especially in the lower tiers," Heather said.

"Yeah, the ones farthest from the Ōmāthäär," Andrew sneered. "But I'm not leaving."

"It shouldn't have been that way," Tom said. "I wish we could have had Ōmāthäär in the lower tiers."

"They've been working too hard to keep us all alive," Tävna reminded him.

"Mär said something about Nŭährnär not being as united as Nrathĕrmĕ," Spalding said. "We haven't had time to be. Nrathĕrmĕ's already solid, and we're having to fight for our lives too much to really care about each other."

"It's a good thing we have homegrown Ōmāthäär right here," John smiled.

"It's a good thing we've all got each other," Tom said.

25: Heritage of Ähänär

"How's Annie doing?" Sarah asked John, as if to deliberately change the subject.

John looked at his assistant beside him, Kōrhas, then managed a grin again.

"Way better than I would've expected," he said. "And better than me.

"She's been appointed two tiers up, right to Peter's old tier. His managers didn't revive, and only three of his assistants did, but now they're Annie's assistants. It's like Annie got put with Peter, as if he were still here."

John fell silent.

"But she's doing well?" Sarah said.

"Yes. I've never seen her like this. She's not after revenge. Not anymore. But it's like she thinks Peter's death will have been in vain somehow if we lose here.

"She's bent on stopping Thahn. She even talks about killing Sĕrĕhahn.

"She blames Sĕrĕhahn for Peter's death. And she credits Mär with their marriage. She's crazy about him now, about Mär.

"I think she'd face Thahn all alone, now, if she thought it could help Mär."

"What about you?" Tom asked.

"I wish I could take it like her," John said bravely. "I don't know.

"They moved me up a tier, Tom. Right into your old tier. I never knew how hard you worked."

"There is a lot more to do now," Tom said.

"But it's not because of me," John said. "It's like Andrew says. We're getting desperate. Too many people at the high tiers won't revive, and too many people at the low tiers are leaving all the time."

"It isn't as clear cut as all that," Lewis said.

"Yeah," John nodded. "But I don't think I can do this, Tom. You got put in your tiers because the Ōmäthäär wanted you there. I'm just here because there's no one else."

"There are billions of elses," Tom said.

John smiled. "I wish you were my manager again."

"I could arrange that," Tom said thoughtfully. "At least, see if you could be assistant to one of my assistants."

"But you don't need us," Sarah cut in. "You're capable of more than you're giving yourself credit for."

"Yeah, I need you guys," John said. "It's like you said, Tom, we'd all go nuts if we didn't have each other.

"It's bad enough knowing I'll never see Peter again."

"That's what I mean," Sarah said earnestly. "We enjoy each other, but we can't rely on each other. I just don't want you to handicap yourself by thinking you can't do anything without our help."

"Or without Peter's," she added.

"You need to stand up, now, John. You need to let yourself be you!"

"I really am not much to rely on," John said to her.

"But you can't just lean on other people forever," Sarah said.

"But Mär doesn't rely on himself, either," Tom said quietly. "He relies on Är, though."

"I wish I were an Ōmäthäär," John sighed.

Tom smiled at him. "Maybe we, and you, it has to be you, can arrange that, too."

John looked surprisedly at him.

"I think Sarah has something," Kōrhas said.

"I do?" Sarah said.

"Yep. You did kind of worship Peter," she said to John. "Now he's not here to lean on. You've lost that support. I remember the way you were when Peter was plotting against Nŭährnär. It was like you couldn't do anything right.

"Well, it was," she smiled as John looked hurt.

"I think Sarah's right. You can't keep yourself from being you, with or without all of us. You said Annie's been inspired by his loss. Shouldn't you be?"

John nodded slowly.

"Maybe that's why Är's letting Peter move on," Kōrhas said. "He's a hero already. Now you better move up into his shoes."

"I'm already into his tier," John said uneasily.

"I like her," Spalding said.

Kōrhas smiled but looked away.

"You're right," Lewis said to Kōrhas. He looked at Andrew. "We can all be heroes. What better opportunity can we ask for? Now we have to let ourselves be heroes, and grow into our responsibilities. Nŭährnär needs us. All of us. We all need each other, to live through this."

"Dad's been talking to Ōmäthäär more," Andrew said.

"It fits," Tom answered.

"I'm glad you say that, Tom," Lewis said.

Andrew sighed. "So maybe you're right, Dad. But what if we do lose here?"

"Then Sĕrĕhahn would win," Tävna said. "That can't happen. If all the Ōmäthäär, and Ōhōnŭäär, get killed—"

25: Heritage of Ähänär

"What if Earth is not Ōhōnüäär?" Andrew said. "What if Mär and the Ōmäthäär made a mistake?"

"They couldn't have," Tävna said.

"Anyone can," Sarah said. "But I'm certain Earth is Ōhōnüäär."

"Maybe," Andrew said. "But what if it isn't? Our world, remember what it was like here, before Nüährnär got here?

"Hunger, war, murder, poverty, disasters happening every day, remember? You call that the seat of Är's power?

"If you want my opinion, I think Earth deserves to be wiped out. Not Nüährnär, not the ones who are staying, but I don't think Earth is this big a deal.

"If there is an Är, and Mär thinks there is, maybe he won't care if Earth gets destroyed. Maybe he's even doing this, so it will get destroyed."

"I don't believe that," Tom said softly.

"I don't believe anything," Andrew said. "And I'm afraid."

"They're all yours, Sarah!" Her manager Äōhäüdär's voice called frantically.

Good luck, she thought for him as her manager joined the Ōmäthäär engaging Thahn's Ämäthōär.

"Keep apart!" she called to her assistants, hurling her ships faster and faster, weaving to avoid the ubiquitous rantha.

Several gargantuan fleets of hundreds of thousands of planet-sized spheres bore down behind her, drawing inexorably closer. Every bolt of rantha annihilated another part of her fleet.

"Now!" she shouted.

She pulled her ships down and around, hoping to arc up in the middle of the charging juggernaut behind her. Every one of her assistants' remaining fleets was streaking to the same point.

There was a bite of piercing cold.

Darkness clouded everything.

She was screaming against the unnatural gale of ghostly fear.

And then the simulation vanished.

Her heart was pounding, and her hands were shaking. The warm peace of the Sanctuary slowly dissipated the chilling horror coursing through every part of her consciousness.

"You lasted longer than I did," Tom said beside her.

Sarah managed a smile.

"Alright you two," Mär's voice called in their heads. "Come meet me outside."

Sarah shook her head.

"Never a break," Tom said.

Sarah followed him past the remaining concentrating Ōmäthäär, and out through the wall, which was just regaining its transcendent color in her eyes.

Mär greeted them looking extremely exhausted, floating no less happily in the air some distance from the nearest Sentinel.

"That can't have been accurate," Sarah said to him.

"Unfortunately, I doubt it was," Mär said. "We tried to reproduce a representation of what we think Ämäthöär might do in a battle like that. But they're hard to predict. And we don't know the exact nature of Thahn's army yet.

"I think it will dwarf what they're fighting right now, but we'll fight a bigger army next time, if we have time."

"Bigger?" Tom gasped.

"It's not military armament that will determine this battle," Mär reminded them.

"Okay," Sarah said.

"The Ämäthöär changed everything," Tom said.

"We Ōmäthäär did a lot to influence that battle against the N'nrathěrmě," Mär said. "We will have to do more this time. We will likely have to use Ärthähr in outright attack, not just in influencing people. The Ämäthöär are going to make this a very different battle."

"It was hard to think," Tom said.

"It will be worse. Remember, we just tried to represent Ämäthöär; of course there weren't any real M'tärnhär or Ämäthöär around in the simulation; we just simulated it.

"Does that motivate you to get a more definitive hold of Ärthähr?"

"Yes," Tom said meaningfully.

"We're trying," Sarah said.

"I know," Mär said. "But anything to squeeze some movement out of you two!"

He shook his shoulders and relaxed, then looked benignly at them.

"Who first?"

Tom looked at Sarah.

"It doesn't matter," she said tiredly. "You go."

"Here we go," Tom said, shaking his shoulders too and stretching out his arms relaxedly. "Let's see what happens."

He closed his eyes. He slowly let himself melt into the Ärthähr around

25: Heritage of Ähänär

him.

It was incredible. Total comfort gradually filled every part of him. Warmth, and peace, and content confidence spread deep into his core.

They would be okay.

He knew they would be okay. Somehow, they were going to be okay. Är cared about them, he cared about Mär, he cared about everyone. And he cared about this cause of theirs.

They were going to be okay.

Nearly ten minutes passed before Tom opened his eyes.

"Still nothing," he said, without the disappointment he would have expected.

"Nothing," Mär said quietly. "You were on fire with Ärthähr. But yeah, you didn't move me at all."

"It was great," Tom said.

"It looked like it," Mär smiled. "We will try again. You have to learn this."

"Do you know what I'm doing wrong?"

"I've been thinking about that," Mär said. "This has never happened before.

"A few other Nōhōnüäär have managed to move things already. But I don't see in them the same magnitude of power I can see every time I see you two. But for the most part, other Nōhōnüäär can't move things either.

"For every Ōmäthäär I've taught, it's been simpler than this. They have affinity with Ärthähr, and they can use it to manipulate matter, and soon enough to manipulate finer stuff.

"There are plenty of Ämäthōär who have far less light than you do, who can do spectacular things. Who kill people, among other things.

"It's not a matter of magnitude of affinity, it's how that affinity's arranged. I have just never met people arranged how most of you Nōhōnüäär are.

"You know that two relatively equally intelligent people can have strengths in different areas. One may be more intelligent interpersonally, the other more intelligent administratively. Or in any number of ways. It depends where their intelligence is allocated.

"I've never tried to train people with intelligence arranged like yours.

"You have so much to work with! I can see it! But I just haven't been able to get to it!

"Don't worry, I'm talking to Är about this as much as I can."

"What does he say?" Sarah asked.

"A lot to make me think," Mär smiled. "But I'm still thinking. The smarter we are, the faster we learn, but I'm still not smart enough to have learned this yet."

"Okay," she said. "I hope you figure it out fast."

"Maybe I won't need to with you," he said, taking a luxuriant breath. "You're up."

Sarah stretched out her arms too.

She concentrated, and relaxed; she could feel the consummate glory of Ärthähr filling her; but after more than ten minutes of pleasurable comfort she let go.

"Or maybe I will have to think a lot more about both of you," Mär said as she opened her eyes.

"I'm sorry," Sarah said.

"It's no fault," Mär said. "Just a new situation for me. We'll figure this out."

"It was great, though," Sarah said.

"Good," Mär smiled. "Now, feel free to practice together, but only inside the Sanctuary."

"Whenever we can get time," Tom said.

"I won't mind feeling that again," Sarah said.

"Why can we practice alone now, when we couldn't before?" Tom asked. "Have we made that much progress?"

"You've made *so much* progress!" Mär said. "Even if you haven't noticed it yet.

"But there are more reasons, now, for giving you two time together," he grinned.

"Oh," Sarah blushed.

"Thank you," Tom laughed, smiling at Sarah's deepening rouge.

"Now, about Nŭährnär," Mär said, still grinning as Sarah tried to blink her attention back to business.

"Oh yeah," Tom said.

"And why we don't call it Ä'ähänärdanär," Mär continued.

"Remember what happened after the Ä'ähänärdanär order had to leave Nrathĕrmĕ. Sĕrĕhahn and his Ämäthōär pursued us. They killed Ahntä, and most of the leading Ōmäthäär.

"Most of us had brought our families with us. We knew we might never return to Nrathĕrmĕ, and we didn't want to be separated from them, nor they from us, even if it meant they had to leave Nrathĕrmĕ.

"The Ämäthōär might have killed many of them anyway, if they had stayed.

25: Heritage of Ähänär

"So now we were the Ä'ähänärdanär order and our unsworn, uninitiated family members.

"Then many of us, including some of the order, determined we should leave Nrathĕrmĕ forever behind. They wanted to use almost all of our energy to accelerate and not look back, so we could find some other land where we could set up Ä'ähänärdanär again.

"The rest of us refused to abandon the N'nrathĕrmĕ.

"You know all this.

"They left, we stayed; that was over a hundred weeks ago. Many uninitiated people whose Ōmäthäär relatives had already been killed went with them, but some such stayed with us.

"Now we were still the Ä'ähänärdanär order accompanied by our families and our friends.

"But we weren't pure Ä'ähänärdanär. We didn't want to deal lightly with that title. We didn't want to include unsworn people under that title.

"Remember, Ä'ähänärdanär means the Light of Är. But 'ähänär' is a very complex word. It means light, but that stands for life, and power, and intelligence. Everything the Ärthähr's made of. 'Glory' is probably more accurate than 'light.'

"Break it apart: 'ä-hä-n-Är.' That suggests to me some piece of Är that comes from Är; the intelligence and power and light we have comes from Är, but it's not the whole, but it's part of it. It's not a half-made adulteration like the incomplete Ämäthöär; that would be 'här,' or even 'ähr' in some cases; it's 'hä,' a work in progress."

"Alright," Tom said, trying to keep up.

"It's light progressively being given from Är to us.

"Now, 'Ä'ähänärdanär' emphasizes that: 'The Ähänär which comes from Är.'

"It's what we call the Grand Event that Är executed on Ōhōnŭäär, since all progression, past and future, comes from that single Event. We just access that Ä'ähänärdanär that Är set in motion down there on the surface so many years ago whenever we progress in any way at all.

"We can't give ourselves what we don't have. Whenever we gain, whenever anything defies its own entropic stupidity, whenever we gain intelligence and, really, permanently shed stupidity, it comes from that Central Pillar: Ä'ähänärdanär.

"The Ärthähr comes from the Ä'ähänärdanär.

"Time has no bearing on it. It did happen, it had to happen, it could not just 'be,' but it affects everything throughout all time and space. Past and future are now for Är, even if we still see time from tiny, ignorant points of view.

"Do you see the magnitude of this word? Of what it means?

"The Ähänär of Är. And since the point of our order is to help people let themselves grow like Är, to help them progress and not regress, to gain, to grow, to use Är's Ä'ähänärdanär to gain infinite awesomeness from him, we called the order itself Ä'ähänärdanär.

"We could not call anyone a part of such an order who was not ready to do all they could to that aim, to help everyone become everything.

"So we thought of other names for our band.

"Some of us termed us 'Äfäsĕrĕhahn;' others, 'Äfäämäthōär.' Or 'M'närdamähr,' or 'Ōhōämhär,' or 'M'tärnär.' 'Nŭährnär' is the one that got most popular.

"I like 'M'närdamähr' or 'M'tärnär' myself.

"But so many of our unsworn family and friends understood so little about Är's Ä'ähänärdanär.

"We tried to teach them everything we could about Ä'ähänärdanär as quickly as we could. But overcoming Sĕrĕhahn's philosophies, which had so thoroughly pervaded them at Nrathĕrmĕ, was as difficult as ever. Many of our family and friends could not understand what we tried to show them.

"Children were being born constantly, many of whom were not taught about Ä'ähänärdanär when they were born. Some of them were taught pretty deeply a lot of Sĕrĕhahn's insidious philosophies.

"It felt like we were falling farther from our hope to be able to rename ourselves Ä'ähänärdanär.

"Now, in Nŭährnär's second hundred weeks, Är and Ä'ähänärdanär are like mere legends among most of us. The sworn Ōmäthäär made up barely a few millionths of a percent of us when we arrived here.

"Many of us Ōmäthäär have been killed.

"Many of our children are more ready to swear to ally with Är. But the majority of new children in Nŭährnär are taught so little about him."

"Okay," Sarah said subduedly.

"But that, I hope, is changing.

"Those who've refused to believe in Är are leaving.

"I don't like that. But it may turn out for good. I will not force anyone to stay with us. But I am afraid that the Ämäthōär will the more easily be able to capture many of them now that they have left the Ōmäthäärs' immediate influence.

"But few who believe about Ä'ähänärdanär are leaving.

25: Heritage of Ähänär

"And, now that we're here at Ōhōnŭäär, it seems that Nŭährnär is being forced by Är to face up to the realities it should have accepted already.

"Our situation here may be one of the best things that's ever happened to Nŭährnär."

"And you really think Nŭährnär will survive this," Tom said.

"I don't know," Mär said. "But I'm confident that Ä'ähänärdanär will survive this, in some way or other. Whether many of the Ōmäthäär or much of Nŭährnär is going to survive this, too, I don't know. I hope so.

"But whatever happens, if we do our best, then Är will make up for everything else. Sĕrĕhahn will not win, whatever that ends up meaning, if we do our best.

"And now," he said more soberly, "I want to tie this personally in to you two.

"No matter what happens to you, or what happens to me, or where you go, or anything, I want you to remember the oaths you've made. Remember Ä'ähänärdanär. Remember 'Ōhä-Ä'ähänärdanär.'

"No matter what happens to the Ōmäthäär, I want you to remember. Always remember everything you can. Gratitude will keep you on track.

"No matter where you go, whom you may fall in with, remember, and make sure you live up to those oaths. Make sure every single tiniest thing you do is directed to helping people in Är's Epic of Ä'ähänärdanär.

"I want you to understand this about people:

"I told you that Är has an Är, who helped him become Infinite. Är's Är, to put it simplistically, executed an Ä'ähänärdanär by which he was able to give Infinity to the finite people, who now are our Är."

"Är is not just one—?" Tom began.

"He is. He's a person, you can see him, you can touch him. That doesn't mean he doesn't have an infinity of companion Ärs. Remember, they're all Ärs together, Infinity together. Är and his Är and his Är, but also every other finite man or woman whom Är's Är helped to become Infinite.

"The togetherness of Infinite people is not like finite togetherness.

"Nor is it a loss of individuality. Är remembers everything he ever did in his finite time as well as everything that Infinity comprehends.

"He is more him, now, in his eternal now, than he was before he accepted all Infinity from his Är."

"Can we actually grow *infinitely*?" Sarah asked. "Do we just approach it until the end of time?"

"Infinite Är can give Infinity. This is not calculus, Sarah. This is no asymptote of infinite approach. This is real.

Light and Glory

"I have spoken with infinite people. People who have not always been infinite, the way Är has, but who have actually let themselves get Infinity."

"According to them, it was a very long road."

"None of them are mortal anymore, if that tells you something of how long it usually takes."

"What are they?" Tom asked.

"Infinite," Mär said. "Think of it! People just like you and me, but now, they are Ärs!

"Think how perfect, how…*perfect* Är's Plan of Ä'ähänärdanär is! That all goodness grows, and evil ends!

"Of course, the chronology of that is our mortal illusion, but the more we grow the less we're bound to the 'surface,' so to speak, of time.

"But, a few days ago, Tom, you asked where we came from before we took up mortality.

"Understand this about people:

"We are Är's own, personal, individual offspring.

"We have to grow still to become like him. But that is exactly how we have the capacity to grow to be like him. Because he is our progenitor!

"The 'he' I talk about is our Father! Literally! We are direct children, not grandchildren, not distant evolutionary descendents, but direct children of infinite Parents!"

"Parents?" Tom asked.

"What, girls can't use Ä'ähänärdanär?" Sarah smirked.

"I told you we Ōmäthäär like marriage," Mär said. "That's because we didn't invent it. No mortal did.

"Anyone who thinks Infinity can be genderless, or only the Man who most often confers with us, has a lot to learn from Infinity."

"So Är is married," Tom said.

"In a total, perfect sense," Mär smiled.

"I just can't wait until I get to be literally hand in hand with Lhĕhûnrĕ again."

He smiled dreamily.

"Anyhow," he said then. "I want you to remember that. No matter where you go, whom you meet, what kind of people you meet, I want you to always remember that every single human, from any world, is a direct, mortalized, son or daughter of Är. No matter how repulsive, no matter how dehumanized, no matter what they've done to themselves or what they do to anyone else, *remember* what they are.

"Being Nōhōnŭäär is so important. But every single man or woman you will know has better heritage than that; the infinite parentage of Infinity!"

"Mär, what are you afraid is going to happen?" Sarah asked.

"I can't say," Mär said. "But tell me you will remember."

"We will," they both said uncertainly.

Mär smiled at them. "We'll be fine.

"Also, be aware that the Ämäthöär will want people like you. And other, nastier people may want you too. Want you to join them.

"Remember Är. Remember the Ōmäthäär.

"Just remember."

"We will," Tom and Sarah said again.

Chapter 26

One of Those Times

Mär emerged from the inner cube and sphere.

"Oh, good," he breathed, catching sight of Tom and Sarah together in the courtyard.

"Everyone else went to direct the exercises already," Sarah said.

"Good," Mär said.

"We thought we should wait for you," Tom explained.

"Why?" Mär said, smiling with a fatigue that was becoming all too characteristic for him.

"We just...I don't know," Sarah said.

"You do," Mär said appreciatively.

"It felt right," Sarah said.

"Excellent," Mär said. "I was kind of actively hoping you would stay."

"What do you need us to do?" Tom asked.

"Thahn isn't here yet," Mär said. "Obviously."

"So we have time for more training."

"If you have time," Sarah said. "Ōhōmhär's address made it sound like you're really busy."

"I still am. This is part of it. Training you is important right now."

"Are fewer people leaving now?" Tom asked.

Mär nodded. "But whether that's because of the Ōmäthäärs' speeches yesterday or because few who are going to flee have not already fled, I don't know.

"I want people to stay, though. If they can be courageous, and take Är seriously, we need them."

"It was different listening to Ŭkan now," Tom said.

"I hope you'll get to know all the other Ōmäthäär better," Mär said.

"But that will have to be for later. For now, every second of our time has to be put to preparing ourselves against Thahn."

"Okay, let's get started then," Sarah said hastily.

"But hurry can be far less productive than calm," Mär said.

"Sorry," Sarah said.

"So, I want you to not hurry, just relax, and move me.

"We are running out of time. Don't let that make you worry, but know how important it is for you to succeed at this.

26: One of Those Times

"That kind of motivation can work wonders."

"Okay," Sarah said.

"You move him first," Tom smiled, rubbing his hands together absently.

A quarter hour later, Tom opened his eyes again impatiently.

"Alright, what now?" he said.

"Just relax, Tom," Mär said. "It's okay. I felt it a lot stronger then than I ever have before from you."

"So we'll just be commanding again," Sarah said with unhidden relief, "Not fighting any Ämäthöär."

"I doubt you will have any choice," Mär said. "But I would never have *made* you face Ämäthöär if you didn't agree to. You're leaders; just do what you think needs to be done."

Tom and Sarah both shivered.

"We will be fine," Mär said compellingly. "No matter what happens, Ä'ähänärdanär will survive here."

They nodded.

"That's all the training we should take time for, now," Mär said. "I understand you've been practicing together some, too."

"With no more success," Tom said, manifestly afraid. "But it does feel amazing."

"It makes everything a lot less dismal," Sarah said. "I can't be afraid, even if I'm still concerned, when we're practicing."

"I wonder," Mär said, "If that's because of the Ärthähr or just the company."

"She's right," Tom said, wrapping an arm around Sarah's waist, "Everyone except the Ōmäthäär is making me feel so hopeless. But Ärthähr makes that go away."

"We are doing all we can to fuel Nŭährnär's courage," Mär said. "I don't appreciate this permeating hopelessness. It's not what we need right now.

"But I can't blame people, either.

"We will be okay," he assured them.

Tom and Sarah nodded again. Neither of them said anything.

"Sarah, can you leave Tom, just for a minute? I want to talk to him alone. Just for a minute."

"Okay," Sarah smiled. She moved toward the wall, but then came back and kissed Tom's cheek.

Then she turned and was gone.

Mär sighed happily as he gazed where she had vanished.

"You never seem all that busy," Tom said complementarily.

"I try," Mär smiled quietly.

Tom waited.

Mär sighed again. He looked at Tom placidly, but there was distinct worry in his eyes.

"What do you need?" Tom asked.

Mär smiled sadly. "How's Sarah doing?"

"Well, really good, considering," Tom said. "Ärthähr's helping us a lot.

"She's helping me a lot. You are right about hurrying; we do so much better when we spend time together than when we just hurry and don't get to see each other.

"So, uh, yeah, she's doing as awesome as ever."

"Okay," Mär said, "You answered my meaning more than my question. So, what do you think of her?"

Tom fished for words for a few seconds. "I love her," he said finally. "But I guess I love a lot of people. I really do love Brittney.

"But I've never felt this…this deeply! It's never been like this."

Mär was beaming, though still sadly.

"I want to marry her," Tom said. He paused.

"I really do. I'll have to talk to her about that. How can I not?"

Mär expelled a whistle of air. "I can't tell you how happy I am to hear that," he said. "Seeing you two together, it's more than I wanted to dare to hope for.

"But listen to me, Tom. You must not ask Sarah to marry you."

"What?"

"I know," Mär said. "This must go against everything you're rightly feeling. It goes against what I wanted to see.

"But you have got to heed this. Don't marry Sarah.

"Don't ask me why. I can't explain much. But you absolutely should not be married.

"At least, not now."

Tom could not be angry at Mär, but still he could not believe what he was hearing. "Why?" he breathed.

"I just told you I couldn't explain much," Mär smiled with sadness that quietly managed to reflect the sudden tempest inside of Tom.

"I am not, not at all, saying you ought to change anything about your relationship for the worse.

"Just don't ask her to marry you."

Tom just barely stopped himself from asking "Why?" again.

"There are very obviously some reasons why neither of you have been able

26: One of Those Times

to handle macro matter with Ärthähr," Mär said, slowly as if carefully choosing his words. "As far as I can say right now, the very same reasons are telling me to tell you to not ask her to marry you."

Yet Tom was adept enough at Ärthähr to feel the sincerity behind Mär's desperate words.

He managed a half a grin through the shattering tumult he was feeling. "It's because you like her, isn't it?"

Mär laughed heartily, and the mood magically lightened. "I do!" he said. "Oh, I do!

"But you know, Tom, Sarah Rose Trotter is way more than a match for me. Or she will be."

He smiled admiringly at Tom. "I really do feel how hard this is for you."

He moved forward and pulled Tom into a hug. Tears started stinging Tom's eyes.

"Know that all this will work out better than we can know yet," Mär said, "If we do what Är's telling us to do."

"I know," Tom whispered. He pulled away from Mär, shaking a little.

"That, Thomas Pratt," Mär said, "Is courage."

Tom smiled. "Thanks for telling me," he said voicelessly.

"Thanks for keeping the oath," Mär said.

"And I will talk to Sarah about this. But I wanted to tell you both this separately."

Tom nodded.

It was okay, he told himself.

It was all going to turn out better than he could know yet.

He hoped Är really could deliver that.

"Mär, my man!"

A grey-skinned man with long, thick black hair and beard slapped his arms around Mär.

"Ärhaōthänär," Mär said fondly, hugging him back. "It's good to see you alive again!"

Millions of vulgar looking men and women were stopping in the midst of the defenses behind the homecome Ōmäthäär.

"We are in a fix," Ärhaōthänär grinned giddily.

"Hōäōhä arrived three days ago," Mär told him. "He hadn't found anything more than the militia."

"It's Thahn, Mär," Ärhaōthänär shrugged.

"You couldn't detect her either?"

"Not a bloody thing. But I did hear tell Vŭt was on her way. I thought she would be here."

"All that time with pirates," a woman's voice called in their minds, "And you still don't talk crypted?"

"It's good to have you back," Mär smiled at Ärhaōthänär.

A hard-faced woman slammed to a stop right beside them.

"And better to have you both to liven each other up," he said.

Vŭt threw her arms around Mär. "Oh, it's great to see you!"

She hopped back. "The clan of S'zahan is at your disposal," she said with a flourish at the ranks of fleets that had stopped behind her.

"Thahn?" Mär asked.

"I like to hope she's still far away," Vŭt said. "But I know better. We wouldn't be able to detect stealth like hers if she were right on top of us."

"Odds say that she is," Ärhaōthänär said. "I do not fancy seeing her again."

"Hey, Annie?"

"Hi, John," Annie called back, turning to face him as he soared from the distant Shell.

John came up beside her. Defenses filled every angle of their view, stretching away in front of them against the ominous dark.

"What are you doing?" he asked.

Annie shrugged. "Trying not to think. What are you doing?"

"I wish I knew," John said. "I wish I knew what Mär's doing."

Annie laughed grimly. "I just keep telling myself, I can trust Mär, I can trust Mär.

"It makes me feel less responsible, and I can get myself to almost stop worrying."

"He knows what he's doing," John said.

Annie looked away. John noticed a tear slip from her eye.

"Annie, we will win here. For Peter."

Annie shuddered.

"We can't give up. It's—"

"John, stop," Annie said quietly.

John stopped.

"I know all that," she said. "I know."

She looked back at him, the tear gone. She smiled fearfully. "Peter died to save us, John," she said, as if to keep him from saying it. "I'm not going to throw that away.

26: One of Those Times

"Mär knows what he is doing. And if he thinks Är's real, and that he'll get involved here, then I won't worry."

"Mär thinks Peter's still there. He said he's rooting for us, and helping us in ways we may not see.

"I trust Peter. My Peter."

John tried to smile.

"I believe Mär. Peter can save our lives again," Annie said.

"If Mär said that," John said, "Then I'll remember it. I can use any hope I can hang onto right now."

"I think it's more than blind hope," Annie said, looking out at the unending space. "Mär has been telling the truth, the whole time."

"Yes, I'm certain," the breathless man said as more Ōmäthäär entered the Sanctuary. "If we could tell anything, we could tell that army was huge. It's Thahn."

Mär took a breath.

"Did she see you?" Vŭt asked.

"No," the man said.

"How did you manage that?" Ŭmäthŭ asked.

"I wasn't in command," the man smiled. "I let Ä'ävär get us here. And his people have some good stealth themselves."

"Not good enough," Ä'ävär, a rough but comparatively clean man said. "I don't know what you all are expecting outside of wholesale slaughter."

"Naŭbärōdä," Mär said, "What did you detect?"

"Zōrd underestimated Thahn," the man Naŭbärōdä said. "A great deal. There was at least a thousand systems' worth of warship there.

"We couldn't tell many details, but the strength of their stealth, and how fast they were coming up on us, has got to fall in line with what kind of armament they have."

"How fast?" Bävän asked.

"Four hundred ten and some times light relative to here. We've got an hour."

"An hour," Ŭdbän repeated steadily.

"Nŭährnär's going to find out," Mär said.

"We're with you, Mär," another newly arrived Ōmäthäär said. "We have half a billion sworn pirates all told."

Mär smiled. "I'm glad."

"It's their oath that'll be of help to us," Ŭkan said, "Not their fleets."

"And maybe we can convince Nŭährnär to make a sort of unofficial oath

Light and Glory

for Är," Mär said. "I want them to understand what they're fighting for."

Sarah found Tom deep under an ocean with his eyes closed, directing a battle with thousands of lower managers.

She streamed down toward him, saying, "Wake up; they'll be okay without you."

Tom opened his eyes as she stopped in front of him.

Sarah threw her arms around his neck, squealing, "You were going to ask me to marry you?!"

"Not surprised, were you?" Tom said, hugging her tightly and kissing her temple.

"Well, no," Sarah said. "But still, you were going to ask me to marry you! You wanted to marry me!"

"I still do!" Tom said, laughing some. "How can't I?"

Sarah smiled and kissed him.

"But, well…"

"Yeah," Sarah said. "He explained that too."

"What do you think?"

Sarah looked surprised at him. "I love you, Tom. But what kind of question is that?"

Tom smiled at her. "Okay," he said, heaving a breath.

"Hey, nothing changes," Sarah shrugged. "I still won't ever leave you alone, and this way we know we both *want* to marry each other…"

"I just wish I knew *why*…" Tom said.

Sarah smiled, and for the first time sadness showed through. "We'll—" she began, but she trailed off. She nodded over past Tom's shoulder.

Tom looked, and saw a frenzied wall of people rising up from deeper in the ocean, flying helter-skelter toward the air. Many of them were crashing through Tom's still concentrating N'nüährnär.

And more people were rocketing around from other directions. It was chaos. And now some of Tom's people were taking off after them.

"What's going on?" Tom called to a plainly panicking woman shooting past.

"Thahn!" the woman shrieked. "She's almost here!"

"So?" Sarah whispered indignantly.

"This doesn't look good," Tom said, and shot up toward the surface. He ended the others' simulation. "Come with me," he told them.

He sliced up out of the water, where the air was boiling with N'nüährnär flying in every direction.

26: One of Those Times

"Tom!" John flew up with Tom's trainees beside him and Sarah. "What is it?"

"Thahn," Sarah said. "Apparently she's almost here."

"Everyone, stop!"

Tom felt like an idiot when he said it, but his voice was backed by a surging power that felt like it commanded everything around. A great many of the nearest people did stop, looking at Tom the Ōmāthäär to hear what to do.

"Tell me what you've heard," he said with the same compelling energy, more gathering with the clump around him Sarah and John.

"You, tell me," Tom said to a man nearest him.

"Thahn's been spotted," the man said. "She's less than an hour away. And she has more forces than we expected."

"How much?"

The man stuttered.

"I heard it was ten thousand systems," another man said.

"That's ridiculous!" a woman said. "I heard five hundred."

"No, a thousand," someone else said.

"Alright," Tom said. "A hundred or a million, it's more than we can imagine."

"We've got to get out of here!" one person said. "We can't win! Of course Mär will—"

"What if Mär doesn't say to leave?" Sarah demanded. "Will you stay?"

"Are you nuts?"

"Of course he'll say to leave!"

"And after all that talk about Ōhōnŭäär—"

"And Är," Tom cut in. His voice was not raised, but inaudible Ärthähr was backing every syllable.

"Mär *will* save Ōhōnŭäär. But that does not require fleeing.

"Remember what Peter Garcia told you: Mär said at the very beginning that Sĕrĕhahn would try to crush us with an unsurvivable blow. The Ōmāthäär have known all along what they've been doing.

"They know Thahn. They know Sĕrĕhahn.

"And they have said we will stay.

"Because, remember, Ōhōnŭäär is not important if it isn't from Är!

"Är is *infinite*! He can defeat the armies of Thahn.

"Do you believe that, or do you believe the Ōmāthäär are lying?"

"Why hasn't Är saved us before, if he can save us now?" one man demanded.

"Are you serious?" Sarah said. "Just a few days ago we were totally outnumbered. How many armies can win against ten to one odds against a better equipped and better trained army? How many times has that ever happened, ever?"

"Think of pirates," Tom said. "Think of the wars in the Wild Lands. There has never been a battle like the one we just *lived through.*

"Do you have no mind? Are you so intent on only believing what you can already comprehend that you'll find any explanation for our success as long as it isn't Är?"

No one answered, though Tom could see the angry disagreement in their eyes.

"Är can do more than keep us alive," Sarah said. "Stay with Mär! He knows Är. He does want the best for all of us."

A few people seemed placated, but most of the rest of Tom and Sarah's audience was already moving off.

"I can't believe this," one of the others with them said. "A week ago, all these people were so ready to stand and fight to the end. Now look at them!"

"We have to save our families," one woman protested pleadingly.

"And I don't?" Sarah demanded contentiously.

The woman shook her head and joined the surging chaos flying by all around them.

"*Nŭährnär!*" A lion-like voice roared in all their hearing.

"Mär," Tom said.

The orderless tides of deserting N'nŭährnär shuddered as many of them momentarily paused in their hurried scrambling.

"Thahn is here," Mär's voice rang out. "She means to destroy us all. I believe she means to destroy Pp'ōhōnŭäär. She has brought an army more than large enough to finish us without any effort.

"And I know she has brought quite a few Ämäthōär with her.

"Nevertheless, *do not be afraid.*"

Far away outside the Shell, Annie Garcia tried to steel her heart as she willed herself to trust Mär. She didn't bother going back.

"I can't beat Thahn. I can't.

"We Ōmäthäär cannot beat these Ämäthōär. Our defenses are trivial against Thahn's army.

"*We* cannot win this battle.

"We Ōmäthäär helped a great deal to turn the tide last week. We will not be able to this time. Thahn's Ämäthōär will turn the tide superfluously against us more than we Ōmäthäär will be able to counteract.

26: One of Those Times

"We can no longer depend on ourselves.

"This is one of those times when we have to steady our breath, relax, and step out into the darkness from which no capacity of our own can deliver us.

"This is one of those times when preparing is past, and we see through action what kind of power we're made of.

"This is when we see who is stupid, and depends on himself, and who is ready to access Eternal Power, and let Eternal Capacity access him!

"I want no part of any R'dōněmär. All you who cannot wrap yourselves around the fact that Är is and always has been right under your nose, everywhere, all around you, the Man, the Infinite, all you who will not believe that an Infinite Savior can make our finite bastion for freedom and hope endure against *anything*, all you who are so afraid of the possibility of truth, who govern everything you do in response to fear, leave!

"Get out!

"See where fear takes you!

"All you who respect yourselves, who value life and yourselves and everyone too, trust me!

"We are not trying to fool you into staying.

"I have never lied to you.

"Believe that as you want to let yourselves believe it, but there really do exist people who aren't liars. I am one.

"Think:

"*I* have nothing to gain if you stay; the chances of survival for all who stay will be nil, regardless of how many of us stay. Neither all of Nŭährnär nor part of Nŭährnär will offer so much as a spot of resistance against these forces.

"But 'chances' are not what we are relying on here.

"Chances will never get anyone beyond the mundane.

"Chances say, over and over, that Nŭährnär should never, ever have survived longer than a day against Sěrěhahn.

"Who among you can still believe in chances, now?"

Lewis's demoralizing battle exercise had ceased in the tumult, and now as he listened to Mär's desperately passionate words, he found himself afraid to hope that they could be any more than just words.

"If you are determined to believe there are no stars, how long will it take you, staring at them day after day, to allow yourselves to acknowledge that there are?

"How long will it take you stubborn, fearful people, staring into Är's intervention for Nŭährnär day after day, to step up to acknowledge that he is?

"Are you just afraid of being wrong? Are you afraid of appearing foolish?

"Because fearing to believe something just for fear of being wrong, far more often than not, leaves us in erroneous disbelief. Failing to act, to make choices, to *do*, just for fear of appearing foolish is so *incredibly* foolish!

"Fear is only motivating, and de-motivating, to weak people.

"Stop being weak!

"If you flee, you die. Do you really think Thahn is going to let you go?

"If you stay, many of you are certain you will die, or be tortured by the Ämäthöär; many of you, who won't risk testing if Är really is.

"Some think they'll at least have a chance if they flee.

"They underestimate Thahn. They underestimate her resources, her ships' speed and the range of their detection.

"If you abandon everything that's worth living for, you will be better off killed by Thahn.

"Many of you are afraid for your families. As you should be. Not afraid, but concerned for their welfare.

"That's better than cowardice for your own lives.

"So I am telling you: you, and your loved ones, we all have no chance anywhere but here with Ōhōnŭäär. If you flee, you will be dead within hours. If we stay, we very well may die, valiantly, in the peaceful fulfillment that worthy death brings, but then we may not. Here is where we at least have a chance.

"Not because of martial capabilities. Not because of strategy, not our own strategies, and not because of Ōmäthäär.

"Är will stop Thahn. And he will preserve us to fight Sĕrĕhahn, *if we are ready to give what such a fight demands.*

"Är knows what Thahn does not.

"Thahn has been known to outthink enemies many times her own strength. Don't you think Är can outthink fallible Thahn?

Rene Trotter steadied herself. Mär was right. She knew he was right.

They were going to be okay.

She leaned into Scott, who put his arm around her.

"I, as head manager of all of you, tell you, do not force any of your assistants, or anyone, to stay.

"If any are still so unthinking as to leave here, still so fearfully blind as to run from the possibility of Är's actuality, then keeping them here will be no better for them. Let them go.

"But I also tell all of you, that *here* is where hope is, and nowhere else!"

Brittney took a steadying breath, holding back her terrified tears. She was going to stay. She was going to stay, no matter what.

26: One of Those Times

She could not believe what her life had become. That it was going to end like this.

"Remember who we are," Mär said. "Remember why we're doing this.

"Remember the Fight we are fighting in. The ongoing War of goodness, and happiness, and glory, against short-sighted chaotic evil, and universal entropic misery.

"Why do we bother? Why do good people try so hard in this War that, to the pessimist, looks like it will never end?

"Back at Nrathĕrmĕ, almost all of Ahntä's Ōmäthäär were slaughtered.

"Was it a failure?

"For every single N'nrathĕrmĕ who was trained and enlivened by their tutoring, who got to enjoy living life instead of grey pointlessness, for every person who was helped or cheered or taught by Ahntä's Ōmäthäär, for them it was no failure.

"To cultivate just a little more happiness, anywhere, is worth it to such people.

"To work against evil, to make the world just a little better, to move the balance just a little more in favor of happiness and away from misery, just a little bit more, is so much more than worth it to such people.

"I have seen The End. The final End of the whole War of good over evil. I know Är, and he's shown me what it'll be like. It's total, it's perfect. It's everything we could ever want to see even if we feared we never really would.

"But now, right now, is enough for me at this moment. Just moving the world a little closer to happiness and farther from darkness is enough for me.

"The Fight has come so far. If you cannot see that, then I think you need to get better involved.

"Think of Nrathĕrmĕ.

"It was once called Närdamähr. Then Sĕrĕhahn arose. We know so little about his start, or about Närdamähr before him, but as long as he has steered Nrathĕrmĕ it has been devoid of the fire and joy that acquaintance with Är gives! The Ämäthōär have directed it behind its peoples' consciousness, and Sĕrĕhahn has swelled his Ämäthōärs' ranks, corrupting some of the most talented people who then serve to keep his enslavement over the sextillions of other wonderful, masterful people.

"They could be so much, but they aren't.

"Think of Earth, and its past."

Spalding, having given up persuading his and Tävna's assistants not to scatter, started paying a little more attention at the mention of Earth.

"From the very beginning, there was oppression and selfishness and fear and pain and cruel darkness.

"Empires, wars, inequality. Man abusing and disregarding man.

"And I'm not just talking about old times. Right up until the time that our Nŭährnär got here, Earth was putrefying in hate and apathy and horrors.

"The crimes of Earthly humanity were at least as vile as the most despicable evils I've witnessed in the Wild Lands. Love was a foreign feeling to so many, to individuals and general societies. Selfishness, ignorance, pride, willing reality to fit their ridiculous notions and desires, that was the way of so many.

"And for many of you Earthmen, that has not changed.

"So, really, why do we bother?

"What's worth fighting for? Närdamähr is benighted, and Earth society is diseased."

Andrew couldn't believe Mär was addressing this openly. What kind of motivational speech was this? He had been ready to give up on Earth himself, only his faith to the Ōmäthäär binding him there. But now what was Mär saying?

"Why do we bother?"

"Think of Närdamähr again:

"As long as there have been Ämäthöär, there have been Ōmäthäär.

"From the earliest fogs of our knowledge, those marvelous, wonderful heroes have given everything they could in every passing day to help move the cause of good. They embraced every opportunity in this great Fight to deliver the world from evil to peace, lighting the way, forging out paths for the, to them, unknown people who might bear off the Fight after them.

"All their hearts, their every energy, was put to making life, and all existence, as much better as they could for everyone around them. Every day, every hour, some progress was made, some gallant, if unnoticed, heroism was executed. Every day they lived and risked and worked and labored and cried and endured and hoped for *everyone*.

"And on Earth, those mighty heroes who gave and give everything, *everything*, to bring joy and reality and everything to everyone around them, and to the unseen hosts to follow them.

"The persecuted who endured, who gave all their substance, their time, everything, who used it all for the helping of everything, for the moving of the world on toward good!

"The unadmired who pressed ever ahead, sacrificing to help the very people who worked against them! Who loved, and lived, and gave; unthanked, unrecognized, even unheard, but never losing their sight of saving

26: One of Those Times

the world, again and again, for the good of *all*, and against the universal misery that evil by its very nature *will* ultimately cause.

"There have been so many noble pioneers in the histories of Närdamähr and of Earth.

"And for what? For making life better for their times only? Or for fighting for the great End, the ultimate Victory that *will come* of liberty and joy embracing *everything* and darkness being consumed, utterly!

"Är is not flawed! His Plan is not second-rate!

"He, and only an Infinite intelligence like his, can bring happiness to everyone!

"But he will never force us to be what we don't want to be.

"Good is going to triumph!

"The day will actually come, it will actually happen, and we will be there just as we are now, whether still mortal like this or not, and we will be there when all good achieves perfection, total victory, and when all evil, all fear, all ignorance, weakness, darkness, all of it will be swallowed up in the understanding of the conquering good, the interlocked happiness of everyone who can be happy! Of all of us, if we are not locked and determined to hate and destroy all happiness, most especially our own.

"Understand: the good brings, through its many apparent convolutions, eventual real happiness to everyone, bringing it to them each in their way.

"The evil is everything that does not do that, that will not bring happiness.

"No matter how much it may appear to in short sight.

"There is a good, there is an evil. This is not a matter of opinion.

"The Ämäthöär and I have opposing goals, but their goals are nonetheless evil; they will lead to misery for the Ämäthöär themselves no less than they will for everyone else. Even more!

"And the good will triumph.

"Through us!

"It must be through us! Good cannot just 'happen;' it is by the great heroism of people!

"Through all our known histories of Närdamähr and of Earth, think of all the miracles, the wonders, the magnificent victories Är has worked for every man or woman who has stepped up to ally himself with everything!

"With Är.

"Remember, remember everything Är's done for people who have given their all to defend good and truth, and happiness.

"G'nhō opened the chasm in the mountains. Moses opened the very water of the sea.

Light and Glory

"Both were miracles beyond the ability, beyond the imagination, of the people they saved! Both were *miracles*, from Är, working through courageous people who knew and trusted him, to save the Nŭährnär, really, of their respective times.

"Remember the fall of the M'närdamähr that G'nhō did so much to save:

"They were like us. Fearful. They didn't know Är. They didn't want to.

"*The Ämäthōär destroyed them because they forfeited the power they could have had.* They did not back the Ōmäthäär who tried to lead them, and they perished.

"Moses's Jacobites, the unlikely Nŭährnär of his time, were fearful, petty, selfish.

"Just as we're being.

"They were the Nŭährnär, the refuge of the truth and of the tattered remnants of the once mighty Ōmäthäär of Earth. They were like us, the families and the families' families of exiled Ōmäthäär, and they, too, had a great deal of—difficulty—in trusting their Ōmäthäär leaders and their Är.

"But they pulled through.

"They trusted Är just enough to survive.

"Remember Enoch, Ŭdhōär, Joseph. Ahntä.

"Remember what our heritage is. Remember what we're involved in!

"Why are we doing this?

"We must restore Närdamähr to peace and good! We must preserve Ōhōnŭäär from the evil that has tried, again and again for so long, to capture it!

"I am going to fight here, to fight as those marvelous people fought for ages before. I am going to fight Thahn; just the most recent attempt of evil against the rising light of good.

"The dawn is coming.

"I mean to be on the good's side when it comes.

"What are we doing?

"Why do we care?

"What are we fighting for? Why?

"*I am going to fight, right here, right now*—and if I have to, I will die—to help to move the struggle of truth over tyranny to, finally, to its long-awaited End.

"I will not leave hope.

"I will not leave those great heroes of our history to fight alone!

"And even if you will not fight for yourselves, I will fight for you!

"I love you, I love our founding saviors, and I will fight for their legacy

26: One of Those Times

and for you!

"I will fight for all good! Regardless of what happens to me in the process.

"Now, do what you know is best."

His voice left a weighty vacuum in the air of the Shell as it finished.

Tom looked at the people yet standing around him and Sarah.

He smiled through his fear.

"And I, I am not going to leave him alone," he said.

"Me neither," Sarah choked through her sniffling tears.

"Nor I," one of the people in front of them said.

"No," another woman said. "You are right."

"Yeah."

"No matter what."

"Yeah, no matter what."

"Well," John said, "At least some of us are staying, then."

"Yeah," another of them nodded.

"I hope it'll be enough," John said.

One of the people shook his head. "It doesn't matter," he said.

"Yeah," Sarah nodded. "Only a miracle will save us."

"I hope Mär has one more in him," a woman whispered.

Chapter 27

Outguessing Thahn

"We've been scanning her fleet as much as we can," Mär went on. "There's no use pretending we don't know she's here; she'd see right through that, anyhow."

Tom tried not to be afraid as he listened with the other Ōmäthäär to this last briefing. Not even the comfort of the Sanctuary made him feel any lighter. He tightened his arm around Sarah.

"Parts of her fleet have slowed down. It's been difficult to see anything definite about her ships, but I've seen her do this kind of thing before."

"Just never with this many forces," he whispered, but then rounded up his shoulders.

"She is going to surround us on every side. She doesn't need the tactical advantage; she just wants to catch as many of us as she can. She doesn't want any N'nüährnär to escape."

"I fear for any who try to flee now. They'll never see her coming."

"Which is yet another problem. Even as close as her fleet's coming, we still cannot detect her ships very well."

"Antr's information leads us to believe that most of her ships are hollow spheres only a few ten thousand athz across."

"That does make some sense. If Ä'ävär's clan's findings were right, that would mean Thahn has almost three hundred thousand such ships. But those will be more than enough."

"Barely a score ships like that would be able to take on all of Nüährnär."

"A few of us were afraid Thahn would put all her matter into only a few hundred ships, with an Ämäthöär on board every one. But this seems to indicate that there will only be Ämäthöär on about one ship in every thousand."

"So the others will be naked."

Tom still didn't know what Mär meant by referring to the ships as 'naked.'

"All of us who are going to board, we will have to work perfectly. There will be no time for any hesitations."

"What does he mean, 'board?'" Sarah's voice asked him.

Tom shook his head bewilderedly. "How do you board an operational ship?" he wondered back to her. "With its energy frame and all?"

"I will board Thahn's ship. Ŭkan, Ärdhär, and Hŭrnhä, you may come with me, if you still want to."

27: Outguessing Thahn

"Absolutely," Hŭrnhä said.

"We will," Ŭkan nodded.

"The rest of you, when we give the word, attack every ship *except* for the ones we designate.

"Those will be the ones we are boarding.

"If the tide turns against us—it most likely will; there are too few of us to engage these Ämäthōär—you will have to direct Nŭährnär to destroy the ships we have boarded. As long as we can destroy the Ämäthōärs' ships before they kill the Ōmäthäär on board, their guard ought to be weakened enough that the destruction of the ship will destroy them.

"There can be no hesitation. If one Ämäthōär escapes, we may not have another chance to effectively, or almost effectively," he smiled grimly, "Engage him. If the Ämäthōär are overcoming the Ōmäthäär on board any ship, that ship must be destroyed immediately.

"Anyone assigned to board who is not willing to give his life to take down these Ämäthōär, tell us now. There is no time."

No one was surprised by the silence.

Thahn closed her eyes.

"He'll know we're encircling them," she continued. "He will try to maneuver his way out of this. He will try to get Hûhōnĕrrŭ itself away from us."

"Ōhōnŭäär will have to join the fight," Mär was saying. "It must move as quickly as the rest of us. Thahn must not capture it, and she must not destroy it."

Thahn skimmed along the treetops within her commanding battleship.

"He knows he cannot fight us. But be ready for his Ōmäthäär to try anything."

"We cannot fight Thahn or her fleet," Mär said. "She will be waiting for us to try anything desperate.

"But she won't be expecting this."

"Watch them," Thahn continued to her R'bathĕrŭ. "Find every one of them and wait for them to try anything.

"As soon as you feel *anything*, alert everyone else!"

* * *

"Everything depends on this next hour.
"Everything depends on surviving this one blow.
"On beating her."

"Mär is dangerous when he's desperate. He will not accept defeat until he's completely defeated.
"Do not let your guard down.
"This is serious."

"I hope," Mär said with the first sign of worry, "That we're interpreting Zōrd's associates' silence correctly."

"I love you all," Thahn smiled, stretching out her arms as she arrived in the center of her ship's cool sky. "Let's do our best!
"For the glory of Hûhōněrrŭ!"

"For Ōhōnŭäär," Mär said.
"For Ä'ähänärdanär."
He clapped his hands together.
"Let's fight."

"No, no one move," Tom said to his assistants. "There's no use trying to confuse Thahn. Save your energy."
"I can't see anything," Määrhan said.
"She's right there," Tom said. "I'm afraid we'll see her ships all too soon."
No others of his assistants said anything. Nŭährnär might have been cut nearly in half, but still he knew his assistants had plenty of people to coordinate.
He shivered, as he thought what must have already happened to the tens of billions who had fled.
"Är, help us," he whispered.

"As soon as Anthŭ's divisions are in place," Thahn's voice said, "Clamp the sphere down on them.
"This time Mär will not have an escape."
Ě'ěthr'rŭ the R'batherŭ felt his body relax entirely.
He could feel Mär's counterfeits. He could feel that they were afraid.
This may work, he thought guardedly. *Oh, this might really work!*
He directed all his energy at the Ōmäthäär.

27: Outguessing Thahn

They were planning something, he could feel that.
"Keep an eye on them," he called to the other R'bathĕrŭ. "Can you feel that?"
"Feel each other," Thahn's voice said. "We have to work in tandem."
"Prepare to attack."
It was a few awful moments of sudden, incredible pain before Ĕ'ĕthr'rŭ realized he was screaming.

Thahn felt the attack just before it came.
Her Ärthähr sealed itself within her as she felt the sudden force trying to tear her apart.
It was coming from her crew, the N'nrathĕrmĕ right there in her ship!
Pä the Ōmäthäär threw everything he had at the now terrifying Ämäthōär whom he had obeyed as his commander for the past five weeks.
Cut off the power! he willed to the others.
He felt Thahn's Ärthähr slice through him.
Then everything in the ship went dark. Pä could still see by rantha, but there was no light anywhere.
He fought back against the horrible scream of terror filling him as Thahn's Ärthähr tore at every corner of his body and mind.
He hoped Mär would know what to do.

Mär was floating with his three companions among the motionless defenses. Nothing was happening.
What if they had guessed wrong? What if no Ōmäthäär had come with Thahn's army, and the silence from the Ōmäthäär who were supposed to be at Nrathĕrmĕ meant something else, something they could not guess?
Är would take care of them, he told himself.
No matter how he was going to do it, he trusted that Är would take care of them.
But then, the thought that the others had disguised aboard Thahn's own strike army had felt so good.
And it was so unlike him; Thahn would never foresee—
And then it happened.
A ship appeared, stealthless and apparently shieldless, a chillingly short distance away.
And before Mär could utter any command, more ships began appearing in every direction.
Thousands, hundreds of thousands of unmoving spheres were emerging

Light and Glory

into view, arranged in a loose cage around Nŭährnär's defenses.

"GO!" Mär shouted.

He and his three friends hurled themselves, instantly reaching more than six hundred times light's speed, straight at Thahn's shieldless, inert command ship.

Thahn was surprised at her surprise. She knew of few who were adept enough at Ärthähr to hide such a plot right under her nose. And for so long!

One more of the N'nrathĕrmĕ Ōmäthäär succumbed. She focused her will on the other twelve.

She could feel the unbearable pain of their assaults against her thin in the tiniest way. She was beating them.

And Mär just wouldn't have done something like this! her assaulted mind raged. He couldn't have! They had kept their voyage secret until they had gone far from Nrathĕrmĕ.

Unless...

There was another traitor among the Ämäthöär.

She bridled her fury and focused more intently on the fading Ärthähr within her foes. She got a better hold of the life within herself.

Then, her fingers flexing with energy, she threw herself at the nearest of them.

Her arms parried his hands away, her hands connected with his terror-struck face, and he fell immediately dead.

She turned and, screaming with focused emotion, pounced on the next pitiful stowaway.

"*Charge!*" Sarah screamed.

Her fleets rampaged forward. Rantha poured from them, crashing into Thahn's nakedly unshielded vessels. Thousands of warships collapsed in eruptions of light, then fell back in on themselves, the fragments of their superdense hulls clumping in harmless hulks.

"Sarah, kill the one at 31°, 178°!" Äōhäŭdär shouted.

"Include 31°, 178 °!" Sarah commanded.

So the Ōmäthäär were already losing.

"And at 28°, 161°!" Äōhäŭdär called.

Sarah's voice shook as she relayed the command.

Another Ōmäthäär crumpled dead in a dark shiver. Thahn sprang to the next. The woman broke before Thahn touched her, dropping her attack and

27: Outguessing Thahn

screaming in abject terror.

Barely a swipe of the fingers slammed the life out of her, and Thahn pivoted gracefully toward the last two.

He was there, she realized.

Mär emerged out of the floor of her warship's unshielded hull, followed by Ŭkan, Ärdhär, and Hŭrnhä.

Thahn instantly engaged the six of them, as the new Ōmäthäärs' power seared through every part of her.

"Mär," she said, forcing the words through her consuming suffering. "What have you done?"

Mär didn't answer. His eyes were focused on the face of his mentor.

"And you, Thardŭ," she added to Ŭkan. "I'm surp—"

"My name is Ŭkan!" he snarled.

Ärdhär screamed and hurled herself at Thahn.

Mär lunged after her.

Thahn deftly knocked Ärdhär's outstretched hand away, grabbed her other arm, then struck her chest.

At that moment, Mär touched Ärdhär's back as he punched straight at Thahn's face.

Ŭkan and Hŭrnhä arced around at the Ämäthōär as Ärdhär choked back to life.

Thahn knocked Mär's furious fist away and clasped his throat.

One of the N'nrathĕrmĕ Ōmäthäär raced up behind Thahn, who released Mär and turned with lightning speed, faster than any inertial speed, and struck the woman's arm away and thrust her other hand over her eyes.

Mär recovered himself almost immediately, the darkness racing back out of him. He screamed passionately as he leapt again at Thahn.

Thahn turned as the woman crumpled, snatching Mär's hand by the wrist as she dodged her legs away from Hŭrnhä's attack.

Mär's vision blackened, and his mind flickered in incomprehensible torment.

Then he heard Ŭkan's scream rise above the receding shriek of unnatural noise, and realized Thahn had had to release him once more.

Opening himself back to enlivening Ärthähr, he felt warmth fill him more slowly; he hurled himself back at the horrifying Thahn, just as Ŭkan's living light went out.

"Watch out! 65°, 287°!" Tom shouted to everyone around.

The warship at 65°, 287° had sprung back to life, fading almost entirely from sight as it roared into the attacking N'nŭährnär armadas.

"Just evade it!" Tom commanded. "We can't do much against it now, but we can still take out the rest!"

The armored sphere of Earth, hardly noticeable amidst the variegated defenses, was rocketing evasively away from the newly revived warship. Tom's assistants were scattering far and wide. The N'nratherme warship was eradicating all N'nŭährnär it could catch.

"Keep spreading out! Take out the naked ones!"

Another ship far away came to life and charged into the thitherto one-sided battle. Tom could see many N'nŭährnär fleets engaging the small vessel, but its superior rantha was decimating them while its shields almost totally repelled any rantha that managed to hit.

Tom veered evasively around. His assistants were doing beautifully.

But then he saw that many of his ships were scattering too far.

"Come back!" he yelled, realizing what they were doing.

To be fair, he had almost wished he had fled himself when Thahn's army had appeared around them. Now that doom was returning, he knew, even those who had stayed this far were breaking and flying away while they still could.

"We can destroy them!" he said, hoping it was true.

Most of his forces were still bearing down on the defenseless warships, but more N'nŭährnär were breaking away every second, scared out of their morals by seemingly inescapable death.

He saw Thahn's command ship. It was still sitting motionlessly.

Mär was having trouble.

Mär lunged forward at Thahn, but a powerful blast of Ärthähr threw him from her. Crashing through treetops he felt his body slam deep into the woodland floor.

He felt more exhausted than he ever had since leaving Nratherme as he flew back to the fight.

Then his heart froze.

"Mänrŭ!" he yelled to the N'nratherme Ōmäthäär as he shot around away from Thahn's lunge. Five Ämäthöär were emerging from the ground behind Mänrŭ.

"Thahn!" one of the Ämäthöär shouted.

Thick darkness filled everything.

Mär could only barely make out Mänrŭ engaging two of the Ämäthöär, his arms flying, his body dodging every way as he darted back from the Ämäthöär

27: Outguessing Thahn

all around the warship's cavernous courtyard.

Thahn was on him. He couldn't see anything, but he could feel her. He pushed out with everything he could.

His senses rose above the terror again as he heard Ärdhär's scream announce her arrival, Thahn's hands releasing his head.

It was only a matter of time, he knew, as he threw himself at Thahn. The Ämäthöär were going to kill them.

It was only a matter of time before their wills broke and the ship's systems were no longer stopped by their Ärthähr.

Nüährnär was doomed.

Är, help!

"It doesn't matter now!" Sarah cried. "Let them go! Take out as many dead ones as we can!"

Three more warships had sprung to life.

"Kill 36°, 234°; 78°, 203°; and 81°, 40°!" Äōhäŭdär shouted desperately.

Soon they'd have to take out Mär, too, she thought.

"Nōath, take out 36°, 234°! Rtōbähn, 78°, 203°! Ppahär, 81°, 40°!"

"Alright," she heard Rtōbähn say miserably.

"They're dying for us!" Sarah made herself say. "We should be able to revive them!"

She hoped that was true.

The N'nrathĕrmĕ warships were guarding their as yet inert companions, destroying almost all N'nüährnär who came close. Earth was maneuvering as far from any of them as it could get.

Sarah felt cold as she realized what those people were who were moving from the operational ship to that dead one.

"Tänthät!" she called. "Go in and blast 21°, 191° when I say!"

If she timed it right, she knew, right when the Ōmäthäär had the Ämäthöärs' Ärthähr occupied enough but before the tide turned totally against them, the Ämäthöär would be distracted enough that rantha would be as deadly to them as to anyone else.

She veered her fleets frantically back and forth, looking for any opening to hit some of the warships nearest her.

"Now, Tänthät!"

Tänthät's fleets forked wide around the guarding warship, pulverizing both the boarded vessel and another naked one before scattering away from the rantha-hurling warship bearing down against them.

More of Sarah's fleets were scattering away, abandoning the survival of their friends and ideals to escape the terror of the warships.

She was glad the Ämäthōär were so occupied; seeing them influencing the battle would have been true terror.

But even without the Ämäthoärs' darkness, Thahn's few operational ships were still pursuing and eradicating the N'nŭährnär fleets with horrible speed. Only the N'nŭährnärs' distance from one another had kept them from already being overwhelmingly exterminated.

She could see Earth darting about to keep distance from the N'nrathĕrmĕ.

"Sarah," she then heard Tom's voice call.

"What," she replied, maneuvering closer to an unattended dead warship.

"Keep them busy! We've got to give Mär time!"

Sarah veered back closer to one of the ravaging warships.

"R'mäbhän!" she called.

Her Ōmäthäär assistant was gone.

"Tänthät!" she called without missing a beat. "Distract that warship by you! Take out as many dead ones as you can; that ought to get his attention!"

She pulled her ships around, spitting rantha at a solitary warship. It exploded and crumpled in the unshielded rantha.

"Vŭ'thōaōaōs, draw them away from Earth!"

"Änathä—"

He and Bähd were gone too.

This could not be happening.

They would revive them, as soon as they saved themselves.

"Aranŭ, go with Vŭ'thōaōaōs!'

She banked sharply down as another of the live warships charged toward her. She was actually grateful as more of her forces fled madly away, the warship following them instead of the ones still with her.

She shot down another of the remaining sitting ducks.

There were only a few left, including Thahn's and one more as yet unsacrificed boarded vessel.

The ships whose energy the Ōmäthäär had stopped up having been almost all destroyed anyway, the guarding N'nrathĕrmĕ apparently gave up defending them.

Now, instead, the seven operational warships converged around Earth.

Two of them had already been chasing the armored planet, the pilots of Earth maneuvering frantically to stay out of range or to dodge what rantha did get released at the world while the two ships tried to trap it between them.

The Shell kept sending off great bursts of rantha, but even what rantha did hit the pursuers did them no visible harm.

Thahn

...r to commandeer those two
...her five warships sped

...rage her at all.

...
...nst him.
...ead.
...'s Ämäthōär cut him off.
...ore.
...hardly noticed as his arms raced,
power into him.
...elt Ärdhär's presence vanish.

[folded corner text: around Earth. powerful broadsides at ...ad on. They weren't ...ally away, spinning ...h flickered out. ...ame a scream of ...ful N'nŭährnär Pp'ŏhŏnŭäär]

...ere!"

...om responded furiously. He could not believe how
...g. "We have to help him! We have to get those ships!"
, Tom," another higher manager said, "Get out while you

... not have time for this, Tom thought enragedly as he wondered
... could do.
...e're with you, Tom," he heard John's voice call. "As many of my
...ple as will come."
Many N'nŭährnär were rushing toward Earth, as if to help somehow. Small though the warships may have been, they paid as little concern to the N'nŭährnär as determined hunters might to buzzing flies while they methodically trapped their quarry.

"We need more!" Tom said. "We can't fight Ämäthōär; we need to overwhelm them!"

People's resolve were breaking every instant; a steady stream of N'nŭährnär was racing out away from the battle, most fleeing away in the opposite direction from Nrathĕrmĕ.

"Then we need to go!" he heard Annie Garcia's voice command. "Now! Let's go!"

"We need more," Sarah insisted.

But Annie was right, Tom knew. They had no time.

Then the other spared boarded warship burst into life. It raced to join the seven others outthinking the desperate N'nŭährnär le

But Tom was amazed to see the new ship fire three
the other seven.

Caught unsuspecting, three of the hunters were hit d
destroyed, but their rantha ceased and they wobbled errati
off in the middle of their racing after the planet as their steal

Tom almost cried out for renewed hope, but his cry be
disbelief.

Relaxing just a hair in its evasion at the sight of the powe
warship, the Earth was instantly caught by three powerful bursts

Rantha sliced terribly through energy, Shell, and planet.
disintegrated in an unreal eruption of fire and light.

Chapter 28

Blaze of Glory

Sarah could not believe what she was seeing.

Earth. Ōhōnŭäär.

It was gone.

"Okay, I'm going to Mär now," Tom's voice called through the haze of horror. "Even if I'm going alone."

"No!" she called. "Meet me before you go in!"

"Me too," John said.

"And me," Annie called. "But I can't give you many of my people."

"Nor mine," came Brittney's voice.

"Everyone's scattering," Tävna said. "Guess they think Mär was wrong..."

"I'm going to save him," Tom said quaveringly. "If you don't want to die, don't—"

"Stop," Sarah said.

"Yeah," another higher manager said, "We have no choice now."

"Everyone, to Mär!" Sarah called to every assistant and assistant's assistant still alive and with her. "To the command ship!"

A heartening number of vessels streaked in from all around, gathering toward Thahn's ship amidst the routing ruins of Nŭährnär.

Two of the seven live warships broke away to chase down the escaping remnants, and the other five engaged the one N'nŭährnär vessel worth any threat. One of them, having left itself open to the N'nŭährnär battleship as it focused on Earth, had been severely damaged, but the four crippled ships with their unhurt companion were more than a match for their solitary foe.

"We have to go in together!" Tom called as he approached the sedentary shape of Thahn's commanding vessel. "We can't fight them, but we may be able to overwhelm them!"

A few score thousand ships were streaking in from every direction.

He had no idea what they were going to do, but that didn't matter.

They just had to do whatever they could for all that was left that was good, which didn't seem to be much more than Mär anymore.

This was the moment.

Mär was the last one left.

Ŭkan, Ărdhär, Hŭrnhä, the moles from Nrathĕrmĕ, all of them had fallen under the Ărthähr of Thahn and the two remaining Ämäthöär.

He was only barely holding on to consciousness. It was pain beyond screaming, beyond any release of any kind. Darkness and sheer terror intensified the torture within him, through every inch of his body and every awareness of his mind.

And yet he was holding on. He could not let go of the energy within the ship. He had to hope that there was some chance, that Nŭährnär would survive, if only he could keep Thahn's ship defenseless.

He dared not let himself wonder why the ship had still not been destroyed, and forced himself to remember that there was still hope, somehow, that there was still Ăr, even as he sensed that Ōhōnŭäär had just been annihilated.

He could feel himself waning. Thahn was inevitably going to gain enough control of his living force to separate it from his body.

But he could hold on a little longer.

There must have been some reason to hold on...

He had to hold on. As long as he could, in any way.

But he was not going to be able to hold on forever...

Thahn could feel the N'nŭährnär pouring toward them, but she saw they were no threat.

Ignore them, she willed to the other two R'bathĕrŭ. *Do* not *slacken!* If any one of them eased the slightest degree in their assault, Mär might be able to recover himself and possibly even kill one of the others, making him that much harder to finally kill.

Hundreds, thousands, tens of thousands of N'nŭährnär then emerged from the spherical ground all around, rantha hitting her from every one of them.

Not a one of the Ämäthöär took any notice, their hands firmly pressed against Mär's head.

He was not moving.

And he took no more notice of his rescuers than the Ämäthöär did. But that was because of the freezing, crushing torrent raging in his deepest soul. He was unaware of anything but the need to hold on.

But then, dimly, as if in the murkiest dream, he felt something warm and beautiful draw near, like a blazing but deeply concealed fire.

And then another.

Tom had rushed right up to Mär. Terror filled his senses; he didn't care that he could hear his voice screaming, that darkness and fear were shrieking

28: Blaze of Glory

through him. His mind just wanted to run, to get away, anywhere. The fear was too much. But he had to help Mär.

He hardly noticed Thahn and the other two live Ämäthōär right there, only aware that the terror and frigidity and agony were worse, worse than he thought he could live through, the closer he came to the three of them right there.

But he reached Mär. He realized his screams had turned into sobs of Mär's name as he made to wrench Thahn's hands off of him.

Sarah was right beside him. She grabbed ahold of Mär's face, screaming with terror and fear, but also with anguish for him. Her skin pushed right up against one of the Ämäthōärs' arms.

Then Mär's limply floating body began to stir.

Thahn instantly realized what was happening as she felt Mär's life start to revive.

And, more than that, she saw in Tom and Sarah exactly what Mär was seeing, however far more clearly and vividly through her less assaulted senses.

Before she could think to stop herself, before she was aware of anything but a surge of fury and fear, she had released Mär entirely.

The full force of Thahn's power divided itself between Tom and Sarah.

It was worse than Mär had said.

Tom and Sarah were filled completely with the most soul-rending, intensely terrifying suffering. It was as if their consciousnesses, their very beings, were going to be destroyed.

They couldn't feel their bodies. They couldn't feel anything.

But they were not dead yet.

Why?

And then determination filled them both like no feeling they had ever felt before, determination and adamant desire to hold on to their selves.

And after an eternal instant of that absolute suffering, it stopped.

No sooner had Thahn released her assault on Mär than he had burst back like a spring at the Ämäthōär.

The three terrible Ämäthōär were now struggling to hold on against his miraculously rejuvenated Ärthähr. Thahn was resisting him far more firmly than he had ever resisted her, but nevertheless she was reduced almost wholly to defense.

She released Tom and Sarah, both of whom by all accounts should have been destroyed instantaneously.

And if Mär had burst back like a spring, it was nothing to Tom and Sarah.

Neither of them had ever succeeded in Ärthähr practices with Mär, but with all their will suddenly adamant against Thahn's attack and just as suddenly released, the power held latent in them for so long, for one flicker, burst out from them straight at her.

A flash of light somehow incomparably more thorough than other light saturated everything.

And Tom, Sarah, and Mär realized that they were floating in front of two dead Ämäthöär, and no trace at all of Thahn.

The light within the ship returned.

Mär laughed, sobbing, grabbing Tom and Sarah in either arm.

"Thank you! Thank you!" he babbled.

Then he dropped them. "Go help the others," he said shortly. "We have a fight to win."

Tom and Sarah looked around.

Their thousands of companions were all crumpled near the walls, almost all of them still cowering in fear.

It was the white horror on their faces that made Tom realize just how unafraid he now felt. Seconds ago, incarnate fear had been standing inches from him, even touching his head.

But, now, everything around him and Sarah felt beautifully easy and bright, and peaceful, as if nothing bad had ever happened there, ever.

"C'mon," Sarah tugged at his elbow, leading him to comfort the traumatized heroes.

Neither of them in their warm bliss noticed Mär moving back to the center of the courtyard; the idea that the battle was still raging was edged out by the light flowing all through them both.

Mär reached out his inertia to take mechanical control of the ship's systems.

The captured N'nüährnär warship was still barely surviving against the other five when Thahn's commanding sphere at last joined the battle.

Hesitating so very slightly at the welcome sight of their leader's arrival, the five N'nratherme vessels were instantly hit by broadsides from not only the N'nüährnär ship, but from Thahn's as well. The four already damaged ships were crippled, the now damaged fifth left all but alone.

Mär was almost as excellent a handler of the ship as Thahn had been. Wherever the operable N'nratherme battleship fired its rantha, Mär's ship had managed to slip away just an instant before.

The other N'nüährnär warship passed in front of Mär's. Mär darted the vessel down, firing four more blasts at the nearly immobilized ships,

28: Blaze of Glory

effectively incapacitating them.

His ship slid ahead just as powerful bolts of rantha streaked past behind.

The other ship swung up around from behind the now harmless hulks, firing rantha at the dancing N'nrathĕrmĕ warship as Mär's ship blasted at it from below.

The ship dodged Mär's bolt, but in so doing moved right into the other ship's broadside.

It swerved in its maneuvering, slowing slightly.

Both N'nŭährnär ships struck at it again.

The ship was broken.

They had won.

"Make sure they're totally disabled," Mär commanded the Ōmäthäär aboard the other ship.

"Ōhärnäth, get the N'nŭährnär out of here! Tell them to look like they're fleeing away as fast as they can. Don't spare any energy, until I tell you to come back.

"Särdnä, take every other Ōmäthäär and get in those ships! Don't let those Ämäthōär get away!"

He closed his eyes, and extended his arms. His fingers moved relaxedly.

This had to be done perfectly.

Ärthähr flowed through him. He was ready.

"Mûhĕn, Nrath'r," he heard himself call the Ämäthōär commanders of the two hunting ships.

"Thahn," Nrath'r's voice answered with relief. "Mär's dead, then?"

"Unfortunately," Mär said with Thahn's own signature of Ärthähr. "Leave the rest. We've scattered the few remaining Ōmäthäär; we'd better get back to Nrathĕrmĕ with our record."

"We did it," Mûhĕn's voice sighed. "I love it when Anhar's warnings are just warnings," she smiled.

"This warning might have been more if he hadn't warned us," Mär said; it felt right to say, even though he had little idea what his own words were meaning. He would have to take time later to think about these things the Ärthähr was intimating him to say.

He ended the connection, and glided back toward the ground.

"How are you doing?" he asked Tom and Sarah quietly.

They were standing a short distance from the ground, Tom telling some others what to do about the residual fear.

"Alive," Sarah said, but her face was glowing.

"Very," Mär smiled at her.

"How did we do that?" she asked.

"I told you I could see it in you," Mär beamed. "Sometimes it just takes something like that to—"

"But I just tried moving some things on the ground," Sarah interrupted, "And I still can't.

"I did try comforting some of my friends by touching their heads the way you do, and I think it helped, but I don't know if it really did anything."

Mär gazed thoughtfully at her. He did still look deeply exhausted.

"But you know you *can* do it," he said at last.

Sarah nodded hesitantly.

"Later," Mär said, patting her head.

"What's happening now?" she asked.

"I'm waiting to kill a few old friends," Mär said heavily. "Again.

"There are two more ships to disable, and then we'll have to kill their Ämäthöär, too.

"No, I never knew any of these, not that I know of," he assured her. "I still think of the Ämäthöär as a nasty kind of friends though; they were my friends; I think of them as nasty old friends who betrayed me in every possible way."

Sarah nodded again.

"We've got a couple minutes, though," Mär said.

"Of course, you betrayed them," Sarah smiled.

Mär sighed. "Yeah.

"But they were living betrayals of everything I had thought they stood for."

"I know," Sarah said.

Mär looked studiously at her. Then he said fervently, "Good can look like evil, and vice-versa. Listen to Ärthähr. Don't...don't oversimplify it.

"Don't oversimplify it. What looks evil can be beautiful good.

"Learn to see with Ärthähr."

Sarah nodded again. "Okay," she said uncertainly.

Mär smiled at her. "Don't talk to me until I come back."

He turned and flew back to the center of the open air.

After a short while, he could see the other two ships returning. The rest of Nüährnär had already fled far into the distance.

"Alright," Mär said as Thahn. "Help us fix up the others, and we'll start back. I've already sent a message off to Lhĕhrha."

"Alright," Nrath'r said.

As soon as the two warships were occupied directing ruined matter back

28: Blaze of Glory

to the other ships, Mär sent off two simultaneous broadsides straight at them.

"What?" Mûhĕn cried. "Thahn?"

Mär blasted another volley at them both. Ōmäthäär poured from the other N'nüährnär warship as the two N'nrathĕrmĕ ships collapsed in on themselves.

"Mär," he corrected her.

Mûhĕn and Nrath'r sped out of the crumpling wreckage, but they were overwhelmed by the outnumbering Ōmäthäär.

Mär extended Ärthähr out at his companions.

He could see several Ōmäthäär engaging each of the terrifying Ämäthöär. They were whizzing around in front of his ship, the Ämäthöär blocking every one of them, though not yet able to break through any of their parries.

He had to work quickly, before any Ōmäthäär fell.

He watched, waited, waited, and then when he saw an opening he shot a concentrated jet of rantha straight at Mûhĕn.

There was a blast of light, and she and her dark terror were gone.

Another precisely timed pulse killed the last Ämäthöär, and finally Nüährnär was safe.

At least for another couple weeks.

"Are you alright, John?" Sarah asked.

John's attempted brave smile stalled.

"I understand why Tom never wanted to talk about...them," he said.

Sarah smiled, then hugged him. She hoped that would help him in some way.

"We won," she assured him. "We actually won!"

Rather than warmth, John felt extremely awkward.

"I, uh, heard you two are getting married," he said as Sarah let go of him.

Sarah frowned sadly. "No," she said. "We want to," she said quickly, "But...it's a long story."

"Oh," John said. "So...what's happening now?"

"I don't know." She looked up at Mär's speck far away in the center of the sky. "I think Mär's fighting the last ships."

John nodded. The thought of deadly battle didn't faze him now, after feeling the Ämäthöär.

"With him piloting, we'll be fine," Sarah said, and John felt more comforted than he would have expected.

"We're good now," she said. "We're safe."

"Okay, Ōhärnäth," Mär said. "It's done! Bring them back. And call back anyone who will listen.

"I'll contact the rest, as many as made it out."

He sent his voice to every fleeing N'nüährnär vessel.

"This is Mär!" he called jubilantly. "I'm alive! *We won!* I told you we'd win!

"Come back! Thahn is dead, the Ämäthöär are all dead, we've captured two of her ships and destroyed all the rest! Come back!

"And trust me.

"If you don't believe I'm Mär, believe this:

"I told you the onslaught Sěrěhahn had spurred Nrathěrmě to send at us would be made to be unsurvivable.

"And we did all we could, and we have survived! Come back!

"I told you that Är knows better strategy than our foes do. I told you we would come out conquerors here if we followed his plans.

"I told you that Är would fight for us in this battle of good over evil, if we fought for good!

"And I told you to stop being weak.

"Stop being weak.

"You know this is me talking. Come back."

He closed the connection.

"Yeah, I know," Tom was saying comfortingly to Claire Neame. "You don't have to think about them, though. Thinking about them makes it worse."

"Usually," Mär said, gliding down behind Tom.

Claire stared, overawed, at Nüährnär's leader.

"Think about people you love," he told her. "That can help a lot."

"Okay," Claire said.

"What's happening now?" Tom asked him.

"It's over," Mär said.

"It's over?" Tom repeated.

Mär smiled at him. "You did believe Är would save us, right?"

"I tried to," Tom said. "It's kind of hard to believe anything when…"

"I know," Mär nodded. "But he saved us anyway. Now it's over. We're safe for now."

"For now?" Tom asked.

Claire and the others nearby were looking worried now as well as intimidated by Mär.

"You don't think that was it, do you?" Mär said. "Thahn is dead—thanks

28: Blaze of Glory

to you," he smiled adoringly, "And we defeated this fleet; and these resources will help us a great deal; but the Ämäthöär are not just going to let that pass.

"The N'nrathĕrmĕs' fury that we destroyed this army, and Thahn whom they loved, is going to be worse than it already is, you can be sure.

"And Sĕrĕhahn is not going to ignore all the Ämäthöär we've just killed."

"No, we're safe only for now."

"This blow was designed to destroy us utterly."

"But Sĕrĕhahn himself didn't come; that means he had doubts. He was testing Ōhōnŭäär. And you Nōhōnŭäär.

"This chapter is only just beginning."

"But Earth, Ōhōnŭäär, it's gone!" Tom said. Several of the Nōhōnŭäär around nodded miserably. "They destroyed it!" Tom said.

Mär raised his eyebrows at them. "Think about that a little more," he said then.

"What?"

"Tom, I just told Bävän and Ŭmäthŭ to revive it! They're rebuilding Ōhōnŭäär as we speak! Just the way it was, or, rather, just how it would be now if it hadn't been destroyed, down to the tiniest anthill, ants and all!"

Over the succeeding days, the debris from Thahn's army was cannibalized into new defenses and a far stronger Shell around the gorgeously glowing Earth, the unspent stuff of nearly four hundred star systems at their fingertips. Detailed analyses of the two captured warships revealed great innovations in inertial manipulation, all of which Nŭährnär was quick to implement in its fortifications.

Many of the N'nŭährnär who had fled returned, but many never came back, retreating as far from Nrathĕrmĕ as they could fly.

"How did I guess?" John grinned. He splashed down into the shallows where Tom and Sarah were floating. "I never see one of you without the other!"

"Hey, John," Tom and Sarah said at the same time.

"Ah, now your minds are merging," John said.

Sarah laughed.

"Hey, I've heard a few things about you, too," Tom said, "And a certain former assistant of yours…"

"You can't believe everything you hear," John shrugged.

"Well, what should we believe?" Sarah pressed.

John smiled as if he couldn't keep it in anymore.

"Kōrhas deserved it," he then said simply. "Getting appointed up a tier. She was amazing keeping her people together last week."

"It's already been a week?" Tom breathed.

"Almost," Sarah said quietly.

"Yeah," John said. "I just wish it were really over. M'närdamähr and Höämhär won't seem to let an hour pass without reminding us how much we still have to do about the N'nrathĕrmĕ."

Tom nodded. "I've been talking to them a lot about that. But don't worry, John. We deserve a rest!"

"Are they all back yet?" Sarah asked.

"Well, like you already know, Kōrhas isn't my assistant anymore. And I don't think Tas and Räm are going to come back. And no one knows what happened to Mayaben; I'm thinking she was killed. But the other four, yeah. I'm going to have to appoint some more, sometime here."

"Do it soon," Tom said seriously. "We need organization. We can rest, but Sĕrĕhahn's going to hit us again."

"I wish I could be as confident about it as you," John said.

"It's Mär, he's rubbing off on me," Tom smiled.

"It's nice knowing what you three were up to all this time," John said. "How's it coming?"

Tom looked at Sarah. "Same as always, pretty much..."

"We are doing better," Sarah said optimistically.

"But no, not like the Ōmäthäär," Tom said to John.

"Not like the *other* Ōmäthäär, you mean," John grinned.

"Yeah," Tom shrugged.

They floated contently in the warm, clear water.

"How's Annie?" Sarah asked after a quiet minute.

"Famous," John said.

"Famous?" Tom asked.

"Yeah." John laughed a little. "Everything's settling down now, so now everyone wants to meet Peter Garcia's wife. He's like a legend now."

"Wow," Tom said.

"That's great," Sarah said. "They deserve it."

"How's Annie handling fame?" Tom asked.

"Well, she's accepting it. Which is more than I can say for either of you Ōmäthäär. You should hear some of the rumors going around about 'Mär's rescuers'!

"But she's busy, you know. But I am surprised with how well she's taking having to talk about Peter this much."

28: Blaze of Glory

"Nŭährnär needs heroes like him," Sarah said. "Like both of them."

"Yeah," Tom nodded. "I hope this will bring Nŭährnär together more. More together than we were this time."

"I hope so," John said. "I'm surprised Mär's been so accepting, welcoming back everyone who left us to die. I hope we'll be more united, if Nrathĕrmĕ attacks us again. Or, *when* they attack us again.

"But how hadn't you heard? About the famous Annie Garcia?"

"We've been busy," Tom said.

"Yeah, I can see that," John smiled at them.

Tom grinned sadly back. "Well, I guess we can tell you."

"We think we're going to be leaving soon. We're going to go out and harvest."

John looked crushed. "You're leaving?"

"Just for a few weeks," Sarah said.

"Mär's letting you leave?"

"He said he thinks he will," Tom said.

"And we think he will," Sarah said.

"But why?"

"We feel like we should," Sarah said simply.

"This an Ōmäthäär thing?" John asked.

Tom smiled. "I'm going to miss you guys. All of you."

"Well, you're going to have all the company you need," John grinned at the two of them. "But call me before you leave."

"Okay," Tom said.

"We'll be back as soon as we can," Sarah said earnestly.

"We promise," Tom said.

The joy filling Nŭährnär was more poignant than had been the fear and despair before Thahn's attack.

On the week anniversary of their victory, Mär addressed all the remaining N'nŭährnär, giving a joyful, triumphant address. The kind of speech to make when an impossible trial has been happily overcome and ended:

"...and here we are!

"Look around! Think of where we are! Look how far we've come!

"I do believe that the very fact that you're hearing me speak right now is nothing less than a miracle of Är!

"A miracle!

"Är's miracles don't have to be spectacular, unexplainable events—

"But I challenge anybody to explain how it is that we're alive today!

"—But miracles are always Är's help to us when we go all the way in doing what needs to be done!...

"...Always, always do better than you have been doing!

"And remember, by what we've just lived, that Är really will never fail us, if only we don't fail out on him!

"Now, it is not over.

"Nrathĕrmĕ will most certainly make us pay dearly for our victory. Sĕrĕhahn will make us pay. He will not forget all the Ämäthöär we've killed.

"But be happy!

"Whatever comes, whatever Sĕrĕhahn contrives to ruin our cause, *whatever may come*, just learn to follow Är's advice! And trust him!

"Är will never fail us, if we do not fail away from his Cause!

"So don't worry! If you're allied with Infinity, you never do worry, no matter what!

"Nothing permanently bad can happen to us, if we're following Är's strategy.

"Believe us Ōmäthäär; we do know Är's strategies, as much as he tells us.

"If you don't believe about Är, you don't believe us.

"We are either deep liars, or this is real!

"There is no other possibility.

"Nothing permanently bad will happen to us if we're allied with Är, listening to what he advises, stepping out into the darkness because we can, because we're capable of doing such impossible, incredible things, because we know Är's plan always works!

"No matter how much it looks like it can't!

"Like this time!

"Always remember what we've just lived through. Never forget. Never, ever forget!

"Be happy! We are going to win!

"Be confident in doing your part!

"Be sure, and at peace, that neither Nrathĕrmĕ nor Sĕrĕhahn and all his Ämäthöär can be of any real trouble to us if we do what we know we're supposed to do!

"And no one can ask more of you than that!...

"...there is, apparently, still enough hope for our cause of Ä'ähänärdanär, for the N'nrathĕrmĕ, for Närdamähr and Pp'ōhōnŭäär, that Är thinks it's worth helping us in.

"There is apparently still enough good in our world for Är to fight for it.

"I don't know about you, but that is more than enough for me!"

28: Blaze of Glory

From "About the Meaning of Joy" by Sarah Pratt

...*that was joy! Progressing, moving onward, getting closer and closer to perfection!*
It was not easy. It was not a simple life, not by any means! Every day life became more complicated, more difficult, more stressful. But that invited us to do better! We grew faster than the difficulties of life could keep up with, because we let Infinity make us!
We became heroes. We became what we had always wanted ourselves to be, through the Är who knew that better than any of us ever could have!
We were just good people doing what we knew how to do. Who could have guessed what was about to come of that simple nobleness? Who could have predicted how many wonderful people were going to be helped, how many lives were going to become lives, how much was going to happen, because of our desperate sacrificings and endurings there?
What a story Är's Perfect Story is! How much better he's made my Life than I could ever have made it! So much better than I could ever have planned it!
I'm Antär, in Ä'ähänärdanär!
Who could have predicted all this? Oh, what our world has become!
And all from just good, normal, real people doing the best they could in what they knew how to do, each playing their unwittingly essential part in the grand Story of Ä'ähänärdanär!